IN SEARCH OF LOST TIME

In Search of Lost Time

Volume II

Within a Budding Grove

Marcel Proust

Translated by
C. K. Scott Moncrieff and Terence Kilmartin
Revised by D. J. Enright

The Modern Library
New York

1992 Modern Library Edition

 Published in the United States by Random House, Inc., New York.

This 1992 edition was published in Great Britain by Chatto & Windus.

This translation is a revised edition of the 1981 translation of *Within a Budding Grove* by C. K. Scott Moncrieff and Terence Kilmartin, published in the United States by Random House, Inc., and in Great Britain by Chatto & Windus. Revisions by D. J. Enright.

Within a Budding Grove first appeared in
The Modern Library in 1930.

Jacket portrait courtesy of Archive Photos.

Printed on recycled, acid-free paper.

Library of Congress Cataloging-in-Publication Number: 92-50224

ISBN 0-679-60006-X

Manufactured in the United States of America

2 4 6 8 9 7 5 3 1

MARCEL PROUST

Marcel Proust was born in the Parisian suburb of Auteuil on July 10, 1871. His father, Adrien Proust, was a doctor celebrated for his work in epidemiology; his mother, Jeanne Weil, was a stockbroker's daughter of Jewish descent. He lived as a child in the family home on Boulevard Malesherbes in Paris, but spent vacations with his aunt and uncle in the town of Illiers near Chartres, where the Prousts had lived for generations and which became the model for the Combray of his great novel. (In recent years it was officially renamed Illiers-Combray.) Sickly from birth, Marcel was subject from the age of nine to violent attacks of asthma, and although he did a year of military service as a young man and studied law and political science, his invalidism disqualified him from an active professional life.

During the 1890s Proust contributed sketches to *Le Figaro* and to a short-lived magazine, *Le Banquet*, founded by some of his school friends in 1892. *Pleasures and Days*, a collection of his stories, essays, and poems, was published in 1896. In his youth Proust led an active social life, penetrating the highest circles of wealth and aristocracy. Artistically and intellectually, his influences included the aesthetic criticism of John Ruskin, the philosophy of Henri Bergson, the music of Wagner, and the fiction of Anatole France (on whom he modeled his character Bergotte). An affair begun in 1894 with the composer and pianist Reynaldo Hahn marked the beginning of Proust's often anguished acknowledgment of his homosexuality. Following the publication of Emile Zola's letter in defense of Colonel Dreyfus in 1898, Proust became "the first Dreyfusard," as he later phrased it. By the time Dreyfus was finally vindicated of charges of treason, Proust's social circles had been torn apart by the anti-Semitism and political hatreds stirred up by the affair.

Proust was very attached to his mother, and after her death in 1905 he spent some time in a sanitorium. His health worsened progressively, and he withdrew almost completely from society and devoted himself to writing. Proust's early work had done nothing to establish his reputation as a major writer. In an unfinished novel, *Jean Santeuil* (not published until 1952), he laid some of the groundwork for *In Search of Lost Time*, and in *Against Sainte-Beuve*, written in 1908–09, he stated as his aesthetic credo: "A book is the product of a different self from the one we manifest in our habits, in society, in our vices. If we mean to try to understand this self it is only in our inmost depths, by endeavoring to reconstruct it there, that the quest can be achieved." He appears to have begun work on his long masterpiece sometime around 1908, and the first volume, *Swann's Way*, was published in 1913. In 1919 the second volume, *Within a Budding Grove*, won the Goncourt Prize, bringing Proust great and instantaneous fame. Two subsequent sections—*The Guermantes Way* (1920–21) and *Sodom and Gomorrah* (1921)—appeared in his lifetime. (Of the depiction of homosexuality in the latter, his friend André Gide complained: "Will you never portray this form of Eros for us in the aspect of youth and beauty?") The remaining volumes were published following Proust's death on November 18, 1922: *The Captive* in 1923, *The Fugitive* in 1925, and *Time Regained* in 1927.

WITHIN A BUDDING GROVE

CONTENTS

Numerals in the text refer the reader to explanatory notes while asterisks indicate the position of textual addenda. The notes and the addenda follow the text.

Part One

MADAME SWANN AT HOME

My mother, when it was a question of our having M. de Norpois to dinner for the first time, having expressed her regret that Professor Cottard was away from home and that she herself had quite ceased to see anything of Swann, since either of these might have helped to entertain the ex-ambassador, my father replied that so eminent a guest, so distinguished a man of science as Cottard could never be out of place at a dinner-table, but that Swann, with his ostentation, his habit of crying aloud from the house-tops the name of everyone he knew, however slightly, was a vulgar show-off whom the Marquis de Norpois would be sure to dismiss as—to use his own epithet—a "pestilent" fellow. Now, this attitude on my father's part may be felt to require a few words of explanation, inasmuch as some of us, no doubt, remember a Cottard of distinct mediocrity and a Swann by whom modesty and discretion, in all his social relations, were carried to the utmost refinement of delicacy. But in his case what had happened was that, to the original "young Swann" and also to the Swann of the Jockey Club, our old friend had added a new personality (which was not to be his last), that of Odette's husband. Adapting to the humble ambitions of that lady the instinct, the desire, the industry which he had always had, he had laboriously constructed for himself, a long way beneath the old, a new position more appropriate to the companion who was to share it with him. In this new position he revealed himself a different man. Since (while continuing to meet his own personal friends by himself, not wishing to impose Odette on them unless they expressly asked to be introduced to her) it was a second life that he had begun to lead, in common with his wife, among a new set of people, it would have been understandable if, in order to gauge the social importance of these new acquaintances and thereby the degree of self-esteem that might be derived from entertaining them, he had used, as a standard of comparison, not the brilliant society in which he himself had moved before his marriage, but former connections of Odette's. But, even when one knew that it was with uncouth functionaries and tainted women, the ornaments of ministerial ball-rooms, that he now wished to associate, it was still astonishing to hear him, who in the old days, and even still, would so gracefully refrain from mentioning an invitation to Twickenham or to Buckingham Palace, proclaim with quite unnecessary emphasis that the wife of some junior minister had returned Mme Swann's call. It will perhaps be objected here that what this really implied was that the simplicity of the fashionable Swann had been simply a more refined form of vanity, and that, like certain other Jews, my parents' old friend had contrived to illustrate in turn all the successive stages through which those of his race had passed, from the most naïve snobbery and the crudest caddishness to the most exquisite good manners. But the chief reason—and one which is applicable to humanity as a whole—was that our virtues themselves are not free and floating qualities over which we retain a permanent control and power of disposal; they come to be so closely linked in our minds with the actions in conjunction with which we have made it our duty to exercise them that if we come to engage in an activity of a different kind, it catches us off guard and without the slightest awareness that it might involve the application of those same virtues. Swann, in his solicitude for these new connections and in the pride with which he referred to them, was like those great artists—modest or generous by nature—who, if in their declining years they take to cooking or to gardening, display a naïve gratification at the compliments that are paid to their dishes or their borders, and will not allow any of the criticism which they readily accept when it is applied to their real achievements; or who, while giving away a canvas for nothing, cannot conceal their annoyance if they lose a couple of francs at dominoes.

As for Professor Cottard, we shall meet him again, at length, much later, with the "Mistress," Mme Verdurin, in her country house La Raspelière. For the present, the following observations must suffice: first of all, whereas in the case of Swann the alteration may indeed be surprising, since it had been accomplished and yet was not suspected by me when I used to see Gilberte's father in the Champs-Elysées, where in any case, as he never spoke to me, he could not very well boast to me of his political connections (it is true that if he had done so, I might not at once have discerned his vanity, for the idea that one has long held of a person is apt to stop one's eyes and ears; my mother, for three whole years, had no more noticed the rouge with which one of her nieces used to paint her lips than if it had been invisibly dissolved in some liquid; until one day a streak too much, or else some other cause, brought about the phenomenon known as super-saturation; all the paint that had hitherto passed unperceived now crystallised, and my mother, in the face of this sudden riot of colour, declared, in the best Combray manner, that it was a perfect scandal, and almost severed relations with her niece). In the case of Cottard, on the other hand, the period when we saw him in attendance at Swann's first meetings with the Verdurins was already fairly remote; and honours, offices and titles come with the passage of the years. Secondly, a man may be illiterate, and make stupid puns, and yet have a special gift which no amount of general culture can replace—such as the gift of a great strategist or physician. And so it was not merely as an obscure practitioner, who had attained in course of time to European celebrity, that the rest of his profession regarded Cottard. The most intelligent of the younger doctors used to assert—for a year or two at least, for fashions change, being themselves begotten of the desire for change—that if they themselves ever fell ill Cottard was the only one of the leading men to whom they would entrust their lives. No doubt they preferred the company of certain others who were better read, more artistic, with whom they could discuss Nietzsche and Wagner. When there was a musical party at Mme Cottard's, on the evenings when—in the hope that it might one day make him Dean of the Faculty—she entertained the colleagues and pupils of her husband, the latter, instead of listening, preferred to play cards in another room. But everyone praised the quickness, the penetration, the unerring judgment of his diagnoses. Thirdly, in considering the general impression which Professor Cottard must have made on a man like my father, we must bear in mind that the character which a man exhibits in the latter half of his life is not always, though it often is, his original character developed or withered, attenuated or enlarged; it is sometimes the exact reverse, like a garment that has been turned. Except from the Verdurins, who were infatuated with him, Cottard's hesitating manner, his excessive shyness and affability had, in his young days, called down upon him endless taunts and sneers. What charitable friend counselled that glacial air? The importance of his professional standing made it all the more easy for him to adopt. Wherever he went, save at the Verdurins', where he instinctively became himself again, he would assume a repellent coldness, remain deliberately silent, adopt a peremptory tone when he was obliged to speak, and never fail to say the most disagreeable things. He had every opportunity of rehearsing this new attitude before his patients, who, seeing him for the first time, were not in a position to make comparisons, and would have been greatly surprised to learn that he was not at all a rude man by nature. Impassiveness was what he strove to attain, and even while visiting his hospital wards, when he allowed himself to utter one of those puns which left everyone, from the house physician to the most junior student, helpless with laughter, he would always make it without moving a muscle of his face, which was itself no longer recognisable now that he had shaved off his beard and moustache.

Who, finally, was the Marquis de Norpois? He had been Minister Plenipotentiary before the War, and was actually an ambassador on the Sixteenth of May;[1] in spite of which, and to the general astonishment, he had since been several times chosen to represent France on special missions—even, as Controller of Debts, in Egypt, where, thanks to his considerable financial skill, he had rendered important services—by Radical cabinets under which a simple bourgeois reactionary would have declined to serve, and in whose eyes M. de Norpois, in view of his past, his connexions and his opinions, ought presumably to have been suspect. But these advanced ministers seemed to be aware that, in making such an appointment, they were showing how broadminded they were when the higher interests of France were at stake, were raising themselves above the general run of politicians to the extent that the *Journal des Débats* itself referred to them as "statesmen," and were reaping direct advantage from the prestige that attaches to an aristocratic name and the dramatic interest always aroused by an unexpected appointment. And they knew also that, in calling upon M. de Norpois, they could reap these advantages without having to fear any want of political loyalty on his part, a fault against which his noble birth not only need not put them on their guard but offered a positive guarantee. And in this calculation the Government of the Republic was not mistaken. In the first place, because an aristocrat of a certain type, brought up from his cradle to regard his name as an innate asset of which no accident can deprive him (and of whose value his peers, or those of even nobler birth, can form a fairly exact estimate), knows that he can dispense with the efforts (since they can in no way enhance his position) in which, without any appreciable result, so many public men of the middle class spend themselves to profess only orthodox opinions and associate only with right-thinking people. Anxious, on the other hand, to enhance his own importance in the eyes of the princely or ducal families which take immediate precedence of his own, he knows that he can do so only by complementing his name with something that it lacked, something that will give it priority over other names heraldically its equals: such as political influence, a literary or an artistic reputation, or a large fortune. And so what he saves by ignoring the ineffectual squires who are sought after by his bourgeois colleagues, but of his sterile friendship with whom a prince would think nothing, he will lavish on the politicians who (freemasons, or worse, though they be) can advance him in diplomacy or support him in elections, and on the artists or scientists whose patronage can help him to "break into" the branches in which they are predominant, on anyone, in fact, who is in a position to confer a fresh distinction or to help bring off a rich marriage.

But in the case of M. de Norpois there was above all the fact that, in the course of a long career in diplomacy, he had become imbued with that negative, methodical, conservative spirit, a "governmental mind," which is common to all governments and, under every government, particularly inspires its foreign service. He had imbibed, during that career, an aversion, a dread, a contempt for the methods of procedure, more or less revolutionary and at the very least improper, which are those of an Opposition. Save in the case of a few illiterates—high or low, it makes no matter—by whom no difference in quality is perceptible, what brings men together is not a community of views but a consanguinity of minds. An Academician of the Legouvé type, an upholder of the classics, would have applauded Maxime Du Camp's or Mézière's eulogy of Victor Hugo with more fervour than that of Boileau by Claudel. A common nationalism suffices to endear Barrès to his electors, who scarcely distinguish between him and

M. Georges Berry, but not to those of his brother Academicians who, with the same political opinions but a different type of mind, will be more partial even to enemies such as M. Ribot and M. Deschanel, with whom, in turn, the most loyal Monarchists feel themselves more at home than with Maurras or Léon Daudet, who nevertheless also desire the King's return. Sparing of his words, not only from a professional habit of prudence and reserve, but because words themselves have more value, present more subtleties of definition to men whose efforts, protracted over a decade, to bring two countries to an understanding are condensed, translated—in a speech or in a protocol—into a single adjective, colourless in all appearance, but to them pregnant with a world of meaning, M. de Norpois was considered very stiff, on the Commission, where he sat next to my father, whom everyone else congratulated on the astonishing way in which the ex-ambassador unbent to him. My father was himself more astonished than anyone. For, being generally somewhat unsociable, he was not used to being sought after outside the circle of his intimates, and frankly admitted it. He realised that these overtures on the part of the diplomat were a reflection of the completely individual standpoint which each of us adopts for himself in making his choice of friends, and from which all a man's intellectual qualities or his sensibility will be a far less potent recommendation to someone who is bored or irritated by him than the frankness and gaiety of another man whom many would consider vapid, frivolous and null. "De Norpois has asked me to dinner again; it's quite extraordinary; everyone on the Commission is amazed, as he has no personal relations with anyone else. I'm sure he's going to tell me some more fascinating things about the 'Seventy war." My father knew that M. de Norpois had warned, had perhaps been alone in warning the Emperor of the growing strength and bellicose designs of Prussia, and that Bismarck rated his intelligence most highly. Only the other day, at the Opera, during the gala performance given for King Theodosius, the newspapers had all drawn attention to the long conversation which that monarch had had with M. de Norpois. "I must ask him whether the King's visit had any real significance," my father went on, for he was keenly interested in foreign policy. "I know old Norpois keeps very close as a rule, but when he's with me he opens out quite charmingly."

As for my mother, perhaps the Ambassador had not the type of mind towards which she felt herself most attracted. And it must be said that his conversation furnished so exhaustive a glossary of the superannuated forms of speech peculiar to a certain profession, class and period—a period which, for that profession and that class, might be said not to have altogether passed away—that I sometimes regret not having kept a literal record simply of the things that I heard him say. I should thus have obtained an effect of old-fashioned usage by the same process and at as little expense as that actor at the Palais-Royal who, when asked where on earth he managed to find his astounding hats, answered, "I do not find my hats. I keep them." In a word, I suppose that my mother considered M. de Norpois a trifle "out-of-date," which was by no means a fault in her eyes, so far as manners were concerned, but attracted her less in the realm, not, in this instance, of ideas—for those of M. de Norpois were extremely modern—but of idiom. She felt, however, that she was paying a delicate compliment to her husband when she spoke admiringly of the diplomat who had shown so remarkable a predilection for him. By reinforcing in my father's mind the good opinion that he already had of M. de Norpois, and so inducing him to form a good opinion of himself also, she knew that she was carrying out that wifely duty which consisted in making life pleasant and comfortable for her husband, just as when she saw to it that his dinner was perfectly cooked and served in silence. And as she was incapable of deceiving my father, she compelled herself to admire the Ambassador in order to be able to praise him with sincerity. In any event she could naturally appreciate his air of kindliness, his somewhat antiquated courtesy (so ceremonious that when, as he was walking along the street, his tall figure rigidly erect, he caught sight of my mother driving past, before raising his hat to her he would fling away the cigar that he had just lighted), his conversation, so elaborately circumspect, in which he referred as seldom as possible to himself and always considered what might interest the person to whom he was speaking, and his promptness in answering a letter, which was so astonishing that whenever my father, just after posting one himself to M. de Norpois, saw his handwriting on an envelope, his first impulse was always one of annoyance that their letters must unfortunately have crossed: it was as though he enjoyed at the post office the special and luxurious privilege of supplementary deliveries and collections at all hours of the day and night. My mother marvelled at his being so punctilious although so busy, so friendly although so much in demand, never realising that "although," with such people, is invariably an unrecognised "because," and that (just as old men are always wonderful for their age, and kings extraordinarily simple, and country cousins astonishingly well-informed) it was the same system of habits that enabled M. de Norpois to meet so many social demands and to be so methodical in answering letters, to go everywhere and to be so friendly when he came to us. Moreover she made the mistake which everyone makes who is unduly modest; she rated everything that concerned herself below, and consequently outside, the range of other people's duties and engagements. The letter which it seemed to her so meritorious in my father's friend to have written us promptly, since in the course of the day he must have had so many letters to write, she excepted from that great number of letters of which it was only one; in the same way she did not consider that dining with us was, for M. de Norpois, merely one of the innumerable activities of his social life: she never guessed that the Ambassador had trained himself, long ago, to look upon dining-out as part of his diplomatic functions, and to display, at table, an inveterate charm which it would have been too much to have expected him specially to discard when he came to dine with us.

The evening on which M. de Norpois first appeared at our table, in a year when I still went to play in the Champs-Elysées, has remained fixed in my memory because the afternoon of the same day was that upon which I at last went to a matinée to see Berma in *Phèdre,* and also because in talking to M. de Norpois I realised suddenly, and in a new and different way, how completely the feelings aroused in me by all that concerned Gilberte Swann and her parents differed from those which the same family inspired in everyone else.

It was no doubt the dejection into which I was plunged by the approach of the New Year holidays during which, as she herself had informed me, I was to see nothing of Gilberte, that prompted my mother to suggest one day, in the hope of distracting my mind: "If you're still longing to see Berma, I think your father might perhaps allow you to go; your grandmother can take you."

But it was because M. de Norpois had told him that he ought to let me see Berma, that it was an experience for a young man to remember in later life, that my father, who had hitherto been so resolutely opposed to my going and wasting my time, with the added risk of my falling ill again, on what he used to shock my grandmother by calling "futilities," was now not far from regarding this outing recommended by the Ambassador as vaguely forming part of a sum of precious formulae for success in a brilliant career. My grandmother, who, in renouncing on my behalf the benefit which, according to her, I should have derived from hearing Berma, had made a considerable sacrifice in the interests of my health, was surprised to find that this last had become of no account at a mere word from M. de Norpois. Reposing the unconquerable hopes of her rationalist spirit in the strict course of fresh air and early hours which had been prescribed for me, she now deplored as something disastrous the infringement of these rules that I was about to commit, and in anguished tones exclaimed "How frivolous you are!" to my father, who replied angrily "What! So now it's you who don't want him to go! It's really a bit much, after your telling us all day and every day that it would be so good for him."

M. de Norpois had also brought about a change in

my father's plans in a matter of far greater importance to myself. My father had always wanted me to be a diplomat, and I could not endure the thought that, even if I were to remain for some years attached to the Ministry, I might run the risk of being sent later on as ambassador to capitals in which there would be no Gilberte. I should have preferred to return to the literary projects which I had formerly planned and abandoned in the course of my wanderings along the Guermantes way. But my father had steadily opposed my devoting myself to literature, which he regarded as vastly inferior to diplomacy, refusing even to dignify it with the title of career, until the day when M. de Norpois, who had little love for the more recent generations of diplomatic officials, assured him that it was quite possible, as a writer, to attract as much attention, to receive as much consideration, to exercise as much influence as in the ambassadorial world, and at the same time to preserve more independence.

"Well, well, I should never have believed it—old Norpois doesn't at all disapprove of the idea of your taking up writing," my father had reported. And as he had a certain amount of influence himself, he imagined that there was nothing that could not be arranged, no problem for which a happy solution might not be found in the conversation of people who counted. "I shall bring him back to dinner, one of these days, from the Commission. You must talk to him a bit, so that he can get some idea of your calibre. Write something good that you can show him; he's a great friend of the editor of the *Deux-Mondes*; he'll get you in there; he'll fix it all, the cunning old fox; and, upon my soul, he seems to think that diplomacy, nowadays . . . !"

My happiness at the prospect of not being separated from Gilberte made me desirous, but not capable, of writing something good which could be shown to M. de Norpois. After a few laboured pages, the tedium of it made the pen drop from my fingers, and I wept with rage at the thought that I should never have any talent, that I was not gifted, that I could not even take advantage of the chance that M. de Norpois's coming visit offered me of spending the rest of my life in Paris. The recollection that I was to be taken to see Berma alone distracted me from my grief. But just as I wished to see storms only on those coasts where they raged with most violence, so I should not have cared to see the great actress except in one of those classic parts in which Swann had told me that she touched the sublime. For when it is in the hope of making a priceless discovery that we desire to receive certain impressions from nature or from works of art, we have qualms lest our soul imbibe inferior impressions which might lead us to form a false estimate of the value of Beauty. Berma in *Andromaque*, in *Les Caprices de Marianne*, in *Phèdre*, was one of those famous spectacles which my imagination had long desired. I should enjoy the same rapture as on the day when a gondola would deposit me at the foot of the Titian of the Frari or the Carpaccios of San Giorgio dei Schiavoni, were I ever to hear Berma recite the lines beginning,

> They say a prompt departure takes you from us,
> Prince . . .

I was familiar with them from the simple reproduction in black and white which was given of them upon the printed page; but my heart beat furiously at the thought—as of the realisation of a long-planned voyage—that I should see them at length bathed and brought to life in the atmosphere and sunshine of the golden voice. A Carpaccio in Venice, Berma in *Phèdre*, masterpieces of pictorial or dramatic art which the glamour, the dignity attaching to them made so vividly alive for me, that is to say so indivisible, that if I had been to see Carpaccios in one of the galleries of the Louvre, or Berma in some piece of which I had never heard, I should not have experienced the same delicious amazement at finding myself at last, with wide-open eyes, before the unique and inconceivable object of so many thousand dreams. Then, expecting as I did from Berma's playing the revelation of certain aspects of nobility and tragic grief, it seemed to me that whatever greatness, whatever truth there might be in her playing must be enhanced if the actress superimposed it upon a work of real value, instead of what would, after all, be but embroidering a pattern of truth and beauty upon a commonplace and vulgar web.

Finally, if I went to see Berma in a new play, it would not be easy for me to assess her art and her diction, since I should be unable to discriminate between a text which was not already familiar to me and what she added to it by her vocal inflexions and gestures, an addition which would seem to me to be an integral part of it; whereas the old plays, the classics which I knew by heart, presented themselves to me as vast and empty walls, reserved and made ready for my inspection, on which I should be able to appreciate without restriction the devices by which Berma would cover them, as with frescoes, with the perpetually fresh discoveries of her inspiration.

Unfortunately, for some years now, since she had abandoned the serious stage to throw in her lot with a commercial theatre where she was the star, she had ceased to appear in classic parts, and in vain did I scan the hoardings, they never advertised any but the newest pieces, written specially for her by authors in fashion at the moment. When, one morning, searching through the column of theatre advertisements to find the afternoon performances for the week of the New Year holidays, I saw there for the first time—at the foot of the bill, after some probably insignificant curtain-raiser, whose title was opaque to me because it contained all the particulars of a plot I did not know—two acts of *Phèdre* with Mme Berma, and, on the following afternoons, *Le Demi-Monde* and *Les Caprices de Marianne*, names which, like that of *Phèdre*, were for me transparent, filled with light only, so familiar were those works to me, illuminated to their very depths by the revealing smile of art. They seemed to me to invest with a fresh nobility Mme Berma herself when I read in the newspapers, after the programme of these performances, that it was she who had decided to show herself once more to the public in some of her early creations. She was conscious, then, that certain roles have an interest which survives the novelty of their first production or the success of a revival; she regarded them, when interpreted by herself, as museum pieces which it might be instructive to set once more before the eyes of the generation which had admired her in them long ago, or of the one which had never yet seen her in them. In thus advertising, in the middle of a column of plays intended only to while away an evening, this *Phèdre*, whose title was no bigger than any of the rest, nor set in different type, she added to it, as it were, the unspoken comment of a hostess who, on introducing you to her other guests before going in to dinner, casually mentions amid the string of names which are the names of guests and nothing more, and without any change of tone:—"M. Anatole France."

The doctor who was attending me—the same who had forbidden me to travel—advised my parents not to let me go to the theatre; I should only be ill again afterwards, perhaps for weeks, and in the long run derive more pain than pleasure from the experience. The fear of this might have availed to stop me, if what I had anticipated from such a spectacle had been only a pleasure which a subsequent pain could offset and annul. But what I demanded from this performance—as from the visit to Balbec and the visit to Venice for which I had so intensely longed—was something quite different from pleasure: verities pertaining to a world more real than that in which I lived, which, once acquired, could never be taken from me again by any trivial incident—even though it were to cause me bodily suffering—of my otiose existence. At most, the pleasure which I might experience during the performance appeared to me as the perhaps necessary form of the perception of these truths; and I hoped only that the predicted ailments would not begin until the play was finished, so that this pleasure should not be in any way compromised or spoiled. I implored my parents, who, after the doctor's visit, were no longer inclined to let me go to *Phèdre*. I recited to myself all day long the speech beginning,

They say a prompt departure takes you from us . . .

trying out every inflexion and intonation that could be put into it, the better to appreciate the unexpected way which Berma would have found of uttering the lines. Concealed, like the Holy of Holies, beneath the veil that screened her from my gaze and behind which I invested her from one moment to the next with a fresh aspect, according to whichever of the words of Bergotte (in the booklet that Gilberte had found for me) came to my mind—"plastic nobility," "Christian hair shirt" or "Jansenist pallor," "Princess of Troezen and of Cleves," "Mycenean drama," "Delphic symbol," "solar myth"—the goddess of beauty whom Berma's acting was to reveal to me was enthroned, night and day, upon an altar perpetually lit, in the sanctuary of my mind—on whose behalf my stern and fickle parents were to decide whether or not it was to enshrine, and for all time, the perfections of the Deity unveiled in that same spot where her invisible form now reigned. And with my eyes fastened on that inconceivable image, I strove from morning to night to overcome the barriers which my family were putting in my way. But when these had at last fallen, when my mother—although this matinée was actually to coincide with the meeting of the Commission from which my father had promised to bring M. de Norpois home to dinner—had said to me, "Very well, we don't want to make you unhappy—if you think you will enjoy it so very much, you must go," when this visit to the theatre, hitherto forbidden and unattainable, depended now on myself alone, then for the first time, being no longer troubled by the wish that it might cease to be impossible, I wondered whether it was desirable, whether there were not other reasons than my parents' prohibition which should have made me abandon it. In the first place, whereas I had hated them for their cruelty, their consent made them now so dear to me that the thought of causing them pain stabbed me also with a pain through which the purpose of life now appeared to me as the pursuit not of truth but of loving-kindness, and life itself seemed good or evil only in so far as my parents were happy or sad. "I would rather not go, if it distresses you," I told my mother, who, on the contrary, strove hard to expel from my mind any lurking fear that she might regret my going, since that, she said, would spoil the pleasure which I should otherwise derive from *Phèdre* and in consideration of which she and my father had reversed their earlier decision. But then this sort of obligation to find pleasure in the performance seemed to me very burdensome. Besides, if I returned home ill, should I be well again in time to be able to go to the Champs-Elysées as soon as the holidays were over and Gilberte returned? Against all these arguments I set, in order to decide which course I should take, the idea, invisible there behind its veil, of Berma's perfection. I placed on one side of the scales "Making Mamma unhappy," "risking not being able to go to the Champs-Elysées," and on the other, "Jansenist pallor," "solar myth," until the words themselves grew dark and clouded in my mind's vision, ceased to say anything to me, lost all their force; and gradually my hesitations became so painful that if I had now opted for the theatre it would have been only in order to bring them to an end and be delivered from them once and for all. It would have been to fix a term to my sufferings, and no longer in the expectation of an intellectual benediction, yielding to the attractions of perfection, that I would have allowed myself to be led, not now to the Wise Goddess, but to the stern, implacable Divinity, faceless and unnamed, who had been surreptitiously substituted for her behind her veil. But suddenly everything was altered. My desire to go and see Berma received a fresh stimulus which enabled me to await the coming of the matinée with impatience and with joy. Having gone to take up my daily station, as excruciating, of late, as that of a stylite, in front of the column on which the playbills were displayed, I had seen there, still moist and wrinkled, the complete bill of *Phèdre*, which had just been pasted up for the first time (and on which, I must confess, the rest of the cast furnished no additional attraction which could help me to decide). But it gave to one of the goals between which my indecision wavered a form at once more concrete and—inasmuch as the bill bore the date not of the day on which I was reading it but that on which the performance would take place, and the very hour at which the curtain would rise—almost imminent, already well on the way to its realisation, so that I jumped for joy before the column at the thought that on that day, and at that hour precisely, I should be sitting there in my seat, ready to hear the voice of Berma; and for fear lest my parents might not now be in time to secure two good seats for my grandmother and myself, I raced back to the house, whipped on by the magic words which had now taken the place in my mind of "Jansenist pallor" and "solar myth": "Ladies will not be admitted to the stalls in hats. The doors will be closed at two o'clock."

Alas! that first matinée was to prove a bitter disappointment. My father offered to drop my grandmother and me at the theatre, on his way to the Commission. Before leaving the house he said to my mother: "Try and have a good dinner for us tonight; you remember I'm bringing de Norpois back with me." My mother had not forgotten. And ever since the day before, Françoise, rejoicing in the opportunity to devote herself to that art of cooking at which she was so gifted, stimulated, moreover, by the prospect of a new guest, and knowing that she would have to compose, by methods known to her alone, a dish of *boeuf à la gelée*, had been living in the effervescence of creation; since she attached the utmost importance to the intrinsic quality of the materials which were to enter into the fabric of her work, she had gone herself to the Halles to procure the best cuts of rump-steak, shin of beef, calves'-feet, just as Michelangelo spent eight months in the mountains of Carrara choosing the most perfect blocks of marble for the monument of Julius II. Françoise expended on these comings and goings so much ardour that Mamma, at the sight of her flaming cheeks, was alarmed lest our old servant should fall ill from overwork, like the sculptor of the Tombs of the Medici in the quarries of Pietrasanta. And overnight Françoise had sent to be cooked in the baker's oven protected with breadcrumbs, like a block of pink marble packed in sawdust, what she called a "Nev'-York ham." Believing the language to be less rich in words than it is, and her own ears untrustworthy, the first time she had heard someone mention York ham she had thought, no doubt—feeling it to be hardly conceivable that the dictionary could be so prodigal as to include at once a "York" and a "New York"—that she had misheard, and that the ham was really called by the name already familiar to her. And so, ever since, the word York was preceded in her ears, or before her eyes when she read it in an advertisement, by the affix "New" which she pronounced "Nev'." And it was with the utmost conviction that she would say to her kitchen-maid: "Go and get me some ham from Olida's. Madame told me especially that it must be Nev'-York."

On that particular day, if Françoise was consumed by the burning certainty of creative genius, my lot was the cruel anxiety of the seeker after truth. No doubt, so long as I had not yet heard Berma speak, I still felt some pleasure. I felt it in the little square that lay in front of the theatre, in which, in two hours' time, the bare boughs of the chestnut-trees would gleam with a metallic lustre as the lighted gas-lamps showed up every detail of their structure; and before the ticket attendants, whose selection, advancement and ultimate fate depended upon the great artist—for she alone held power in this administration at the head of which ephemeral and purely nominal managers followed one after the other in an obscure succession—who took our tickets without even glancing at us, so preoccupied were they in seeing that all Mme Berma's instructions had been duly transmitted to the new members of the staff, that it was clearly understood that the hired applause must never sound for her, that the windows must all be kept open so long as she was not on the stage and every door closed tight the moment she appeared, that a bowl of hot water must be concealed somewhere close to her to make the dust settle. And, indeed, at any moment now her carriage, drawn by a pair of horses with flowing manes, would be stopping outside the theatre, she would alight from it muffled in furs, and, crossly acknowledging people's salutes, would send one of her attendants to find out whether a stage box had been kept for her friends, what the temperature was "in front," who were in the other boxes, how the programme sellers were turned out; theatre and audience being to her no more than a second, outer cloak which she would put on, and the medium, the more or less good conductor, through which her talent would have to pass. I was happy, too, in the theatre itself; since I had made the discovery that—contrary to the notion so long entertained by my childish imagination—there was but one stage for everybody, I had supposed that I should be prevented from seeing it properly by the presence of the other spectators, as one is when in the thick of a crowd; now I registered the fact that, on the contrary, thanks to an arrangement which is, as it were, symbolical of all spectatorship, everyone feels himself to be the centre of the theatre; which explained to me why, when Françoise had been sent once to see some melodrama from the top gallery, she had assured us on her return that her seat had been the best in the house, and that instead of finding herself too far from the stage she had been positively frightened by the mysterious and living proximity of the curtain. My pleasure increased further when I began to distinguish behind this lowered curtain such obscure noises as one hears through the shell of an egg before the chicken emerges, sounds which presently grew louder and suddenly, from that world which, impenetrable to our eyes, yet scrutinised us with its own, addressed themselves indubitably to us in the imperious form of three consecutive thumps as thrilling as any signals from the planet Mars. And—once this curtain had risen—when on the stage a writing-table and a fireplace, in no way out of the ordinary, had indicated that the persons who were about to enter would be, not actors come to recite as I had once seen some of them do at an evening party, but real people, just living their lives at home, on whom I was thus able to spy without their seeing me, my pleasure still endured. It was broken by a momentary uneasiness: just as I was pricking up my ears in readiness before the piece began, two men appeared on the stage obviously furious with one another since they were talking so loud that in this auditorium where there were at least a thousand people one could hear every word, whereas in quite a small café one is obliged to ask the waiter what two individuals who appear to be quarrelling are saying; but at that moment, while I sat astonished to find that the audience was listening to them without protest, submerged as it was in a unanimous silence upon which presently a little wave of laughter broke here and there, that these insolent fellows were the actors, and that the short piece known as "the curtain-raiser" had now begun. It was followed by an interval so long that the audience, having returned to their seats, grew impatient and began to stamp their feet. I was terrified at this; for just as in the report of a criminal trial, when I read that some noble-minded person was coming, in defiance of his own interests, to testify on behalf of an innocent man, I was always afraid that they would not be nice enough to him, would not show enough gratitude, would not recompense him lavishly, and that he, in disgust, would then range himself on the side of injustice, so now, assimilating genius with virtue, I was afraid lest Berma, vexed by the bad behaviour of so ill-bred an audience—in which, on the contrary, I should have liked her to recognise with gratification a few celebrities to whose judgment she would be bound to attach importance—should express her displeasure and disdain by acting badly. And I looked round imploringly at these stamping brutes, who were about to shatter, in their insensate rage, the rare and fragile impression which I had come to seek. The last moments of my pleasure were during the opening scenes of the *Phèdre*. The heroine herself does not appear in these first scenes of the second act; and yet, as soon as the curtain rose, and another curtain, of red velvet this time, was drawn aside (a curtain which was used to halve the depth of the stage in all the plays in which the star appeared), an actress entered from the back who had the face and voice which, I had been told, were those of Berma. The cast must therefore have been changed; all the trouble that I had taken in studying the part of the wife of Theseus was wasted. But a second actress now responded to the first. I must have been mistaken in supposing that the first was Berma, for the second resembled her even more closely and, more than the other, had her diction. Both of them, moreover, embellished their roles with noble gestures—which I could clearly distinguish, and could appreciate in their relation to the text, while they raised and let fall the folds of their beautiful robes—and also with skilful changes of tone, now passionate, now ironical, which made me understand the significance of lines that I had read to myself at home without paying sufficient attention to what they really meant. But all of a sudden, in the cleft of the red curtain that veiled her sanctuary, as in a frame, a woman appeared, and instantly, from the fear that seized me, far more anxious than Berma's own fear could be, lest someone should upset her by opening a window, or drown one of her lines by rustling a programme, or annoy her by applauding the others and by not applauding her enough, from the way in which, from that moment, more absolutely than Berma herself, I considered theatre, audience, play and my own body only as an acoustic medium of no importance save in the degree to which it was favourable to the inflexions of that voice, I realised that the two actresses whom I had been admiring for some minutes bore not the least resemblance to her whom I had come to hear. But at the same time all my pleasure had ceased; in vain did I strain towards Berma eyes, ears, mind, so as not to let one morsel escape me of the reasons which she would give me for admiring her, I did not succeed in gleaning a single one. I could not even, as I could with her companions, distinguish in her diction and in her playing intelligent modulations or beautiful gestures. I listened to her as though I were reading *Phèdre*, or as though Phaedra herself had at that moment uttered the words that I was hearing, without its appearing that Berma's talent had added anything at all to them. I could have wished—in order to be able to explore them fully, to try to discover what it was in them that was beautiful—to arrest, to immobilise for a time before my senses every inflexion of the artist's voice, every expression of her features; at least I did attempt, by dint of mental agility, by having, before a line came, my attention ready and tuned to catch it, not to waste upon preparations any morsel of the precious time that each word, each gesture occupied, and, thanks to the intensity of my observation, to contrive to penetrate as far into them as if I had had whole hours to spend upon them by myself. But how short their duration was! Scarcely had a sound been received by my ear than it was displaced there by another. In one scene, where Berma stands motionless for a moment, her arm raised to the level of her face, bathed, by some artifice of lighting, in a greenish glow, before a back-cloth painted to represent the sea, the whole house broke out in applause; but already the actress had moved, and the tableau that I should have liked to study existed no longer. I told my grandmother that I could not see very well, and she handed me her glasses. But when one believes in the reality of things, making them visible by artificial means is not quite the same as feeling that they are close at hand. I thought that it was no longer Berma but her image that I was seeing in the magnifying lenses. I put the glasses down. But perhaps the image that my eye received of her, diminished by distance, was no more exact; which of the two Bermas was the real one? As for her declaration to Hippolyte, I had greatly counted on that, since, to judge by the ingenious significance which her companions were disclosing to me every moment in less beautiful passages, she would certainly render it with modulations more surprising than any which, when reading the play at home, I had contrived to imagine; but she did not attain even to the heights which Oenone or Aricie would naturally have reached, she planed down into a uniform chant the whole of a speech in which there were mingled together contrasts so striking that the least intelligent of actresses, even the pupils of an academy, could not have missed their effect; besides which, she delivered it so rapidly that it was only when she had come to the last line that my mind became aware of the deliberate monotony which she had imposed on it throughout.

Then at last I felt my first impulse of admiration, which was provoked by the frenzied applause of the audience. I mingled my own with theirs, endeavouring to prolong it so that Berma, in her gratitude, should surpass herself, and I be certain of having heard her on one of her great days. A curious thing, by the way, was that the moment when this storm of enthusiasm broke loose was, as I afterwards learned, that in which Berma has one of her finest inspirations. It would appear that certain transcendent realities emit all around them a sort of radiation to which the crowd is sensitive. Thus it is that when any great event occurs, when on a distant frontier an army is in jeopardy, or defeated, or victorious, the vague and conflicting reports from which an educated man can derive little enlightenment stimulate in the crowd an emotion which surprises him and in which, once the experts have informed him of the actual military situation, he recognises the popular perception of that "aura" which surrounds momentous happenings and which may be visible hundreds of miles away. One learns of a victory either after the event, when the war is over, or at once, from the hilarious joy of one's hall porter. One discovers the touch of genius in Berma's acting either a week after one has heard her, from a review, or else on the spot, from the thundering acclamation of the stalls. But this immediate recognition by the crowd being mingled with a hundred others, all erroneous, the applause came most often at wrong moments, apart from the fact that it was mechanically produced by the effect of the applause that had gone before, just as in a storm, once the sea is sufficiently disturbed, it will continue to swell even after the wind has begun to subside. No matter; the more I applauded, the better, it seemed to me, did Berma act. "I say," a fairly ordinary-looking woman sitting next to me was saying, "she fairly gives it you, she does; you'd think she'd do herself an injury, the way she runs about. I call that acting, don't you?" And happy to find these reasons for Berma's superiority, though not without a suspicion that they no more accounted for it than a peasant's gawping exclamations—"That's a good bit of work. It's all gold, look! Fine, ain't it?"—would for that of the Gioconda or Benvenuto's Perseus, I greedily imbibed the rough wine of this popular enthusiasm. Nevertheless, when the curtain had fallen for the last time, I was disappointed that the pleasure for which I had so longed had not been greater, but at the same time I felt the need to prolong it, not to relinquish for ever, by leaving the auditorium, this strange life of the theatre which for a few hours had been mine, and from which I should have torn myself away as though I were being dragged into exile by going straight home, had I not hoped there to learn a great deal more about Berma from her admirer M. de Norpois, to whom I was indebted already for having been permitted to go to *Phèdre*.

I was introduced to him before dinner by my father, who summoned me into his study for the purpose. As I entered, the Ambassador rose, held out his hand, bowed his tall figure and fixed his blue eyes attentively on my face. As the foreign visitors who used to be presented to him, in the days when he still represented France abroad, were all more or less (even the famous singers) persons of note, with regard to whom he therefore knew that he would be able to say later on, when he heard their names mentioned in Paris or in Petersburg, that he remembered perfectly the evening he had spent with them in Munich or Sofia, he had formed the habit of impressing upon them, by his affability, the pleasure he felt in making their acquaintance; but in addition to this, being convinced that in the life of foreign capitals, in contact at once with all the interesting personalities that passed through them and with the manners and customs of the native populations, one acquired a deeper insight than could be gleaned from books into the history, the geography, the traditions of the different nations, and into the intellectual trends of Europe, he would exercise upon each newcomer his keen power of observation, so as to decide at once with what manner of man he had to deal. It was some time since the Government had entrusted him with a post abroad, but as soon as anyone was introduced to him, his eyes, as though they had not yet received notification of their master's retirement, began their fruitful observation, while by his whole attitude he endeavoured to convey that the stranger's name was not unknown to him. And so, while speaking to me kindly and with the air of self-importance of a man who is conscious of the vastness of his experience, he never ceased to examine me with a sagacious curiosity for his own profit, as though I had been some exotic custom, some historic and instructive monument or some star on tour. And in this way he gave proof, in his attitude towards me, at once of the majestic benevolence of the sage Mentor and of the zealous curiosity of the young Anacharsis.

He offered me absolutely no opening to the *Revue des Deux-Mondes*, but put a number of questions to me about my life and my studies, and about my tastes which I heard thus spoken of for the first time as though it might be a reasonable thing to obey their promptings, whereas hitherto I had always supposed it to be my duty to suppress them. Since they inclined me towards literature, he did not dissuade me from it; on the contrary, he spoke of it with deference, as of some venerable and charming personage whose select circle, in Rome or at Dresden, one remembers with pleasure and regrets only that one's multifarious duties in life enable one to revisit so seldom. He appeared to envy me, with an almost rakish smile, the delightful hours which, more fortunate than himself and more free, I should be able to spend with such a mistress. But the very terms that he employed showed me Literature as something entirely different from the image that I had formed of it at Combray, and I realised that I had been doubly right in renouncing it. Until now, I had concluded only that I had no gift for writing; now M. de Norpois took away from me even the desire to write. I wanted to express to him what had been my dreams; trembling with emotion, I was painfully anxious that all the words I uttered would be the sincerest possible equivalent of what I had felt and had never yet attempted to formulate; which is to say that my words were very unclear. Perhaps from a professional habit, perhaps by virtue of the calm that is acquired by every important personage whose advice is commonly sought, and who, knowing that he will keep the control of the conversation in his own hands, allows his interlocutor to fret, to struggle, to toil to his heart's content, perhaps also to show off the character of his face (Greek, according to himself, despite his sweeping whiskers), M. de Norpois, while anything was being expounded to him, would preserve a facial immobility as absolute as if you had been addressing some ancient—and deaf—bust in a museum. Until suddenly, falling upon you like an auctioneer's hammer or a Delphic oracle, the Ambassador's voice, as he replied to you, would be all the more striking in that nothing in his face had allowed you to guess what sort of impression you had made on him, or what opinion he was about to express.

"Precisely," he suddenly began, as though the case were now heard and judged, after having allowed me to stammer incoherently beneath those motionless eyes which never for an instant left my face; "a friend of mine has a son whose case, *mutatis mutandis*, is very much like yours." He adopted in speaking of our common predisposition the same reassuring tone as if it had been a predisposition not for literature but for rheumatism, and he had wished to assure me that it would not necessarily prove fatal. "He too chose to leave the Quai d'Orsay, although the way had been paved for him there by his father, and without caring what people might say, he settled down to write. And certainly, he's had no reason to regret it. He published two years ago—of course, he's much older than you—a book about the Sense of the Infinite on the western shore of Lake Victoria Nyanza, and this year he has brought out a short treatise, less weighty but written with a lively, not to say cutting pen, on the Repeating Rifle in the Bulgarian Army; and these have put him quite in a class by himself. He's already gone pretty far, and he's not the sort of man to stop halfway. I happen to know that (without any suggestion, of course, of his standing for election) his name has been mentioned several times in conversation, and not at all unfavourably, at the Academy of Moral Sciences. And so, though one can't say yet, of course, that he's exactly at the pinnacle, he has fought his way by sheer merit to a very fine position indeed, and success—which doesn't always come only to the pushers and the muddlers, the fusspots who are generally show-offs—success has crowned his efforts."

My father, seeing me already, in a few years' time, an Academician, exuded a satisfaction which M. de Norpois raised to the highest pitch when, after a momentary hesitation during which he appeared to be calculating the possible consequences of his act, he handed me his card and said: "Why not go and see him yourself? Tell him I sent you. He may be able to give you some good advice," plunging me by these words into as painful a state of anxiety as if he had told me that I was to embark next day as cabin-boy on board a wind-jammer.

My aunt Léonie had bequeathed to me, together with a multiplicity of objects and furniture which were something of an embarrassment, almost all her liquid assets—revealing thus after her death an affection for me which I had little suspected in her lifetime. My father, who was trustee of this estate until I came of age, now consulted M. de Norpois with regard to a number of investments. He recommended certain stocks bearing a low rate of interest, which he considered particularly sound, notably English consols and Russian four per cents. "With absolutely first-class securities such as those," said M. de Norpois, "even if your income from them is nothing very great, you may be certain of never losing any of your capital." My father then gave him a rough indication of what else he had bought. M. de Norpois gave a just perceptible smile of congratulation; like all capitalists, he regarded wealth as an enviable thing, but thought it more delicate to compliment people upon their possessions only by an inconspicuous sign of intelligent sympathy; at the same time, as he was himself colossally rich, he thought it in good taste to seem to regard as considerable the inferior incomes of his friends, with, however, a happy and comforting reference to the superiority of his own. On the other hand, he did not hesitate to congratulate my father on the "composition" of his portfolio, selected "with so sure, so delicate, so fine a taste." It was as though he attributed to the relative values of shares, and even to shares themselves, something akin to aesthetic merit. Of one, comparatively recent and still little known, which my father mentioned, M. de Norpois, like the people who have always read the books of which you imagined you alone had ever heard, said at once, "Ah, yes, I used to amuse myself for a time following it in the share index; it was not uninteresting," with the retrospective smile of a regular subscriber who has read the latest novel already, in monthly instalments, in his magazine. "It wouldn't be at all a bad idea to apply for some of this new issue. It's distinctly attractive; they're offering it at a most tempting discount." But when he came to some of the older investments, my father, who could not remember their exact names, which it was easy to confuse with others of the same kind, opened a drawer and showed the securities themselves to the Ambassador. The sight of them enchanted me. They were ornamented with cathedral spires and allegorical figures, like some of the old romantic editions that I had pored over as a child. All the products of one period resemble one another; the artists who illustrate the poetry of their generation are the same artists who are employed by the big financial houses. And nothing reminds me more strongly of the instalments of *Notre-Dame de Paris* and of various works of Gérard de Nerval, that used to hang outside the grocer's door at Combray, than does, in its rectangular and flowery border, supported by recumbent river-gods, a registered share in the Water Company.

The contempt which my father had for my kind of intelligence was so far tempered by affection that, in practice, his attitude towards everything I did was one of blind indulgence. And so he had no qualm about sending me to fetch a little prose poem which I had made up years before at Combray on coming home from a walk. I had written it in a state of exaltation which must, I felt certain, communicate itself to everyone who read it. But it was not destined to captivate M. de Norpois, for he handed it back to me without a word.

My mother, who was full of respect for all my father's occupations, came in now to ask timidly whether dinner might be served. She was afraid to interrupt a conversation in which she herself could have no part. And indeed my father was continually reminding the Marquis of some useful measure which they had decided to support at the next meeting of the Commission, speaking in the peculiar tone always adopted in a strange environment by a pair of colleagues—akin, in this respect, to a pair of schoolfellows—whose professional routine has furnished them with a common fund of memories to which others have no access and to which they apologise for referring in their presence.

But the absolute control over his facial muscles to which M. de Norpois had attained allowed him to listen without seeming to hear a word. At length my father became uneasy: "I had thought," he ventured, after an endless preamble, "of asking the advice of the Commission . . ." Then from the face of the noble virtuoso, who had maintained the passivity of an orchestral player whose moment has not yet come, there emerged with an even delivery, on a sharp note, and as though they were no more than the completion (but scored for a different voice) of the phrase that my father had begun, the words: "of which you will not hesitate, of course, to call a meeting, more especially as the members are all known to you personally and can easily make themselves available." It was not in itself a very remarkable ending. But the immobility that had preceded it made it detach itself with the crystal clarity, the almost mischievous unexpectedness of those phrases with which the piano, silent until then, takes over, at a given moment, from the cello to which one has just been listening, in a Mozart concerto.

"Well, did you enjoy your matinée?" asked my father as we moved to the dining-room, hoping to draw me out and with the idea that my enthusiasm would give M. de Norpois a good opinion of me. "He has just been to see Berma. You remember we talked about it the other day," he went on, turning towards the diplomat, in the same tone of retrospective, technical and mysterious allusiveness as if he had been referring to a meeting of the Commission.

"You must have been enchanted, especially if you had never seen her before. Your father was alarmed at the possible repercussions that this little jaunt might have upon your health, which is none too good, I am told, none too robust. But I soon set his mind at rest. Theatres today are not what they were even twenty years ago. You have more or less comfortable seats now, and a certain amount of ventilation, although we have still a long way to go before we come up to the standard of Germany or England, who in that respect as in many others are immeasurably ahead of us. I have never seen Mme Berma in *Phèdre*, but I have always heard that she is excellent in the part. You were charmed with her, of course?"

M. de Norpois, a man a thousand times more intelligent than myself, must know that hidden truth which I had failed to extract from Berma's playing, and would reveal it to me; in answering his question I would ask him to let me know in what that truth consisted; and he would thereby justify me in the longing that I had felt to see and hear the actress. I had only a moment; I must take advantage of it and bring my cross-examination to bear upon the essential points. But what were they? Fastening my whole attention upon my own so confused impressions, with no thought of winning the admiration of M. de Norpois but only that of learning from him the truth that I had still to discover, I made no attempt to substitute ready-made phrases for the words that failed me but stood there stammering until finally, in the hope of provoking him into declaring what was so admirable about Berma, I confessed that I had been disappointed.

"What's that?" cried my father, annoyed at the bad impression which this admission of my failure to appreciate the performance must make on M. de Norpois, "How can you possibly say that you didn't enjoy it? Why, your grandmother has been telling us that you sat there hanging on every word that Berma uttered, with your eyes starting out of your head; that everyone else in the theatre seemed quite bored beside you."

"Oh, yes, I listened as hard as I could, trying to find out what it was that was supposed to be so wonderful about her. Of course, she's frightfully good . . ."

"If she is frightfully good, what more do you want?"

"One of the things that have undoubtedly contributed to the success of Mme Berma," said M. de Norpois, turning with application towards my mother, so as not to leave her out of the conversation, and in conscientious fulfilment of his duty of politeness to the lady of the house, "is the perfect taste that she shows in her choice of roles, which always assures her of complete success, and success of the right sort. She hardly ever appears in anything trivial. Look how she has thrown herself into the part of Phèdre. And then, she brings the same good taste to the choice of her costumes, and to her acting. In spite of her frequent and lucrative tours in England and America, the vulgarity—I will not say of John Bull, which would be unjust, at any rate as regards the England of the Victorian era—but of Uncle Sam has not infected her. No loud colours, no rant. And then that admirable voice, which serves her so well and upon which she plays so ravishingly—I should almost be tempted to describe it as a musical instrument!"

My interest in Berma's acting had continued to grow ever since the fall of the curtain because it was no longer compressed within the limits of reality; but I felt the need to find explanations for it; moreover it had been concentrated with equal intensity, while Berma was on the stage, upon everything that she offered, in the indivisibility of a living whole, to my eyes and ears; it had made no attempt to separate or discriminate; accordingly it welcomed the discovery of a reasonable cause for itself in these tributes paid to the simplicity, to the good taste of the actress, it drew them to itself by its power of absorption, seized upon them as the optimism of a drunken man seizes upon the actions of his neighbour, in each of which he finds an excuse for maudlin emotion. "It's true!" I told myself, "what a beautiful voice, what an absence of shrillness, what simple costumes, what intelligence to have chosen *Phèdre*! No, I have not been disappointed!"

The cold spiced beef with carrots made its appearance, couched by the Michelangelo of our kitchen upon enormous crystals of aspic, like transparent blocks of quartz.

"You have a first-rate cook, Madame," said M. de Norpois, "and that is no small matter. I myself, who have had, when abroad, to maintain a certain style in housekeeping, I know how difficult it often is to find a perfect chef. This is a positive banquet that you have set before us!"

And indeed Françoise, in the excitement of her ambition to make a success, for so distinguished a guest, of a dinner the preparation of which had been sown with difficulties worthy of her powers, had put herself out as she no longer did when we were alone, and had recaptured her incomparable Combray manner.

"That is a thing you don't get in a chophouse, not even in the best of them: a spiced beef in which the aspic doesn't taste of glue and the beef has caught the flavour of the carrots. It's admirable! Allow me to come again," he went on, making a sign to show that he wanted more of the aspic. "I should be interested to see how your chef managed a dish of quite a different kind; I should like, for instance, to see him tackle a *bœuf Stroganoff*."

To add his own contribution to the pleasures of the repast, M. de Norpois entertained us with a number of the stories with which he was in the habit of regaling his diplomatic colleagues, quoting now some ludicrous period uttered by a politician notorious for long sentences packed with incoherent images, now some lapidary epigram of a diplomat sparkling with Attic salt. But, to tell the truth, the criterion which for him set the two kinds of sentence apart in no way resembled that which I was in the habit of applying to literature. Most of the finer shades escaped me; the words which he recited with derision seemed to me not to differ very greatly from those which he found remarkable. He belonged to the class of men who, had we come to discuss the books I liked, would have said: "So you understand that, do you? I must confess that I don't; I'm not initiated," but I could have retaliated in kind, for I did not grasp the wit or folly, the eloquence or pomposity which he found in a retort or in a speech, and the absence of any perceptible reason for this being good and that bad made that sort of literature seem more mysterious, more obscure to me than any other. All that I grasped was that to repeat what everybody else was thinking was, in politics, the mark not of an inferior but of a superior mind. When M. de Norpois used certain expressions which were common currency in the newspapers, and uttered them with emphasis, one felt that they became an official pronouncement by the mere fact of his having employed them, and a pronouncement which would provoke widespread comment.

My mother was counting greatly upon the pineapple and truffle salad. But the Ambassador, after fastening for a moment on the confection the penetrating gaze of a trained observer, ate it with the inscrutable discretion of a diplomat, without disclosing his opinion. My mother insisted on his taking some more, which he did, but saying only, in place of the compliment for which she was hoping: "I obey, Madame, for I can see that it is, on your part, a positive ukase."

"We saw in the papers that you had a long talk with King Theodosius," my father ventured.

"Why, yes, the King, who has a wonderful memory for faces, was kind enough to remember, when he noticed me in the stalls, that I had had the honour to meet him on several occasions at the Court of Bavaria, at a time when he had never dreamed of his oriental throne—to which, as you know, he was summoned by a European Congress, and indeed had grave doubts about accepting, regarding that particular sovereignty as unworthy of his race, the noblest, heraldically speaking, in the whole of Europe. An aide-de-camp came down to bid me pay my respects to His Majesty, whose command I hastened, naturally, to obey."

"And I trust you are satisfied with the results of his visit?"

"Enchanted! One was justified in feeling some apprehension as to the manner in which a sovereign who is still so young would handle such an awkward situation, particularly at this highly delicate juncture. For my own part, I had complete confidence in the King's political sense. But I must confess that he far surpassed my expectations. The speech that he made at the Elysée, which, according to information that has come to me from a most authoritative source, was composed from beginning to end by the King himself, was fully deserving of the interest that it has aroused in all quarters. It was simply masterly; a trifle daring, I quite admit, but it was an audacity which, after all, was fully justified by the event. Traditional diplomacy is all very well in its way, but in practice it has made his country and ours live in a hermetically sealed atmosphere in which it was no longer possible to breathe. Very well! There is one method of letting in fresh air, obviously not a method that one could officially recommend, but one which King Theodosius could allow himself to adopt—and that is to break the windows. Which he accordingly did, with a spontaneous good humour that delighted everybody, and also with an aptness in his choice of words in which one could at once detect the race of scholarly princes from whom he is descended through his mother. There can be no question that when he spoke of the 'affinities' that bind his country to France, the expression, unusual though it be in the vocabulary of the chancelleries, was a singularly happy one. You see that literary ability is no drawback, even in diplomacy, even upon a throne," he added, turning to me. "The community of interests had long been apparent, I quite admit, and relations between the two powers were excellent. Still, it needed saying. The word was awaited; it was chosen with marvellous aptitude; you have seen the effect it had. For my part, I thoroughly applaud it."

"Your friend M. de Vaugoubert will be pleased, after preparing for the agreement all these years."

"All the more so in that His Majesty, who is quite incorrigible in some ways, had taken care to spring it on him as a surprise. And it did come as a complete surprise, incidentally, to everyone concerned, beginning with the Foreign Minister himself, who—I have heard—did not find it at all to his liking. It appears that when someone spoke to him about it he replied pretty sharply, and loud enough to be overheard by people in the vicinity: 'I was neither consulted nor informed,' indicating clearly that he declined to accept any responsibility in the matter. I must own that the incident has caused a great furore, and I should not go so far as to deny," he went on with a mischievous smile, "that certain of my colleagues, who are only too inclined to take the line of least resistance, may have been shaken from their habitual repose. As for Vaugoubert, you are aware that he has been bitterly attacked for his policy of bringing that country into closer relations with France, and this must have been more than ordinarily painful to him since he is a sensitive and tender-hearted man. I can amply testify to that, since, for all that he is considerably my junior, I have had many dealings with him, we are friends of long standing and I know him intimately. Besides, who could help knowing him? His is a heart of crystal. Indeed, that is the one fault to be found with him; it is not necessary for the heart of a diplomat to be as transparent as his. Nevertheless there is talk of his being sent to Rome, which would be a splendid promotion, but a pretty big plum to swallow. Between ourselves, I fancy that Vaugoubert, utterly devoid of ambition as he is, would be extremely pleased, and would by no means ask for that cup to pass from him. For all we know, he may do wonders down there; he is the chosen candidate of the Consulta, and for my part I can see him perfectly well, with his artistic leanings, in the setting of the Farnese Palace and the Caracci Gallery. You would suppose that at least it was impossible for anyone to hate him; but there is a whole camarilla collected round King Theodosius which is more or less pledged to the Wilhelmstrasse, whose suggestions it slavishly follows, and which did everything in its power to spike his guns. Not only did Vaugoubert have to face these backstairs intrigues, he also had to endure the insults of a gang of paid hacks who later on, being like every hireling journalist the most arrant cowards, were the first to cry quits, but in the interval did not shrink from hurling at our representative the most fatuous accusations that the wit of irresponsible fools could invent. For a month and more Vaugoubert's enemies danced around him howling for his scalp" (M. de Norpois detached this word with sharp emphasis). "But forewarned is forearmed; he treated their insults with the contempt they deserved," he added even more forcibly, and with so fierce a glare in his eye that for a moment we forgot our food. "In the words of a fine Arab proverb, 'The dogs bark, but the caravan moves on!' "

After launching this quotation M. de Norpois paused and examined our faces, to see what effect it had had upon us. The effect was great, the proverb being familiar to us already. It had taken the place, that year, among the men of consequence, of "He who sows the wind shall reap the whirlwind," which was sorely in need of a rest, not having the perennial freshness of "Working for the King of Prussia." For the culture of these eminent men was an alternating one, usually triennial. Of course, the use of quotations such as these, with which M. de Norpois excelled in sprinkling his articles in the *Revue*, was in no way essential to their appearing sound and well-informed. Even without the ornament which the quotations supplied, it sufficed that M. de Norpois should write at a suitable point (as he never failed to do): "The Court of St James was not the last to be sensible of the peril," or "Feeling ran high on the Singers' Bridge, where the selfish but skilful policy of the Dual Monarchy was being followed with anxious eyes," or "A cry of alarm sounded from Montecitorio," or yet again, "That perpetual double dealing which is so characteristic of the Ballplatz."[2] By these expressions the lay reader had at once recognised and acknowledged the career diplomat. But what had made people say that he was something more than that, that he was endowed with a superior culture, had been his judicious use of quotations, the perfect example of which, at that date, was still: "Give me a good policy and I will give you good finances, to quote the favourite words of Baron Louis": for we had not yet imported from the Far East: "Victory is on the side that can hold out a quarter of an hour longer than the other, as the Japanese say." This reputation as a literary man, combined with a positive genius for intrigue which he concealed beneath a mask of indifference, had secured the election of M. de Norpois to the Académie des Sciences Morales. And there were some who even thought that he would not be out of place in the Académie Française, on the famous day when, wishing to indicate that it was only by strengthening the Russian Alliance that we could hope to arrive at an understanding with Great Britain, he had not hesitated to write: "Let it be clearly understood in the Quai d'Orsay, let it be taught henceforward in all the manuals of geography, which appear to be incomplete in this respect, let his certificate of graduation be remorselessly withheld from every candidate who has not learned to say, 'If all roads lead to Rome, on the other hand the way from Paris to London runs of necessity through St Petersburg.' "

"In short," M. de Norpois went on, addressing my father, "Vaugoubert has brought off a considerable triumph, and one that even surpassed his expectations. He expected, you understand, a formal toast (which, after the storm-clouds of recent years, would have been already an achievement) but nothing more. Several persons who had the honour to be present have assured me that it is impossible merely from reading the speech to form any conception of the effect that it produced when articulated with marvellous clearness of diction by the King, who is a master of the art of public speaking and underlined in passing every delicate intention, every subtle courtesy. In this connection, one of my informants told me a little anecdote which brings out once again that frank, boyish charm by which King Theodosius has won so many hearts. I am assured that, precisely at that word 'affinities,' which was, on the whole, the great innovation of the speech, and one that, you will see, will be the talk of the chancelleries for years to come, His Majesty, anticipating the delight of our ambassador, who would see it as the just consummation of his efforts—of his dreams, one might almost say—and, in a word, his marshal's baton, made a half turn towards Vaugoubert and fixing upon him the arresting gaze so characteristic of the Oettingens, brought out that admirably chosen word 'affinities,' a veritable brain-wave, in a tone which made it plain to all his hearers that it was employed of set purpose and with full knowledge of its implications. It appears that Vaugoubert found some difficulty in mastering his emotion, and I must confess that, to a certain extent, I can well understand it. Indeed, a person worthy of absolute credence confided to me that the King came up to Vaugoubert after the dinner, when His Majesty was holding informal court, and was heard to say, 'Are you satisfied with your pupil, my dear Marquis?' "

"One thing, however," M. de Norpois concluded, "is certain; and that is that a speech of such a nature has done more than twenty years of negotiation towards bringing the two countries together, uniting their 'affinities,' to borrow the picturesque expression of Theodosius II. It is no more than a word, if you like, but look what success it has had, how the whole of the European press is repeating it, what interest it has aroused, what a new note it has struck. Besides, it is entirely in keeping with the young sovereign's style. I will not go so far as to say that he lights upon a diamond of that water every day. But it is very seldom, that, in his prepared speeches, or better still in the spontaneous flow of his conversation, he does not reveal his character—I was on the point of saying 'does not affix his signature'—by the use of some incisive word. I myself am quite free from any suspicion of partiality in this respect since I am opposed to all innovations in terminology. Nine times out of ten they are most dangerous."

"Yes, I was thinking only the other day that the recent telegram from the Emperor of Germany could not be much to your liking," said my father.

M. de Norpois raised his eyes to heaven, as who should say, "Oh, that fellow!" before he replied: "In the first place, it is an act of ingratitude. It is more than a crime, it's a blunder, and one of a crassness which I can describe only as pyramidal! Indeed, unless someone puts a check on his activities, the man who got rid of Bismarck is quite capable of repudiating by degrees the whole of the Bismarckian policy; after which it will be a leap in the dark."

"My husband tells me, Monsieur, that you may perhaps take him to Spain one summer. I'm delighted for his sake."

"Why yes, it's an idea that greatly appeals to me. I should very much like to make this journey with you, my dear fellow. And you, Madame, have you decided yet how you are going to spend your holidays?"

"I shall perhaps go with my son to Balbec, but I'm not certain."

"Ah! Balbec is quite charming. I was down that way a few years ago. They are beginning to build some very attractive little villas there; I think you'll like the place. But may I ask what made you choose Balbec?"

"My son is very anxious to visit some of the churches in that neighbourhood, and Balbec church in particular. I was a little afraid that the tiring journey there and the discomfort of staying in the place might be too much for his health. But I hear that they have just opened an excellent hotel, in which he will be able to get all the comfort that he requires."

"Indeed! I must make a note of that for a certain person who will not turn up her nose at a comfortable hotel."

"The church at Balbec is very beautiful, is it not, Monsieur?" I inquired, repressing my sorrow at learning that one of the attractions of Balbec consisted in its pretty little villas.

"No, it's not bad; but it cannot be compared for a moment with such positive jewels in stone as the cathedrals of Rheims and Chartres, or with what is to my mind the pearl among them all, the Sainte-Chapelle here in Paris."

"But Balbec church is partly Romanesque, is it not?"

"Why, yes, it is in the Romanesque style, which is to say very cold and lifeless, with not the slightest hint of the grace, the fantasy of the later Gothic builders, who worked their stone as if it had been so much lace. Balbec church is well worth a visit if one is in the neighbourhood; it is decidedly quaint. On a wet day, when you have nothing better to do, you might look inside; you'll see the tomb of Tourville."[3]

"Tell me, were you at the Foreign Ministry dinner last night?" asked my father. "I couldn't go."

"No," M. de Norpois smiled, "I must confess that I renounced it for a party of a very different sort. I was dining with a lady of whom you may possibly have heard, the beautiful Mme Swann."

My mother repressed a shudder of apprehension, for, being more rapid in perception than my father, she grew alarmed on his account over things which only began to vex him a moment later. Whatever might cause him annoyance was first noticed by her, just as bad news of France is always known abroad sooner than among ourselves. But being curious to know what sort of people the Swanns might entertain, she inquired of M. de Norpois as to whom he had met there.

"Why, my dear lady, it is a house which (or so it struck me) is especially attractive to . . . gentlemen. There were several married men there last night, but their wives were all, as it happened, unwell, and so had not come with them," replied the Ambassador with a slyness veiled by good-humour, casting round the table a glance the gentleness and discretion of which appeared to be tempering while in reality intensifying its malice.

"In all fairness," he went on, "I must add that women do go to the house, but women who . . . belong rather—what shall I say—to the Republican world than to Swann's" (he pronounced it "Svann's") "circle. Who knows? Perhaps it will turn into a political or a literary salon some day. Anyhow, they appear to be quite content as they are. Indeed, I feel that Swann advertises his contentment just a trifle too blatantly. He told us the names of all the people who had asked him and his wife out for the next week, people whose friendship there is no reason to be proud of, with a want of reserve, of taste, almost of tact, which I was astonished to remark in so refined a man. He kept on repeating, 'We haven't a free evening!' as though that was a thing to boast of, positively like a parvenu, and he is certainly not that. For Swann had always plenty of friends, women as well as men, and without seeming over-bold, without the least wish to appear indiscreet, I think I may safely say that not all of them, of course, nor even the majority of them, but one at least, who is a lady of the very highest rank, would perhaps not have shown herself inexorably averse from the idea of entering into relations with Mme Swann, in which case it is safe to assume that more than one sheep of the social flock would have followed her lead. But it seems that there has been no indication of any approach on Swann's part in that direction . . . What do I see? A Nesselrode pudding! As well! I declare I shall need a course at Carlsbad after such a Lucullan feast as this . . . Possibly Swann felt that there would be too much resistance to overcome. The marriage—so much is certain—was not well received. There has been some talk of his wife's having money, but that's the grossest fallacy. At all events, the whole affair has been looked upon with disfavour. And then, Swann has an aunt who is excessively rich and in an admirable position socially, married to a man who, financially speaking, is a power in the land. Not only did she refuse to meet Mme Swann, she conducted an out-and-out campaign to force her friends and acquaintances to do the same. I don't mean to say that any well-bred Parisian has shown actual incivility to Mme Swann . . . No! A hundred times no! Quite apart from her husband's being eminently a man to take up the gauntlet. At all events, the odd thing is to see the alacrity with which Swann, who knows so many of the most select people, cultivates a society of which the best that can be said is that it is extremely mixed. I myself, who knew him in the old days, must admit that I felt more astonished than amused at seeing a man so well-bred as he, so much at home in the most exclusive circles, effusively thanking the Principal Private Secretary to the Minister of Posts for coming to their house, and asking him whether Mme Swann might *take the liberty* of calling upon his wife. He must feel like a fish out of water, don't you know; obviously, it's quite a different world. All the same, I don't think Swann is unhappy. It's true that for some years before the marriage she was always trying to blackmail him in a rather disgraceful way; she would take the child away whenever Swann refused her anything. Poor Swann, who is as ingenuous as he is in other ways discerning, believed every time that the child's disappearance was a coincidence, and declined to face the facts. Apart from that, she made such continual scenes that everyone expected that, as soon as she achieved her object and was safely married, nothing could possibly restrain her and that their life would be a hell on earth. Instead of which, just the opposite has happened. People are inclined to laugh at the way Swann speaks of his wife; it's become a standing joke. Of course one hardly expected that, more or less aware of being . . . (you know Molière's word),[4] he would go and proclaim it *urbi et orbi*; all the same, people find it a little excessive when he says that she's an excellent wife. And yet that is not so far from the truth as people imagine. In her own way—which is not, perhaps, what all husbands would choose, but then, between you and me, I find it difficult to believe that Swann, who has known her for a long time and is far from being an utter fool, did not know what to expect—there can be no denying that she does seem to have a certain regard for him. I don't say she isn't flighty, and Swann himself is not noted for his constancy, if one is to believe the charitable tongues which, as you may suppose, continue to wag. But she is grateful to him for what he has done for her, and, contrary to the fears that were generally expressed, her temper seems to have become angelic."

This alteration was perhaps not so extraordinary as M. de Norpois professed to find it. Odette had not believed that Swann would ever consent to marry her; each time she made the tendentious announcement that some man about town had just married his mistress she had seen him stiffen into a glacial silence, or at the most, if she challenged him directly by asking: "Don't you think it's very good and very right, what he's done for a woman who sacrificed all her youth to him?" had heard him answer dryly: "But I don't say that there's anything wrong in it. Everyone does as he thinks fit." She came very near, indeed, to believing that (as he used to threaten in moments of anger) he would leave her altogether, for she had heard it said, not long since, by a woman sculptor, that "You can't be surprised at anything men do, they're such cads," and impressed by the profundity of this pessimistic maxim she had appropriated it for herself, and repeated it on every possible occasion with a despondent air that seemed to imply: "After all, it's not at all impossible; it would be just my luck." Meanwhile all the virtue had gone from the optimistic maxim which had hitherto guided Odette through life: "You can do anything with men when they're in love with you, they're such idiots!", a doctrine which was expressed on her face by the same flicker of the eyelids that might have accompanied such words as: "Don't be frightened; he won't break anything." While she waited, Odette was tormented by the thought of what such and such a friend of hers, who had been married by a man who had not lived with her for nearly so long as she herself had lived with Swann, and had no child by him, and who was now relatively esteemed, invited to balls at the Elysée and so forth, must think of Swann's behaviour. A consultant more discerning than M. de Norpois would doubtless have been able to diagnose that it was this feeling of shame and humiliation that had embittered Odette, that the infernal temper she displayed was not an essential part of her nature, was not an incurable disease, and so would easily have foretold what had indeed come to pass, namely that a new regimen, that of matrimony, would put an end with almost magic swiftness to those painful incidents, of daily occurrence but in no sense organic. Almost everyone was surprised at the marriage, and that in itself is surprising. No doubt very few people understand the purely subjective nature of the phenomenon that we call love, or how it creates, so to speak, a supplementary person, distinct from the person whom the world knows by the same name, a person most of whose constituent elements are derived from ourselves. And so there are very few who can regard as natural the enormous proportions that a person comes to assume in our eyes who is not the same as the person that they see. It would seem, none the less, that so far as Odette was concerned people could have taken into account the fact that if, indeed, she had never entirely understood Swann's mentality, at least she was acquainted with the titles and with all the details of his studies, so much so that the name of Vermeer was as familiar to her as that of her own dressmaker; while as for Swann himself, she knew intimately those traits of character of which the rest of the world is ignorant or which it scoffs at, and of which only a mistress or a sister possesses the true and cherished image; and so strongly are we attached to such idiosyncrasies, even to those of them which we are most anxious to correct, that it is because a woman comes in time to acquire an indulgent, an affectionately mocking familiarity with them, such as we ourselves or our relatives have, that love affairs of long standing have something of the sweetness and strength of family affection. The bonds that unite us to another human being are sanctified when he or she adopts the same point of view as ourselves in judging one of our imperfections. And among these special traits there were others, besides, which belonged as much to Swann's intellect as to his character, but which nevertheless, because they had their roots in the latter, Odette had been able more easily to discern. She complained that when Swann turned author, when he published his essays, these characteristics were not to be found in them to the same extent as in his letters or in his conversation, where they abounded. She urged him to give them a more prominent place. She wanted this because it was these things that she herself most liked in him, but since she liked them because they were the things most typical of him, she was perhaps not wrong in wishing that they might be found in his writings. Perhaps also she thought that his work, if endowed with more vitality, so that it ultimately brought him success, might enable her also to form what at the Verdurins' she had been taught to value above everything else in the world—a salon.

Among the people to whom this sort of marriage appeared ridiculous, people who in their own case would ask themselves, "What will M. de Guermantes think, what will Bréauté say, when I marry Mlle de Montmorency?", among the people who cherished that sort of social ideal, would have figured, twenty years earlier, Swann himself, the Swann who had taken endless pains to get himself elected to the Jockey Club and had reckoned at that time on making a brilliant marriage which, by consolidating his position, would have made him one of the most prominent figures in Paris. However, the visions which such a marriage suggests to the mind of the interested party need, like all visions, if they are not to fade away and be altogether lost, to receive sustenance from without. Your most ardent longing is to humiliate the man who has insulted you. But if you never hear of him any more, having removed to some other place, your enemy will come to have no longer the slightest importance to you. If for twenty years one has lost sight of all the people on whose account one would have liked to be elected to the Jockey Club or the Institute, the prospect of becoming a member of one or other of those establishments will have ceased to tempt one. Now, fully as much as retirement, ill-health or religious conversion, a protracted love affair will substitute fresh visions for the old. There was no renunciation on Swann's part, when he married Odette, of his social ambitions, for from those ambitions Odette had long ago, in the spiritual sense of the word, detached him. Besides, had he not been so detached, his marriage would have been all the more creditable. It is because they entail the sacrifice of a more or less advantageous position to a purely private happiness that, as a general rule, ignominious marriages are the most estimable of all. (One cannot very well include among ignominious marriages those that are made for money, there being no instance on record of a couple, of whom the wife or else the husband has thus sold himself, who have not sooner or later been admitted into society, if only by tradition, and on the strength of so many precedents, and so as not to have, as it were, one law for the rich and another for the poor.) Perhaps, on the other hand, the artistic, if not the perverse side of Swann's nature would in any event have derived a certain pleasure from coupling himself, in one of those crossings of species such as Mendelians practise and mythology records, with a creature of a different race, archduchess or prostitute—from contracting a royal alliance or marrying beneath him. There had been but one person in all the world whose opinion he took into consideration whenever he thought of his possible marriage with Odette; this was, and from no snobbish motive, the Duchesse de Guermantes—with whom Odette, on the contrary, was but little concerned, thinking only of those people whose position was immediately above her own rather than in so vague an empyrean. But when Swann in his day-dreams saw Odette as already his wife he invariably pictured to himself the moment when he would take her—her, and above all his daughter—to call upon the Princesse des Laumes (who was shortly, on the death of her father-in-law, to become Duchesse de Guermantes). He had no desire to introduce them anywhere else, but his heart would soften as he imagined—articulating to himself their actual words—all the things that the Duchess would say of him to Odette, and Odette to the Duchess, the affection that she would show for Gilberte, spoiling her, making him proud of his child. He enacted to himself the scene of this introduction with the same precision in each of its imaginary details that people show when they consider how they would spend, supposing they were to win it, a lottery prize the amount of which they have arbitrarily determined. In so far as a mental picture which accompanies one of our resolutions may be said to motivate it, so it might be said that if Swann married Odette it was in order to introduce her, together with Gilberte, without anyone else being present, without, if need be, anyone else ever coming to know of it, to the Duchesse de Guermantes. We shall see how this sole social ambition that he had entertained for his wife and daughter was precisely the one whose realisation proved to be forbidden him, by a veto so absolute that Swann died in the belief that the Duchess could never come to know them. We shall see too that, on the contrary, the Duchesse de Guermantes did strike up a friendship with Odette and Gilberte after Swann's death. And doubtless he would have been wiser—in so far as he could attach such importance to so small a matter—not to have formed too dark a picture of the future in this connexion, but to have consoled himself with the hope that the desired meeting might indeed take place when he was no longer there to enjoy it. The laborious process of causation which sooner or later will bring about every possible effect, including, consequently, those which one had believed to be least possible, naturally slow at times, is rendered slower still by our desire (which in seeking to accelerate only obstructs it), by our very existence, and comes to fruition only when we have ceased to desire, and sometimes ceased to live. Was not Swann conscious of this from his own experience, and was there not already in his lifetime—as it were a prefiguration of what was to happen after his death—a posthumous happiness in this marriage with Odette whom he had passionately loved—even if she had not attracted him at first sight—whom he had married when he no longer loved her, when the person who, in Swann, had so longed to live and so despaired of living all his life with Odette, when that person was dead?

I began to talk about the Comte de Paris, to ask whether he was not one of Swann's friends, for I was afraid lest the conversation should drift away from him.

"Why, yes!" replied M. de Norpois, turning towards me and fixing upon my modest person the azure gaze in which there floated, as in their vital element, his immense capacity for work and his power of assimilation. "And upon my word," he added, once more addressing my father, "I do not think that I shall be over-stepping the bounds of the respect which I have always professed for the Prince (without, however, maintaining any personal relations with him, which would inevitably compromise my position, unofficial though it may now be) if I tell you of a little episode which is not unintriguing. No more than four years ago, at a small railway station in one of the countries of Central Europe, the Prince happened to set eyes on Mme Swann. Naturally, none of his circle ventured to ask His Royal Highness what he thought of her. That would not have been seemly. But when her name came up by chance in conversation, by certain signs—barely perceptible, if you like, but quite unmistakable—the Prince appeared willing enough to let it be understood that his impression of her had on the whole been far from unfavourable."

"But there could have been no possibility, surely, of her being presented to the Comte de Paris?" inquired my father.

"Well, we don't know; with princes one never does know," replied M. de Norpois. "The most exalted, those who know best how to secure what is due to them, are as often as not the last to let themselves be embarrassed by the decrees of popular opinion, even by those for which there is most justification, especially when it is a question of their rewarding a personal attachment to themselves. And it is certain that the Comte de Paris has always most graciously acknowledged the devotion of Swann, who is moreover a man of wit if ever there was one."

"And what was your own impression, Your Excellency?" my mother asked, from politeness as well as from curiosity.

All the vigour of an old connoisseur broke through the habitual moderation of his speech as he answered: "Quite excellent!"

And knowing that the admission that a strong impression has been made on one by a woman takes its place, provided that one makes it in a playful tone, in a certain form of the art of conversation that is highly appreciated, he broke into a little laugh that lasted for several moments, moistening the old diplomat's blue eyes and making his nostrils, with their network of tiny scarlet veins, quiver. "She is altogether charming!"

"Was there a writer of the name of Bergotte at this dinner, Monsieur?" I asked timidly, still trying to keep the conversation to the subject of the Swanns.

"Yes, Bergotte was there," replied M. de Norpois, inclining his head courteously towards me, as though in his desire to be agreeable to my father he attached to everything connected with him a genuine importance, even to the questions of a boy of my age who was not accustomed to see such politeness shown to him by persons of his. "Do you know him?" he went on, fastening on me that clear gaze the penetration of which had won the admiration of Bismarck.

"My son does not know him, but he admires his work immensely," my mother explained.

"Good heavens!" exclaimed M. de Norpois, inspiring me with doubts of my own intelligence far graver than those that ordinarily tormented me, when I saw that what I valued a thousand times more than myself, what I regarded as the most exalted thing in the world, was for him at the bottom of the scale of admiration, "I do not share your son's point of view. Bergotte is what I call a flute-player: one must admit that he plays very agreeably, although with a great deal of mannerism, of affectation. But when all is said, there's no more to it than that, and that is not much. Nowhere does one find in his flaccid works what one might call structure. No action—or very little—but above all no range. His books fail at the foundation, or rather they have no foundation at all. At a time like the present, when the ever-increasing complexity of life leaves one scarcely a moment for reading, when the map of Europe has undergone radical alterations and is on the eve, perhaps, of undergoing others more drastic still, when so many new and threatening problems are arising on every side, you will allow me to suggest that one is entitled to ask that a writer should be something more than a clever fellow who lulls us into forgetting, amid otiose and byzantine discussions of the merits of pure form, that we may be overwhelmed at any moment by a double tide of barbarians, those from without and those from within our borders. I am aware that this is to blaspheme against the sacrosanct school of what these gentlemen term 'Art for Art's sake,' but at this period of history there are tasks more urgent than the manipulation of words in a harmonious manner. I don't deny that Bergotte's manner can be quite seductive at times, but taken as a whole, it is all very precious, very thin, and altogether lacking in virility. I can now understand more easily, when I bear in mind your altogether excessive regard for Bergotte, the few lines that you showed me just now, which it would be ungracious of me not to overlook, since you yourself told me in all simplicity that they were merely a childish scribble." (I had indeed said so, but I did not mean a word of it.) "For every sin there is forgiveness, and especially for the sins of youth. After all, others as well as yourself have such sins upon their conscience, and you are not the only one who has believed himself a poet in his idle moments. But one can see in what you showed me the unfortunate influence of Bergotte. You will not, of course, be surprised when I say that it had none of his qualities, since he is a past-master in the art—entirely superficial by the by—of handling a certain style of which, at your age, you cannot have acquired even the rudiments. But already there is the same fault, that nonsense of stringing together fine-sounding words and only afterwards troubling about what they mean. That is putting the cart before the horse. Even in Bergotte's books, all those Chinese puzzles of form, all those subtleties of a deliquescent mandarin seem to me to be quite futile. Given a few fireworks let off prettily enough by an author, and up goes the shout of masterpiece. Masterpieces are not so common as all that! Bergotte cannot place to his credit—does not carry in his baggage, if I may use the expression—a single novel that is at all lofty in its conception, one of those books which one keeps in a special corner of one's library. I cannot think of one such in the whole of his work. But that does not mean that, in his case, the work is not infinitely superior to the author. Ah! there's a man who justifies the wit who insisted that one ought never to know an author except through his books. It would be impossible to imagine an individual who corresponded less to his—more pretentious, more pompous, more ill-bred. Vulgar at times, at others talking like a book, and not even like one of his own, but like a boring book, which his, to do them justice, are not—such is your Bergotte. He has the most confused and convoluted mind, what our forebears called sesquipedalian, and he makes the things that he says even more unpleasing by the manner in which he says them. I forget for the moment whether it is Loménie or Sainte-Beuve who tells us that Vigny repelled people by the same failing. But Bergotte has never given us a *Cinq-Mars*, or a *Cachet rouge*, certain pages of which are veritable anthology pieces."

Shattered by what M. de Norpois had just said to me with regard to the fragment which I had submitted to him, and remembering at the same time the difficulties that I experienced when I attempted to write an essay or merely to devote myself to serious thought, I felt conscious once again of my intellectual nullity and that I was not cut out for the literary life. Doubtless in the old days at Combray certain impressions of a very humble order, or a few pages of Bergotte, had plunged me into a state of reverie which had appeared to me to be of great value. But this state was what my prose poem reflected; there could be no doubt that M. de Norpois had at once grasped and seen through the fallacy of what I had thought to be beautiful simply through a deceptive mirage, since the Ambassador had not been taken in by it. He had shown me, on the contrary, what an infinitely unimportant place was mine when I was judged from outside, objectively, by the best-disposed and most intelligent of experts. I felt dismayed, diminished; and my mind, like a fluid which is without dimensions save those of the vessel that is provided for it, just as it had expanded in the past to fill the vast capacity of genius, contracted now, was entirely contained within the straitened mediocrity in which M. de Norpois had of a sudden enclosed and sealed it.

"Our first introduction—I speak of Bergotte and myself," he resumed, turning to my father, "was somewhat beset with thorns (which is, after all, only another way of saying that it was piquant). Bergotte—some years ago, now—paid a visit to Vienna while I was Ambassador there; he was introduced to me by the Princess Metternich, came and wrote his name in the Embassy book, and made it known that he wished to be invited. Now, being when abroad the representative of France, to which he has after all done some honour by his writings, to a certain extent (let us say, to be precise, to a very slight extent), I was prepared to set aside the unfavourable opinion that I hold of his private life. But he was not travelling alone, and moreover he let it be understood that he was not to be invited without his companion. I trust that I am no more of a prude than most men, and, being a bachelor, I was perhaps in a position to throw open the doors of the Embassy a little wider than if I had been married and the father of a family. Nevertheless, I confess that there are depths of ignominy to which I refuse to accommodate myself and which are made more repulsive still by the tone, more than just moral, but frankly moralising, that Bergotte adopts in his books, where one finds nothing but perpetual and, between ourselves, somewhat wearisome analyses, painful scruples, morbid remorse, and, for the merest peccadilloes, veritable preachifying (one knows what that's worth), while all the time he is showing such frivolity and cynicism in his private life. To cut a long story short, I avoided answering, the Princess returned to the charge, but with no greater success. So that I do not suppose that I appear exactly in the odour of sanctity to the gentleman, and I am not sure how far he appreciated Swann's kindness in inviting him and myself on the same evening. Unless of course it was he who asked for the invitation. One can never tell, for really he is a sick man. Indeed that is his sole excuse."

"And was Mme Swann's daughter at the dinner?" I asked M. de Norpois, taking advantage, to put this question, of a moment in which, as we all moved towards the drawing-room, I could more easily conceal my emotion than would have been possible at table, where I was held fast in the glare of the lamplight.

M. de Norpois appeared to be trying for a moment to remember:

"Ah, yes, you mean a young person of fourteen or fifteen? Yes, of course, I remember now that she was introduced to me before dinner as the daughter of our Amphitryon. I'm afraid that I saw little of her; she retired to bed early. Or else she went out to see some friends—I forget which. But I can see that you are very intimate with the Swann household."

"I play with Mlle Swann in the Champs-Elysées, and she's delightful."

"Oh! so that's it? But I assure you, I too thought her charming. I must confess to you, however, that I do not believe that she will ever come anywhere near her mother, if I may say as much without hurting your feelings."

"I prefer Mlle Swann's face, but I admire her mother, too, enormously. I go for walks in the Bois simply in the hope of seeing her pass."

"Ah! But I must tell them that; they will be highly flattered."

While he was uttering these words, and for a few seconds after he had uttered them, M. de Norpois was still in the same position as anyone else who, hearing me speak of Swann as an intelligent man, of his family as respectable stockbrokers, of his house as a fine house, imagined that I would speak just as readily of another man equally intelligent, of other stockbrokers equally respectable, of another house equally fine; it was the moment in which a sane man who is talking to a lunatic has not yet perceived that he is a lunatic. M. de Norpois knew that there is nothing unnatural in the pleasure one derives from looking at pretty women, that it is good manners, when someone speaks to you of a pretty woman with any warmth, to pretend to think that he is in love with her, and to promise to further his designs. But in saying that he would speak of me to Gilberte and her mother (which would enable me, like an Olympian deity who has taken on the fluidity of a breath of wind, or rather the aspect of the old greybeard whose form Minerva borrows, to insinuate myself, unseen, into Mme Swann's drawing-room, to attract her attention, to occupy her thoughts, to arouse her gratitude for my admiration, to appear before her as the friend of an important person, to seem to her worthy to be invited by her in the future and to enter into the intimate life of her family), this important person who was going to use on my behalf the great influence which he must have with Mme Swann inspired in me suddenly an affection so compelling that I had difficulty in restraining myself from kissing his soft, white, wrinkled hands, which looked as though they had been left lying too long in water. I almost made as if to do so, in an impulsive movement which I believed that I alone had noticed. For it is difficult for any of us to calculate exactly the extent to which our words or gestures are apparent to others. Partly from the fear of exaggerating our own importance, and also because we enlarge to enormous proportions the field over which the impressions formed by other people in the course of their lives are obliged to extend, we imagine that the incidentals of our speech and of our postures scarcely penetrate the consciousness, still less remain in the memory of those with whom we converse. It is, no doubt, to a supposition of this sort that criminals yield when they touch up the wording of a statement already made, thinking that the new variant cannot be confronted with any existing version. But it is quite possible that, even with respect to the millennial existence of the human race, the philosophy of the journalist, according to which everything is doomed to oblivion, is less true than a contrary philosophy which would predict the conservation of everything. In the same newspaper in which the moralist of the leader column says to us of an event, of a work of art, *a fortiori* of a singer who has enjoyed her "hour of fame": "Who will remember this in ten years' time?", does not the report of the Académie des Inscriptions overleaf speak often of a fact in itself of smaller importance, of a poem of little merit, which dates from the epoch of the Pharaohs and is still known in its entirety? Perhaps this does not quite hold true for the brief life of a human being. And yet, some years later, in a house in which M. de Norpois, who was also a guest there, seemed to me the most solid support that I could hope to find, because he was a friend of my father, indulgent, inclined to wish us all well, and moreover, by profession and upbringing trained to discretion, when, after the Ambassador had gone, I was told that he had alluded to an evening long ago when he had "seen the moment in which I was about to kiss his hand," not only did I blush to the roots of my hair but I was stupefied to learn how different from what I might have believed was not only the manner in which M. de Norpois spoke of me but also the composition of his memory. This piece of gossip enlightened me as to the incalculable proportions of absence and presence of mind, of recollection and forgetfulness, of which the human mind is composed; and I was as marvellously surprised as on the day on which I read for the first time, in one of Maspero's books, that there existed a precise list of the sportsmen whom Assurbanipal used to invite to his hunts a thousand years before the birth of Christ.

"Oh, Monsieur," I assured M. de Norpois, when he told me that he would inform Gilberte and her mother how much I admired them, "if you would do that, if you would speak of me to Mme Swann my whole life would not be long enough to prove my gratitude, and that life would be all at your service. But I feel bound to point out to you that I do not know Mme Swann, and that I have never been introduced to her."

I had added these last words from a scruple of conscience, and so as not to appear to be boasting of an acquaintance which I did not possess. But as I uttered them I sensed that they were already superfluous, for from the beginning of my speech of thanks, with its chilling ardour, I had seen flitting across the face of the Ambassador an expression of hesitation and displeasure, and in his eyes that vertical, narrow, slanting look (like, in the drawing of a solid body in perspective, the receding line of one of its surfaces), that look which one addresses to the invisible interlocutor whom one has within oneself at the moment when one is telling him something that one's other interlocutor, the person to whom one has been talking up till then—myself, in this instance—is not meant to hear. I realised in a flash that the words I had pronounced, which, feeble as they were when measured against the flood of gratitude that was coursing through me, had seemed to me bound to touch M. de Norpois and to confirm his decision upon an intervention which would have given him so little trouble and me so much joy, were perhaps (out of all those that could have been chosen with diabolical malice by persons anxious to do me harm) the only ones that could result in his abandoning his intention. Indeed, on hearing them, in the same way as when a stranger with whom we have been pleasantly exchanging impressions which we might have supposed to be similar about passers-by whom we agreed in regarding as vulgar, reveals suddenly the pathological abyss that divides him from us by adding carelessly as he feels his pocket: "What a pity I haven't got my revolver with me; I could have picked off the lot of them," M. de Norpois, who knew that nothing was less costly or more simple than to be commended to Mme Swann and taken to her house, and saw that to me, on the contrary, such favours bore so high a price and must consequently be very difficult to obtain, thought that the desire I had expressed, though ostensibly normal, must cloak some different motive, some suspect intention, some prior transgression, on account of which, in the certainty of displeasing Mme Swann, no one had hitherto been willing to undertake the responsibility for conveying a message to her from me. And I realised that this mission was one he would never discharge, that he might see Mme Swann daily, for years to come, without ever mentioning my name. He did indeed ask her, a few days later, for some information which I required, and charged my father to convey it to me. But he had not thought fit to tell her on whose behalf he was inquiring. So she would never discover that I knew M. de Norpois and that I so longed to be asked to her house; and this was perhaps a lesser misfortune than I supposed. For the second of these discoveries would probably not have added much to the efficacy of the first, which was in any event dubious: for Odette, the idea of her own life and of her own home awakened no mysterious uneasiness, and a person who knew her, who came to her house, did not seem to her a fabulous creature such as he seemed to me who would have flung a stone through Swann's windows if I could have written upon it that I knew M. de Norpois; I was convinced that such a message, even when transmitted in so brutal a fashion, would have given me far more prestige in the eyes of the lady of the house than it would have prejudiced her against me. But even if I had been capable of understanding that the mission which M. de Norpois did not perform must have remained futile, indeed that it might have damaged my credit with the Swanns, I should not have had the courage, had he proved himself willing, to relieve the Ambassador of it and to renounce the pleasure—however fatal its consequences might prove—of feeling that my name and my person were thus brought for a moment into Gilberte's presence, into her unknown life and home.

After M. de Norpois had gone my father cast an eye over the evening paper, and I thought once more of Berma. The pleasure which I had experienced in listening to her required all the more to be reinforced in that it had fallen far short of what I had promised myself; and so it at once assimilated everything that was capable of giving it nourishment, for instance those merits which M. de Norpois had ascribed to her and which my mind had imbibed at a single draught, like a dry lawn when water is poured on it. Then my father handed me the newspaper, pointing out to me a paragraph which ran more or less as follows:—

> The performance of *Phèdre*, given this afternoon before an enthusiastic audience which included the foremost representatives of the artistic and critical world, was for Mme Berma, who played the heroine, the occasion of a triumph as brilliant as any that she has known in the course of her phenomenal career. We shall return at greater length to this performance, which is indeed an event in the history of the stage; suffice it to say here that the best qualified judges were unanimous in declaring that this interpretation shed an entirely new light on the role of Phèdre, which is one of the finest and most complex of Racine's creations, and that it constituted the purest and most exalted manifestation of dramatic art which it has been the privilege of our generation to witness.

As soon as my mind had conceived this new idea of "the purest and most exalted manifestation of dramatic art," it, the idea, sped to join the imperfect pleasure which I had felt in the theatre, adding to it a little of what it lacked, and the combination formed something so exalting that I exclaimed to myself: "What a great artist!" It will doubtless be argued that I was not absolutely sincere. But let us bear in mind, rather, the countless writers who, dissatisfied with the passage they have just written, read some eulogy of the genius of Chateaubriand, or evoke the spirit of some great artist whose equal they aspire to be, humming to themselves, for instance, a phrase of Beethoven the melancholy of which they compare with what they have been trying to express in their prose, and become so imbued with this idea of genius that they add it to their own productions when they return to them, no longer see them in the light in which they appeared at first, and, hazarding an act of faith in the value of their work, say to themselves: "After all!" without taking into account that, into the total which determines their ultimate satisfaction, they have introduced the memory of marvellous pages of Chateaubriand which they assimilate to their own but which, after all, they did not write; let us bear in mind the numberless men who believe in the love of a mistress who has done nothing but betray them; all those, too, who are sustained by the alternative hopes, on the one hand of an incomprehensible survival after death, when they think, inconsolable husbands, of the wives whom they have lost but have not ceased to love, or, artists, of the posthumous glory which they may thus enjoy, and on the other of a reassuring void, when their thoughts turn to the misdeeds that otherwise they must expiate after their death; let us bear in mind also the travellers who come home enraptured by the over-all splendour of a journey from which day by day they experienced nothing but tedium; and let us then declare whether, in the communal life that is led by our ideas in the enclosure of our minds, there is a single one of those that makes us most happy which has not first sought, like a real parasite, and won from an alien but neighbouring idea the greater part of the strength that it originally lacked.

My mother appeared none too pleased that my father no longer thought of a diplomatic career for me. I fancy that, anxious above all else that a definite rule of life should discipline the vagaries of my nervous system, what she regretted was not so much seeing me abandon diplomacy as the prospect of my devoting myself to literature. "Don't worry," my father told her, "the main thing is that a man should find pleasure in his work. He's no longer a child. He knows pretty well now what he likes, it's very unlikely that he will change, and he's quite capable of deciding for himself what will make him happy in life."

That evening, as I waited for the time to arrive when, thanks to the freedom of choice which they allowed me, I should or should not begin to be happy in life, my father's words caused me great uneasiness. His unexpected kindnesses, when they occurred, had always made me long to kiss his glowing cheeks above his beard, and if I did not yield to the impulse, it was simply because I was afraid of annoying him. Now, as an author becomes alarmed when he sees the fruits of his own meditations, which do not appear to him to be of great value since he does not separate them from himself, oblige a publisher to choose a brand of paper, to employ a type-face finer, perhaps, than they deserve, I asked myself whether my desire to write was of sufficient importance to justify my father in dispensing so much generosity. But apart from that, in speaking of my inclinations as no longer liable to change, and of what was destined to make my life happy, he aroused in me two very painful suspicions. The first was that (at a time when, every day, I regarded myself as standing upon the threshold of a life which was still intact and would not enter upon its course until the following morning) my existence had already begun, and that, furthermore, what was yet to follow would not differ to any extent from what had gone before. The second suspicion, which was really no more than a variant of the first, was that I was not situated somewhere outside Time, but was subject to its laws, just like those characters in novels who, for that reason, used to plunge me into such gloom when I read of their lives, down at Combray, in the fastness of my hooded wicker chair. In theory one is aware that the earth revolves, but in practice one does not perceive it, the ground upon which one treads seems not to move, and one can rest assured. So it is with Time in one's life. And to make its flight perceptible novelists are obliged, by wildly accelerating the beat of the pendulum, to transport the reader in a couple of minutes over ten, or twenty, or even thirty years. At the top of one page we have left a lover full of hope; at the foot of the next we meet him again, a bowed old man of eighty, painfully dragging himself on his daily walk around the courtyard of a hospital, scarcely replying to what is said to him, oblivious of the past. In saying of me, "He's no longer a child," "His tastes won't change now," and so forth, my father had suddenly made me conscious of myself in Time, and caused me the same kind of depression as if I had been, not yet the enfeebled old pensioner, but one of those heroes of whom the author, in a tone of indifference which is particularly galling, says to us at the end of a book: "He very seldom comes up from the country now. He has finally decided to end his days there."

Meanwhile my father, in order to forestall any criticism that we might feel tempted to make of our guest, said to my mother: "Upon my word, old Norpois was a bit 'stuffy,' as you call it, this evening, wasn't he? When he said that it wouldn't have been 'seemly' to ask the Comte de Paris a question, I was quite afraid you would burst out laughing."

"Not at all!" answered my mother. "I was delighted to see a man of his standing and his age with that sort of simplicity, which is really a sign of decency and good breeding."

"I dare say. But that doesn't prevent him from having a shrewd and discerning mind—as I know very well since I see him on the Commission, remember, where he's very different from what he was here," exclaimed my father, who was glad to see that Mamma appreciated M. de Norpois, and anxious to persuade her that he was even better than she supposed, because a cordial nature exaggerates a friend's qualities with as much pleasure as a mischievous one finds in depreciating them. "What was it that he said, again—'With princes one never does know' . . . ?"

"Yes, that was it. I noticed it at the time; it was very shrewd. You can see that he has a profound experience of life."

"It's extraordinary that he should have dined with the Swanns, and that he seems to have found quite respectable people there, government officials. How on earth can Mme Swann have managed to get hold of them?"

"Did you notice the malicious way he said: 'It is a house which is especially attractive to gentlemen!'?"

And each of them attempted to reproduce the manner in which M. de Norpois had uttered these words, as they might have attempted to capture some intonation of Bressant's voice or of Thiron's in *L'Aventurière* or in *Le Gendre de M. Poirier*. But of all his sayings there was none so keenly relished as one was by Françoise, who, years afterwards, could not "keep a straight face" if we reminded her that she had been described by the Ambassador as "a first-rate chef," a compliment which my mother had gone in person to transmit to her, like a War Minister passing on the congratulations of a visiting sovereign after reviewing the troops. I had, as it happened, preceded my mother to the kitchen. For I had extorted from Françoise, who though a pacifist was cruel, a promise that she would cause no undue suffering to the rabbit which she had to kill, and I had had no report yet of its death. Françoise assured me that it had passed away as peacefully as could be desired, and very swiftly. "I've never seen a beast like it; it died without saying a blessed word; you would have thought it was dumb." Being but little versed in the language of beasts, I suggested that rabbits perhaps did not squeal like chickens. "Just wait till you see," said Françoise, filled with contempt for my ignorance, "if rabbits don't squeal every bit as much as chickens. Why, their voices are even louder."

Françoise received the compliments of M. de Norpois with the proud simplicity, the joyful and (if only momentarily) intelligent expression of an artist when someone speaks to him of his art. My mother had sent her when she first came to us to several of the big restaurants to see how the cooking there was done. I had the same pleasure, that evening, in hearing her dismiss the most famous of them as mere cookshops, that I had had long ago when I learned with regard to theatrical artists that the hierarchy of their merits did not at all correspond to that of their reputations. "The Ambassador," my mother told her, "assured me that he knows nowhere where one can get cold beef and soufflés as good as yours." Françoise, with an air of modesty and of paying just homage to the truth, agreed, but seemed not at all impressed by the title "Ambassador"; she said of M. de Norpois, with the friendliness due to a man who had taken her for a chef: "He's a good old soul, like me." She had indeed hoped to catch sight of him as he arrived, but knowing that Mamma hated people lurking behind doors and at windows, and thinking that she would get to know from the other servants or from the porter that she had been keeping watch (for Françoise saw everywhere nothing but "jealousies" and "tale-bearings," which played the same baleful and perennial role in her imagination as, for certain other people, the intrigues of the Jesuits or the Jews), she had contented herself with a peep from the kitchen window, "so as not to have words with Madame," and from her momentary glimpses of M. de Norpois had "thought it was Monsieur Legrandin," because of what she called his "agelity" and in spite of their having not a single point in common.

"Well then," inquired my mother, "and how do you explain that nobody else can make an aspic as well as you—when you choose?" "I really couldn't say how that becomes about," replied Françoise, who had established no very clear line of demarcation between the verb "to come," in certain of its meanings, and the verb "to become." She was speaking the truth, moreover, if only in part, being scarcely more capable—or desirous—of revealing the mystery which ensured the superiority of her aspics or her creams than a well-dressed woman the secrets of her toilettes or a great singer those of her voice. Their explanations tell us little; it was the same with the recipes of our cook. "They do it in too much of a hurry," she went on, alluding to the great restaurants, "and then it's not all done together. You want the beef to become like a sponge, then it will drink up all the juice to the last drop. Still, there was one of those cafés where I thought they did know a little bit about cooking. I don't say it was altogether my aspic, but it was very nicely done, and the soufflés had plenty of cream."

"Do you mean Henry's?" asked my father (who had now joined us), for he greatly enjoyed that restaurant in the Place Gaillon where he went regularly to regimental dinners. "Oh, dear no!" said Françoise with a mildness which cloaked a profound contempt. "I meant a little restaurant. At that Henry's it's all very good, sure enough, but it's not a restaurant, it's more like a—soup-kitchen." "Weber's, then?" "Oh, no, Monsieur, I meant a good restaurant. Weber's, that's in the Rue Royale; that's not a restaurant, it's a brasserie. I don't know that the food they give you there is even served. I think they don't even have any table-cloths; they just shove it down in front of you like that, with a take it or leave it." "Ciro's?" Françoise smiled. "Oh! there I should say the main dishes are ladies of the world." (*Monde* meant for Françoise the *demi-monde*.) "Lord! they need them to fetch the boys in."

We could see that, with all her air of simplicity, Françoise was for the celebrities of her profession a more ferocious "colleague" than the most jealous, the most self-infatuated of actresses. We felt, all the same, that she had a proper feeling for her art and a respect for tradition, for she added: "No, I mean a restaurant where it looked like they kept a very good little family table. It's a place of some consequence, too. Plenty of custom there. Oh, they raked in the coppers, there, all right." (Françoise, being thrifty, reckoned in coppers, where your plunger would reckon in gold.) "Madame knows the place well enough, down there to the right along the main boulevards, a little way back." The restaurant of which she spoke with this blend of pride and good-humoured tolerance was, it turned out, the Café Anglais.

When New Year's Day came, I first of all paid a round of family visits with Mamma who, so as not to tire me, had planned them beforehand (with the aid of an itinerary drawn up by my father) according to district rather than degree of kinship. But no sooner had we entered the drawing-room of the distant cousin whose claim to being visited first was that her house was at no distance from ours, than my mother was horrified to see standing there, his present of marrons glacés or déguisés in his hand, the bosom friend of the most sensitive of all my uncles, to whom he would at once go and report that we had not begun our round with him. And this uncle would certainly be hurt; he would have thought it quite natural that we should go from the Madeleine to the Jardin des

Plantes, where he lived, before stopping at Saint-Augustin, on our way to the Rue de l'Ecole de Médecine.

Our visits ended (my grandmother had dispensed us from the duty of calling on her, since we were to dine there that evening), I ran all the way to the Champs-Elysées to give to our own special stall-keeper, with instructions to hand it over to the person who came to her several times a week from the Swanns to buy gingerbread, the letter which, on the day when my beloved had caused me so much pain, I had decided to send her at the New Year, and in which I told her that our old friendship was vanishing with the old year, that I would now forget my grievances and disappointments, and that, from this first day of January, it was a new friendship that we were going to build, so solid that nothing could destroy it, so wonderful that I hoped Gilberte would go out of her way to preserve it in all its beauty and to warn me in time, as I promised to warn her, should either of us detect the least sign of a peril that might endanger it.

On the way home Françoise made me stop at the corner of the Rue Royale, before an open-air stall from which she selected for her own stock of presents photographs of Pius IX and Raspail, while for myself I purchased one of Berma. The wholesale admiration which that artist excited gave an air of slight impoverishment to this one face that she had to respond with, immutable and precarious like the garments of people who have none "spare," this face on which she must continually expose to view only the tiny dimple upon her upper lip, the arch of her eyebrows, and a few other physical characteristics, always the same, which, after all, were at the mercy of a burn or a blow. This face, moreover, would not in itself have seemed to me beautiful, but it gave me the idea and consequently the desire to kiss it, by reason of all the kisses that it must have sustained and for which, from its page in the album, it seemed still to be appealing with that coquettishly tender gaze, that artfully ingenuous smile. For Berma must indeed have felt for many young men those desires which she confessed under cover of the character of Phèdre, desires which everything, even the glamour of her name which enhanced her beauty and prolonged her youth, must make it so easy for her to appease. Night was falling; I stopped before a column of playbills, on which was posted the performance in which she was to appear on January 1. A moist and gentle breeze was blowing. It was a weather with which I was familiar; I suddenly had a feeling and a presentiment that New Year's Day was not a day different from the rest, that it was not the first day of a new world in which I might, by a chance that was still intact, have made Gilberte's acquaintance anew as at the time of the Creation, as though the past did not yet exist, as though, together with the lessons I could have drawn from them for my future guidance, the disappointments which she had sometimes brought me had been obliterated; a new world in which nothing should subsist from the old—save one thing, my desire that Gilberte should love me. I realised that if my heart hoped for such a regeneration all around it of a universe that had not satisfied it before, it was because it, my heart, had not altered, and I told myself that there was no reason to suppose that Gilberte's had altered either; I felt that this new friendship was the same, just as there is no boundary ditch between their fore-runners and those new years which our desire, without being able to reach and so to modify them, invests, unknown to themselves, with a different name. For all that I might dedicate this new year to Gilberte, and, as one superimposes a religion on the blind laws of nature, endeavour to stamp New Year's Day with the particular image that I had formed of it, it was in vain. I felt that it was not aware that people called it New Year's Day, that it was passing in a wintry dusk in a manner that was not new to me: in the gentle breeze that blew around the column of playbills, I had recognised, had sensed the reappearance of, the eternal common substance, the familiar moisture, the unheeding fluidity of the old days and years.

I returned home. I had just spent the New Year's Day of old men, who differ on that day from their juniors, not because people have ceased to give them presents but because they themselves have ceased to believe in the New Year. Presents I had indeed received, but not that present which alone could bring me pleasure, namely a line from Gilberte. I was nevertheless still young, since I had been able to write her one, by means of which I hoped, in telling her of my solitary dreams of love and longing, to arouse similar dreams in her. The sadness of men who have grown old lies in their no longer even thinking of writing such letters, the futility of which their experience has shown.

When I was in bed, the noises of the street, unduly prolonged on this festive evening, kept me awake. I thought of all the people who would end the night in pleasure, of the lover, the troop of debauchees perhaps, who would be going to meet Berma at the stage-door after the performance that I had seen announced for this evening. I was not even able, to calm the agitation which this idea engendered in me during my sleepless night, to assure myself that Berma was not, perhaps, thinking about love, since the lines that she recited, which she had long and carefully rehearsed, reminded her at every moment that love is an exquisite thing, as of course she already knew, and knew so well that she displayed its familiar pangs—only enriched with a new violence and an unsuspected sweetness—to her astonished audience, each member of which had felt them for himself. I lighted my candle again, to look at her face once more. At the thought that it was no doubt at that very moment being caressed by those men whom I could not prevent from giving to Berma and receiving from her joys superhuman but vague, I felt an emotion more cruel than voluptuous, a longing that was presently intensified by the sound of the horn, as one hears it on the nights of the mid-Lent festival and often of other public holidays, which, because it then lacks all poetry, is more saddening, coming from a tavern, than "at evening, in the depths of the woods." At that moment, a message from Gilberte would perhaps not have been what I wanted. Our desires cut across one another, and in this confused existence it is rare for happiness to coincide with the desire that clamoured for it.

I continued to go to the Champs-Elysées on fine days, along streets whose elegant pink houses seemed to be washed (because exhibitions of water-colours were then the height of fashion) in a lightly floating atmosphere. It would be untrue to say that in those days the palaces of Gabriel struck me as being of greater beauty than, or even of another period from, the neighbouring houses. I found more style and should have supposed more antiquity if not in the Palais de l'Industrie at any rate in the Trocadéro. Plunged in a restless sleep, my adolescence embraced in one uniform vision the whole of the quarter through which it guided it, and I had never dreamed that there could be an eighteenth-century building in the Rue Royale, just as I should have been astonished to learn that the Porte Saint-Martin and the Porte Saint-Denis, those glories of the age of Louis XIV, were not contemporary with the most recently built tenements in the sordid districts that bore their names. Once only one of Gabriel's palaces made me stop for more than a moment; this was because, night having fallen, its columns, dematerialised by the moonlight, had the appearance of having been cut out in pasteboard, and by reminding me of a set from the operetta *Orphée aux Enfers*, gave me for the first time an impression of beauty.

Meanwhile Gilberte never came to the Champs-Elysées. And yet it was imperative that I should see her, for I could not so much as remember her face. The questing, anxious, exacting way that we have of looking at the person we love, our eagerness for the word which will give us or take from us the hope of an appointment for the morrow, and, until that word is uttered, our alternate if not simultaneous imaginings of joy and despair, all this makes our attention in the presence of the beloved too tremulous to be able to carry away a very clear impression of her. Perhaps, also, that activity of all the senses at once which yet endeavours to discover with the eyes alone what lies beyond them is over-indulgent to the myriad forms, to the different savours, to the movements of the living person whom as a rule, when we are not in love, we immobilise. Whereas the beloved model does not stay still; and our mental photographs of it are always blurred.

I no longer really knew how Gilberte's features were composed, except in the heavenly moments when she unfolded them to me: I could remember nothing but her smile. And being unable to visualise that beloved face, despite every effort that I might make to recapture it, I was disgusted to find, etched on my memory with a maddening precision of detail, the meaningless, emphatic faces of the roundabout man and the barley-sugar woman; just as those who have lost a loved one whom they never see again in sleep, are enraged at meeting incessantly in their dreams any number of insupportable people whom it is quite enough to have known in the waking world. In their inability to form an image of the object of their grief they are almost led to accuse themselves of feeling no grief. And I was not far from believing that, since I could not recall Gilberte's features, I had forgotten Gilberte herself, and no longer loved her.

At last she returned to play there almost every day, setting before me fresh pleasures to desire, to demand of her for the morrow, in this sense indeed making my love for her each day a new love. But an incident was to change once again, and abruptly, the manner in which, at about two o'clock every afternoon, the problem of my love confronted me. Had M. Swann intercepted the letter that I had written to his daughter, or was Gilberte merely confessing to me long after the event, and so that I should be more prudent in future, a state of affairs already long established? As I was telling her how greatly I admired her father and mother, she assumed that vague air, full of reticence and secrecy, which she invariably wore when one spoke to her of what she was going to do, her walks, drives, visits, then suddenly said to me: "You know, they can't stand you!" and, slipping from me like the water-sprite that she was, burst out laughing. Often her laughter, out of harmony with her words, seemed, as music seems, to be tracing an invisible surface on another plane. M. and Mme Swann did not require Gilberte to give up playing with me, but they would have been just as well pleased, she thought, if we had never begun. They did not look upon our relations with a kindly eye, believed me to be a person of low moral standard and imagined that I could only be a bad influence on their daughter. This type of unscrupulous youth whom Swann thought I resembled, I pictured to myself as detesting the parents of the girl he loves, flattering them to their faces but, when he is alone with her, making fun of them, urging her on to disobey them and, when once he has completed his conquest, preventing them even from seeing her. With these characteristics (though they are never those under which the basest of scoundrels recognises himself) how vehemently did my heart contrast the sentiments by which it was animated with regard to Swann, so passionate, on the contrary, that I had no doubt that had he had an inkling of them he would have repented of his judgment of me as of a judicial error. All that I felt towards him I made bold to express to him in a long letter which I entrusted to Gilberte with the request that she deliver it to him. She agreed to do so. Alas! he must have seen in me an even greater impostor than I had feared; he must have suspected the sentiments which I had supposed myself to be portraying, in sixteen pages, with such conviction and truth: in short, the letter that I wrote to him, as ardent and as sincere as the words that I had uttered to M. de Norpois, met with no more success. Gilberte told me next day, after taking me aside behind a clump of laurels, on a little path where we sat down on a couple of chairs, that as he read my letter, which she had now brought back to me, her father had shrugged his shoulders and said: "All this means nothing; it only goes to prove how right I was." I who knew the purity of my intentions, the goodness of my soul, was furious that my words should not even have impinged upon the surface of Swann's ridiculous error. For it was an error; of that I had then no doubt. I felt that I had described with such accuracy certain irrefutable characteristics of my generous sentiments that, if Swann had not at once recognised their authenticity, had not come to ask my forgiveness and to admit that he had been mistaken, it must be because he himself had never experienced these noble sentiments, and this would make him incapable of understanding their existence in other people.

But perhaps it was simply that Swann knew that nobility is often no more than the inner aspect which our egotistical feelings assume when we have not yet named and classified them. Perhaps he had recognised in the regard that I expressed for him simply an effect—and the strongest possible proof—of my love for Gilberte, by which—and not by my secondary veneration for himself—my subsequent actions would be inevitably controlled. I was unable to share his predictions, since I had not succeeded in abstracting my love from myself, in fitting it into the common experience of humanity and computing, experimentally, its consequences; I was in despair. I was obliged to leave Gilberte for a moment; Françoise had called me. I had to accompany her into a little pavilion covered in a green trellis, not unlike one of the disused toll-houses of old Paris, in which had recently been installed what in England they call a lavatory but in France, by an ill-judged piece of Anglomania, "water-closets." The old, damp walls of the entrance, where I stood waiting for Françoise, emitted a cool, fusty smell which, relieving me at once of the anxieties that Swann's words, as reported by Gilberte, had just awakened in me, filled me with a pleasure of a different kind from other pleasures, which leave one more unstable, incapable of grasping them, of possessing them, a pleasure that was solid and consistent, on which I could lean for support, delicious, soothing, rich with a truth that was lasting, unexplained and sure. I should have liked, as, long ago, in my walks along the Guermantes way, to endeavour to penetrate the charm of this impression which had seized hold of me, and, remaining there motionless, to explore this antiquated emanation which invited me not to enjoy the pleasure which it was offering me only as a bonus, but to descend into the underlying reality which it had not yet disclosed to me. But the keeper of the establishment, an elderly dame with painted cheeks and an auburn wig, began to talk to me. Françoise thought her "a proper lady." Her young "missy" had married what Françoise called "a young man of family," which meant that he differed more, in her eyes, from a workman than, in Saint-Simon's, a duke did from a man "risen from the dregs of the people." No doubt the keeper, before entering upon her tenancy, had suffered setbacks. But Françoise was positive that she was a "marquise," and belonged to the Saint-Ferréol family. This "marquise" now warned me not to stand outside in the cold, and even opened one of her doors for me, saying: "Won't you go inside for a minute? Look, here's a nice clean one, and I shan't charge *you* anything." Perhaps she made this offer simply in the spirit in which the young ladies at Gouache's, when we went in there to order something, used to offer me one of the sweets which they kept on the counter under glass bells, and which, alas, Mamma would never allow me to accept; perhaps, less innocently, like the old florist whom Mamma used to have in to replenish her flower-stands, who rolled languishing eyes at me as she handed me a rose. In any event, if the "marquise" had a weakness for little boys, when she threw open to them the hypogean doors of those cubicles of stone in which men crouch like sphinxes, she must have been moved to that generosity less by the hope of corrupting them than by the pleasure which all of us feel in displaying a needless prodigality to those whom we love, for I never saw her with any other visitor except an old park-keeper.

A moment later I said good-bye to the "marquise," and went out accompanied by Françoise, whom I left to return to Gilberte. I caught sight of her at once, on a chair, behind the clump of laurels. She was there so as not to be seen by her friends: they were playing hide-and-seek. I went and sat down beside her. She had on a flat cap which came low over her eyes, giving her the same "underhand," brooding, sly look which I had remarked in her that first time at Combray. I asked her if there was not some way for me to have it out with her father face to face. Gilberte said that she had suggested that to him, but that he had thought it pointless. "Here," she went on, "don't go away without your letter. I must run along to the others, as they haven't found me."

Had Swann appeared on the scene then before I had

recovered this letter by the sincerity of which I felt that he had been so unreasonable in not letting himself be convinced, perhaps he would have seen that it was he who had been in the right. For, approaching Gilberte, who, leaning back in her chair, told me to take the letter but did not hold it out to me, I felt myself so irresistibly attracted by her body that I said to her: "I say, why don't you try to stop me from getting it; we'll see who's the stronger."

She thrust it behind her back; I put my arms round her neck, raising the plaits of hair which she wore over her shoulders, either because she was still of an age for it or because her mother chose to make her look a child for a little longer so as to make herself seem younger; and we wrestled, locked together. I tried to pull her towards me, and she resisted; her cheeks, inflamed by the effort, were as red and round as two cherries; she laughed as though I were tickling her; I held her gripped between my legs like a young tree which I was trying to climb; and, in the middle of my gymnastics, when I was already out of breath with the muscular exercise and the heat of the game, I felt, like a few drops of sweat wrung from me by the effort, my pleasure express itself in a form which I could not even pause for a moment to analyse; immediately I snatched the letter from her. Whereupon Gilberte said good-naturedly: "You know, if you like, we might go on wrestling a bit longer."

Perhaps she was dimly conscious that my game had another object than the one I had avowed, but too dimly to have been able to see that I had attained it. And I who was afraid that she had noticed (and a slight movement of recoil and constraint as of offended modesty which she made and checked a moment later made me think that my fear had not been unfounded) agreed to go on wrestling, lest she should suppose that I had indeed had no other object in view than the one after which I wished only to sit quietly by her side.

On my way home I perceived, I suddenly recalled the impression, concealed from me until then, of which, without letting me distinguish or recognise it, the cold and almost sooty smell of the trellised pavilion had reminded me. It was that of my uncle Adolphe's little sitting-room at Combray, which had indeed exhaled the same odour of humidity. But I could not understand, and I postponed until later the attempt to discover why the recollection of so trivial an impression had filled me with such happiness. Meanwhile it struck me that I did indeed deserve the contempt of M. de Norpois: I had preferred hitherto to all other writers one whom he styled a mere "flute-player," and a positive rapture had been conveyed to me, not by some important idea, but by a musty smell.

For some time past, in certain households, the name of the Champs-Elysées, if a visitor mentioned it, would be greeted by the mothers with that baleful air which they reserve for a physician of established reputation whom they claim to have seen make too many false diagnoses to have any faith left in him; people insisted that these gardens were not good for children, that they knew of more than one sore throat, more than one case of measles and any number of feverish chills for which they must be held responsible. Without venturing openly to doubt the maternal affection of Mamma, who continued to let me play there, several of her friends deplored her inability to see what was as plain as daylight.

Neurotic subjects are perhaps less addicted than any, despite the time-honoured phrase, to "listening to their insides": they hear so many things going on by which they realise later that they were wrong to let themselves be alarmed, that they end by paying no attention to any of them. Their nervous systems have so often cried out to them for help, as though with some serious malady, when it was simply going to start snowing or they were going to move house, that they have acquired the habit of paying no more heed to these warnings than a soldier who in the heat of battle perceives them so little that he is capable, although dying, of carrying on for some days still the life of a man in perfect health. One morning, bearing within me all my habitual ailments, from whose constant internal circulation I kept my mind turned as resolutely away as from the circulation of my blood, I came running blithely into the dining-room where my parents were already at table, and—having assured myself, as usual, that to feel cold may mean not that one ought to warm oneself but that, for instance, one has received a scolding, and not to feel hungry may mean that it is going to rain and not that one ought to fast—had taken my place between them when in the act of swallowing the first mouthful of a particularly tempting cutlet, a nausea and dizziness brought me to a halt, the feverish reaction of an illness that had already begun, the symptoms of which had been masked and retarded by the ice of my indifference, but which obstinately refused the nourishment that I was not in a fit state to absorb. Then, at the same moment, the thought that I would be prevented from going out if I was seen to be unwell gave me, as the instinct of self-preservation gives a wounded man, the strength to crawl to my own room, where I found that I had a temperature of 104, and then to get ready to go to the Champs-Elysées. Through the languid and vulnerable shell which encased them, my eager thoughts were urging me towards, were clamouring for the soothing delight of a game of prisoner's base with Gilberte, and an hour later, barely able to keep on my feet, but happy in being by her side, I had still the strength to enjoy it.

Françoise, on our return, declared that I had been "taken bad," that I must have caught a "hot and cold," while the doctor, who was called in at once, declared that he "preferred" the "severity," the "virulence" of the rise in temperature which accompanied my congestion of the lungs, and would be no more than "a flash in the pan," to other symptoms, more "insidious" and "masked." For some time now I had been liable to fits of breathlessness, and our doctor, braving the disapproval of my grandmother, who saw me already dying a drunkard's death, had recommended me to take, as well as the caffeine which had been prescribed to help me to breathe, beer, champagne or brandy when I felt an attack coming. These attacks would subside, he said, in the "euphoria" brought on by the alcohol. I was often obliged, so that my grandmother should allow it to be given to me, instead of disguising, almost to make a display of my state of suffocation. On the other hand, as soon as I felt it coming, never being quite certain what proportions it would assume, I would grow distressed at the thought of my grandmother's anxiety, of which I was far more afraid than of my own sufferings. But at the same time my body, either because it was too weak to keep those sufferings secret, or because it feared lest, in their ignorance of the imminent attack, people might demand of me some exertion which it would have found impossible or dangerous, gave me the need to warn my grandmother of my symptoms with a precision into which I put a sort of physiological punctiliousness. If I observed in myself a disturbing symptom which I had not previously discerned, my body was in distress so long as I had not communicated it to my grandmother. If she pretended to take no notice, it made me insist. Sometimes I went too far; and that beloved face, which was no longer able always to control its emotion as in the past, would betray an expression of pity, a painful contraction. Then my heart was wrung by the sight of her grief; as if my kisses had the power to expel that grief, as if my affection could give my grandmother as much joy as my recovery, I flung myself into her arms. And its scruples being at the same time calmed by the certainty that she was now aware of the discomfort that I felt, my body offered no opposition to my reassuring her. I protested that this discomfort was not really painful, that I was in no sense to be pitied, that she might be quite sure that I was now happy; my body had wished to secure exactly the amount of pity that it deserved, and, provided that someone knew that it had a pain in its right side, it could see no harm in my declaring that this pain was of no consequence and was not an obstacle to my happiness; for my body did not pride itself on its philosophy; that was outside its province. Almost every day during my convalescence I had some of these fits of suffocation. One evening, after my grandmother had left me comparatively well, she returned to my room very late and, seeing me struggling for breath, "Oh, my poor boy," she exclaimed, her face quivering with sympathy, "you must be in dreadful pain." She left me at once; I heard the street door open, and in a little while she came back with some brandy which she had gone out to buy since there was none in the house. Presently I began to feel better. My grandmother, who was rather flushed, seemed somehow embarrassed, and her eyes had a look of weariness and dejection.

"I shall leave you alone now, and let you take advantage of this improvement," she said, rising suddenly to go. I detained her, however, for a kiss, and could feel on her cold cheek something moist, but did not know whether it was the dampness of the night air through which she had just passed. Next day, she did not come to my room until the evening, having had, she told me, to go out. I considered that this showed a surprising indifference to my well-being, and I had to restrain myself in order not to reproach her with it.

My suffocations having persisted long after any congestion remained that could account for them, my parents brought in Professor Cottard. It is not enough that a physician who is called in to treat cases of this sort should be learned. Confronted with symptoms which may be those of three or four different complaints, it is in the long run his flair, his instinctive judgment, that must decide with which, despite the more or less similar appearance of them all, he has to deal. This mysterious gift does not imply any superiority in the other departments of the intellect, and a person of the utmost vulgarity, who admires the worst pictures, the worst music, who is without the slightest intellectual curiosity, may perfectly well possess it. In my case, what was physically evident might well have been caused by nervous spasms, by incipient tuberculosis, by asthma, by a toxi-alimentary dyspnoea with renal insufficiency, by chronic bronchitis, or by a complex state into which more than one of these factors entered. Now, nervous spasms required to be treated firmly, and discouraged, tuberculosis with infinite care and the sort of "feeding-up" which would have been bad for an arthritic condition such as asthma and might indeed have been dangerous in a case of toxi-alimentary dyspnoea, this last calling for a strict diet which, in turn, would be fatal to a tubercular patient. But Cottard's hesitations were brief and his prescriptions imperious: "Purges, violent and drastic purges; milk for some days, nothing but milk. No meat. No alcohol." My mother murmured that I needed, all the same, to be "built up," that I was already very nervy, that drenching me like a horse and restricting my diet would make me worse. I could see in Cottard's eyes, as anxious as if he was afraid of missing a train, that he was wondering whether he had not succumbed to his natural gentleness. He was trying to think whether he had remembered to put on his mask of coldness, as one looks for a mirror to see whether one has forgotten to tie one's tie. In his uncertainty, and in order to compensate just in case, he replied brutally: "I am not in the habit of repeating my prescriptions. Give me a pen. Now remember, milk! Later on, when we've got the breathlessness and the agrypnia under control, I'm prepared to let you take a little clear soup, and then a little broth, but always with milk; *au lait!* You'll enjoy that, since Spain is all the rage just now; *olé, olé!*" (His pupils knew this joke well, for he made it at the hospital whenever he had to put a heart or liver case on a milk diet.) "After that, you'll gradually return to your normal life.

But whenever there's any coughing or choking—purges, enemas, bed, milk!" He listened with icy calm, and without replying, to my mother's final objections, and as he left us without having condescended to explain the reasons for this course of treatment, my parents concluded that it had no bearing on my case, and would weaken me to no purpose, and so they did not make me try it. Naturally they sought to conceal their disobedience from the Professor, and to make sure of it avoided all the houses in which they might have run across him. Then, as my health deteriorated, they decided to make me follow Cottard's prescriptions to the letter; in three days my rattle and cough had ceased, I could breathe freely. Whereupon we realised that Cottard, while finding, as he told us later on, that I was distinctly asthmatic, and above all "batty," had discerned that what was really the matter with me at the moment was toxaemia, and that by loosening my liver and washing out my kidneys he would clear my bronchial tubes and thus give me back my breath, my sleep and my strength. And we realised that this imbecile was a great physician.

At last I was able to get up. But there was talk of my no longer being allowed to go to the Champs-Elysées. The reason given was that the air there was bad; but I felt sure that this was only a pretext so that I should no longer be able to see Mlle Swann, and I forced myself to repeat the name of Gilberte all the time, like the native tongue which peoples in captivity endeavour to preserve among themselves so as not to forget the land that they will never see again.

Sometimes my mother would stroke my forehead, saying: "So little boys don't tell Mamma their troubles any more?" And Françoise used to come up to me every day and say: "What a face, to be sure! If you could just see yourself! You look like death!" It is true that, if I had simply had a cold in the head, Françoise would have assumed the same funereal air. These lamentations pertained rather to her "class" than to the state of my health. I could not at the time distinguish whether this pessimism was due to sorrow or to satisfaction. I decided provisionally that it was social and professional.

One day, after the postman had called, my mother laid a letter upon my bed. I opened it carelessly, since it could not bear the one signature that would have made me happy, the name of Gilberte, with whom I had no relations outside the Champs-Elysées. But there, at the foot of the page, which was embossed with a silver seal representing a helmeted head above a scroll with the device *Per viam rectam*, beneath a letter written in a large and flowing hand in which almost every phrase appeared to be underlined, simply because the crosses of the "t"s ran not across but over them, and so drew a line beneath the corresponding letters of the word above, it was precisely Gilberte's signature that I saw. But because I knew this to be impossible in a letter addressed to me, the sight of it unaccompanied by any belief in it gave me no pleasure. For a moment it merely gave an impression of unreality to everything around me. With dizzy speed the improbable signature danced about my bed, the fireplace, the four walls. I saw everything reel, as one does when one falls from a horse, and I asked myself whether there was not an existence altogether different from the one I knew, in direct contradiction to it, but itself the real one, which, being suddenly revealed to me, filled me with that hesitation which sculptors, in representing the Last Judgment, have given to the awakening dead who find themselves at the gates of the next world. "My dear friend," said the letter, "I hear that you have been very ill and have given up going to the Champs-Elysées. I hardly ever go there either because there has been such an enormous lot of illness. But my friends come to tea here every Monday and Friday. Mamma asks me to tell you that it will be a great pleasure to us all if you will come too as soon as you are well again, and we can have some more nice talks here as we did in the Champs-Elysées. Good-bye, my dear friend; I hope that your parents will allow you to come to tea very often. With all my kindest regards. GILBERTE."

While I was reading these words, my nervous system received, with admirable promptitude, the news that a great happiness had befallen me. But my mind, that is to say myself, in other words the party principally concerned, was still unaware of it. Happiness, happiness through Gilberte, was a thing I had never ceased to think of, a thing wholly in my mind—as Leonardo said of painting, *cosa mentale*. Now, a sheet of paper covered with writing is not a thing that the mind assimilates at once. But as soon as I had finished reading the letter, I thought of it, it became an object of reverie, it too became *cosa mentale*, and I loved it so much now that every few minutes I had to re-read it and kiss it. Then at last I was conscious of my happiness.

Life is strewn with these miracles for which people who love can always hope. It is possible that this one had been artificially brought about by my mother who, seeing that for some time past I had lost all interest in life, may have suggested to Gilberte to write to me, just as, when I first went sea-bathing, in order to make me enjoy diving which I hated because it took away my breath, she used secretly to hand to my bathing instructor marvellous boxes made of shells, and branches of coral, which I believed that I myself discovered lying at the bottom of the sea. However, with every occurrence in life and its contrasting situations that relates to love, it is best to make no attempt to understand, since in so far as these are as inexorable as they are unlooked-for, they appear to be governed by magic rather than by rational laws. When a multi-millionaire—who for all his millions is a charming man—sent packing by a poor and unattractive woman with whom he has been living, calls to his aid, in his despair, all the resources of wealth and brings every worldly influence to bear without succeeding in making her take him back, it is wiser for him, in the face of the implacable obstinacy of his mistress, to suppose that Fate intends to crush him and to make him die of an affection of the heart rather than to seek any logical explanation. These obstacles against which lovers have to contend and which their imagination, over-excited by suffering, seeks in vain to analyse, are to be found, as often as not, in some peculiar characteristic of the woman whom they cannot win back—in her stupidity, in the influence acquired over her and the fears suggested to her by people whom the lover does not know, in the kind of pleasures which at that moment she demands of life, pleasures which neither her lover nor her lover's wealth can procure for her. In any event, the lover is not in the best position to discover the nature of these obstacles which the woman's guile conceals from him and his own judgment, distorted by love, prevents him from estimating exactly. They may be compared with those tumours which the doctor succeeds in reducing, but without having traced them to their source. Like them these obstacles remain mysterious but are temporary. Only they last, as a rule, longer than love itself. And as the latter is not a disinterested passion, the lover who no longer loves does not seek to know why the woman, neither rich nor virtuous, with whom he was in love refused obstinately for years to let him continue to keep her.

Now the same mystery which often veils from our eyes the reason for a catastrophe envelops just as frequently, when love is in question, the suddenness of certain happy solutions, such as had been brought to me by Gilberte's letter. Happy, or at least seemingly happy, for there are few that can really be happy when we are dealing with a sentiment of such a kind that any satisfaction we can give it does no more, as a rule, than dislodge some pain. And yet sometimes a respite is granted us, and we have for a little while the illusion of being healed.

As regards this letter, at the foot of which Françoise refused to recognise Gilberte's name because the elaborate capital "G" leaning against the undotted "i" looked more like an "A," while the final syllable was indefinitely prolonged by a waving flourish, if we persist in looking for a rational explanation of the sudden change of feeling towards me which it reflected, and which made me so radiantly happy, we may perhaps find that I was to some extent indebted for it to an incident which I should have supposed, on the contrary, to be calculated to ruin me for ever in the eyes of the Swann family. A short while back, Bloch had come to see me at a time when Professor Cottard, who, now that I was following his prescriptions, had again been called in, happened to be in my room. As his examination was over and he was sitting with me simply as a visitor because my parents had invited him to stay to dinner, Bloch was allowed to come in. While we were all talking, Bloch having mentioned that he had been told by a lady with whom he had been dining the day before, and who was a great friend of Mme Swann's, that the latter was very fond of me, I should have liked to reply that he was most certainly mistaken, and to establish the fact (from the same scruple of conscience that had made me proclaim it to M. de Norpois, and for fear that Mme Swann might take me for a liar) that I did not know her and had never spoken to her. But I did not have the heart to correct Bloch's mistake, because I realised that it was deliberate, and that, if he had made up something that Mme Swann could not possibly have said, it was simply to let us know (what he considered flattering to himself, and was not true either) that he had been dining with one of that lady's friends. And thus it came about that whereas M. de Norpois, on learning that I did not know but would very much like to know Mme Swann, had taken good care to avoid speaking to her about me, Cottard, who was her doctor, having gathered from what he had heard Bloch say that she knew me quite well and thought highly of me, concluded that to remark, when next he saw her, that I was a charming young fellow and a great friend of his could not be of the smallest use to me and would be advantageous to himself, two reasons which induced him to speak of me to Odette whenever an opportunity arose.

Thus at length I came to know that house from which was wafted even on to the staircase the scent that Mme Swann used, but which was more redolent still of the peculiar, disturbing charm that emanated from the life of Gilberte. The implacable concierge, transformed into a benevolent Eumenid, adopted the habit, when I asked him if I might go upstairs, of indicating to me, by raising his cap with a propitious hand, that he granted my prayer. Those windows which, seen from outside, used to interpose between me and the treasures within, which were not destined for me, a polished, distant and superficial stare, which seemed to me the very stare of the Swanns themselves, it fell to my lot, when in the warm weather I had spent a whole afternoon with Gilberte in her room, to open myself so as to let in a little air and even to lean out of beside her, if it was her mother's "at home" day, to watch the visitors arrive who would often look up as they stepped out of their carriages and greet me with a wave of the hand, taking me for some nephew of their hostess. At such moments Gilberte's plaits used to brush my cheek. They seemed to me, in the fineness of their grain, at once natural and supernatural, and in the strength of their skilfully woven tracery, a matchless work of art in the composition of which had been used the very grass of Paradise. To a section of them, however infinitesimal, what celestial herbarium would I not have given as a reliquary? But since I never hoped to obtain an actual fragment of those plaits, if at least I had been able to have a photograph of them, how far more precious than one of a sheet of flowers drawn by Leonardo! To acquire one, I stooped to servilities, with friends of the Swanns and even with photographers, which not only failed to procure for me what I wanted, but tied me for life to a number of extremely boring people.

Gilberte's parents, who for so long had prevented me from seeing her, now—when I entered the dark hall in which hovered perpetually, more formidable and more to be desired than, at Versailles, the apparition of the King, the possibility of my encountering them, in which too, invariably, after bumping into an enormous seven-branched hat-stand, like the Candlestick in Holy Writ, I would begin bowing profusely to a footman, seated among the skirts of his long grey coat upon the wood chest, whom in the dim light I had mistaken for Mme Swann—Gilberte's parents, if one of them happened to be passing at the moment of my arrival, so far from seeming annoyed would come and shake hands with me with a smile, and say: "How d'ye do?" (which they both pronounced in the same clipped way, which, as may be imagined, I made it my incessant and delightful task to imitate when I was back at home). "Does Gilberte know you're here? She does? Then I'll leave you to her."

Better still, the tea-parties themselves to which Gilberte invited her friends, parties which for so long had seemed to me the most insurmountable of the barriers heaped up between her and myself, became now an opportunity for bringing us together of which she would inform me in a few lines written (because I was still a comparative stranger) on writing-paper that was always different. Once it was adorned with a poodle embossed in blue, above a humorous inscription in English with an exclamation mark after it; another time it would be engraved with an anchor, or with the initials G. S. preposterously elongated in a rectangle which ran from top to bottom of the page, or else with the name Gilberte, now traced across one corner in letters of gold which imitated her signature and ended with a flourish, beneath an open umbrella printed in black, now enclosed in a monogram in the shape of a Chinaman's hat which contained all the letters of the name in capitals without its being possible to make out a single one of them. Finally, as the series of different writing-papers which Gilberte possessed, numerous though it was, was not unlimited, after a certain number of weeks I saw reappear the sheet that bore (like the first letter she had written me) the motto *Per viam rectam*, and over it the helmeted head set in a medallion of tarnished silver. And each of them was chosen for one day rather than another by virtue of a certain ritual, as I then supposed, but more probably, I now think, because she tried to remember which of them she had already used, so as never to send the same one twice to any of her correspondents, of those at least whom she took special pains to please, save at the longest possible intervals. As, on account of the different times of their lessons, some of the friends whom Gilberte used to invite to her parties were obliged to leave just as the rest were arriving, while I was still on the stairs I could hear emanating from the hall a murmur of voices which, such was the emotion aroused in me by the imposing ceremony in which I was to take part, suddenly broke the bonds that connected me with my previous life long before I had reached the landing, so that I did not even remember that I was to take off my muffler as soon as I felt too hot and to keep an eye on the clock so as not to be late in getting home. That staircase, too, all of wood as they were built about that time in certain apartment houses in that Henri II style which had for so long been Odette's ideal though she was shortly to abandon it, and furnished with a placard, to which there was no equivalent at home, on which one read the words: " NOTICE. Do not use the lift when going down," seemed to me a thing so marvellous that I told my parents that it was an antique staircase brought from ever so far away by M. Swann. My regard for the truth was so great that I should not have hesitated to give them this information even if I had known it to be false, for it alone could enable them to feel for the dignity of the Swanns' staircase the same respect that I felt myself—just as when one is talking to some ignorant person who cannot understand what constitutes the genius of a great doctor, it is well not to admit that he does not know how to cure a cold in the head. But since I was extremely unobservant, and since, as a general rule, I never knew either the name or the nature of the things I came across and could understand only that when they were connected with the Swanns they must be extraordinary, it did not seem absolutely certain to me that in notifying my parents of the artistic value and remote origin of the staircase I was guilty of a falsehood. It did not seem certain; but it must have seemed probable, for I felt myself turn very red when my father interrupted me with: "I know those houses. I've been in one of them. They're all alike; Swann just has several floors in one; it was Berlier built them all." He added that he had thought of taking a flat in one of them, but that he had changed his mind, finding that they were not conveniently arranged, and that the landings were too dark. So he said; but I felt instinctively that I must make the sacrifices necessary to the glory of the

Swanns and to my own happiness, and by an internal decree, in spite of what I had just heard, I banished for ever from my mind, as a good Catholic banishes Renan's *Vie de Jésus*, the corrupting thought that their house was just an ordinary flat in which we ourselves might have been living.

Meanwhile, on those tea-party days, pulling myself up the staircase step by step, reason and memory already cast off like outer garments, and myself no more now than the sport of the basest reflexes, I would arrive in the zone in which the scent of Mme Swann greeted my nostrils. I could already visualise the majesty of the chocolate cake, encircled by plates heaped with biscuits, and by tiny napkins of patterned grey damask, as required by convention but peculiar to the Swanns. But this ordered and unalterable design seemed, like Kant's necessary universe, to depend on a supreme act of free will. For when we were all together in Gilberte's little sitting-room, suddenly she would look at the clock and exclaim:

"I say! It's getting a long time since luncheon, and we aren't having dinner till eight. I feel as if I could eat something. What do you say?"

And she would usher us into the dining-room, as sombre as the interior of an Asiatic temple painted by Rembrandt, in which an architectural cake, as urbane and familiar as it was imposing, seemed to be enthroned there on the off-chance as on any other day, in case the fancy seized Gilberte to discrown it of its chocolate battlements and to hew down the steep brown slopes of its ramparts, baked in the oven like the bastions of the palace of Darius. Better still, in proceeding to the demolition of that Ninevite pastry, Gilberte did not consider only her own hunger; she inquired also after mine, while she extracted for me from the crumbling monument a whole glazed slab jewelled with scarlet fruits, in the oriental style. She would even ask me what time my parents dined, as if I still knew, as if the agitation which overwhelmed me had allowed the sensation of satiety or of hunger, the notion of dinner or the image of my family, to persist in my empty memory and paralysed stomach. Alas, its paralysis was but momentary. A time would come when I should have to digest the cakes that I took without noticing them. But that time was still remote. Meanwhile Gilberte was making "my" tea. I would go on drinking it indefinitely, although a single cup would keep me awake for twenty-four hours. As a consequence of which my mother used always to say: "What a nuisance it is; this child can never go to the Swanns' without coming home ill." But was I aware even, when I was at the Swanns', that it was tea that I was drinking? Had I known, I should have drunk it just the same, for even supposing that I had recovered for a moment the sense of the present, that would not have restored to me the memory of the past or the apprehension of the future. My imagination was incapable of reaching to the distant time in which I might have the idea of going to bed and the need to sleep.

Gilberte's girl friends were not all plunged in that state of intoxication in which it is impossible to make any decisions. Some of them even refused tea! Then Gilberte would say, using a phrase that was very popular that year: "I can see I'm not having much of a success with my tea!" And to eradicate even more completely any notion of ceremony, she would disarrange the chairs that were drawn up round the table, saying: "It's just like a wedding breakfast. Goodness, how stupid servants are!"

She would nibble away, perched sideways upon a cross-legged seat placed at an angle to the table. And then, just as though she could have had all those cakes at her disposal without having asked her mother's permission, when Mme Swann, whose "day" coincided as a rule with Gilberte's tea-parties, having shown one of her visitors to the door, came sweeping in a moment later, dressed sometimes in blue velvet, more often in a black satin gown draped with white lace, she would say with an air of astonishment: "I say, that looks good, what you've got there. It makes me quite hungry to see you all eating cake."

"But, Mamma, do! We invite you," Gilberte would answer.

"Thank you, no, my precious; what would my visitors say? I've still got Mme Trombert and Mme Cottard and Mme Bontemps. You know dear Mme Bontemps never pays very short visits, and she has only just come. What would all those good people say if I didn't go back to them? If no one else calls, I'll come back and have a chat with you (which will be far more amusing) after they've all gone. I really think I've earned a little rest. I've had forty-five different people today, and forty-two of them have told me about Gérôme's picture! But you must come along one of these days," she turned to me, "and take 'your' tea with Gilberte. She'll make it for you just as you like it, as you have it in your own little 'den'," she added as she rushed off to her visitors and as if it had been something as familiar to me as my own habits (such as the habit I might have had of drinking tea, had I ever done so; as for my "den," I was uncertain whether I had one or not) that I had come to seek in this mysterious world. "When can you come? Tomorrow? We'll make you some toast that's every bit as good as you get at Colombin's. No? You are horrid!"—for, since she too had begun to form a salon, she was adopting Mme Verdurin's mannerisms, and notably her tone of simpering autocracy. "Toast" being as unfamiliar to me as "Colombin's," this further promise could not have added to my temptation. It will appear stranger, now that everyone uses such expressions—perhaps even at Combray—that I had not at first understood who Mme Swann was speaking of when I heard her sing the praises of our old "nurse." I did not know any English; I soon gathered, however, that the word was intended to denote Françoise. Having been so terrified in the Champs-Elysées of the bad impression that she must make, I now learned from Mme Swann that it was all the things that Gilberte had told them about my "nurse" that had attracted her husband and her to me. "One feels that she is so devoted to you, that she must be so nice!" (At once my opinion of Françoise was diametrically changed. Conversely, to have a governess equipped with a waterproof and a feather in her hat no longer appeared quite so essential.) Finally I learned from some words which Mme Swann let fall with regard to Mme Blatin (whose good nature she acknowledged but whose visits she dreaded) that personal relations with that lady would have been of less value to me than I had supposed, and would not in any way have improved my standing with the Swanns.

If I had now begun to explore with tremors of reverence and joy the enchanted domain which, against all expectations, had opened to me its hitherto impenetrable approaches, this was still only in my capacity as a friend of Gilberte. The realm into which I was admitted was itself contained within another, more mysterious still, in which Swann and his wife led their supernatural existence and towards which they made their way, after shaking my hand, when they crossed the hall at the same moment as myself but in the other direction. But soon I was to penetrate also to the heart of the Sanctuary. For instance, Gilberte might be out when I called, but M. or Mme Swann was at home. They would ask who had rung, and on being told that it was I, would send out to ask me to come in for a moment and talk to them, desiring me to use in one way or another, with this or that object in view, my influence over their daughter. I remembered the letter, so complete and so persuasive, which I had written to Swann only the other day, and which he had not deigned even to acknowledge. I marvelled at the impotence of the mind, the reason and the heart to effect the least conversion, to solve a single one of those difficulties which subsequently life, without one's so much as knowing how it went about it, so easily unravels. My new position as the friend of Gilberte, endowed with an excellent influence over her, now enabled me to enjoy the same favours as if, having had as a companion at some school where I was always at the top of my class the son of a king, I had owed to that accident the right of informal entry into the palace and to audiences in the throne-room. Swann, with an infinite benevolence and as though he were not over-burdened with glorious occupations, would take me into his library and there allow me for an hour on end to respond in stammered monosyllables, timid silences broken by brief and incoherent bursts of courage, to observations of which my excitement prevented me from understanding a single word; would show me works of art and books which he thought likely to interest me, things as to which I had no doubt that they infinitely surpassed in beauty anything that the Louvre or the Bibliothèque Nationale possessed, but at which I found it impossible to look. At such moments I should have been delighted if Swann's butler had demanded from me my watch, my tie-pin, my boots, and made me sign a deed acknowledging him as my heir; in the admirable words of a popular expression of which, as of the most famous epics, we do not know the author, although, like these epics, and with all deference to Wolf and his theory,[5] it most certainly had one (one of those inventive and modest souls such as we come across every year, who light upon such gems as "putting a name to a face," though their own names they never reveal), *I no longer knew what I was doing*. The most I was capable of was astonishment, when my visit was at all prolonged, at the nullity of achievement, at the utter inconclusiveness of those hours spent in the enchanted dwelling. But my disappointment arose neither from the inadequacy of the works of art that were shown to me nor from the impossibility of fixing upon them my distracted gaze. For it was not the intrinsic beauty of the objects themselves that made it miraculous for me to be sitting in Swann's library, it was the attachment to those objects—which might have been the ugliest in the world—of the particular feeling, melancholy and voluptuous, which I had for so many years located in that room and which still impregnated it; similarly the multitude of mirrors, of silver-backed brushes, of altars to Saint Anthony of Padua carved and painted by the most eminent artists, her friends, counted for nothing in the feeling of my own unworthiness and of her regal benevolence which was aroused in me when Mme Swann received me for a moment in her bedroom, in which three beautiful and impressive creatures, her first, second and third lady's-maids, smilingly prepared for her the most marvellous toilettes, and towards which, on the order conveyed to me by the footman in knee-breeches that Madame wished to say a few words to me, I would make my way along the tortuous path of a corridor perfumed for the whole of its length with the precious essences which ceaselessly wafted from her dressing-room their fragrant exhalations.

When Mme Swann had returned to her visitors, we could still hear her talking and laughing, for even with only two people in the room, and as though she had to cope with all the "chums" at once, she would raise her voice, ejaculate her words, as she had so often in the "little clan" heard the "Mistress" do, at the moments when she "led the conversation." The expressions which we have recently borrowed from other people being those which, for a time at least, we are fondest of using, Mme Swann used to select sometimes those which she had learned from distinguished people whom her husband had not been able to avoid introducing to her (it was from them that she derived the mannerism which consists in suppressing the article or demonstrative pronoun before an adjective qualifying a person's name), sometimes others more vulgar (such as "He's a mere nothing!"—the favourite expression of one of her friends), and tried to place them in all the stories which, from a habit formed in the "little clan," she loved to tell. She would follow these up automatically with, "I do love that story!" or "Do admit, it's a very *good* story!" which came to her, through her husband, from the Guermantes whom she did not know.

Mme Swann had left the dining-room, but her husband, having just returned home, would make his appearance among us in turn. "Do you know if your mother is alone, Gilberte?" "No, Papa, she still has some visitors." "What, still? At seven o'clock! It's appalling. The poor woman must be absolutely broken. It's odious." (At home I had always heard the first syllable of this word pronounced with a long "o," like "ode," but M. and Mme Swann made it short, as in "odd.") "Just think of it; ever since two o'clock this afternoon!" he went on, turning to me. "And Camille tells me that between four and five he let in at least a dozen people. Did I say a dozen? I believe he told me fourteen. No, a dozen; I don't remember. When I came home I had quite forgotten it was her 'day,' and when I saw all those carriages outside the door I thought there must be a wedding in the house. And just now, while I've been in the library for a short while, the bell has never stopped ringing; upon my word, it's given me quite a headache. And are there a lot of them in there still?" "No; only two." "Who are they, do you know?" "Mme Cottard and Mme Bontemps." "Oh! the wife of the Chief Secretary to the Minister of Public Works." "I know her husband works in some Ministry or other, but I don't know what as," Gilberte would say in a babyish manner.

"What's that? You silly child, you talk as if you were

two years old. What do you mean: 'works in some Ministry or other' indeed! He's nothing less than Chief Secretary, head of the whole show, and what's more—what on earth am I thinking of? Upon my word, I'm getting as stupid as yourself: he isn't the Chief Secretary, he's the Permanent Secretary."

"How should I know? Is that supposed to mean a lot, being Permanent Secretary?" answered Gilberte, who never let slip an opportunity of displaying her own indifference to anything that gave her parents cause for vanity. (She may, of course, have considered that she only enhanced the brilliance of such an acquaintance by not seeming to attach any undue importance to it.)

"I should think it did 'mean a lot'!" exclaimed Swann, who preferred to this modesty, which might have left me in doubt, a more explicit parlance. "Why it means simply that he's the first man after the Minister. In fact, he's more important than the Minister, because it's he who does all the work. Besides, it appears that he's immensely able, a man quite of the first rank, a most distinguished individual. He's an Officer of the Legion of Honour. A delightful man, and very good-looking too."

(This man's wife, incidentally, had married him against everyone's wishes and advice because he was a "charming creature." He had, what may be sufficient to constitute a rare and delicate whole, a fair, silky beard, good features, a nasal voice, bad breath, and a glass eye.)

"I may tell you," he added, turning to me, "that I'm greatly amused to see that lot serving in the present government, because they are Bontemps of the Bontemps-Chenut family, typical of the old-fashioned bourgeoisie, reactionary, clerical, tremendously straitlaced. Your grandfather knew quite well, at least by name and by sight, old Chenut, the father, who never tipped cabmen more than a sou, though he was a rich man for those days, and the Baron Bréau-Chenut. All their money went in the Union Générale smash—you're too young to remember that, of course—and, gad! they've had to get it back as best they could."

"He's the uncle of a girl who used to come to my lessons, in a class a long way below mine, the famous 'Albertine.' She's certain to be dreadfully 'fast' when she's older, but meanwhile she's an odd fish."

"She is amazing, this daughter of mine. She knows everyone."

"I don't know her. I only used to see her about, and hear them calling 'Albertine' here and 'Albertine' there. But I do know Mme Bontemps, and I don't like her much either."

"You are quite wrong; she's charming, pretty, intelligent. She's even quite witty. I shall go in and say how d'ye do to her, and ask her if her husband thinks we're going to have a war, and whether we can rely on King Theodosius. He's bound to know, don't you think, since he's in the counsels of the gods."

It was not thus that Swann used to talk in days gone by; but which of us cannot call to mind some quite unpretentious royal princess who has let herself be carried off by a footman, and then, ten years later, trying to get back into society and sensing that people are not very willing to call on her, spontaneously adopts the language of all the old bores, and, when a fashionable duchess is mentioned, can be heard to say: "She came to see me only yesterday," or "I live a very quiet life"? Thus it is superfluous to make a study of social mores, since we can deduce them from psychological laws.

The Swanns shared this failing of people who are not much sought after; a visit, an invitation, a mere friendly word from anyone at all prominent was for them an event to which they felt the need to give full publicity. If bad luck would have it that the Verdurins were in London when Odette gave a rather smart dinner-party, it would be arranged for some common friend to cable a report to them across the Channel. The Swanns were incapable even of keeping to themselves the complimentary letters and telegrams received by Odette. They spoke of them to their friends, passed them from hand to hand. Thus the Swanns' drawing-room was reminiscent of a seaside hotel where telegrams are posted up on a board.

Moreover, people who had known the old Swann not merely outside society, as I had, but in society, in that Guermantes set which, with certain concessions to Highnesses and Duchesses, was infinitely exacting in the matter of wit and charm, from which banishment was sternly decreed for men of real eminence whom its members found boring or vulgar,—such people might have been astonished to observe that the old Swann had ceased not only to be discreet when he spoke of his acquaintance, but particular when it came to choosing it. How was it that Mme Bontemps, so common, so ill-natured, failed to exasperate him? How could he possibly describe her as attractive? The memory of the Guermantes set must, one would suppose, have prevented him; in fact it encouraged him. There was certainly among the Guermantes, as compared with the great majority of groups in society, a degree of taste, even refined taste, but also a snobbishness from which there arose the possibility of a momentary interruption in the exercise of that taste. In the case of someone who was not indispensable to their circle, of a Minister of Foreign Affairs, a slightly pompous Republican, or an Academician who talked too much, their taste would be brought to bear heavily against him; Swann would condole with Mme de Guermantes on having had to sit next to such people at dinner at one of the embassies; and they would a thousand times rather have a man of fashion, that is to say a man of the Guermantes kind, good for nothing, but endowed with the wit of the Guermantes, someone who belonged to the same clique. Only, a Grand Duchess, a Princess of the Blood, should she dine often with Mme de Guermantes, would soon find herself enrolled in that clique also, without having any right to be there, without being at all so endowed. But with the naïvety of society people, from the moment they had her in their houses they went out of their way to find her agreeable, since they were unable to say to themselves that it was because she was agreeable that they invited her. Swann, coming to the rescue of Mme de Guermantes, would say to her after the Highness had gone: "After all, she's not such a bad sort; really, she has quite a sense of humour. I don't suppose for a moment she has mastered the *Critique of Pure Reason*; still, she's not unpleasant." "Oh, I do so entirely agree with you!" the Duchess would reply. "Besides, she was a little shy: you'll see that she can be charming." "She is certainly a great deal less boring than Mme X" (the wife of the talkative Academician, who was in fact a remarkable woman) "who quotes twenty volumes at you." "Oh, but there's no comparison." The faculty of saying such things as these, and of saying them sincerely, Swann had acquired from the Duchess, and had never lost. He made use of it now with reference to the people who came to his house. He went out of his way to discern and to admire in them the qualities that every human being will display if we examine him with a prejudice in his favour and not with the distaste of the nice-minded; he extolled the merits of Mme Bontemps as he had once extolled those of the Princesse de Parme, who must have been excluded from the Guermantes set if there had not been privileged terms of admission for certain Highnesses, and if, when they too presented themselves for election, the only consideration had been wit and a certain charm. We have seen already, moreover, that Swann had always an inclination (which he was now putting into practice merely in a more lasting fashion) to exchange his social position for another which, in certain circumstances, might suit him better. It is only people incapable of dissecting what at first sight appears indivisible in their perception who believe that one's position is an integral part of one's person. One and the same man, taken at successive points in his life, will be found to breathe, on different rungs of the social ladder, in atmospheres that do not of necessity become more and more refined; whenever, in any period of our existence, we form or re-form associations with a certain circle, and feel cherished and at ease in it, we begin quite naturally to cling to it by putting down human roots.

Where Mme Bontemps was concerned, I believe also that Swann, in speaking of her with so much emphasis, was not sorry to think that my parents would hear that she had been to see his wife. To tell the truth, in our house the names of the people whom Mme Swann was gradually getting to know aroused more curiosity than admiration. At the name of Mme Trombert, my mother exclaimed: "Ah! there's a new recruit who will bring in others." And as though she found a similarity between the somewhat summary, rapid, and violent manner in which Mme Swann conquered her new connections and a colonial expedition, Mamma went on to observe: "Now that the Tromberts have been subdued, the neighbouring tribes will soon surrender." If she had passed Mme Swann in the street, she would tell us when she came home: "I saw Mme Swann in all her war-paint; she must have been embarking on some triumphant offensive against the Massachutoes, or the Singhalese, or the Tromberts." And so with all the new people whom I told her that I had seen in that somewhat composite and artificial society, to which they had often been brought with some difficulty and from widely different worlds, Mamma would at once divine their origin, and, speaking of them as of trophies dearly bought, would say: "Brought back from the expedition against the so-and-so!"

As for Mme Cottard, my father was astonished that Mme Swann could see anything to be gained from inviting so utterly undistinguished a woman to her house, and said: "In spite of the Professor's position, I must say that I cannot understand it." Mamma, on the other hand, understood very well; she knew that a great deal of the pleasure which a woman finds in entering a class of society different from that in which she has previously lived would be lacking if she had no means of keeping her old associates informed of those others, relatively more brilliant, with whom she has replaced them. For this, she requires an eye-witness who may be allowed to penetrate this new, delicious world (as a buzzing, browsing insect bores its way into a flower) and will then, so it is hoped, as the course of her visits may carry her, spread abroad the tidings, the latent germ of envy and of wonder. Mme Cottard, who might have been created on purpose to fulfil this role, belonged to that special category in a visiting list which Mamma (who inherited certain facets of her father's turn of mind) used to call "Go tell the Spartans" people. Besides—apart from another reason which did not come to our knowledge until many years later—Mme Swann, in inviting this good-natured, reserved and modest friend to her "at homes," had no need to fear lest she might be introducing into her drawing-room a traitor or a rival. She knew what a vast number of bourgeois calyxes that busy worker, armed with her plume and card-case, could visit in a single afternoon. She knew her power of pollination, and, basing her calculations upon the law of probability, was justified in thinking that almost certainly some intimate of the Verdurins would be bound to hear, within two or three days, how the Governor of Paris had left cards upon her, or that M. Verdurin himself would be told how M. Le Hault de Pressagny, the President of the Horse Show, had taken them, Swann and herself, to the King Theodosius gala; she imagined the Verdurins to be informed of these two events, both so flattering to herself, and of these alone, because the particular manifestations in which we envisage and pursue fame are but few in number, through the deficiency of our own minds, which are incapable of imagining at one and the same time all the forms which we none the less hope—on the whole—that fame will not fail simultaneously to assume for our benefit.

Mme Swann had, however, met with no success outside what was called the "official world." Elegant women did not go to her house. It was not the presence there of Republican notables that frightened them away. In the days of my early childhood, everything that pertained to conservative society was worldly, and no respectable salon would ever have opened its doors to a Republican. The people who lived in such an atmosphere imagined that the impossibility of ever inviting an "opportunist"—still, more a "horrid radical"—was something that would endure for ever, like oil-lamps and horse-drawn omnibuses. But, like a kaleidoscope which is every now and then given a turn, society arranges successively in different orders elements which one would have supposed immutable, and composes a new pattern. Before I had made my first Communion, right-minded ladies had had the stupefying experience of meeting an elegant Jewess while paying a social call. These new arrangements of the kaleidoscope are produced by what a philosopher would call a "change of criterion." The Dreyfus case brought about another, at a period rather later than that in which I began to go to Mme Swann's, and the kaleidoscope once more reversed its coloured lozenges. Everything Jewish, even the elegant lady herself, went down, and various obscure nationalists rose to take its place. The most brilliant salon in Paris was that of an ultra-Catholic Austrian prince. If instead of the Dreyfus case there had come a war with Germany, the pattern of the kaleidoscope would have taken a turn in the other direction. The Jews having shown, to the general astonishment, that they were patriots, would have kept their position, and no one would any longer have cared to go, or even to admit that he had ever gone any longer to the Austrian prince's. None of this alters the fact, however, that whenever society is momentarily stationary, the people who live in it imagine that no further change will occur, just as, in spite of having witnessed the birth of the telephone, they decline to believe in the aeroplane. Meanwhile the philosophers of journalism are at work castigating the preceding epoch, and not only the kind of pleasures in which it indulged, which seem to them to be the last word in corruption, but even the work of its artists and philosophers, which have no longer the least value in their eyes, as though they were indissolubly linked to the successive moods of fashionable frivolity. The one thing that does not change is that at any and every time it appears that there have been "great changes." At the time when I went to Mme Swann's the Dreyfus storm had not yet broken, and some of the more prominent Jews were extremely powerful—none more so than Sir Rufus Israels, whose wife, Lady Israels, was Swann's aunt. She herself had no intimate connections as distinguished as those of her nephew, who, since he did not care for her, had never much cultivated her society, although he was presumed to be her heir. But she was the only one of Swann's relations who had any idea of his social position, the others having always remained in the state of ignorance, in that respect, which had long been our own. When one of the members of a family emigrates into high society—which to him appears a feat without parallel until after the lapse of a decade he observes that it has been performed in other ways and for different reasons by more than one young man whom he knew as a boy—he draws round about himself a zone of shadow, a *terra incognita*, which is clearly visible in its minutest details to all those who inhabit it but is darkest night, pure nothingness, to those who do not penetrate it but touch its fringe without the least suspicion of its existence in their midst. There being no news agency to furnish Swann's cousins with intelligence of the people with whom he consorted, it was (before his appalling marriage, of course) with a smile of condescension that they would tell one another over family dinner-tables that they had spent a "virtuous" Sunday in going to see "cousin Charles," whom (regarding him as a poor relation who was inclined to envy their prosperity) they used wittily to name, playing upon the title of Balzac's novel, "Le Cousin Bête." Lady Israels, however, knew exactly who the people were who lavished upon Swann a friendship of which she was frankly jealous. Her husband's family, which was roughly the equivalent of the Rothschilds, had for several generations managed the affairs of the Orléans princes. Lady Israels, being immensely rich, exercised a wide influence, and had employed it so as to ensure that no one whom she knew should be "at home" to Odette. One alone had disobeyed her, in secret, the Comtesse de Marsantes. And then, as ill luck would have it, Odette having gone to call upon Mme de Marsantes, Lady Israels had entered the room almost at her heels. Mme de Marsantes was on tenterhooks.* With the cowardice of those who are nevertheless in a position to act as they choose, she did not address a single word to Odette, who thus found little encouragement to pursue any further an incursion into a world which was not in any case the one into which she wished to be received. In her complete detachment from the Faubourg Saint-Germain, Odette continued to be the illiterate courtesan, utterly different from those bourgeois snobs, "well up" in all the minutest points of genealogy, who endeavour to quench by reading old memoirs their thirst for the aristocratic connections with which real life has omitted to provide them. And Swann, for his part, continued no doubt to be the lover in whose eyes all these peculiarities of an old mistress seem lovable or at least inoffensive, for I often heard his wife perpetuate veritable social heresies without his attempting to correct them, whether from lingering affection, lack of esteem, or weariness of the effort to improve her. It was perhaps also another form of the simplicity which for so long had misled us at Combray, and which now had the effect that, while he continued to know, on his own account at least, very grand people, he had no wish for them to appear to be regarded as of any importance in conversation in his wife's drawing-room. They had, indeed, less importance than ever for Swann, the centre of gravity of his life having shifted. In any case, Odette's ignorance in social matters was such that if the name of the Princesse de Guermantes were mentioned in conversation after that of the Duchess, her cousin, "Those ones are princes, are they?" she would exclaim; "So they've gone up a step?" Were anyone to say "the Prince," in speaking of the Duc de Chartres, she would put him right: "The Duke, you mean; he's Duc de Chartres, not Prince." As for the Duc d'Orléans, son of the Comte de Paris: "That's funny; the son is higher than the father!" she would remark, adding, for she was afflicted with Anglomania, "Those *Royalties* are so dreadfully confusing!"—while to someone who asked her from what province the Guermantes family came she would reply: "From the Aisne."

But so far as Odette was concerned, Swann was quite blind, not merely to these deficiencies in her education but to the general mediocrity of her intelligence. More than that; whenever Odette told a silly story Swann would sit listening to his wife with a complacency, a merriment, almost an admiration in which some vestige of desire for her must have played a part; while in the same conversation, anything subtle or even profound that he himself might say would be listened to by Odette with an habitual lack of interest, rather curtly, with impatience, and would at times be sharply contradicted. And we may conclude that this subservience of refinement to vulgarity is the rule in many households, when we think, conversely, of all the superior women who yield to the blandishments of a boor, merciless in his censure of their most delicate utterances, while they themselves, with the infinite indulgence of love, are enraptured by the feeblest of his witticisms. To return to the reasons which prevented Odette, at this period, from gaining admittance to the Faubourg Saint-Germain, it must be observed that the latest turn of the social kaleidoscope had been actuated by a series of scandals. Women to whose houses one had been going with perfect confidence had been discovered to be common prostitutes or British spies. For some time thereafter one expected people to be (such at least was one's intention) staid and solidly based. Odette represented exactly what one had just severed relations with, only, incidentally, to renew them at once (for men, their natures not altering overnight, seek in every new order a continuance of the old), though seeking it under another form which would allow one to be taken in, and to believe that it was no longer the same society as before the crisis. However, the "branded" women of that society and Odette were too closely alike. Society people are very short-sighted; at the moment when they cease to have any relations with the Jewish ladies they know, while they are wondering how they are to fill the gap thus made in their lives, they perceive, thrust into it as by the windfall of a night of storm, a new lady, also Jewish; but by virtue of her novelty she is not associated in their minds with her predecessors, with what they are convinced that they must abjure. She does not ask that they shall respect her God. They take her up. There was no question of anti-Semitism at the time when I used first to visit Odette. But she resembled what people wished for a time to avoid.

As for Swann himself, he still often called on some of his former acquaintances, who, of course, belonged to the very highest society. And yet when he spoke to us of the people whom he had just been to see I noticed that, among those whom he had known in the old days, the choice that he made was dictated by the same kind of taste, partly artistic, partly historic, that inspired him as a collector. And remarking that it was often some Bohemian noblewoman who interested him because she had been the mistress of Liszt or because one of Balzac's novels had been dedicated to her grandmother (as he would purchase a drawing if Chateaubriand had written about it), I conceived a suspicion that we had, at Combray, replaced one error, that of regarding Swann as a rich bourgeois who did not go into society, by another, when we supposed him to be one of the smartest men in Paris. To be a friend of the Comte de Paris means nothing at all. Is not the world full of such "friends of princes," who would not be received in any house that was at all exclusive? Princes know themselves to be princes, and are not snobs; besides, they believe themselves to be so far above everything that is not of their blood royal that noblemen and commoners appear, in the depths beneath them, to be practically on a level.

But Swann was not content with seeking in society, and fastening on the names which the past has inscribed on its roll and which are still to be read there, a simple artistic and literary pleasure; he indulged in the slightly vulgar diversion of arranging as it were social nosegays by grouping heterogeneous elements, by bringing together people taken at random here, there and everywhere. These amusing (to Swann) sociological experiments did not always provoke an identical reaction from all his wife's friends. "I'm thinking of asking the Cottards to meet the Duchesse de Vendôme," he would say to Mme Bontemps with a laugh, in the zestful tone of an epicure who has thought of and intends to try substituting cayenne pepper for cloves in a sauce. But this plan, which might indeed appear agreeable to the Cottards, was calculated to infuriate Mme Bontemps. She herself had recently been introduced by the Swanns to the Duchesse de Vendôme, and had found this as agreeable as it seemed to her natural. The thought of being able to boast about it at the Cottards' had been by no means the least savoury ingredient of her pleasure. But like those persons recently decorated who, their investiture once accomplished, would like to see the fountain of honour turned off at the main, Mme Bontemps would have preferred that, after herself, no one else in her own circle should be made known to the Princess. She inwardly cursed the depraved taste which caused Swann, in order to gratify a wretched aesthetic whim, to destroy at one swoop the dazzling impression she had made on the Cottards when she told them about the Duchesse de Vendôme. How was she even to dare to announce to her husband that the Professor and his wife were in their turn to partake of this pleasure of which she had boasted to him as though it were unique. If only the Cottards could be made to know that they were being invited not seriously but for the amusement of their host! It is true that the Bontemps had been invited for the same reason, but Swann, having acquired from the aristocracy that eternal Donjuanism which, in treating with two women of no importance, makes each of them believe that it is she alone who is seriously loved, had spoken to Mme Bontemps of the Duchesse de Vendôme as of a person with whom it was essential for her to dine. "Yes, we're having the Princess here with the Cottards," said Mme Swann a few weeks later. "My husband thinks that we might get something quite amusing out of the conjunction." For if she had retained from the "little nucleus" certain habits dear to Mme Verdurin, such as that of shouting things aloud so as to be heard by all the faithful, she made use, at the same time, of certain expressions, such as "conjunction," which were dear to the Guermantes circle, of which she was thus undergoing the attraction, unconsciously and at a distance, as the sea is swayed by the moon, though without being drawn perceptibly closer to it. "Yes, the Cottards and the Duchesse de Vendôme. Don't you think that might be rather fun?" asked Swann.

"I think it will go very badly, and can only lead to a lot of bother. People oughtn't to play with fire," snapped Mme Bontemps, furious. She and her husband, and also the Prince d'Agrigente, were, as it happened, invited to this dinner, which Mme Bontemps and Cottard had each two alternative ways of describing, according to whom they were addressing. To some Mme Bontemps for her part, and Cottard for his, would say casually, when asked who else had been of the party: "Only the Prince d'Agrigente; it was very intimate." But there were others who might, alas, be better informed (once, indeed, someone had challenged Cottard with: "But weren't the Bontemps there too?" "Oh, I forgot them," Cottard had blushingly admitted to the tactless questioner whom he ever afterwards classified among the mischief-makers). For these the Bontemps and the Cottards had each adopted, without any mutual arrangement, a version the framework of which was identical for both parties, their own names being interchanged. "Let me see," Cottard would say, "there were our host and hostess, the Duc and Duchesse de Vendôme—" (with a self-satisfied smile) "Professor and Mme Cottard, the Prince d'Agrigente, and, upon my soul, heaven only knows how they got there, for they were like fish out of water, M. and Mme Bontemps!" Mme Bontemps would recite exactly the same "piece," only it was M. and Mme Bontemps who were named with self-satisfied emphasis between the Duchesse de Vendôme and the Prince d'Agrigente, while the scurvy lot, whom she wound up by accusing of having invited themselves, and who completely spoiled the picture, were the Cottards.

When he had been paying social calls Swann would often come home with little time to spare before dinner. At that point in the evening, around six o'clock, when in the old days he used to feel so wretched, he no longer asked himself what Odette might be about, and was hardly at all concerned to hear that she had people with her or had gone out. He recalled at times that he had once, years ago, tried to read through its envelope a letter addressed by Odette to Forcheville. But this memory was not pleasing to him, and rather than plumb the depths of shame that he felt in it he preferred to indulge in a little grimace, twisting up the corners of his mouth and adding, if need be, a shake of the head which signified "What do I care about it?" True, he considered now that the hypothesis on which he had often dwelt at that time, according to which it was his jealous imagination alone that blackened what was in reality the innocent life of Odette—that this hypothesis (which after all was beneficent, since, so long as his amorous malady had lasted, it had diminished his sufferings by making them seem imaginary) was not the correct one, that it was his jealousy that had seen things in the correct light, and that if Odette had loved him more than he supposed, she had also deceived him more. Formerly, while his sufferings were still keen, he had vowed that, as soon as he had ceased to love Odette and was no longer afraid either of vexing her or of making her believe that he loved her too much, he would give himself the satisfaction of elucidating with her, simply from his love of truth and as a point of historical interest, whether or not Forcheville had been in bed with her that day when he had rung her bell and rapped on her window in vain, and she had written to Forcheville that it was an uncle of hers who had called. But this so interesting problem, which he was only waiting for his jealousy to subside before clearing up, had precisely lost all interest in Swann's eyes when he had ceased to be jealous. Not immediately, however. Long after he had ceased to feel any jealousy with regard to Odette, the memory of that day, that afternoon spent knocking vainly at the little house in the Rue La Pérouse, had continued to torment him. It was as though his jealousy, not dissimilar in that respect from those maladies which appear to have their seat, their centre of contagion, less in certain persons than in certain places, in certain houses, had had for its object not so much Odette herself as that day, that hour in the irrevocable past when Swann had knocked at every entrance to her house in turn, as though that day, that hour alone had caught and preserved a few last fragments of the amorous personality which had once been Swann's, that there alone could he now recapture them. For a long time now it had been a matter of indifference to him whether Odette had been, or was being, unfaithful to him. And yet he had continued for some years to seek out old servants of hers, to such an extent had the painful curiosity persisted in him to know whether on that day, so long ago, at six o'clock, Odette had been in bed with Forcheville. Then that curiosity itself had disappeared, without, however, his abandoning his investigations. He went on trying to discover what no longer interested him, because his old self, though it had shrivelled to extreme decrepitude, still acted mechanically, in accordance with preoccupations so utterly abandoned that Swann could not now succeed even in picturing to himself that anguish—so compelling once that he had been unable to imagine that he would ever be delivered from it, that only the death of the woman he loved (though death, as will be shown later on in this story by a cruel corroboration, in no way diminishes the sufferings caused by jealousy) seemed to him capable of smoothing the path of his life which then seemed impassably obstructed.

But to bring to light, some day, those passages in the life of Odette to which he had owed his sufferings had not been Swann's only ambition; he had also resolved to avenge himself for his sufferings when, being no longer in love with Odette, he should no longer be afraid of her; and the opportunity of gratifying this second ambition had now presented itself, for Swann was in love with another woman, a woman who gave him no grounds for jealousy but none the less made him jealous, because he was no longer capable of altering his mode of loving, and it was the mode he had employed with Odette that must serve him now for another. To make Swann's jealousy revive it was not necessary for this woman to be unfaithful; it sufficed that for some reason or other she should have been away from him, at a party for instance, and should have appeared to enjoy herself. That was enough to reawaken in him the old anguish, that lamentable and contradictory excrescence of his love, which alienated Swann from what was in fact a sort of need to attain (the real feelings this young woman had for him, the hidden longing that absorbed her days, the secret places of her heart), for between Swann and the woman whom he loved this anguish piled up an unyielding mass of previous suspicions, having their cause in Odette, or in some other perhaps who had preceded Odette, which allowed the ageing lover to know his mistress of today only through the old, collective spectre of the "woman who aroused his jealousy" in which he had arbitrarily embodied his new love. Often, however, Swann would accuse his jealousy of making him believe in imaginary infidelities; but then he would remember that he had given Odette the benefit of the same argument, and wrongly. And so everything that the young woman whom he loved did in the hours when he was not with her ceased to appear innocent. But whereas at that other time he had made a vow that if ever he ceased to love the woman who, though he did not then know it, was to be his future wife, he would show her an implacable indifference that would at last be sincere, in order to avenge his pride that had so long been humiliated, now that he could enforce those reprisals without risk to himself (for what harm could it do him to be taken at his word and deprived of those intimate moments with Odette that had once been so necessary to him?), he no longer wished to do so; with his love had vanished the desire to show that he no longer loved. And he who, when he was suffering at the hands of Odette, so longed to let her see one day that he had fallen for another, now that he was in a position to do so took infinite precautions lest his wife should suspect the existence of this new love.

It was not only in those tea-parties, on account of which I had formerly had the sorrow of seeing Gilberte leave me and go home earlier than usual, that I was henceforth to take part, but the excursions she made with her mother which, by preventing her from coming to the Champs-Elysées, had deprived me of her on those days when I loitered alone upon the lawn in front of the roundabout—in these also M. and Mme Swann now included me: I had a seat in their landau, and indeed it was me that they asked if I would rather go to the theatre, to a dancing lesson at the house of one of Gilberte's friends, to some social gathering given by a friend of Mme Swann's (what the latter called "a little *meeting*") or to visit the tombs at Saint-Denis.

On the days when I was to go out with the Swanns I would arrive at their house in time for what Mme Swann called "le lunch." As one was not expected before half-past twelve, while my parents in those days had their meal at a quarter past eleven, it was not until they had risen from table that I made my way towards that sumptuous quarter, deserted enough at any time, but more particularly at that hour, when everyone had gone home. Even on frosty days in winter if the weather was fine, tightening every few minutes the knot of a gorgeous Charvet tie and looking to see that my patent-leather boots were not getting dirty, I would wander up and down the avenues, waiting until twenty-seven minutes past the hour. I could see from afar in the Swanns' little garden-plot the sunlight glittering like hoar-frost from the bare-boughed trees. It is true that the garden boasted only two. The unusual hour presented the scene in a new light. These pleasures of nature (intensified by the suppression of habit and indeed by my physical hunger), were infused by the thrilling prospect of sitting down to lunch with Mme Swann. It did not diminish them, but dominated and subdued them, made of them social accessories; so that if, at this hour when ordinarily I did not notice them, I seemed now to be discovering the fine weather, the cold, the wintry sunlight, it was all as a sort of preface to the creamed eggs, as a patina, a cool pink glaze applied to the decoration of that mystic chapel which was the habitation of Mme Swann, and in the heart of which there was by contrast so much warmth, so many scents and flowers.

At half-past twelve I would finally make up my mind to enter the house which, like an immense Christmas stocking, seemed ready to bestow upon me supernatural delights. (The French name "Noël" was, by the way, unknown to Mme Swann and Gilberte, who had substituted for it the English "Christmas," and would speak of nothing but "Christmas pudding," what people had given them as "Christmas presents," of going away—the thought of which maddened me with grief—"for Christmas." Even at home I should have thought it degrading to use the word "Noël," and always said "Christmas," which my father considered extremely silly.)

I encountered no one at first but a footman who, after leading me through several large drawing-rooms, showed me into one that was quite small, empty, its windows beginning to dream already in the blue light of afternoon. I was left alone there in the company of orchids, roses and violets, which, like people waiting beside you who do not know you, preserved a silence which their individuality as living things made all the more striking, and warmed themselves in the heat of a glowing coal fire, preciously ensconced behind a crystal screen, in a basin of white marble over which it spilled from time to time its dangerous rubies.

I had sat down, but rose hurriedly on hearing the door open; it was only another footman, and then a third, and the slender result that their vainly alarming entrances and exits achieved was to put a little more coal on the fire or water in the vases. They departed, and I found myself alone again, once that door was shut which Mme Swann was surely soon to open. Of a truth, I should have been less ill at ease in a magician's cave than in this little waiting-room where the fire appeared to me to be performing alchemical transmutations as in Klingsor's laboratory. Footsteps sounded afresh, but I did not get up; it was sure to be yet another footman. It was M. Swann. "What! all by yourself? What is one to do? That poor wife of mine has never been able to remember what time means! Ten minutes to one. She gets later every day. And as you'll see, she will come sailing in without the least hurry, and imagine she's in heaps of time." And since he was still subject to neuritis, and was becoming a trifle ridiculous, the fact of possessing so unpunctual a wife, who came in so late from the Bois, forgot everything at her dressmaker's and was never in time for lunch, made Swann anxious for his digestion but flattered his self-esteem.

He would show me his latest acquisitions and explain to me the interesting points about them, but my emotion, added to the unfamiliarity of being still unfed at this hour, stirred my mind while leaving it void, so that while I was capable of speech I was incapable of hearing. In any event, as far as the works of art in Swann's possession were concerned, it was enough for me that they were contained in his house, formed a part there of the delicious hour that preceded luncheon. The Gioconda herself might have appeared there without giving me any more pleasure than one of Mme Swann's indoor gowns, or her bottles of smelling-salts.

I continued to wait, alone, or with Swann and often Gilberte, who came in to keep us company. The arrival of Mme Swann, prepared for me by all those majestic apparitions, must, I felt, be something truly immense. I strained my ears to catch the slightest sound. But one never finds a cathedral, a wave in a storm, a dancer's leap in the air quite as high as one has been expecting; after those liveried footmen, suggesting the chorus whose processional entry upon the stage leads up to and at the same time diminishes the final appearance of the queen, Mme Swann, creeping furtively in, in a little otter-skin coat, her veil lowered to cover a nose pink-tipped by the cold, did not fulfil the promises lavished upon my imagination during my vigil.

But if she had stayed at home all morning, when she arrived in the drawing-room she would be clad in a brightly coloured crêpe-de-Chine housecoat which seemed to me more exquisite than any of her dresses.

Sometimes the Swanns decided to remain in the house all afternoon, and then, as we had lunched so late, very soon I would see, beyond the garden-wall, the sun setting on that day which had seemed to me bound to be different from other days; and in vain might the servants bring in lamps of every size and shape, burning each upon the consecrated altar of a console, a wall-bracket, a corner-cupboard, an occasional table, as though for the celebration of some strange and secret rite, nothing extraordinary transpired in the conversation, and I went home disappointed, as one often is in one's childhood after midnight mass.

But that disappointment was scarcely more than spiritual. I was radiant with happiness in this house where Gilberte, when she was not yet with us, was about to appear and would bestow on me in a moment, and for hours to come, her speech, her smiling and attentive gaze as I had glimpsed it for the first time at Combray. At the most I was a trifle jealous when I saw her so often disappear into vast rooms above, reached by an interior staircase. Obliged myself to remain in the drawing-room, like a man in love with an actress who is confined to his stall and wonders anxiously what is going on behind the scenes, in the green-room, I put to Swann some artfully veiled questions with regard to this other part of the house, but in a tone from which I could not succeed in banishing a slight uneasiness. He explained to me that the room to which Gilberte had gone was the linen-room, offered to show it to me himself, and promised me that whenever Gilberte had occasion to go there again he would insist on her taking me with her. By these last words and the relief which they brought me, Swann at once abolished for me one of those terrifying inner perspectives at the end of which a woman with whom we are in love appears so remote. At that moment I felt for him an affection which I believed to be deeper than my affection for Gilberte. For he, his daughter's master, was giving her to me, whereas she withheld herself at times; I had not the same direct control over her as I had indirectly through Swann. Besides, it was she whom I loved and whom I could not therefore see without that anxiety, without that desire for something more, which destroys in us, in the presence of the person we love, the sensation of loving.

As a rule, however, we did not stay indoors but went out. Sometimes, before going to dress, Mme Swann would sit down at the piano. Her lovely hands emerging from the pink, or white, or, often, vividly coloured sleeves of her crêpe-de-Chine housecoat, drooped over the keys with that same melancholy which was in her eyes but was not in her heart. It was on one of those days that she happened to play for me the passage in Vinteuil's sonata that contained the little phrase of which Swann had been so fond. But often one hears nothing when one listens for the first time to a piece of music that is at all complicated. And yet when, later on, this sonata had been played to me two or three times I found that I knew it perfectly well. And so it is not wrong to speak of hearing a thing for the first time. If one had indeed, as one supposes, received no impression from the first hearing, the second, the third would be equally "first hearings" and there would be no reason why one should understand it any better after the tenth. Probably what is wanting, the first time, is not comprehension but memory. For our memory, relative to the complexity of the impressions which it has to face while we are listening, is infinitesimal, as brief as the memory of a man who in his sleep thinks of a thousand things and at once forgets them, or as that of a man in his second childhood who cannot recall a minute afterwards what one has just said to him. Of these multiple impressions our memory is not capable of furnishing us with an immediate picture. But that picture gradually takes shape in the memory, and, with regard to works we have heard more than once, we are like the schoolboy who has read several times over before going to sleep a lesson which he supposed himself not to know, and finds that he can repeat it by heart next morning. But I had not, until then, heard a note of the sonata, and where Swann and his wife could make out a distinct phrase, it was as far beyond the range of my perception as a name which one endeavours to recall and in place of which one discovers only a void, a void from which, an hour later, when one is not thinking about them, will spring of their own accord, at one bound, the syllables that one has solicited in vain. And not only does one not grasp at once and remember works that are truly rare, but even within those works (as happened to me in the case of Vinteuil's sonata) it is the least precious parts that one at first perceives. So much so that I was mistaken not only in thinking that this work held nothing further in store for me (so that for a long time I made no effort to hear it again) from the moment Mme Swann had played me its most famous passage (I was in this respect as stupid as people are who expect to feel no astonishment when they stand in Venice before the façade of Saint Mark's, because photography has already acquainted them with the outline of its domes); far more than that, even when I had heard the sonata from beginning to end, it remained almost wholly invisible to me, like a monument of which distance or a haze allows us to catch but a faint and fragmentary glimpse. Hence the melancholy inseparable from one's knowledge of such works, as of everything that takes place in time. When the least obvious beauties of Vinteuil's sonata were revealed to me, already, borne by the force of habit beyond the grasp of my sensibility, those that I had from the first distinguished and preferred in it were beginning to escape, to elude me. Since I was able to enjoy everything that this sonata had to give me only in a succession of hearings, I never possessed it in its entirety: it was like life itself. But, less disappointing than life, great works of art do not begin by giving us the best of themselves. In a work such as Vinteuil's sonata the beauties that one discovers soonest are also those of which one tires most quickly, and for the same reason, no doubt—namely, that they are less different from what one already knows. But when those first impressions have receded, there remains for our enjoyment some passage whose structure, too new and strange to offer anything but confusion to our mind, had made it indistinguishable and so preserved intact; and this, which we had passed every day without knowing it, which had held itself in reserve for us, which by the sheer power of its beauty had become invisible and remained unknown, this comes to us last of all. But we shall also relinquish it last. And we shall love it longer than the rest because we have taken longer to get to love it. The time, moreover, that a person requires—as I required in the case of this sonata—to penetrate a work of any depth is merely an epitome, a symbol, one might say, of the years, the centuries even, that must elapse before the public can begin to cherish a masterpiece that is really new. So that the man of genius, to spare himself the ignorant contempt of the world, may say to himself that, since one's contemporaries are incapable of the necessary detachment, works written for posterity should be read by posterity alone, like certain pictures which one cannot appreciate when one stands too close to them. But in reality any such cowardly precaution to avoid false judgments is doomed to failure; they are unavoidable. The reason why a work of genius is not easily admired from the first is that the man who has created it is extraordinary, that few other men resemble him. It is his work itself that, by fertilising the rare minds capable of understanding it, will make them increase and multiply. It was Beethoven's quartets themselves (the Twelfth, Thirteenth, Fourteenth and Fifteenth) that devoted half a century to forming, fashioning and enlarging the audience for Beethoven's quartets, thus marking, like every great work of art, an advance if not in the quality of artists at least in the community of minds, largely composed today of what was not to be found when the work first appeared, that is to say of persons capable of appreciating it. What is called posterity is the posterity of the work of art. It is essential that the work (leaving out of account, for simplicity's sake, the contingency that several men of genius may at the same time be working along parallel lines to create a more instructed public in the future, from which other men of genius will benefit) should create its own posterity. For if the work were held in reserve, were revealed only to posterity, that audience, for that particular work, would be not posterity but a group of contemporaries who were merely living half-a-century later in time. And so it is essential that the artist (and this is what Vinteuil had done), if he wishes his work to be free to follow its own course, should launch it, there where there is sufficient depth, boldly into the distant future. And yet, if leaving out of account this time to come, the true perspective in which to appreciate a work of art, is the mistake made by bad judges, taking it into account is at times a dangerous precaution of good ones. No doubt it is easy to imagine, by an illusion similar to that which makes everything on the horizon appear equidistant, that all the revolutions which have hitherto occurred in painting or in music did at least respect certain rules, whereas that which immediately confronts us, be it Impressionism, the pursuit of dissonance, an exclusive use of the Chinese scale, Cubism, Futurism or what you will, differs outrageously from all that has occurred before. This is because everything that went before we are apt to regard as a whole, forgetting that a long process of assimilation has converted it into a substance that is varied of course but, taken as a whole, homogeneous, in which Hugo is juxtaposed with Molière. Let us try to imagine the shocking disparities we should find, if we did not take account of the future and the changes that it must bring, in a horoscope of our own riper years cast for us in our youth. Only horoscopes are not always accurate, and the necessity, when judging a work of art, of including the temporal factor in the sum total of its beauty introduces into our judgment something as conjectural, and consequently as barren of interest, as any prophecy the non-fulfilment of which will in no way imply any inadequacy on the prophet's part, for the power to summon possibilities into existence or to exclude them from it is not necessarily within the competence of genius; one may have had genius and yet not have believed in the future of railways or of flight, or, although a brilliant psychologist, in the infidelity of a mistress or of a friend whose treachery persons far less gifted would have foreseen.

If I did not understand the sonata, I was enchanted to hear Mme Swann play. Her touch appeared to me (like her wrapper, like the scent of her staircase, like her coats, like her chrysanthemums) to form part of an individual and mysterious whole, in a world infinitely superior to that in which reason is capable of analysing talent. "Isn't it beautiful, that Vinteuil sonata?" Swann asked me. "The moment when night is falling among the trees, when the arpeggios of the violin call down a cooling dew upon the earth. You must admit it's lovely; it shows all the static side of moonlight, which is the essential part. It's not surprising that a course of radiant heat such as my wife is taking should act on the muscles, since moonlight can prevent the leaves from stirring. That's what is expressed so well in that little phrase, the Bois de Boulogne plunged in a cataleptic trance. By the sea it's even more striking, because you have there the faint response of the waves, which, of course, you can hear quite distinctly since nothing else can move. In Paris it's the other way round: at most, you may notice unfamiliar lights among the old buildings, the sky lit up as though by a colourless and harmless conflagration, a sort of vast news item of which you get a hint here and there. But in Vinteuil's little phrase, and in the whole sonata for that matter, it's not like that; the scene is laid in the Bois; in the *gruppetto* you can distinctly hear a voice saying: 'I can almost see to read the paper!' "

These words of Swann's might have distorted, later on, my impression of the sonata, music being too little exclusive to dismiss absolutely what other people suggest that we should find in it. But I understood from other remarks he made that this nocturnal foliage was simply that beneath whose shade, in many a restaurant on the outskirts of Paris, he had listened on so many evenings to the little phrase. In place of the profound meaning that he had so often sought in it, what it now recalled to Swann were the leafy boughs, ordered, wreathed, painted round about it (which it gave him the desire to see again because it seemed to him to be their inner, their hidden self, as it were their soul), was the whole of one spring season which he had not been able to enjoy at the time, not having had—feverish and sad as he then was—the requisite physical and mental well-being, and which (as one puts by for an invalid the dainties that he has not been able to eat) it had kept for him. The charm that he had been made to feel by certain evenings in the Bois, a charm of which Vinteuil's sonata served to remind him, he could not have recaptured by questioning Odette, although she, as well as the little phrase, had been his companion there. But Odette had been merely by his side, not (as the phrase had been) within him, and so had seen nothing—nor would have, had she been a thousand times as comprehending—of that vision which for none of us (or at least I was long under the impression that this rule admitted of no exception) can be externalised.

"It's rather a charming thought, don't you think," Swann continued, "that sound can reflect, like water, like a mirror. And it's curious, too, that Vinteuil's phrase now shows me only the things to which I paid no attention then. Of my troubles, my loves of those days, it recalls nothing, it has swapped things around." "Charles, I don't think that's very polite to me, what you're saying." "Not polite? Really, you women are superb! I was simply trying to explain to this young man that what the music shows—to me, at least—is not 'the triumph of the Will' or 'In Tune with the Infinite,' but shall we say old Verdurin in his frock-coat in the palmhouse in the Zoological Gardens. Hundreds of times, without my leaving this room, the little phrase has carried me off to dine with it at Armenonville. Good God, it's less boring, anyhow, than having to go there with Mme de Cambremer."

Mme Swann laughed. "That is a lady who's supposed to have been very much in love with Charles," she explained, in the same tone in which, shortly before, when we were speaking of Vermeer of Delft, of whose existence I had been surprised to find her informed, she had replied to me: "I ought to explain that Monsieur Swann was very much taken up with that painter at the time he was courting me. Isn't that so, Charles dear?" "You're not to start saying things about Mme de Cambremer," Swann checked her, secretly flattered. "But I'm only repeating what I've been told. Besides, it seems that she's extremely clever; I don't know her myself. I believe she's very *pushing*, which surprises me rather in a clever woman. But everyone says that she was quite mad about you; there's nothing hurtful in that." Swann remained silent as a deaf-mute, which was a sort of confirmation, and a proof of his self-complacency.

"Since what I'm playing reminds you of the Zoo," his wife went on, with a playful pretence of being offended, "we might drive this boy there this afternoon if it would amuse him. The weather's lovely now, and you can recapture your fond impressions! Which reminds me, talking of the Zoo, do you know, this young man thought that we were devotedly attached to a person whom I cut as a matter of fact whenever I possibly can, Mme Blatin. I think it's rather humiliating for us that she should be taken for a friend of ours. Just fancy, dear Dr Cottard, who never says a harsh word about anyone, declares that she's positively repellent." "A frightful woman! The one thing to be said for her is that she's exactly like Savonarola. She's the very image of that portrait of Savonarola by Fra Bartolommeo."

This mania of Swann's for finding likenesses to people in pictures was defensible, for even what we call individual expression is—as we so painfully discover when we are in love and would like to believe in the unique reality of the beloved—something diffused and general, which can be found existing at different periods. But if one had listened to Swann, the retinues of the Magi, already so anachronistic when Benozzo Gozzoli introduced in their midst various Medicis, would have been even more so, since they would have included the portraits of a whole crowd of men, contemporaries not of Gozzoli but of Swann, subsequent, that is to say, not only by fifteen centuries to the Nativity but by four to the painter himself. There was not missing from those cortèges, according to Swann, a single living Parisian of note, any more than there was from that act in one of Sardou's plays, in which, out of friendship for the author and for the leading lady, and also because it was the fashion, all the notabilities of Paris, famous doctors, politicians, barristers, amused themselves, each on a different evening, by "walking on."

"But what has she got to do with the Zoo?" "Everything!" "What? You don't suggest that she's got a sky-blue behind, like the monkeys?" "Charles, you really are too dreadful! I was thinking of what the Singhalese said to her. Do tell him, Charles, it really is a gem." "Oh, it's too silly. You know Mme Blatin loves accosting people, in a tone which she thinks friendly, but which is really condescending." "What our good friends on the Thames call *patronising*," interrupted Odette. "Exactly. Well, she went the other day to the Zoo, where they have some blackamoors—Singhalese I think I heard my wife say—she is much better at ethnology than I am." "Now, Charles, don't mock." "I'm not mocking at all. Well, to continue, she went up to one of these black fellows with 'Good morning, nigger!' . . ." "She's a nothing!" Mme Swann interjected. "Anyhow, this classification seems to have displeased the black. 'Me nigger,' he said angrily to Mme

Blatin, 'me nigger; you old cow!' " "I do think that's so delightful! I adore that story. Don't you think it's a good one. Can't you see old Blatin standing there?: 'Me nigger; you old cow!' "

I expressed an intense desire to go there and see these Singhalese, one of whom had called Mme Blatin an old cow. They did not interest me in the least. But I reflected that on the way to the Zoo, and again on our way home, we should pass through the Allée des Acacias in which I used to gaze so admiringly at Mme Swann, and that perhaps Coquelin's mulatto friend, to whom I had never managed to exhibit myself in the act of saluting her, would see me there, seated at her side, as the victoria swept by.

During those minutes in which Gilberte, having gone to get ready, was not in the room with us, M. and Mme Swann would take delight in revealing to me all the rare virtues of their child. And everything that I myself observed seemed to prove the truth of what they said. I remarked that, as her mother had told me, she had not only for her friends but for the servants, for the poor, the most delicate attentions, carefully thought out, a desire to give pleasure, a fear of causing displeasure, expressed in all sorts of little things over which she often took a great deal of trouble. She had done a piece of needlework for our stall-keeper in the Champs-Elysées, and went out in the snow to give it to her with her own hands, so as not to lose a day. "You have no idea how kind-hearted she is, since she never lets it be seen," her father assured me. Young as she was, she appeared far more sensible already than her parents. When Swann boasted of his wife's grand friends Gilberte would turn away and remain silent, but without any appearance of reproaching him, for it seemed inconceivable to her that her father could be the object of the slightest criticism. One day, when I had spoken to her of Mlle Vinteuil, she said to me:

"I never want to know her, for a very good reason, and that is that she was not nice to her father, from what one hears, and made him very unhappy. You can't understand that any more than I, can you? I'm sure you could no more live without your papa than I could, which is quite natural after all. How can one ever forget a person one has loved all one's life?"

And once when she was being particularly loving with Swann, and I mentioned this to her when he was out of the room:

"Yes, poor Papa, it's the anniversary of his father's death round about now. You can understand what he must be feeling. You do understand, don't you—you and I feel the same about things like that. So I just try to be a little less naughty than usual." "But he doesn't ever think you naughty. He thinks you're quite perfect." "Poor Papa, that's because he's far too good himself."

But her parents were not content with singing the praises of Gilberte—that same Gilberte who, even before I had set eyes on her, used to appear to me standing in front of a church, in a landscape of the Ile-de-France, and later, awakening in me not dreams now but memories, was embowered always in a hedge of pink hawthorn, in the little lane that I took when I was going the Méséglise way. Once when I had asked Mme Swann (making an effort to assume the indifferent tone of a friend of the family, curious to know the preferences of a child) which among all her playmates Gilberte liked the best, Mme

Swann replied: "But you ought to know a great deal better than I do, since you're in her confidence, the great favourite, the *crack,* as the English say."

Doubtless, in such perfect coincidences as this, when reality folds back and overlays what we have long dreamed of, it completely hides it from us, merges with it, like two equal superimposed figures which appear to be one, whereas, to give our happiness its full meaning, we would rather preserve for all those separate points of our desire, at the very moment in which we succeed in touching them—and to be quite certain that it is indeed they—the distinction of being intangible. And our thoughts cannot even reconstruct the old state in order to compare it with the new, for it has no longer a clear field: the acquaintance we have made, the memory of those first, unhoped-for moments, the talk we have heard, are there now to block the passage of our consciousness, and as they control the outlets of our memory far more than those of our imagination, they react more forcibly upon our past, which we are no longer able to visualise without taking them into account, than upon the form, still unshaped, of our future. For years I had believed that the notion of going to Mme Swann's was a vague, chimerical dream to which I should never attain; after I had spent a quarter of an hour in her drawing-room, it was the time when I did not yet know her that had become chimerical and vague like a possibility which the realisation of an alternative possibility has destroyed. How could I ever dream again of her dining-room as of an inconceivable place, when I could not make the least movement in my mind without crossing the path of that inextinguishable ray cast backwards ad infinitum, into my own most distant past, by the lobster *à l'Américaine* which I had just been eating. And Swann must have observed in his own case a similar phenomenon: for this house in which he now entertained me might be regarded as the place into which had flowed, to merge and coincide, not only the ideal dwelling that my imagination had constructed, but another still, which his jealous love, as inventive as any fantasy of mine, had so often depicted to him, that dwelling common to Odette and himself which had appeared to him so inaccessible once, on an evening when Odette had taken him home with Forcheville to drink orangeade with her; and what had flowed in to be absorbed, for him, in the walls and furniture of the dining-room in which we now sat down to lunch was that unhoped-for paradise in which, in the old days, he could not without a pang imagine that he would one day be saying to *their* butler the very words, "Is Madame ready yet?" which I now heard him utter with a touch of impatience mingled with self-satisfaction. No more, probably, than Swann himself could I succeed in knowing my own happiness, and when Gilberte herself once broke out: "Who would ever have said that the little girl you watched playing prisoner's base, without daring to speak to her, would one day be your greatest friend whose home you could go to whenever you liked?", she spoke of a change which I could verify only by observing it from without, finding no trace of it within myself, for it was composed of two separate states which I could not, without their ceasing to be distinct from one another, succeed in imagining at one and the same time.

And yet this house, because it had been so passionately desired by Swann, must have kept for him some of its sweetness, if I was to judge by myself for whom it had not lost all its mystery. That singular charm in which I had for so long supposed the life of the Swanns to be bathed had not been entirely exorcised from their house on my being admitted to it: I had made it draw back, overwhelmed as it was by the sight of the stranger, the pariah that I had been, to whom now Mme Swann graciously pushed forward an exquisite, hostile and scandalised armchair for him to sit in; but all around me in my memory, I can perceive it still. Is it because, on the days when M. and Mme Swann invited me to lunch, to go out afterwards with them and Gilberte, I imprinted with my gaze—while I sat waiting for them alone—on the carpet, the sofas, the tables, the screens, the pictures, the idea engraved upon my mind that Mme Swann, or her husband, or Gilberte was about to enter? Is it because those objects have dwelt ever since in my memory side by side with the Swanns, and have gradually acquired something of their identity? Is it because, knowing that they spent their existence among these things, I made of them all as it were emblems of the life and habits of the Swanns from which I had too long been excluded for them not to continue to appear strange to me, even when I was allowed the privilege of sharing in them? However it may be, whenever I think of that drawing-room which Swann (not that the criticism implied on his part any intention to find fault with his wife's taste) found so amorphous—because, while it was still conceived in the style, half conservatory half studio, which had been that of the rooms in which he had first known Odette, she had none the less begun to replace in this jumble a number of the Chinese ornaments which she now felt to be rather sham, a trifle dowdy, by a swarm of little chairs and stools and things draped in old Louis XVI silks; not to mention the works of art brought by Swann himself from his house on the Quai d'Orléans—it has kept in my memory, that composite, heterogeneous room, a cohesion, a unity, an individual charm that are not to be found even in the most complete, the least spoiled of the collections that the past has bequeathed to us, or the most modern, alive and stamped with the imprint of a living personality; for we alone, by our belief that they have an existence of their own, can give to certain things we see a soul which they afterwards keep and which they develop in our minds. All the ideas that I had formed of the hours, different from those that exist for other men, passed by the Swanns in that house which was to their everyday life what the body is to the soul, and whose singularity it must have expressed, all those ideas were distributed, amalgamated—equally disturbing and indefinable throughout—in the arrangement of the furniture, the thickness of the carpets, the position of the windows, the ministrations of the servants. When, after lunch, we went to drink our coffee in the sunshine of the great bay window of the drawing-room, as Mme Swann was asking me how many lumps of sugar I took, it was not only the silk-covered stool which she pushed towards me that exuded, together with the agonising charm that I had long ago discerned—first among the pink hawthorn and then beside the clump of laurels—in the name of Gilberte, the hostility that her parents had shown to me and which this little piece of furniture seemed to have so well understood and shared that I felt myself unworthy and found myself almost reluctant to set my feet on its defenceless cushion; a personality, a soul was latent there which linked it secretly to the afternoon light, so different from any other light in the gulf which spread beneath our feet its sparkling tide of gold out of which the bluish sofas and vaporous tapestries emerged like enchanted islands; and there was nothing, not even the painting by Rubens that hung above the chimney-piece, that was not endowed with the same quality and almost the same intensity of charm as the laced boots of M. Swann and the hooded cape the like of which I had so dearly longed to wear, whereas Odette would now beg her husband to go and put on another, so as to appear smarter, whenever I did them the honour of driving out with them. She too went away to dress—not heeding my protestations that no "outdoor" clothes could be nearly so becoming as the marvellous garment of crêpe-de-Chine or silk, old rose, cherry-coloured, Tiepolo pink, white, mauve, green, red or yellow, plain or patterned, in which Mme Swann had sat down to lunch and which she was now going to take off. When I told her that she ought to go out in that costume, she laughed, either in mockery of my ignorance or from delight in my compliment. She apologised for having so many housecoats, explaining that they were the only kind of dress in which she felt comfortable, and left us to go and array herself in one of those regal toilettes which imposed their majesty on all beholders, and yet among which I was sometimes summoned to decide which I would prefer her to put on.

In the Zoo, how proud I was, when we had left the carriage, to be walking by the side of Mme Swann! As she strolled negligently along, letting her cloak stream in the air behind her, I kept eyeing her with an admiring gaze to which she coquettishly responded in a lingering smile. And now, were we to meet one or other of Gilberte's friends, boy or girl, who greeted us from afar, it was my turn to be looked upon by them as one of those happy creatures whose lot I had envied, one of those friends of Gilberte who knew her family and had a share in that other part of her life, the part which was not spent in the Champs-Elysées.

Often upon the paths of the Bois or the Zoo we would be greeted by some distinguished lady who was a friend of Swann's, whom sometimes he had not at first seen and who would be pointed out to him by his wife: "Charles! Don't you see Mme de Montmorency?" And Swann, with that amicable smile bred of a long and intimate friendship, would none the less doff his hat with a sweeping gesture, and with a grace peculiarly his own. Sometimes the lady would stop, glad of an opportunity to show Mme Swann a courtesy which would set no tiresome precedent, of which they all knew that she would never take advantage, so thoroughly had Swann trained her in reserve. She had even so acquired all the manners of polite society, and however elegant, however stately the lady might be, Mme Swann was invariably a match for her; halting for a moment before the friend whom her husband had recognised and was addressing, she would introduce us, Gilberte and myself, with so much ease of manner, would remain so free, so relaxed in her affability, that it would have been hard to say, looking at them both, which of the two was the aristocrat.

The day on which we went to inspect the Singhalese, on our way home we saw coming in our direction, and followed by two others who seemed to be acting as her escort, an elderly but still handsome lady enveloped in a dark overcoat and wearing a little bonnet tied beneath her chin with a pair of ribbons. "Ah! here's someone who will interest you!" said Swann. The old lady, who was now within a few yards of us, smiled at us with a caressing sweetness. Swann doffed his hat. Mme Swann swept to the ground in a curtsey and made as if to kiss the hand of the lady, who, standing there like a Winterhalter portrait, drew her up again and kissed her cheek. "Come, come, will you put your hat on, you!" she scolded Swann in a thick and almost growling voice, speaking like an old and familiar friend. "I'm going to present you to Her Imperial Highness," Mme Swann whispered.

Swann drew me aside for a moment while his wife talked to the Princess about the weather and the animals recently added to the Zoo. "That is the Princesse Mathilde," he told me, "you know who I mean, the friend of Flaubert, Sainte-Beuve, Dumas. Just fancy, she's the niece of Napoleon I. She had offers of marriage from Napoleon III and the Emperor of Russia. Isn't that interesting? Talk to her a little. But I hope she won't keep us standing here for an hour! . . . I met Taine the other day," he went on, addressing the Princess, "and he told me Your Highness was vexed with him." "He's behaved like a perfect peeg!" she said gruffly, pronouncing the word *cochon* as though she referred to Joan of Arc's contemporary, Bishop Cauchon. "After his article on the Emperor I left my card on him with p. p. c. on it."[6]

I felt the surprise that one feels on opening the correspondence of that Duchesse d'Orléans who was by birth a Princess Palatine. And indeed Princesse Mathilde, animated by sentiments so entirely French, expressed them with a straightforward bluntness that recalled the Germany of an older generation, and was inherited, doubtless, from her Württemberger mother. This somewhat rough and almost masculine frankness she softened, as soon as she began to smile, with an Italian languor. And the whole person was clothed in an outfit so typically Second Empire that—for all that the Princess wore it simply and solely, no doubt, from attachment to the fashions that she had loved when she was young—she seemed to have deliberately planned to avoid the slightest discrepancy in historic colour, and to be satisfying the expectations of those who looked to her to evoke the memory of another age. I whispered to Swann to ask her whether she had known Musset. "Very slightly, Monsieur," was the answer, given in a tone which seemed to feign annoyance at the question, and of course it was by way of a joke that she called Swann Monsieur, since they were intimate friends. "I had him to dine once. I had invited him for seven o'clock. At half-past seven, as he had not appeared, we sat down to dinner. He arrived at eight, bowed to me, took his seat, never opened his lips, and went off after dinner without letting me hear the sound of his voice. Of course he was dead drunk. That hardly encouraged me to make another attempt." We were standing a little way off, Swann and I. "I hope this little audience is not going to last much longer," he muttered, "the soles of my feet are hurting. I can't think why my wife keeps on making conversation. When we get home it will be she who complains of being tired, and she knows I simply cannot go on standing like this."

For Mme Swann, who had had the news from Mme Bontemps, was in the process of telling the Princess that the Government, having at last begun to realise the depth of its shoddiness, had decided to send her an invitation to be present on the platform in a few days' time, when the Tsar Nicholas was to visit the Invalides. But the Princess who, in spite of appearances, in spite of the character of her entourage, which consisted mainly of artists and literary people, had remained at heart and showed herself, whenever she had to take action, the niece of Napoleon, replied: "Yes, Madame, I received it this morning and I sent it back to the Minister, who must have had it by now. I told him that I had no need of an invitation to go to the Invalides. If the Government desires my presence there, it will not be on the platform but in our vault, where the Emperor's tomb is. I have no need of a card to admit me there. I have my own keys. I go in and out when I choose. The Government has only to let me know whether it wishes me to be present or not. But if I do go to the Invalides, it will be down below or nowhere at all."

At that moment we were saluted, Mme Swann and I, by a young man who greeted her without stopping, and whom I was not aware that she knew; it was Bloch. When I asked her about him, she told me that he had been introduced to her by Mme Bontemps, and that he was employed in the Minister's secretariat, which was news to me. At all events, she could not have seen him often—or perhaps she had not cared to utter the name Bloch, hardly "smart" enough for her liking, for she told me that he was called M. Moreul. I assured her that she was mistaken, that his name was Bloch.

The Princess gathered up the train that flowed out behind her, and Mme Swann gazed at it with admiring eyes. "Yes, as it happens, it's a fur that the Emperor of Russia sent me," she explained, "and as I've just been to see him I put it on to show him that I'd managed to have it made up as a coat." "I hear that Prince Louis has joined the Russian Army; the Princess will be very sad at losing him," went on Mme Swann, not noticing her husband's signs of impatience. "He *would* go and do that! As I said to him, 'Just because there's been a soldier in the family there's no need to follow suit,'" replied the Princess, alluding with this abrupt simplicity to Napoleon the Great.

But Swann could hold out no longer: "Ma'am, it is I that am going to play the Royal Highness and ask your permission to retire; but you see, my wife hasn't been too well, and I don't like her to stand around for too long." Mme Swann curtseyed again, and the Princess conferred upon us all a celestial smile, which she seemed to have summoned out of the past, from among the graces of her girlhood, from the evenings at Compiègne, a smile which stole, sweet and unbroken, over her hitherto surly face. Then she went on her way, followed by the two ladies in waiting, who had confined themselves, in the manner of interpreters, of children's or invalids' nurses, to punctuating our conversation with meaningless remarks and superfluous explanations. "You should go and write your name in her book one day this week," Mme Swann counselled me. "One doesn't leave cards upon these 'Royalties,' as the English call them, but she will invite you to her house if you put your name down."

Sometimes in those last days of winter, before proceeding on our expedition we would go into one of the small picture-shows that were beginning to open and where Swann, as a collector of note, was greeted with special deference by the dealers in whose galleries they were held. And in that still wintry weather the old longing to set out for the South of France and Venice would be reawakened in me by those rooms in which a springtime, already well advanced, and a blazing sun cast violet shadows upon the roseate Alpilles and gave the intense transparency of emeralds to the Grand Canal. If the weather was bad, we would go to a concert or a theatre, and afterwards to one of the fashionable tea-rooms. There, whenever Mme Swann had anything to say to me which she did not wish the people at the next table or even the waiters who brought our tea to understand, she would say it in English, as though that had been a secret language known to our two selves alone. As it happened everyone in the place knew English—I alone had not yet learned the language, and was obliged to say so to Mme Swann in order that she might cease to make, about the people who were drinking tea or serving us with it, remarks which I guessed to be uncomplimentary without either my understanding or the person referred to missing a single word.

Once, in connexion with a matinée at the theatre, Gilberte gave me a great surprise. It was precisely the day of which she had spoken to me in advance, on which fell the anniversary of her grandfather's death. We were to go, she and I, with her governess, to hear selections from an opera, and Gilberte had dressed with a view to attending this performance, wearing the air of indifference with which she was in the habit of treating whatever we might be going to do, saying that it might be anything in the world, no matter what, provided that it amused me and had her parents' approval. Before lunch, her mother drew us aside to tell her that her father was vexed at the thought of our going to a concert on that particular day.

This seemed to be only natural. Gilberte remained impassive, but grew pale with an anger which she was unable to conceal, and uttered not a word. When M. Swann joined us his wife took him to the other end of the room and said something in his ear. He called Gilberte, and they went together into the next room. We could hear their raised voices. Yet I could not bring myself to believe that Gilberte, so submissive, so loving, so thoughtful, would resist her father's appeal, on such a day and for so trifling a matter. At length Swann reappeared with her, saying: "You heard what I said. Now do as you like."

Gilberte's features remained contracted in a frown throughout luncheon, after which she retired to her room. Then suddenly, without hesitating and as though she had never at any point hesitated over her course of action: "Two o'clock!" she exclaimed, "You know the concert begins at half-past." And she told her governess to make haste.

"But," I reminded her, "won't your father be cross with you?"

"Not the least little bit!"

"Surely he was afraid it would look odd, because of the anniversary."

"What do I care what people think? I think it's perfectly absurd to worry about other people in matters of sentiment. We feel things for ourselves, not for the public. Mademoiselle has very few pleasures, and she's been looking forward to going to this concert. I'm not going to deprive her of it just to satisfy public opinion."

"But, Gilberte," I protested, taking her by the arm, "it's not to satisfy public opinion, it's to please your father."

"You're not going to start scolding me, I hope," she said sharply, plucking her arm away.

A favour still more precious than their taking me with them to the Zoo or a concert, the Swanns did not exclude me even from their friendship with Bergotte, which had been at the root of the attraction that I had found in them when, before I had even seen Gilberte, I reflected that her intimacy with that godlike elder would have made her, for me, the most enthralling of friends, had not the disdain that I was bound to inspire in her forbidden me to hope that she would ever take me, in his company, to visit the towns that he loved. And then, one day, Mme Swann invited me to a big luncheon-party. I did not know who the guests were to be. On my arrival I was disconcerted, as I crossed the hall, by an alarming incident. Mme Swann seldom missed an opportunity of adopting any of those customs which are thought fashionable for a season, and then, failing to catch on, are presently abandoned (as, for instance, many years before, she had had her *hansom cab*, or had printed in English upon a card inviting people to luncheon the words *To meet*, followed by the name of some more or less important personage). Often enough these usages implied nothing mysterious and required no initiation. For instance, a minor innovation of those days, imported from England: Odette had made her husband have some visiting cards printed on which the name Charles Swann was preceded by "Mr." After the first visit that I paid her, Mme Swann had left at my door one of these "pasteboards," as she called them. No one had ever left a card on me before, and I felt at once so much pride, emotion and gratitude that, scraping together all the money I possessed, I ordered a superb basket of camellias and sent it round to Mme Swann. I implored my father to go and leave a card on her, but first, quickly, to have some printed on which his name should bear the prefix "Mr." He complied with neither of my requests. I was in despair for some days, and then asked myself whether he might not after all have been right. But this use of "Mr.," if it meant nothing, was at least intelligible. Not so with another that was revealed to me on the occasion of this luncheon-party, but revealed without any indication of its purport. At the moment when I was about to step from the hall into the drawing-room, the butler handed me a thin, oblong envelope upon which my name was inscribed. In my surprise I thanked him; but I eyed the envelope with misgivings. I no more knew what I was expected to do with it than a foreigner knows what to do with one of those little utensils that they lay in his place at a Chinese banquet. Noticing that it was gummed down, I was afraid of appearing indiscreet were I to open it then and there, and so I thrust it into my pocket with a knowing air. Mme Swann had written to me a few days before, asking me to come to "a small, informal luncheon." There were, however, sixteen people, among whom I never suspected for a moment that I was to find Bergotte. Mme Swann, who had already "named" me, as she called it, to several of her guests, suddenly, after my name, in the same tone that she had used in uttering it (and as though we were merely two of the guests at her luncheon who ought to each feel equally flattered on meeting the other), pronounced that of the gentle Bard with the snowy locks. The name Bergotte made me start, like the sound of a revolver fired at me point blank, but instinctively, to keep my countenance, I bowed: there, in front of me, like one of those conjurers whom we see standing whole and unharmed, in their frock-coats, in the smoke of a pistol shot out of which a pigeon had just fluttered, my greeting was returned by a youngish, uncouth, thickset and myopic little man, with a red nose curled like a snail-shell and a goatee beard. I was cruelly disappointed, for what had just vanished in the dust of the explosion was not only the languorous old man, of whom no vestige now remained, but also the beauty of an immense work which I had contrived to enshrine in the frail and hallowed organism that I had constructed, like a temple, expressly for it, but for which no room was to be found in the squat figure, packed tight with blood-vessels, bones, glands, sinews, of the little man with the snub nose and black beard who stood before me. The whole of the Bergotte whom I had slowly and delicately elaborated for myself, drop by drop, like a stalactite, out of the transparent beauty of his books, ceased (I could see at once) to be of any possible use, the moment I was obliged to include in him the snail-shell nose and to utilise the goatee beard—just as we must reject as worthless the solution we have found for a problem the terms of which we had not read in full and so failed to observe that the total must amount to a specified figure. The nose and beard were elements similarly ineluctable, and all the more aggravating in that, while forcing me to reconstruct entirely the personage of Bergotte, they seemed further to imply, to produce, to secrete incessantly a certain quality of mind, alert and self-satisfied, which was not fair, for such a mind had no connexion whatever with the sort of intelligence that was diffused throughout those books, so intimately familiar to me, which were permeated by a gentle and godlike wisdom. Starting from them, I should never have arrived at that snail-shell nose; but starting from the nose, which did not appear to be in the slightest degree ashamed of itself, but stood out alone there like a grotesque ornament fastened on his face, I found myself proceeding in a totally different direction from the work of Bergotte, and must arrive, it would seem, at the mentality of a busy and preoccupied engineer, of the sort who when you accost them in the street think it correct to say: "Thanks, and you?" before you have actually inquired of them how they are, or else, if you assure them that you have been delighted to make their acquaintance, respond with an abbreviation which they imagine to be smart, intelligent and up-to-date, inasmuch as it avoids any waste of precious time on vain formalities: "Same here!" Names, no doubt, are whimsical draughtsmen, giving us of people as well as of places sketches so unlike the reality that we often experience a kind of stupor when we have before our eyes, in place of the imagined, the visible world (which, for that matter, is not the real world, our senses being little more endowed than our imagination with the art of portraiture—so little, indeed, that the final and approximately lifelike pictures which we manage to obtain of reality are at least as different from the visible world as that was from the imagined). But in Bergotte's case, my preconceived idea of him from his name troubled me far less than my familiarity with his work, to which I was obliged to attach, as to the cord of a balloon, the man with the goatee beard, without knowing whether it would still have the strength to raise him from the ground. It seemed clear, however, that it really was he who had written the books that I had so loved, for Mme Swann having thought it incumbent upon her to tell him of my admiration for one of these, he showed no surprise that she should have mentioned this to him rather than to any other guest, and did not seem to regard it as due to a misapprehension, but, swelling out the frock-coat which he had put on in honour of all these distinguished guests with a body avid for the coming meal, while his mind was completely occupied by other, more important realities, it was only as at some finished episode in his life, and as though one had alluded to a costume as the Duc de Guise which he had worn, one season, at a fancy dress ball, that he smiled as he bore his mind back to the idea of his books; which at once began to fall in my estimation (bringing down with them the whole value of Beauty, of the world, of life itself), until they seemed to have been merely the casual recreation of a man with a goatee beard. I told myself that he must have taken pains over them, but that, if he had lived on an island surrounded by beds of pearl-oysters, he would instead have devoted himself with equal success to the pearling trade. His work no longer appeared to me so inevitable. And then I asked myself whether originality did indeed prove that great writers are gods, ruling each over a kingdom that is his alone, or whether there is not an element of sham in it all, whether the differences between one man's books and another's were not the result of their respective labours rather than the expression of a radical and essential difference between diverse personalities.

Meanwhile we had taken our places at table. By the side of my plate I found a carnation, the stalk of which was wrapped in silver paper. It embarrassed me less than the envelope that had been handed to me in the hall, which, however, I had completely forgotten. Its use, strange as it was to me, seemed to me more intelligible when I saw all the male guests take up the similar carnations that were lying by their plates and slip them into their buttonholes. I did as they had done, with the air of naturalness that a free-thinker assumes in church when he is not familiar with the mass but rises when everyone else rises and kneels a moment after everyone else is on his knees. Another usage, equally strange to me but less ephemeral, disquieted me more. On the other side of my plate was a smaller plate, on which was heaped a blackish substance which I did not then know to be caviare. I was ignorant of what was to be done with it but firmly determined not to let it enter my mouth.

Bergotte was sitting not far from me and I could hear quite clearly everything that he said. I understood then the impression that M. de Norpois had formed of him. He had indeed a peculiar "organ"; there is nothing that so alters the material qualities of the voice as the presence of thought behind what is being said: the resonance of the diphthongs, the energy of the labials are profoundly affected—as is the diction. His seemed to me to differ entirely from his way of writing, and even the things that he said from those with which he filled his books. But the voice issues from a mask behind which it is not powerful enough to make us recognise at first sight a face which we have seen uncovered in the speaker's literary style. At certain points in the conversation when Bergotte was in the habit of talking in a manner which not only M. de Norpois would have thought affected or unpleasant, it was a long time before I discovered an exact correspondence with the parts of his books in which his form became so poetic and so musical. At those points he could see in what he was saying a plastic beauty independent of whatever his sentences might mean, and as human speech reflects the human soul, though without expressing it as does literary style, Bergotte appeared almost to be talking nonsense, intoning certain words and, if he were pursuing, beneath them, a single image, stringing them together uninterruptedly on one continuous note, with a wearisome monotony. So that a pretentious, turgid and monotonous delivery was a sign of the rare aesthetic value of what he was saying, and an effect, in his conversation, of the same power which, in his books, produced that harmonious flow of imagery. I had had all the more difficulty in discovering this at first since what he said at such moments, precisely because it was the authentic utterance of Bergotte, did not appear to be typical Bergotte. It was a profusion of precise ideas, not included in that "Bergotte manner" which so many essayists had appropriated to themselves; and this dissimilarity was probably but another aspect—seen in a blurred way through the stream of conversation, like an image seen through smoked glass—of the fact that when one read a page of Bergotte it was never what would have been written by any of those lifeless imitators who, nevertheless, in newspapers and in books, adorned their prose with so many "Bergottish" images and ideas. This difference in style arose from the fact that what was meant by "Bergottism" was, first and foremost, a priceless element of truth hidden in the heart of each thing, whence it was extracted by that great writer by virtue of his genius, and that this extraction, rather than the perpetration of "Bergottisms," was the aim of the gentle Bard. Though, it must be added, he continued to perpetrate them in spite of himself because he was Bergotte, and so in this sense every fresh beauty in his work was the little drop of Bergotte buried at the heart of a thing and which he had distilled from it. But if, for that reason, each of those beauties was related to all the rest and recognisable, yet each remained separate and individual, as was the act of discovery that had brought it to the light of day; new, and consequently different from what was known as the Bergotte manner, which was a loose synthesis of all the "Bergottisms" already thought up and written down by him, with no indication by which men who lacked genius might foresee what would be his next discovery. So it is with all great writers: the beauty of their sentences is as unforeseeable as is that of a woman whom we have never seen; it is creative, because it is applied to an external object which they have thought of—as opposed to thinking about themselves—and to which they have not yet given expression. An author of memoirs of our time, wishing to write without too obviously seeming to be writing like Saint-Simon, might at a pinch give us the first line of his portrait of Villars: "He was a rather tall man, dark . . . with an alert, open, expressive physiognomy," but what law of determinism could bring him to the discovery of Saint-Simon's next line, which begins with "and, to tell the truth, a trifle mad"? The true variety is in this abundance of real and unexpected elements, in the branch loaded with blue flowers which shoots up, against all reason, from the spring hedgerow that seemed already overcharged with blossoms, whereas the purely formal imitation of variety (and one might advance the same argument for all the other qualities of style) is but a barren uniformity, that is to say the very antithesis of variety, and cannot, in the work of imitators, give the illusion or recall the memory of it save to a reader who has not acquired the sense of it from the masters themselves.

And so—just as Bergotte's way of speaking would no doubt have charmed the listener if he himself had been merely an amateur reciting imitation Bergotte, whereas it was attached to the thought of Bergotte, at work and in action, by vital links which the ear did not at once distinguish—so it was because Bergotte applied that thought with precision to the reality which pleased him that his language had in it something down-to-earth, something over-nourishing, which disappointed those who expected to hear him speak only of the "eternal torrent of forms" and of the "mysterious tremors of beauty." Moreover the quality, always rare and new, of what he wrote was expressed in his conversation by so subtle a manner of approaching a question, ignoring every aspect of it that was already familiar, that he appeared to be seizing hold of an unimportant detail, to be off the point, to be indulging in paradox, so that his ideas seemed as often as not to be confused, for each of us sees clarity only in those ideas which have the same degree of confusion as his own. Besides, as all novelty depends upon the prior elimination of the stereotyped attitude to which we had grown accustomed, and which seemed to us to be reality itself, any new form of conversation, like all original painting and music, must always appear complicated and exhausting. It is based on figures of speech with which we are not familiar, the speaker appears to us to be talking entirely in metaphors; and this wearies us, and gives us the impression of a want of truth. (After all, the old forms of speech must also in their time have been images difficult to follow, when the listener was not yet cognisant of the universe which they depicted. But for a long time it has been taken to be the real universe, and is instinctively relied upon.) So when Bergotte—and his figures appear simple enough today—said of Cottard that he was a mannikin in a bottle, trying to find his balance, and of Brichot that "for him even more than for Mme Swann the arrangement of his hair was a matter for anxious deliberation, because, in his twofold preoccupation with his profile and his reputation, he had always to make sure that it was so brushed as to give him the air at once of a lion and of a philosopher," people immediately felt the strain, and sought a foothold upon something which they called more concrete, meaning by that more usual. It was indeed to the writer whom I admired that the unrecognisable words issuing from the mask I had before my eyes must be attributed, and yet they could not have been inserted among his books like pieces in a jigsaw puzzle, they were on another plane and required a transposition by means of which, one day, when I was repeating to myself certain phrases that I had heard Bergotte use, I discovered in them the whole framework of his written style, the different elements of which I was able to recognise and to name in this spoken discourse which had struck me as being so different.

From a more subsidiary point of view the special way, a little too meticulous, too intense, that he had of pronouncing certain words, certain adjectives which constantly recurred in his conversation and which he never uttered without a certain emphasis, giving to each of their syllables a separate force and intoning the last (as for instance the word *visage* which he always used in preference to *figure* and enriched with a number of superfluous v's and s's and g's, which seemed all to explode from his outstretched palm at such moments), corresponded exactly to the fine passages where, in his prose, he brought out those favourite words, preceded by a sort of pause and composed in such a way in the metrical whole of the sentence that the reader was obliged, if he was not to make a false quantity, to give to each of them its full value. And yet one did not find in Bergotte's speech a certain luminosity which in his books, as in those of some other writers, often modified in the written sentence the appearance of its words. This was doubtless because that light issues from so profound a depth that its rays do not penetrate to our spoken words in the hours in which, thrown open to others by the act of conversation, we are to a certain extent closed to ourselves. In this respect, there was more modulation, more stress in his books than in his talk: stress independent of beauty of style, which the author himself has possibly not perceived, since it is not separable from his most intimate personality. It was this stress which, at the moments when, in his books, Bergotte was entirely natural, gave a rhythm to the words—often at such times quite insignificant—that he wrote. This stress is not marked on the printed page, there is nothing there to indicate it, and yet it imposes itself of its own accord on the writer's sentences, one cannot pronounce them in any other way, it is what was most ephemeral and at the same time most profound in the writer, and it is what will bear witness to his true nature, what will ultimately say whether, despite all the asperities he expressed, he was gentle, or despite all his sensualities, sentimental.

Certain peculiarities of elocution, faint traces of which were to be found in Bergotte's conversation, were not exclusively his own; for when, later on, I came to know his brothers and sisters I found those peculiarities much more pronounced in them. There was something abrupt and harsh in the closing words of a cheerful sentence, something faint and dying at the end of a sad one. Swann, who had known the Master as a boy, told me that in those days one used to hear on his lips, just as much as on his brothers' and sisters', those family inflexions, shouts of violent merriment interspersed with murmurings of a long-drawn melancholy, and that in the room in which they all played together he used to perform his part, better than any of them, in their symphonies, alternately deafening and subdued. However characteristic it may be, the sound that escapes from a person's lips is fugitive and does not survive him. But it was not so with the pronunciation of the Bergotte family. For if it is difficult ever to understand, even in the *Meistersinger*, how an artist can invent music by listening to the twittering of birds, yet Bergotte had transposed and perpetuated in his prose that manner of dwelling on words which repeat themselves in shouts of joy or fall drop by drop in melancholy sighs. There are in his books just such closing phrases where the accumulated sonorities are prolonged (as in the last chords of the overture of an opera which cannot bring itself to a close and repeats several times over its final cadence before the conductor finally lays down his baton), in which, later on, I was to find a musical equivalent for those phonetic "brasses" of the Bergotte family. But in his own case, from the moment when he transferred them to his books, he ceased instinctively to make use of them in his speech. From the day on which he had begun to write—and thus all the more markedly later, when I first knew him—his voice had abandoned this orchestration for ever.

These young Bergottes—the future writer and his brothers and sisters—were doubtless in no way superior, far from it, to other young people, more refined, more intellectual than themselves, who found the Bergottes rather noisy, not to say a trifle vulgar, irritating in their witticisms which characterised the tone, at once pretentious and asinine, of the household. But genius, and even great talent, springs less from seeds of intellect and social refinement superior to those of other people than from the faculty of transforming and transposing them. To heat a liquid with an electric lamp requires not the strongest lamp possible, but one of which the current can cease to illuminate, can be diverted so as to give heat instead of light. To mount the skies it is not necessary to have the most powerful of motors, one must have a motor which, instead of continuing to run along the earth's surface, intersecting with a vertical line the horizontal which it began by following, is capable of converting its speed into lifting power. Similarly, the men who produce works of genius are not those who live in the most delicate atmosphere, whose conversation is the most brilliant or their culture the most extensive, but those who have had the power, ceasing suddenly to live only for themselves, to transform their personality into a sort of mirror, in such a way that their life, however mediocre it may be socially and even, in a sense, intellectually, is reflected by it, genius consisting in reflecting power and not in the intrinsic quality of the scene reflected. The day on which the young Bergotte succeeded in showing to the world of his readers the tasteless household in which he had spent his childhood, and the not very amusing conversations between himself and his brothers, was the day on which he rose above the friends of his family, more intellectual and more distinguished than himself; they in their fine Rolls-Royces might return home expressing due contempt for the vulgarity of the Bergottes; but he, in his modest machine which had at last "taken off," soared above their heads.

There were other characteristics of his elocution which he shared not with the members of his family, but with certain contemporary writers. Younger men who were beginning to repudiate him and disclaimed any intellectual affinity with him nevertheless displayed it willy-nilly by employing the same adverbs, the same prepositions that he incessantly repeated, by constructing their sentences in the same way, speaking in the same quiescent, subdued tone, in reaction against the eloquent and facile language of an earlier generation. Perhaps these young men—we shall come across some of whom this may be said—had never known Bergotte. But his way of thinking, inoculated into them, had led them to those alterations of syntax and accentuation which bear a necessary relation to originality of mind. A relation which, incidentally, requires to be traced. Thus Bergotte, if he owed nothing to anyone in his manner of writing, derived his manner of speaking from one of his early associates, a marvellous talker to whose spell he had succumbed, whom he imitated unwittingly in his conversation, but who himself, being less gifted, had never written any really outstanding book. So that if one had been in quest of originality in speech, Bergotte must have been labelled a disciple, a second-hand writer, whereas, influenced by his friend only in the domain of conversation, he had been original and creative in his writings. Doubtless again to distinguish himself from the previous generation, too fond as it had been of abstractions, of weighty commonplaces, when Bergotte wished to speak favourably of a book, what he would emphasise, what he would quote with approval would always be some scene that furnished the reader with an image, some picture that had no rational meaning. "Ah, yes!" he would exclaim, "it's good! There's a little girl in an orange shawl. It's excellent!" or again, "Oh yes, there's a passage in which there's a regiment marching along the street; yes, it's good!" As for style, he was not altogether of his time (and remained quite exclusively French, abominating Tolstoy, George Eliot, Ibsen and Dostoievsky), for the word that always came to his lips when he wished to praise the style of any writer was "mellow." "Yes, you know I like Chateaubriand better in *Atala* than in *Rancé*; it seems to me to be mellower." He said the word like a doctor who, when his patient assures him that milk will give him indigestion, answers, "But, you know, it's quite mellow." And it is true that there was in Bergotte's style a kind of harmony similar to that for which the ancients used to praise certain of their orators in terms which we now find hard to understand, accustomed as we are to our own modern tongues in which effects of that kind are not sought.

He would say also, with a shy smile, of pages of his own for which someone had expressed admiration: "I think it's more or less true, more or less accurate; it may be of some value perhaps," but he would say this simply from modesty, as a woman to whom one has said that her dress or her daughter is beautiful replies, "It's comfortable," or "She's a good girl." But the instinct of the maker, the builder, was too deeply implanted in Bergotte for him not to be aware that the sole proof that he had built both usefully and truthfully lay in the pleasure that his work had given, to himself first of all and afterwards to his readers. Only, many years later, when he no longer had any talent, whenever he wrote anything with which he was not satisfied, in order not to have to suppress it, as he ought to have done, in order to be able to publish it, he would repeat, but to himself this time: "After all, it's more or less accurate, it must be of some value to my country." So that the phrase murmured long ago among his admirers by the crafty voice of modesty came in the end to be whispered in the secrecy of his heart by the uneasy tongue of pride. And the same words which had served Bergotte as a superfluous excuse for the excellence of his early works became as it were an ineffective consolation to him for the mediocrity of the last.

A kind of austerity of taste which he had, a kind of determination to write nothing of which he could not say that it was "mellow," which had made people for so many years regard him as a sterile and precious artist, a chiseller of trifles, was on the contrary the secret of his strength, for habit forms the style of the writer just as much as the character of the man, and the author who has more than once been content to attain, in the expression of his thoughts, to a certain kind of attractiveness, in so doing lays down unalterably the boundaries of his talent, just as, in succumbing too often to pleasure, to laziness, to the fear of being put to trouble, one traces for oneself, on a character which it will finally be impossible to retouch, the lineaments of one's vices and the limits of one's virtue.

If, however, despite all the similarities which I was to perceive later on between the writer and the man, I had not at first sight, in Mme Swann's drawing-room, believed that this could be Bergotte, the author of so many divine books, who stood before me, perhaps I was not altogether wrong, for he himself did not, in the strict sense of the word, "believe" it either. He did not believe it since he showed some alacrity in ingratiating himself with fashionable people (though he was not a snob), and with literary men and journalists who were vastly inferior to himself. Of course he had long since learned, from the suffrage of his readers, that he had genius, compared to which social position and official rank were as nothing. He had learned that he had genius, but he did not believe it since he continued to simulate deference towards mediocre writers in order to succeed, shortly, in becoming an Academician, when the Academy and the Faubourg Saint-Germain have no more to do with that part of the Eternal Mind which is the author of the works of Bergotte than with the law of causality or the idea of God. That also he knew, but as a kleptomaniac knows, without profiting by the knowledge, that it is wrong to steal. And the man with the goatee beard and snail-shell nose knew and used all the tricks of the gentleman who pockets your spoons, in his efforts to reach the coveted academic chair, or some duchess or other who could command several votes at the election, but to do so in a way that ensured that no one who would consider the pursuit of such a goal a vice in him would see what he was doing. He was only half-successful; one could hear, alternating with the speech of the true Bergotte, that of the other, selfish and ambitious Bergotte who talked only of his powerful, rich or noble friends in order to enhance himself, he who in his books, when he was really himself, had so well portrayed the charm, pure as a mountain spring, of the poor.

As for those other vices to which M. de Norpois had alluded, that almost incestuous love affair, which was made still worse, people said, by a want of delicacy in the matter of money, if they contradicted in a shocking manner the trend of his latest novels, filled with such a painfully scrupulous concern for what was right and good that the most innocent pleasures of their heroes were poisoned by it, and that even for the reader himself it exhaled a sense of anguish in the light of which even the quietest of lives seemed scarcely bearable, those vices did not necessarily prove, supposing that they were fairly imputed to Bergotte, that his literature was a lie and all his sensitiveness mere play-acting. Just as in pathology certain conditions similar in appearance are due, some to an excess, others to an insufficiency of blood pressure, of glandular secretion and so forth, there may be vice arising from hypersensitiveness just as much as from the lack of it. Perhaps it is only in really vicious lives that the problem of morality can arise in all its disquieting strength. And to this problem the artist offers a solution in the terms not of his own personal life but of what is for him his true life, a general, a literary solution. As the great Doctors of the Church began often, while remaining good, by experiencing the sins of all mankind, out of which they drew their own personal sanctity, so great artists often, while being wicked, make use of their vices in order to arrive at a conception of the moral law that is binding upon us all. It is the vices (or merely the weaknesses and follies) of the circle in which they live, the meaningless conversation, the frivolous or shocking lives of their daughters, the infidelity of their wives, or their own misdeeds that writers have most often castigated in their books, without, however, thinking to alter their way of life or improve the tone of their household. But this contrast had never before been so striking as it was in Bergotte's time, because, on the one hand, in proportion as society grew more corrupt, notions of morality became increasingly refined, and on the other hand the public became a great deal more conversant than it had ever been before with the private lives of literary men; and on certain evenings in the theatre people would point out the author whom I had so greatly admired at Combray, sitting at the back of a box the very composition of which seemed an oddly humorous or poignant comment on, an impudent denial of, the thesis which he had just been maintaining in his latest book. Nothing that this or that casual informant might tell me was of much use in helping me to settle the question of the goodness or wickedness of Bergotte. An intimate friend would furnish proofs of his hardheartedness; then a stranger would cite some instance (touching, since it had evidently been destined to remain hidden) of his real depth of feeling. He had behaved cruelly to his wife. But, in a village inn where he had gone to spend the night, he had sat up with a poor woman who had tried to drown herself, and when he was obliged to go had left a large sum of money with the landlord, so that he should not turn the poor creature out but see that she got proper attention. Perhaps the more the great writer developed in Bergotte at the expense of the little man with the beard, the more his own personal life was drowned in the flood of all the lives that he imagined, until he no longer felt himself obliged to perform certain practical duties, for which he had substituted the duty of imagining those other lives. But at the same time, because he imagined the feelings of others as completely as if they had been his own, whenever the occasion arose for him to have to deal with an unfortunate person, at least in a transitory way, he would do so not from his own personal standpoint but from that of the sufferer himself, a standpoint from which he would have been horrified by the language of those who continue to think of their own petty concerns in the presence of another's grief. With the result that he gave rise everywhere to justifiable rancour and to undying gratitude.

Above all, he was a man who in his heart of hearts only really loved certain images and (like a miniature set in the floor of a casket) composing and painting them in words. For a trifle that someone had sent him, if that trifle gave him the opportunity of weaving a few images round it, he would be prodigal in the expression of his gratitude, while showing none whatever for an expensive present. And if he had had to plead before a tribunal, he would inevitably have chosen his words not for the effect that they might have on the judge but with an eye to certain images which the judge would certainly never have perceived.

That first day on which I met him with Gilberte's parents, I mentioned to Bergotte that I had recently been to see Berma in *Phèdre*; and he told me that in the scene in which she stood with her arm raised to the level of her shoulders—one of those very scenes that had been greeted with such applause—she had managed to suggest with great nobility of art certain classical figures which quite possibly she had never even seen, a Hesperid carved in the same attitude upon a metope at Olympia, and also the beautiful primitive virgins on the Erechtheum.

"It may be sheer divination, and yet I fancy that she goes to museums. It would be interesting to 'log' that." ("Log" was one of those regular Bergotte expressions, and one which various young men who had never met him had caught from him, speaking like him by some sort of telepathic suggestion.)

"Do you mean the Caryatids?" asked Swann.

"No, no," said Bergotte, "except in the scene where she confesses her passion to Oenone, where she moves her hand exactly like Hegeso on the stele in the Ceramicus, it's a far more primitive art that she evokes. I was referring to the Korai of the old Erechtheum, and I admit that there is perhaps nothing quite so remote from the art of Racine, but there are so many things already in *Phèdre* . . . that one more . . . Oh, and then, yes, she's really charming, that little sixth-century Phaedra, the rigidity of the arm, the lock of hair 'frozen into marble,' yes, you know, it's wonderful of her to have discovered all that. There is a great deal more antiquity in it than in most of the books they're labelling 'antique' this year."

Since Bergotte had in one of his books addressed a famous invocation to these archaic statues, the words that he was now uttering were quite intelligible to me, and gave me a fresh reason for taking an interest in Berma's acting. I tried to picture her again in my mind, as she had looked in that scene in which I remembered that she had raised her arm to the level of her shoulder. And I said to myself: "There we have the Hesperid of Olympia; there we have the sister of those adorable suppliants on the Acropolis; there indeed is nobility in art!" But in order for these thoughts to enhance for me the beauty of Berma's gesture, Bergotte would have had to put them into my head before the performance. Then, while that attitude of the actress actually existed in flesh and blood before my eyes, at that moment when the thing that is happening still has the plenitude of reality, I might have tried to extract from it the idea of archaic sculpture. But all that I retained of Berma in that scene was a memory which was no longer susceptible of modification; as meagre as an image devoid of those deep layers of the present in which one can delve and genuinely discover something new, an image on which one cannot retrospectively impose an interpretation that is not subject to verification and objective sanction.

At this point Mme Swann chipped into the conversation, asking me whether Gilberte had remembered to give me what Bergotte had written about *Phèdre*, and adding, "My daughter is such a scatterbrain!" Bergotte smiled modestly and protested that they were only a few pages of no importance. "But it's absolutely delightful, that little booklet, that little 'tract' of yours," Mme Swann assured him, to show that she was a good hostess, to give the impression that she had read Bergotte's essay, and also because she liked not merely to flatter Bergotte, but to pick and choose from what he wrote, to influence him. And it must be admitted that she did inspire him, though not in the way that she supposed. But when all is said there are, between what constituted the elegance of Mme Swann's drawing-room and a whole aspect of Bergotte's work, connexions such that each of them may serve, among elderly men today, as a commentary upon the other.

I let myself go in telling him what my impressions had been. Often Bergotte disagreed, but he allowed me to go on talking. I told him that I had liked the green light which was turned on when Phèdre raised her arm. "Ah! the designer will be glad to hear that; he's a real artist, and I shall tell him you liked it, because he is very proud of that effect. I must say, myself, that I don't care for it much, it bathes everything in a sort of sea-green glow, little Phèdre standing there looks too like a branch of coral on the floor of an aquarium. You will tell me, of course, that it brings out the cosmic aspect of the play. That's quite true. All the same, it would be more appropriate if the scene were laid in the Court of Neptune. Oh yes, I know the Vengeance of Neptune does come into the play. I don't suggest for a moment that we should think only of Port-Royal, but after all Racine isn't telling us a story about love among the sea-urchins. Still, it's what my friend wanted, and it's very well done, right or wrong, and really quite pretty. Yes, so you liked it, did you; you understood what he was after. We feel the same about it, don't we, really: it's a bit crazy, what he's done, you agree with me, but on the whole it's very clever." And when Bergotte's opinion was thus contrary to mine, he in no way reduced me to silence, to the impossibility of framing any reply, as M. de Norpois would have done. This does not prove that Bergotte's opinions were less valid than the Ambassador's; far from it. A powerful idea communicates some of its power to the man who contradicts it. Partaking of the universal community of minds, it infiltrates, grafts itself on to, the mind of him whom it refutes, among other contiguous ideas, with the aid of which, counter-attacking, he complements and corrects it; so that the final verdict is always to some extent the work of both parties to a discussion. It is to ideas which are not, strictly speaking, ideas at all, to ideas which, based on nothing, can find no foothold, no fraternal echo in the mind of the adversary, that the latter, grappling as it were with thin air, can find no word to say in answer. The arguments of M. de Norpois (in the matter of art) were unanswerable simply because they were devoid of reality.

Since Bergotte did not sweep aside my objections, I confessed to him that they had been treated with contempt by M. de Norpois. "But he's an old goose!" was the answer. "He keeps on pecking at you because he imagines all the time that you're a piece of cake, or a slice of cuttle-fish." "What, you know Norpois?" asked Swann. "He's as dull as a wet Sunday," interrupted his wife, who had great faith in Bergotte's judgment, and was no doubt afraid that M. de Norpois might have spoken ill of her to us. "I tried to make him talk after dinner; I don't know if it's his age or his digestion, but I found him too sticky for words. I really thought I should have to 'dope' him." "Yes, isn't he?" Bergotte chimed in. "You see, he has to keep his mouth shut half the time so as not to use up all the stock of inanities that keep his shirt-front starched and his waistcoat white."

"I think that Bergotte and my wife are both very hard on him," came from Swann, who took the "line," in his own house, of being a plain, sensible man. "I quite see that Norpois cannot interest you very much, but from another point of view," (for Swann made a hobby of collecting scraps of "real life") "he is quite remarkable, quite a remarkable instance of a 'lover.' When he was Counsellor in Rome," he went on, after making sure that Gilberte could not hear him, "he had a mistress here in Paris with whom he was madly in love, and he found time to make the double journey twice a week to see her for a couple of hours. She was, as it happens, a most intelligent woman, and remarkably beautiful then; she's a dowager now. And he has had any number of others since. I'm sure I should have gone stark mad if the woman I was in love with lived in Paris and I had to be in Rome. Highly strung people ought always to love, as the lower orders say, 'beneath' them, so that their women have a material inducement to be at their disposal."

As he spoke, Swann realised that I might be applying this maxim to himself and Odette, and as, even among superior people, at the moment when they seem to be soaring with you above the plane of life, their personal pride is still basely human, he was overcome with profound irritation towards me. But it manifested itself only in the uneasiness of his glance. He said nothing to me at the time. Not that this need surprise us. When Racine (according to a story that is in fact apocryphal though its substance may be found recurring every day in Parisian life) made an allusion to Scarron in front of Louis XIV, the most powerful monarch on earth said nothing to the poet that evening. It was on the following day that he fell from grace.

But since a theory requires to be stated as a whole, Swann, after this momentary irritation, and after wiping his eyeglass, completed his thought in these words, words which were to assume later on in my memory the importance of a prophetic warning which I had not had the sense to heed: "The danger of that kind of love, however, is that the woman's subjection calms the man's jealousy for a time but also makes it more exacting. After a while he will force his mistress to live like one of those prisoners whose cells are kept lighted day and night to prevent their escaping. And that generally ends in trouble."

I reverted to M. de Norpois. "You must never trust him; he has the most wicked tongue," said Mme Swann in a tone which seemed to me to indicate that M. de Norpois had spoken ill of her, especially as Swann looked across at his wife with an air of rebuke, as though to stop her before she went too far.

Meanwhile Gilberte, who had twice been told to go and get ready to go out, remained listening to our conversation, sitting between her mother and her father, her head resting affectionately against the latter's shoulder. Nothing, at first sight, could be in greater contrast to Mme Swann, who was dark, than this child with her red hair and golden skin. But after a while one saw in Gilberte many of the features—for instance, the nose cut short with a sharp, unerring decision by the invisible sculptor whose chisel repeats its work upon successive generations—the expression, the movements of her mother; to take an illustration from another art, she recalled a portrait that was as yet a poor likeness of Mme Swann, whom the painter, from some colourist's whim, had posed in a partial disguise, dressed to go out to a party in Venetian "character." And since not only was she wearing a fair wig, but every atom of darkness had been evicted from her flesh which, stripped of its brown veils, seemed more naked, covered simply in rays shed by an internal sun, this "make-up" was not just superficial but incarnate: Gilberte had the air of embodying some fabulous animal or of having assumed a mythological fancy dress. This reddish skin was so exactly that of her father that nature seemed to have had, when Gilberte was being created, to solve the problem of how to reconstruct Mme Swann piecemeal, without any material at its disposal save the skin of M. Swann. And nature had utilised this to perfection, like a master carver who makes a point of leaving the grain, the knots of his wood in evidence. On Gilberte's face, at the corner of a perfect reproduction of Odette's nose, the skin was raised so as to preserve intact M. Swann's two moles. It was a new variety of Mme Swann that was thus obtained, growing there by her side like a white lilac-tree beside a purple. At the same time it would be wrong to imagine the line of demarcation between these two likenesses as absolutely clear-cut. Now and then, when Gilberte smiled, one could distinguish the oval of her father's cheek upon her mother's face, as though they had been put together to see what would result from the blend; this oval took shape as an embryo forms; it lengthened obliquely, swelled, and a moment later had disappeared. In Gilberte's eyes there was the frank and honest gaze of her father; this was how she had looked at me when she gave me the agate marble and said "Keep it as a souvenir of our friendship." But were one to question Gilberte about what she had been doing, then one saw in those same eyes the embarrassment, the uncertainty, the prevarication, the misery that Odette used in the old days to betray, when Swann asked her where she had been and she gave him one of those lying answers which in those days drove the lover to despair and now made him abruptly change the conversation as an incurious and prudent husband. Often, in the Champs-Elysées, I was disturbed to see this look in Gilberte's eyes. But as a rule my fears were unfounded. For in her, a purely physical survival of her mother, this look (if no other) had ceased to have any meaning. It was when she had been to her classes, when she must go home for some lesson, that Gilberte's pupils executed that movement which, in the past, in Odette's eyes, had been caused by the fear of disclosing that she had opened the door that day to one of her lovers, or was at that moment in a hurry to get to some assignation. Thus did one see the two natures of M. and Mme Swann ripple and flow and overlap one upon the other in the body of this Mélusine.

It is, of course, common knowledge that a child takes after both its father and its mother. And yet the distribution of the qualities and defects which it inherits is so oddly planned that, of two good qualities which seemed inseparable in one of the parents, only one will be found in the child, and allied to the very fault in the other parent which seemed most irreconcilable with it. Indeed, the embodiment of a good moral quality in an incompatible physical blemish is often one of the laws of filial resemblance. Of two sisters, one will combine with the proud bearing of her father the mean little soul of her mother; the other, abundantly endowed with the paternal intelligence, will present it to the world in the aspect which her mother has made familiar; her mother's shapeless nose and puckered belly and even her voice have become the bodily vestment of gifts which one had learned to recognise beneath a superb presence. With the result that of each of the sisters one can say with equal justification that it is she who takes more after one or other of her parents. It is true that Gilberte was an only child, but there were, at the least, two Gilbertes. The two natures, her father's and her mother's, did more than just blend themselves in her; they disputed the possession of her—and even that would be not entirely accurate since it would give the impression that a third Gilberte was in the meantime suffering from being the prey of the two others. Whereas Gilberte was alternately one and then the other, and at any given moment only one of the two, that is to say incapable, when she was not being good, of suffering accordingly, the better Gilberte being unable at the time, on account of her momentary absence, to detect the other's lapse from virtue. And so the less good of the two was free to enjoy pleasures of an ignoble kind. When the other spoke to you with her father's heart she held broad and generous views, and you would have liked to engage with her upon a fine and beneficent enterprise; you told her so, but, just as your arrangements were being completed, her mother's heart would already have claimed its turn, and hers was the voice that answered; and you would be disappointed and vexed—almost baffled, as though by the substitution of one person for another—by a mean remark, a sly snigger, in which Gilberte would take delight, since they sprang from what she herself at that moment was. Indeed, the disparity was at times so great between the two Gilbertes that you asked yourself, though without finding an answer, what on earth you could have said or done to her to find her now so different. When she herself had suggested meeting you somewhere, not only would she fail to appear and would offer no excuse afterwards, but, whatever the influence might have been that had made her change her mind, she would appear so different that you might well have supposed that, taken in by a resemblance such as forms the plot of the *Menaechmi*, you were now talking to a different person from the one who had so sweetly expressed a desire to see you, had she not shown signs of an ill-humour which revealed that she felt herself to be in the wrong and wished to avoid entering into explanations.

"Now then, run along and get ready; you're keeping us waiting," her mother reminded her.

"I'm so happy here with my little Papa; I want to stay just for a minute," replied Gilberte, burying her head beneath the arm of her father, who passed his fingers lovingly through her fair hair.

Swann was one of those men who, having lived for a long time amid the illusions of love, have seen the blessings they have brought to a number of women increase the happiness of those women without exciting in them any gratitude, any tenderness towards their benefactors; but who believe that in their children they can feel an affection which, being incarnate in their own name, will enable them to survive after their death. When there should no longer be any Charles Swann, there would still be a Mlle Swann, or a Mme X, *née* Swann, who would continue to love the vanished father. Indeed, to love him too well perhaps, Swann may have been thinking, for he acknowledged Gilberte's caress with a "You're a good girl," in the tone softened by uneasiness to which, when we think of the future, we are prompted by the too passionate affection of a person who is destined to survive us. To conceal his emotion, he joined in our talk about Berma. He pointed out to me, but in a detached, bored tone, as though he wished to remain somehow detached from what he was saying, with what intelligence, with what an astonishing fitness the actress said to Oenone, "You knew it!" He was right. That intonation at least had a validity that was really intelligible, and might thereby have satisfied my desire to find incontestable reasons for admiring Berma. But it was because of its very clarity that it did not in the least satisfy me. Her intonation was so ingenious, so definite in intention and meaning, that it seemed to exist by itself, so that any intelligent actress might have acquired it. It was a fine idea; but whoever else might express it as fully must possess it equally. It remained to Berma's credit that she had discovered it, but can one use the word "discover" when the object in question is something that would not be different if one had been given it, something that does not belong essentially to one's own nature since someone else may afterwards reproduce it?

"Upon my soul, your presence among us does raise the tone of the conversation!" Swann observed to me, as though to excuse himself to Bergotte; for he had formed the habit, in the Guermantes set, of entertaining great artists as if they were just ordinary friends whom one seeks only to provide with the opportunity to eat the dishes or play the games they like, or, in the country, indulge in whatever form of sport they please. "It seems to me that we're talking a great deal about *art*," he went on. "But it's so nice, I do love it!" said Mme Swann, throwing me a look of gratitude, from good nature as well as because she had not abandoned her old aspirations towards intellectual conversation. After this it was to others of the party, and principally to Gilberte, that Bergotte addressed himself. I had told him everything that I felt with a freedom which had astonished me and which was due to the fact that, having acquired with him, years before (in the course of all those hours of solitary reading, in which he was to me merely the better part of myself), the habit of sincerity, of frankness, of confidence, I found him less intimidating than a person with whom I was talking for the first time. And yet, for the same reason, I was very uneasy about the impression that I must have been making on him, the contempt that I had supposed he would feel for my ideas dating not from that afternoon but from the already distant time in which I had begun to read his books in our garden at Combray. I ought perhaps to have reminded myself nevertheless that since it was in all sincerity, abandoning myself to the train of my thoughts, that I had felt on the one hand so intensely in sympathy with the work of Bergotte and on the other hand, in the theatre, a disappointment the reasons for which I did not know, those two instinctive impulses could not be so very different from one another, but must be obedient to the same laws; and that that mind of Bergotte's which I had loved in his books could not be entirely alien and hostile to my disappointment and to my inability to express it. For my intelligence must be one—

perhaps indeed there exists but a single intelligence of which everyone is a co-tenant, an intelligence towards which each of us from out of his own separate body turns his eyes, as in a theatre where, if everyone has his own separate seat, there is on the other hand but a single stage. Doubtless the ideas which I was tempted to seek to disentangle were not those which Bergotte usually explored in his books. But if it was one and the same intelligence which we had, he and I, at our disposal, he must, when he heard me express those ideas, be reminded of them, cherish them, smile upon them, keeping probably, in spite of what I supposed, before his mind's eye, quite a different part of his intelligence than that of which an excerpt had passed into his books, an excerpt upon which I had based my notion of his whole mental universe. Just as priests, having the widest experience of the human heart, are best able to pardon the sins which they do not themselves commit, so genius, having the widest experience of the human intelligence, can best understand the ideas most directly in opposition to those which form the foundation of its own works. I ought to have told myself all this (though in fact it is none too consoling a thought, for the benevolent condescension of great minds has as a corollary the incomprehension and hostility of small; and one derives far less happiness from the amiability of a great writer, which one can find after all in his books, than suffering from the hostility of a woman whom one did not choose for her intelligence but cannot help loving). I ought to have told myself all this, but I did not; I was convinced that I had appeared a fool to Bergotte, when Gilberte whispered in my ear:

"You can't think how overjoyed I am, because you've made a conquest of my great friend Bergotte. He's been telling Mamma that he found you extremely intelligent."

"Where are we going?" I asked her.

"Oh, wherever you like. You know it's all the same to me."

But since the incident that had occurred on the anniversary of her grandfather's death I had begun to wonder whether Gilberte's character was not other than I had supposed, whether that indifference to what was to be done, that docility, that calm, that gentle and constant submissiveness did not indeed conceal passionate longings which her pride would not allow her to reveal and which she disclosed only by her sudden resistance whenever by any chance they were thwarted.

As Bergotte lived in the same neighbourhood as my parents, we left the house together. In the carriage he spoke to me of my health: "Our friends were telling me that you had been ill. I'm very sorry. And yet, after all, I'm not too sorry, because I can see quite well that you are able to enjoy the pleasures of the mind, and they are probably what means most to you, as to everyone who has known them."

Alas, how little I felt that what he was saying applied to me, whom all reasoning, however exalted it might be, left cold, who was happy only in moments of pure idleness, when I was comfortable and well. I felt how purely material was everything that I desired in life, and how easily I could dispense with the intellect. As I made no distinction among my pleasures between those that came to me from different sources, of varying depth and permanence, I thought, when the moment came to answer him, that I should have liked an existence in which I was on intimate terms with the Duchesse de Guermantes and often came across, as in the old toll-house in the Champs-Elysées, a fusty coolness that would remind me of Combray. And in this ideal existence which I dared not confide to him, the pleasures of the mind found no place.

"No, Monsieur, the pleasures of the mind count for very little with me; it is not them that I seek after; indeed I don't even know that I have ever tasted them."

"You really think not?" he replied. "Well, you know, after all, that must be what you like best—at least that's my guess, that's what I think."

He did not convince me, of course, and yet I already felt happier, less constricted. After what M. de Norpois had said to me, I had regarded my moments of day-dreaming, of enthusiasm, of self-confidence as purely subjective and false. But according to Bergotte, who appeared to understand my case, it seemed that it was quite the contrary, that the symptom I ought to disregard was, in fact, my doubts, my disgust with myself. Moreover, what he had said about M. de Norpois took most of the sting out of a sentence from which I had supposed that no appeal was possible.

"Are you being properly looked after?" Bergotte asked me. "Who is treating you?" I told him that I had seen, and should probably go on seeing, Cottard. "But that's not at all the sort of man you want!" he told me. "I know nothing about him as a doctor. But I've met him at Mme Swann's. The man's an imbecile. Even supposing that that doesn't prevent his being a good doctor, which I hesitate to believe, it does prevent his being a good doctor for artists, for intelligent people. People like you must have suitable doctors, I would almost go so far as to say treatment and medicines specially adapted to themselves. Cottard will bore you, and that alone will prevent his treatment from having any effect. Besides, the proper course of treatment cannot possibly be the same for you as for any Tom, Dick or Harry. Nine tenths of the ills from which intelligent people suffer spring from their intellect. They need at least a doctor who understands *that* disease. How do you expect Cottard to be able to treat you? He has made allowances for the difficulty of digesting sauces, for gastric trouble, but he has made no allowance for the effect of reading Shakespeare. So that his calculations are inaccurate in your case, the balance is upset; you see, always the little bottle-imp bobbing up again. He will find that you have a distended stomach; he has no need to examine you for it, since he has it already in his eye. You can see it there, reflected in his glasses."

This manner of speaking tired me greatly. I said to myself with the stupidity of common sense: "There's no more a distended stomach reflected in Professor Cottard's glasses than there are inanities stored behind M. de Norpois's white waistcoat."

"I should recommend you, instead," went on Bergotte, "to consult Dr du Boulbon, who is an extremely intelligent man." "He's a great admirer of your books," I replied.

I saw that Bergotte knew this, and I concluded that kindred spirits soon come together, that one has few really "unknown friends." What Bergotte had said to me with respect to Cottard impressed me, while running contrary to everything that I myself believed. I was in no way disturbed at finding my doctor a bore; what I expected of him was that, thanks to an art whose laws escaped me, he should pronounce on the subject of my health an infallible oracle after consultation of my entrails. And I did not at all require that, with the aid of an intelligence in which I could compete with him, he should seek to understand mine, which I pictured to myself merely as a means, of no importance in itself, of trying to attain to certain external verities. I very much doubted whether intelligent people required a different form of hygiene from imbeciles, and I was quite prepared to submit myself to the latter.

"I'll tell you who does need a good doctor, and that's our friend Swann," said Bergotte. And on my asking whether he was ill, "Well, don't you see, he's typical of the man who has married a whore, and has to pocket a dozen insults a day from women who refuse to meet his wife or men who have slept with her. Just look, one day when you're there, at the way he lifts his eyebrows when he comes in, to see who's in the room."

The malice with which Bergotte spoke thus to a stranger of the friends in whose house he had for so long been received as a welcome guest was as new to me as the almost tender tone he invariably adopted towards them in their presence. Certainly a person like my great-aunt, for instance, would have been incapable of treating any of us to the blandishments which I had heard Bergotte lavishing upon Swann. Even to the people whom she liked, she enjoyed saying disagreeable things. But behind their backs she would never have uttered a word to which they might not have listened. There was nothing less like the social world than our society at Combray. The Swanns' was already a step on the way to it, towards its inconstant waters. If they had not yet reached the open sea, they were certainly in the estuary. "This is all between ourselves," said Bergotte as he left me outside my own door. A few years later I should have answered: "I never repeat things." That is the ritual phrase of society people, from which the slanderer always derives a false reassurance. It is what I would have said then and there to Bergotte—for one does not invent everything one says, especially when one is acting merely as a social being—but I did not yet know the formula. What my great-aunt, on the other hand, would have said on a similar occasion was: "If you don't wish it to be repeated, why do you say it?" That is the answer of the unsociable, of the dissenter. I was nothing of that sort: I bowed my head in silence.

Men of letters who were in my eyes persons of considerable importance had to intrigue for years before they succeeded in forming with Bergotte relations which remained always dimly literary and never emerged beyond the four walls of his study, whereas I had now been installed among the friends of the great writer, straight off and without any effort, like someone who, instead of standing in a queue for hours in order to secure a bad seat in a theatre, is shown in at once to the best, having entered by a door that is closed to the public. If Swann had thus opened such a door to me, it was doubtless because, just as a king finds himself naturally inviting his children's friends into the royal box, or on board the royal yacht, so Gilberte's parents received their daughter's friends among all the precious things that they had in their house and the even more precious intimacies that were enshrined there. But at the time I thought, and perhaps was right in thinking, that this friendliness on

Swann's part was aimed indirectly at my parents. I seemed to remember having heard once at Combray that he had suggested to them that, in view of my admiration for Bergotte, he should take me to dine with him, and that my parents had declined, saying that I was too young and too highly strung to "go out." My parents doubtless represented to certain other people (precisely those who seemed to me the most wonderful) something quite different from what they were to me, so that, just as when the lady in pink had paid my father a tribute of which he had shown himself so unworthy, I should have wished them to understand what an inestimable present I had just received and, to show their gratitude to that generous and courteous Swann who had offered it to me, or to them rather, without seeming any more conscious of its value than the charming Mage with the arched nose and fair hair in Luini's fresco, to whom, it was said, Swann had at one time been thought to bear a striking resemblance.

Unfortunately, this favour that Swann had done me, which, on returning home, before I had even taken off my greatcoat, I reported to my parents in the hope that it would awaken in their hearts an emotion equal to my own and would determine them upon some immense and decisive gesture towards the Swanns, did not appear to be greatly appreciated by them. "Swann introduced you to Bergotte? An excellent acquaintance, a charming relationship!" exclaimed my father sarcastically: "That really does crown it all!" Alas, when I went on to say that Bergotte was by no means inclined to admire M. de Norpois:

"I dare say!" retorted my father. "That simply proves that he's a false and malevolent fellow. My poor boy, you never had much common sense, but I'm sorry to see that you've fallen among people who will send you off the rails altogether."

Already the mere fact of my associating with the Swanns had far from delighted my parents. This introduction to Bergotte seemed to them a fatal but natural consequence of an original mistake, namely their own weakness, which my grandfather would have called a "want of circumspection." I felt that in order to put the finishing touch to their ill humour, it only remained for me to tell them that this perverse fellow who did not appreciate M. de Norpois had found me extremely intelligent. For I had observed that whenever my father decided that anyone, one of my school friends for instance, was going astray—as I was at that moment—if that person had the approval of somebody whom my father did not respect, he would see in this testimony the confirmation of his own stern judgment. The evil merely seemed to him the greater. Already I could hear him exclaiming, "Of course, it all hangs together," an expression that terrified me by the vagueness and vastness of the reforms the introduction of which into my quiet life it seemed to threaten. But since, even if I did not tell them what Bergotte had said of me, nothing could anyhow efface the impression my parents had already formed, that it should be made slightly worse mattered little. Besides, they seemed to me so unfair, so completely mistaken, that not only had I no hope, I had scarcely any desire to bring them to a more equitable point of view. However, sensing, as the words were passing my lips, how alarmed my parents would be at the thought that I had found favour in the sight of a person who dismissed clever men as fools, who had earned the contempt of all decent people, and praise from whom, since it seemed to me a thing to be desired, would only encourage me in wrongdoing, it was in faltering tones and with a slightly shamefaced air that I reached the coda: "He told the Swanns that he had found me extremely intelligent." Just as a poisoned dog in a field flings itself without knowing why at the grass which is precisely the antidote to the toxin that it has swallowed, so I, without in the least suspecting it, had said the one thing in the world that was capable of overcoming in my parents this prejudice with respect to Bergotte, a prejudice which all the best arguments that I could have put forward, all the tributes that I could have paid him, must have proved powerless to defeat. Instantly the situation changed.

"Oh! he said that he found you intelligent," repeated my mother. "I'm glad to hear that, because he's a man of talent."

"What! he said that, did he?" my father joined in . . . "I don't for a moment deny his literary distinction, before which the whole world bows; only it's a pity that he should lead that disreputable existence to which old Norpois made a guarded allusion," he went on, not seeing that against the sovereign virtue of the magic words which I had just pronounced, the depravity of Bergotte's morals was scarcely more capable of holding out any longer than the falsity of his judgment.

"But, my dear," Mamma interrupted, "we've no proof that it's true. People say all sorts of things. Besides, M. de Norpois may have the most perfect manners in the world, but he's not always very good-natured, especially about people who are not exactly his sort."

"That's quite true; I've noticed it myself," my father admitted.

"And then, too, a great deal ought to be forgiven Bergotte since he thinks well of my little son," Mamma went on, stroking my hair and fastening upon me a long and pensive gaze.

My mother had not in fact awaited this verdict from Bergotte before telling me that I might ask Gilberte to tea whenever I had friends coming. But I dared not do so for two reasons. The first was that at Gilberte's nothing else but tea was ever served. Whereas at home Mamma insisted on there being hot chocolate as well. I was afraid that Gilberte might regard this as common and so conceive a great contempt for us. The other reason was a formal difficulty, a question of procedure which I could never succeed in settling. When I arrived at Mme Swann's she used to ask me: "And how is your mother?"

I had made several overtures to Mamma to find out whether she would do the same when Gilberte came to us, a point which seemed to me more serious than, at the Court of Louis XIV, the use of "Monseigneur." But Mamma would not hear of it for a moment.

"Certainly not. I do not know Mme Swann."

"But neither does she know you."

"I never said she did, but we're not obliged to behave in exactly the same way about everything. I shall find other ways of being nice to Gilberte than Mme Swann does with you."

But I remained unconvinced, and preferred not to invite Gilberte.

Leaving my parents, I went upstairs to change my clothes and on emptying my pockets came suddenly upon the envelope which the Swann's butler had handed me before showing me into the drawing-room. I was now alone. I opened it; inside was a card on which was indicated the name of the lady whom I ought to have taken in to luncheon.

It was about this period that Bloch overthrew my conception of the world and opened for me fresh possibilities of happiness (which, as it happened, were to change later on into possibilities of suffering), by assuring me that, contrary to all that I had believed at the time of my walks along the Méséglise way, women never asked for anything better than to make love. He added to this service a second, the value of which I was not to appreciate until much later: it was he who took me for the first time into a house of assignation. He had indeed told me that there were any number of pretty women whom one might enjoy. But I could see them only in a vague outline for which those houses were to enable me to substitute actual human features. So that if I owed to Bloch—for his "good tidings" that happiness and the enjoyment of beauty were not inaccessible things that we have made a meaningless sacrifice in renouncing for ever—a debt of gratitude of the same kind as that we owe to an optimistic physician or philosopher who has given us reason to hope for longevity in this world and not to be entirely cut off from it when we shall have passed into another, the houses of assignation which I frequented some years later—by furnishing me with samples of happiness, by allowing me to add to the beauty of women that element which we are powerless to invent, which is something more than a mere summary of former beauties, that present indeed divine, the only one that we cannot bestow upon ourselves, before which all the logical creations of our intellect pale, and which we can seek from reality alone: an individual charm—deserved to be ranked by me with those other benefactors more recent in origin but of comparable utility (before finding which we used to imagine without any warmth the seductive charms of Mantegna, of Wagner, of Siena, on the basis of our knowledge of other painters, other composers, other cities): namely illustrated editions of the Old Masters, symphony concerts, and guidebooks to historic towns. But the house to which Bloch took me (and which he himself in fact had long ceased to visit) was of too inferior a grade and its personnel too mediocre and too little varied to be able to satisfy my old or to stimulate new curiosities. The mistress of this house knew none of the women with whom one asked her to negotiate, and was always suggesting others whom one did not want. She boasted to me of one in particular, of whom, with a smile full of promise (as though this was a great rarity and a special treat), she would say: "She's Jewish. How about that?" (It was doubtless for this reason that she called her Rachel.) And with an inane affectation of excitement which she hoped would prove contagious, and which ended in a hoarse gurgle, almost of sensual satisfaction: "Think of that, my boy, a Jewess! Wouldn't that be thrilling? Rrrr!" This Rachel, of whom I caught a glimpse without her seeing me, was dark, not pretty, but intelligent-looking, and would pass the tip of her tongue over her lips as she smiled with a look of boundless impertinence at the customers who were introduced to her and whom I could hear making conversation. Her thin and narrow face was framed with curly black hair, irregular as though outlined in pen-strokes upon a wash-drawing in Indian ink. Every evening I promised the madame, who offered her to me with a special insistence, boasting of her superior intelligence and her education, that I would not fail to come some day on purpose to make the acquaintance of Rachel, whom I had nicknamed "Rachel when from the Lord."[7] But the first evening I had heard her say to the madame as she was leaving the house: "That's settled then. I shall be free tomorrow, so if you have anyone you won't forget to send for me."

And these words had prevented me from recognising her as a person because they had made me classify her at once in a general category of women whose habit, common to all of them, was to come there in the evening to see whether there might not be a louis or two to be earned. She would simply vary her formula, saying indifferently: "If you need me" or "If you need anybody."

The madame, who was not familiar with Halévy's opera, did not know why I always called the girl "Rachel when from the Lord." But failure to understand a joke has never yet made anyone find it less amusing, and it was always with a wholehearted laugh that she would say to me:

"Then there's nothing doing tonight? When am I going to fix you up with 'Rachel when from the Lord'? How do you say that: 'Rachel when from the Lord'? Oh, that's a nice one, that is. I'm going to make a match of you two. You won't regret it, you'll see."

Once I nearly made up my mind, but she had "gone to press," another time she was in the hands of the "hairdresser," an old gentleman who never did anything to the women except pour oil on their loosened hair and then comb it. And I grew tired of waiting, even though several of the humbler denizens of the place (so-called working girls, though they always seemed to be out of work) had come to make tea for me and to hold long conversations to which, despite the gravity of the subjects discussed, the partial or total nudity of my interlocutors gave an attractive simplicity. I ceased moreover to go to this house because, anxious to present a token of my good-will to the woman who kept it and was in need of furniture, I had given her a few pieces—notably a big sofa—which I had inherited from my aunt Léonie. I used never to see them, for want of space had prevented my parents from taking them in at home, and they were stored in a warehouse. But as soon as I saw them again in the house where these women were putting them to their own uses, all the virtues that pervaded my aunt's room at Combray at once appeared to me, tortured by the cruel contact to which I had abandoned them in their defencelessness! Had I outraged the dead, I would not have suffered such remorse. I returned no more to visit their new mistress, for they seemed to me to be alive and to be appealing to me, like those apparently inanimate objects in a Persian fairy-tale, in which imprisoned human souls are undergoing martyrdom and pleading for deliverance. Besides, as our memory does not as a rule present things to us in their chronological sequence but as it were by a reflection in which the order of the parts is reversed, I remembered only long afterwards that it was upon that same sofa that, many years before, I had tasted for the first time the delights of love with one of my girl cousins, with whom I had not known where to go until she somewhat rashly suggested our taking advantage of a moment in which aunt Léonie had left her room.

A whole lot more of my aunt Léonie's things, and notably a magnificent set of old silver plate, I sold, against my parents' advice, so as to have more money to spend, and to be able to send more flowers to Mme Swann who would greet me, after receiving an immense basket of orchids, with: "If I were your father, I should have you up before the magistrate for this." How could I suppose that one day I might particularly regret the loss of my silver plate, and rank certain other pleasures more highly than that (which might perhaps have shrunk to nothing) of paying courtesies to Gilberte's parents. Similarly, it was with Gilberte in my mind, and in order not to be separated from her, that I had decided not to enter upon a career of diplomacy abroad. It is always thus, impelled by a state of mind which is destined not to last, that we make our irrevocable decisions. I could scarcely imagine that that strange substance which was housed in Gilberte, and which radiated from her parents and her home, leaving me indifferent to all things else, could be liberated, could migrate into another person. Unquestionably the same substance, and yet one that would have a wholly different effect on me. For the same sickness evolves; and a delicious poison can no longer be taken with the same impunity when, with the passing of the years, the heart's resistance has diminished.

My parents meanwhile would have liked to see the intelligence that Bergotte had discerned in me made manifest in some outstanding piece of work. When I still did not know the Swanns I thought that I was prevented from working by the state of agitation into which I was thrown by the impossibility of seeing Gilberte when I chose. But now that their door stood open to me, scarcely had I sat down at my desk than I would get up and hurry round to them. And after I had left them and was back at home, my isolation was apparent only, my mind was powerless to swim against the stream of words on which I had allowed myself mechanically to be borne for hours on end. Sitting alone, I continued to fashion remarks such as might have pleased or amused the Swanns, and to make this pastime more entertaining I myself took the parts of those absent players, putting to myself fictitious questions so chosen that my brilliant epigrams served simply as apt repartee. Though conducted in silence, this exercise was none the less a conversation and not a meditation, my solitude a mental social round in which it was not I myself but imaginary interlocutors who controlled my choice of words, and in which, as I formulated, instead of the thoughts that I believed to be true, those that came easily to my mind and involved no retrogression from the outside inwards, I experienced the sort of pleasure, entirely passive, which sitting still affords to anyone who is burdened with a sluggish digestion.

Had I been less firmly resolved upon settling down definitively to work, I should perhaps have made an effort to begin at once. But since my resolution was explicit, since within twenty-four hours, in the empty frame of the following day where everything was so well arranged because I myself was not yet in it, my good intentions would be realised without difficulty, it was better not to start on an evening when I felt ill-prepared. The following days were not, alas, to prove more propitious. But I was reasonable. It would have been puerile, on the part of one who had waited now for years, not to put up with a postponement of two or three days. Confident that by the day after tomorrow I should have written several pages, I said not a word more to my parents of my decision; I preferred to remain patient for a few hours and then to bring to a convinced and comforted grandmother a sample of work that was already under way. Unfortunately the next day was not that vast, extraneous expanse of time to which I had feverishly looked forward. When it drew to a close, my laziness and my painful struggle to overcome certain internal obstacles had simply lasted twenty-four hours longer. And at the end of several days, my plans not having matured, I had no longer the same hope that they would be realised at once, and hence no longer the heart to subordinate everything else to their realisation: I began again to stay up late, having no longer, to oblige me to go to bed early one evening, the certain hope of seeing my work begun next morning. I needed, before I could recover my creative energy, a few days of relaxation, and the only time my grandmother ventured, in a gentle and disillusioned tone, to frame the reproach: "Well, this famous work, don't we even speak about it any more?", I resented her intrusion, convinced that in her inability to see that my decision was irrevocably made, she had further and perhaps for a long time postponed its execution by the shock which her denial of justice had administered to my nerves and under the impact of which I should be disinclined to begin my work. She felt that her scepticism had stumbled blindly against a genuine intention. She apologised, kissing me: "I'm sorry, I shan't say another word," and, so that I should not be discouraged, assured me that as soon as I was quite well again, the work would come of its own accord to boot.

Besides, I said to myself, in spending all my time with the Swanns, am I not doing exactly what Bergotte does? To my parents it seemed almost as though, idle as I was, I was leading, since it was spent in the same salon as a great writer, the life most favourable to the growth of talent. And yet the assumption that anyone can be dispensed from having to create that talent for himself, from within himself, and can acquire it from someone else, is as erroneous as to suppose that a man can keep himself in good health (in spite of neglecting all the rules of hygiene and of indulging in the worst excesses) merely by dining out often in the company of a physician. The person, incidentally, who was most completely taken in by this illusion which misled me as well as my parents, was Mme Swann. When I explained to her that I was unable to come, that I must stay at home and work, she looked as though she felt that I was making a great fuss about nothing, that I was being rather stupidly pretentious:

"After all, Bergotte's coming. Do you mean you don't think what he writes is any good? It will be even better very soon," she went on, "because he's sharper and pithier in newspaper articles than in his books, where he's apt to pad a bit. I've arranged that in future he's to do the *leaders* in the *Figaro*. He'll be distinctly *the right man in the right place* there." And finally she added: "Do come! He'll tell you better than anyone what you ought to do."

And so, just as one invites a gentleman ranker with his colonel, it was in the interests of my career, and as though masterpieces arose out of "getting to know" people, that she told me not to fail to come to dinner next day with Bergotte.

Thus, no more from the Swanns than from my parents, that is to say from those who, at different times, had seemed bound to resist it, was there any further opposition to that delectable existence in which I might see Gilberte as often as I chose, with enchantment if not with peace of mind. There can be no peace of mind in love, since what one has obtained is never anything but a new starting-point for further desires. So long as I had been unable to go to her house, with my eyes fixed upon that inaccessible happiness, I could not even imagine the fresh grounds for anxiety that lay in wait for me there. Once the resistance of her parents was broken, and the problem solved at last, it began to set itself anew, each time in different terms. In this sense it was indeed a new friendship that began each day. Each evening, on arriving home, I reminded myself that I had things to say to Gilberte of prime importance, things upon which our whole friendship hung, and these things were never the same. But at least I was happy, and no further threat arose to endanger my happiness. One was to appear, alas, from a quarter in which I had never detected any peril, namely from Gilberte and myself. And yet I should have been tormented by what, on the contrary, reassured me, by what I mistook for happiness. We are, when we love, in an abnormal state, capable of giving at once to the most apparently simple accident, an accident which may at any moment occur, a seriousness which in itself it would not entail. What makes us so happy is the presence in our hearts of an unstable element which we contrive perpetually to maintain and of which we cease almost to be aware so long as it is not displaced. In reality, there is in love a permanent strain of suffering which happiness neutralises, makes potential only, postpones, but which may at any moment become, what it would long since have been had we not obtained what we wanted, excruciating.

On several occasions I sensed that Gilberte was anxious to put off my visits. It is true that when I was at all anxious to see her I had only to get myself invited by her parents who were increasingly persuaded of my excellent influence over her. "Thanks to them," I thought, "my love is in no danger; seeing that I have them on my side, I can set my mind at rest since they have complete authority over Gilberte." Until, alas, detecting certain signs of impatience which she betrayed when her father asked me to the house almost against her will, I wondered whether what I had regarded as a protection for my happiness was not in fact the secret reason why that happiness could not last.

The last time I came to see Gilberte, it was raining; she had been asked to a dancing lesson in the house of some people whom she knew too slightly to be able to take me there with her. In view of the dampness of the air I had taken rather more caffeine than usual. Perhaps on account of the weather, perhaps because she had some objection to the house in which this party was being given, Mme Swann, as her daughter was about to leave, called her back in the sharpest of tones: "Gilberte!" and pointed to me, to indicate that I had come there to see her and that she ought to stay with me. This "Gilberte!" had been uttered, or shouted rather, with the best of intentions towards myself, but from the way in which Gilberte shrugged her shoulders as she took off her outdoor clothes I divined that her mother had unwittingly hastened a process, which until then it might perhaps have been possible to arrest, which was gradually drawing my beloved away from me. "One doesn't have to go out dancing every day," Odette told her daughter, with a sagacity acquired no doubt in earlier days from Swann. Then, becoming once more Odette, she began to speak to her daughter in English. At once it was as though a wall had sprung up to hide from me a part of Gilberte's life, as though an evil genius had spirited her far away. In a language that we know, we have substituted for the opacity of sounds the transparency of ideas. But a language which we do not know is a fortress sealed, within whose walls the one we love is free to play us false, while we, standing outside, desperately keyed up in our impotence, can see, can prevent nothing. So this conversation in English, at which a month earlier I should merely have smiled, interspersed with a few proper names in French which served only to intensify and pinpoint my anxieties, and conducted within a few feet of me by two motionless persons, was as painful to me, left me as much abandoned and alone, as the forcible abduction of my companion. At length Mme Swann left us. That day, perhaps from resentment against me, the involuntary cause of her not going out to enjoy herself, perhaps also because, guessing her to be angry with me, I was pre-emptively colder than usual with her, Gilberte's face, divested of every sign of joy, bleak, bare, ravaged, seemed all afternoon to be harbouring a melancholy regret for the pas-de-quatre which my arrival had prevented her from going to dance, and to be defying every living creature, beginning with myself, to understand the subtle reasons that had induced in her a sentimental attachment to the boston. She confined herself to exchanging with me now and again, on the weather, the increasing violence of the rain, the fastness of the clock, a conversation punctuated with silences and monosyllables, in which I myself persisted, with a sort of desperate rage, in destroying those moments which we might have devoted to friendship and happiness. And on each of our remarks a sort of transcendent harshness was conferred by the paroxysm of their stupefying insignificance, which at the same time consoled me, for it prevented Gilberte from being taken in by the banality of my observations and the indifference of my tone. In vain did I say: "I thought the other day that the clock was slow, if anything," she clearly understood me to mean: "How nasty you are!" Obstinately as I might protract, over the whole length of that rain-sodden afternoon, the dull cloud of words through which no fitful ray shone, I knew that my coldness was not so unalterably fixed as I pretended, and that Gilberte must be fully aware that if, after already saying it to her three times, I had hazarded a fourth repetition of the statement that the evenings were drawing in, I should have had difficulty in restraining myself from bursting into tears. When she was like this, when no smile filled her eyes or opened up her face, I cannot describe the devastating monotony that stamped her melancholy eyes and sullen features. Her face, grown almost ugly, reminded me then of those dreary beaches where the sea, ebbing far out, wearies one with its faint shimmering, everywhere the same, encircled by an immutable low horizon. At length, seeing no sign in Gilberte of the happy change for which I had been waiting now for some hours, I told her that she was not being nice. "It's you who are not being nice," was her answer. "Yes I am!" I wondered what I could have done, and, finding no answer, put the question to her. "Naturally, you think yourself nice!" she said to me with a laugh, and went on laughing. Whereupon I felt how agonising it was for me not to be able to attain to that other, more elusive plane of her mind which her laughter reflected. It seemed, that laughter, to mean: "No, no, I'm not going to be taken in by anything that you say, I know you're mad about me, but that leaves me neither hot nor cold, for I don't care a rap for you." But I told myself that, after all, laughter was not a language so well defined that I could be certain of understanding what this laugh really meant. And Gilberte's words were affectionate. "But how am I not being nice," I asked her, "tell me—I'll do anything you want." "No; that wouldn't be any good. I can't explain." For a moment I was afraid that she thought that I did not love her, and this was for me a fresh agony, no less acute, but one that required a different dialectic. "If you knew how much you were hurting me you would tell me." But this pain which, had she doubted my love, must have rejoiced her, seemed instead to irritate her the more. Then, realising my mistake, making up my mind to pay no more attention to what she had said, letting her (without believing her) assure me: "I really did love you; you'll see one day" (that day on which the guilty are convinced that their innocence will be made clear, and which, for some mysterious reason, never happens to be the day on which their evidence is taken), I suddenly had the courage to resolve never to see her again, and without telling her yet since she would not have believed me.

Grief that is caused by a person one loves can be bitter, even when it is interspersed with preoccupations, occupations, pleasures in which that person is not involved and from which our attention is diverted only now and again to return to the beloved. But when such a grief has its birth—as was the case with mine—at a moment when the happiness of seeing that person fills us to the exclusion of all else, the sharp depression that then affects our spirits, hitherto sunny, sustained and calm, lets loose in us a raging storm against which we feel we may not be capable of struggling to the end. The storm that was blowing in my heart was so violent that I made my way home battered and bruised, feeling that I could recover my breath only by retracing my steps, by returning, upon whatever pretext, into Gilberte's presence. But she would have said to herself: "Back again! Evidently I can do what I like with him: he'll come back every time, and the more wretched he is when he leaves me the more docile he'll be." Besides, I was irresistibly drawn towards her by my thoughts, and those alternative orientations, that wild spinning of my inner compass, persisted after I had reached home, and expressed themselves in the mutually contradictory letters to Gilberte which I began to draft.

I was about to pass through one of those difficult crises which we generally find that we have to face at various stages in life, and which, for all that there has been no change in our character, in our nature (that nature which itself creates our loves, and almost creates the women we love, down to their very faults), we do not face in the same way on each occasion, that is to say at every age. At such moments our life is divided, and so to speak distributed over a pair of scales, in two counterpoised pans which between them contain it all. In one there is our desire not to displease, not to appear too humble to the person whom we love without being able to understand, but whom we find it more astute at times to appear almost to disregard, so that she shall not have that sense of her own indispensability which may turn her from us; in the other scale there is a feeling of pain—and one that is not localised and partial only—which cannot be assuaged unless, abandoning every thought of pleasing the woman and of making her believe that we can do without her, we go to her at once. If we withdraw from the pan that holds our pride a small quantity of the willpower which we have weakly allowed to wither with age, if we add to the pan that holds our suffering a physical pain which we have acquired and have allowed to get worse, then, instead of the brave solution that would have carried the day at twenty, it is the other, grown too heavy and insufficiently counter-balanced, that pulls us down at fifty. All the more because situations, while repeating themselves, tend to alter, and there is every likelihood that, in middle life or in old age, we shall have had the fatal self-indulgence of complicating our love by an intrusion of habit which adolescence, detained by too many other duties, less free to choose, knows nothing of.

I had just written Gilberte a letter in which I allowed my fury to thunder, not however without throwing her the lifebuoy of a few words disposed as though by accident on the page, by clinging to which my beloved might be brought to a reconciliation. A moment later, the wind having changed, they were phrases full of love that I addressed to her, chosen for the sweetness of certain forlorn expressions, those "nevermores" so touching to those who pen them, so wearisome to her who will have to read them, whether she believes them to be false and translates "nevermore" by "this very evening, if you want me," or believes them to be true and so to be breaking the news to her of one of those final separations to which we are so utterly indifferent when the person concerned is one with whom we are not in love. But since we are incapable, while we are in love, of acting as fit predecessors of the person whom we shall presently have become and who will be in love no longer, how are we to imagine the actual state of mind of a woman whom, even when we are conscious that we are of no account to her, we have perpetually represented in our musings as uttering, in order to lull us into a happy dream or to console us for a great sorrow, the same words that she would use if she loved us. Faced with the thoughts, the actions of a woman whom we love, we are as completely at a loss as the world's first natural philosophers must have been, face to face with the phenomena of nature, before their science had been elaborated and had cast a ray of light over the unknown. Or, worse still, we are like a person in whose mind the law of causality barely exists, a person who would be incapable, therefore, of establishing a connexion between one phenomenon and another and to whose eyes the spectacle of the world would appear as unstable as a dream. Of course I made efforts to emerge from this incoherence, to find reasons for things. I tried even to be "objective" and, to that end, to bear in mind the disproportion that existed between the importance which Gilberte had in my eyes and that, not only which I had in hers, but which she herself had in the eyes of other people, a disproportion which, had I failed to remark it, might have caused me to mistake mere friendliness on her part for a passionate avowal, and a grotesque and debasing display on mine for the simple and amiable impulse that directs us towards a pretty face. But I was afraid also of falling into the opposite excess, whereby I should have seen in Gilberte's unpunctuality in keeping an appointment, merely on a bad-tempered impulse, an irremediable hostility. I tried to discover between these two perspectives, equally distorting, a third which would enable me to see things as they really were; the calculations I was obliged to make with that object helped to take my mind off my sufferings; and whether in obedience to the laws of arithmetic or because I had made them give me the answer that I desired, I made up my mind to go round to the Swanns' next day, happy, but happy in the same way as people who, having long been tormented by the thought of a journey which they have not wished to make, go no further than the station and then return home to unpack their boxes. And since, while one is hesitating, the mere idea of a possible decision (unless one has rendered that idea sterile by deciding that one will make no decision) develops, like a seed in the ground, the lineaments, the minutiae, of the emotions that would spring from the performance of the action, I told myself that it had been quite absurd of me to go to as much trouble, in planning never to see Gilberte again, as if I had really had to put this plan into effect and that since, on the contrary, I was to end by returning to her side, I might have spared myself all those painful velleities and acceptances.

But this resumption of friendly relations lasted only so long as it took me to reach the Swanns'; not because their butler, who was really fond of me, told me that Gilberte had gone out (a statement the truth of which was confirmed to me, as it happened, the same evening, by people who had seen her somewhere), but because of the manner in which he said it: "Sir, the young lady is not at home; I can assure you, sir, that I am speaking the truth. If you wish to make any inquiries I can fetch the young lady's maid. You know very well, sir, that I would do everything in my power to oblige you, and that if the young lady was at home I would take you to her at once." These words being of the only kind that is really important, that is to say involuntary, the kind that gives us a sort of X-ray photograph of the unimaginable reality which would be wholly concealed beneath a prepared speech, proved that in Gilberte's household there was an impression that she found me importunate; and so, scarcely had the man uttered them than they had aroused in me a hatred of which I preferred to make him rather than Gilberte the victim; he drew upon his own head all the angry feelings that I might have had for my beloved; relieved of them thanks to his words, my love subsisted alone; but his words had at the same time shown me that I must cease for the present to attempt to see Gilberte. She would be certain to write to me to apologise. In spite of which, I should not return at once to see her, so as to prove to her that I was capable of living without her. Besides, once I had received her letter, Gilberte's society was a thing with which I could more easily dispense for a time, since I should be certain of finding her ready to receive me whenever I chose. All that I needed in order to support less gloomily the pain of a voluntary separation was to feel that my heart was rid of the terrible uncertainty as to whether we were not irreconcilably sundered, whether she had not become engaged, left Paris, been taken away by force. The days that followed resembled the first week of that previous New Year which I had had to spend without Gilberte. But when that week had dragged to its end, for one thing my beloved would be coming again to the Champs-Elysées, I should be seeing her as before, of that I had been sure; for another thing, I had known with no less certainty that so long as the New Year holidays lasted there was no point in my going to the Champs-Elysées, which meant that during that miserable week, which was already ancient history, I had endured my wretchedness with a quiet mind because it was mixed with neither fear nor hope. Now, on the other hand, it was the latter of these which, almost as much as fear, made my suffering intolerable.

Not having had a letter from Gilberte that evening, I had attributed this to her negligence, to her other occupations, and I did not doubt that I should find one from her in the morning's post. This I awaited, every day, with a throbbing of the heart that subsided, leaving me utterly prostrate, when I found in it only letters from people who were not Gilberte, or else nothing at all, which was no worse, the proofs of another's friendship making all the more cruel those of her indifference. I transferred my hopes to the afternoon post. Even between the times at which letters were delivered I dared not leave the house, for she might be sending hers by a messenger. Then, the time coming at last when neither the postman nor a footman from the Swanns' could possibly appear that night, I had to postpone till the morrow my hope of being reassured, and thus, because I believed that my sufferings were not destined to last, I was obliged, so to speak, incessantly to renew them. My disappointment was perhaps the same, but instead of just uniformly prolonging, as formerly it had, an initial emotion, it began again several times daily, starting each time with an emotion so frequently renewed that it ended—it, so purely physical, so instantaneous a state—by becoming stabilised, so that the strain of waiting having hardly time to subside before a fresh reason for waiting supervened, there was no longer a single minute in the day during which I was not in that state of anxiety which it is so difficult to bear even for an hour. Thus my suffering was infinitely more cruel than in those former New Year holidays, because this time there was in me, instead of the acceptance, pure and simple, of that suffering, the hope, at every moment, of seeing it come to an end.

And yet I did ultimately arrive at this acceptance: then I realised that it must be final, and I renounced Gilberte for ever, in the interests of my love itself and because I hoped above all that she would not retain a contemptuous memory of me. Indeed, from that moment, so that she should not be led to suppose any sort of lover's spite on my part, when she made appointments for me to see her I used often to accept them and then, at the last moment, write to her to say that I could not come, but with the same protestations of disappointment as I should have made to someone whom I had not wished to see. These expressions of regret, which we reserve as a rule for people who do not matter, would do more, I imagined, to persuade Gilberte of my indifference than would the tone of indifference which we affect only towards those we love. When, better than by mere words, by a course of action indefinitely repeated, I should have proved to her that I had no inclination to see her, perhaps she would discover once again an inclination to see me. Alas! I was doomed to failure; to attempt, by ceasing to see her, to reawaken in her that inclination to see me was to lose her for ever; first of all because, when it began to revive, if I wished it to last I must not give way to it at once; besides, the most agonising hours would then have passed; it was at this very moment that she was indispensable to me, and I should have liked to be able to warn her that what presently she would assuage, by seeing me again, would be a grief so far diminished as to be no longer (as now it would still be), in order to put an end to it, a motive for surrender, reconciliation and further meetings. And later on, when I should at last be able safely to confess to Gilberte (so much would her feeling for me have regained its strength) my feeling for her, the latter, not having been able to resist the strain of so long a separation, would have ceased to exist; I should have become indifferent to Gilberte. I knew this, but I could not explain it to her; she would have assumed that if I was claiming that I would cease to love her if I remained for too long without seeing her, that was solely to persuade her to summon me back to her at once. In the meantime, what made it easier for me to sentence myself to this separation was the fact that (in order to make it quite clear to her that despite my protestations to the contrary it was my own free will and not any extraneous obstacle, not the state of my health, that prevented me from seeing her), whenever I knew beforehand that Gilberte would not be in the house, was going out somewhere with a friend and would not be home for dinner, I went to see Mme Swann, who had once more become to me what she had been at the time when I had such difficulty in seeing her daughter and (on days when the latter was not coming to the Champs-Elysées) used to repair to the Allée des Acacias. In this way I should hear about Gilberte, and could be certain that she would in due course hear about me, and in terms which would show her that I was not hankering after her. And I found, as all those who suffer find, that my melancholy situation might have been worse. For, being free at any time to enter the house in which Gilberte lived, I constantly reminded myself, for all that I was firmly resolved to make no use of that privilege, that if ever my pain grew too sharp there was a way of making it cease. I was not unhappy, except one day at a time. And even that is an exaggeration. How many times an hour (but now without that anxious expectancy which had strained my every nerve in the first weeks after our quarrel, before I had gone again to the Swanns') did I not recite to myself the words of the letter which, one day soon, Gilberte would surely send, would perhaps even bring to me herself! The perpetual vision of that imagined happiness helped me to endure the destruction of my real happiness. With women who do not love us, as with the "dear departed," the knowledge that there is no hope left does not prevent us from continuing to wait. We live in expectancy, constantly on the alert; the mother whose son has gone to sea on some perilous voyage of discovery sees him in imagination every moment, long after the fact of his having perished has been established, striding into the room, saved by a miracle and in the best of health. And this expectancy, according to the strength of her memory and the resistance of her bodily organs, either helps her on her journey through the years, at the end of which she will be able to endure the knowledge that her son is no more, to forget gradually and to survive his loss—or else it kills her.

At the same time, my grief found consolation in the idea that my love must profit by it. Every visit that I paid to Mme Swann without seeing Gilberte was painful to me, but I felt that it correspondingly enhanced the idea that Gilberte had of me. Besides, if I always took care, before going to see Mme Swann, to ensure that her daughter was absent, this arose not only from my determination to break with her, but no less perhaps from the hope of reconciliation which overlay my intention to renounce her (very few of such intentions are absolute, at least in a continuous form, in this human soul of ours, one of whose laws, confirmed by the unlooked-for wealth of illustration that memory supplies, is intermittence), and hid from me something of its cruelty. I knew how chimerical was this hope. I was like a pauper who moistens his dry crust with fewer tears if he assures himself that at any moment a total stranger is perhaps going to leave him his entire fortune. We are all of us obliged, if we are to make reality endurable, to nurse a few little follies in ourselves. And my hope remained more intact—while at the same time our separation became more ineluctable—if I refrained from meeting Gilberte. If I had found myself face to face with her in her mother's drawing room, we might perhaps have exchanged irrevocable words which would have rendered our breach final, killed my hope and, at the same time, by creating a fresh anxiety, reawakened my love and made resignation harder.

Long before my break with her daughter, Mme Swann had said to me: "It's all very well your coming to see Gilberte but I should like you to come sometimes for my sake, not to my 'do's,' which would bore you because there's such a crowd, but on the other days, when you will always find me at home if you come fairly late." So that I might be thought, when I came to see her, to be belatedly complying with a wish that she had expressed in the past. And very late in the afternoon, when it was already dark, almost at the hour at which my parents would be sitting down to dinner, I would set out to pay Mme Swann a visit during the course of which I knew that I should not see Gilberte and yet should be thinking only of her. In that quarter, then looked upon as remote, of a Paris darker than it is today, where even in the centre there was no electric light in the public thoroughfares and very little in private houses, the lamps of a drawing-room situated on the ground floor or a low mezzanine (as were the rooms in which Mme Swann generally received her visitors) were enough to lighten the street and to make the passer-by raise his eyes and connect with the glow from the windows, as with its apparent though veiled cause, the presence outside the door of a string of smart broughams. This passer-by was led to believe, not without a certain excitement, that a modification had been effected in this mysterious cause, when he saw one of the carriages begin to move; but it was merely a coachman who, afraid that his horses might catch cold, started them now and again on a brisk walk, all the more impressive because the rubber-tired wheels gave the sound of their hooves a background of silence from which it stood out more distinct and more explicit.

The "winter-garden," of which in those days the passer-by generally caught a glimpse, in whatever street he might be walking, if the apartment did not stand too high above the pavement, is to be seen today only in photogravures in the gift-books of P. J. Stahl, where, in contrast to the infrequent floral decorations of the Louis XVI drawing-rooms now in fashion—a single rose or a Japanese iris in a long-necked vase of crystal into which it would be impossible to squeeze a second—it seems, because of the profusion of indoor plants which people had then, and of the absolute lack of stylisation in their arrangement, as though it must have responded in the ladies whose houses it adorned to some lively and delightful passion for botany rather than to any cold concern for lifeless decoration. It suggested to one, only on a larger scale, in the houses of those days, those tiny, portable hothouses laid out on New Year's morning beneath the lighted lamp—for the children were always too impatient to wait for daylight—among all the other New Year presents but the loveliest of them all, consoling them, with its real plants which they could tend as they grew, for the bareness of the winter soil; and even more than those little houses themselves, those winter gardens were like the hothouse that the children could see there at the same time, portrayed in a delightful book, another New Year present and one which, for all that it was given not to them but to Mlle Lili, the heroine of the story, enchanted them to such a pitch that even now, when they are almost old men and women, they ask themselves whether, in those fortunate years, winter was not the loveliest of the seasons. And finally, beyond the winter-garden, through the various kinds of arborescence which from the street made the lighted window appear like the glass front of one of those children's playthings, pictured or real, the passer-by, drawing himself up on tiptoe, would generally observe a man in a frock-coat, a gardenia or a carnation in his buttonhole, standing before a seated lady, both vaguely outlined like two intaglios cut in a topaz, in the depths of the drawing-room atmosphere clouded by the samovar—then a recent importation—with steam which may escape from it still today, but to which, if it does, we have grown so accustomed now that no one notices it. Mme Swann attached great importance to her "tea"; she thought that she showed her originality and expressed her charm when she said to a man: "You'll find me at home any day, fairly late; come to tea," and so would accompany with a sweet and subtle smile these words which she pronounced with a fleeting trace of an English accent, and which her listener duly noted, bowing solemnly in acknowledgment, as though the invitation had been something important and uncommon which commanded deference and required attention. There was another reason, apart from those given already, for the flowers' having more than a merely ornamental significance in Mme Swann's drawing-room, and this reason pertained not to the period but, in some degree, to the life that Odette had formerly led. A great courtesan, such as she had been, lives largely for her lovers, that is to say at home, which means that she comes in time to live for her home. The things that one sees in the house of a respectable woman, things which may of course appear to her also to be of importance, are those which are in any event of the utmost importance to the courtesan. The culminating point of her day is not the moment in which she dresses herself for society, but that in which she undresses herself for a man. She must be as elegant in her dressing-gown, in her night-dress, as in her outdoor attire. Other women display their jewels, but she lives in the intimacy of her pearls. This kind of existence imposes on her the obligation, and ends by giving her the taste, for a luxury which is secret, that is to say which comes near to being disinterested. Mme Swann extended this to include her flowers. There was always beside her chair an immense crystal bowl filled to the brim with Parma violets or with long white daisy-petals floating in the water, which seemed to testify, in the eyes of the arriving guest, to some favourite occupation now interrupted, as would also have been the cup of tea which Mme Swann might have been drinking there alone for her own pleasure; an occupation more intimate still and more mysterious, so much so that one wanted to apologise on seeing the flowers exposed there by her side, as one would have apologised for looking at the title of the still open book which would have revealed to one Odette's recent reading and hence perhaps her present thoughts. And even more than the book, the flowers were living things; one was embarrassed, when one entered the room to pay Mme Swann a visit, to discover that she was not alone, or if one came home with her, not to find the room empty, so enigmatic a place, intimately associated with hours in the life of their mistress of which one knew nothing, did those flowers assume, those flowers which had not been arranged for Odette's visitors but, as it were forgotten there by her, had held and would hold with her again intimate talks which one was afraid of disturbing, the secret of which one tried in vain to read by staring at the washed-out, liquid, mauve and dissolute colour of the Parma violets. From the end of October Odette would begin to come home with the utmost punctuality for tea (which was still known at that time as "five-o'clock tea") having once heard it said, and being fond of repeating, that if Mme Verdurin had been able to form a salon it was because people were always certain of finding her at home at the same hour. She imagined that she herself had one also, of the same kind, but freer, *senza rigore* as she liked to say. She saw herself figuring thus as a sort of Lespinasse, and believed that she had founded a rival salon by taking from the du Deffand of the little group several of her most attractive men, notably Swann himself, who had followed her in her secession and into her retirement, according to a version for which one can understand that she had succeeded in gaining credit among newcomers who were ignorant of the past, though without convincing herself. But certain favourite roles are played by us so often before the public and rehearsed so carefully when we are alone that we find it easier to refer to their fictitious testimony than to that of a reality which we have almost entirely forgotten. On days when Mme Swann had not left the house, one found her in a crêpe-de-Chine dressing-gown, white as the first snows of winter, or, it might be, in one of those long pleated chiffon garments, which looked like nothing so much as a shower of pink or white petals, and would be regarded today as highly inappropriate for winter—though quite wrongly, for these light fabrics and soft colours gave to a woman—in the stifling warmth of the drawing-rooms of those days, with their heavily curtained doors, rooms of which the most elegant thing that the society novelists of the time could find to say was that they were "cosily padded"—the same air of coolness that they gave to the roses which were able to stay in the room there beside her, despite the winter, in the glowing flesh tints of their nudity, as though it were already spring. Because of the muffling of all sound by the carpets, and of her withdrawal into a recess, the lady of the house, not being apprised of your entry as she is today, would continue to read almost until you were standing before her chair, which enhanced still further that sense of the romantic, that charm as of detecting a secret, which we can recapture today in the memory of those gowns, already out of fashion even then, which Mme Swann was perhaps alone in not having discarded, and which give us the feeling that the woman who wore them must have been the heroine of a novel because most of us have scarcely set eyes on them outside the pages of certain of Henry Gréville's novels. Odette had now in her drawing-room, at the beginning of winter, chrysanthemums of enormous size and of a variety of colours such as Swann, in the old days, certainly never saw in her drawing-room in the Rue La Pérouse. My admiration for them—when I went to pay Mme Swann one of those melancholy visits during which, prompted by my sorrow, I discovered in her all the mysterious poetry of her character as the mother of that Gilberte to whom she would say next day: "Your friend came to see me yesterday"—sprang, no doubt, from my sense that, pale pink like the Louis XV silk that covered her chairs, snow-white like her crêpe-de-Chine dressing-gown, or of a metallic red like her samovar, they superimposed upon the decoration of the room another, a supplementary scheme of decoration, as rich and as delicate in its colouring, but one that was alive and would last for a few days only. But I was touched to find that these chrysanthemums appeared not so much ephemeral as relatively durable compared with the tones, equally pink or equally coppery, which the setting sun so gorgeously displays amid the mists of a November afternoon, and which, after seeing them fading from the sky before I had entered the house, I found again inside, prolonged, transposed in the flaming palette of the flowers. Like the fires caught and fixed by a great colourist from the impermanence of the atmosphere and the sun, so that they should enter and adorn a human dwelling, they invited me, those chrysanthemums, to put away all my sorrows and to taste with a greedy rapture during that tea-time hour the all-too-fleeting pleasures of November, whose intimate and mysterious splendour they set ablaze all around me. Alas, it was not in the conversations which I heard that I could hope to attain to that splendour; they had little in common with it. Even with Mme Cottard, and although it was growing late, Mme Swann would assume her most caressing manner to say: "Oh, no, it's quite early really; you mustn't look at the clock; that's not the right time; it's stopped; you can't possibly have anything very urgent to do," as she pressed a final tartlet upon the Professor's wife, who was gripping her card-case in readiness for flight.

"One simply can't tear oneself away from this house," observed Mme Bontemps to Mme Swann, while Mme Cottard, in her astonishment at hearing her own thought put into words, exclaimed: "Why, that's just what I always say to myself, in my common-sensical little way, in my heart of hearts!" winning the approval of the gentlemen from the Jockey Club, who had been profuse in their salutations, as though overwhelmed by such an honour, when Mme Swann had introduced them to this graceless little bourgeois woman, who, when confronted with Odette's brilliant friends, remained on her guard, if not on what she herself called "the defensive," for she always used stately language to describe the simplest things.

"I should never have suspected it," was Mme Swann's comment, "three Wednesdays running you've let me down." "That's quite true, Odette; it's *simply ages, it's an eternity* since I saw you last. You see I plead guilty; but I must tell you," she went on with a vague and prudish air (for although a doctor's wife she would never have dared to speak without periphrasis of rheumatism or of a chill on the kidneys), "that I have a lot of little *troubles.* As we all have, I dare say. And besides that I've had a crisis among my masculine staff. Without being more imbued than most with a sense of my own authority, I've been obliged, just to make an example you know, to give my Vatel notice;[8] I believe he was looking out anyhow for a more remunerative place. But his departure nearly brought about the resignation of the entire Ministry. My own maid refused to stay in the house a moment longer; oh, we have had some Homeric scenes. However, I held fast to the helm through thick and thin; the whole affair's been a perfect object lesson, which won't be lost on me, I can tell you. I'm afraid I'm boring you with all these stories about servants, but you know as well as I do what a business it is when one is obliged to set about rearranging one's household."

"Aren't we to see anything of your delicious daughter?" she wound up. "No, my delicious daughter is dining with a friend," replied Mme Swann, and then, turning to me: "I believe she's written to you, asking you to come and see her tomorrow. And your *babies*?" she went on to Mme Cottard.

I breathed a sigh of relief. These words of Mme Swann's, which proved to me that I could see Gilberte whenever I chose, gave me precisely the comfort which I had come to seek, and which at that time made my visits to Mme Swann so necessary. "No, I shall write her a note this evening. Besides, Gilberte and I can no longer see one another," I added, pretending to attribute our separation to some mysterious cause, which gave me a further illusion of love, sustained as well by the affectionate way in which I spoke of Gilberte and she of me.

"You know she's simply devoted to you," said Mme Swann. "Really, you won't come tomorrow?"

Suddenly I was filled with elation; the thought had just struck me—"After all, why not, since it's her own mother who suggests it?" But at once I relapsed into my gloom. I was afraid lest Gilberte, on seeing me, might think that my indifference of late had been feigned, and it seemed wiser to prolong our separation. During these asides Mme Bontemps had been complaining of the insufferable dullness of politicians' wives, for she affected to find everyone too deadly or too stupid for words, and to deplore her husband's official position.

"Do you mean to say you can shake hands with fifty doctors' wives, like that, one after the other?" she exclaimed to Mme Cottard, who, on the contrary, was full of benevolence towards everybody, and determined to do her duty in every respect. "Ah! you're a woman of virtue! As for me, at the Ministry, of course I have my obligations. Well, it's more than I can stand. You know what those officials' wives are like, it's all I can do not to put my tongue out at them. And my niece Albertine is just like me. You've no idea how insolent she is, that child. Last week, during my 'at home,' I had the wife of the Under Secretary of State for Finance, who told us that she knew nothing at all about cooking. 'But surely, ma'am,' my niece chipped in with her most winning smile, 'you ought to know all about it, since your father was a scullion.' "

"Oh, I do love that story; I think it's simply exquisite!" cried Mme Swann. "But certainly for the Doctor's consultation days you should make a point of having a little *home*, with your flowers and books and all your pretty things," she urged Mme Cottard.

"Straight out like that! Slap-bang, right in the face! She made no bones about it, I can tell you! And she didn't give me a word of warning, the little minx; she's as cunning as a monkey. You're lucky to be able to hold yourself back; I do envy people who can hide what's in their minds." "But I've no need to do that, Mme Bontemps, I'm not so hard to please," Mme Cottard gently expostulated. "For one thing, I'm not in such a privileged position as you," she went on, slightly raising her voice as was her custom, as though to underline the remark, whenever she slipped into the conversation one of those delicate courtesies, those skilful flatteries which won her the admiration and assisted the career of her husband. "And besides I'm only too glad to do anything that can be of use to the Professor."

"But Madame, it's what one is able to do! I expect you're not highly strung. Do you know, whenever I see the War Minister's wife grimacing, I start imitating her at once. It's a dreadful thing to have a temperament like mine."

"Ah, yes," said Mme Cottard, "I've heard that she had a twitch. My husband knows someone else who occupies a very high position, and it's only natural, when these gentlemen get talking together . . ."

"And then you know, it's just the same with the Head of Protocol, who's a hunchback. He has only to be in my house five minutes before my fingers are itching to stroke his hump. I can't help it. My husband says I'll cost him his place. What if I do! Pooh to the Ministry! Yes, pooh to the Ministry! I should like to have that printed as a motto on my notepaper. I can see I'm shocking you; you're so good, but I must say there's nothing amuses me like a little devilry now and then. Life would be dreadfully monotonous without it."

And she went on talking about the Ministry all the time, as though it had been Mount Olympus. To change the subject, Mme Swann turned to Mme Cottard: "But you're looking very elegant today. Redfern *fecit*?"

"No, you know I always swear by Raudnitz. Besides, it's only an old thing I've had done up."

"Well, well! it's really smart!"

"Guess how much . . . No, change the first figure!"

"You don't say so! Why, it's dirt cheap, it's a gift! Three times that at least, I was told."

"That's how history comes to be written," concluded the doctor's wife. And pointing to a neck-ribbon which had been a present from Mme Swann: "Look, Odette! Do you recognise it?"

Through the gap between a pair of curtains a head peeped with ceremonious deference, making a playful pretence of being afraid of disturbing the party: it was Swann. "Odette, the Prince d'Agrigente is with me in my study and wants to know if he may pay his respects to you. What am I to tell him?" "Why, that I shall be delighted," Odette replied, secretly flattered but without losing anything of the composure which came to her all the more easily since she had always, even as a cocotte, been accustomed to entertain men of fashion. Swann disappeared to deliver the message, to return presently with the Prince, unless in the meantime Mme Verdurin had arrived.

When he married Odette Swann had insisted on her ceasing to frequent the little clan. (He had several good reasons for this stipulation, and even if he had had none, would have made it none the less in obedience to a law of ingratitude which admits of no exception and proves that every go-between is either lacking in foresight or else singularly disinterested.) He had conceded only that Odette might exchange visits with Mme Verdurin once a year, and even this seemed excessive to some of the "faithful," indignant at the insult offered to the Mistress who for so many years had treated Odette and even Swann himself as the spoiled children of her house. For if it contained false brethren who defaulted on certain evenings in order that they might secretly accept an invitation from Odette, ready, in the event of discovery, with the excuse that they were curious to meet Bergotte (although the Mistress assured them that he never went to the Swanns' and was totally devoid of talent—in spite of which she made the most strenuous efforts, to quote one of her favourite expressions, to "attract" him), the little group had its "die-hards" too. And these—though ignorant of those refinements of convention which often dissuade people from the extreme attitude one would like to see them adopt in order to annoy someone else—would have wished Mme Verdurin but had never managed to prevail upon her to sever all relations with Odette and thus deprive her of the satisfaction of saying with a laugh: "We seldom go to the Mistress's now, since the Schism. It was all very well while my husband was still a bachelor, but when one is married, you know, it isn't always so easy . . . If you must know, M. Swann can't abide old Ma Verdurin, and he wouldn't much like the idea of my going there regularly as I used to. And I, dutiful spouse . . ." Swann would accompany his wife to their annual evening there but would take care not to be in the room when Mme Verdurin came to call on Odette. And so, if the Mistress was in the drawing-room, the Prince d'Agrigente would enter it alone. Alone, too, he was presented to her by Odette, who preferred that Mme Verdurin should be left in ignorance of the names of her humbler guests and, seeing more than one strange face in the room, might be led to believe that she was mixing with the cream of the aristocracy, a device which proved so successful that Mme Verdurin said to her husband that evening with profound contempt: "Charming people, her friends! I met all the flower of Reaction!"

Odette was living, with respect to Mme Verdurin, under a converse illusion. Not that the latter's salon had even begun, at that time, to develop into what we shall one day see it become. Mme Verdurin had not yet reached the period of incubation in which one dispenses with the big parties where the few brilliant specimens recently acquired would be lost in the crowd, and prefers to wait until the generative force of the ten just men whom one has succeeded in attracting shall have multiplied those ten seventy-fold. As Odette was not to be long now in doing, Mme Verdurin did indeed entertain the idea of "society" as her final objective, but her zone of attack was as yet so restricted, and moreover so remote from that by way of which Odette stood some chance of arriving at an identical goal, of breaking through, that the latter remained in total ignorance of the strategic plans which the Mistress was elaborating. And it was with the most perfect sincerity that Odette, when anyone spoke to her of Mme Verdurin as a snob, would answer, laughing: "Oh, no, quite the opposite! For one thing, she hasn't the basis for it: she doesn't know anyone. And then, to do her justice, I must say that she seems quite content with things as they are. No, what she likes are her Wednesdays, good talkers." And in her heart of hearts she envied Mme Verdurin (for all that she did not despair of having herself, in so eminent a school, succeeded in acquiring them) those arts to which the Mistress attached such paramount importance, although they did no more than discriminate between shades of the non-existent, sculpture the void, and were, strictly speaking, the Arts of Nonentity: to wit those, in the lady of a house, of knowing how to "bring people together," how to "group," to "draw out," to "keep in the background," to act as a "connecting link."

At all events Mme Swann's friends were impressed when they saw in her house a lady of whom they were accustomed to think only as in her own, in an inseparable setting of guests, in the midst of her little group which they were astonished to behold thus evoked, summarised, compressed into a single armchair in the bodily form of the Mistress, the hostess turned visitor, muffled in her cloak with its grebe trimming, as fluffy as the white furs that carpeted that drawing-room, embowered in which Mme Verdurin was a drawing-room in herself. The more timid among the women thought it prudent to retire, and using the plural, as people do when they mean to hint to the rest of the room that it is wiser not to tire a convalescent who is out of bed for the first time, "Odette," they murmured, "we're going to leave you." They envied Mme Cottard, whom the Mistress called by her Christian name.

"Can I drop you anywhere?" Mme Verdurin asked her, unable to bear the thought that one of the faithful was going to remain behind instead of following her from the room.

"Oh, but this lady has been so very kind as to say she'll take me," replied Mme Cottard, not wishing to appear to be forgetting, when approached by a more illustrious personage, that she had accepted the offer which Mme Bontemps had made to drive her home behind her cockaded coachman. "I must say that I'm always specially grateful to the friends who are so kind as to take me with them in their vehicles. It's a regular godsend to me who have no charioteer."

"Especially," broke in the Mistress, hardly daring to say anything, since she knew Mme Bontemps slightly and had just invited her to her Wednesdays, "as at Mme de Crécy's house you're not very near home. Oh, good gracious, I shall never get into the habit of saying Mme Swann!" It was a recognised joke in the little clan, among those who were not over-endowed with wit, to pretend that they could never grow used to saying "Mme Swann":

"I've been so accustomed to saying Mme de Crécy that I nearly went wrong again!" Only Mme Verdurin, when she spoke to Odette, was not content with the nearly, but went wrong on purpose.

"Don't you feel afraid, Odette, living out in the wilds like this? I'm sure I shouldn't feel at all comfortable, coming home after dark. Besides, it's so damp. It can't be at all good for your husband's eczema. You haven't rats in the house, I hope!" "Oh, dear no. What a horrid idea!" "That's a good thing; I was told you had. I'm glad to know it's not true, because I have a perfect horror of the creatures, and I should never have come to see you again. Good-bye, my dear child, we shall meet again soon; you know what a pleasure it is to me to see you. You don't know how to arrange chrysanthemums," she added as she prepared to leave the room, Mme Swann having risen to escort her. "They are Japanese flowers; you must arrange them the same way as the Japanese."

"I do not agree with Mme Verdurin, although she is the fount of wisdom to me in all things! There's no one like you, Odette, for finding such lovely chrysanthemums, or chrysanthema rather, for it seems that's what we ought to call them now," declared Mme Cottard as soon as the Mistress had shut the door behind her.

"Dear Mme Verdurin is not always very kind about other people's flowers," said Odette sweetly. "Whom do you go to, Odette," asked Mme Cottard, to forestall any further criticism of the Mistress. "Lemaître? I must confess, the other day in Lemaître's window I saw a lovely pink shrub which made me commit the wildest extravagance." But modesty forbade her to give any more precise details as to the price of the shrub, and she said merely that the Professor, "and you know, he's not at all a quick-tempered man," had "flown off the handle" and told her that she "didn't know the value of money."

"No, no, I've no regular florist except Debac." "Me too," said Mme Cottard, "but I confess that I forsake him now and then for Lachaume." "Oh, you're unfaithful to him with Lachaume, are you? I must tell him that," replied Odette, always anxious to show her wit, and to lead the conversation in her own house, where she felt more at her ease than in the little clan. "Besides, Lachaume is really becoming too dear; his prices are quite excessive, don't you know; I find his prices indecent!" she added, laughing.

Meanwhile Mme Bontemps, who had been heard a hundred times to declare that nothing would induce her to go to the Verdurins', delighted at being asked to the famous Wednesdays, was working out how she could manage to attend as many of them as possible. She was not aware that Mme Verdurin liked people not to miss a single one; moreover she was one of those people whose company is but little sought after who, when a hostess invites them to a series of "at homes," instead of going to her house without more ado—like those who know that it is always a pleasure to see them—whenever they have a moment to spare and feel inclined to go out, deny themselves for example the first evening and the third, imagining that their absence will be noticed, and save themselves up for the second and fourth, unless it should happen that, having heard from a trustworthy source that the third is to be a particularly brilliant party, they reverse the original order, assuring their hostess that "most unfortunately, we had another engagement last week." So Mme

Bontemps was calculating how many Wednesdays there could still be left before Easter, and by what means she might manage to secure an extra one and yet not appear to be thrusting herself upon her hostess. She relied upon Mme Cottard, whom she would have with her in the carriage going home, to give her a few hints.

"Oh, Mme Bontemps, I see you getting up to go; it's very bad of you to give the signal for flight like that! You owe me some compensation for not turning up last Thursday . . . Come, sit down again, just for a minute. You can't possibly be going anywhere else before dinner. Really, you won't let yourself be tempted?" went on Mme Swann, and, as she held out a plate of cakes, "You know, they're not at all bad, these little horrors. They may not be much to look at, but just you taste one and you'll see."

"On the contrary, they look quite delicious," broke in Mme Cottard. "In your house, Odette, one is never short of victuals. I have no need to ask to see the trade-mark; I know you get everything from Rebattet. I must say that I am more eclectic. For sweets and cakes and so forth I repair, as often as not, to Bourbonneux. But I agree that they simply don't know what an ice means. Rebattet for everything iced, and syrups and sorbets; they're past masters. As my husband would say, they're the *ne plus ultra*."

"Oh, but these are home-made. You won't, really?"

"I shan't be able to eat a scrap of dinner," pleaded Mme Bontemps, "but I'll sit down again for a moment. You know, I adore talking to a clever woman like you."

"You'll think me highly indiscreet, Odette, but I should so like to know what you thought of the hat Mme Trombert had on. I know, of course, that big hats are the fashion just now. All the same, wasn't it just the least little bit exaggerated? And compared to the hat she came to see me in the other day, the one she was wearing just now was microscopic!" "Oh no, I'm not at all clever," said Odette, thinking that this sounded well. "I am a perfect simpleton, I believe everything people say, and worry myself to death over the least thing." And she insinuated that she had, just at first, suffered terribly from having married a man like Swann who had a separate life of his own and was unfaithful to her.

Meanwhile the Prince d'Agrigente, having caught the words "I'm not at all clever," thought it incumbent on him to protest, but unfortunately lacked the gift of repartee. "Fiddlesticks!" cried Mme Bontemps, "not clever, you!" "That's just what I was saying to myself—'What do I hear?'," the Prince clutched at this straw. "My ears must have played me false!"

"No, I assure you," went on Odette, "I'm really just an ordinary woman, very easily shocked, full of prejudices, living in my own little groove and dreadfully ignorant." And then, in case he had any news of the Baron de Charlus, "Have you seen our dear Baronet?" she asked him.

"You, ignorant!" cried Mme Bontemps. "Then I wonder what you'd say of the official world, all those wives of Excellencies who can talk of nothing but their frocks . . . Just imagine, not more than a week ago I happened to mention *Lohengrin* to the Education Minister's wife. She stared at me and said '*Lohengrin*? Oh, yes, the new review at the Folies-Bergère. I hear it's a perfect scream!' Well, I ask you! When people say things like that it makes your blood boil. I could have hit her. Because I have a bit of a temper of my own. What do you say, Monsieur," she added, turning to me, "was I not right?"

"But still," said Mme Cottard, "it's forgivable to be a little off the mark when you're asked a thing like that point blank, without any warning. I know something about it, because Mme Verdurin also has a habit of putting a pistol to your head."

"Speaking of Mme Verdurin," Mme Bontemps asked Mme Cottard, "do you know who will be there on Wednesday? Oh, I've just remembered that we've accepted an invitation for next Wednesday. You wouldn't care to dine with us on Wednesday week? We could go on together to Mme Verdurin's. I should never dare to go there by myself. I don't know why it is, that great lady always terrifies me."

"I'll tell you what it is," replied Mme Cottard, "that frightens you about Mme Verdurin: it's her voice. But you see everyone can't have such a charming voice as Mme Swann. Once you've found your tongue, as the Mistress says, the ice will soon be broken. For she's a very easy person, really, to get on with. But I can quite understand what you feel; it's never pleasant to find oneself for the first time in strange surroundings."

"Won't you dine with us, too?" said Mme Bontemps to Mme Swann. "After dinner we could all go to the Verdurins' together, 'do a Verdurin'; and even if it means that the Mistress will glare at me and never ask me to the house again, once we are there we'll just sit by ourselves and have a quiet talk, I'm sure that's what I should like best." But this assertion can hardly have been quite truthful, for Mme Bontemps went on to ask: "Who do you think will be there on Wednesday week? What will be happening? There won't be too big a crowd, I hope!"

"I certainly shan't be there," said Odette. "We'll just put in a brief appearance on the last Wednesday of all. If you don't mind waiting till then . . ." But Mme Bontemps did not appear to be tempted by the proposal.

Granted that the intellectual distinction of a salon and its elegance are generally in inverse rather than direct ratio, one must suppose, since Swann found Mme Bontemps agreeable, that any forfeiture of position once accepted has the consequence of making people less particular with regard to those among whom they have resigned themselves to move, less particular with regard to their intelligence as to everything else about them. And if this is true, men, like nations, must see their culture and even their language disappear with their independence. One of the effects of this indulgence is to aggravate the tendency people have after a certain age to derive pleasure from words that are a homage to their own turn of mind, to their weaknesses, and an encouragement to them to yield to them; that is the age at which a great artist prefers to the company of original minds that of pupils who have nothing in common with him save the letter of his doctrine, who listen to him and offer incense; at which a man or woman of distinction who lives exclusively for love will think the most intelligent person in a gathering the one who, however inferior, has shown by some remark that he can understand and approve an existence devoted to gallantry, and has thus pleasantly flattered the voluptuous instincts of the lover or mistress; it was the age, too, at which Swann, inasmuch as he had become the husband of Odette, enjoyed hearing Mme Bontemps say how silly it was to have nobody in one's house but duchesses (concluding from that, contrary to what he would have done in the old days at the Verdurins', that she was a good creature, extremely witty and not at all a snob) and telling her stories which made her "die laughing," because she had not heard them before and moreover "saw the point" of them at once, since she enjoyed flattering and exchanging jokes.

"So the Doctor is not mad about flowers, like you?" Mme Swann asked Mme Cottard.

"Oh, well, you know, my husband is a sage; he practises moderation in all things. Wait, though, he does have one passion."

Her eye aflame with malice, joy, curiosity, "And what is that, pray?" inquired Mme Bontemps.

Artlessly Mme Cottard replied: "Reading." "Oh, that's a very restful passion in a husband!" cried Mme Bontemps, suppressing a diabolical laugh.

"When the Doctor gets a book in his hands, you know!"

"Well, that needn't alarm you much . . ."

"But it does, for his eyesight. I must go now and look after him, Odette, and I shall come back at the very first opportunity and knock at your door. Talking of eyesight, have you heard that the new house Mme Verdurin has just bought is to be lighted by electricity? I didn't get that from my own little secret service, you know, but from quite a different source; it was the electrician himself, Mildé, who told me. You see, I quote my authorities! Even the bedrooms, he says, are to have electric lamps with shades which will filter the light. It's obviously a charming luxury for those who can afford it. But it seems that our contemporaries must absolutely have the newest thing if it's the only one of its kind in the world. Just fancy, the sister-in-law of a friend of mine has had the telephone installed in her house! She can order things from tradesmen without having to go out! I confess that I've indulged in the most bare-faced intrigues to get permission to go there one day, just to speak into the instrument. It's very tempting, but rather in a friend's house than at home. I don't think I should like to have the telephone in my establishment. Once the first excitement is over, it must be a real headache. Now, Odette, I must be off; you're not to keep Mme Bontemps any longer, she's looking after me. I must absolutely tear myself away: a nice way you're making me behave—I shall be getting home after my husband!"

And for myself also it was time to return home, before I had tasted those wintry delights of which the chrysanthemums had seemed to me to be the brilliant envelope. These pleasures had not appeared, and yet Mme Swann did not look as though she expected anything more. She allowed the servants to carry away the tea-things, as who should say "Time, please, gentlemen!" And finally she said to me: "Really, must you go? Well then, *good-bye*!" I felt that I might have stayed there without encountering those unknown pleasures, and that my sadness was not the only cause of my having to forgo them. Were they to be found, then, situated not upon that beaten track of hours which leads one always so rapidly to the moment of departure, but rather upon some unknown by-road along which I ought to have digressed? At least the object of my visit had been attained; Gilberte would know that I had come to her parents' house when she was not at home, and that I had, as Mme Cottard had incessantly assured me, "made a complete conquest, first shot, of Mme Verdurin" (whom, she added, she had never seen "make so much" of anyone: "You and she must be soulmates"). She would know that I had spoken of her as was fitting, with affection, but that I had not that incapacity for living without our seeing one another which I believed to be at the root of the boredom that she had shown at our last meetings. I had told Mme Swann that I could not be with Gilberte any more. I had said this as though I had finally decided not to see her again. And the letter which I was going to send Gilberte would be framed on those lines. Only to myself, to fortify my courage, I proposed no more than a final, concentrated effort, lasting a few days only. I said to myself: "This is the last time that I shall refuse an invitation to meet her; I shall accept the next one." To make our separation less difficult to realise, I did not picture it to myself as final. But I knew very well that it would be.

The first of January was exceptionally painful to me that winter. So, no doubt, is everything that marks a date and an anniversary, when we are unhappy. But if our unhappiness is due to the loss of someone dear to us, our suffering consists merely in an unusually vivid comparison of the present with the past. Added to this, in my case, was the unformulated hope that Gilberte, having wished to leave me to take the first steps towards a reconciliation, and discovering that I had not taken them, had been waiting only for the excuse of New Year's Day to write to me, saying: "What is the matter? I'm mad about you, so come and have it out frankly, I can't live without seeing you." As the last days of the old year went by, such a letter began to seem probable. It was, perhaps, nothing of the sort, but to make us believe that such a thing is probable the desire, the need that we have for it suffices. The soldier is convinced that a certain interval of time, capable of being indefinitely prolonged, will be allowed him before the bullet finds him, the thief before he is caught, men in general before they have to die. That is the amulet which preserves people—and sometimes peoples—not from danger but from the fear of danger, in reality from the belief in danger, which in certain cases allows them to brave it without actually needing to be brave. It is confidence of this sort, and with as little foundation, that sustains the lover who is counting on a reconciliation, on a letter. For me to cease to expect a reconciliation, it would have sufficed that I should have ceased to wish for one. However indifferent to us we may know the beloved to be, we attribute to her a series of thoughts (though their sum-total be indifference), the intention to express those thoughts, a complication of her inner life in which one is the object of her antipathy, perhaps, but also of her constant attention. But to imagine what was going on in Gilberte's mind I should have required simply the power to anticipate on that New Year's Day what I should feel on the first day of any of the following years, when the attention or the silence or the affection or the coldness of Gilberte would pass almost unnoticed by me and I should not dream, should not even be able to dream, of seeking a solution to problems which would have ceased to perplex me. When we are in love, our love is too big a thing for us to be able altogether to contain it within ourselves. It radiates towards the loved one, finds there a surface which arrests it, forcing it to return to its starting-point, and it is this repercussion of our own feeling which we call the other's feelings and which charms us more then than on its outward journey because we do not recognise it as having originated in ourselves.

New Year's Day went by, hour after hour, without bringing me that letter from Gilberte. And as I received a few others containing greetings belated or retarded by the congestion of the mails at that season, on the third and fourth of January I still hoped, but more and more faintly. On the days that followed, I wept a great deal. True, this was due to the fact that, having been less sincere than I thought in my renunciation of Gilberte, I had clung to the hope of a letter from her in the New Year. And seeing that hope exhausted before I had had time to shelter myself behind another, I suffered like an invalid who has emptied his phial of morphia without having another within his reach. But perhaps also in my case—and these two explanations are not mutually exclusive, for a single feeling is often made up of contrary elements—the hope that I entertained of ultimately receiving a letter had brought to my mind's eye once again the image of Gilberte, had reawakened the emotions which the expectation of finding myself in her presence, the sight of her, her behaviour towards me, had aroused in me before. The immediate possibility of a reconciliation had suppressed in me that faculty the immense importance of which we are apt to overlook: the faculty of resignation. Neurasthenics find it impossible to believe the friends who assure them that they will gradually recover their peace of mind if they will stay in bed and receive no letters, read no newspapers. They imagine that such a regime will only exasperate their twitching nerves. And similarly lovers, contemplating it from within a contrary state of mind, not having yet begun to put it to the test, are unable to believe in the healing power of renunciation.

Because of the violence of my heart-beats, my doses of caffeine were reduced; the palpitations ceased. Whereupon I asked myself whether it was not to some extent the drug that had been responsible for the anguish I had felt when I had fallen out with Gilberte, an anguish which I had attributed, whenever it recurred, to the pain of not seeing her any more or of running the risk of seeing her only when she was a prey to the same ill-humour. But if this drug had been at the root of the sufferings which my imagination must in that case have interpreted wrongly (not that there would be anything extraordinary in that, seeing that, for lovers, the most acute mental suffering often has its origin in the physical presence of the woman with whom they are living), it had been, in that sense, like the philtre which, long after they have absorbed it, continues to bind Tristan to Isolde. For the physical improvement which the reduction of my caffeine effected almost at once did not arrest the evolution of that grief which my absorption of the toxin had perhaps, if not created, at any rate contrived to render more acute.

Only, as the middle of the month of January approached, once my hopes of a New Year letter had been disappointed, once the additional pang that had come with their disappointment had been assuaged, it was my old sorrow, that of "before the holidays," which began again. What was perhaps the most cruel thing about it was that I myself was its architect, unconscious, wilful, merciless and patient. The one thing that mattered to me was my relationship with Gilberte, and it was I who was labouring to make it impossible by gradually creating out of this prolonged separation from my beloved, not indeed her indifference, but what would come to the same thing in the end, my own. It was to a slow and painful suicide of that self which loved Gilberte that I was goading myself with untiring energy, with a clear sense not only of what I was doing in the present but of what must result from it in the future: I knew not only that after a certain time I should cease to love Gilberte, but also that she herself would regret it and that the attempts which she would then make to see me would be as vain as those that she was making now, no longer because I loved her too much but because I should certainly be in love with some other woman whom I should continue to desire, to wait for, through hours of which I should not dare to divert a single particle of a second to Gilberte who would be nothing to me then. And no doubt at that very moment in which (since I was determined not to see her again, barring a formal request for a reconciliation, a complete declaration of love on her part, neither of which was in the least degree likely to be forthcoming) I had already lost Gilberte, and loved her more than ever since I could feel all that she was to me better than in the previous year when, spending all my afternoons in her company, or as many as I chose, I believed that no peril threatened our friendship—no doubt at that moment the idea that I should one day entertain identical feelings for another was odious to me, for that idea deprived me, not only of Gilberte, but of my love and my suffering: my love, my suffering, in which through my tears I was attempting to grasp precisely what Gilberte was, and yet was obliged to recognise that they did not pertain exclusively to her but would, sooner or later, be some other woman's fate. So that—or such, at least, was my way of thinking then—we are always detached from our fellow-creatures: when we love, we sense that our love does not bear a name, that it may spring up again in the future, could have sprung up already in the past, for another person rather than this one; and during the time when we are not in love, if we resign ourselves philosophically to love's inconsistencies and contradictions, it is because we do not at that moment feel the love which we speak about so freely, and hence do not know it, knowledge in these matters being intermittent and not outlasting the actual presence of the sentiment. Of course there would still have been time to warn Gilberte that that future in which I should no longer love her, which my suffering helped me to divine although my imagination was not yet able to form a clear picture of it, would gradually take shape, that its coming was, if not imminent, at least inevitable, if she herself did not come to my rescue and nip my future indifference in the bud. How often was I not on the point of writing, or of going to Gilberte to tell her: "Take care. My mind is made up. This is my final attempt. I am seeing you now for the last time. Soon I shall love you no longer!" But to what end? By what right could I reproach her for an indifference which, without considering myself guilty on that account, I myself manifested towards everything that was not Gilberte? The last time! To me, that appeared as something of immense significance, because I loved Gilberte. On her it would doubtless have made just as much impression as those letters in which our friends ask whether they may pay us a visit before they finally leave the country, requests which, like those made by tiresome women who are in love with us, we decline because we have pleasures of our own in prospect. The time which we have at our disposal every day is elastic; the passions that we feel expand it, those that we inspire contract it; and habit fills up what remains.

Besides, what good would it have done if I had spoken to Gilberte? She would not have heard me. We imagine always when we speak that it is our own ears, our own mind, that are listening. My words would have come to her only in a distorted form, as though they had had to pass through the moving curtain of a waterfall before they reached my beloved, unrecognisable, sounding false and absurd, having no longer any kind of meaning. The truth which one puts into one's words does not carve out a direct path for itself, is not irresistibly self-evident. A considerable time must elapse before a truth of the same order can take shape in them. Then the political opponent who, despite every argument, every proof, condemns the votary of the rival doctrine as a traitor, himself comes to share the hated conviction, in which he who once sought in vain to disseminate it no longer believes. Then the masterpiece of literature whose excellence seemed self-evident to the admirers who read it aloud, while to those who listened it presented only a senseless or commonplace image, will by those too be proclaimed a masterpiece, but too late for the author to learn of their conversion. Similarly, in love, the barriers, do what he may, cannot be broken down from without by the despairing lover; it is when he no longer cares about them that suddenly, as the result of an effort directed from elsewhere, accomplished within the heart of the one who did not love, those barriers which he has charged in vain will fall to no avail. If I had come to Gilberte to tell her of my future indifference and the means of preventing it, she would have assumed that my love for her, the need that I had of her, were even greater than she had supposed, and her reluctance to see me would thereby have been increased. And it is all too true, moreover, that it was that love for her which helped me, by the disparate states of mind which it successively produced in me, to foresee, more clearly than she herself could, the end of that love. And yet some such warning I might perhaps have addressed, by letter or by word of mouth, to Gilberte, after a long enough interval, which would render her, it is true, less indispensable to me, but might also have proved to her that she was not so indispensable. Unfortunately certain well or ill intentioned persons spoke of me to her in a fashion which must have led her to think that they were doing so at my request. Whenever I thus learned that Cottard, my own mother, even M. de Norpois had by a few ill-chosen words nullified the whole sacrifice that I had just been making, wasted all the advantage of my reserve by wrongly making me appear to have emerged from it, I had a double grievance. In the first place I now had to date from that day only my laborious and fruitful abstention which these tiresome people had, unknown to me, interrupted and consequently brought to nothing. But in addition I should now have less pleasure in seeing Gilberte, who would think of me no longer as containing myself in dignified resignation, but as plotting in the dark for an interview which she had scorned to grant me. I cursed all this idle chatter of people who so often, without any intention either of hurting us or of doing us a service, for no reason, for talking's sake, sometimes because we ourselves have not been able to refrain from talking in their presence and because they are indiscreet (as we ourselves are), do us, at a crucial moment, so much harm. It is true that in the baleful task of destroying our love they are far from playing a part comparable to that played by two persons who are in the habit, one from excess of good-will and the other from excess of ill-will, of undoing everything at the moment when everything is on the point of being settled. But against these two persons we bear no such grudge as against the inopportune Cottards of this world, for one of them is the person whom we love and the other is ourself.

Meanwhile, since almost every time I went to see her Mme Swann would invite me to come to tea with her daughter and tell me to reply to the latter direct, I was constantly writing to Gilberte, and in this correspondence I did not choose the expressions which might, I felt, have won her over, but sought only to carve out the easiest channel for the flow of my tears. For regret, like desire, seeks not to analyse but to gratify itself. When one begins to love, one spends one's time, not in getting to know what one's love really is, but in arranging for tomorrow's rendezvous. When one renounces love one seeks not to know one's grief but to offer to the person who is its cause the expression of it which seems most moving. One says the things which one feels the need to say, and which the other will not understand: one speaks for oneself alone. I wrote: "I had thought that it would not be possible. Alas, I see now that it is not so difficult." I said also: "I shall probably never see you again," and said it while continuing to avoid showing a coldness which she might think feigned, and the words, as I wrote them, made me weep because I felt that they expressed not what I should have liked to believe but what was probably going to happen. For at the next request for a meeting which she would convey to me I should have again, as I had now, the courage not to yield, and, with one refusal after another, I should gradually come to the moment when, by virtue of not having seen her again, I should no longer wish to see her. I wept, but I found courage enough to sacrifice, I savoured the melancholy pleasure of sacrificing, the happiness of being with her to the possibility of being pleasing in her eyes one day—a day, alas, when being pleasing in her eyes would be immaterial to me. Even the supposition, improbable though it was, that at this moment, as she had claimed during the last visit that I had paid her, she loved me, that what I took for the boredom which one feels in the company of a person of whom one has grown tired had been due only to a jealous susceptibility, to a feigned indifference analogous to my own, only rendered my decision less painful. It seemed to me that in years to come, when we had forgotten one another, when I should be able to look back and tell her that this letter which I was now in the course of writing to her had not been for one moment sincere, she would answer: "What, you really did love me, did you? If you only knew how I waited for that letter, how I longed for us to meet, how I cried when I read it." The thought, while I was writing it, immediately on my return from her mother's house, that I was perhaps consummating that very misunderstanding, that thought, by its very sadness, by the pleasure of imagining that I was loved by Gilberte, gave me the impulse to continue my letter.

If, at the moment of leaving Mme Swann, when her

tea-party ended, I was thinking of what I was going to write to her daughter, Mme Cottard, as she departed, had been filled with thoughts of a wholly different kind. On her little "tour of inspection" she had not failed to congratulate Mme Swann on the new furnishings, the recent "acquisitions" which caught the eye in her drawing-room. She could also see among them some, though only a very few, of the things that Odette had had in the old days in the Rue La Pérouse, for instance her animals carved in precious stones, her mascots.

For since Mme Swann had picked up from a friend whose opinion she valued the word "trashy"—which had opened to her new horizons because it denoted precisely those things which a few years earlier she had considered "smart"—all those things had, one after another, followed into retirement the gilded trellis that had served as background to her chrysanthemums, innumerable bonbonnières from Giroux's, and the coroneted note-paper (not to mention the coins of gilt pasteboard littered about on the mantelpieces, which, even before she had come to know Swann, a man of taste had advised her to jettison). Moreover in the artistic disorder, the studio-like jumble of the rooms, whose walls were still painted in sombre colours which made them as different as possible from the white-enamelled drawing-rooms Mme Swann was to favour a little later, the Far East was retreating more and more before the invading forces of the eighteenth century; and the cushions which, to make me "comfortable," Mme Swann heaped up and buffeted into position behind my back were sprinkled with Louis XV garlands and not, as of old, with Chinese dragons. In the room in which she was usually to be found, and of which she would say,

"Yes, I like this room; I use it a great deal. I couldn't live with a lot of hostile, pompous things; this is where I do my work" (though she never stated precisely at what she was working, whether a picture, or perhaps a book, for the hobby of writing was beginning to become common among women who liked to do something, not to be quite useless), she was surrounded by Dresden pieces (having a fancy for that sort of porcelain, which she pronounced with an English accent, saying in any connexion: "How pretty that is; it reminds me of Dresden flowers"), and dreaded for them even more than in the old days for her grotesque figures and her vases the ignorant handling of her servants who were made to expiate the anxiety that they had caused her by submitting to outbursts of rage at which Swann, the most courteous and considerate of masters, looked on without being shocked. Not that the clear perception of certain weaknesses in those we love in any way diminishes our affection for them; rather that affection makes us find those weaknesses charming. Nowadays it was rarely in Japanese kimonos that Odette received her intimates, but rather in the bright and billowing silk of a Watteau housecoat whose flowering foam she would make as though to rub gently over her bosom, and in which she basked, lolled, disported herself with such an air of well-being, of cool freshness, taking such deep breaths, that she seemed to look on these garments not as something decorative, a mere setting for herself, but as necessary, in the same way as her "tub" or her daily "constitutional," to satisfy the requirements of her physiognomy and the niceties of hygiene. She used often to say that she would go without bread rather than give up art and cleanliness, and that the burning of the "Gioconda" would distress her infinitely more than the destruction, by the same element, of the "fulltitudes" of people she knew. Theories which seemed paradoxical to her friends, but made them regard her as a superior woman, and earned her a weekly visit from the Belgian Minister, so that in the little world of which she was the sun everyone would have been greatly astonished to learn that elsewhere—at the Verdurins', for instance—she was reckoned a fool. It was this vivacity of mind that made Mme Swann prefer men's society to women's. But when she criticised the latter it was always from the courtesan's standpoint, singling out the blemishes that might lower them in the esteem of men, thick ankles, a bad complexion, inability to spell, hairy legs, foul breath, pencilled eyebrows. But towards a woman who had shown her kindness or indulgence in the past she was more lenient, especially if this woman was now in trouble. She would defend her warmly, saying: "People are not fair to her. I assure you, she's quite a nice woman really."

It was not only the furniture of Odette's drawing-room, it was Odette herself whom Mme Cottard and all those who had frequented the society of Mme de Crécy would have found it difficult, if they had not seen her for some little time, to recognise. She seemed to be so much younger. No doubt this was partly because she had put on a little weight, was in better health, seemed at once calmer, cooler, more restful, and also because the new way in which she braided her hair gave more breadth to a face which was animated by an application of pink powder, and into which her eyes and profile, formerly too prominent, seemed now to have been reabsorbed. But another reason for this change lay in the fact that, having reached the turning-point of life, Odette had at length discovered, or invented, a physiognomy of her own, an unalterable "character," a "style of beauty," and on her uncoordinated features—which for so long, exposed to the dangerous and futile vagaries of the flesh, putting on momentarily years, a sort of fleeting old age, as a result of the slightest fatigue, had composed for her somehow or other, according to her mood and her state of health, a dishevelled, changeable, formless, charming face—had now set this fixed type, as it were an immortal youthfulness.

Swann had in his room, instead of the handsome photographs that were now taken of his wife, in all of which the same enigmatic and winning expression enabled one to recognise, whatever dress and hat she was wearing, her triumphant face and figure, a little daguerreotype of her, quite plain, taken long before the appearance of this new type, from which the youthfulness and beauty of Odette, which she had not yet discovered when it was taken, appeared to be missing. But doubtless Swann, having remained constant, or having reverted, to a different conception of her, enjoyed in the frail young woman with pensive eyes and tired features, caught in a pose between stillness and motion, a more Botticellian charm. For he still liked to see his wife as a Botticelli figure. Odette, who on the contrary sought not to bring out but to compensate for, to cover and conceal the points about her looks that did not please her, what might perhaps to an artist express her "character" but in her woman's eyes were blemishes, would not have that painter mentioned in her presence. Swann had a wonderful scarf of oriental silk, blue and pink, which he had bought because it was exactly that worn by the Virgin in the *Magnificat*. But Mme

Swann refused to wear it. Once only she allowed her husband to order her a dress covered all over with daisies, cornflowers, forget-me-nots and bluebells, like that of the Primavera. And sometimes in the evening, when she was tired, he would quietly draw my attention to the way in which she was giving, quite unconsciously, to her pensive hands the uncontrolled, almost distraught movement of the Virgin who dips her pen into the inkpot that the angel holds out to her, before writing upon the sacred page on which is already traced the word "*Magnificat*." But he added: "Whatever you do, don't say anything about it to her; if she knew she was doing it, she would change her pose at once."

Except at these moments of involuntary relaxation in which Swann sought to recapture the melancholy Botticellian droop, Odette's body seemed now to be cut out in a single silhouette wholly confined within a "line" which, following the contours of the woman, had abandoned the ups and downs, the ins and outs, the reticulations, the elaborate dispersions of the fashions of former days, but also, where it was her anatomy that went wrong by making unnecessary digressions within or without the ideal form traced for it, was able to rectify, by a bold stroke, the errors of nature, to make good, along a whole section of its course, the lapses of the flesh as well as of the material. The pads, the preposterous "bustle" had disappeared, as well as those tailed bodices which, overlapping the skirt and stiffened by rods of whalebone, had so long amplified Odette with an artificial stomach and had given her the appearance of being composed of several disparate pieces which there was no individuality to bind together. The vertical fall of the fringes, the curve of the ruches had made way for the inflexion of a body which made silk palpitate as a siren stirs the waves and gave to cambric a human expression, now that it had been liberated, like an organic and living form, from the long chaos and nebulous envelopment of fashions at last dethroned. But Mme Swann had chosen, had contrived to preserve some vestiges of certain of these, in the very midst of those that had supplanted them. When, in the evening, finding myself unable to work and knowing that Gilberte had gone to the theatre with friends, I paid a surprise visit to her parents, I used often to find Mme Swann in an elegant dishabille the skirt of which, of one of those rich dark colours, blood-red or orange, which seemed to have a special meaning because they were no longer in fashion, was crossed diagonally, though not concealed, by a broad band of black lace which recalled the flounces of an earlier day. When, on a still chilly afternoon in spring, she had taken me (before my break with her daughter) to the Zoo, under her jacket, which she opened or buttoned up according as the exercise made her feel warm, the dog-toothed edging of her blouse suggested a glimpse of the lapel of some non-existent waistcoat such as she had been accustomed to wear some years earlier, when she had liked their edges to have the same slight indentations; and her scarf—of that same "tartan" to which she had remained faithful, but whose tones she had so far softened, red becoming pink and blue lilac, that one might almost have taken it for one of those pigeon's-breast taffetas which were the latest novelty—was knotted in such a way under her chin, without one's being able to make out where it was fastened, that one was irresistibly reminded of those bonnet-strings which were now no longer worn.

She need only "hold out" like this for a little longer and young men attempting to understand her theory of dress would say: "Mme Swann is quite a period in herself, isn't she?" As in a fine literary style which superimposes different forms but is strengthened by a tradition that lies concealed behind them, so in Mme Swann's attire those half-tinted memories of waistcoats or of ringlets, sometimes a tendency, at once repressed, towards the "all aboard," or even a distant and vague allusion to the "follow-me-lad," kept alive beneath the concrete form the unfinished likeness of other, older forms which one would not have been able to find effectively reproduced by the milliner or the dressmaker, but about which one's thoughts incessantly hovered, and enveloped Mme Swann in a sort of nobility—perhaps because the very uselessness of these fripperies made them seem designed to serve some more than utilitarian purpose, perhaps because of the traces they preserved of vanished years, or else because of a vestimentary personality peculiar to this woman, which gave to the most dissimilar of her costumes a distinct family likeness. One felt that she did not dress simply for the comfort or the adornment of her body; she was surrounded by her garments as by the delicate and spiritualised machinery of a whole civilisation.

When Gilberte, who, as a rule, gave her tea-parties on the days when her mother was "at home," had for some reason to go out and I was therefore free to attend Mme Swann's "do," I would find her dressed in one or other of her beautiful dresses, some of which were of taffeta, others of grosgrain, or of velvet, or of crêpe-de-Chine, or satin or silk, dresses which, not being loose like the gowns she generally wore in the house but pulled together as though she were just going out in them, gave to her stay-at-home laziness on those afternoons something alert and energetic. And no doubt the bold simplicity of their cut was singularly appropriate to her figure and to her movements, which her sleeves appeared to be symbolising in colours that varied from day to day: one felt that there was a sudden determination in the blue velvet, an easy-going good humour in the white taffeta, and that a sort of supreme discretion full of dignity in her way of holding out her arm had, in order to become visible, put on the appearance, dazzling with the smile of one who had made great sacrifices, of the black crêpe-de-Chine. But at the same time, to these animated dresses the complication of their trimmings, none of which had any practical utility or served any visible purpose, added something detached, pensive, secret, in harmony with the melancholy which Mme Swann still retained, at least in the shadows under her eyes and the drooping arches of her hands. Beneath the profusion of sapphire charms, enamelled four-leaf clovers, silver medals, gold medallions, turquoise amulets, ruby chains and topaz chestnuts there would be on the dress itself some design carried out in colour which pursued across the surface of an inserted panel a preconceived existence of its own, some row of little satin buttons which buttoned nothing and could not be unbuttoned, a strip of braid that sought to please the eye with the minuteness, the discretion of a delicate reminder; and these, as well as the jewels, gave the impression—having otherwise no possible justification—of disclosing a secret intention, being a pledge of affection, keeping a secret, ministering to a superstition, commemorating a recovery from sickness, a granted wish, a love affair or a philopena. And now and then in the blue velvet of the bodice a hint of "slashes," in the Henri II style, or in the gown of black satin a slight swelling which, if it was in the sleeves, just below the shoulders, made one think of the "leg of mutton" sleeves of 1830, or if, on the other hand, it was beneath the skirt, of Louis XV "panniers," gave the dress a just perceptible air of being a "fancy dress" costume and at all events, by insinuating beneath the life of the present day a vague reminiscence of the past, blended with the person of Mme Swann the charm of certain heroines of history or romance. And if I were to draw her attention to this: "I don't play golf," she would answer, "like so many of my friends. So I should have no excuse for going about in *sweaters* as they do."

In the confusion of her drawing-room, on her way from showing out one visitor, or with a plateful of cakes to tempt another, Mme Swann as she passed by me would take me aside for a moment: "I've been specially charged by Gilberte to invite you to luncheon the day after tomorrow. As I wasn't sure of seeing you here, I was going to write to you if you hadn't come." I continued to resist. And this resistance was costing me gradually less and less, because, however much we may love the poison that is destroying us, when necessity has deprived us of it for some time past, we cannot help attaching a certain value to the peace of mind which we had ceased to know, to the absence of emotion and suffering. If we are not altogether sincere in telling ourselves that we never wish to see the one we love again, we would not be a whit more sincere in saying that we do. For no doubt we can endure her absence only by promising ourselves that it will not be for long, and thinking of the day when we shall see her again, but at the same time we feel how much less painful are those daily recurring dreams of an imminent and constantly postponed meeting than would be an interview which might be followed by a spasm of jealousy, with the result that the news that we are shortly to see her would create a disagreeable turmoil in our mind. What we now put off from day to day is no longer the end of the intolerable anxiety caused by separation, it is the dreaded renewal of emotions which can lead to nothing. How infinitely we prefer to any such interview the docile memory which we can supplement at will with dreams in which she who in reality does not love us seems, on the contrary, to be making protestations of her love, when we are all alone! How infinitely we prefer that memory which, by blending gradually with it a great deal of what we desire, we can contrive to make as sweet as we choose, to the deferred interview in which we would have to deal with a person to whom we could no longer dictate at will the words that we want to hear on her lips, but from whom we can expect to meet with new coldness, unforeseen aggressions! We know, all of us, when we no longer love, that forgetfulness, or even a vague memory, does not cause us so much suffering as an ill-starred love. It was the reposeful tranquillity of such forgetfulness that in anticipation I preferred, without acknowledging it to myself.

Moreover, however painful such a course of psychical detachment and isolation may be, it grows steadily less so for another reason, namely that it weakens while it is in process of healing that fixed obsession which is a state of love. Mine was still strong enough for me to wish to recapture my old position in Gilberte's estimation, which in view of my voluntary abstention must, it seemed to me, be steadily increasing, so that each of those calm and melancholy days on which I did not see her, coming one after the other without interruption, continuing too without prescription (unless some busy-body were to meddle in my affairs), was a day not lost but gained. Gained to no purpose, perhaps, for presently I might be pronounced cured. Resignation, modulating our habits, allows certain elements of our strength to be indefinitely increased. Those—so wretchedly inadequate—that I had had to support my grief, on the first evening of my rupture with Gilberte, had since multiplied to an incalculable power. Only, the tendency of everything that exists to prolong its own existence is sometimes interrupted by sudden impulses to which we allow ourselves to surrender with all the fewer qualms because we know for how many days, for how many months even, we have been able, and might still be able to abstain. And often it is when the purse in which we hoard our savings is nearly full that we suddenly empty it, it is without waiting for the result of our treatment and when we have succeeded in growing accustomed to it that we abandon it. And so, one day, when Mme Swann repeated her familiar words about the pleasure it would be to Gilberte to see me, thus putting the happiness of which I had now for so long been depriving myself as it were within arm's reach, I was stupefied by the realisation that it was still possible for me to enjoy it; and I could hardly wait until next day; for I had made up my mind to pay a surprise visit to Gilberte before her dinner.

What helped me to remain patient throughout the long day that followed was a little plan that I made. As soon as everything was forgotten, as soon as I was reconciled with Gilberte, I no longer wished to visit her except as a lover. Every day she would receive from me the finest flowers that grew. And if Mme Swann, although she had no right to be too severe a mother, should forbid my making a daily offering of flowers, I should find other gifts, more precious and less frequent. My parents did not give me enough money for me to be able to buy expensive things. I thought of a big vase of old Chinese porcelain which had been left to me by aunt Léonie, and of which Mamma prophesied daily that Françoise would come to her and say "Oh, it's all come to pieces!" and that would be the end of it. Would it not be wiser, in that case, to part with it, to sell it so as to be able to give Gilberte all the pleasure I could. I felt sure that I could easily get a thousand francs for it. I had it wrapped up; I had grown so used to it that I had ceased altogether to notice it: parting with it had at least the advantage of making me realise what it was like. I took it with me on my way to the Swanns', and, giving the driver their address, told him to go by the Champs-Elysées, at one end of which was the shop of a big dealer in oriental objects whom my father knew. Greatly to my surprise he offered me there and then not one thousand but ten thousand francs for the vase. I took the notes with rapture: every day, for a whole year, I could smother Gilberte in roses and lilac. When I left the shop and got back into the carriage the driver (naturally enough, since the Swanns lived out by the Bois) instead of taking the ordinary way began to drive along the Avenue des Champs-Elysées. He had just passed the corner of the Rue de Berri when, in the failing light, I thought I saw, close to the Swanns' house but going in the other direction, away from it, Gilberte, who was walking slowly, though with a firm step, by the side of a young man with whom she was conversing and whose face I could not distinguish. I stood up in the cab, meaning to tell the driver to stop; then hesitated. The strolling couple were already some way away, and the two parallel lines which their leisurely progress was quietly drawing were on the verge of disappearing in the Elysian gloom. A moment later, I had reached Gilberte's door. I was received by Mme Swann. "Oh! she will be sorry!" was my greeting, "I can't think why she isn't in. But she was complaining of the heat just now after a lesson, and said she might go out for a breath of fresh air with one of her girl friends." "I thought I saw her in the Avenue des Champs-Elysées." "Oh, I don't think it can have been her. Anyhow, don't mention it to her father; he doesn't approve of her going out at this time of night. Must you go? *Good-bye.*" I left her, told my driver to go back the same way, but found no trace of the two walkers. Where had they been? What were they saying to one another in the darkness with that confidential air?

I returned home, despairingly clutching my windfall of ten thousand francs, which would have enabled me to arrange so many pleasant surprises for that Gilberte whom now I had made up my mind never to see again. No doubt my call at the dealer's had brought me happiness by allowing me to hope that in future, whenever I saw my beloved, she would be pleased with me and grateful. But if I had not called there, if the carriage had not taken the Avenue des Champs-Elysées, I should not have seen Gilberte with that young man. Thus a single action may have two contradictory effects, and the misfortune that it engenders cancel the good fortune it had brought one. What had happened to me was the opposite of what so frequently occurs. We desire some pleasure, and the material means of obtaining it are lacking. "It is sad," La Bruyère tells us, "to love without an ample fortune." There is nothing for it but to try to eradicate little by little our desire for that pleasure. In my case, however, the material means had been forthcoming, but at the same moment, if not by a logical effect, at any rate as a fortuitous consequence of that initial success, my pleasure had been snatched from me. As, for that matter, it seems as though it must always be. As a rule, however, not on the same evening as we have acquired what makes it possible. Usually, we continue to struggle and hope for a little longer. But happiness can never be achieved. If we succeed in overcoming the force of circumstances, nature at once shifts the battle-ground, placing it within ourselves, and effects a gradual change in our hearts until they desire something other than what they are about to possess. And if the change of fortune has been so rapid that our hearts have not had time to change, nature does not on that account despair of conquering us, in a manner more gradual, it is true, more subtle, but no less efficacious. It is then at the last moment that the possession of our happiness is wrested from us, or rather it is that very possession which nature, with diabolical cunning, uses to destroy our happiness. Having failed in everything related to the sphere of life and action, it is a final impossibility, the psychological impossibility of happiness, that nature creates. The phenomenon of happiness either fails to appear, or at once gives rise to the bitterest reactions.

I put my ten thousand francs in a drawer. But they

were no longer of any use to me. I ran through them, as it happened, even more rapidly than if I had sent flowers every day to Gilberte, for when evening came I was always too wretched to stay at home and went to drown my sorrows in the arms of women whom I did not love. As for seeking to give any sort of pleasure to Gilberte, I no longer thought of that; to visit her house again now could only give me pain. Even the sight of Gilberte, which would have been so exquisite a pleasure only yesterday, would no longer have sufficed me. For I should have been anxious all the time that I was not actually with her. That is how a woman, by every fresh torture that she inflicts on us, often quite unwittingly, increases her power over us and at the same time our demands upon her. With each injury that she does us, she encircles us more and more completely, redoubles our chains, but also those which hitherto we had thought adequate to bind her in order to keep our minds at rest. Only yesterday, had I not been afraid of annoying Gilberte, I should have been content to ask for no more than occasional meetings, which now would no longer have sufficed me and for which I should now have substituted quite different terms. For in this respect love is not like war; after each battle we renew the fight with keener ardour, which we never cease to intensify the more thoroughly we are defeated, provided always that we are still in a position to give battle. This was not my case with regard to Gilberte. Hence I preferred at first not to return to her mother's house. I continued, it is true, to assure myself that Gilberte did not love me, that I had known this for some time, that I could see her again if I chose, and, if I did not choose, forget her in the long run. But these ideas, like a remedy which has no effect upon certain complaints, had no power whatsoever to obliterate those two parallel lines which I kept on seeing, traced by Gilberte and the young man as they slowly disappeared along the Avenue des Champs-Elysées. This was a new malady, which like the rest would gradually lose its force, a fresh image which would one day present itself to my mind's eye completely purged of every noxious element that it now contained, like those deadly poisons which one can handle without danger, or like a crumb of dynamite which one can use to light one's cigarette without fear of an explosion. Meanwhile there was in me another force which strove with all its might to overpower that unwholesome force which still showed me, without alteration, the figure of Gilberte walking in the dusk: to meet and to break the shock of the renewed assaults of memory, I had, toiling effectively in the opposite direction, imagination. The first of these two forces did indeed continue to show me that couple walking in the Champs-Elysées, and offered me other disagreeable pictures drawn from the past, as for instance Gilberte shrugging her shoulders when her mother asked her to stay and entertain me. But the second force, working upon the canvas of my hopes, outlined a future far more attractively developed than this meagre past which was on the whole so restricted. For one minute in which I saw Gilberte's sullen face, how many were there in which I devised steps she might take with a view to our reconciliation, perhaps even to our engagement! It is true that this force, which my imagination was focusing upon the future, it drew, after all, from the past. As my vexation at Gilberte's having shrugged her shoulders gradually faded, the memory of her charm, a memory that made me wish for her to return to me, would diminish too. But I was still a long way from such a death of the past. I was still in love with her, even though I believed that I detested her. Whenever anyone told me that I was looking well, or was nicely dressed, I wished that she could have been there to see me. I was irritated by the desire that many people showed about this time to ask me to their houses, and refused all their invitations. There was a scene at home because I did not accompany my father to an official dinner at which the Bontemps were to be present with their niece Albertine, a young girl still hardly more than a child. So it is that the different periods of our lives overlap one another. We scornfully decline, because of one whom we love and who will some day be of so little account, to see another who is of no account today, whom we shall love tomorrow, whom we might perhaps, had we consented to see her now, have loved a little sooner and who would thus have put an end to our present sufferings, bringing others, it is true, in their place. Mine were steadily growing less. I was amazed to observe deep down inside me, one sentiment one day, another the next, generally inspired by some hope or some fear relative to Gilberte. To the Gilberte whom I carried within me. I ought to have reminded myself that the other, the real Gilberte, was perhaps entirely different from mine, knew nothing of the regrets that I ascribed to her, thought probably much less about me, not merely than I thought about her but than I made her think about me when I was closeted alone with my fictitious Gilberte, wondering what really were her feelings towards me, and imagining her thus, her attention as constantly directed towards myself.

During those periods in which grief and bitterness of spirit, though steadily diminishing, still persist, a distinction must be drawn between the pain which comes to us from the constant thought of the beloved herself and that which is revived by certain memories, some cruel remark, some verb used in a letter that we have had from her. Pending the description, in the context of another and later love affair, of the various forms that pain can assume, suffice it to say that, of these two kinds, the former is infinitely the less cruel. That is because our conception of the person, still living within us, is there adorned with the halo with which we are bound before long to invest her, and is imprinted if not with the frequent solace of hope, at any rate with the tranquillity of a permanent sadness. (It must also be observed that the image of a person who makes us suffer counts for little in those complications which aggravate the unhappiness of love, prolong it and prevent our recovery, just as in certain maladies the cause is out of proportion to the fever which follows it and the slowness of the process of convalescence.) But if the idea of the person we love is reflected in the light of an intelligence that is on the whole optimistic, the same is not true of those particular memories, those cruel remarks, that hostile letter (I received only one that could be so described from Gilberte); it is as though the person herself dwelt in those fragments, however limited, multiplied to a power which she is far from possessing in the habitual image we form of her as a whole. Because the letter has not—as the image of the loved one has—been contemplated by us in the melancholy calm of regret; we have read it, devoured it in the fearful anguish with which we were wrung by an unforeseen misfortune. Sorrows of this sort come to us in another way—from without—and it is by way of the most cruel suffering that they have penetrated to our hearts. The picture of the beloved in our minds which we believe to be old, original, authentic, has in reality been refashioned by us many times over. The cruel memory, on the other hand, is not contemporaneous with the restored picture, it is of another age, it is one of the rare witnesses to a monstrous past. But inasmuch as this past continues to exist, save in ourselves who have been pleased to substitute for it a miraculous golden age, a paradise in which all mankind shall be reconciled, those memories, those letters carry us back to reality, and cannot but make us feel, by the sudden pang they give us, what a long way we have been borne from that reality by the baseless hopes engendered by our daily expectation. Not that the said reality is bound always to remain the same, though that does indeed happen at times. There are in our lives any number of women whom we have never sought to see again, and who have quite naturally responded to our in no way calculated silence with a silence as profound. Only in their case, since we never loved them, we have never counted the years spent apart from them, and this instance, which would invalidate our whole argument, we are inclined to forget when we consider the healing effect of isolation, just as people who believe in presentiments forget all the occasions on which their own have not come true.

But after a time, absence may prove efficacious. The desire, the appetite for seeing us again may after all be reborn in the heart which at present contemns us. Only, we must allow time. But our demands as far as time is concerned are no less exorbitant than those which the heart requires in order to change. For one thing, time is the very thing that we are least willing to allow, for our suffering is acute and we are anxious to see it brought to an end. And then, too, the time which the other heart will need in order to change will have been spent by our own heart in changing itself too, so that when the goal we had set ourselves becomes attainable it will have ceased to be our goal. Besides, the very idea that it will be attainable, that there is no happiness that, when it has ceased to be a happiness for us, we cannot ultimately attain, contains an element, but only an element, of truth. It falls to us when we have grown indifferent to it. But the very fact of our indifference will have made us less exacting, and enabled us in retrospect to feel convinced that it would have delighted us had it come at a time when perhaps it would have seemed to us miserably inadequate. One is not very particular, nor a very good judge, about things which no longer matter to one. The friendly overtures of a person whom we no longer love, overtures which in our indifference strike us as excessive, would perhaps have fallen a long way short of satisfying our love. Those tender words, that offer to meet us, we think only of the pleasure which they would have given us, and not of all those other words and meetings by which we should have wished to see them immediately followed, and which by this greed of ours we might perhaps have prevented from ever happening. So that we can never be certain that the happiness which comes to us too late, when we can no longer enjoy it, when we are no longer in love, is altogether the same as that same happiness the lack of which made us at one time so unhappy. There is only one person who could decide this—our then self; it is no longer with us, and were it to reappear, no doubt our happiness—identical or not—would vanish.

Pending these belated fulfilments of a dream about which I should by then have ceased to care, by dint of inventing, as in the days when I still hardly knew Gilberte, words or letters in which she implored my forgiveness, swore that she had never loved anyone but myself and besought me to marry her, a series of pleasant images incessantly renewed came by degrees to hold a larger place in my mind than the vision of Gilberte and the young man, which had nothing now to feed upon. At this point I should perhaps have resumed my visits to Mme Swann but for a dream I had in which one of my friends, who was not, however, one that I could identify, behaved with the utmost treachery towards me and appeared to believe that I had been treacherous to him. Abruptly awakened by the pain which this dream had caused me, and finding that it persisted after I was awake, I turned my thoughts back to the dream, racked my brains to remember who the friend was that I had seen in my sleep and whose name—a Spanish name—was no longer distinct. Combining Joseph's part with Pharaoh's, I set to work to interpret my dream. I knew that in many cases it is a mistake to pay too much attention to the appearance of the people one saw in one's dream, who may perhaps have been disguised or have exchanged faces, like those mutilated saints in cathedrals which ignorant archaeologists have restored, fitting the head of one to the body of another and jumbling all their attributes and names. Those that people bear in a dream are apt to mislead us. The person whom we love is to be recognised only by the intensity of the pain that we suffer. From mine I learned that, transformed while I was asleep into a young man, the person whose recent betrayal still hurt me was Gilberte. I remembered then that, the last time I had seen her, on the day when her mother had forbidden her to go out to a dancing lesson, she had, whether in sincerity or in pretence, declined, laughing in a strange manner, to believe in the genuineness of my feelings for her. And by association this memory brought back to me another. Long before that, it was Swann who had not wished to believe in my sincerity, or that I was a suitable friend for Gilberte. In vain had I written to him, Gilberte had brought back my letter and had returned it to me with the same incomprehensible laugh. She had not returned it to me at once: I remembered now the whole of that scene behind the clump of laurels. One becomes moral as soon as one is unhappy. Gilberte's present antipathy for me seemed to me a punishment meted out to me by life for my conduct that afternoon. One thinks one can escape such punishments because one is careful when crossing the street, and avoids obvious dangers. But there are others that take effect within us. The accident comes from the direction one least expected, from inside, from the heart. Gilberte's words: "If you like, we might go on wrestling," made me shudder. I imagined her behaving like that, at home perhaps, in the linen-room, with the young man whom I had seen escorting her along the Avenue des Champs-Elysées. And so, just as much as to believe (as I had a little time back) that I was calmly established in a state of happiness, it had been foolish in me, now that I had abandoned all thought of happiness, to take it for granted that at least I had become and would be able to remain calm. For, so long as our heart keeps enshrined with any permanence the image of another person, it is not only our happiness that may at any moment be destroyed; when that happiness has vanished, when we have suffered and then succeeded in anaesthetising our sufferings, the thing then that is as elusive, as precarious as ever our happiness was, is calm. Mine returned to me in the end, for the cloud which, affecting one's spirits, one's desires, has entered one's mind under cover of a dream, will also in course of time dissolve: permanence and stability being assured to nothing in this world, not even to grief. Besides, those who suffer through love are, as we say of certain invalids, their own physicians. Since consolation can come to them only from the person who is the cause of their grief, and since their grief is an emanation from that person, it is in their grief itself that they must in the end find a remedy: which it will disclose to them at a given moment, for as long as they turn it over in their minds, this grief will continue to show them fresh aspects of the loved, the regretted person, at one moment so intensely hateful that one has no longer the slightest desire to see her since before finding enjoyment in her company one would have to make her suffer, at another so sweet and gentle that one gives her credit for the virtue one attributes to her, and finds in it a fresh reason for hope. But even though the anguish that had re-awakened in me did at length subside, I no longer wished—except rarely—to visit Mme Swann. In the first place because, in those who love and have been forsaken, the state of incessant—even if unconfessed—expectancy in which they live undergoes a spontaneous transformation, and, while to all appearances unchanged, substitutes for its original state a second that is precisely the opposite. The first was the consequence, the reflection of the painful incidents which had upset us. Expectation of what may happen is mingled with fear, all the more since we desire at that moment, should we hear nothing new from the loved one, to act ourselves, and are none too confident of the success of a step which, once we have taken it, we may find it impossible to follow up. But presently, without our having noticed any change, expectation, which still endures, is sustained, we discover, no longer by our recollection of the painful past but by anticipation of an imaginary future. From then on, it is almost pleasant. Besides, the first state, by continuing for some time, has accustomed us to living in expectation. The pain we felt during those last meetings survives in us still, but is already lulled to sleep. We are in no hurry to arouse it, especially as we do not see very clearly what to ask for now. The possession of a little more of the woman we love would only make more necessary to us the part that we do not possess, which would inevitably remain, in spite of everything, since our requirements are begotten of our satisfactions, an irreducible quantity.

Another, final reason came later on to reinforce this, and to make me discontinue altogether my visits to Mme Swann. This reason, slow in revealing itself, was not that I had yet forgotten Gilberte but that I must make every effort to forget her as speedily as possible. No doubt, now that the keen edge of my suffering was dulled, my visits to Mme Swann had become once again, for the residue of my sadness, the sedative and distraction which had been so precious to me at first. But the reason for the efficacy of the former was the drawback of the latter, namely that with these visits the memory of Gilberte was intimately blended. The distraction would be of no avail to me unless it set up, in opposition to a feeling no longer nourished by Gilberte's presence, thoughts, interests, passions in which Gilberte had no part. These states of consciousness to which the person whom we love remains a stranger then occupy a place which, however small it may be at first, is always that much reconquered from the love that had been in unchallenged possession of our whole soul. We must seek to encourage these thoughts, to make them grow, while the sentiment which is no more now than a memory dwindles, so that the new elements introduced into the mind contest with that sentiment, wrest from it an ever-increasing portion of our soul, until at last the victory is complete. I realised that this was the only way in which my love could be killed, and I was still young enough and brave enough to undertake the attempt, to subject myself to that most cruel grief which springs from the certainty that, however long it may take us, we shall succeed in the end. The reason I now gave in my letters to Gilberte for refusing to see her was an allusion to some mysterious misunderstanding, wholly fictitious, which was supposed to have arisen between her and myself, and as to which I had hoped at first that Gilberte would demand an explanation. But, in fact, never, even in the most insignificant relations in life, does a request for enlightenment come from a correspondent who knows that an obscure, untruthful, incriminating sentence has been introduced on purpose, so that he shall protest against it; he is only too happy to feel thereby that he possesses—and to keep in his own hands—the initiative in the matter. All the more so is this true in our more tender relations, in which love is endowed with so much eloquence, indifference with so little curiosity. Gilberte never having questioned or sought to learn about this misunderstanding, it became for me a real entity, to which I referred anew in every letter. And there is in these baseless situations, in the affectation of coldness, a sort of fascination which tempts one to persevere in them. By dint of writing: "Now that our hearts are sundered," so that Gilberte might answer: "But they're not. Do let's talk it over," I had gradually come to believe that they were. By constantly repeating, "Life may have changed for us, but it will never destroy the feeling that we had for one another," in the hope of at last hearing the answer: "But there has been no change, the feeling is stronger now than it ever was," I was living with the idea that life had indeed changed, that we should keep the memory of the feeling which no longer existed, as certain neurotics, from having at first pretended to be ill, end by becoming chronic invalids. Now, whenever I had to write to Gilberte, I brought my mind back to this imagined change, which, being now tacitly admitted by the silence which she preserved with regard to it in her replies, would in future subsist between us. Then Gilberte ceased to confine herself to preterition. She too adopted my point of view; and, as in the speeches at official banquets, when the Head of State who is being entertained adopts more or less the same expressions as have just been used by the Head of State who is entertaining him, whenever I wrote to Gilberte: "Life may have parted us, but the memory of the days when we knew one another will endure," she never failed to respond: "Life may have parted us, but it cannot make us forget those happy hours which will always be dear to us both" (though we should have found it hard to say why or how "Life" had parted us, or what change had occurred). My sufferings were no longer excessive. And yet, one day when I was telling her in a letter that I had heard of the death of our old barley-sugar woman in the Champs-Elysées, as I wrote the words: "I felt that this would grieve you; in me it awakened a host of memories," I could not restrain myself from bursting into tears when I saw that I was speaking in the past tense, as though it were of some dead friend, now almost forgotten, of that love of which in spite of myself I had never ceased to think as something still alive, or at least capable of reviving. Nothing could have been more tender than this correspondence between friends who did not wish to see one another any more. Gilberte's letters to me had all the delicacy of those which I used to write to people who did not matter to me, and showed me the same apparent marks of affection, which it was so soothing for me to receive from her.

But, little by little, every refusal to see her grieved me less. And as she became less dear to me, my painful memories were no longer strong enough to destroy by their incessant return the growing pleasure which I found in thinking of Florence or of Venice. I regretted, at such moments, that I had abandoned the idea of diplomacy and had condemned myself to a sedentary existence, in order not to be separated from a girl whom I should never see again and had already almost forgotten. We construct our lives for one person, and when at length it is ready to receive her that person does not come; presently she is dead to us, and we live on, prisoners within the walls which were intended only for her. If Venice seemed to my parents to be too far away and its climate too treacherous for me, it would be at least quite easy and not too tiring to go and settle down at Balbec. But to do that I should have had to leave Paris, to forgo those visits thanks to which, infrequent as they were, I might sometimes hear Mme Swann talk to me about her daughter. Besides, I was beginning to find in them various pleasures in which Gilberte had no part.

When spring arrived, and with it the cold weather, during an icy Lent and the hailstorms of Holy Week, as Mme Swann declared that it was freezing in her house, I used often to see her entertaining her guests in her furs, her shivering hands and shoulders buried beneath the gleaming white carpets of an immense rectangular muff and a cape, both of ermine, which she had not taken off on coming in from her drive, and which suggested the last patches of the snows of winter, more persistent than the rest, which neither the heat of the fire nor the advancing season had succeeded in melting. And the all-embracing truth about these glacial but already flowering weeks was suggested to me in this drawing-room, which soon I should be entering no more, by other more intoxicating forms of whiteness, that for example of the guelder-roses clustering, at the summits of their tall bare stalks, like the rectilinear trees in pre-Raphaelite paintings, their balls of blossom, divided yet composite, white as annunciating angels and exhaling a fragrance as of lemons. For the mistress of Tansonville knew that April, even an ice-bound April, is not barren of flowers, that winter, spring, summer are not held apart by barriers as hermetic as might be supposed by the town-dweller who, until the first hot day, imagines the world as containing nothing but houses that stand naked in the rain. That Mme Swann was content with the consignments furnished by her Combray gardener, that she did not, through the medium of her own "regular" florist, fill the gaps in an inadequate display with borrowings from a precocious Mediterranean shore, I do not for a moment suggest, nor did it worry me at the time. It was enough to fill me with longing for country scenes that, overhanging the loose snowdrifts of the muff in which Mme Swann kept her hands, the guelder-rose snow-balls (which served very possibly in the mind of my hostess no other purpose than to compose, on the advice of Bergotte, a "Symphony in White" with her furniture and her garments) should remind me that the Good Friday music in *Parsifal* symbolises a natural miracle which one could see performed every year if one had the sense to look for it, and, assisted by the acid and heady perfume of other kinds of blossom which, although their names were unknown to me, had brought me so often to a standstill on my walks round Combray, should make Mme Swann's drawing-room as virginal, as candidly in blossom without the least trace of verdure, as overladen with genuine scents of flowers, as was the little lane by Tansonville.

But it was still too much for me that these memories should be revived. There was a risk of their fostering what little remained of my love for Gilberte. And so, though I no longer felt the least distress during these visits to Mme Swann, I spaced them out even more and endeavoured to see as little of her as possible. At most, since I continued not to go out of Paris, I allowed myself an occasional walk with her. The fine weather had come at last, and the sun was hot. As I knew that before luncheon Mme Swann used to go out every day for an hour's stroll in the Avenue du Bois, near the Etoile—a spot which at that time, because of the people who used to collect there to gaze at the "swells" whom they knew only by name, was known as the "Down-and-outs Club"—I persuaded my parents, on Sunday (for on weekdays I was busy all morning) to let me postpone my lunch until long after theirs, until a quarter past one, and go for a walk before it. During that month of May I never missed a Sunday, Gilberte having gone to stay with friends in the country. I used to arrive at the Arc-de-Triomphe about noon. I kept watch at the entrance to the Avenue, never taking my eyes off the corner of the side-street along which Mme Swann, who had only a few yards to walk, would come from her house. Since by this time many of the people who had been strolling there were going home to lunch, those who remained were few in number and, for the most part, fashionably dressed. Suddenly, on the gravelled path, unhurrying, cool, luxuriant, Mme Swann would appear, blossoming out in a costume which was never twice the same but which I remember as being typically mauve; then she would hoist and unfurl at the end of its long stalk, just at the moment when her radiance was at its zenith, the silken banner of a wide parasol of a shade that matched the showering petals of her dress. A whole troop of people escorted her; Swann himself, four or five clubmen who had been to call upon her that morning or whom she had met in the street: and their black or grey agglomeration, obedient to her every gesture, performing the almost mechanical movements of a lifeless setting in which Odette was framed, gave to this woman, in whose eyes alone was there any intensity, the air of looking out in front of her, from among all those men, as from a window behind which she had taken her stand, and made her loom there, frail but fearless, in the nudity of her delicate colours, like the apparition of a creature of a different species, of an unknown race, and of almost martial power, by virtue of which she seemed by herself a match for all her multiple escort. Smiling, rejoicing in the fine weather, in the sunshine which had not yet become trying, with the air of a calm assurance of a creator who has accomplished his task and takes no thought for anything besides, certain that her clothes—even though the vulgar herd should fail to appreciate them—were the most elegant of all, wearing them for herself and for her friends, naturally, without exaggerated attention to them but also without absolute detachment, not preventing the little bows of ribbon on her bodice and skirt from floating buoyantly upon the air before her like creatures of whose presence she was not unaware and whom she indulgently permitted to disport themselves in accordance with their own rhythm, provided that they followed where she led, and even upon her mauve parasol, which, as often as not, she still held closed when she appeared on the scene, letting fall now and then, as though upon a bunch of Parma violets, her happy gaze, so kindly that, when it was fastened no longer upon her friends but on some inanimate object, it still seemed to smile. She thus reserved, kept open for her wardrobe, this interval of elegance of which the men with whom she was on the most familiar terms respected both the extent and the necessity, not without a certain deference, as of profane visitors to a shrine, an admission of their own ignorance, and over which they acknowledged (as to an invalid over the special precautions that he has to take, or a mother over the bringing up of her children) their friend's competence and jurisdiction. No less than by the court which encircled her and seemed not to observe the passers-by, Mme Swann, by the belatedness of her appearance, evoked those rooms in which she had spent so long, so leisurely a morning and to which she must presently return for luncheon; she seemed to indicate their proximity by the sauntering ease of her progress, like the stroll one takes up and down one's own garden; of those rooms one would have said that she carried about her still the cool, the indoor shade. But for that very reason the sight of her made me feel the more strongly a sensation of open air and warmth—all the more so because, already persuaded as I was that, by virtue of the liturgy and ritual in which Mme Swann was so profoundly versed, her clothes were connected with the season and the hour by a bond both necessary and unique, the flowers on the flexible straw brim of her hat, the ribbons on her dress, seemed to me to spring from the month of May even more naturally than the flowers of garden or woodland; and to learn what latest change there was in weather or season, I did not raise my eyes higher than to her parasol, open and outstretched like another, a nearer sky, round, clement, mobile and blue. For these rites, sovereign though they were, subjugated their glory (and, consequently, Mme Swann her own) in condescending obedience to the day, the spring, the sun, none of which struck me as being sufficiently flattered that so elegant a woman had deigned not to ignore their existence, and had chosen on their account a dress of a brighter, thinner fabric, suggesting to me, by a splaying at the collar and sleeves, the moist warmness of the throat and wrists that they exposed—in a word, had taken for them all the pains of a great lady who, having gaily condescended to pay a visit to common folk in the country, and whom everyone, even the most plebeian, knows, yet makes a point of donning for the occasion suitably pastoral attire. On her arrival I would greet Mme Swann, and she would stop me and say (in English) "*Good morning*" with a smile. We would walk a little way together. And I realised that it was for herself that she obeyed these canons in accordance with which she dressed, as though yielding to a superior wisdom of which she herself was the high priestess: for if it should happen that, feeling too warm, she threw open or even took off altogether and gave me to carry the jacket which she had intended to keep buttoned up, I would discover in the blouse beneath it a thousand details of execution which had had every chance of remaining unobserved, like those parts of an orchestral score to which the composer has devoted infinite labour although they may never reach the ears of the public: or, in the sleeves of the jacket that lay folded across my arm I would see, and would lengthily gaze at, for my own pleasure or from affection for its wearer, some exquisite detail, a deliciously tinted strap, a lining of mauve satinette which, ordinarily concealed from every eye, was yet just as delicately fashioned as the outer parts, like those Gothic carvings on a cathedral, hidden on the inside of a balustrade eighty feet from the ground, as perfect as the bas-reliefs over the main porch, and yet never seen by any living man until, happening to pass that way upon his travels, an artist obtains leave to climb up there among them, to stroll in the open air, overlooking the whole town, between the soaring towers.

What enhanced this impression that Mme Swann walked in the Avenue du Bois as though along the paths of her own garden, was—for people ignorant of her habit of taking a "constitutional"—the fact that she had come there on foot, without any carriage following, she whom, once May had begun, they were accustomed to see, behind the most brilliant "turn-out," the smartest liveries in Paris, indolently and majestically seated, like a goddess, in the balmy open air of an immense victoria on eight springs. On foot, Mme Swann had the appearance—especially when her step was slowed by the heat of the sun—of having yielded to curiosity, of committing an elegant breach of the rules of protocol, like those crowned heads who, without consulting anyone, accompanied by the slightly scandalised admiration of a suite which dares not venture any criticism, step out of their boxes during a gala performance and visit the lobby of the theatre, mingling for a moment or two with the rest of the audience. So between Mme Swann and themselves the crowd felt that there existed those barriers of a certain kind of opulence which seem to them the most insurmountable of all. The Faubourg Saint-Germain may have its barriers too, but these are less telling to the eyes and imagination of the "down-and-out." These latter, in the presence of an aristocratic lady who is simpler, more easily mistaken for an ordinary middle-class woman, less remote from the people, will not feel the same sense of inequality, almost of unworthiness, as they do before a Mme Swann. Of course women of this sort are not themselves dazed, as the crowd are, by the splendour in which they are surrounded; they have ceased to pay any attention to it, but only because they have grown used to it, that is to say have come to look upon it more and more as natural and necessary, to judge their fellow creatures according as they are more or less initiated into these luxurious ways: so that (the grandeur which they allow themselves to display or discover in others being wholly material, easily verified, slowly acquired, the lack of it hard to compensate) if such women place a passer-by in the lowest rank, it is by the same process that has made them appear to him as in the highest, that is to say instinctively, at first sight, and without possibility of appeal. Perhaps that social class which included in those days women like Lady Israels, who mixed with the women of the aristocracy, and Mme Swann, who was to get to know them later on, that intermediate class, inferior to the Faubourg Saint-Germain, since it courted the latter, but superior to everything that was not of the Faubourg Saint-Germain, possessing this peculiarity that, while already detached from the world of the merely rich, it was riches still that it represented, but riches that had become ductile, obedient to a conscious artistic purpose, malleable gold, chased with a poetic design and taught to smile; perhaps that class—in the same form, at least, and with the same charm—exists no longer. In any event, the women who were its members would not satisfy today what was the primary condition on which they reigned, since with advancing age they have lost—almost all of them—their beauty. Whereas it was from the glorious zenith of her ripe and still so fragrant summer as much as from the pinnacle of her noble wealth that Mme Swann, majestic, smiling, benign, advancing along the Avenue du Bois, saw, like Hypatia, worlds revolving beneath the slow tread of her feet. Young men as they passed looked at her anxiously, not knowing whether their vague acquaintance with her (especially since, having been introduced only once, at the most, to Swann, they were afraid that he might not remember them) was sufficient excuse for their venturing to doff their hats. And they trembled to think of the consequences as they made up their minds to do so, wondering whether this audaciously provocative and sacrilegious gesture, challenging the inviolable supremacy of a caste, would not let loose the catastrophic forces of nature or bring down upon them the vengeance of a jealous god. It provoked only, like the winding of a piece of clockwork, a series of gesticulations from little, bowing figures, who were none other than Odette's escort, beginning with Swann himself, who raised his tall hat lined in green leather with a smiling courtesy which he had acquired in the Faubourg Saint-Germain but to which was no longer wedded the indifference that he would at one time have shown. Its place was now taken (for he had been to some extent permeated by Odette's prejudices) at once by irritation at having to acknowledge the salute of a person who was none too well dressed and by satisfaction at his wife's knowing so many people, a mixed sensation to which he gave expression by saying to the smart friends who walked by his side: "What, another one! Upon my word, I can't imagine where my wife picks all these fellows up!" Meanwhile, having acknowledged with a nod the greeting of some terrified young man who had already passed out of sight though his heart was still beating furiously, Mme Swann turned to me: "Then it's all over?" she said. "You aren't ever coming to see Gilberte again? I'm glad you make an exception of me, and are not going to *drop* me completely. I like seeing you, but I also liked the influence you had over my daughter. I'm sure she's very sorry about it, too. However, I mustn't bully you, or you'll make up your mind at once that you never want to set eyes on me again." "Odette, there's Sagan saying good-day to you," Swann pointed out to his wife. And there indeed was the Prince, as in some grand finale at the theatre or the circus or in an old painting, wheeling his horse round so as to face her, and doffing his hat with a sweeping theatrical and, as it were, allegorical flourish in which he displayed all the chivalrous courtesy of the great nobleman bowing in token of respect for Womanhood, even if it was embodied in a woman whom it was impossible for his mother or his sister to know. And in fact at every turn, recognised in the depths of the liquid transparency and of the luminous glaze of the shadow which her parasol cast over her, Mme Swann received the salutations of the last belated horsemen, who passed as though filmed at the gallop in the blinding glare of the Avenue, clubmen whose names, those of celebrities for the public—Antoine de Castellane, Adalbert de Montmorency and the rest—were for Mme Swann the familiar names of friends. And as the average span of life, the relative longevity of our memories of poetical sensations is much greater than that of our memories of what the heart has suffered, now that the sorrows that I once felt on Gilberte's account have long since faded and vanished, there has survived them the pleasure that I still derive—

whenever I close my eyes and read, as it were upon the face of a sundial, the minutes that are recorded between a quarter past twelve and one o'clock in the month of May—from seeing myself once again strolling and talking thus with Mme Swann, beneath her parasol, as though in the coloured shade of a wistaria bower.

Part Two

PLACE-NAMES · THE PLACE

I had arrived at a state of almost complete indifference to Gilberte when, two years later, I went with my grandmother to Balbec. When I succumbed to the attraction of a new face, when it was with the help of some other girl that I hoped to discover the Gothic cathedrals, the palaces and gardens of Italy, I said to myself sadly that this love of ours, in so far as it is a love for one particular creature, is not perhaps a very real thing, since, though associations of pleasant or painful musings can attach it for a time to a woman to the extent of making us believe that it has been inspired by her in a logically necessary way, if on the other hand we detach ourselves deliberately or unconsciously from those associations, this love, as though it were in fact spontaneous and sprang from ourselves alone, will revive in order to bestow itself on another woman. At the time, however, of my departure for Balbec, and during the earlier part of my stay there, my indifference was still only intermittent. Often, our life being so careless of chronology, interpolating so many anachronisms into the sequence of our days, I found myself living in those—far older days than yesterday or last week—when I still loved Gilberte. And then no longer seeing her became suddenly painful, as it would have been at that time. The self that had loved her, which another self had already almost entirely supplanted, would reappear, stimulated far more often by a trivial than by an important event. For instance, if I may anticipate for a moment my arrival in Normandy, I heard someone who passed me on the sea-front at Balbec refer to "the head of the Ministry of Posts and his family." Now, since I as yet knew nothing of the influence which that family was to have on my life, this remark ought to have passed unheeded; instead, it gave me at once an acute twinge, which a self that had for the most part long since been outgrown in me felt at being parted from Gilberte. For I had never given another thought to a conversation which Gilberte had had with her father in my hearing, in which allusion was made to the Secretary to the Ministry of Posts and his family. Now the memories of love are no exception to the general laws of memory, which in turn are governed by the still more general laws of Habit. And as Habit weakens everything, what best reminds us of a person is precisely what we had forgotten (because it was of no importance, and we therefore left it in full possession of its strength). That is why the better part of our memories exists outside us, in a blatter of rain, in the smell of an unaired room or of the first crackling brushwood fire in a cold grate: wherever, in short, we happen upon what our mind, having no use for it, had rejected, the last treasure that the past has in store, the richest, that which, when all our flow of tears seems to have dried at the source, can make us weep again. Outside us? Within us, rather, but hidden from our eyes in an oblivion more or less prolonged. It is thanks to this oblivion alone that we can from time to time recover the person that we were, place ourselves in relation to things as he was placed, suffer anew because we are no longer ourselves but he, and because he loved what now leaves us indifferent. In the broad daylight of our habitual memory the images of the past turn gradually pale and fade out of sight, nothing remains of them, we shall never recapture it. Or rather we should never recapture it had not a few words (such as this "head of the Ministry of Posts") been carefully locked away in oblivion, just as an author deposits in the National Library a copy of a book which might otherwise become unobtainable.

But this pain and this recrudescence of my love for Gilberte lasted no longer than such things last in a dream, and this time, on the contrary, because at Balbec the old Habit was no longer there to keep them alive. And if these effects of Habit appear to be incompatible, that is because Habit is bound by a diversity of laws. In Paris I had grown more and more indifferent to Gilberte, thanks to Habit. The change of habit, that is to say the temporary cessation of Habit, completed Habit's work when I set out for Balbec. It weakens, but it stabilises; it leads to disintegration but it makes the scattered elements last indefinitely. Day after day, for years past, I had modelled my state of mind as best I could upon that of the day before. At Balbec a strange bed, to the side of which a tray was brought in the morning that differed from my Paris breakfast tray, could no longer sustain the thoughts upon which my love for Gilberte had fed: there are cases (fairly rare, it is true) where, one's days being paralysed by a sedentary life, the best way to gain time is to change one's place of residence. My journey to Balbec was like the first outing of a convalescent who needed only that to convince him that he was cured.

The journey was one that would now no doubt be made by motor-car, with a view to making it more agreeable. We shall see that, accomplished in such a way, it would even be in a sense more real, since one would be following more closely, in a more intimate contiguity, the various gradations by which the surface of the earth is diversified. But after all the specific attraction of a journey lies not in our being able to alight at places on the way and to stop altogether as soon as we grow tired, but in its making the difference between departure and arrival not as imperceptible but as intense as possible, so that we are conscious of it in its totality, intact, as it existed in us when our imagination bore us from the place in which we were living right to the very heart of a place we longed to see, in a single sweep which seemed miraculous to us not so much because it covered a certain distance as because it united two distinct individualities of the world, took us from one name to another name, and which is schematised (better than in a form of locomotion in which, since one can disembark where one chooses, there can scarcely be said to be any point of arrival) by the mysterious operation performed in those peculiar places, railway stations, which scarcely form part of the surrounding town but contain the essence of its personality just as upon their sign-boards they bear its painted name.

But in this respect as in every other, our age is infected with a mania for showing things only in the environment that properly belongs to them, thereby suppressing the essential thing, the act of the mind which isolated them from that environment. A picture is nowadays "presented" in the midst of furniture, ornaments, hangings of the same period, stale settings which the hostess who but yesterday was so crassly ignorant but who now spends her time in archives and libraries excels at composing in the houses of today, and in the midst of which the masterpiece we contemplate as we dine does not give us the exhilarating delight that we can expect from it only in a public gallery, which symbolises far better, by its bareness and by the absence of all irritating detail, those innermost spaces into which the artist withdrew to create it.

Unhappily those marvellous places, railway stations, from which one sets out for a remote destination, are tragic places also, for if in them the miracle is accomplished whereby scenes which hitherto have had no existence save in our minds are about to become the scenes among which we shall be living, for that very reason we must, as we emerge from the waiting-room, abandon any thought of presently finding ourselves once more in the familiar room which but a moment ago still housed us. We must lay aside all hope of going home to sleep in our own bed, once we have decided to penetrate into the pestiferous cavern through which we gain access to the mystery, into one of those vast, glass-roofed sheds, like that of Saint-Lazare into which I went to find the train for Balbec, and which extended over the eviscerated city one of those bleak and boundless skies, heavy with an accumulation of dramatic menace, like certain skies painted with an almost Parisian modernity by Mantegna or Veronese, beneath which only some terrible and solemn act could be in process, such as a departure by train or the erection of the Cross.

So long as I had been content to look out from the warmth of my own bed in Paris at the Persian church of Balbec, shrouded in driving sleet, no sort of objection to this journey had been offered by my body. Its objections began only when it realised that it would be of the party, and that on the evening of my arrival I should be shown to "my" room which would be unknown to it. Its revolt was all the more profound in that on the very eve of my departure I learned that my mother would not be coming with us, my father, who would be kept busy at the Ministry until it was time for him to set off for Spain with M. de Norpois, having preferred to take a house in the neighbourhood of Paris. On the other hand, the contemplation of Balbec seemed to me none the less desirable because I must purchase it at the price of a discomfort which, on the contrary, seemed to me to symbolise and to guarantee the reality of the impression which I was going there to seek, an impression which no allegedly equivalent spectacle, no "panorama" which I might have gone to see without being thereby precluded from returning home to sleep in my own bed, could possibly have replaced. It was not for the first time that I felt that those who love and those who enjoy are not always the same. I believed that I hankered after Balbec just as much as the doctor who was treating me and who said to me on the morning of our departure, surprised to see me looking so unhappy: "I don't mind telling you that if I could only manage a week to go down and get a blow by the sea, I shouldn't have to be asked twice. You'll be having races, regattas, it will be delightful." But I had already learned the lesson—long before I was taken to see Berma—that, whatever it might be that I loved, it would never be attained, save at the end of a long and painful pursuit, in the course of which I should have first to sacrifice my pleasure to that paramount good instead of seeking it therein.

My grandmother, naturally enough, looked upon our exodus from a somewhat different point of view, and (anxious as ever that the presents which were made me should take some artistic form) had planned, in order to offer me a "print" of this journey that was old in part, for us to repeat, partly by rail and partly by road, the itinerary that Mme de Sévigné had followed when she went from Paris to "L'Orient" by way of Chaulnes and "the Pont-Audemer." But my grandmother had been obliged to abandon this project at the instance of my father, who knew, whenever she organised any expedition with a view to extracting from it the utmost intellectual benefit that it was capable of yielding, what could be anticipated in missed trains, lost luggage, sore throats and broken rules. She was free at least to rejoice in the thought that never, when the time came for us to sally forth to the beach, would we be exposed to the risk of being kept indoors by the sudden appearance of what her beloved Sévigné calls a "beast of a coachload," since we should know not a soul at Balbec, Legrandin having refrained from offering us a letter of introduction to his sister. (This abstention had not been so well appreciated by my aunts Céline and Flora, who, having known that lady as a girl and always hitherto referred to her, to commemorate this early intimacy, as "Renée de Cambremer," and still possessing a number of gifts from her, the kind which continue to ornament a room or a conversation but to which the present reality no longer corresponds, imagined themselves to be avenging the insult by never uttering the name of her daughter again, when they called upon Mme Legrandin senior, confining themselves to mutual congratulations, once they were safely out of the house, such as: "I made no reference to you know whom. I think it went home!")

And so we were simply to leave Paris by that 1.22 train which I had too often beguiled myself by looking up in the railway time-table, where it never failed to give me the emotion, almost the illusion of departure, not to feel that I already knew it. As the delineation in our minds of the features of any form of happiness depends more on the nature of the longings that it inspires in us than on the accuracy of the information which we have about it, I felt that I already knew this happiness in all its details, and had no doubt that I should feel in my compartment a special delight as the day began to cool, should contemplate this or that view as the train approached one or another station; so much so that this train, which always brought to my mind's eye the images of the same towns which I swathed in the light of those afternoon hours through which it sped, seemed to me to be different from every other train; and I had ended—as we are apt to do with a person whom we have never seen but whose friendship we like to believe that we have won—by giving a distinct and unalterable cast of countenance to the fair, artistic traveller who would thus have taken me with him upon his journey, and to whom I should bid farewell beneath the Cathedral of Saint-Lô before he disappeared towards the setting sun.

As my grandmother could not bring herself to go "purely and simply" to Balbec, she was to break the journey half-way, staying the night with one of her friends, from whose house I was to proceed the same evening, so as not to be in the way there and also in order that I might arrive by daylight and see Balbec church, which, we had learned, was at some distance from Balbec-Plage, and which I might not have a chance to visit later on, when I had begun my course of bathing. And perhaps it was less painful for me to feel that the admirable goal of my journey stood between me and that cruel first night on which I should have to enter a new habitation and consent to dwell there. But I had had first to leave the old; my mother had arranged to move in that very afternoon at Saint-Cloud, and had made, or pretended to make, all the arrangements for going there directly after she had seen us off at the station, without having to call again at our own house, to which she was afraid that I might otherwise feel impelled to return with her at the last moment, instead of going to Balbec. In fact, on the pretext of having so much to see to in the house which she had just taken and of being pressed for time, but in reality so as to spare me the cruel ordeal of a long-drawn parting, she had decided not to wait with us until the moment of the train's departure when, concealed amidst comings and goings and preparations that involve no final commitment, a separation suddenly looms up, impossible to endure when it is no longer possible to avoid, concentrated in its entirety in one enormous instant of impotent and supreme lucidity.

For the first time I began to feel that it was possible that my mother might live another kind of life, without me, otherwise than for me. She was going to live on her own with my father, whose existence it may have seemed to her that my ill-health, my nervous excitability, made somewhat complicated and gloomy. This separation made me all the more wretched because I told myself that for my mother it was probably the outcome of the successive disappointments which I had caused her, of which she had never said a word to me but which had made her realise the difficulty of our taking our holidays together; and perhaps also a preliminary trial for a form of existence to which she was beginning, now, to resign herself for the future, as the years crept on for my father and herself, an existence in which I should see less of her, in which (a thing that not even in my nightmares had yet been revealed to me) she would already have become something of a stranger to me, a lady who might be seen going home by herself to a house in which I should not be, asking the concierge whether there was a letter for her from me.

I could scarcely answer the porter who offered to take my bag. My mother tried to comfort me by the methods which seemed to her most efficacious. Thinking it useless to appear not to notice my unhappiness, she gently teased me about it: "Well, and what would Balbec church say if it knew that people pulled long faces like that when they were going to see it? Surely this is not the enraptured traveller Ruskin speaks of. In any case I shall know if you have risen to the occasion, even when we're miles apart I shall still be with my little man. You shall have a letter tomorrow from your Mamma."

"My dear," said my grandmother, "I picture you like Mme de Sévigné, your eyes glued to the map, and never losing sight of us for an instant."

Then Mamma sought to distract me by asking what I thought of having for dinner and drawing my attention to Françoise, whom she complimented on a hat and coat which she did not recognise, although they had horrified her long ago when she first saw them, new, upon my great-aunt, the one with an immense bird towering over it, the other decorated with a hideous pattern and jet beads. But the cloak having grown too shabby to wear, Françoise had had it turned, exposing an "inside" of plain cloth and quite a good colour. As for the bird, it had long since come to grief and been discarded. And just as it is disturbing, sometimes, to find the effects which the most conscious artists have to strive for in a folk-song or on the wall of some peasant's cottage where above the door, at precisely the right spot in the composition, blooms a white or yellow rose—so with the velvet band, the loop of ribbon that would have delighted one in a portrait by Chardin or Whistler, which Françoise had set with simple but unerring taste upon the hat, which was now charming.

To take a parallel from an earlier age, the modesty and integrity which often gave an air of nobility to the face of our old servant having extended also to the clothes which, as a discreet but by no means servile woman, who knew how to hold her own and to keep her place, she had put on for the journey so as to be fit to be seen in our company without at the same time seeming or wishing to make herself conspicuous, Françoise, in the faded cherry-coloured cloth of her coat and the discreet nap of her fur collar, brought to mind one of those miniatures of Anne of Brittany painted in Books of Hours by an old master, in which everything is so exactly in the right place, the sense of the whole is so evenly distributed throughout the parts, that the rich and obsolete singularity of the costume expresses the same pious gravity as the eyes, the lips and the hands.

Of thought, in relation to Françoise, one could hardly speak. She knew nothing, in that absolute sense in which to know nothing means to understand nothing, except the rare truths to which the heart is capable of directly attaining. The vast world of ideas did not exist for her. But when one studied the clearness of her gaze, the delicate lines of the nose and the lips, all those signs lacking from so many cultivated people in whom they would have signified a supreme distinction, the noble detachment of a rare mind, one was disquieted, as one is by the frank, intelligent eyes of a dog, to which nevertheless one knows that all our human conceptions are alien, and one might have been led to wonder whether there may not be, among those other humbler brethren, the peasants, individuals who are as it were the élite of the world of the simple-minded, or rather who, condemned by an unjust fate to live among the simple-minded, deprived of enlightenment and yet more naturally, more essentially akin to the chosen spirits than most educated people, are members as it were, dispersed, strayed, robbed of their heritage of reason, of the sacred family, kinsfolk, left behind in infancy, of the loftiest minds, in whom—as is apparent from the unmistakable light in their eyes, although it is applied to nothing—there has been lacking, to endow them with talent, only the gift of knowledge.

My mother, seeing that I was having difficulty in keeping back my tears, said to me: " 'Regulus was in the habit, when things looked grave . . .' Besides, it isn't very nice for your Mamma! What does Mme de Sévigné say? Your grandmother will tell you: 'I shall be obliged to draw upon all the courage that you lack.' " And remembering that affection for another distracts one's attention from selfish griefs, she endeavoured to beguile me by telling me that she expected the removal to Saint-Cloud to go without a hitch, that she was pleased with the cab, which she had kept waiting, that the driver seemed civil and the seats comfortable. I made an effort to smile at these trifles, and bowed my head with an air of acquiescence and contentment. But they helped me only to picture to myself the more accurately Mamma's imminent departure, and it was with a heavy heart that I gazed at her as though she were already torn from me, beneath that wide-brimmed straw hat which she had bought to wear in the country, in a flimsy dress which she had put on in view of the long drive through the sweltering midday heat; hat and dress making her someone else, someone who belonged already to the Villa Montretout, in which I should not see her.

To prevent the suffocating fits which the journey might bring on, the doctor had advised me to take a stiff dose of beer or brandy at the moment of departure, so as to begin the journey in a state of what he called "euphoria," in which the nervous system is for a time less vulnerable. I had not yet made up my mind whether to do this, but I wished at least that my grandmother should acknowledge that, if I did so decide, I should have wisdom and authority on my side. I spoke about it therefore as if my hesitation were concerned only with where I should go for my drink, to the platform buffet or to the bar on the train. But immediately, at the air of reproach which my grandmother's face assumed, an air of not wishing even to entertain such an idea for a moment, "What!" I cried, suddenly resolving upon this action of going to get a drink, the performance of which became necessary as a proof of my independence since the verbal announcement of it had not succeeded in passing unchallenged, "What! You know how ill I am, you know what the doctor ordered, yet look at the advice you give me!"

When I had explained to my grandmother how unwell I felt, her distress, her kindness were so apparent as she replied, "Run along then, quickly; get yourself some beer or a liqueur if it will do you good," that I flung myself upon her and smothered her with kisses. And if after that I went and drank a great deal too much in the bar of the train it was because I felt that otherwise I should have too violent an attack, which was what would distress her most. When at the first stop I clambered back into our compartment I told my grandmother how pleased I was to be going to Balbec, that I felt that everything would go off splendidly, that after all I should soon grow used to being without Mamma, that the train was most comfortable, the barman and the attendants so friendly that I should like to make the journey often so as to have the opportunity of seeing them again. My grandmother, however, did not appear to be quite so overjoyed at all these good tidings. She answered, without looking me in the face: "Why don't you try to get a little sleep?" and turned her eyes to the window, the blind of which, though we had lowered it, did not completely cover the glass, so that the sun could shed on the polished oak of the door and the cloth of the seat (like a far more persuasive advertisement for a life shared with nature than those hung high up on the wall of the compartment by the railway company, representing landscapes whose names I could not make out from where I sat) the same warm and slumbrous light which drowsed in the forest glades.

But when my grandmother thought that my eyes were shut I could see her now and again, from behind her spotted veil, steal a glance at me, then withdraw it, then look back again, like a person trying to make himself perform some exercise that hurts him in order to get into the habit.

Thereupon I spoke to her, but that did not seem to please her. And yet to myself the sound of my own voice was agreeable, as were the most imperceptible, the innermost movements of my body. And so I endeavoured to prolong them. I allowed each of my inflexions to linger lazily upon the words, I felt each glance from my eyes pause pleasurably on the spot where it came to rest and remain there beyond its normal time. "Now, now, sit still and rest," said my grandmother. "If you can't manage to sleep, read something." And she handed me a volume of Mme de Sévigné which I opened, while she buried herself in the *Mémoires de Madame de Beausergent.*[9] She never travelled anywhere without a volume of each. They were her two favourite authors. Unwilling to move my head for the moment, and experiencing the greatest pleasure from maintaining a position once I was in it, I sat holding the volume of Mme de Sévigné without looking at it, without even lowering my eyes, which were confronted with nothing but the blue window-blind. But the contemplation of this blind appeared to me an admirable thing, and I should not have troubled to answer anyone who might have sought to distract me from contemplating it. The blue of this blind seemed to me, not perhaps by its beauty but by its intense vividness, to efface so completely all the colours that had passed before my eyes from the day of my birth up to the moment when I had gulped down the last of my drink and it had begun to take effect, that compared with this blue they were as drab, as null, as the darkness in which he has lived must be in retrospect to a man born blind whom a subsequent operation has at length enabled to see and to distinguish colours. An old ticket-collector came to ask for our tickets. I was charmed by the silvery gleam that shone from the metal buttons of his tunic. I wanted to ask him to sit down beside us. But he passed on to the next carriage, and I thought with longing of the life led by railwaymen for whom, since they spent all their time on the line, hardly a day could pass without their seeing this old collector. The pleasure that I found in staring at the blind, and in feeling that my mouth was half-open, began at length to diminish. I became more mobile; I shifted in my seat; I opened the book that my grandmother had given me and turned its pages casually, reading whatever caught my eye. And as I read I felt my admiration for Mme de Sévigné grow.

One must not be taken in by purely formal characteristics, idioms of the period or social conventions, the effect of which is that certain people believe that they have caught the Sévigné manner when they have said: "Acquaint me, my dear," or "That count struck me as being a man of parts," or "Haymaking is the sweetest thing in the world." Mme de Simiane imagines already that she resembles her grandmother because she can write: "M. de la Boulie is flourishing, sir, and in perfect condition to hear the news of his death," or "Oh, my dear Marquis, how your letter enchanted me! What can I do but answer it?" or "Meseems, sir, that you owe me a letter, and I owe you some boxes of bergamot. I discharge my debt to the number of eight; others shall follow . . . Never has the soil borne so many—evidently for your gratification." And she writes in this style also her letter on bleeding, on lemons and so forth, supposing it to be typical of the letters of Mme de Sévigné. But my grandmother, who had come to the latter from within, from love of her family and of nature, had taught me to enjoy the real beauties of her correspondence, which are altogether different. They were soon to strike me all the more forcibly inasmuch as Mme de Sévigné is a great artist of the same family as a painter whom I was to meet at Balbec and who had such a profound influence on my way of seeing things: Elstir. I realised at Balbec that it was in the same way as he that she presented things to her readers, in the order of our perception of them, instead of first explaining them in relation to their several causes. But already that afternoon in the railway carriage, on re-reading that letter in which the moonlight appears—"I could not resist the temptation: I put on all my bonnets and cloaks, though there is no need of them, I walk along this mall, where the air is as sweet as that of my chamber; I find a thousand phantasms, *monks white and black, nuns grey and white, linen cast here and there on the ground, men enshrouded upright against the tree-trunks*"—I was enraptured by what, a little later, I should have described (for does not she draw landscapes in the same way as he draws characters?) as the Dostoievsky side of Mme de Sévigné's Letters.

When, that evening, after having accompanied my grandmother to her destination and spent some hours in her friend's house, I had returned by myself to the train, at any rate I found nothing to distress me in the night which followed; this was because I did not have to spend it imprisoned in a room whose somnolence would have kept me awake; I was surrounded by the soothing activity of all those movements of the train which kept me company, offered to stay and talk to me if I could not sleep, lulled me with their sounds which I combined—like the chime of the Combray bells—now in one rhythm, now in another (hearing as the whim took me first four equal semi-quavers, then one semi-quaver furiously dashing against a crotchet); they neutralised the centrifugal force of my insomnia by exerting on it contrary pressures which kept me in equilibrium and on which my immobility and presently my drowsiness seemed to be borne with the same sense of relaxation that I should have felt had I been resting under the protecting vigilance of powerful forces in the heart of nature and of life, had I been able for a moment to metamorphose myself into a fish that sleeps in the sea, carried along in its slumber by the currents and the waves, or an eagle outstretched upon the buoyant air of the storm.

Sunrise is a necessary concomitant of long railway journeys, like hard-boiled eggs, illustrated papers, packs of cards, rivers upon which boats strain but make no progress. At a certain moment, when I was counting over the thoughts that had filled my mind during the preceding minutes, so as to discover whether I had just been asleep or not (and when the very uncertainty which made me ask myself the question was about to furnish me with an affirmative answer), in the pale square of the window, above a small black wood, I saw some ragged clouds whose fleecy edges were of a fixed, dead pink, not liable to change, like the colour that dyes the feathers of a wing that has assimilated it or a pastel on which it has been deposited by the artist's whim. But I felt that, unlike them, this colour was neither inertia nor caprice, but necessity and life. Presently there gathered behind it reserves of light. It brightened; the sky turned to a glowing pink which I strove, glueing my eyes to the window, to see more clearly, for I felt that it was related somehow to the most intimate life of Nature, but, the course of the line altering, the train turned, the morning scene gave place in the frame of the window to a nocturnal village, its roofs still blue with moonlight, its pond encrusted with the opalescent sheen of night, beneath a firmament still spangled with all its stars, and I was lamenting the loss of my strip of pink sky when I caught sight of it anew, but red this time, in the opposite window which it left at a second bend in the line; so that I spent my time running from one window to the other to reassemble, to collect on a single canvas the intermittent, antipodean fragments of my fine, scarlet, ever-changing morning, and to obtain a comprehensive view and a continuous picture of it.

The scenery became hilly and steep, and the train stopped at a little station between two mountains. Far down the gorge, on the edge of a hurrying stream, one could see only a solitary watch-house, embedded in the water which ran past on a level with its windows. If a person can be the product of a soil to the extent of embodying for us the quintessence of its peculiar charm, more even than the peasant girl whom I had so desperately longed to see appear when I wandered by myself along the Méséglise way, in the woods of Roussainville, such a person must have been the tall girl whom I now saw emerge from the house and, climbing a path lighted by the first slanting rays of the sun, come towards the station carrying a jar of milk. In her valley from which the rest of the world was hidden by these heights, she must never see anyone save in these trains which stopped for a moment only. She passed down the line of windows, offering coffee and milk to a few awakened passengers. Flushed with the glow of morning, her face was rosier than the sky. I felt on seeing her that desire to live which is reborn in us whenever we become conscious anew of beauty and of happiness. We invariably forget that these are individual qualities, and, mentally substituting for them a conventional type at which we arrive by striking a sort of mean among the different faces that have taken our fancy, among the pleasures we have known, we are left with mere abstract images which are lifeless and insipid because they lack precisely that element of novelty, different from anything we have known, that element which is peculiar to beauty and to happiness. And we deliver on life a pessimistic judgment which we suppose to be accurate, for we believed that we were taking happiness and beauty into account, whereas in fact we left them out and replaced them by syntheses in which there is not a single atom of either. So it is that a well-read man will at once begin to yawn with boredom when one speaks to him of a new "good book," because he imagines a sort of composite of all the good books that he has read, whereas a good book is something special, something unforeseeable, and is made up not of the sum of all previous masterpieces but of something which the most thorough assimilation of every one of them would not enable him to discover, since it exists not in their sum but beyond it. Once he has become acquainted with this new work, the well-read man, however jaded his palate, feels his interest awaken in the reality which it depicts. So, completely unrelated to the models of beauty which I was wont to conjure up in my mind when I was by myself, this handsome girl gave me at once the taste for a certain happiness (the sole form, always different, in which we may acquire a taste for happiness), for a happiness that would be realised by my staying and living there by her side. But in this again the temporary cessation of Habit played a great part. I was giving the milk-girl the benefit of the fact that it was the whole of my being, fit to taste the keenest joys, which confronted her. As a rule it is with our being reduced to a minimum that we live; most of our faculties lie dormant because they can rely upon Habit, which knows what there is to be done and has no need of their services. But on this morning of travel, the interruption of the routine of my existence, the unfamiliar place and time, had made their presence indispensable. My habits, which were sedentary and not matutinal, for once were missing, and all my faculties came hurrying to take their place, vying with one another in their zeal, rising, each of them, like waves, to the same unaccustomed level, from the basest to the most exalted, from breath, appetite, the circulation of my blood to receptivity and imagination. I cannot say whether, in making me believe that this girl was unlike the rest of women, the rugged charm of the locality added to her own, but she was equal to it. Life would have seemed an exquisite thing to me if only I had been free to spend it, hour after hour, with her, to go with her to the stream, to the cow, to the train, to be always at her side, to feel that I was known to her, had my place in her thoughts. She would have initiated me into the delights of country life and of early hours of the day. I signalled to her to bring me some of her coffee. I felt the need to be noticed by her. She did not see me; I called to her. Above her tall figure, the complexion of her face was so burnished and so glowing that it was as if one were seeing her through a lighted window. She retraced her steps. I could not take my eyes from her face which grew larger as she approached, like a sun which it was somehow possible to stare at and which was coming nearer and nearer, letting itself be seen at close quarters, dazzling you with its blaze of red and gold. She fastened on me her penetrating gaze, but doors were being closed and the train had begun to move. I saw her leave the station and go down the hill to her home; it was broad daylight now; I was speeding away from the dawn. Whether my exaltation had been produced by this girl or had on the other hand been responsible for most of the pleasure that I had found in her presence, in either event she was so closely associated with it that my desire to see her again was above all a mental desire not to allow this state of excitement to perish utterly, not to be separated for ever from the person who, however unwittingly, had participated in it. It was not only that this state was a pleasant one. It was above all that (just as increased tension upon a string or the accelerated vibration of a nerve produces a different sound or colour) it gave another tonality to all that I saw, introduced me as an actor upon the stage of an unknown and infinitely more interesting universe; that handsome girl whom I still could see, as the train gathered speed, was like part of a life other than the life I knew, separated from it by a clear boundary, in which the sensations aroused in me by things were no longer the same, from which to emerge now would be, as it were, to die to myself. To have the consolation of feeling that I had at least an attachment to this new life, it would suffice that I should live near enough to the little station to be able to come to it every morning for a cup of coffee from the girl. But alas, she must be for ever absent from the other life towards which I was being borne with ever increasing speed, a life which I could resign myself to accept only by weaving plans that would enable me to take the same train again some day and to stop at the same station, a project which had the further advantage of providing food for the selfish, active, practical, mechanical, indolent, centrifugal tendency which is that of the human mind, for it turns all too readily aside from the effort which is required to analyse and probe, in a general and disinterested manner, an agreeable impression which we have received. And since, at the same time, we wish to continue to think of that impression, the mind prefers to imagine it in the future tense, to continue to bring about the circumstances which may make it recur—which, while giving us no clue as to the real nature of the thing, saves us the trouble of re-creating it within ourselves and allows us to hope that we may receive it afresh from without.

Certain names of towns, Vézelay or Chartres, Bourges or Beauvais, serve to designate, by abbreviation, their principal churches. This partial acceptation comes at length—if the names in question are those of places that we do not yet know—to mould the name as a whole which henceforth, whenever we wish to introduce into it the idea of the town—the town which we have never seen—will impose on it the same carved outlines, in the same style, will make of it a sort of vast cathedral. It was, however, in a railway-station, above the door of a refreshment-room in white letters on a blue panel, that I read the name—almost Persian in style—of Balbec. I strode buoyantly through the station and across the avenue that led up to it, and asked the way to the shore, so as to see nothing in the place but its church and the sea. People seemed not to understand what I meant. Old Balbec, Balbec-en-Terre, at which I had arrived, had neither beach nor harbour. True, it was indeed in the sea that the fishermen, according to the legend, had found the miraculous Christ, a discovery recorded in a window in the church a few yards away from me; it was indeed from cliffs battered by the waves that the stone of its nave and towers had been quarried. But this sea, which for those reasons I had imagined as coming to expire at the foot of the window, was twelve miles away and more, at Balbec-Plage, and, rising beside its cupola, that steeple which, because I had read that it was itself a rugged Norman cliff round which the winds howled and the sea-birds wheeled, I had always pictured to myself as receiving at its base the last dying foam of the uplifted waves, stood on a square which was the junction of two tramway routes, opposite a café which bore, in letters of gold, the legend "Billiards," against a background of houses with the roofs of which no upstanding mast was blended. And the church—impinging on my attention at the same time as the café, the passing stranger of whom I had had to ask my way, the station to which presently I should have to return—merged with all the rest, seemed an accident, a by-product of this summer afternoon, in which the mellow and distended dome against the sky was like a fruit of which the same light that bathed the chimneys of the houses ripened the pink, glowing, luscious skin. But I wished only to consider the eternal significance of the carvings when I recognised the Apostles, of which I had seen casts in the Trocadéro museum, and which on either side of the Virgin, before the deep bay of the porch, were awaiting me as though to do me honour. With their benign, blunt, mild faces and bowed shoulders they seemed to be advancing upon me with an air of welcome, singing the Alleluia of a fine day. But it was evident that their expression was as unchanging as that of a corpse, and altered only if one walked round them. I said to myself: "Here I am: this is the Church of Balbec. This square, which looks as though it were conscious of its glory, is the only place in the world that possesses Balbec church. All that I have seen so far have been photographs of this church—and of these famous Apostles, this Virgin of the Porch, mere casts only. Now it is the church itself, the statue itself, they, the only ones—this is something far greater."

It was also something less, perhaps. As a young man on the day of an examination or of a duel feels the question that he has been asked, the shot that he has fired, to be very insignificant when he thinks of the reserves of knowledge and of valour that he would like to have displayed, so my mind, which had lifted the Virgin of the Porch far above the reproductions that I had had before my eyes, invulnerable to the vicissitudes which might threaten them, intact even if they were destroyed, ideal, endowed with a universal value, was astonished to see the statue which it had carved a thousand times, reduced now to its own stone semblance, occupying, in relation to the reach of my arm, a place in which it had for rivals an election poster and the point of my stick, fettered to the square, inseparable from the opening of the main street, powerless to hide from the gaze of the café and of the omnibus office, receiving on its face half of the ray of the setting sun (and presently, in a few hours' time, of the light of the street lamp) of which the savings bank received the other half, invaded simultaneously with that branch office of a loan society by the smells from the pastry-cook's oven, subjected to the tyranny of the Particular to such a point that, if I had chosen to scribble my name upon that stone, it was she, the illustrious Virgin whom until then I had endowed with a general existence and an intangible beauty, the Virgin of Balbec, the unique (which meant, alas, the only one), who, on her body coated with the same soot as defiled the neighbouring houses, would have displayed—powerless to rid herself of them—to all the admiring strangers come there to gaze upon her, the marks of my piece of chalk and the letters of my name, and it was she, finally, the immortal work of art so long desired, whom I found transformed, as was the church itself, into a little old woman in stone whose height I could measure and whose wrinkles I could count. But time was passing; I must return to the station, where I was to wait for my grandmother and Françoise, so that we should all go on to Balbec-Plage together. I reminded myself of what I had read about Balbec, of Swann's saying: "It's exquisite; as beautiful as Siena." And casting the blame for my disappointment upon various accidental causes, such as the state of my health, my exhaustion after the journey, my incapacity for looking at things properly, I endeavoured to console myself with the thought that other towns still remained intact for me, that I might soon, perhaps, be making my way, as into a shower of pearls, into the cool babbling murmur of watery Quimperlé, or traversing the roseate glow in which verdant Pont-Aven was bathed; but as for Balbec, no sooner had I set foot in it than it was as though I had broken open a name which ought to have been kept hermetically closed, and into which, seizing at once the opportunity that I had imprudently given them, expelling all the images that had lived in it until then, a tramway, a café, people crossing the square, the branch of the savings bank, irresistibly propelled by some external pressure, by a pneumatic force, had come surging into the interior of those two syllables which, closing over them, now let them frame the porch of the Persian church and would henceforth never cease to contain them.

I found my grandmother in the little train of the local railway which was to take us to Balbec-Plage, but found her alone—for she had had the idea of sending Françoise on ahead of her, so that everything should be ready before we arrived, but having given her the wrong instructions, had succeeded only in sending her off in the wrong direction, so that Françoise at that moment was being carried down all unsuspectingly at full speed to Nantes, and would probably wake up next morning at Bordeaux. No sooner had I taken my seat in the carriage, which was filled with the fleeting light of sunset and with the lingering heat of the afternoon (the former enabling me, alas, to see written clearly upon my grandmother's face how much the latter had tired her), than she began: "Well, and Balbec?" with a smile so brightly illuminated by her expectation of the great pleasure which she supposed me to have experienced that I dared not at once confess to her my disappointment. Besides, the impression which my mind had been seeking occupied it steadily less as the place to which my body would have to become accustomed drew nearer. At the end—still more than an hour away—of this journey I was trying to form a picture of the manager of the hotel at Balbec, for whom I, at that moment, did not exist, and I should have liked to be presenting myself to him in more impressive company than that of my grandmother, who would be certain to ask for a reduction of his terms. He appeared to me to be endowed with an indubitable haughtiness, but its contours were very vague.

Every few minutes the little train brought us to a standstill at one of the stations which came before Balbec-Plage, stations the mere names of which (Incarville, Marcouville, Douville, Pont-à-Couleuvre, Arambouville, Saint-Mars-le-Vieux, Hermonville, Maineville) seemed to me outlandish, whereas if I had come upon them in a book I should at once have been struck by their affinity to the names of certain places in the neighbourhood of Combray. But to the ear of a musician two themes, substantially composed of the same notes, will present no similarity whatever if they differ in the colour of their harmony and orchestration. In the same way, nothing could have reminded me less than these dreary names, redolent of sand, of space too airy and empty, and of salt, out of which the suffix "ville" emerged like "fly" in "butterfly"—nothing could have reminded me less of those other names, Roussainville or Martinville, which, because I had heard them pronounced so often by my great-aunt at table, in the dining-room, had acquired a certain sombre charm in which were blended perhaps extracts of the flavour of preserves, the smell of the log fire and of the pages of one of Bergotte's books, or the colour of the sandstone front of the house opposite, and which even today, when they rise like a gaseous bubble from the depths of my memory, preserve their own specific virtue through all the successive layers of different environments which they must traverse before reaching the surface.

Overlooking the distant sea from the crests of their dunes or already settling down for the night at the foot of hills of a harsh green and a disagreeable shape, like that of the sofa in one's bedroom in an hotel at which one has just arrived, each composed of a cluster of villas whose line was extended to include a tennis court and occasionally a casino over which a flag flapped in the freshening, hollow, uneasy wind, they were a series of little watering-places which now showed me for the first time their denizens, but showed them only through their habitual exterior—tennis players in white hats, the station-master living there on the spot among his tamarisks and roses, a lady in a straw "boater" who, following the everyday routine of an existence which I should never know, was calling to her dog which had stopped to examine something in the road before going in to her bungalow where the lamp was already lighted—and which with these strangely ordinary and disdainfully familiar sights cruelly stung my unconsidered eyes and stabbed my homesick heart. But how much more were my sufferings increased when we had finally landed in the hall of the Grand Hotel at Balbec, and I stood there in front of the monumental staircase of imitation marble, while my grandmother, regardless of the growing hostility and contempt of the strangers among whom we were about to live, discussed "terms" with the manager, a pot-bellied figure with a face and a voice alike covered with scars (left by the excision of countless pustules from the one, and from the other of the divers accents acquired from an alien ancestry and a cosmopolitan upbringing), a smart dinner-jacket, and the air of a psychologist who, whenever the "omnibus" discharged a fresh load, invariably took the grandees for haggling skinflints and the flashy crooks for grandees! Forgetting, doubtless, that he himself was not drawing five hundred francs a month, he had a profound contempt for people to whom five hundred francs—or, as he preferred to put it, "twenty-five louis"—was "a lot of money," and regarded them as belonging to a race of pariahs for whom the Grand Hotel was certainly not intended. It is true that even within its walls there were people who did not pay very much and yet had not forfeited the manager's esteem, provided that he was assured that they were watching their expenditure not from poverty so much as from avarice. For this could in no way lower their standing, since it is a vice and may consequently be found at every grade in the social hierarchy. Social position was the one thing by which the manager was impressed—social position, or rather the signs which seemed to him to imply that it was exalted, such as not taking one's hat off when one came into the hall, wearing knickerbockers or an overcoat with a waist, and taking a cigar with a band of purple and gold out of a crushed morocco case—to none of which advantages could I, alas, lay claim. He would also adorn his business conversation with choice expressions, to which, as a rule, he gave the wrong meaning.

While I heard my grandmother, who betrayed no sign of annoyance at his listening to her with his hat on his head and whistling through his teeth, ask him in an artificial tone of voice "And what are . . . your charges? . . . Oh! far too high for my little budget," waiting on a bench, I took refuge in the innermost depths of my being, strove to migrate to a plane of eternal thoughts, to leave nothing of myself, nothing living, on the surface of my body—anaesthetised like those of certain animals, which, by inhibition, feign death when they are wounded—so as not to suffer too keenly in this place, my total unfamiliarity with which was impressed upon me all the more forcibly by the familiarity with it that seemed to be evinced at the same moment by a smartly dressed lady to whom the manager showed his respect by taking liberties with the little dog that followed her across the hall, the young dandy with a feather in his hat who came in asking if there were "any letters," all these people for whom climbing those imitation marble stairs meant going home. And at the same time the triple stare of Minos, Aeacus and Rhadamanthus (into which I plunged my naked soul as into an unknown element where there was nothing now to protect it) was bent sternly upon me by a group of gentlemen who, though little versed perhaps in the art of receiving, yet bore the title "reception clerks," while beyond them again, behind a glass partition, were people sitting in a reading-room for the description of which I should have had to borrow from Dante alternately the colours in which he paints Paradise and Hell, according as I was thinking of the happiness of the elect who had the right to sit and read there undisturbed, or of the terror which my grandmother would have inspired in me if, in her insensibility to this sort of impression, she had asked me to go in there.

My sense of loneliness was further increased a moment later. When I had confessed to my grandmother that I did not feel well, that I thought that we should be obliged to return to Paris, she had offered no protest, saying merely that she was going out to buy a few things which would be equally useful whether we left or stayed (and which, I afterwards learned, were all intended for me, Françoise having gone off with certain articles which I might need). While I waited for her I had taken a turn through the streets, which were packed with a crowd of people who imparted to them a sort of indoor warmth, and in which the hairdresser's shop and the pastry-cook's were still open, the latter filled with customers eating ices opposite the statue of Duguay-Trouin. This crowd gave me just about as much pleasure as a photograph of it in one of the "illustrateds" might give a patient who was turning its pages in the surgeon's waiting-room. I was astonished to find that there were people so different from myself that this stroll through the town had actually been recommended to me by the manager as a diversion, and also that the torture chamber which a new place of residence is could appear to some people a "delightful abode," to quote the hotel prospectus, which might perhaps exaggerate but was none the less addressed to a whole army of clients to whose tastes it must appeal. True, it invoked, to make them come to the Grand Hotel, Balbec, not only the "exquisite fare" and the "magical view across the Casino gardens," but also the "ordinances of Her Majesty Queen Fashion, which no one may violate with impunity without being taken for a philistine, a charge that no well-bred man would willingly incur."

The need that I now felt for my grandmother was enhanced by my fear that I had shattered another of her illusions. She must be feeling discouraged, feeling that if I could not stand the fatigue of this journey there was no hope that any change of air could ever do me good. I decided to return to the hotel and to wait for her there; the manager himself came forward and pressed a button, whereupon a personage whose acquaintance I had not yet made, known as "lift" (who at the highest point in the building, where the skylight would be in a Norman church, was installed like a photographer behind his curtain or an organist in his loft) began to descend towards me with the agility of a domestic, industrious and captive squirrel. Then, gliding upwards again along a steel pillar, he bore me aloft in his wake towards the dome of this temple of Mammon. On each floor, on either side of a narrow communicating stair, a range of shadowy galleries opened out fanwise, along one of which came a chambermaid carrying a bolster. I applied to her face, which was blurred in the twilight, the mask of my most impassioned dreams, but read in her eyes as they turned towards me the horror of my own nonentity. Meanwhile, to dissipate, in the course of this interminable ascent, the mortal anguish which I felt in traversing in silence the mystery of this chiaroscuro so devoid of poetry, lighted by a single vertical line of little windows which were those of the solitary water-closet on each landing, I addressed a few words to the young organist, artificer of my journey and my partner in captivity, who continued to manipulate the registers of his instrument and to finger the stops. I apologised for taking up so much room, for giving him so much trouble, and asked whether I was not obstructing him in the practice of an art in regard to which, in order to flatter the virtuoso, more than displaying curiosity, I confessed my strong attachment. But he vouchsafed no answer, whether from astonishment at my words, preoccupation with his work, regard for etiquette, hardness of hearing, respect for holy ground, fear of danger, slowness of understanding, or the manager's orders.

There is perhaps nothing that gives us so strong an impression of the reality of the external world as the difference in the position, relative to ourselves, of even a quite unimportant person before we have met him and after. I was the same man who had taken, that afternoon, the little train from Balbec to the coast; I carried in my body the same consciousness. But on that consciousness, in the place where at six o'clock there had been, together with the impossibility of forming any idea of the manager, the Grand Hotel or its staff, a vague and timorous anticipation of the moment at which I should reach my destination, were to be found now the pustules excised from the face of the cosmopolitan manager (he was, in fact, a naturalised Monegasque, although—as he himself put it, for he was always using expressions which he thought distinguished without noticing that they were incorrect—"of Romanian originality"), his action in ringing for the lift, the lift-boy himself, a whole frieze of puppet-show characters issuing from that Pandora's box which was the Grand Hotel, undeniable, irremovable, and, like everything that is realised, jejune. But at least this change which I had done nothing to bring about proved to me that something had happened which was external to myself—however devoid of interest that thing might be in itself—and I was like a traveller who, having had the sun in his face when he started, concludes that he has been for so many hours on the road when he finds the sun behind him. I was half dead with exhaustion, I was burning with fever; I would gladly have gone to bed, but I had no night-things. I should have liked at least to lie down for a little while on the bed, but to what purpose, since I should not have been able to procure any rest for that mass of sensations which is for each of us his conscious if not his physical body, and since the unfamiliar objects which encircled that body, forcing it to place its perceptions on the permanent footing of a vigilant defensive, would have kept my sight, my hearing, all my senses in a position as cramped and uncomfortable (even if I had stretched out my legs) as that of Cardinal La Balue in the cage in which he could neither stand nor sit? It is our noticing them that puts things in a room, our growing used to them that takes them away again and clears a space for us. Space there was none for me in my bedroom (mine in name only) at Balbec; it was full of things which did not know me, which flung back at me the distrustful glance I cast at them, and, without taking any heed of my existence, showed that I was interrupting the humdrum course of theirs. The clock—whereas at home I heard mine tick only a few seconds in a week, when I was coming out of some profound meditation—continued without a moment's interruption to utter, in an unknown tongue, a series of observations which must have been most uncomplimentary to myself, for the violet curtains listened to them without replying, but in an attitude such as people adopt who shrug their shoulders to indicate that the sight of a third person irritates them. They gave to this room with its lofty ceiling a quasi-historical character which might have made it a suitable place for the assassination of the Duc de Guise, and afterwards for parties of tourists personally conducted by one of Thomas Cook's guides, but for me to sleep in—no. I was tormented by the presence of some little bookcases with glass fronts which ran along the walls, but especially by a large cheval-glass which stood across one corner and before the departure of which I felt there could be no possibility of rest for me there. I kept raising my eyes—which the things in my room in Paris disturbed no more than did my eyelids themselves, for they were merely extensions of my organs, an enlargement of myself—towards the high ceiling of this belvedere planted upon the summit of the hotel which my grandmother had chosen for me; and deep down in that region more intimate than that in which we see and hear, in that region where we experience the quality of smells, almost in the very heart of my inmost self, the scent of flowering grasses next launched its offensive against my last feeble line of trenches, an offensive against which I opposed, not without exhausting myself still further, the futile and unremitting riposte of an alarmed sniffling. Having no world, no room, no body now that was not menaced by the enemies thronging round me, penetrated to the very bones by fever, I was alone, and longed to die. Then my grandmother came in, and to the expansion of my constricted heart there opened at once an infinity of space.

She was wearing a loose cambric dressing-gown which she put on at home whenever any of us was ill (because she felt more comfortable in it, she used to say, for she always ascribed selfish motives to her actions), and which was, for tending us, for watching by our beds, her servant's smock, her nurse's uniform, her nun's habit. But whereas the attentions of servants, nurses and nuns, their kindness to us, the merits we find in them and the gratitude we owe them, increase the impression we have of being, in their eyes, someone else, of feeling that we are alone, keeping in our own hands the control over our thoughts, our will to live, I knew, when I was with my grandmother, that however great the misery that there was in me, it would be received by her with a pity still more vast, that everything that was mine, my cares, my wishes, would be buttressed, in my grandmother, by a desire to preserve and enhance my life that was altogether stronger than was my own; and my thoughts were continued and extended in her without undergoing the slightest deflection, since they passed from my mind into hers without any change of atmosphere or of personality. And—like a man who tries to fasten his tie in front of a glass and forgets that the end which he sees reflected is not on the side to which he raises his hand, or like a dog that chases along the ground the dancing shadow of an insect in the air—misled by her appearance in the body as we are apt to be in this world where we have no direct perception of people's souls, I threw myself into the arms of my grandmother and pressed my lips to her face as though I were thus gaining access to that immense heart which she opened to me. And when I felt my mouth glued to her cheeks, to her brow, I drew from them something so beneficial, so nourishing, that I remained as motionless, as solemn, as calmly gluttonous as a babe at the breast.

Afterwards I gazed inexhaustibly at her large face, outlined like a beautiful cloud, glowing and serene, behind which I could discern the radiance of her tender love. And everything that received, in however slight a degree, any share of her sensations, everything that could be said to belong in any way to her was at once so spiritualised, so sanctified that with outstretched hands I smoothed her beautiful hair, still hardly grey, with as much respect, precaution and gentleness as if I had actually been caressing her goodness. She found such pleasure in taking any trouble that saved me one, and in a moment of immobility and rest for my weary limbs something so exquisite, that when, having seen that she wished to help me undress and go to bed, I made as though to stop her and to undress myself, with an imploring gaze she arrested my hands as they fumbled with the top buttons of my jacket and my boots.

"Oh, do let me!" she begged. "It's such a joy for your Granny. And be sure you knock on the wall if you want anything in the night. My bed is just on the other side, and the partition is quite thin. Just give a knock now, as soon as you're in bed, so that we shall know where we are."

And, sure enough, that evening I gave three knocks—a signal which, a week later, when I was ill, I repeated every morning for several days, because my grandmother wanted me to have some milk early. Then, when I thought that I could hear her stirring—so that she should not be kept waiting but might, the moment she had brought me the milk, go to sleep again—I would venture three little taps, timidly, faintly, but for all that distinctly, for if I was afraid of disturbing her in case I had been mistaken and she was still asleep, neither did I wish her to lie awake listening for a summons which she had not at once caught and which I should not have the heart to repeat. And scarcely had I given my taps than I heard three others, in a different tone from mine, stamped with a calm authority, repeated twice over so that there should be no mistake, and saying to me plainly: "Don't get agitated; I've heard you; I shall be with you in a minute!" and shortly afterwards my grandmother would appear. I would explain to her that I had been afraid she would not hear me, or might think that it was someone in the room beyond who was tapping; at which she would smile: "Mistake my poor pet's knocking for anyone else's! Why, Granny could tell it a mile away! Do you suppose there's anyone else in the world who's such a silly-billy, with such febrile little knuckles, so afraid of waking me up and of not making me understand? Even if it just gave the tiniest scratch, Granny could tell her mouse's sound at once, especially such a poor miserable little mouse as mine is. I could hear it just now, trying to make up its mind, and rustling the bedclothes, and going through all its tricks."

She would push open the shutters, and where a wing of the hotel jutted out at right angles to my window, the sun would already have settled on the roof, like a slater who is up betimes, and starts early and works quietly so as not to rouse the sleeping town whose stillness makes him seem more agile. She would tell me what time it was, what sort of day it would be, that it was not worth while my getting up and coming to the window, that there was a mist over the sea, whether the baker's shop had opened yet, what the vehicle was that I could hear passing—that whole trifling curtain-raiser, that insignificant *introit* of a new day which no one attends, a little scrap of life which was only for our two selves, but which I should have no hesitation in evoking, later on, to Françoise or even to strangers, speaking of the fog "which you could have cut with a knife" at six o'clock that morning, with the ostentation of one who was boasting not of a piece of knowledge that he had acquired but of a mark of affection shown to himself alone; sweet morning moment which opened like a symphony with the rhythmical dialogue of my three taps, to which the thin wall of my bedroom, steeped in love and joy, grown melodious, incorporeal, singing like the angelic choir, responded with three other taps, eagerly awaited, repeated once and again, in which it contrived to waft to me the soul of my grandmother, whole and perfect, and the promise of her coming, with the swiftness of an annunciation and a musical fidelity. But on this first night after our arrival, when my grandmother had left me, I began again to suffer as I had suffered the day before, in Paris, at the moment of leaving home. Perhaps this fear that I had—and that is shared by so many others—of sleeping in a strange room, perhaps this fear is only the most humble, obscure, organic, almost unconscious form of that great and desperate resistance put up by the things that constitute the better part of our present life against our mentally acknowledging the possibility of a future in which they are to have no part; a resistance which was at the root of the horror that I had so often been made to feel by the thought that my parents would die some day, that the stern necessity of life might oblige me to live far from Gilberte, or simply to settle permanently in a place where I should never see any of my old friends; a resistance which was also at the root of the difficulty that I found in imagining my own death, or a survival such as Bergotte used to promise to mankind in his books, a survival in which I should not be allowed to take with me my memories, my frailties, my character, which did not easily resign themselves to the idea of ceasing to be, and desired for me neither extinction nor an eternity in which they would have no part.

When Swann had said to me in Paris one day when I felt particularly unwell: "You ought to go off to one of those glorious islands in the Pacific; you'd never come back again if you did," I should have liked to answer: "But then I shall never see your daughter again, I shall be living among people and things she has never seen." And yet my reason, my better judgment whispered: "What difference can that make, since you won't be distressed by it? When M. Swann tells you that you won't come back he means by that that you won't want to come back, and if you don't want to that is because you'll be happier out there." For my reason was aware that Habit—Habit which was even now setting to work to make me like this unfamiliar lodging, to change the position of the mirror, the shade of the curtains, to stop the clock—undertakes as well to make dear to us the companions whom at first we disliked, to give another appearance to their faces, to make the sound of their voices attractive, to modify the inclinations of their hearts. It is true that these new friendships for places and people are based upon forgetfulness of the old; my reason precisely thought that I could envisage without dread the prospect of a life in which I should be for ever separated from people all memory of whom I should lose, and it was by way of consolation that it offered my heart a promise of oblivion which in fact succeeded only in sharpening the edge of its despair. Not that the heart, too, is not bound in time, when separation is complete, to feel the analgesic effect of habit; but until then it will continue to suffer. And our dread of a future in which we must forgo the sight of faces and the sound of voices which we love and from which today we derive our dearest joy, this dread, far from being dissipated, is intensified, if to the pain of such a privation we feel that there will be added what seems to us now in anticipation more painful still: not to feel it as a pain at all—to remain indifferent; for then our old self would have changed, it would then be not merely the charm of our family, our mistress, our friends that had ceased to environ us, but our affection for them would have been so completely eradicated from our hearts, of which today it is so conspicuous an element, that we should be able to enjoy a life apart from them, the very thought of which today makes us recoil in horror; so that it would be in a real sense the death of the self, a death followed, it is true, by resurrection, but in a different self, to the love of which the elements of the old self that are condemned to die cannot bring themselves to aspire. It is they—even the meanest of them, such as our obscure attachments to the dimensions, to the atmosphere of a bedroom—that take fright and refuse, in acts of rebellion which we must recognise to be a secret, partial, tangible and true aspect of our resistance to death, of the long, desperate, daily resistance to the fragmentary and continuous death that insinuates itself throughout the whole course of our life, detaching from us at each moment a shred of ourself, dead matter on which new cells will multiply and grow. And for a neurotic nature such as mine—one, that is to say, in which the intermediaries, the nerves, perform their functions badly, fail to arrest on its way to the consciousness, allow indeed to reach it, distinct, exhausting, innumerable and distressing, the plaints of the most humble elements of the self which are about to disappear—the anxiety and alarm which I felt as I lay beneath that strange and too lofty ceiling were but the protest of an affection that survived in me for a ceiling that was familiar and low. Doubtless this affection too would disappear, another having taken its place (when death, and then another life, had, in the guise of Habit, performed their double task); but until its annihilation, every night it would suffer afresh, and on this first night especially, confronted with an irreversible future in which there would no longer be any place for it, it rose in revolt, it tortured me with the sound of its lamentations whenever my straining eyes, powerless to turn from what was wounding them, endeavoured to fasten themselves upon that inaccessible ceiling.

But next morning!—after a servant had come to call me and to bring me hot water, and while I was washing and dressing myself and trying in vain to find the things that I needed in my trunk, from which I extracted, pell-mell, only a lot of things that were of no use whatever, what a joy it was to me, thinking already of the pleasure of lunch and a walk along the shore, to see in the window, and in all the glass fronts of the bookcases, as in the portholes of a ship's cabin, the open sea, naked, unshadowed, and yet with half of its expanse in shadow, bounded by a thin, fluctuating line, and to follow with my eyes the waves that leapt up one behind another like jumpers on a trampoline. Every other moment, holding in my hand the stiff starched towel with the name of the hotel printed upon it, with which I was making futile efforts to dry myself, I returned to the window to have another look at that vast, dazzling, mountainous amphitheatre, and at the snowy crests of its emerald waves, here and there polished and translucent, which with a placid violence and a leonine frown, to which the sun added a faceless smile, allowed their crumbling slopes to topple down at last. It was at this window that I was later to take up my position every morning, as at the window of a stage-coach in which one has slept, to see whether, during the night, a longed-for mountain range has come nearer or receded—only here it was those hills of the sea which, before they come dancing back towards us, are apt to withdraw so far that often it was only at the end of a long, sandy plain that I would distinguish, far off, their first undulations in a transparent, vaporous, bluish distance, like the glaciers that one sees in the backgrounds of the Tuscan Primitives. On other mornings it was quite close at hand that the sun laughed upon those waters of a green as tender as that preserved in Alpine pastures (among mountains on which the sun displays himself here and there like a giant who may at any moment come leaping gaily down their craggy sides) less by the moisture of the soil than by the liquid mobility of the light. Moreover, in that breach which the shore and the waves open up in the midst of the rest of the world for the passage or the accumulation of light, it is above all the light, according to the direction from which it comes and along which our eyes follow it, it is the light that displaces and situates the undulations of the sea. Diversity of lighting modifies no less the orientation of a place, erects no less before our eyes new goals which it inspires in us the yearning to attain, than would a distance in space actually traversed in the course of a long journey. When, in the morning, the sun came from behind the hotel, disclosing to me the sands bathed in light as far as the first bastions of the sea, it seemed to be showing me another side of the picture, and to be inviting me to pursue, along the winding path of its rays, a motionless but varied journey amid all the fairest scenes of the diversified landscape of the hours. And on this first morning, it pointed out to me far off, with a jovial finger, those blue peaks of the sea which bear no name on any map, until, dizzy with its sublime excursion over the thundering and chaotic surface of their crests and avalanches, it came to take shelter from the wind in my bedroom, lolling across the unmade bed and scattering its riches over the splashed surface of the basin-stand and into my open trunk, where, by its very splendour and misplaced luxury, it added still further to the general impression of disorder. Alas for that sea-wind: an hour later, in the big dining-room—while we were having lunch, and from the leathern gourd of a lemon were sprinkling a few golden drops on to a pair of soles which presently left on our plates the plumes of their picked skeletons, curled like stiff feathers and resonant as citherns—it seemed to my grand-mother a cruel deprivation not to be able to feel its life-giving breath on her cheek, on account of the glass partition, transparent but closed, which, like the front of a glass case in a museum, separated us from the beach while allowing us to look out upon its whole expanse, and into which the sky fitted so completely that its azure had the effect of being the colour of the windows and its white clouds so many flaws in the glass. Imagining that I was "sitting on the mole" or at rest in the "boudoir" of which Baudelaire speaks, I wondered whether his "sun's rays upon the sea" were not—a very different thing from the evening ray, simple and superficial as a tremulous golden shaft—just what at that moment was scorching the sea topaz-yellow, fermenting it, turning it pale and milky like beer, frothy like milk, while now and then there hovered over it great blue shadows which, for his own amusement, some god seemed to be shifting to and fro by moving a mirror in the sky. Unfortunately, it was not only in its outlook that this dining-room at Balbec—bare-walled, filled with a sunlight green as the water in a pond, while a few feet away from it the high tide and broad daylight erected as though before the gates of the heavenly city an indestructible and mobile rampart of emerald and gold—differed from our dining-room at Combray which gave on to the houses across the street. At Combray, since we were known to everyone, I took heed of no one. In seaside life one does not know one's neighbours. I was not yet old enough, and was still too sensitive to have outgrown the desire to find favour in the sight of other people and to possess their hearts. Nor had I acquired the more noble indifference which a man of the world would have felt towards the people who were eating in the dining-room or the boys and girls who strolled past the window, with whom I was pained by the thought that I should never be allowed to go on expeditions, though not so pained as if my grandmother, contemptuous of social formalities and concerned only with my health, had gone to them with the request, humiliating for me, that they should consent to allow me to accompany them. Whether they were returning to some villa beyond my ken, or had emerged from one, racquet in hand, on their way to a tennis court, or were riding horses whose hooves trampled my heart, I gazed at them with a passionate curiosity, in that blinding light of the beach by which social distinctions are altered, I followed all their movements through the transparency of that great bay of glass which allowed so much light to flood the room. But it intercepted the wind, and this was a defect in the eyes of my grandmother, who, unable to endure the thought that I was losing the benefit of an hour in the open air, surreptitiously opened a pane and at once sent flying, together with the menus, the newspapers, veils and hats of all the people at the other tables, while she herself, fortified by the celestial draught, remained calm and smiling like Saint Blandina amid the torrent of invective which, increasing my sense of isolation and misery, those contemptuous, dishevelled, furious visitors combined to pour on us.

To a certain extent—and this, at Balbec, gave to the population, as a rule monotonously rich and cosmopolitan, of that sort of "grand" hotel a quite distinctive local character—they were composed of eminent persons from the departmental capitals of that region of France, a senior judge from Caen, a president of the Cherbourg bar, a notary public from Le Mans, who annually, when the holidays came round, starting from the various points over which, throughout the working year, they were scattered like snipers on a battlefield or draughtsmen upon a board, concentrated their forces in this hotel. They always reserved the same rooms, and with their wives, who had pretensions to aristocracy, formed a little group which was joined by a leading barrister and a leading doctor from Paris, who on the day of their departure would say to the others: "Oh, yes, of course; you don't go by our train. You're privileged, you'll be home in time for lunch."

"Privileged, you say? You who live in the capital, in

Paris, while I have to live in a wretched county town of a hundred thousand souls (it's true we managed to muster a hundred and two thousand at the last census, but what is that compared to your two and a half millions?), going back, too, to asphalt streets and all the glamour of Paris life."

They said this with a rustic burring of their "r"s, without acrimony, for they were leading lights each in his own province, who could like others have gone to Paris had they chosen—the senior judge from Caen had several times been offered a seat on the Court of Appeal—but had preferred to stay where they were, from love of their native towns, or of obscurity, or of fame, or because they were reactionaries, and enjoyed being on friendly terms with the country houses of the neighbourhood. Besides, several of them were not going back at once to their county towns.

For—inasmuch as the Bay of Balbec was a little world apart in the midst of the great, a basketful of the seasons in which good days and bad, and the successive months, were clustered in a ring, so that not only on days when one could make out Rivebelle, which was a sign of storm, could one see the sunlight on the houses there while Balbec was plunged in darkness, but later on, when the cold weather had reached Balbec, one could be certain of finding on that opposite shore two or three supplementary months of warmth—those of the regular visitors to the Grand Hotel whose holidays began late or lasted long gave orders, when the rains and the mists came and autumn was in the air, for their boxes to be packed and loaded on to a boat, and set sail across the bay to find the summer again at Rivebelle or Costedor. This little group in the Balbec hotel looked at each new arrival with suspicion, and, while affecting to take not the least interest in him, hastened, all of them, to interrogate their friend the head waiter about him. For it was the same head waiter—Aimé—who returned every year for the season, and kept their tables for them; and their lady-wives, having heard that his wife was expecting a baby, would sit after meals each working on a part of the layette, while weighing up through their lorgnettes my grandmother and myself because we were eating hard-boiled eggs in salad, which was considered common and was not done in the best society of Alençon. They affected an attitude of contemptuous irony with regard to a Frenchman who was called "His Majesty" and who had indeed proclaimed himself king of a small island in the South Seas peopled only by a few savages. He was staying in the hotel with his pretty mistress, whom, as she crossed the beach to bathe, the little boys would greet with "Long live the Queen!" because she would reward them with a shower of small silver. The judge and the president went so far as to pretend not to see her, and if any of their friends happened to look at her, felt bound to warn him that she was only a little shop-girl.

"But I was told that at Ostend they used the royal bathing-hut."

"Well, and why not? It's on hire for twenty francs. You can take it yourself, if you care for that sort of thing. Anyhow, I know for a fact that the fellow asked for an audience with the King, who sent back word that he wasn't interested in pantomime princes."

"Really, that's interesting! What queer people there are in the world, to be sure!"

And no doubt all this was true; but it was also from resentment of the thought that, to many of their fellow-visitors, they were themselves simply solid middle-class citizens who did not know this king and queen who were so prodigal with their small change, that the notary, the judge, the president, when what they were pleased to call the "Carnival" went by, felt so much annoyance and expressed aloud an indignation that was quite understood by their friend the head waiter who, obliged to show proper civility to these generous if not authentic sovereigns, would nevertheless, as he took their orders, glance across the room at his old patrons and give them a meaningful wink. Perhaps there was also something of the same resentment at being erroneously supposed to be less "smart" and unable to explain that they were more, at the bottom of the "Fine specimen!" with which they referred to a young toff, the consumptive and dissipated son of an industrial magnate, who appeared every day in a new suit of clothes with an orchid in his buttonhole, drank champagne at luncheon, and then went off to the Casino, pale, impassive, a smile of complete indifference on his lips, to throw away at the baccarat table enormous sums "which he could ill afford to lose," as the notary said with a knowing air to the senior judge, whose wife had it "on good authority" that this "decadent" young man was bringing his parents' grey hair in sorrow to the grave.

Furthermore, the president and his friends were inexhaustibly sarcastic on the subject of a wealthy old lady of title, because she never moved anywhere without taking her whole household with her. Whenever the wives of the notary and the judge saw her in the dining-room at meal-times, they put up their lorgnettes and gave her an insolent scrutiny, as meticulous and distrustful as if she had been some dish with a pretentious name but a suspicious appearance which, after the adverse result of a systematic study, is sent away with a lofty wave of the hand and a grimace of disgust.

No doubt by this behaviour they meant only to show that, if there were things in the world which they themselves lacked—in this instance, certain prerogatives which the old lady enjoyed, and the privilege of her acquaintance—it was not because they could not, but because they did not choose to acquire them. But they had ended up by convincing themselves that this really was what they felt; and the suppression of all desire for, of all curiosity about, ways of life which are unfamiliar, of all hope of endearing oneself to new people, for which, in these women, had been substituted a feigned contempt, a spurious jubilation, had the disagreeable effect of obliging them to label their discontent satisfaction and to lie everlastingly to themselves, two reasons why they were unhappy. But everyone else in the hotel was no doubt behaving in a similar fashion, though under different forms, and sacrificing, if not to self-esteem, at any rate to certain inculcated principles or mental habits, the disturbing thrill of being involved in an unfamiliar way of life. Of course the microcosm in which the old lady isolated herself was not poisoned with virulent rancour, as was the group in which the wives of the notary and the judge sat sneering with rage. It was indeed embalmed with a delicate and old-world fragrance which, however, was no less artificial. For at heart the old lady would probably have discovered, in attracting, in attaching to herself (and, in doing so, renewing herself) the mysterious sympathy of new people, a charm which is altogether lacking from the pleasure that is to be derived from mixing only with the people of one's own world, and reminding oneself that, this being the best of all possible worlds, the ill-informed contempt of others may be disregarded. Perhaps she felt that if she arrived incognito at the Grand Hotel, Balbec, she would, in her black woollen dress and old-fashioned bonnet, bring a smile to the lips of some old reprobate, who from the depths of his rocking chair would glance up and murmur, "What a scarecrow!" or, still worse, to those of some worthy man who had, like the judge, kept between his pepper-and-salt whiskers a fresh complexion and a pair of sparkling eyes such as she liked to see, and who would at once bring the magnifying lens of the conjugal glasses to bear upon so quaint a phenomenon; and perhaps it was in unconscious apprehension of those first few minutes which one knows will be brief but which are none the less dreaded—like one's first header into the sea—that this lady sent a servant down in advance to inform the hotel of the personality and habits of his mistress, and, cutting short the manager's greetings with an abruptness in which there was more shyness than pride, made straight for her room, where her own curtains, replacing those that draped the hotel windows, her own screens and photographs, set up so effectively between her and the outside world, to which otherwise she would have had to adapt herself, the barrier of her private life and habits, that it was her home (in the cocoon of which she had remained) that travelled rather than herself.

Thenceforward, having placed, between herself on the one hand and the hotel staff and the tradesmen on the other, her own servants who bore instead of her the shock of contact with all this strange humanity and kept up the familiar atmosphere around their mistress, having set her prejudices between herself and the other visitors, indifferent whether or not she gave offence to people whom her friends would not have had in their houses, it was in her own world that she continued to live, by correspondence with her friends, by memories, by her intimate awareness of her own position, the quality of her manners, the adroitness of her courtesy. And every day, when she came downstairs to go for a drive in her own carriage, the lady's-maid who came after her carrying her wraps, and the footman who preceded her, seemed like sentries who, at the gate of an embassy, flying the flag of the country to which she belonged, assured to her upon foreign soil the privilege of extra-territoriality. She did not leave her room until the middle of the afternoon on the day after our arrival, so that we did not see her in the dining-room, into which the manager, since we were newcomers, conducted us at the lunch hour, taking us under his wing, as a corporal takes a squad of recruits to the master-tailor to have them fitted; we did however see a moment later a country squire and his daughter, of an obscure but very ancient Breton family, M. and Mlle de Stermaria, whose table had been allotted to us in the belief that they had gone out and would not be back until the evening. Having come to Balbec only to see various owners of manors whom they knew in that neighbourhood, they spent in the hotel dining-room, what with the invitations they accepted and the visits they paid, only such time as was strictly unavoidable. It was their haughtiness that preserved them intact from all human sympathy, from arousing the least interest in the strangers seated round about them, among whom M. de Stermaria kept up the glacial, preoccupied, distant, stiff, touchy and ill-intentioned air that we assume in a railway refreshment-room in the midst of fellow-passengers whom we have never seen before and will never see again, and with whom we can conceive of no other relations than to defend from their onslaught our cold chicken and our corner seat in the train. No sooner had we begun our lunch than we were asked to leave the table on the instructions of M. de Stermaria who had just arrived and, without the faintest attempt at an apology to us, requested the head waiter in our hearing to see that such a mistake did not occur again, for it was repugnant to him that "people whom he did not know" should have taken his table.

And certainly the feeling which impelled a young actress (better known in fact for her smart clothes, her wit, her collection of German porcelain, than for the occasional parts that she had played at the Odéon), her lover, an immensely rich young man for whose sake she had acquired her culture, and two sprigs of the aristocracy at that time much in the public eye, to form an exclusive group, to travel only together, to come down to luncheon—when at Balbec—very late, after everyone else had finished, to spend the whole day in their sitting-room playing cards, reflected no sort of ill-will towards the rest of us but simply the requirements of the taste that they had formed for a certain type of witty conversation, for certain refinements of good living, which made them find pleasure in spending their time, in taking their meals, only by themselves, and would have rendered intolerable a life in common with people who had not been initiated. Even at a dinner-table or a card table, each of them had to be certain that in the diner or partner who sat opposite to him there were, latent and in abeyance, a certain brand of knowledge which would enable him to identify the rubbish which so many houses in Paris boast of as genuine mediaeval or Renaissance "pieces" and, whatever the subject of discussion, criteria common to them all wherewith to distinguish the good from the bad. No doubt by now, at such moments, it was merely by some rare and amusing interjection flung into the general silence of meal or game, or by the new and charming frock which the young actress had put on for lunch or for poker, that the special kind of existence in which these four friends desired everywhere to remain plunged was made apparent. But by engulfing them thus in a system of habits which they knew by heart it sufficed to protect them from the mystery of the life that was going on all round them. All the long afternoon, the sea was suspended there before their eyes only as a canvas of attractive colouring might hang on the wall of a wealthy bachelor's flat, and it was only in the intervals between hands that one of the players, finding nothing better to do, raised his eyes to it to seek some indication of the weather or the time, and to remind the others that tea was ready. And at night they did not dine in the hotel, where, hidden springs of electricity flooding the great dining-room with light, it became as it were an immense and wonderful aquarium against whose glass wall the working population of Balbec, the fishermen and also the tradesmen's families, clustering invisibly in the outer darkness, pressed their faces to watch the luxurious life of its occupants gently floating upon the golden eddies within, a thing as extraordinary to the poor as the life of strange fishes or molluscs (an important social question, this: whether the glass wall will always protect the banquets of these weird and wonderful creatures, or whether the obscure folk who watch them hungrily out of the night will not break in some day to gather them from their aquarium and devour them). Meanwhile, perhaps, amid the dumbfounded stationary crowd out there in the dark, there may have been some writer, some student of human ichthyology, who, as he watched the jaws of old feminine monstrosities close over a mouthful of submerged food, was amusing himself by classifying them by race, by innate characteristics, as well as by those acquired characteristics which bring it about that an old Serbian lady whose buccal appendage is that of a great sea-fish, because from her earliest years she has moved in the fresh waters of the Faubourg Saint-Germain, eats her salad for all the world like a La Rochefoucauld.

At that hour the three young men in dinner-jackets could be observed waiting for the young woman, who was as usual late but presently, wearing a dress that was almost always different and one of a series of scarves chosen to gratify some special taste in her lover, after having rung for the lift from her landing, would emerge from it like a doll coming out of its box. And then all four, finding that the international phenomenon of the "de luxe" hotel, having taken root at Balbec, had blossomed there in material luxury rather than in food that was fit to eat, climbed into a carriage and went off to dine a mile away in a little restaurant of repute where they held endless discussions with the cook about the composition of the menu and the cooking of its various dishes. During their drive, the road bordered with apple-trees that led out of

Balbec was no more to them than the distance that must be traversed—barely distinguishable in the darkness from that which separated their homes in Paris from the Café Anglais or the Tour d'Argent—before they arrived at the fashionable little restaurant where, while the rich young man's friends envied him because he had such a smartly dressed mistress, the latter's scarves hung before the little company a sort of fragrant, flowing veil, but one that kept it apart from the outer world.

Alas for my peace of mind, I had none of the detachment that all these people showed. To many of them I gave constant thought; I should have liked not to pass unobserved by a man with a receding forehead and eyes that dodged between the blinkers of his prejudices and his upbringing, the grandee of the district, who was none other than the brother-in-law of Legrandin. He came every now and then to see somebody at Balbec, and on Sundays, by reason of the weekly garden-party that his wife and he gave, robbed the hotel of a large number of its occupants, because one or two of them were invited to these entertainments and the others, so as not to appear not to have been invited, chose that day for an expedition to some distant spot. He had had, as it happened, an exceedingly bad reception at the hotel on the first day of the season, when the staff, freshly imported from the Riviera, did not yet know who or what he was. Not only was he not wearing white flannels, but, with old-fashioned French courtesy and in his ignorance of the ways of grand hotels, on coming into the hall in which there were ladies sitting, he had taken off his hat at the door, with the result that the manager had not so much as raised a finger to his own in acknowledgment, concluding that this must be someone of the most humble extraction, what he called "sprung from the ordinary." The notary's wife alone had felt attracted to the stranger, who exhaled all the starched vulgarity of the really respectable, and she had declared, with the unerring discernment and the indisputable authority of a person for whom the highest society of Le Mans held no secrets, that one could see at a glance that one was in the presence of a gentleman of great distinction, of perfect breeding, a striking contrast to the sort of people one usually saw at Balbec, whom she condemned as impossible to know so long as she did not know them. This favourable judgment which she had pronounced on Legrandin's brother-in-law was based perhaps on the lacklustre appearance of a man about whom there was nothing to intimidate anyone; perhaps also she had recognised in this gentleman farmer with the look of a sacristan the Masonic signs of her own clericalism.

Even though I knew that the young men who went past the hotel every day on horseback were the sons of the shady proprietor of a fancy goods shop whom my father would never have dreamed of knowing, the glamour of "seaside life" exalted them in my eyes to equestrian statues of demi-gods, and the best thing that I could hope for was that they would never allow their proud gaze to fall upon the wretched boy who was myself, who left the hotel dining-room only to sit upon the sands. I should have been glad to arouse some response even from the adventurer who had been king of a desert island in the South Seas, even from the young consumptive, of whom I liked to think that he concealed beneath his insolent exterior a shy and tender heart, which might perhaps have lavished on me, and on me alone, the treasures of its affection. Besides (contrary to what is usually said about travelling acquaintances) since being seen in certain company can invest us, in a watering-place to which we shall return another year, with a coefficient that has no equivalent in real social life, there is nothing that, far from keeping resolutely at a distance, we cultivate with such assiduity after our return to Paris as the friendships that we have formed by the sea. I was concerned about the impression I might make on all these temporary or local celebrities whom my tendency to put myself in the place of other people and to re-create their state of mind made me place not in their true rank, that which they would have occupied in Paris for instance and which would have been quite low, but in that which they must imagine to be theirs and which indeed was theirs at Balbec, where the want of a common denominator gave them a sort of relative superiority and unwonted interest. Alas, none of these people's contempt was so painful to me as that of M. de Stermaria.

For I had noticed his daughter the moment she came into the room, her pretty face, her pallid, almost bluish complexion, the distinctiveness in the carriage of her tall figure, in her gait, which suggested to me, with reason, her heredity, her aristocratic upbringing, all the more vividly because I knew her name—like those expressive themes invented by musicians of genius which paint in splendid colours the glow of fire, the rush of water, the peace of fields and woods, to audiences who, having glanced through the programme in advance, have their imaginations trained in the right direction. "Pedigree," by adding to Mlle de Stermaria's charms the idea of their origin, made them more intelligible, more complete. It made them more desirable also, advertising their inaccessibility as a high price enhances the value of a thing that has already taken our fancy. And its stock of heredity gave to her complexion, in which so many selected juices had been blended, the savour of an exotic fruit or of a famous vintage.

Now, chance had suddenly put into our hands, my grandmother's and mine, the means of acquiring instantaneous prestige in the eyes of all the other occupants of the hotel. For on that first afternoon, at the moment when the old lady came downstairs from her room, producing, thanks to the footman who preceded her and the maid who came running after her with a book and a rug that she had forgotten, a marked effect upon all who beheld her and arousing in each of them a curiosity from which it was evident that none was so little immune as M. de Stermaria, the manager leaned across to my grandmother and out of kindness (as one might point out the Shah or Queen Ranavalo to an obscure onlooker who could obviously have no sort of connexion with such mighty potentates, but might all the same be interested to know that he had been standing within a few feet of one) whispered in her ear, "The Marquise de Villeparisis!" while at the same moment the old lady, catching sight of my grandmother, could not repress a start of pleased surprise.

It may be imagined that the sudden appearance, in the guise of a little old woman, of the most powerful of fairies would not have given me more pleasure, destitute as I was of any means of access to Mlle de Stermaria, in a strange place where I knew no one: no one, that is to say, for any practical purpose. Aesthetically, the number of human types is so restricted that we must constantly, wherever we may be, have the pleasure of seeing people we know, even without looking for them in the works of the old masters, like Swann. Thus it happened that in the first few days of our visit to Balbec I had succeeded in encountering Legrandin, Swann's hall porter, and Mme Swann herself, transformed respectively into a waiter, a foreign visitor whom I never saw again, and a bathing superintendent. And a sort of magnetisation attracts and retains so inseparably, one beside another, certain characteristics of physiognomy and mentality, that when Nature thus introduces a person into a new body she does not mutilate him unduly. Legrandin turned waiter kept intact his stature, the outline of his nose, part of his chin; Mme Swann, in the masculine gender and the calling of a bathing superintendent, had been accompanied not only by her familiar features but even by certain mannerisms of speech. Only she could be of little if any more use to me, standing upon the beach there in the red sash of her office, and hoisting at the first gust of wind the flag which forbade us to bathe (for these superintendents are prudent men, seldom knowing how to swim), than she would have been in that fresco of the *Life of Moses* in which Swann had long ago identified her in the person of Jethro's daughter. Whereas this Mme de Villeparisis was her real self; she had not been the victim of a magic spell which had robbed her of her power, but was capable, on the contrary, of putting at the disposal of mine a spell which would multiply it a hundredfold, and thanks to which, as though I had been swept through the air on the wings of a fabulous bird, I was about to cross in a few moments the infinitely wide social gulf which separated me—at least at Balbec—from Mlle de Stermaria.

Unfortunately, if there was one person who, more than anyone else, lived shut up in a world of her own, it was my grandmother. She would not even have despised me, she would simply not have understood what I meant, if she had known that I attached importance to the opinions, that I felt an interest in the persons, of people the very existence of whom she never noticed and of whom, when the time came to leave Balbec, she would not remember the names. I dared not confess to her that if these same people had seen her talking to Mme de Villeparisis, I should have been immensely gratified, because I felt that the Marquise enjoyed some prestige in the hotel and that her friendship would have given us status in the eyes of Mlle de Stermaria. Not that my grandmother's friend represented to me, in any sense of the word, a member of the aristocracy: I was too accustomed to her name, which had been familiar to my ears before my mind had begun to consider it, when as a child I had heard it uttered in conversation at home; while her title added to it only a touch of quaintness, as some uncommon Christian name would have done, or as in the names of streets, among which we can see nothing more noble in the Rue Lord Byron, in the plebeian and even squalid Rue Rochechouart, or in the Rue de Gramont than in the Rue Léonce-Reynaud or the Rue Hippolyte-Lebas. Mme de Villeparisis no more made me think of a person who belonged to a special social world than did her cousin MacMahon, whom I did not clearly distinguish from M. Carnot, likewise President of the Republic, or from Raspail, whose photograph Françoise had bought with that of Pius IX. It was one of my grandmother's principles that, when away from home, one should cease to have any social intercourse, that one did not go to the seaside to meet people, having plenty of time for that sort of thing in Paris, that they would make one waste in polite exchanges, in pointless conversation, the precious time which ought all to be spent in the open air, beside the waves; and finding it convenient to assume that this view was shared by everyone else, and that it authorised, between old friends whom chance brought face to face in the same hotel, the fiction of a mutual incognito, on hearing her friend's name from the manager she merely looked the other way and pretended not to see Mme de Villeparisis, who, realising that my grandmother did not want to be recognised, likewise gazed into space. She went past, and I was left in my isolation like a shipwrecked mariner who has seen a vessel apparently approaching, which has then vanished under the horizon.

She, too, had her meals in the dining-room, but at the other end of it. She knew none of the people who were staying in the hotel or who came there to call, not even M. de Cambremer; indeed, I noticed that he gave her no greeting one day when, with his wife, he had accepted an invitation to lunch with the president, who, intoxicated with the honour of having the nobleman at his table, avoided his habitual friends and confined himself to a distant twitch of the eyelid, so as to draw their attention to this historic event but so discreetly that his signal could not be interpreted as an invitation to join the party.

"Well, I hope you've done yourself proud, I hope you feel smart enough," the judge's wife said to him that evening.

"Smart? Why should I?" asked the president, concealing his rapture in an exaggerated astonishment. "Because of my guests, do you mean?" he went on, feeling that it was impossible to keep up the farce any longer. "But what is there smart about having a few friends to lunch? After all, they must feed somewhere!"

"Of course it's smart! They were the *de* Cambremers, weren't they? I recognised them at once. She's a Marquise. And quite genuine, too. Not through the females."

"Oh, she's a very simple soul, she's charming, no standoffishness about her. I thought you were coming to join us. I was making signals to you . . . I would have introduced you!" he asserted, tempering with a hint of irony the vast generosity of the offer, like Ahasuerus when he says to Esther: "Of all my Kingdom must I give you half?"

"No, no, no, no! We lie hidden, like the modest violet."

"But you were quite wrong, I assure you," replied the president emboldened now that the danger point was passed. "They weren't going to eat you. I say, aren't we going to have our little game of bezique?"

"Why, of course! We didn't dare suggest it, now that you go about entertaining marquises."

"Oh, get along with you; there's nothing so very wonderful about them. Why, I'm dining there tomorrow. Would you care to go instead of me? I mean it. Honestly, I'd just as soon stay here."

"No, no! I should be removed from the bench as a reactionary," cried the senior judge, laughing till the tears came to his eyes at his own joke. "But you go to Féterne too, don't you?" he went on, turning to the notary.

"Oh, I go there on Sundays—in one door and out

the other. But they don't come and have lunch with me as they do with the president."

M. de Stermaria was not at Balbec that day, to the president's great regret. But he managed to say a word in season to the head waiter:

"Aimé, you can tell M. de Stermaria that he's not the only nobleman you've had in here. You saw the gentleman who was with me today at lunch? Eh? A small moustache, looked like a military man. Well, that was the Marquis de Cambremer!"

"Was it indeed? I'm not surprised to hear it."

"That will show him that he's not the only man who's got a title. That'll teach him! It's not a bad thing to take 'em down a peg or two, those noblemen. I say, Aimé, don't say anything to him unless you want to. I mean to say, it's no business of mine; besides, they know each other already."

And next day M. de Stermaria, who remembered that the president had once represented one of his friends, came up and introduced himself.

"Our friends in common, the de Cambremers, were anxious that we should meet, the days didn't fit—I don't know quite what went wrong," said the president who, like most liars, imagined that other people do not take the trouble to investigate an unimportant detail which, for all that, may be sufficient (if chance puts you in possession of the humble facts of the case, and they contradict it) to show the liar in his true colours and to inspire a lasting mistrust.

As usual, but more easily now that her father had left her to talk to the president I was gazing at Mlle de Stermaria. No less than the bold and always graceful distinctiveness of her attitudes, as when, leaning her elbows on the table, she raised her glass in both hands over her forearms, the dry flame of a glance at once extinguished, the ingrained, congenital hardness that one could sense, ill-concealed by her own personal inflexions, in the depths of her voice, and that had shocked my grandmother, a sort of atavistic ratchet to which she returned as soon as, in a glance or an intonation, she had finished expressing her own thoughts—all this brought the thoughts of the observer back to the long line of ancestors who had bequeathed to her that inadequacy of human sympathy, those gaps in her sensibility, a lack of fullness in the stuff of which she was made. But from a certain look which flooded for a moment the wells—instantly dry again—of her eyes, a look in which one sensed that almost humble docility which the predominance of a taste for sensual pleasures gives to the proudest of women, who will soon come to recognise but one form of personal magic, that which any man will enjoy in her eyes who can make her feel those pleasures, an actor or a mountebank for whom, perhaps, she will one day leave her husband, and from a certain pink tinge, warm and sensual, which flushed her pallid cheeks, like the colour that stained the hearts of the white water-lilies in the Vivonne, I thought I could discern that she might readily have consented to my coming to seek in her the savour of that life of poetry and romance which she led in Brittany, a life to which, whether from over-familiarity or from innate superiority, or from disgust at the penury or the avarice of her family, she seemed to attach no great value, but which, for all that, she held enclosed in her body. In the meagre stock of will-power that had been transmitted to her, and gave her expression a hint of weakness, she would not perhaps have found the strength to resist. And, crowned by a feather that was a trifle old-fashioned and pretentious, the grey felt hat which she invariably wore at meals made her all the more attractive to me, not because it was in harmony with her silver and rose complexion, but because, by making me suppose her to be poor, it brought her closer to me. Obliged by her father's presence to adopt a conventional attitude, but already bringing to the perception and classification of the people who passed before her eyes other principles than his, perhaps she saw in me not my humble rank, but the right sex and age. If one day M. de Stermaria had gone out leaving her behind, if, above all, Mme de Villeparisis, by coming to sit at our table, had given her an opinion of me which might have emboldened me to approach her, perhaps then we might have contrived to exchange a few words, to arrange a meeting, to form a closer tie. And for a whole month during which she would be left alone without her parents in her romantic Breton castle, we should perhaps have been able to wander by ourselves at evening, she and I together in the twilight through which the pink flowers of the bell heather would glow more softly above the darkening water, beneath oak trees beaten and stunted by the pounding of the waves. Together we should have roamed that island impregnated with so intense a charm for me because it had enclosed the everyday life of Mlle de Stermaria and was reflected in the memory of her eyes. For it seemed to me that I should truly have possessed her only there, when I had traversed those regions which enveloped her in so many memories—a veil which my desire longed to tear aside, one of those veils which nature interposes between woman and her pursuers (with the same intention as when, for all of us, she places the act of reproduction between ourselves and our keenest pleasure, and for insects, places before the nectar the pollen which they must carry away with them) in order that, tricked by the illusion of possessing her thus more completely, they may be forced to occupy first the scenes among which she lives and which, of more service to their imagination than sensual pleasure can be, yet would not without that pleasure have sufficed to attract them.

But I was obliged to take my eyes from Mlle de Stermaria, for already, considering no doubt that making the acquaintance of an important person was an odd, brief act which was sufficient in itself and, to bring out all the interest that was latent in it, required only a handshake and a penetrating stare, without either immediate conversation or any subsequent relations, her father had taken leave of the president and returned to sit down facing her, rubbing his hands like a man who has just made a valuable acquisition. As for the president, once the first emotion of this interview had subsided, he could be heard, as on other days, addressing the head waiter every other minute: "But I'm not a king, Aimé; go and attend to the king! I say, Chief, those little trout don't look at all bad, do they? We must ask Aimé to let us have some. Aimé, that little fish you have over there looks to me highly commendable: will you bring us some, please, Aimé, and don't be sparing with it."

He repeated the name "Aimé" all the time, with the result that when he had anyone to dinner the guest would remark "I can see you're quite at home in this place," and would feel himself obliged to keep on saying "Aimé" also, from that tendency, combining elements of timidity, vulgarity and silliness, which many people have, to believe that it is smart and witty to imitate slavishly the people in whose company they happen to be. The president repeated the name incessantly, but with a smile, for he wanted to exhibit at one and the same time his good relations with the head waiter and his own superior station. And the head waiter, whenever he caught the sound of his own name, smiled too, as though touched and at the same time proud, showing that he was conscious of the honour and could appreciate the joke.

Intimidating as I always found these meals, in that vast restaurant, generally full, of the Grand Hotel, they became even more so when there arrived for a few days the proprietor (or he may have been the general manager, appointed by a board of directors) not only of this palace but of seven or eight more besides, situated at all the four corners of France, in each of which, shuttling from one to the other, he would spend a week now and again. Then, just after dinner had begun, there appeared every evening at the entrance to the dining-room this small man with the white hair and a red nose, astonishingly neat and impassive, who was known, it appeared, as well in London as at Monte Carlo, as one of the leading hoteliers in Europe. Once when I had gone out for a moment at the beginning of dinner, as I came in again I passed close by him, and he bowed to me, no doubt to acknowledge that he was my host, but with a coldness in which I could not distinguish whether it was attributable to the reserve of a man who could never forget what he was, or to his contempt for a customer of so little importance. To those, on the other hand, whose importance was considerable, the general manager would bow with quite as much coldness but more deeply, lowering his eyelids with a sort of bashful respect, as though he had found himself confronted, at a funeral, with the father of the deceased or with the Blessed Sacrament. Except for these icy and infrequent salutations, he made not the slightest movement, as if to show that his glittering eyes, which appeared to be starting out of his head, saw everything, controlled everything, ensured for the "Dinner at the Grand Hotel" perfection in every detail as well as an overall harmony. He felt, evidently, that he was more than the producer, more than the conductor, nothing less than the generalissimo. Having decided that a contemplation raised to the maximum degree of intensity would suffice to assure him that everything was in readiness, that no mistake had been made which could lead to disaster, and enable him at last to assume his responsibilities, he abstained not merely from any gesture but even from moving his eyes, which, petrified by the intensity of their gaze, took in and directed operations as a whole. I felt that even the movements of my spoon did not escape him, and were he to vanish after the soup, for the whole of dinner, the inspection he had held would have taken away my appetite. His own was exceedingly good, as one could see at luncheon, which he took like an ordinary guest of the hotel at the same hour as everyone else in the public dining-room. His table had this peculiarity only, that by his side, while he was eating, the other manager, the resident one, remained standing all the time making conversation. For, being subordinate to the general manager, he was anxious to please a man of whom he lived in constant fear. My own fear of him diminished during these luncheons, for being then lost in the crowd of visitors he would exercise the discretion of a general sitting in a restaurant where there are also private soldiers, in not seeming to take any notice of them. Nevertheless when the porter, from the midst of his cluster of bell-hops, announced to me: "He leaves tomorrow morning for Dinard. Then he's going down to Biarritz, and after that to Cannes," I began to breathe more freely.

My life in the hotel was rendered not only gloomy because I had made no friends there but uncomfortable because Françoise had made many. It might be thought that they would have made things easier for us in various respects. Quite the contrary. The proletariat, if they succeeded only with great difficulty in being treated as people she knew by Françoise, and could not succeed at all unless they fulfilled certain exacting conditions of politeness towards her, were, on the other hand, once they had reached that point, the only people who mattered to her. Her time-honoured code taught her that she was in no way beholden to the friends of her employers, that she might, if she was busy, shut the door without ceremony in the face of a lady who had come to call on my grandmother. But towards her own acquaintance, that is to say the select handful of the lower orders whom she admitted to her fastidious friendship, her actions were regulated by the most subtle and most stringent of protocols. Thus Françoise, having made the acquaintance of the man in the coffee-shop and of a young lady's-maid who did dressmaking for a Belgian lady, no longer went upstairs immediately after lunch to get my grandmother's things ready, but came an hour later, because the coffee-man had wanted to make her a cup of coffee or a tisane in his shop, or the maid had invited her to go and watch her sew, and to refuse either of them would have been impossible, one of those things that were not done. Moreover, particular regard was due to the little sewing-maid, who was an orphan and had been brought up by strangers to whom she still went occasionally for a few days' holiday. Her situation aroused Françoise's pity, and also her benevolent contempt. She who had a family, a little house that had come to her from her parents, with a field in which her brother kept a few cows, could not regard so uprooted a creature as her equal. And since this girl hoped, on Assumption Day, to be allowed to pay her benefactors a visit, Françoise kept on repeating: "She does make me laugh! She says, 'I hope to be going home for the Assumption.' Home, says she! It isn't just that it's not her own place, it's people as took her in from nowhere, and the creature says 'home' just as if it really was her home. Poor thing! What a misery it must be, not to know what it is to have a home." Still, if Françoise had associated only with the ladies'-maids brought to the hotel by other visitors, who fed with her in the "service" quarters and, seeing her grand lace cap and her fine profile, took her perhaps for some lady of noble birth, whom reduced circumstances or a personal attachment had driven to serve as companion to my grandmother, if in a word Françoise had known only people who did not belong to the hotel, no great harm would have been done, since she could not have prevented them from being of some service to us, for the simple reason that in no circumstances, even without her knowledge, would it have been possible for them to be of service to us at all. But she had formed connexions also with one of the wine waiters, with a man in the kitchen, and with the head chamber-maid of our landing. And the result of this in our everyday life was that Françoise—who on the day of her arrival, when she still did not know anyone, would set all the bells jangling for the slightest thing, at hours when my grandmother and I would never have dared to ring, and if we offered some gentle admonition would answer: "Well, we're paying enough for it, aren't we?" as though it were she herself that would have to pay—now that she had made friends with a personage in the kitchen, which had appeared to us to augur well for our future comfort, were my grandmother or I to complain of cold feet, Françoise, even at an hour that was quite normal, dared not ring, assuring us that it would give offence because they would have to relight the boilers, or because it would interrupt the servants' dinner and they would be annoyed. And she ended with a formula that, in spite of the dubious way in which she pronounced it, was none the less clear and put us plainly in the wrong: "The fact is . . ." We did not insist, for fear of bringing upon ourselves another, far more serious: "It's a bit much . . . !" So that what it amounted to was that we could no longer have any hot water because Françoise had become a friend of the person who heated it.

In the end we too made a social connexion, in spite of but through my grandmother, for she and Mme de Villeparisis collided one morning in a doorway and were obliged to accost each other, not without having first exchanged gestures of surprise and hesitation, performed movements of withdrawal and uncertainty, and finally broken into protestations of joy and greeting, as in certain scenes in Molière where two actors who have been delivering long soliloquies each on his own account, a few feet apart, are supposed not yet to have seen each other, and then suddenly catching sight of each other, cannot believe their eyes, break off what they are saying, and then simultaneously find their tongues again (the chorus meanwhile having kept the dialogue going) and fall into each other's arms. Mme de Villeparisis tactfully made as if to leave my grandmother to herself after the first greetings, but my grandmother insisted on staying to talk to her until lunch-time, being anxious to discover how her friend managed to get her letters earlier than we got ours, and to get such nice grilled dishes (for Mme de Villeparisis, who took a keen interest in her food, had the poorest opinion of the hotel kitchen which served us with meals that my grandmother, still quoting Mme de Sévigné, described as "of a sumptuousness to make you die of hunger"). And the Marquise formed the habit of coming every day, while waiting to be served, to sit down for a moment at our table in the dining-room, insisting that we should not rise from our chairs or in any way put ourselves out. At the most we would occasionally linger, after finishing our lunch, to chat to her, at that sordid moment when the knives are left littering the tablecloth among crumpled napkins. For my own part, in order to preserve (so that I might be able to enjoy Balbec) the idea that I was on the uttermost promontory of the earth, I compelled myself to look further afield, to notice only the sea, to seek in it the effects described by Baudelaire and to let my gaze fall upon our table only on days when there was set on it some gigantic fish, some marine monster, which unlike the knives and forks was contemporary with the primitive epochs in which the Ocean first began to teem with life, at the time of the Cimmerians, a fish whose body with its numberless vertebrae, its blue and pink veins, had been constructed by nature, but according to an architectural plan, like a polychrome cathedral of the deep.

As a barber, seeing an officer whom he is accustomed to shave with special deference and care recognise a customer who has just entered the shop and stop for a moment to talk to him, rejoices in the thought that these are two men of the same social order, and cannot help smiling as he goes to fetch the bowl of soap, for he knows that in his establishment, to the vulgar routine of a mere barber's-shop are being added social, not to say aristocratic pleasures, so Aimé, seeing that Mme de Villeparisis had found in us old friends, went to fetch our finger-bowls with the proudly modest and knowingly discreet smile of a hostess who knows when to leave her guests to themselves. He suggested also a pleased and loving father who watches silently over the happy pair who have plighted their troth at his hospitable board. Besides, it was enough merely to utter the name of a person of title for Aimé to appear pleased, unlike Françoise, in whose presence you could not mention Count So-and-so without her face darkening and her speech becoming dry and curt, which meant that she cherished the aristocracy not less than Aimé but more. But then Françoise had that quality which in others she condemned as the worst possible fault: she was proud. She was not of that amenable and good-natured race to which Aimé belonged. They feel and they exhibit an intense delight when you tell them a piece of news which may be more or less sensational but is at any rate new, and not to be found in the papers. Françoise would refuse to appear surprised. You might have announced in her hearing that the Archduke Rudolf—not that she had the least suspicion of his having ever existed—was not, as was generally supposed, dead, but alive and kicking, and she would have answered only "Yes," as though she had known it all the time. It may, however, have been that if, even from our own lips, from us whom she so meekly called her masters and who had so nearly succeeded in taming her, she could not hear the name of a nobleman without having to restrain an impulse of anger, this was because the family from which she had sprung occupied in its own village a comfortable and independent position, unlikely to be disturbed in the consideration which it enjoyed save by those same nobles in whose households, meanwhile, from his boyhood, an Aimé would have been domiciled as a servant, if not actually brought up by their charity. Hence, for Françoise, Mme de Villeparisis had to make amends for being noble. But (in France, at any rate) that is precisely the talent, in fact the sole occupation of the aristocracy. Françoise, following the common tendency of servants, who pick up incessantly from the conversation of their masters with other people fragmentary observations from which they are apt to draw erroneous conclusions—as humans do with respect to the habits of animals—was constantly discovering that somebody had slighted us, a conclusion to which she was easily led not so much, perhaps, by her extravagant love for us as by the delight that she took in being disagreeable to us. But having once established, without possibility of error, the endless consideration and kindness shown to us, and shown to herself also, by Mme de Villeparisis, Françoise forgave her for being a marquise, and, as she had never ceased to admire her for being one, preferred her thenceforward to all our other friends. It must be added that no one else took the trouble to be so continually nice to us. Whenever my grandmother remarked on a book that Mme de Villeparisis was reading, or said she had been admiring the fruit which someone had just sent to our friend, within an hour the footman would come to our rooms with book or fruit. And the next time we saw her, in response to our thanks she would simply say, as though trying to find an excuse for her present in some special use to which it might be put: "It's nothing wonderful, but the newspapers come so late here; one must have something to read," or "It's always wiser to have fruit one can be quite certain of, at the seaside."

"But I don't believe I've ever seen you eating oysters," she said to us one day (increasing the sense of disgust which I felt at that moment, for the living flesh of oysters revolted me even more than the viscosity of the stranded jelly-fish defiled the Balbec beach for me). "They're quite delicious down here! Oh, let me tell my maid to fetch your letters when she goes for mine. What, your daughter writes to you *every day*? But what on earth can you find to say to each other?"

My grandmother was silent, but it may be assumed that her silence was due to disdain, for she used to repeat, when she wrote to Mamma, the words of Mme de Sévigné: "As soon as I have received a letter, I want another at once; I sigh for nothing else. There are few who are worthy to understand what I feel." And I was afraid that she might apply to Mme de Villeparisis the conclusion: "I seek out those who are of this chosen few, and I avoid the rest." She fell back upon praise of the fruit which Mme de Villeparisis had sent us the day before. And it had indeed been so fine that the manager, in spite of the jealousy aroused by our neglect of his official offerings, had said to me: "I am like you; I am sweeter for fruit than any other kind of dessert." My grandmother told her friend that she had enjoyed them all the more because the fruit which we got in the hotel was generally horrid. "I cannot," she went on, "say with Mme de Sévigné that if we should take a sudden fancy for bad fruit we should be obliged to order it from Paris." "Oh yes, of course, you read Mme de Sévigné. I've seen you with her letters ever since the day you came." (She forgot that she had never officially seen my grandmother in the hotel before meeting her in that doorway.) "Don't you find it rather exaggerated, her constant anxiety about her daughter? She refers to it too often to be really sincere. She's not very natural." My grandmother felt that any discussion would be futile, and so as not to be obliged to speak of the things she loved to a person incapable of understanding them, concealed the *Mémoires de Madame de Beausergent* by laying her bag upon them.

Were she to encounter Françoise at the moment (which Françoise called "the noon") when, wearing her fine cap and surrounded with every mark of respect, she was coming downstairs to "feed with the service," Mme Villeparisis would stop her to ask after us. And Françoise, when transmitting to us the Marquise's message: "She said to me, 'You'll be sure and bid them good day,' she said," would counterfeit the voice of Mme de Villeparisis, whose exact words she imagined herself to be quoting textually, whereas in fact she was distorting them no less than Plato distorts the words of Socrates or St John the words of Jesus. Françoise was naturally deeply touched by these attentions. Only she did not believe my grandmother, but supposed that she must be lying in the interests of class (the rich always supporting one another) when she assured us that Mme de Villeparisis had been lovely as a young woman. It was true that of this loveliness only the faintest trace remained, from which no one—unless he happened to be a great deal more of an artist than Françoise—would have been able to reconstitute her ruined beauty. For in order to understand how beautiful an elderly woman may once have been one must not only study but translate every line of her face.

"I must remember some time to ask her whether I'm not right, after all, in thinking that there's some connexion with the Guermantes," said my grandmother, to my great indignation. How could I be expected to believe in a common origin uniting two names which had entered my consciousness, one through the low and shameful gate of experience, the other by the golden gate of imagination?

We had several times, in the last few days, seen driving past us in a stately equipage, tall, red-haired, handsome, with a rather prominent nose, the Princesse de Luxembourg, who was staying in the neighbourhood for a few weeks. Her carriage had stopped outside the hotel, a footman had come in and spoken to the manager, had gone back to the carriage and had reappeared with the most amazing armful of fruit (which combined a variety of seasons in a single basket, like the bay itself) with a card: "La Princesse de Luxembourg," on which were scrawled a few words in pencil. For what princely traveller, sojourning here incognito, could they be intended, those plums, glaucous, luminous and spherical as was at that moment the circumfluent sea, those transparent grapes clustering on the shrivelled wood, like a fine day in autumn, those pears of a heavenly ultramarine? For it could not be on my grandmother's friend that the Princess had meant to pay a call. And yet on the following evening Mme de Villeparisis sent us the bunch of grapes, cool, liquid, golden, and plums and pears which we remembered too, though the plums had changed, like the sea at our dinner-hour, to a dull purple, and in the ultramarine of the pears there floated the shapes of a few pink clouds.

A few days later we met Mme de Villeparisis as we came away from the symphony concert that was given every morning on the beach. Convinced that the music that I heard there (the Prelude to *Lohengrin*, the Overture to *Tannhäuser* and suchlike) expressed the loftiest of truths, I tried to raise myself in so far as I could in order to reach and grasp them, I drew from myself, in order to understand them, and put back into them all that was best and most profound in my own nature at that time. But, as we came out of the concert, and, on our way back to the hotel, had stopped for a moment on the front, my grandmother and I, to exchange a few words with Mme de Villeparisis who told us that she had ordered some *croque-monsieurs* and a dish of creamed eggs for us at the hotel, I saw, in the distance, coming in our direction, the Princesse de Luxembourg, half leaning upon a parasol in such a way as to impart to her tall and wonderful form that slight inclination, to make it trace that arabesque, so dear to the women who had been beautiful under the Empire and knew how, with drooping shoulders, arched backs, concave hips and taut legs, to make their bodies float as softly as a silken scarf about the rigid armature of an invisible shaft which might be supposed to have transfixed it. She went out every morning for a stroll on the beach almost at the time when everyone else, after bathing, was coming home to lunch, and as hers was not until half past one she did not return to her villa until long after the hungry bathers had left the scorching beach a desert. Mme de Villeparisis introduced my grandmother and was about to introduce me, but had first to ask me my name, which she could not remember. She had perhaps never known it, or if she had must have forgotten years ago to whom my grandmother had married her daughter. The name appeared to make a sharp impression on Mme de Villeparisis. Meanwhile the Princesse de Luxembourg had offered us her hand and from time to time, while she chatted to the Marquise, turned to bestow a kindly glance on my grandmother and myself, with that embryonic kiss which we put into our smiles when they are addressed to a baby out with its "Nana." Indeed, in her anxiety not to appear to be enthroned in a higher sphere than ours, she had probably miscalculated the distance, for by an error in adjustment her eyes became infused with such benevolence that I foresaw the moment when she would put out her hand and stroke us like two lovable beasts who had poked our heads out at her through the bars of our cage in the Zoo. And immediately, as it happened, this idea of caged animals and the Bois de Boulogne received striking confirmation. It was the time of day when the beach is crowded by itinerant and clamorous vendors, hawking cakes and sweets and biscuits. Not knowing quite what to do to show her affection for us, the Princess hailed the next one to come by;

he had nothing left but a loaf of rye bread, of the kind one throws to the ducks. The Princess took it and said to me: "For your grandmother." And yet it was to me that she held it out, saying with a friendly smile, "You shall give it to her yourself," thinking that my pleasure would thus be more complete if there were no intermediary between myself and the animals. Other vendors came up, and she stuffed my pockets with everything that they had, tied up in packets, comfits, sponge-cakes, sugar-sticks. "You will eat some yourself," she told me, "and give some to your grandmother," and she had the vendors paid by the little negro page, dressed in red satin, who followed her everywhere and was a nine days' wonder on the beach. Then she said good-bye to Mme de Villeparisis and held out her hand to us with the intention of treating us in the same way as she treated her friend, as people whom she knew, and of bringing herself within our reach. But this time she must have reckoned our level as not quite so low in the scale of creation, for her equality with us was indicated by the Princess to my grandmother by that tender and maternal smile which one bestows upon a little boy when one says good-bye to him as though to a grown-up person. By a miraculous stride in evolution, my grandmother was no longer a duck or an antelope, but had already become what Mme Swann would have called a "*baby*." Finally, having taken leave of us all, the Princess resumed her stroll along the sunlit esplanade, curving and inflecting her splendid form, which, like a serpent coiled about a wand, twined itself round the white parasol patterned in blue which she carried unopened in her hand. She was my first Royalty—I say my first, for the Princesse Mathilde was not at all royal in her ways. The second, as we shall see in due course, was to astonish me no less by her graciousness. One aspect of the benevolence of the nobility, kindly intermediaries between commoners and kings, was revealed to me next day when Mme de Villeparisis reported: "She thought you quite charming. She is a woman of the soundest judgment, the warmest heart. Not like so many queens and highnesses. She has real merit." And Mme de Villeparisis added in a tone of conviction, and quite thrilled to be able to say it to us: "I think she would be delighted to see you again."

But on that previous morning, after we had parted from the Princesse de Luxembourg, Mme de Villeparisis said a thing which impressed me far more and was not prompted merely by friendly feeling.

"Are you," she had asked me, "the son of the Permanent Secretary at the Ministry? Indeed! I'm told your father is a most charming man. He is having a splendid holiday just now."

A few days earlier we had heard, in a letter from Mamma, that my father and his travelling-companion M. de Norpois had lost their luggage.

"It has been found, or rather it was never really lost. I can tell you what happened," explained Mme de Villeparisis, who, without our knowing how, seemed to be far better informed than ourselves about my father's travels. "I think your father is now planning to come home earlier, next week, in fact, as he will probably give up the idea of going to Algeciras. But he's anxious to spend a day longer in Toledo, since he's an admirer of a pupil of Titian—I forget the name—whose work can only be seen properly there."

And I wondered by what strange accident, in the impartial telescope through which Mme de Villeparisis considered, from a safe distance, the minuscule, perfunctory, vague agitation of the host of people whom she knew, there had come to be inserted at the spot through which she observed my father a fragment of glass of prodigious magnifying power which made her see in such high relief and in the fullest detail everything that was agreeable about him, the contingencies that obliged him to return home, his difficulties with the customs, his admiration for El Greco, and, altering the scale of her vision, showed her this one man, so large among all the rest so small, like that Jupiter to whom Gustave Moreau, when he portrayed him by the side of a weak mortal, gave a superhuman stature.

My grandmother bade Mme de Villeparisis good-bye, so that we might stay and imbibe the fresh air for a little while longer outside the hotel, until they signalled to us through the glazed partition that our lunch was ready. There were sounds of uproar. The young mistress of the King of the Cannibal Island had been down to bathe and was now coming back to the hotel.

"Really and truly, it's a perfect plague, it's enough to make one decide to emigrate!" cried the president in a towering rage as he crossed her path.

Meanwhile the notary's wife was following the bogus queen with eyes that seemed ready to start from their sockets.

"I can't tell you how angry Mme Blandais makes me when she stares at those people like that," said the president to the judge, "I feel I want to slap her. That's just the way to make the wretches appear important, which is of course the very thing they want. Do ask her husband to tell her what a fool she's making of herself. I swear I won't go out with them again if they stop and gape at those masqueraders."

As to the coming of the Princesse de Luxembourg, whose carriage, on the day she had left the fruit, had drawn up outside the hotel, it had not passed unobserved by the little group of wives, the notary's, the president's and the judge's, who had already for some time past been extremely anxious to know whether that Mme de Villeparisis whom everyone treated with so much respect—which all these ladies were burning to hear that she did not deserve—was a genuine marquise and not an adventuress. Whenever Mme de Villeparisis passed through the hall the judge's wife, who scented irregularities everywhere, would lift her nose from her needlework and stare at the intruder in a way that made her friends die with laughter.

"Oh, well, you know," she proudly explained, "I always begin by believing the worst. I will never admit that a woman is properly married until she has shown me her birth certificate and her marriage lines. But never fear—just wait till I've finished my little investigation."

And so day after day the ladies would come together and laughingly ask: "Any news?"

But on the evening of the Princesse de Luxembourg's call the judge's wife laid a finger on her lips.

"I've discovered something."

"Oh, isn't Mme Poncin simply wonderful? I never saw . . . But do tell us! What's happened?"

"Just listen to this. A woman with yellow hair and six inches of paint on her face and a carriage which reeked of harlot a mile away—which only a creature like that would dare to have—came here today to call on the so-called Marquise!"

"Oh-yow-yow! Crash bang! Did you ever! Why, it must be the woman we saw—you remember, President—we said at the time we didn't at all like the look of her, but we didn't know that it was the 'Marquise' she'd come to see. A woman with a nigger-boy, you mean?"

"That's the one."

"You don't say! Do you happen to know her name?"

"Yes, I made a mistake on purpose. I picked up her card. She *trades* under the name of the 'Princesse de Luxembourg'! Wasn't I right to have my doubts about her? It's a nice thing to have to fraternise with a Baronne d'Ange like that?"[10]

The president quoted Mathurin Régnier's *Macette* to the judge.

It must not, however, be supposed that this misunderstanding was merely temporary, like those that occur in the second act of a farce to be cleared up before the final curtain. Mme de Luxembourg, a niece of the King of England and of the Emperor of Austria, and Mme de Villeparisis, when one called to take the other for a drive, always appeared like two "old trots" of the kind one has always such difficulty in avoiding at a watering-place. Nine tenths of the men of the Faubourg Saint-Germain appear to a large section of the middle classes as crapulous paupers (which, individually, they not infrequently are) whom no respectable person would dream of asking to dinner. The middle classes pitch their standards in this respect too high, for the failings of these men would never prevent their being received with every mark of esteem in houses which they themselves will never enter. And so fondly do the aristocracy imagine that the middle classes know this that they affect a simplicity in speaking of themselves, a disparagement of friends of theirs who are particularly "on their beam-ends," that compounds the misunderstanding. If, by chance, a man of the fashionable world has dealings with the petty bourgeoisie because, having more money than he knows what to do with, he finds himself elected chairman of all sorts of important financial concerns, his business associates who at last see a nobleman worthy to be ranked with the professional classes, would take their oaths that such a man would not consort with the Marquis ruined by gambling whom the said business associates assume to be all the more destitute of friends the more friendly he makes himself. And they cannot get over their surprise when the duke who is Chairman of the Board of Directors of the colossal undertaking arranges a marriage for his son with the daughter of that very marquis, who may be a gambler but who bears the oldest name in France, just as a sovereign would sooner see his son marry the daughter of a dethroned king than that of a president still in office. In other words, the two worlds have as fanciful a view of one another as the inhabitants of the resort situated at one end of Balbec Bay have of the resort at the other end: from Rivebelle you can just see Marcouville-l'Orgueilleuse; but even that is deceptive, for you imagine that you are seen from Marcouville, where, as a matter of fact, the splendours of Rivebelle are almost wholly invisible.

The Balbec doctor, called in to cope with a sudden feverish attack, gave the opinion that I ought not to stay out all day on the beach in the blazing sun during the hot weather, and wrote out various prescriptions for me. My grandmother took these with a show of respect in which I could at once discern her firm resolve to ignore them all, but did pay attention to the advice on the question of hygiene, and accepted an offer from Mme de Villeparisis to take us for drives in her carriage. After this I would spend the mornings going to and fro between my own room and my grandmother's. Hers did not look out directly on the sea, as mine did, but was open on three of its four sides—on to a strip of the esplanade, a courtyard, and a view of the country inland—and was furnished differently from mine, with armchairs embroidered with metallic filigree and pink flowers from which the cool and pleasant odour that greeted one on entering seemed to emanate. And at that hour when the sun's rays, drawn from different exposures and, as it were, from different hours of the day, broke the angles of the wall, projected on to the chest of drawers, side by side with a reflection of the beach, a festal altar as variegated as a bank of field-flowers, hung on the fourth wall the folded, quivering, warm wings of a radiance ready at any moment to resume its flight, warmed like a bath a square of provincial carpet before the window overlooking the courtyard which the sun festooned and patterned like a climbing vine, and added to the charm and complexity of the room's furniture by seeming to pluck and scatter the petals of the silken flowers on the chairs and to make their silver threads stand out from the fabric, this room in which I lingered for a moment before going to get ready for our drive suggested a prism in which the colours of the light that shone outside were broken up, a hive in which the sweet juices of the day which I was about to taste were distilled, scattered, intoxicating and visible, a garden of hope which dissolved in a quivering haze of silver threads and rose petals. But before all this I had drawn back my own curtains, impatient to know what Sea it was that was playing that morning by the shore, like a Nereid. For none of those Seas ever stayed with us longer than a day. The next day there would be another, which sometimes resembled its predecessor. But I never saw the same one twice.

There were some that were of so rare a beauty that my pleasure on catching sight of them was enhanced by surprise. By what privilege, on one morning rather than another, did the window on being uncurtained disclose to my wondering eyes the nymph Glauconome, whose lazy beauty, gently breathing, had the transparency of a vaporous emerald through which I could see teeming the ponderable elements that coloured it? She made the sun join in her play, with a smile attenuated by an invisible haze which was no more than a space kept vacant about her translucent surface, which, thus curtailed, was rendered more striking, like those goddesses whom the sculptor carves in relief upon a block of marble the rest of which he leaves unchiselled. So, in her matchless colour, she invited us out over those rough terrestrial roads, from which, sitting with Mme de Villeparisis in her barouche, we should glimpse, all day long and without ever reaching it, the coolness of her soft palpitation.

Mme de Villeparisis used to order her carriage early, so that we should have time to reach Saint-Mars-le-Vêtu, or the rocks of Quetteholme, or some other goal which, for a somewhat lumbering vehicle, was far enough off to require the whole day. In my joy at the thought of the long drive we were going to take I would hum some tune that I had heard recently as I strolled up and down until Mme de Villeparisis was ready. If it was Sunday, hers would not be the only carriage drawn up outside the hotel; several hired cabs would be waiting there, not only for the people who had been invited to Féterne by Mme de Cambremer, but for those who, rather than stay at home all day like children in disgrace, declared that Sunday was always quite impossible at Balbec and set off immediately after lunch to hide themselves in some neighbouring watering-place or to visit one of the "sights" of the neighbourhood. And indeed whenever (which was often) Mme Blandais was asked if she had been to the Cambremers', she would answer emphatically: "No, we went to the Falls of the Bec," as though that were the sole reason for her not having spent the day at Féterne. And the president would charitably remark: "I envy you. I wish I had gone there instead. They must be well worth seeing."

Beside the row of carriages, in front of the porch in which I stood waiting, was planted, like some shrub of a rare species, a young page who attracted the eye no less by the unusual and harmonious colouring of his hair than by his plant-like epidermis. Inside, in the hall, corresponding to the narthex, or Church of the Catechumens in a primitive basilica, through which the persons who were not staying in the hotel were entitled to pass, the comrades of the "outside" page did not indeed work much harder than he but did at least execute certain movements. It is probable that in the early morning they helped with the cleaning. But in the afternoon they stood there only like a chorus who, even when there is nothing for them to do, remain upon the stage in order to strengthen the representation. The general manager, the same who had so terrified me, reckoned on increasing their number considerably next year, for he had "big ideas." And this prospect greatly afflicted the manager of the hotel, who found that all these boys were simply "busybodies," by which he meant that they got in the visitors' way and were of no use to anyone. But between lunch and dinner at least, between the exits and entrances of the visitors, they did fill an otherwise empty stage, like those pupils of Mme de Maintenon who, in the garb of young Israelites, carry on the action whenever Esther or Joad "goes off." But the outside page, with his delicate tints, his slender, fragile frame, in proximity to whom I stood waiting for the Marquise to come down, preserved an immobility mixed with a certain melancholy, for his elder brothers had left the hotel for more brilliant careers elsewhere, and he felt isolated upon this alien soil. At last Mme de Villeparisis appeared. To stand by her carriage and to help her into it ought perhaps to have been part of the young page's duties. But he knew that a person who brings her own servants to an hotel expects them to wait on her and is not as a rule lavish with her tips, and that the same was true also of the nobility of the old Faubourg Saint-Germain. Mme de Villeparisis belonged to both these categories. The arborescent page concluded therefore that he could expect nothing from her, and leaving her own maid and footman to pack her and her belongings into the carriage, he continued to dream sadly of the enviable lot of his brothers and preserved his vegetable immobility.

We would set off; some time after rounding the railway station, we came into a country road which soon became as familiar to me as the roads round Combray, from the bend where it took off between charming orchards to the turning at which we left it where there were tilled fields on either side. Among these we could see here and there an apple-tree, stripped it was true of its blossom and bearing no more than a fringe of pistils, but sufficient even so to enchant me since I could imagine, seeing those inimitable leaves, how their broad expanse, like the ceremonial carpet spread for a wedding that was now over, had been only recently swept by the white satin train of their blushing flowers.

How often in Paris, during the month of May of the following year, was I to bring home a branch of apple-blossom from the florist and afterwards to spend the night in company with its flowers in which bloomed the same creamy essence that still powdered with its froth the burgeoning leaves and between whose white corollas it seemed almost as though it had been the florist who, from generosity towards me, from a taste for invention too and as an effective contrast, had added on either side the supplement of a becoming pink bud: I sat gazing at them, I grouped them in the light of my lamp—for so long that I was often still there when the dawn brought to their whiteness the same flush with which it must at that moment have been tingeing their sisters on the Balbec road—and I sought to carry them back in my imagination to that roadside, to multiply them, to spread them out within the frame prepared for them, on the canvas already primed, of those fields and orchards whose outline I knew by heart, which I so longed to see, which one day I must see, again, at the moment when, with the exquisite fervour of genius, spring covers their canvas with its colours.

Before getting into the carriage, I had composed the seascape which I was going to look out for, which I hoped to see with Baudelaire's "radiant sun" upon it, and which at Balbec I could distinguish only in too fragmentary a form, broken by so many vulgar adjuncts that had no place in my dream—bathers, cabins, pleasure yachts. But when, Mme de Villeparisis's carriage having reached the top of a hill, I caught a glimpse of the sea through the leafy boughs of the trees, then no doubt at such a distance those temporal details which had set it apart, as it were, from nature and history disappeared, and I could try to persuade myself as I looked down upon its waters that they were the same which Leconte de Lisle describes for us in his *Orestie*, where "like a flight of birds of prey, at break of day" the long-haired warriors of heroic Hellas "with oars a hundred thousand sweep the resounding deep." But on the other hand I was no longer near enough to the sea, which seemed to me not alive but congealed, I no longer felt any power beneath its colours, spread like those of a picture between the leaves, through which it appeared as insubstantial as the sky and only of an intenser blue.

Mme de Villeparisis, seeing that I was fond of churches, promised me that we should visit several of them, and especially the church at Carqueville "quite buried in all its old ivy," as she said with a gesture of her hand which seemed tastefully to be clothing the absent façade in an invisible and delicate screen of foliage. Mme de Villeparisis would often, with this little descriptive gesture, find just the right word to define the charm and distinctiveness of an historic building, always avoiding technical terms, but incapable of concealing her thorough understanding of the things to which she referred. She appeared to seek an excuse for this erudition in the fact that one of her father's country houses, the one in which she had lived as a girl, was situated in a region where there were churches similar in style to those round Balbec, so that it would have been shameful if she had not acquired a taste for architecture, this house being, incidentally, one of the finest examples of that of the Renaissance. But as it was also a regular museum, as moreover Chopin and Liszt had played there, Lamartine recited poetry, all the most famous artists for fully a century written thoughts, dashed off melodies, made sketches in the family album, Mme de Villeparisis ascribed, whether from delicacy, good breeding, true modesty or want of speculative intelligence, only this purely material origin to her acquaintance with all the arts, and had seemingly come to regard painting, music, literature, and philosophy as the appanage of a young lady brought up on the most aristocratic lines in an historic building that was classified and starred. One got the impression that for her there were no other pictures than those that have been inherited. She was pleased that my grandmother liked a necklace which she wore, and which hung over her dress. It appeared in the portrait of an ancestress of hers, by Titian, which had never left the family. So that one could be certain of its being genuine. She would not hear a word about pictures bought, heaven knew where, by a Croesus; she was persuaded in advance that they were fakes, and had no desire to see them. We knew that she herself painted flowers in water-colour, and my grandmother, who had heard these praised, spoke to her of them. Mme de Villeparisis modestly changed the subject, but without showing any more surprise or pleasure than would an artist of established reputation to whom compliments mean nothing. She said merely that it was a delightful pastime because, even if the flowers that sprang from the brush were nothing wonderful, at least the work made you live in the company of real flowers, of the beauty of which, especially when you were obliged to study them closely in order to draw them, you could never grow tired. But at Balbec Mme de Villeparisis was giving herself a holiday, in order to rest her eyes.

We were astonished, my grandmother and I, to find how much more "liberal" she was than even the majority of the middle class. She did not understand how anyone could be scandalised by the expulsion of the Jesuits, saying that it had always been done, even under the Monarchy, in Spain even. She defended the Republic, reproaching it for its anti-clericalism only to this extent: "I should find it just as bad to be prevented from going to mass when I wanted to, as to be forced to go to it when I didn't!" and even startled us with such remarks as: "Oh! the aristocracy in these days, what does it amount to?" or, "To my mind, a man who doesn't work doesn't count!"—perhaps only because she sensed how much they gained in spice and piquancy, how memorable they became, on her lips.

When we heard these advanced opinions—though never so far advanced as to amount to socialism, which Mme de Villeparisis held in abhorrence—expressed so frequently and with so much frankness precisely by one of those people in consideration of whose intelligence our scrupulous and timid impartiality would refuse to condemn outright the ideas of conservatives, we came very near, my grandmother and I, to believing that in the pleasant companion of our drives was to be found the measure and the pattern of truth in all things. We took her word for it when she pronounced judgment on her Titians, the colonnade of her country house, the conversational talent of Louis-Philippe. But—like those learned people who hold us spellbound when we get them on to Egyptian painting or Etruscan inscriptions, and yet talk so tritely about modern work that we wonder whether we have not overestimated the interest of the sciences in which they are versed since they do not betray therein the mediocrity of mind which they must have brought to those studies just as much as to their fatuous essays on Baudelaire—Mme de Villeparisis, questioned by me about Chateaubriand, about Balzac, about Victor Hugo, each of whom in his day had been the guest of her parents and had been glimpsed by her, smiled at my reverence, told amusing anecdotes about them such as she had just been telling us about dukes and statesmen, and severely criticised those writers precisely because they had been lacking in that modesty, that self-effacement, that sober art which is satisfied with a single precise stroke and does not over-emphasise, which avoids above all else the absurdity of grandiloquence, in that aptness, those qualities of moderation, of judgment and simplicity to which she had been taught that real greatness aspired and attained. It was evident that she had no hesitation in placing above them men who might after all, perhaps, by virtue of those qualities, have had the advantage over a

Balzac, a Hugo, a Vigny in a drawing-room, an academy, a cabinet council, men like Molé, Fontanes, Vitrolles, Bersot, Pasquier, Lebrun, Salvandy or Daru.

"Like those novels of Stendhal which you seem to admire. You would have given him a great surprise, I assure you, if you had spoken to him in that tone. My father, who used to meet him at M. Mérimée's—now he was a man of talent, if you like—often told me that Beyle (that was his real name) was appallingly vulgar, but quite good company at dinner, and not in the least conceited about his books. Why, you must have seen for yourself how he just shrugged his shoulders at the absurdly extravagant compliments of M. de Balzac. There at least he showed that he knew how to behave like a gentleman."

She possessed the autographs of all these great men, and seemed, presuming on the personal relations which her family had had with them, to think that her judgment of them must be better founded than that of young people who, like myself, had had no opportunity of meeting them. "I think I have a right to speak about them, since they used to come to my father's house; and as M. Sainte-Beuve, who was a most intelligent man, used to say, in forming an estimate you must take the word of people who saw them close to and were able to judge more exactly their real worth."

Sometimes, as the carriage laboured up a steep road through ploughlands, making the fields more real, adding to them a mark of authenticity like the precious floweret with which certain of the old masters used to sign their pictures, a few hesitant cornflowers, like those of Combray, would follow in our wake. Presently the horses outdistanced them, but a little way on we would glimpse another which while awaiting us had pricked up its azure star in front of us in the grass. Some made so bold as to come and plant themselves by the side of the road, and a whole constellation began to take shape, what with my distant memories and these domesticated flowers.

We began to go down the hill; and then we would meet, climbing it on foot, on a bicycle, in a cart or carriage, one of those creatures—flowers of a fine day but unlike the flowers of the field, for each of them secretes something that is not to be found in another and that will prevent us from gratifying with any of her peers the desire she has aroused in us—a farm-girl driving her cow or reclining on the back of a waggon, a shopkeeper's daughter taking the air, a fashionable young lady erect on the back seat of a landau, facing her parents. Certainly Bloch had been the means of opening a new era and had altered the value of life for me on the day when he had told me that the dreams which I had entertained on my solitary walks along the Méséglise way, when I hoped that some peasant girl might pass whom I could take in my arms, were not a mere fantasy which corresponded to nothing outside myself but that all the girls one met, whether villagers or "young ladies," were alike ready and willing to give heed to such yearnings. And even if I were fated, now that I was ill and did not go out by myself, never to be able to make love to them, I was happy all the same, like a child born in a prison or a hospital who, having long supposed that the human organism was capable of digesting only dry bread and medicines, has learned suddenly that peaches, apricots and grapes are not simply part of the decoration of the country scene but delicious and easily assimilated food. Even if his gaoler or his nurse does not allow him to pluck those tempting fruits, still the world seems to him a better place and existence in it more clement. For a desire seems to us more attractive, we repose on it with more confidence, when we know that outside ourselves there is a reality which conforms to it, even if, for us, it is not to be realised. And we think more joyfully of a life in which (on condition that we eliminate for a moment from our mind the tiny obstacle, accidental and special, which prevents us personally from doing so) we can imagine ourselves to be assuaging that desire. As to the pretty girls who went past, from the day on which I had first known that their cheeks could be kissed, I had became curious about their souls. And the universe had appeared to me more interesting.

Mme de Villeparisis's carriage moved fast. I scarcely had time to see the girl who was coming in our direction; and yet—since the beauty of human beings is not like the beauty of things, and we feel that it is that of a unique creature, endowed with consciousness and free-will—as soon as her individuality, a soul still vague, a will unknown to me, presented a tiny picture of itself, enormously reduced but complete, in the depths of her indifferent eyes, at once, by a mysterious response of the pollen ready in me for the pistils that should receive it, I felt surging through me the embryo, equally vague, equally minute, of the desire not to let this girl pass without forcing her mind to become aware of my person, without preventing her desires from wandering to someone else, without insinuating myself into her dreams and taking possession of her heart. Meanwhile our carriage had moved on; the pretty girl was already behind us; and as she had—of me—none of those notions which constitute a person in one's mind, her eyes, which had barely seen me, had forgotten me already. Was it because I had caught but a momentary glimpse of her that I had found her so attractive? It may have been. In the first place, the impossibility of stopping when we meet a woman, the risk of not meeting her again another day, give her at once the same charm as a place derives from the illness or poverty that prevents us from visiting it, or the lustreless days which remain to us to live from the battle in which we shall doubtless fall. So that, if there were no such thing as habit, life must appear delightful to those of us who are continually under the threat of death—that is to say, to all mankind. Then, if our imagination is set going by the desire for what we cannot possess, its flight is not limited by a reality perceived in these casual encounters in which the charms of the passing stranger are generally in direct ratio to the swiftness of our passage. If night is falling and the carriage is moving fast, whether in town or country, there is not a single torso, disfigured like an antique marble by the speed that tears us away and the dusk that blurs it, that does not aim at our heart, from every crossing, from the lighted interior of every shop, the arrows of Beauty, that Beauty of which we are sometimes tempted to ask ourselves whether it is, in this world, anything more than the complementary part that is added to a fragmentary and fugitive stranger by our imagination, overstimulated by regret.

Had I been free to get down from the carriage and to speak to the girl whom we were passing, I might perhaps have been disillusioned by some blemish on her skin which from the carriage I had not distinguished. (Whereupon any attempt to penetrate into her life would have seemed suddenly impossible. For beauty is a sequence of hypotheses which ugliness cuts short when it bars the way that we could already see opening into the unknown.) Perhaps a single word which she might have uttered, or a smile, would have furnished me with an unexpected key or clue with which to read the expression on her face, to interpret her bearing, which would at once have become commonplace. It is possible, for I have never in real life met any girls so desirable as on days when I was with some solemn person from whom, despite the myriad pretexts that I invented, I could not tear myself away: some years after the one in the course of which I went for the first time to Balbec, as I was driving through Paris with a friend of my father, and had caught sight of a woman walking quickly along the dark street, I felt that it was unreasonable to forfeit, for a purely conventional scruple, my share of happiness in what may very well be the only life there is, and jumping from the carriage without a word of apology I went in search of the stranger, lost her at the junction of two streets, caught up with her again in a third, and arrived at last, breathless, beneath a street lamp, face to face with old Mme Verdurin whom I had been carefully avoiding for years, and who, in her delight and surprise, exclaimed: "But how very nice of you to have run all this way just to say how d'ye do to me!"

That year at Balbec, on the occasion of such encounters, I would assure my grandmother and Mme de Villeparisis that I had so severe a headache that the best thing for me would be to go home alone on foot. But they would never let me get out of the carriage. And I must add the pretty girl (far harder to find again than an historic monument, for she was nameless and had the power of locomotion) to the collection of all those whom I promised myself that I would examine more closely at a later date. One of them, however, happened to pass more than once before my eyes in circumstances which allowed me to believe that I should be able to get to know her as fully as I wished. This was a milk-girl who came from a farm with an additional supply of cream for the hotel. I fancied that she had recognised me also; and she did indeed look at me with an attentiveness which was perhaps due only to the surprise which my attentiveness caused her. And next day, a day on which I had been resting all morning, when Françoise came in about noon to draw my curtains, she handed me a letter which had been left for me downstairs. I knew no one at Balbec. I had no doubt that the letter was from the milk-girl. Alas, it was only from Bergotte who, as he happened to be passing, had tried to see me, but on hearing that I was asleep had scribbled a few charming lines for which the lift-boy had addressed an envelope which I had supposed to have been written by the milk-girl. I was bitterly disappointed, and the thought that it was more difficult and more flattering to get a letter from Bergotte did not in the least console me for this one's not being from her. As for the girl, I never came across her again, any more than I came across those whom I had seen only from Mme de Villeparisis's carriage. Seeing and then losing them all thus increased the state of agitation in which I was living, and I found a certain wisdom in the philosophers who recommend us to set a limit to our desires (if, that is, they refer to our desire for people, for that is the only kind that leads to anxiety, having for its object something unknown but conscious. To suppose that philosophy could be referring to the desire for wealth would be too absurd). At the same time I was inclined to regard this wisdom as incomplete, for I told myself that these encounters made me find even more beautiful a world which thus caused to grow along all the country roads flowers at once rare and common, fleeting treasures of the day, windfalls of the drive, of which the contingent circumstances that might not, perhaps, recur had alone prevented me from taking advantage, and which gave a new zest to life.

But perhaps in hoping that, one day, with greater freedom, I should be able to find similar girls on other roads, I was already beginning to falsify what is exclusively individual in the desire to live in the company of a woman whom one has found attractive, and by the mere fact that I admitted the possibility of bringing it about artificially, I had implicitly acknowledged its illusoriness.

On the day when Mme de Villeparisis took us to Carqueville to see the ivy-covered church of which she had spoken to us and which, built upon rising ground, dominated both the village and the river that flowed beneath it with its little mediaeval bridge, my grandmother, thinking that I would like to be left alone to study the building at my leisure, suggested to her friend that they should go on and wait for me at the pastry-cook's, in the village square which was clearly visible from where we were and beneath its mellow patina seemed like another part of a wholly ancient object. It was agreed that I should join them there later. In the mass of verdure in front of which I was left standing I was obliged, in order to recognise a church, to make a mental effort which involved my grasping more intensely the idea "Church." In fact, as happens to schoolboys who gather more fully the meaning of a sentence when they are made, by translating or by paraphrasing it, to divest it of the forms to which they are accustomed, I was obliged perpetually to refer back to this idea of "Church," which as a rule I scarcely needed when I stood beneath steeples that were recognisable in themselves, in order not to forget, here that the arch of this clump of ivy was that of a Gothic window, there that the salience of the leaves was due to the carved relief of a capital. Then came a breath of wind, sending a tremor through the mobile porch, which was traversed by eddies flickering and spreading like light; the leaves unfurled against one another; and, quivering, the arboreal façade bore away with it the undulant, rustling, fugitive pillars.

As I came away from the church I saw by the old bridge a cluster of girls from the village who, probably because it was Sunday, were standing about in their best clothes, hailing the boys who went past. One of them, a tall girl not so well dressed as the others but seeming to enjoy some ascendancy over them—for she scarcely answered when they spoke to her—with a more serious and a more self-willed air, was sitting on the parapet of the bridge with her feet hanging down, and holding on her lap a bowl full of fish which she had presumably just caught. She had a tanned complexion, soft eyes but with a look of disdain for her surroundings, and a small nose, delicately and attractively modelled. My eyes alighted upon her skin; and my lips, at a pinch, might have believed that they had followed my eyes. But it was not only to her body that I should have liked to attain; it was also the person that lived inside it, and with which there is but one form of contact, namely to attract its attention, but one sort of penetration, to awaken an idea in it.

And this inner being of the handsome fisher-girl seemed to be still closed to me; I was doubtful whether I had entered it, even after I had seen my own image furtively reflected in the twin mirrors of her gaze, following an index of refraction that was as unknown to me as if I had been placed in the field of vision of a doe. But just as it would not have sufficed that my lips should find pleasure in hers without giving pleasure to them too, so I could have wished that the idea of me which entered this being and took hold in it should bring me not merely her attention but her admiration, her desire, and should compel her to keep me in her memory until the day when I should be able to meet her again. Meanwhile I could see, within a stone's-throw, the square in which Mme de Villeparisis's carriage must be waiting for me. I had not a moment to lose; and already I could feel that the girls were beginning to laugh at the sight of me standing there before them. I had a five-franc piece in my pocket. I drew it out, and, before explaining to the girl the errand on which I proposed to send her, in order to have a better chance of her listening to me I held the coin for a moment before her eyes.

"Since you seem to belong to the place," I said to her, "I wonder if you would be so good as to take a message for me. I want you to go to a pastry-cook's—which is apparently in a square, but I don't know where that is—where there is a carriage waiting for me. One moment! To make quite sure, will you ask if the carriage belongs to the Marquise de Villeparisis? But you can't miss it; it's a carriage and pair."

That was what I wished her to know, so that she should regard me as someone of importance. But when I had uttered the words "Marquise" and "carriage and pair," suddenly I had a sense of enormous assuagement. I felt that the fisher-girl would remember me, and together with my fear of not being able to see her again, a part of my desire to do so evaporated too. It seemed to me that I had succeeded in touching her person with invisible lips, and that I had pleased her. And this forcible appropriation of her mind, this immaterial possession, had robbed her of mystery as much as physical possession would have done.

We came down towards Hudimesnil; and suddenly I was overwhelmed with that profound happiness which I had not often felt since Combray, a happiness analogous to that which had been given me by—among other things—the steeples of Martinville. But this time it remained incomplete. I had just seen, standing a little way back from the hog's-back road along which we were travelling, three trees which probably marked the entry to a covered driveway and formed a pattern which I was not seeing for the first time. I could not succeed in reconstructing the place from which they had been as it were detached, but I felt that it had been familiar to me once; so that, my mind having wavered between some distant year and the present moment, Balbec and its surroundings began to dissolve and I wondered whether the whole of this drive were not a make-believe, Balbec a place to which I had never gone except in imagination, Mme de Villeparisis a character in a story and the three old trees the reality which one recaptures on raising one's eyes from the book which one has been reading and which describes an environment into which one has come to believe that one has been bodily transported.

I looked at the three trees; I could see them plainly, but my mind felt that they were concealing something which it could not grasp, as when an object is placed out of our reach, so that our fingers, stretched out at arm's-length, can only touch for a moment its outer surface, without managing to take hold of anything. Then we rest for a little while before thrusting out our arm with renewed momentum, and trying to reach an inch or two further. But if my mind was thus to collect itself, to gather momentum, I should have to be alone. What would I not have given to be able to draw aside as I used to do on those walks along the Guermantes way, when I detached myself from my parents! I felt indeed that I ought to do so. I recognised that kind of pleasure which requires, it is true, a certain effort on the part of the mind, but in comparison with which the attractions of the indolence which inclines us to renounce that pleasure seem very slight. That pleasure, the object of which I could only dimly feel, which I must create for myself, I experienced only on rare occasions, but on each of these it seemed to me that the things that had happened in the meantime were of little importance, and that in attaching myself to the reality of that pleasure alone could I at length begin to lead a true life. I put my hand for a moment across my eyes, so as to be able to shut them without Mme de Villeparisis's noticing. I sat there thinking of nothing, then with my thoughts collected, compressed and strengthened I sprang further forward in the direction of the trees, or rather in that inner direction at the end of which I could see them inside myself. I felt again behind them the same object, known to me and yet vague, which I could not bring nearer. And yet all three of them, as the carriage moved on, I could see coming towards me. Where had I looked at them before? There was no place near Combray where an avenue opened off the road like that. Nor was there room for the site which they recalled to me in the scenery of the place in Germany where I had gone one year with my grandmother to take the waters. Was I to suppose, then, that they came from years already so remote in my life that the landscape which surrounded them had been entirely obliterated from my memory and that, like the pages which, with a sudden thrill, we recognise in a book that we imagined we had never read, they alone survived from the forgotten book of my earliest childhood? Were they not rather to be numbered among those dream landscapes, always the same, at least for me in whom their strange aspect was only the objectivation in my sleeping mind of the effort I made while awake either to penetrate the mystery of a place beneath the outward appearance of which I was dimly conscious of there being something more, as had so often happened to me on the Guermantes way, or to try to put mystery back into a place which I had longed to know and which, from the day when I had come to know it, had seemed to me to be wholly superficial, like Balbec? Or were they merely an image freshly extracted from a dream of the night before, but already so worn, so faded that it seemed to me to come from somewhere far more distant? Or had I indeed never seen them before, and did they conceal beneath their surface, like certain trees on tufts of grass that I had seen beside the Guermantes way, a meaning as obscure, as hard to grasp, as is a distant past, so that, whereas they were inviting me to probe a new thought, I imagined that I had to identify an old memory? Or again, were they concealing no hidden thought, and was it simply visual fatigue that made me see them double in time as one sometimes sees double in space? I could not tell. And meanwhile they were coming towards me; perhaps some fabulous apparition, a ring of witches or of Norns who would propound their oracles to me. I chose rather to believe that they were phantoms of the past, dear companions of my childhood, vanished friends who were invoking our common memories. Like ghosts they seemed to be appealing to me to take them with me, to bring them back to life. In their simple and passionate gesticulation I could discern the helpless anguish of a beloved person who has lost the power of speech, and feels that he will never be able to say to us what he wishes to say and we can never guess. Presently, at a cross-roads, the carriage left them. It was bearing me away from what alone I believed to be true, what would have made me truly happy; it was like my life.

I watched the trees gradually recede, waving their despairing arms, seeming to say to me: "What you fail to learn from us today, you will never know. If you allow us to drop back into the hollow of this road from which we sought to raise ourselves up to you, a whole part of yourself which we were bringing to you will vanish for ever into thin air." And indeed if, in the course of time, I did discover the kind of pleasure and disquiet which I had just felt once again, and if one evening—too late, but then for all time—I fastened myself to it, of those trees themselves I was never to know what they had been trying to give me nor where else I had seen them. And when, the road having forked and the carriage with it, I turned my back on them and ceased to see them, while Mme de Villeparisis asked me what I was dreaming about, I was as wretched as if I had just lost a friend, had died myself, had broken faith with the dead or repudiated a god.

It was time to be thinking of home. Mme de Villeparisis, who had a certain feeling for nature, colder than that of my grandmother but capable of recognising, even outside museums and noblemen's houses, the simple and majestic beauty of certain old and venerable things, told her coachman to take us back by the old Balbec road, a road little used but planted with old elm-trees which we thought magnificent.

Once we had got to know this road, for a change we would return—unless we had taken it on the outward journey—by another which ran through the woods of Chantereine and Canteloup. The invisibility of the numberless birds that took up one another's song close beside us in the trees gave me the same sense of being at rest that one has when one shuts one's eyes. Chained to my flap-seat like Prometheus on his rock, I listened to my Oceanides. And whenever I caught a glimpse of one of those birds as it flitted from one leaf to another, there was so little apparent connexion between it and the songs I heard that I could not believe I was beholding their cause in that little body, fluttering, startled and blank.

This road was like many others of the same kind which are to be found in France, climbing on a fairly steep gradient and then gradually descending over a long stretch. At that particular moment, I found no great attraction in it; I was only glad to be going home. But it became for me later on a frequent source of joy by remaining in my memory as a lure to which all the similar roads that I was to take, on walks or drives or journeys, would at once attach themselves without breach of continuity and would be able, thanks to it, to communicate immediately with my heart. For as soon as the carriage or the motor-car turned into one of these roads that seemed to be the continuation of the road along which I had driven with Mme de Villeparisis, what I found my present consciousness immediately dwelling upon, as upon the most recent event in my past, would be (all the intervening years being quietly obliterated) the impressions that I had had on those bright summer afternoons and evenings, driving in the neighbourhood of Balbec, when the leaves smelt good, the mist was rising from the ground, and beyond the nearby village one could see through the trees the sun setting as though it had been some place further along the road, distant and forested, which we should not have time to reach that evening. Linked up with those I was experiencing now in another place, on a similar road, surrounded by all the incidental sensations of breathing fresh air, of curiosity, indolence, appetite, gaiety which were common to them both, and excluding all others, these impressions would be reinforced, would take on the consistency of a particular type of pleasure, and almost of a framework of existence which, as it happened, I rarely had the luck to come across, but in which these awakened memories introduced, amid the reality that my senses could perceive, a large enough element of evoked, dreamed, unseizable reality to give me, among these regions through which I was passing, more than an aesthetic feeling, a fleeting but exalted ambition to stay and live there for ever. How often since then, at a mere whiff of green leaves, has not being seated on a folding-seat opposite Mme de Villeparisis, meeting the Princesse de Luxembourg who waved a greeting to her from her own carriage, coming back to dinner at the Grand Hotel, appeared to me as one of those ineffable moments of happiness which neither the present nor the future can restore to us and which we taste only once in a lifetime!

Often dusk would have fallen before we reached the hotel. Shyly I would quote to Mme de Villeparisis, pointing to the moon in the sky, some memorable expression of Chateaubriand or Vigny or Victor Hugo: "She shed all around her that ancient secret of melancholy" or "Weeping like Diana by the brink of her streams" or "The shadows nuptial, solemn and august."

"And you think that good, do you?" she would ask, "inspired, as you call it. I must confess that I am always surprised to see people taking things seriously nowadays which the friends of those gentlemen, while giving them full credit for their qualities, were the first to laugh at. People weren't so free then with the word 'genius' as they are now, when if you say to a writer that he has talent he takes it as an insult. You quote me a fine phrase of M. de Chateaubriand's about moonlight. You shall see that I have my own reasons for being resistant to it. M. de Chateaubriand used often to come to see my father. He was quite a pleasant person when you were alone with him, because then he was simple and amusing, but the moment he had an audience he would begin to pose, and then he became absurd. Once, in my father's presence, he claimed that he had flung his resignation in the King's face, and that he had controlled the Conclave, forgetting that he had asked my father to beg the King to take him back, and that my father had heard him make the most idiotic forecasts of the Papal election. You ought to have heard M. de Blacas on that famous Conclave; he was a very different kind of man from M. de Chateaubriand. As for his fine phrases about the moon, they had quite simply become a family joke. Whenever the moon was shining, if there was anyone staying with us for the first time he would be told to take M. de Chateaubriand for a stroll after dinner. When they came in, my father would take his guest aside and say: 'Well, and was M. de Chateaubriand very eloquent?'—'Oh, yes.' 'He talked to you about the moonlight.'—'Yes, how did you know?'—'One moment, didn't he say—' and then my father would quote the phrase. 'He did; but how in the world . . . ?'—'And he spoke to you of the moonlight on the Roman Campagna?'—'But, my dear sir, you're a magician.' My father was no magician, but M. de Chateaubriand had the same little speech about the moon which he served up every time."

At the mention of Vigny she laughed: "The man who said: 'I am the Comte Alfred de Vigny!' One is either a count or one isn't; it is not of the slightest importance."

And then perhaps she discovered that it was, after all, of some slight importance, for she went on: "For one thing I'm by no means sure that he was, and in any case he was of very inferior stock, that gentleman who speaks in his verses of his 'esquire's crest.' In such charming taste, is it not, and so interesting to his readers! Like Musset, a plain citizen of Paris, who laid so much stress on 'The golden falcon that surmounts my helm.' As if you would ever hear a real gentleman say a thing like that! At least Musset had some talent as a poet. But except for *Cinq-Mars*, I've never been able to read a thing by M. de Vigny. I get so bored that the book falls from my hands. M. Molé, who had all the wit and tact that were wanting in M. de Vigny, put him properly in his place when he welcomed him to the Academy. What, you don't know the speech? It's a masterpiece of irony and impertinence."

She found fault with Balzac, whom she was surprised to find her nephews admiring, for having presumed to describe a society "in which he was never received" and of which his descriptions were wildly improbable. As for Victor Hugo, she told us that M. de Bouillon, her father, who had friends among the young Romantics thanks to whom he had attended the first performance of *Hernani*, had been unable to sit through it, so ridiculous had he found the verse of that gifted but extravagant writer who had acquired the title of "major poet" only by virtue of having struck a bargain, and as a reward for the not disinterested indulgence that he showed towards the dangerous aberrations of the socialists.

We had now come in sight of the hotel, with its lights, so hostile that first evening on our arrival, now protective and kind, speaking to us of home. And when the carriage drew up outside the door, the porter, the bell-hops, the lift-boy, attentive, clumsy, vaguely uneasy at our lateness, massed on the steps to receive us, were numbered, now that they had grown familiar, among those beings who change so many times in the course of our lives, as we ourselves change, but in whom, when they are for the time being the mirror of our habits, we find comfort in the feeling that we are being faithfully and amicably reflected. We prefer them to friends whom we have not seen for some time, for they contain more of what we are at present. Only the outside page, exposed to the sun all day, had been taken indoors for protection from the cold night air and swaddled in thick woollen garments which, combined with the orange effulgence of his locks and the curiously red bloom of his cheeks, made one, seeing him there in the glassed-in hall, think of a hot-house plant muffled up for protection from the frost. We got out of the carriage with the help of a great many more servants than were required, but they were conscious of the importance of the scene and each felt obliged to take some part in it. I was always very hungry. And so, often, in order not to keep dinner waiting, I would not go upstairs to the room which had succeeded in becoming so really mine that to catch sight of its long violet curtains and low bookcases was to find myself alone again with that self of which things, like people, gave me a reflected image; and we would all wait together in the hall until the head waiter came to tell us that our dinner was ready. This gave us another opportunity of listening to Mme de Villeparisis.

"But you must be tired of us by now," my grandmother would protest.

"Not at all! Why, I'm delighted, what could be nicer?" replied her friend with a winning smile, drawing out, almost intoning her words in a way that contrasted markedly with her customary simplicity of speech.

And indeed at such moments as this she was not natural; her mind reverted to her early training, to the aristocratic manner in which a great lady is supposed to show commoners that she is glad to be with them, that she is not at all arrogant. And her one and only failure in true politeness lay in this excess of politeness—which it was easy to identify as the professional bent of a lady of the Faubourg Saint-Germain, who, always seeing in her humbler friends the latent discontent that she must one day arouse in their bosoms, greedily seizes every possible opportunity to establish in advance, in the ledger in which she keeps her social account with them, a credit balance which will enable her presently to enter on the debit side the dinner or reception to which she will not invite them. And so, having long ago taken effect in her once and for all, and oblivious of the fact that now both the circumstances and the people concerned were different, and that in Paris she would wish to see us often at her house, the spirit of her caste was urging Mme de Villeparisis on with feverish ardour, as if the time that was allowed her for being amiable to us was limited, to step up, while we were at Balbec, her gifts of roses and melons, loans of books, drives in her carriage and verbal effusions. And for that reason, quite as much as the dazzling splendour of the beach, the many-coloured flamboyance and subaqueous light of the rooms, as much even as the riding-lessons by which tradesmen's sons were deified like Alexander of Macedon, the daily kindnesses shown us by Mme de Villeparisis, and also the unaccustomed, momentary, holiday ease with which my grandmother accepted them, have remained in my memory as typical of life at the seaside.

"Give them your coats to take upstairs."

My grandmother handed them to the manager, and

because he had been so nice to me I was distressed by this want of consideration, which seemed to pain him.

"I think you've hurt his feelings," said the Marquise. "He probably fancies himself too great a gentleman to carry your wraps. I remember the Duc de Nemours, when I was still quite little, coming to see my father who was living then on the top floor of the Hôtel Bouillon, with a fat parcel under his arm, and letters and newspapers. I can see the Prince now, in his blue coat, framed in our doorway, which had such pretty panelling—I think it was Bagard who used to do it—you know those fine laths that they used to cut, so supple that the joiner would twist them sometimes into little shells and flowers, like the ribbons round a nosegay. 'Here you are, Cyrus,' he said to my father, 'look what your porter's given me to bring you. He said to me: Since you're going up to see the Count, it's not worth my while climbing all those stairs; but take care you don't break the string.'—Now that you've got rid of your things, why don't you sit down," she said to my grandmother, taking her by the hand. "Here, take this chair."

"Oh, if you don't mind, not that one! It's too small for two, and too big for me by myself. I shouldn't feel comfortable."

"You remind me, for it was exactly like this one, of an armchair I had for many years, until at last I couldn't keep it any longer, because it had been given to my mother by the unfortunate Duchesse de Praslin. My mother, though she was the simplest person in the world, really, had ideas that belonged to another generation, which even in those days I could scarcely understand; and at first she had not been at all willing to let herself be introduced to Mme de Praslin, who had been plain Mlle Sebastiani, while she, because she was a Duchess, felt that it was not for her to be introduced to my mother. And really, you know," Mme de Villeparisis went on, forgetting that she herself did not understand these fine shades of distinction, "even if she had just been Mme de Choiseul, there was a good deal to be said for her claim. The Choiseuls are everything you could want; they spring from a sister of Louis the Fat; they were real sovereigns down in Bassigny. I admit that we beat them in marriages and in distinction, but the seniority is pretty much the same. This little matter of precedence gave rise to several comic incidents, such as a luncheon party which was kept waiting a whole hour or more before one of these ladies could make up her mind to let herself be introduced to the other. In spite of which they became great friends, and she gave my mother a chair like this one, in which people always refused to sit, as you've just done, until one day my mother heard a carriage drive into the courtyard. She asked a young servant who it was. 'The Duchesse de La Rochefoucauld, ma'am.' 'Very well, say that I am at home.' A quarter of an hour passed; no one came. 'What about the Duchesse de La Rochefoucauld?' my mother asked, 'where is she?' 'She's on the stairs, ma'am, getting her breath,' said the young servant, who had not been long up from the country, where my mother had the excellent habit of getting all her servants. Often she had seen them born. That's the only way to get really good ones. And they're the rarest of luxuries. And sure enough the Duchesse de La Rochefoucauld had the greatest difficulty in getting upstairs, for she was an enormous woman, so enormous, indeed, that when she did come into the room my mother was quite at a loss for a moment to know where to put her. And then the seat that Mme de Praslin had given her caught her eye. 'Won't you sit down?' she said, bringing it forward. And the Duchess filled it from side to side. She was quite a pleasant woman, for all her . . . imposingness. 'She still creates a certain effect when she comes in,' one of our friends said once. 'She certainly creates an effect when she goes out,' said my mother, who was rather more free in her speech than would be thought proper nowadays. Even in Mme de La Rochefoucauld's own drawing-room people didn't hesitate to make fun of her to her face (and she was always the first to laugh at it) over her ample proportions. 'But are you all alone?' my mother once asked M. de La Rochefoucauld, when she had come to pay a call on the Duchess, and being met at the door by him had not seen his wife who was in an alcove at the other end of the room. 'Is Mme de La Rochefoucauld not at home? I don't see her.'—'How charming of you!' replied the Duke, who had about the worst judgment of any man I have ever known, but was not altogether lacking in humour."

After dinner, when I had gone upstairs with my grandmother, I said to her that the qualities which attracted us in Mme de Villeparisis, her tact, her shrewdness, her discretion, her self-effacement, were not perhaps of very great value since those who possessed them in the highest degree were merely people like Molé and Loménie, and that if the want of them can make everyday social relations disagreeable yet it did not prevent conceited fellows who had no judgment—whom it was easy to deride, like Bloch—from becoming Chateaubriand, Vigny, Hugo, Balzac . . . But at the name of Bloch, my grandmother expostulated. And she proceeded to sing the praises of Mme de Villeparisis. As we are told that it is the preservation of the species which guides our individual preferences in love and, so that the child may be constituted in the most normal fashion, sends fat men in pursuit of lean women and vice versa, so in some dim way it was the requirements of my happiness, threatened by my disordered nerves, by my morbid tendency to melancholy and solitude, that made her allot the highest place to the qualities of balance and judgment, peculiar not only to Mme de Villeparisis but to a society in which I might find distraction and assuagement—a society similar to the one in which our ancestors saw the minds of a Doudan, a M. de Rémusat flourish, not to mention a Beausergent, a Joubert, a Sévigné, a type of mind that invests life with more happiness, with greater dignity than the converse refinements which had led a Baudelaire, a Poe, a Verlaine, a Rimbaud to sufferings, to a disrepute such as my grandmother did not wish for her daughter's child. I interrupted her with a kiss and asked her if she had noticed such and such a remark Mme de Villeparisis had made which seemed to point to a woman who thought more of her noble birth than she was prepared to admit. In this way I used to submit my impressions of life to my grandmother, for I was never certain what degree of respect was due to anyone until she had pointed it out to me. Every evening I would come to her with the mental sketches that I had made during the day of all those non-existent people who were not her.

Once I said to her: "I couldn't live without you."

"But you mustn't speak like that," she replied in a troubled voice. "We must be a bit pluckier than that. Otherwise, what would become of you if I went away on a journey? But I hope that you would be quite sensible and quite happy."

"I could manage to be sensible if you went away for a few days, but I should count the hours."

"But if I were to go away for months . . ." (at the mere thought my heart turned over) ". . . for years . . . for . . ."

We both fell silent. We dared not look one another in the face. And yet I was suffering more keenly from her anguish than from my own. And so I walked across to the window and said to her distinctly, with averted eyes:

"You know what a creature of habit I am. For the first few days after I've been separated from the people I love best, I'm miserable. But though I go on loving them just as much, I get used to their absence, my life becomes calm and smooth. I could stand being parted from them for months, for years . . ."

I was obliged to stop speaking and look straight out of the window. My grandmother left the room for a moment. But next day I began to talk to her about philosophy, and, speaking in the most casual tone but at the same time taking care that my grandmother should pay attention to my words, I remarked what a curious thing it was that, according to the latest scientific discoveries, the materialist position appeared to be crumbling, and what was again most likely was the immortality of souls and their future reunion.

Mme de Villeparisis gave us warning that presently she would not be able to see so much of us. A young nephew who was preparing for Saumur, and was meanwhile stationed in the neighbourhood, at Doncières, was coming to spend a few weeks' leave with her, and she would be devoting most of her time to him. In the course of our drives together she had spoken highly of his intelligence and above all his kindheartedness, and already I imagined that he would take a liking to me, that I should be his best friend; and when, before his arrival, his aunt gave my grandmother to understand that he had unfortunately fallen into the clutches of an appalling woman with whom he was infatuated and who would never let him go, since I was persuaded that that sort of love was doomed to end in mental derangement, crime and suicide, thinking how short a time was reserved for our friendship, already so great in my heart although I had not yet set eyes on him, I wept for that friendship and for the misfortunes that were in store for it, as we weep for someone we love when we learn that he is seriously ill and that his days are numbered.

One afternoon of scorching heat I was in the dining-room of the hotel, plunged in semi-darkness to shield it from the sun, which gilded the drawn curtains through the gaps between which twinkled the blue of the sea, when along the central gangway leading from the beach to the road I saw approaching, tall, slim, bare-necked, his head held proudly erect, a young man with penetrating eyes whose skin was as fair and his hair as golden as if they had absorbed all the rays of the sun. Dressed in a suit of soft, whitish material such as I could never have believed that any man would have the audacity to wear, the thinness of which suggested no less vividly than the coolness of the dining-room the heat and brightness of the glorious day outside, he was walking fast. His eyes, from one of which a monocle kept dropping, were the colour of the sea. Everyone looked at him with interest as he passed, knowing that this young Marquis de Saint-Loup-en-Bray was famed for his elegance. All the newspapers had described the suit in which he had recently acted as second to the young Duc d'Uzès in a duel. One felt that the distinctive quality of his hair, his eyes, his skin, his bearing, which would have marked him out in a crowd like a precious vein of opal, azure-shot and luminous, embedded in a mass of coarser substance, must correspond to a life different from that led by other men. So that when, before the attachment which Mme de Villeparisis had been deploring, the prettiest women in society had disputed the possession of him, his presence, at a watering-place for instance, in the company of the beauty of the season to whom he was paying court, not only brought her into the limelight, but attracted every eye fully as much to himself. Because of his "tone," because he had the insolent manner of a young "blood," above all because of his extraordinary good looks, some even thought him effeminate-looking, though without holding it against him since they knew how virile he was and how passionately fond of women. This was the nephew about whom Mme de Villeparisis had spoken to us. I was delighted at the thought that I was going to enjoy his company for some weeks, and confident that he would bestow on me all his affection. He strode rapidly across the whole width of the hotel, seeming to be in pursuit of his monocle, which kept darting away in front of him like a butterfly. He was coming from the beach, and the sea which filled the lower half of the glass front of the hall made a background against which he stood out full-length, as in certain portraits whose painters attempt, without in any way falsifying the most accurate observation of contemporary life, but by choosing for their sitter an appropriate setting—a polo ground, golf links, a race-course, the bridge of a yacht—to furnish a modern equivalent of those canvases on which the old masters used to present the human figure in the foreground of a landscape. A carriage and pair awaited him at the door; and, while his monocle resumed its gambollings on the sunlit road, with the elegance and mastery which a great pianist contrives to display in the simplest stroke of execution, where it did not seem possible that he could reveal his superiority to a performer of the second class, Mme de Villeparisis's nephew, taking the reins that were handed him by the coachman, sat down beside him and, while opening a letter which the manager of the hotel brought out to him, started up his horses.

How disappointed I was on the days that followed, when, each time that I met him outside or in the hotel—his head erect, perpetually balancing the movements of his limbs round the fugitive and dancing monocle which seemed to be their centre of gravity—I was forced to acknowledge that he had evidently no desire to make our acquaintance, and saw that he did not bow to us although he must have known that we were friends of his aunt. And calling to mind the friendliness that Mme de Villeparisis, and before her M. de Norpois, had shown me, I thought that perhaps they were only mock aristocrats and that there must be a secret article in the laws that govern the nobility which allowed women, perhaps, and certain diplomats to discard, in their relations with commoners, for a reason which was beyond me, the haughtiness which must, on the other hand, be pitilessly maintained by a young marquis. My intelligence might have told me the opposite. But the characteristic feature of the ridiculous age I was going through—awkward indeed but by no means infertile—is that we do not consult our intelligence and that the most trivial attributes of other people seem to us to form an inseparable part of their personality. In a world thronged with monsters and with gods, we know little peace of mind. There is hardly a single action we perform in that phase which we would not give anything, in later life, to be able to annul. Whereas what we ought to regret is that we no longer possess the spontaneity which made us perform them. In later life we look at things in a more practical way, in full conformity with the rest of society, but adolescence is the only period in which we learn anything.

This insolence which I surmised in M. de Saint-Loup, and all that it implied of innate hardness, received confirmation from his attitude whenever he passed us, his body as inflexibly erect as ever, his head held as high, his gaze as impassive, not to say as implacable, devoid of that vague respect which one has for the rights of other people, even if they do not know one's aunt, in accordance with which I did not behave in quite the same way towards an old lady as towards a gas lamp. These frigid manners were as far removed from the charming letters which, only a few days before, I had still imagined him writing to me to express his regard as, from the enthusiasm of the Chamber and of the populace which he has pictured himself rousing by an imperishable speech, is the humble, dull, obscure position of the dreamer who, after rehearsing it thus by himself, for himself, aloud, finds himself, once the imaginary applause has died away, just the same Tom, Dick or Harry as before. When Mme de Villeparisis, doubtless in an attempt to counteract the bad impression that had been made on us by an exterior indicative of an arrogant and unfriendly nature, spoke to us again of the inexhaustible kindness of her great-nephew (he was the son of one of her nieces, and a little older than myself), I marvelled how the gentry, with an utter disregard of truth, ascribe tenderness of heart to people whose hearts are in reality so hard and dry, provided only that they behave with common courtesy to the brilliant members of their own set. Mme de Villeparisis herself confirmed, though indirectly, my diagnosis, which was already a conviction, of the essential points of her nephew's character one day when I met them both coming along a path so narrow that she could not do otherwise than introduce me to him. He seemed not to hear that a person's name was being announced to him; not a muscle of his face moved; his eyes, in which there shone not the faintest gleam of human sympathy, showed merely, in the insensibility, in the inanity of their gaze an exaggeration failing which there would have been nothing to distinguish them from lifeless mirrors. Then, fastening on me those hard eyes as though he wished to examine me before returning my salute, with an abrupt gesture which seemed to be due rather to a reflex action of his muscles than to an exercise of will, keeping between himself and me the greatest possible interval, he stretched his arm out to its full extension and, at the end of it, offered me his hand. I supposed that it must mean, at the very least, a duel when, next day, he sent me his card. But he spoke to me when we met only of literature, and declared after a long talk that he would like immensely to spend several hours with me every day. He had not only, in this encounter, given proof of an ardent zest for the things of the mind; he had shown a regard for me which was little in keeping with his greeting of the day before. After I had seen him repeat the same process every time someone was introduced to him, I realised that it was simply a social usage peculiar to his branch of the family, to which his mother, who had seen to it that he should be perfectly brought up, had moulded his limbs; he went through those motions without thinking about them any more than he thought about his beautiful clothes or hair; they were a thing devoid of the moral significance which I had at first ascribed to them, a thing purely acquired, like that other habit that he had of at once demanding an introduction to the family of anyone he knew, which had become so instinctive in him that, seeing me again the day after our meeting, he bore down on me and without further ado asked to be introduced to my grandmother who was with me, with the same feverish haste as if the request had been due to some instinct of self-preservation, like the act of warding off a blow or of shutting one's eyes to avoid a stream of boiling water, without the protection of which it would have been dangerous to remain a moment longer.

The first rites of exorcism once performed, as a cantankerous fairy discards her preliminary guise and assumes all the most enchanting graces, I saw this disdainful creature become the most friendly, the most considerate young man that I had ever met. "Right," I said to myself, "I've been mistaken about him once already. I was the victim of a mirage. But I've got over the first only to fall for a second, for he must be a dyed-in-the-wool grandee who's trying to hide it." As a matter of fact it was not long before all the exquisite breeding, all the friendliness of Saint-Loup were indeed to let me see another person, but one very different from what I had suspected.

This young man who had the air of a disdainful aristocrat and sportsman had in fact no respect or curiosity except for the things of the mind, and especially those modern manifestations of literature and art which seemed so ridiculous to his aunt; he was imbued, moreover, with what she called "socialistic spoutings," was filled with the most profound contempt for his caste, and spent long hours in the study of Nietzsche and Proudhon. He was one of those "intellectuals" easily moved to admiration, who shut themselves up in a book and are interested only in the higher thought. Indeed in Saint-Loup the expression of this highly abstract tendency, which removed him so far from my customary preoccupations, while it seemed to me touching, also annoyed me a little. I may say that when I fully realised who his father had been, on days when I had been reading memoirs rich in anecdotes of that famous Comte de Marsantes in whom were embodied the special graces of a generation already remote, my mind full of speculations, and anxious to obtain fuller details of the life that M. de Marsantes had led, I was infuriated that Robert de Saint-Loup, instead of being content to be the son of his father, instead of being able to guide me through the old-fashioned romance which his father's existence had been, had raised himself to a passion for Nietzsche and Proudhon. His father would not have shared my regret. He had been himself a man of intelligence, who had transcended the narrow confines of his life as a man of the world. He had hardly had time to know his son, but had hoped that he would prove a better man than himself. And I dare say that, unlike the rest of the family, he would have admired his son, would have rejoiced at his abandoning what had been his own small diversions for austere meditations, and without saying a word, in his modesty as a nobleman of wit, would have read in secret his son's favourite authors in order to appreciate how far Robert was superior to himself.

There was, however, this rather painful consideration: that if M. de Marsantes, with his extremely open mind, would have appreciated a son so different from himself, Robert de Saint-Loup, because he was one of those people who believe that merit is attached only to certain forms of art and of life, had an affectionate but slightly contemptuous memory of a father who had spent all his time hunting and racing, who yawned at Wagner and raved over Offenbach. Saint-Loup was not intelligent enough to understand that intellectual worth has nothing to do with adhesion to any one aesthetic formula, and regarded the "intellectuality" of M. de Marsantes with much the same sort of scorn as might have been felt for Boieldieu or Labiche by sons of Boieldieu or Labiche who had become adherents of the most extreme symbolist literature and the most complicated music. "I scarcely knew my father," he used to say. "He seems to have been a charming man. His tragedy was the deplorable age in which he lived. To have been born in the Faubourg Saint-Germain and to have to live in the days of *La Belle Hélène* would be enough to wreck any existence. Perhaps if he'd been some little shopkeeper mad about the *Ring* he'd have turned out quite different. Indeed they tell me that he was fond of literature. But it's impossible to know, because literature to him meant only the most antiquated stuff." And in my own case, if I found Saint-Loup a trifle earnest, he could not understand why I was not more earnest still. Never judging anything except by its intellectual weightiness, never perceiving the magic appeal to the imagination that I found in things which he condemned as frivolous, he was astonished that I—to whom he imagined himself to be so utterly inferior—could take any interest in them.

From the first Saint-Loup made a conquest of my grandmother, not only by the incessant kindness which he went out of his way to show to us both, but by the naturalness which he put into it as into everything else. For naturalness—doubtless because through the artifice of man it allows a feeling of nature to permeate—was the quality which my grandmother preferred to all others, whether in gardens, where she did not like there to be, as in our Combray garden, too formal flower-beds, or in cooking, where she detested those dressed-up dishes in which you can hardly detect the foodstuffs that have gone to make them, or in piano-playing, which she did not like to be too finicking, too polished, having indeed had a special weakness for the discords, the wrong notes of Rubinstein. This naturalness she found and appreciated even in the clothes that Saint-Loup wore, of a loose elegance, with nothing "swagger" or "dressed-up" about them, no stiffness or starch. She appreciated this rich young man still more highly for the free and careless way that he had of living in luxury without "smelling of money," without giving himself airs; she even discovered the charm of this naturalness in the incapacity which Saint-Loup had kept—though as a rule it is outgrown with childhood, at the same time as certain physiological peculiarities of that age—for preventing his face from at once reflecting every emotion. Something, for instance, that he wanted to have but had not expected, if only a compliment, induced in him a pleasure so quick, so glowing, so volatile, so expansive that it was impossible for him to contain and to conceal it; a grin of delight seized irresistible hold of his face, the too delicate skin of his cheeks allowed a bright red glow to shine through them, his eyes sparkled with confusion and joy; and my grandmother was infinitely touched by this charming show of innocence and frankness, which indeed in Saint-Loup—at any rate at the time of our first friendship—was not misleading. But I have known another person, and there are many such, in whom the physiological sincerity of that fleeting blush in no way excluded moral duplicity; as often as not it proves nothing more than the intensity with which pleasure may be felt—to the extent of disarming them and forcing them publicly to confess it—by natures capable of the vilest treachery. But where my grandmother especially adored Saint-Loup's naturalness was in his way of confessing without the slightest reservation his affection for me, to give expression to which he found words than which she herself, she told me, could not have thought of any more appropriate, more truly loving, words to which "Sévigné and Beausergent" might have set their signatures. He was not afraid to make fun of my weaknesses—which he had discerned with a shrewdness that made her smile—but as she herself would have done, affectionately, at the same time extolling my good qualities with a warmth, an impulsive freedom that showed no sign of the reserve, the coldness by means of which young men of his age are apt to suppose that they give themselves importance. And he evinced, in anticipating my every discomfort, however slight, in covering my legs if the day had turned cold without my noticing it, in arranging (without telling me) to stay later with me in the evening if he thought I was sad or gloomy, a vigilance which, from the point of view of my health, for which a more hardening discipline would perhaps have been better, my grandmother found almost excessive, though as a proof of his affection for me she was deeply touched by it.

It was promptly settled between us that he and I were to be great friends for ever, and he would say "our friendship" as though he were speaking of some important and delightful thing which had an existence independent of ourselves, and which he soon called—apart from his love for his mistress—the great joy of his life. These words filled me with a sort of melancholy and I was at a loss for an answer, for I felt when I was with him, when I was talking to him—and no doubt it would have been the same with anyone else—none of that happiness which it was possible for me to experience when I was by myself. Alone, at times, I felt surging from the depths of my being one or other of those impressions which gave me a delicious sense of well-being. But as soon as I was with someone else, as soon as I was talking to a friend, my mind as it were faced about, it was towards this interlocutor and not towards myself that it directed its thoughts, and when they followed this outward course they brought me no pleasure. Once I had left Saint-Loup, I managed, with the help of words, to put some sort of order into the confused minutes that I had spent with him; I told myself that I had a good friend, that a good friend was a rare thing, and I savoured, when I felt myself surrounded by assets that were difficult to acquire, what was precisely the opposite of the pleasure that was natural to me, the opposite of the pleasure of having extracted from myself and brought to light something that was hidden in my inner darkness. If I had spent two or three hours in conversation with Saint-Loup and he had expressed his admiration of what I had said to him, I felt a sort of remorse, or regret, or weariness at not having remained alone and settled down to work at last. But I told myself that one is not intelligent for oneself alone, that the greatest of men have wanted to be appreciated, that hours in which I had built up a lofty idea of myself in my friend's mind could not be considered wasted. I had no difficulty in persuading myself that I ought to be happy in consequence, and I hoped all the more keenly that this happiness might never be taken from me because I had not actually felt it. We fear more than the loss of anything else the disappearance of possessions that have remained outside ourselves, because our hearts have not taken possession of them. I felt that I was capable of exemplifying the virtues of friendship better than most people (because I should always place the good of my friends before those personal interests to which other people are devoted but which did not count for me), but not of finding happiness in a feeling which, instead of increasing the differences that there were between my nature and those of other people—as there are between all of us—would eliminate them. On the other hand there were moments when my mind distinguished in Saint-Loup a personality more generalised than his own, that of the "nobleman," which like an indwelling spirit moved his limbs, ordered his gestures and his actions; then, at such moments, although in his company, I was alone, as I should have been in front of a landscape the harmony of which I could understand. He was no more then than an object the properties of which, in my musings, I sought to explore. The discovery in him of this pre-existent, this immemorial being, this aristocrat who was precisely what Robert aspired not to be, gave me intense joy, but a joy of the mind rather than the feelings. In the moral and physical agility which gave so much grace to his kindnesses, in the ease with which he offered my grandmother his carriage and helped her into it, in the alacrity with which he sprang from the box when he was afraid that I might be cold, to spread his own cloak over my shoulders, I sensed not only the inherited litheness of the mighty hunters who had been for generations the ancestors of this young man who had no pretensions except to intellectuality, their scorn of wealth which, subsisting in him side by side with his enjoyment of it simply because it enabled him to entertain his friends more lavishly, made him so carelessly shower his riches at their feet; I sensed in it above all the certainty or the illusion in the minds of those great lords of being "better than other people," thanks to which they had not been able to hand down to Saint-Loup that anxiety to show that one is "just as good as the next man," that dread of seeming too assiduous of which he was indeed wholly innocent and which mars with so much stiffness and awkwardness the most sincere plebeian civility. Sometimes I reproached myself for thus taking pleasure in considering my friend as a work of art, that is to say in regarding the play of all the parts of his being as harmoniously ordered by a general idea from which they depended but of which he was unaware and which consequently added nothing to his own qualities, to that personal value, intellectual and moral, which he prized so highly.

And yet that idea was to a certain extent their determining cause. It was because he was a gentleman that that mental activity, those socialist aspirations, which made him seek the company of arrogant and ill-dressed young students, connoted in him something really pure and disinterested which was not to be found in them. Looking upon himself as the heir of an ignorant and selfish caste, he was sincerely anxious that they should forgive in him that aristocratic origin which they, on the contrary, found irresistibly attractive and on account of which they sought his acquaintance while simulating coldness and indeed insolence towards him. He was thus led to make advances to people from whom my parents, faithful to the sociological theories of Combray, would have been stupefied at his not turning away in disgust. One day when we were sitting on the sands, Saint-Loup and I, we heard issuing from a canvas tent against which we were leaning a torrent of imprecation against the swarm of Jews that infested Balbec. "You can't go a yard without meeting them," said the voice. "I am not in principle irremediably hostile to the Jewish race, but here there is a plethora of them. You hear nothing but, 'I thay, Apraham, I've chust theen Chacop.' You would think you were in the Rue d'Aboukir." The man who thus inveighed against Israel emerged at last from the tent, and we raised our eyes to behold this anti-Semite. It was my old friend Bloch. Saint-Loup at once asked me to remind him that they had met each other at the *concours général*, when Bloch had carried off the prize of honour, and since then at a people's university course.[11]

At the most I may have smiled now and then, to discover in Robert the marks of his Jesuit schooling in the embarrassment which the fear of hurting people's feelings at once provoked in him whenever one of his intellectual friends made a social error or did something silly to which Saint-Loup himself attached no importance but felt that the other would have blushed if anybody had noticed it. And it was Robert who used to blush as though he were the guilty party, for instance on the day when Bloch, after promising to come and see him at the hotel, went on: "As I cannot endure to be kept waiting among all the false splendour of these great caravanserais, and the Hungarian band would make me ill, you must tell the 'lighft-boy' to make them shut up, and to let you know at once."

Personally, I was not particularly anxious that Bloch should come to the hotel. He was at Balbec, not by himself, unfortunately, but with his sisters, and they in turn had innumerable relatives and friends staying there. Now this Jewish colony was more picturesque than pleasing. Balbec was in this respect like such countries as Russia or Romania, where the geography books teach us that the Jewish population does not enjoy the same esteem and has not reached the same stage of assimilation as, for instance, in Paris. Always together, with no admixture of any other element, when the cousins and uncles of Bloch or their co-religionists male or female repaired to the Casino, the ladies to dance, the gentlemen branching off towards the baccarat-tables, they formed a solid troop, homogeneous within itself, and utterly dissimilar to the people who watched them go by and found them there again every year without ever exchanging a word or a greeting, whether these were the Cambremer set, or the senior judge's little group, professional or "business" people, or even simple corn-chandlers from Paris, whose daughters, handsome, proud, mocking and French as the statues at Rheims, would not care to mix with that horde of ill-bred sluts who carried their zeal for "seaside fashions" so far as to be always apparently on their way home from shrimping or out to dance the tango. As for the men, despite the brilliance of their dinner-jackets and patent-leather shoes, the exaggeration of their type made one think of the so-called "bright ideas" of those painters who, having to illustrate the Gospels or the Arabian Nights, consider the country in which the scenes are laid, and give to St Peter or to Ali Baba the identical features of the heaviest "punter" at the Balbec tables. Bloch introduced his sisters, who, though he silenced their chatter with the utmost rudeness, screamed with laughter at the mildest sallies of this brother who was their blindly worshipped idol. Although it is probable that this set of people contained, like every other, perhaps more than any other, plenty of attractions, qualities and virtues, in order to experience these one would first have had to penetrate it. But it was not popular, it sensed this, and saw there the mark of an anti-Semitism to which it presented a bold front in a compact and closed phalanx into which, as it happened, no one dreamed of trying to force his way.

As regards the word "lighft," I had all the less reason to be surprised at Bloch's pronunciation in that, a few days before, when he had asked me why I had come to

Balbec (although it seemed to him perfectly natural that he himself should be there) and whether it had been "in the hope of making grand friends," and I had explained to him that this visit was a fulfilment of one of my earliest longings, though one not so deep as my longing to see Venice, he had replied: "Yes, of course, to sip iced drinks with the pretty ladies, while pretending to read the *Stones of Venighce* by Lord John Ruskin, a dreary bore, in fact one of the most tedious old prosers you could find." Thus Bloch evidently thought that in England not only were all the inhabitants of the male sex called "Lord," but the letter "i" was invariably pronounced "igh." As for Saint-Loup, this mistake in pronunciation seemed to him all the more venial inasmuch as he saw in it pre-eminently a want of those almost "society" notions which my new friend despised as fully as he was versed in them. But the fear lest Bloch, discovering one day that one says "Venice" and that Ruskin was not a lord, should retrospectively imagine that Robert had thought him ridiculous, made the latter feel as guilty as if he had been found wanting in the indulgence with which, as we have seen, he overflowed, so that the blush which would doubtless one day dye the cheek of Bloch on the discovery of his error, Robert already, by anticipation and reversibility, could feel mounting to his own. For he assumed that Bloch attached more importance than he to this mistake—an assumption which Bloch confirmed some days later, when he heard me pronounce the word "lift," by breaking in with: "Oh, one says 'lift,' does one?" And then, in a dry and lofty tone: "Not that it's of the slightest importance." A phrase that is like a reflex action, the same in all proud and susceptible men, in the gravest circumstances as well as in the most trivial, betraying there as clearly as on this occasion how important the thing in question seems to him who declares that it is of no importance; a tragic phrase at times, the first to escape (and then how heart-breakingly) the lips of any man who is at all proud from whom we have just removed the last hope to which he still clung by refusing to do him a service: "Oh, well, it's not of the slightest importance; I shall make some other arrangement": the other arrangement which it is not of the slightest importance that he should be driven to adopt being sometimes suicide.

Thereupon Bloch made me the prettiest speeches. He was certainly anxious to be on the best of terms with me. And yet he asked me: "Is it because you've taken a fancy to the minor aristocracy that you run after de Saint-Loup-en-Bray? You must be suffering from a severe attack of snobbery. Tell me, are you a snob? I think so, what?" Not that his desire to be friendly had suddenly changed. But what is called in not too correct language "ill breeding" was his defect, therefore the defect which he was bound to overlook, and *a fortiori* the defect by which he did not believe that other people could be shocked.

In the human race, the frequency of the virtues that are identical in us all is not more wonderful than the multiplicity of the defects that are peculiar to each one of us. Undoubtedly, it is not common sense that is "the commonest thing in the world"; it is human kindness. In the most distant, the most desolate corners of the earth, we marvel to see it blossom of its own accord, as in a remote valley a poppy like all the poppies in the rest of the world, which it has never seen as it has never known anything but the wind that occasionally stirs the folds of its lonely scarlet cloak. Even if this human kindness, paralysed by self-interest, is not put into practice, it exists none the less, and whenever there is no selfish motive to restrain it, for example when reading a novel or a newspaper, it will blossom, even in the heart of one who, cold-blooded in real life, has retained a tender heart as a lover of serial romances, and turn towards the weak, the just and the persecuted. But the variety of our defects is no less remarkable than the similarity of our virtues. The most perfect person in the world has a certain defect which shocks us or makes us angry. One man is of rare intelligence, sees everything from the loftiest viewpoint, never speaks ill of anyone, but will pocket and forget letters of supreme importance which he himself asked you to let him post for you, and so make you miss a vital engagement without offering you any excuse, with a smile, because he prides himself upon never knowing the time. Another is so refined, so gentle, so delicate in his conduct that he never says anything to you about yourself that you would not be glad to hear, but you feel that he suppresses, that he keeps buried in his heart, where they turn sour, other, quite different opinions, and the pleasure that he derives from seeing you is so dear to him that he will let you faint with exhaustion sooner than leave you to yourself. A third has more sincerity, but carries it so far that he feels bound to let you know, when you have pleaded the state of your health as an excuse for not having been to see him, that you were seen going to the theatre and were reported to be looking well, or else that he has not been able to turn to full advantage the step you took on his behalf, which in any case three other people had already offered to take, so that he is only moderately indebted to you. In similar circumstances the previous friend would have pretended not to know that you had gone to the theatre, or that other people could have done him the same service. But this last friend feels himself obliged to repeat or to reveal to somebody the very thing that is most likely to give offence; is delighted with his own frankness and tells you, emphatically: "I am like that." While others infuriate you by their exaggerated curiosity, or by a want of curiosity so absolute that you can speak to them of the most sensational happenings without their knowing what it is all about; and others again take months to answer you if your letter has been about something that concerns yourself and not them, or else, if they write that they are coming to ask you for something and you dare not leave the house for fear of missing them, do not appear, but leave you in suspense for weeks because, not having received from you the answer which their letter did not in the least call for, they have concluded that you must be cross with them. And others, considering their own wishes and not yours, talk to you without letting you get a word in if they are in good spirits and want to see you, however urgent the work you may have in hand, but if they feel exhausted by the weather or out of humour, you cannot drag a word out of them, they greet your efforts with an inert languor and no more take the trouble to reply, even in monosyllables, to what you say to them than if they had not heard you. Each of our friends has his defects, to such an extent that to continue to love him we are obliged to console ourselves for them—by thinking of his talent, his kindness, his affection—or rather by ignoring them, for which we need to deploy all our good will. Unfortunately our obliging obstinacy in refusing to see the defect in our friend is surpassed by the obstinacy with which he persists in that defect, from his own blindness to it or the blindness that he attributes to other people. For he does not notice it himself or imagines that it is not noticed. Since the risk of giving offence arises principally from the difficulty of appreciating what does and what does not pass unnoticed, we ought at least, from prudence, never to speak of ourselves, because that is a subject on which we may be sure that other people's views are never in accordance with our own. If, when we discover the true lives of other people, the real world beneath the world of appearance, we get as many surprises as on visiting a house of plain exterior which inside is full of hidden treasures, torture-chambers or skeletons, we are no less surprised if, in place of the image that we have of ourselves as a result of all the things that people have said to us, we learn from the way they speak of us in our absence what an entirely different image they have been carrying in their minds of us and of our lives. So that whenever we have spoken about ourselves, we may be sure that our inoffensive and prudent words, listened to with apparent politeness and hypocritical approbation, have given rise afterwards to the most exasperated or the most mirthful, but in either case the least favourable comments. At the very least we run the risk of irritating people by the disproportion between our idea of ourselves and the words that we use, a disproportion which as a rule makes people's talk about themselves as ludicrous as the performances of those self-styled music-lovers who when they feel the need to hum a favourite tune compensate for the inadequacy of their inarticulate murmurings by a strenuous mimicry and an air of admiration which is hardly justified by what they let us hear. And to the bad habit of speaking about oneself and one's defects there must be added, as part of the same thing, that habit of denouncing in other people defects precisely analogous to one's own. For it is always of those defects that one speaks, as though it were a way of speaking of oneself indirectly, and adding to the pleasure of absolving oneself the pleasure of confession. Moreover it seems that our attention, always attracted by what is characteristic of ourselves, notices it more than anything else in other people. One short-sighted man says of another: "But he can scarcely open his eyes!"; a consumptive has his doubts as to the pulmonary integrity of the most robust; an unwashed man speaks only of the baths that other people do not take; an evil-smelling man insists that other people smell; a cuckold sees cuckolds everywhere, a light woman light women, a snob snobs. Then, too, every vice, like every profession, requires and develops a special knowledge which we are never loath to display. The invert sniffs out inverts; the tailor asked out to dine has hardly begun to talk to you before he has already appraised the cloth of your coat, which his fingers are itching to feel; and if after a few words of conversation you were to ask a dentist what he really thought of you, he would tell you how many of your teeth wanted filling. To him nothing appears more important, or to you, who have noticed his, more absurd. And it is not only when we speak of ourselves that we imagine other people to be blind; we behave as though they were. Each one of us has a special god in attendance who hides from him or promises him the concealment of his defect from other people, just as he closes the eyes and nostrils of people who do not wash to the streaks of dirt which they carry in their ears and the smell of sweat that emanates from their armpits, and assures them that they can with impunity carry both of these about a world that will notice nothing. And those who wear artificial pearls, or give them as presents, imagine that people will take them to be genuine.

Bloch was ill-bred, neurotic and snobbish, and since he belonged to a family of little repute, had to support, as on the floor of the ocean, the incalculable pressures imposed on him not only by the Christians at the surface but by all the intervening layers of Jewish castes superior to his own, each of them crushing with its contempt the one that was immediately beneath it. To pierce his way through to the open air by raising himself from Jewish family to Jewish family would have taken Bloch many thousands of years. It was better to seek an outlet in another direction.

When Bloch spoke to me of the attack of snobbery from which I must be suffering, and bade me confess that I was a snob, I might well have replied: "If I were, I shouldn't be going about with you." I said merely that he was not being very polite. Then he wanted to apologise, but in the way that is typical of the ill-bred man who is only too happy, in retracting his words, to find an opportunity to aggravate his offence. "Forgive me," he would now say to me whenever we met, "I've distressed you, tormented you, I've been wantonly mischievous. And yet—man in general and your friend in particular is so singular an animal—you cannot imagine the affection that I, I who tease you so cruelly, have for you. It brings me often, when I think of you, to the verge of tears." And he gave an audible sob.

What astonished me more in Bloch than his bad manners was to find how the quality of his conversation varied. This youth, so hard to please that of authors who were at the height of their fame he would say: "He's a dismal fool; he's a sheer imbecile," would every now and then recount with immense gusto anecdotes that were simply not funny or would instance as a "really remarkable person" someone who was completely insignificant. This double scale of measuring the wit, the worth, the interest of people continued to puzzle me until I was introduced to M. Bloch, senior.

I had not supposed that we should ever be allowed to meet him, for Bloch junior had spoken ill of me to Saint-Loup and of Saint-Loup to me. In particular, he had said to Robert that I was (still) a frightful snob. "Yes, really, he's thrilled to know M. LLLLegrandin." This trick of Bloch's of isolating a word was a sign at once of irony and literature. Saint-Loup, who had never heard the name Legrandin, was bewildered: "But who is he?" "Oh, he's a *very distinguished* person," Bloch replied with a laugh, thrusting his hands into his pockets as though for warmth, convinced that he was at that moment engaged in contemplation of the picturesque aspect of an extraordinary country gentleman compared to whom those of Barbey d'Aurevilly were as nothing. He consoled himself for his inability to portray M. Legrandin by giving him a string of capital L's and smacking his lips over the name as over a wine of the finest vintage. But these subjective enjoyments remained hidden from other people. If he spoke ill of me to Saint-Loup he made up for it by speaking no less ill of Saint-Loup to me. We had each of us learned these slanders in detail the very next day, not that we had repeated them to each other, a thing which would have seemed to us very wrong but to Bloch appeared so natural and almost inevitable that in his natural anxiety, in the certainty moreover that he would be telling us only what each of us was bound sooner or later to learn, he preferred to anticipate the disclosure and, taking Saint-Loup aside, admitted that he had spoken ill of him, on purpose, so that it might be repeated to him, swore to him "by Zeus Kronion, binder of oaths" that he loved him dearly, that he would lay down his life for him, and wiped away a tear. The same day, he contrived to see me alone, made his confession, declared that he had acted in my interest, because he felt that a certain kind of social intercourse was fatal to me and that I was "worthy of better things." Then, clasping me by the hand with the sentimentality of a drunkard, although his drunkenness was purely nervous: "Believe me," he said, "and may the black Ker seize me this instant and bear me across the portals of Hades, hateful to men, if yesterday, when I thought of you, of Combray, of my boundless affection for you, of afternoon hours in class which you do not even remember, I did not lie awake sobbing all night long. Yes, all night long, I swear it, and alas, I know—for I know the human soul—you will not believe me." I did indeed "not believe" him, and to these words which I felt he was making up on the spur of the moment and developing as he went on, his swearing "by Ker" added no great weight, the Hellenic cult being in Bloch purely literary. Besides, whenever he began to get emotional over a falsehood and wanted one to share his emotion, he would say "I swear it," more for the hysterical pleasure of lying than to make one think that he was speaking the truth. I did not believe what he was saying, but I bore him no ill-will on that account, for I had inherited from my mother and grandmother their incapacity for rancour even against far worse offenders, and their habit of never condemning anyone.

Besides, Bloch was not altogether a bad fellow: he was capable of being extremely nice. And now that the race of Combray, the race from which sprang creatures as absolutely unspoiled as my grandmother and my mother, seems almost extinct, since I no longer have much choice except between decent brutes, frank and insensitive, the mere sound of whose voices shows at once that they take absolutely no interest in your life—and another kind of men who so long as they are with you understand you, cherish you, grow sentimental to the point of tears, then make up for it a few hours later with some cruel joke at your expense, but come back to you, always just as understanding, as charming, as in tune with you for the moment, I think that it is of this latter sort that I prefer, if not the moral worth, at any rate the society.

"You cannot imagine my grief when I think of you," Bloch went on. "Actually, I suppose it's a rather Jewish side of my nature coming out," he added ironically, contracting his pupils as though measuring out under the microscope an infinitesimal quantity of "Jewish blood," as a French nobleman might (but never would) have said who among his exclusively Christian ancestry nevertheless numbered Samuel Bernard, or further back still, the Blessed Virgin from whom, it is said, the Lévy family claim descent. "I rather like," he continued, "to take into account the element in my feelings (slight though it is) which may be ascribed to my Jewish origin." He made this statement because it seemed to him at once clever and courageous to speak the truth about his race, a truth which at the same time he managed to water down to a remarkable extent, like misers who decide to discharge their debts but cannot bring themselves to pay more than half of them. This kind of deceit which consists in having the boldness to proclaim the truth, but only after mixing with it an ample measure of lies which falsify it, is commoner than people think, and even among those who do not habitually practise it certain crises in life, especially those in which a love affair is involved, give them occasion to indulge in it.

All these confidential diatribes by Bloch to Saint-Loup against me and to me against Saint-Loup ended in an invitation to dinner. I am by no means sure that he did not first make an attempt to secure Saint-Loup by himself. It would have been so like Bloch to do so that probably he did; but if so, success did not crown his effort, for it was to myself and Saint-Loup both that he said one day: "Dear master, and you, O horseman beloved of Ares, de Saint-Loup-en-Bray, tamer of horses, since I have encountered you by the shore of Amphitrite, resounding with foam, hard by the tents of the swift-shipped Meniers, will both of you come to dinner one day this week with my illustrious sire, of blameless heart?" He proffered this invitation because he desired to attach himself more closely to Saint-Loup who would, he hoped, secure him the right of entry into aristocratic circles. Formed by me, for myself, this ambition would have seemed to Bloch the mark of the most hideous snobbery, quite in keeping with the opinion that he already held of a whole side of my nature which he did not regard—or at least had not hitherto regarded—as the most important side; but the same ambition in himself seemed to him the proof of a finely developed curiosity in a mind anxious to carry out certain social explorations from which he might perhaps glean some literary benefit. M. Bloch senior, when his son had told him that he was going to bring one of his friends in to dinner, and had in a sarcastic but self-satisfied tone enunciated the name and title of that friend: "The Marquis de Saint-Loup-en-Bray," had been thrown into great commotion. "The Marquis de Saint-Loup-en-Bray! I'll be jiggered!" he had exclaimed, using the oath which was with him the strongest indication of social deference. And he gazed at a son capable of having formed such an acquaintance with an admiring look which seemed to say: "He really is astounding. Can this prodigy be indeed a child of mine!" which gave my friend as much pleasure as if his monthly allowance had been increased by fifty francs. For Bloch was not in his element at home and felt that his father treated him like a black sheep because of his inveterate admiration for Leconte de Lisle, Heredia and other "Bohemians." But to have got to know Saint-Loup-en-Bray, whose father had been chairman of the Suez Canal board ("I'll be jiggered!") was an indisputable "score." What a pity that they had left the stereoscope in Paris for fear of its being broken on the journey. M. Bloch senior alone had the skill, or at least the right, to manipulate it. He did so, moreover, on rare occasions only, and then to good purpose, on evenings when there was a full-dress affair, with hired waiters. So that from these stereoscope sessions there emanated, for those who were present, as it were a special distinction, a privileged position, and for the master of the house who gave them, a prestige such as talent confers on a man—which could not have been greater had the pictures been taken by M. Bloch himself and the machine his own invention. "You weren't invited to Solomon's yesterday?" one of the family would ask another. "No! I wasn't one of the elect. What was on?" "Oh, a great how-d'ye-do, the stereoscope, the whole box of tricks!" "Indeed! If they had the stereoscope I'm sorry I wasn't there; they say Solomon is quite amazing when he works it."

"Ah, well," said M. Bloch now to his son, "it's a mistake to let him have everything at once. Now he'll have something else to look forward to."

He had actually thought, in his paternal affection and in the hope of touching his son's heart, of sending for the instrument. But it was not "physically possible" in the time, or rather they had thought it would not be; for we were obliged to put off the dinner because Saint-Loup could not leave the hotel, where he was expecting an uncle who was coming to spend a few days with Mme de Villeparisis. Since he was greatly addicted to physical culture, and especially to long walks, it was largely on foot, spending the night in wayside farms, that this uncle was to make the journey from the country house in which he was staying, and the precise moment of his arrival at Balbec was somewhat uncertain. Indeed Saint-Loup, afraid to stir out of doors, even entrusted me with the duty of taking to Incarville, where the nearest telegraph-office was, the messages that he sent every day to his mistress. The uncle in question was called Palamède, a Christian name that had come down to him from his ancestors the Princes of Sicily. And later on, when I found, in the course of my historical reading, belonging to this or that

Podestà or Prince of the Church, the same Christian name, a fine Renaissance medal—some said a genuine antique—that had always remained in the family, having passed from generation to generation, from the Vatican cabinet to the uncle of my friend, I felt the pleasure that is reserved for those who, unable from lack of means to start a medal collection or a picture gallery, look out for old names (names of localities, instructive and picturesque as an old map, a bird's-eye view, a sign-board or an inventory of customs; baptismal names whose fine French endings echo the defect of speech, the intonation of an ethnic vulgarity, the corrupt pronunciation whereby our ancestors made Latin and Saxon words undergo lasting mutilations which in due course became the august lawgivers of our grammar books) and, in short, by drawing upon these collections of ancient sonorities, give themselves concerts like the people who acquire violas da gamba and violas d'amore to perform the music of the past on old instruments. Saint-Loup told me that even in the most exclusive aristocratic society his uncle Palamède stood out as being particularly unapproachable, scornful, obsessed with his nobility, forming with his brother's wife and a few other chosen spirits what was known as the Phoenix Club. Even there his insolence was so dreaded that it had happened more than once that society people who had been anxious to meet him and had applied to his own brother for an introduction had met with a refusal: "Really, you mustn't ask me to introduce you to my brother Palamède. Even if my wife and the whole lot of us put ourselves to the task it would be no good. Or else you'd run the risk of his being rude to you, and I shouldn't like that." At the Jockey Club he had, with a few of his friends, marked a list of two hundred members whom they would never allow to be introduced to them. And in the Comte de Paris's circle he was known by the nickname of "The Prince" because of his elegance and his pride.

Saint-Loup told me about his uncle's early life, now long since past. Every day he used to take women to a bachelor establishment which he shared with two of his friends, as good-looking as himself, on account of which they were known as "the three Graces."

"One day, a man who is now one of the brightest luminaries of the Faubourg Saint-Germain, as Balzac would have said, but who at a rather unfortunate stage of his early life displayed bizarre tastes, asked my uncle to let him come to this place. But no sooner had he arrived than it was not to the ladies but to my uncle Palamède that he began to make overtures. My uncle pretended not to understand, and took his two friends aside on some pretext or other. They reappeared on the scene, seized the offender, stripped him, thrashed him till he bled, and then in ten degrees of frost kicked him outside where he was found more dead than alive; so much so that the police started an inquiry which the poor devil had the greatest difficulty in getting them to abandon. My uncle would never go in for such drastic methods now—in fact you can't imagine the number of working men he takes under his wing, only to be repaid quite often with the basest ingratitude—though he's so haughty with society people. It may be a servant who has looked after him in a hotel, for whom he will find a place in Paris, or a farm-labourer whom he will pay to have taught a trade. It's a really rather nice side of his character, in contrast to his social side." For Saint-Loup belonged to that type of young men of fashion, situated at an altitude at which it has been possible to cultivate such expressions as "what is really rather nice about him," "his nicer side," precious seeds which produce very rapidly a way of looking at things in which one counts oneself as nothing and the "people" as everything; the exact opposite, in a word, of plebeian pride. "I'm told it was quite extraordinary to what extent he set the tone, to what extent he laid down the law for the whole of society when he was a young man. As far as he was concerned, in any circumstance he did whatever seemed most agreeable or most convenient to himself, but immediately it was imitated by all the snobs. If he felt thirsty at the theatre, and had a drink brought to him in his box, a week later the little sitting-rooms behind all the boxes would be filled with refreshments. One wet summer when he had a touch of rheumatism, he ordered an overcoat of a loose but warm vicuna wool, which is generally used for travelling rugs, and insisted on the blue and orange stripes. The big tailors at once received orders from their customers for blue overcoats, fringed and shaggy. If for some reason he wanted to remove every aspect of ceremony from a dinner in a country house where he was spending the day, and to underline the distinction had come without evening clothes and sat down to table in the suit he had been wearing that afternoon, it became the fashion not to dress for dinner in the country. If instead of taking a spoon to eat a pudding he used a fork, or a special implement of his own invention which he had had made for him by a silversmith, or his fingers, it was no longer permissible to eat it in any other way. He wanted once to hear some

Beethoven quartets again (for with all his preposterous ideas he is far from being a fool and has great gifts) and arranged for some musicians to come and play them to him and a few friends once a week. The ultra-fashionable thing that season was to give quite small parties with chamber music. I should say he's not done at all badly out of life. With his looks, he must have had any number of women! I couldn't tell you exactly which, because he's very discreet. But I do know that he was thoroughly unfaithful to my poor aunt. Which doesn't mean that he wasn't always perfectly charming to her, that she didn't adore him, and that he didn't go on mourning her for years. When he's in Paris, he still goes to the cemetery nearly every day."

The morning after Robert had told me all these things about his uncle while waiting for him (as it happened in vain), as I was passing the Casino alone on my way back to the hotel, I had the sensation of being watched by somebody who was not far off. I turned my head and saw a man of about forty, very tall and rather stout, with a very black moustache, who, nervously slapping the leg of his trousers with a switch, was staring at me, his eyes dilated with extreme attentiveness. From time to time these eyes were shot through by a look of restless activity such as the sight of a person they do not know excites only in men in whom, for whatever reason, it inspires thoughts that would not occur to anyone else—madmen, for instance, or spies. He darted a final glance at me that was at once bold, prudent, rapid and profound, like a last shot which one fires at an enemy as one turns to flee, and, after first looking all round him, suddenly adopting an absent and lofty air, with an abrupt revolution of his whole person he turned towards a playbill in the reading of which he became absorbed, while he hummed a tune and fingered the moss-rose in his button-hole. He drew from his pocket a note-book in which he appeared to be taking down the title of the performance that was announced, looked at his watch two or three times, pulled down over his eyes a black straw hat the brim of which he extended with his hand held out over it like an eye-shade, as though to see whether someone was coming at last, made the perfunctory gesture of annoyance by which people mean to show that they have waited long enough, although they never make it when they are really waiting, then pushing back his hat and exposing a scalp cropped close except at the sides where he allowed a pair of waved "pigeon's-wings" to grow quite long, he emitted the loud panting breath that people exhale not when they are too hot but when they wish it to be thought that they are too hot. He gave me the impression of a hotel crook who, having been watching my grandmother and myself for some days, and planning to rob us, had just discovered that I had caught him in the act of spying on me. Perhaps he was only seeking by his new attitude to express abstractedness and detachment in order to put me off the scent, but it was with an exaggeration so aggressive that his object appeared to be—at least as much as the dissipating of the suspicions he might have aroused in me—to avenge a humiliation which I must unwittingly have inflicted on him, to give me the idea not so much that he had not seen me as that I was an object of too little importance to attract his attention. He threw back his shoulders with an air of bravado, pursed his lips, twisted his moustache, and adjusted his face into an expression that was at once indifferent, harsh, and almost insulting. So much so that I took him at one moment for a thief and at another for a lunatic. And yet his scrupulously ordered attire was far more sober and far more simple than that of any of the summer visitors I saw at Balbec, and reassured me as to my own suit, so often humiliated by the usual dazzling whiteness of their holiday garb. But my grandmother was coming towards me, we took a turn together, and I was waiting for her, an hour later, outside the hotel into which she had gone for a moment, when I saw emerge from it Mme de Villeparisis with Robert de Saint-Loup and the stranger who had stared at me so intently outside the Casino. Swift as a lightning-flash his look shot through me, just as at the moment when I had first noticed him, and returned, as though he had not seen me, to hover, slightly lowered, before his eyes, deadened, like the neutral look which feigns to see nothing without and is incapable of reporting anything to the mind within, the look which expresses merely the satisfaction of feeling round it the eyelids which it keeps apart with its beatific roundness, the devout and sanctimonious look that we see on the faces of certain hypocrites, the smug look on those of certain fools. I saw that he had changed his clothes. The suit he was wearing was darker even than the other; and no doubt true elegance lies nearer to simplicity than false; but there was something more: from close at hand one felt that if colour was almost entirely absent from these garments it was not because he who had banished it from them was indifferent to it but rather because for some reason he forbade himself the enjoyment of it. And the sobriety which they displayed seemed to be of the kind that comes from obedience to a rule of diet rather than from lack of appetite. A dark green thread harmonised, in the stuff of his trousers, with the stripe on his socks, with a refinement which betrayed the vivacity of a taste that was everywhere else subdued, to which this single concession had been made out of tolerance, while a spot of red on his tie was imperceptible, like a liberty which one dares not take.

"How are you? Let me introduce my nephew, the Baron de Guermantes," Mme de Villeparisis said to me, while the stranger, without looking at me, muttering a vague "Charmed!" which he followed with a "H'm, h'm, h'm," to make his affability seem somehow forced, and crooking his little finger, forefinger and thumb, held out to me his middle and ring fingers, destitute of rings, which I clasped through his suede glove; then, without lifting his eyes to my face, he turned towards Mme de Villeparisis.

"Good gracious, I shall be forgetting my own name next!" she exclaimed with a laugh. "Here am I calling you Baron de Guermantes. Let me introduce the Baron de Charlus. But after all, it's not a very serious mistake," she went on, "for you're a thorough Guermantes all the same."

By this time my grandmother had reappeared, and we all set out together. Saint-Loup's uncle declined to honour me not only with a word but with so much as a look in my direction. If he stared strangers out of countenance (and during this short excursion he two or three times hurled his terrible and searching scrutiny like a sounding-lead at insignificant people of the most humble extraction who happened to pass), on the other hand he never for a moment, if I was to judge by myself, looked at persons whom he knew—as a detective on a secret mission might except his personal friends from his professional vigilance. Leaving my grandmother, Mme de Villeparisis and him to talk to one another, I fell behind with Saint-Loup.

"Tell me, am I right in thinking I heard Mme de Villeparisis say just now to your uncle that he was a Guermantes?"

"Of course he is: Palamède de Guermantes."

"Not the same Guermantes who have a place near Combray, and claim descent from Geneviève de Brabant?"

"Most certainly: my uncle, who is the very last word in heraldry and all that sort of thing, would tell you that our 'cry,' our war-cry, that is to say, which was changed afterwards to 'Passavant,' was originally 'Combraysis,'" he said, smiling so as not to appear to be priding himself on this prerogative of a "cry," which only the quasi-royal houses, the great chiefs of feudal bands, enjoyed. "It's his brother who has the place now."

So she was related, and very closely, to the Guermantes, this Mme de Villeparisis who had for so long been for me the lady who had given me a duck filled with chocolates when I was small, more remote then from the Guermantes way than if she had been shut up somewhere on the Méséglise way, less brilliant, less highly placed by me than was the Combray optician, and who now suddenly went through one of those fantastic rises in value, parallel to the no less unforeseen depreciations of other objects in our possession, which—rise and fall alike—introduce in our youth, and in those periods of our life in which a trace of youth persists, changes as numerous as the Metamorphoses of Ovid.*

"Haven't they got the busts of all the old lords of Guermantes down there?"

"Yes, and a lovely sight they are!" Saint-Loup was ironical. "Between you and me, I look on all that sort of thing as rather a joke. But what they have got at Guermantes, which is a little more interesting, is quite a touching portrait of my aunt by Carrière. It's as fine as Whistler or Velasquez," went on Saint-Loup, who in his neophyte zeal was not always very exact about degrees of greatness. "There are also some stunning pictures by Gustave Moreau. My aunt is the niece of your friend Mme de Villeparisis; she was brought up by her, and married her cousin, who was a nephew, too, of my aunt Villeparisis, the present Duc de Guermantes."

"Then what is your uncle?"

"He bears the title of Baron de Charlus. Strictly, when my great-uncle died, my uncle Palamède ought to have taken the title of Prince des Laumes, which was that of his brother before he became Duc de Guermantes—in that family they change their names as often as their shirts. But my uncle has peculiar ideas about all that sort of thing. And as he feels that people are rather apt to overdo the Italian Prince and Grandee of Spain business nowadays, and although he had half-a-dozen princely titles to choose from, he has remained Baron de Charlus, as a protest, and with an apparent simplicity which really covers a good deal of pride. 'In these days,' he says, 'everybody is a prince; one really must have something to distinguish one; I shall call myself Prince when I wish to travel incognito.' According to him there is no older title than the Charlus barony; to prove to you that it's earlier than the Montmorency title, though they used to claim, quite wrongly, to be the premier barons of France when they were only premier in the Ile-de-France, where their fief was, my uncle will hold forth to you for hours on end and enjoy doing so because, although he's a most intelligent man, really gifted, he regards that sort of thing as quite a live topic of conversation." Saint-Loup smiled again. "But as I'm not like him, you mustn't ask me to talk pedigrees. I know nothing more deadly, more outdated; really, life's too short."

I now recognised in the hard look which had made me turn round outside the Casino the same that I had seen fixed on me at Tansonville at the moment when Mme Swann had called Gilberte away.

"Wasn't Mme Swann one of the numerous mistresses you told me your uncle M. de Charlus had had?"

"Good lord, no! That is to say, my uncle's a great friend of Swann, and has always stood up for him. But no one has ever suggested that he was his wife's lover. You would cause the utmost astonishment in Parisian society if people thought you believed that."

I dared not reply that it would have caused even greater astonishment in Combray society if people had thought that I did not believe it.

My grandmother was delighted with M. de Charlus. No doubt he attached an extreme importance to all questions of birth and social position, and my grandmother had remarked this, but without any trace of that severity which as a rule embodies a secret envy and irritation, at seeing another person enjoy advantages which one would like but cannot oneself possess. Since, on the contrary, my grandmother, content with her lot and not for a moment regretting that she did not move in a more brilliant sphere, employed only her intellect in observing the eccentricities of M. de Charlus, she spoke of Saint-Loup's uncle with that detached, smiling, almost affectionate benevolence with which we reward the object of our disinterested observation for the pleasure that it has given us, all the more so because this time the object was a person whose pretensions, if not legitimate at any rate picturesque, made him stand out in fairly vivid contrast to the people whom she generally had occasion to see. But it was above all in consideration of his intelligence and sensibility, qualities which it was easy to see that M. de Charlus, unlike so many of the society people whom Saint-Loup derided, possessed in a marked degree, that my grandmother had so readily forgiven him his aristocratic prejudice. And yet this prejudice had not been sacrificed by the uncle, as it had been by the nephew, to higher qualities. Rather, M. de Charlus had reconciled it with them. Possessing, by virtue of his descent from the Ducs de Nemours and the Princes de Lamballe, documents, furniture, tapestries, portraits painted for his ancestors by Raphael, Velasquez, Boucher, justified in saying that he was "visiting" a museum and a matchless library when he was merely going over his family mementoes, he still placed the whole heritage of the aristocracy in the high position from which Saint-Loup had toppled it. Perhaps also, being less ideological than Saint-Loup, less satisfied with words, a more realistic observer of men, he did not care to neglect an essential element of prestige in their eyes which, if it gave certain disinterested pleasures to his imagination, could often be a powerfully effective aid to his utilitarian activities. No agreement can ever be reached between men of his sort and those who obey an inner ideal which drives them to rid themselves of such advantages so that they may seek only to realise that ideal, resembling in that respect the painters and writers who renounce their virtuosity, the artistic people who modernise themselves, the warrior people who initiate universal disarmament, the absolute governments which turn democratic and repeal their harsh laws, though as often as not the sequel fails to reward their noble efforts; for the artists lose their talent, the nations their age-old predominance; pacifism often breeds wars and tolerance criminality. If Saint-Loup's strivings towards sincerity and emancipation could not but be regarded as extremely noble, to judge by their visible result, one could still be thankful that they had failed to bear fruit in M. de Charlus, who had transferred to his own home much of the admirable furniture from the Hôtel Guermantes instead of replacing it, like his nephew, with Art Nouveau furniture, pieces by Lebourg or Guillaumin. It was none the less true that M. de Charlus's ideal was highly artificial, and, if the epithet can be applied to the word ideal, as much social as artistic. In certain women of great beauty and rare culture whose ancestresses, two centuries earlier, had shared in all the glory and grace of the old order, he found a distinction which made him capable of taking pleasure in their society alone, and doubtless his admiration for them was sincere, but countless reminiscences, historical and artistic, evoked by their names played a considerable part in it, just as memories of classical antiquity are one of the reasons for the pleasure which a literary man finds in reading an ode by Horace that is perhaps inferior to poems of our own day which would leave him cold. Any of these women by the side of a pretty commoner was for him what an old picture is to a contemporary canvas representing a procession or a wedding—one of those old pictures the history of which we know, from the Pope or King who ordered them, through the hands of the eminent persons whose acquisition of them, by gift, purchase, conquest or inheritance, recalls to us some event or at least some alliance of historic interest, and consequently some knowledge that we ourselves have acquired, gives it new meaning, increases our sense of the richness of the possessions of our memory or of our erudition. M. de Charlus was thankful that a prejudice similar to his own, by preventing these few great ladies from mixing with women whose blood was less pure, presented them for his veneration intact, in their unadulterated nobility, like some eighteenth-century façade supported on its flat columns of pink marble, in which the passage of time has wrought no change.

M. de Charlus extolled the true "nobility" of mind and heart which characterised these women, playing upon the word in a double sense by which he himself was taken in, and in which lay the falsehood of this bastard conception, of this medley of aristocracy, generosity and art, but also its seductiveness, dangerous to people like my grandmother, to whom the less refined but more innocent prejudice of a nobleman who cared only about quarterings and took no thought for anything besides would have appeared too silly for words, whereas she was defenceless as soon as a thing presented itself under the externals of an intellectual superiority, so much so, indeed, that she regarded princes as enviable above all other men because they were able to have a La Bruyère or a Fénelon as their tutors.

Outside the Grand Hotel the three Guermantes left us; they were going to luncheon with the Princesse de Luxembourg. While my grandmother was saying goodbye to Mme de Villeparisis and Saint-Loup to my grandmother, M. de Charlus, who up till then had not addressed a single word to me, drew back from the group and arriving at my side, said to me: "I shall be taking tea this evening after dinner in my aunt Villeparisis's room. I hope that you will give me the pleasure of seeing you there with your grandmother." With which he rejoined the Marquise.

Although it was Sunday, there were no more carriages waiting outside the hotel now than at the beginning of the season. The notary's wife, in particular, had decided that it was not worth the expense of hiring one every time simply because she was not going to the Cambremers', and simply stayed in her room.

"Is Mme Blandais not well?" her husband was asked. "We haven't seen her all morning."

"She has a slight headache—the heat, you know, this thundery weather. The least thing upsets her. But I expect you'll see her this evening. I've told her she ought to come down. It can do her nothing but good."

I had supposed that in thus inviting us to take tea with his aunt, whom I never doubted that he would have warned of our coming, M. de Charlus wished to make amends for the impoliteness which he had shown me during our walk that morning. But when, on our entering Mme de Villeparisis's room, I attempted to greet her nephew, for all that I walked right round him while in shrill accents he was telling a somewhat spiteful story about one of his relatives, I could not succeed in catching his eye. I decided to say "Good evening" to him, and fairly loud, to warn him of my presence; but I realised that he had observed it, for before ever a word had passed my lips, just as I was beginning to bow to him, I saw his two fingers held out for me to shake without his having turned to look at me or paused in his story. He had evidently seen me, without letting it appear that he had, and I noticed then that his eyes, which were never fixed on the person to whom he was speaking, strayed perpetually in all directions, like those of certain frightened animals, or those of street hawkers who, while delivering their patter and displaying their illicit merchandise, keep a sharp look-out, though without turning their heads, on the different points of the horizon from which the police may appear at any moment. At the same time I was a little surprised to find that Mme de Villeparisis, while glad to see us, did not seem to have been expecting us, and I was still more surprised to hear M. de Charlus say to my grandmother: "Ah! what a capital idea of yours to come and pay us a visit! Charming of them, is it not, my dear aunt?" No doubt he had noticed his aunt's surprise at our entry and thought, as a man accustomed to set the tone, that it would be enough to transform that surprise into joy were he to show that he himself felt it, that it was indeed the feeling which our arrival there ought to prompt. In which he calculated wisely; for Mme de Villeparisis, who had a high opinion of her nephew and knew how difficult it was to please him, appeared suddenly to have found new attractions in my grandmother and welcomed her with open arms. But I failed to understand how M. de Charlus could, in the space of a few hours, have forgotten the invitation—so curt but apparently so intentional, so premeditated—which he addressed to me that same morning, or why he called a "capital idea" on my grandmother's part an idea that had been entirely his own. With a regard for accuracy which I retained until I had reached the age at which I realised that it is not by questioning him that one learns the truth of what another man has had in his mind, and that the risk of a misunderstanding which will probably pass unobserved is less than that which may come from a purblind insistence: "But, Monsieur," I reminded him, "you remember, surely, that it was you who asked me if we would come round this evening?" Not a sound, not a movement betrayed that M. de Charles had so much as heard my question. Seeing which, I repeated it, like diplomats or like young men after a misunderstanding who endeavour, with untiring and unrewarded zeal, to obtain an explanation which their adversary is determined not to give them. Still M. de Charlus answered me not a word. I seemed to see hovering upon his lips the smile of those who from a great height pass judgment on the character and breeding of their inferiors.

Since he refused all explanation, I tried to provide one for myself, but succeeded only in hesitating between several, none of which might have been the right one. Perhaps he did not remember, or perhaps it was I who had failed to understand what he had said to me that morning . . . More probably, in his pride, he did not wish to appear to have sought the company of people he despised, and preferred to cast upon them the responsibility for their intrusion. But then, if he despised us, why had he been so anxious that we should come, or rather that my grandmother should come, for of the two of us it was to her alone that he spoke that evening, and never once to me? Talking with the utmost animation to her, as also to Mme de Villeparisis, hiding, so to speak, behind them as though he were seated at the back of a theatre-box, he merely turned from them every now and then the searching gaze of his penetrating eyes and fastened it on my face, with the same gravity, the same air of preoccupation, as if it had been a manuscript difficult to decipher.

No doubt, had it not been for those eyes, M. de Charlus's face would have been similar to the faces of many good-looking men. And when Saint-Loup, speaking to me of various other Guermantes, said on a later occasion: "Admittedly, they don't have that thoroughbred air, that look of being noblemen to their finger-tips, that uncle Palamède has," confirming my suspicion that a thoroughbred air and aristocratic distinction were not something mysterious and new but consisted in elements which I had recognised without difficulty and without receiving any particular impression from them, I was to feel that another of my illusions had been shattered. But however much M. de Charlus tried to seal hermetically the expression on that face, to which a light coating of powder lent a faintly theatrical aspect, the eyes were like two crevices, two loop-holes which alone he had failed to block, and through which, according to one's position in relation to him, one suddenly felt oneself in the path of some hidden weapon which seemed to bode no good, even to him who, without being altogether master of it, carried it within himself in a state of precarious equilibrium and always on the verge of explosion; and the circumspect and unceasingly restless expression of those eyes, with all the signs of exhaustion which the heavy pouches beneath them stamped upon his face, however carefully he might compose and regulate it, made one think of some incognito, some disguise assumed by a powerful man in danger, or merely by a dangerous—but tragic—individual. I should have liked to divine what was this secret which other men did not carry in their breasts and which had already made M. de Charlus's stare seem to me so enigmatic when I had seen him that morning outside the Casino. But with what I now knew of his family I could no longer believe that it was that of a thief, nor, after what I had heard of his conversation, of a madman. If he was so cold towards me, while making himself so agreeable to my grandmother, this did not perhaps arise from any personal antipathy, for in general, to the extent that he was kindly disposed towards women, of whose faults he spoke without, as a rule, departing from the utmost tolerance, he displayed towards men, and especially young men, a hatred so violent as to suggest that of certain misogynists for women. Of two or three "gigolos," relatives or intimate friends of Saint-Loup, who happened to mention their names, M. de Charlus remarked with an almost ferocious expression in sharp contrast to his usual coldness: "Young scum!" I gathered that the particular fault which he found in the young men of the day was their effeminacy. "They're nothing but women," he said with scorn. But what life would not have appeared effeminate beside that which he expected a man to lead, and never found energetic or virile enough? (He himself, when he walked across country, after long hours on the road would plunge his heated body into frozen streams.) He would not even concede that a man should wear a single ring.

But this obsession with virility did not prevent his having also the most delicate sensibilities. When Mme de Villeparisis asked him to describe to my grandmother some country house in which Mme de Sévigné had stayed, adding that she could not help feeling that there was something rather "literary" about that lady's distress at being parted from "that tiresome Mme de Grignan":

"On the contrary," he retorted, "I can think of nothing more genuine. Besides, it was a time in which feelings of that sort were thoroughly understood. The inhabitant of La Fontaine's Monomotapa, running round to see his friend who had appeared to him in a dream looking rather sad, the pigeon finding that the greatest of evils is the absence of the other pigeon, seem to you perhaps, my dear aunt, as exaggerated as Mme de Sévigné's impatience for the moment when she will be alone with her daughter. It's so beautiful, what she says when she leaves her: 'This parting gives a pain to my soul which I feel like an ache in my body. In absence one is liberal with the hours. One anticipates a time for which one is longing.' "

My grandmother was delighted to hear the Letters thus spoken of, exactly as she would have spoken of them herself. She was astonished that a man could understand them so well. She found in M. de Charlus a delicacy, a sensibility that were quite feminine. We said to each other afterwards, when we were by ourselves and discussed him together, that he must have come under the strong influence of a woman—his mother, or in later life his daughter if he had any children. "A mistress," I thought to myself, remembering the influence which Saint-Loup's seemed to have had over him and which enabled me to realise the degree to which men can be refined by the women with whom they live.

"Once she was with her daughter, she had probably nothing to say to her," put in Mme de Villeparisis.

"Most certainly she had: if it was only what she calls 'things so slight that nobody else would notice them but you and I.' And anyhow she was with her. And La Bruyère tells us that that is everything: 'To be with the people one loves, to speak to them, not to speak to them, it is all the same.' He is right: that is the only true happiness," added M. de Charlus in a mournful voice, "and alas, life is so ill arranged that one very rarely experiences it. Mme de Sévigné was after all less to be pitied than most of us. She spent a great part of her life with the person whom she loved."

"You forget that it wasn't 'love' in her case, since it was her daughter."

"But what matters in life is not whom or what one loves," he went on, in a judicial, peremptory, almost cutting tone, "it is the fact of loving. What Mme de Sévigné felt for her daughter has a far better claim to rank with the passion that Racine described in *Andromaque* or *Phèdre* than the commonplace relations young Sévigné had with his mistresses. It's the same with a mystic's love for his God. The hard and fast lines with which we circumscribe love arise solely from our complete ignorance of life."

"You like *Andromaque* and *Phèdre* that much?" Saint-Loup asked his uncle in a faintly contemptuous tone.

"There is more truth in a single tragedy of Racine than in all the dramatic works of Monsieur Victor Hugo," replied M. de Charlus.

"Society people really are appalling," Saint-Loup murmured in my ear. "Say what you like, to prefer Racine to Victor is a bit thick!" He was genuinely distressed by his uncle's words, but the satisfaction of saying "say what you like" and better still "a bit thick" consoled him.

In these reflexions upon the sadness of having to live apart from those one loves (which were to lead my grandmother to say to me that Mme de Villeparisis's nephew understood certain things a great deal better than his aunt, and moreover had something about him that set him far above the average clubman) M. de Charlus not only revealed a refinement of feeling such as men rarely show; his voice itself, like certain contralto voices in which the middle register has not been sufficiently cultivated, so that when they sing it sounds like an alternating duet between a young man and a woman, mounted, when he expressed these delicate sentiments, to its higher notes, took on an unexpected sweetness and seemed to embody choirs of betrothed maidens, of sisters, pouring out their fond feelings. But the bevy of young girls whom M. de Charlus in his horror of every kind of effeminacy would have been so distressed to learn that he gave the impression of sheltering thus within his voice did not confine themselves to the interpretation, the modulation of sentimental ditties. Often while M. de Charlus was talking one could hear their laughter, the shrill, fresh laughter of school-girls or coquettes twitting their companions with all the mischievousness of sharp tongues and quick wits.

He told us about a house that had belonged to his family, in which Marie-Antoinette had slept, with a park laid out by Le Nôtre, which now belonged to the Israels, the wealthy financiers, who had bought it. "Israel—at least that is the name these people go by, though it seems to me a generic, an ethnic term rather than a proper name. One cannot tell; possibly people of that sort do not have names, and are designated only by the collective title of the tribe to which they belong. It is of no importance! To have been the abode of the Guermantes and to belong to the Israels!!!" His voice rose. "It reminds me of a room in the Château of Blois where the caretaker who was showing me round said to me: 'This is where Mary Stuart used to say her prayers. I use it to keep my brooms in.' Naturally I wish to know no more of this house that has disgraced itself, any more than of my cousin Clara de Chimay who has left her husband. But I keep a photograph of the house, taken when it was still unspoiled, just as I keep one of the Princess before her large eyes had learned to gaze on anyone but my cousin. A photograph acquires something of the dignity which it ordinarily lacks when it ceases to be a reproduction of reality and shows us things that no longer exist. I could give you a copy, since you are interested in that style of architecture," he said to my grandmother. At that moment, noticing that the embroidered handkerchief which he had in his pocket was exhibiting its coloured border, he thrust it sharply down out of sight with the scandalised air of a prudish but far from innocent lady concealing attractions which, by an excess of scrupulosity, she regards as indecent.

"Would you believe it?" he went on. "The first thing

these people did was to destroy Le Nôtre's park, which is as bad as slashing a picture by Poussin. For that alone, these Israels ought to be in prison. It is true," he added with a smile, after a moment's silence, "that there are probably plenty of other reasons why they should be there! In any case, you can imagine the effect of an English garden with that architecture."

"But the house is in the same style as the Petit Trianon," said Mme de Villeparisis, "and Marie-Antoinette had an English garden laid out there."

"Which, after all, ruins Gabriel's façade," replied M. de Charlus. "Obviously, it would be an act of vandalism now to destroy the Hameau. But whatever may be the spirit of the age, I beg leave to doubt whether, in that respect, a whim of Mme Israels has the same justification as the memory of the Queen."

Meanwhile my grandmother had been making signs to me to go up to bed, in spite of the urgent appeals of Saint-Loup who, to my utter shame, had alluded in front of M. de Charlus to the depression which used often to come upon me at night before I went to sleep, and which his uncle must regard as betokening a sad want of virility. I lingered a few moments still, then went upstairs, and was greatly surprised when, a little later, having heard a knock at my bedroom door and asked who was there, I heard the voice of M. de Charlus saying dryly: "It is Charlus. May I come in, Monsieur? Monsieur," he continued in the same tone as soon as he had shut the door, "my nephew was saying just now that you were apt to be a little upset at night before going to sleep, and also that you were an admirer of Bergotte's books. As I had one here in my luggage which you probably do not know, I have brought it to you to while away these moments during which you are unhappy."

I thanked M. de Charlus warmly and told him that I had been afraid that what Saint-Loup had said to him about my distress at the approach of night would have made me appear in his eyes even more stupid than I was.

"Not at all," he answered in a gentler voice. "You have not, perhaps, any personal merit—I've no idea, so few people have! But for a time at least you have youth, and that is always an attraction. Besides, Monsieur, the greatest folly of all is to mock or to condemn in others what one does not happen to feel oneself. I love the night, and you tell me that you dread it. I love the scent of roses, and I have a friend whom it throws into a fever. Do you suppose that for that reason I consider him inferior to me? I try to understand everything and I take care to condemn nothing. In short, you must not be too sorry for yourself; I do not say that these moods of depression are not painful, I know how much one can suffer from things which others would not understand. But at least you have placed your affection wisely in your grandmother. You see a great deal of her. And besides, it is a legitimate affection, I mean one that is repaid. There are so many of which that cannot be said!"

He walked up and down the room, looking at one thing, picking up another. I had the impression that he had something to tell me, and could not find the right words to express it.

"I have another volume of Bergotte here. I will have it fetched for you," he went on, and rang the bell. Presently a page came. "Go and find me your head waiter. He is the only person here who is capable of performing an errand intelligently," said M. de Charlus stiffly. "Monsieur Aimé, sir?" asked the page. "I cannot tell you his name. Ah yes, I remember now, I did hear him called Aimé. Run along, I'm in a hurry." "He won't be a minute, sir, I saw him downstairs just now," said the page, anxious to appear efficient. A few minutes went by. The page returned. "Sir, M. Aimé has gone to bed. But I can take a message." "No, you must get him out of bed." "But I can't do that, sir; he doesn't sleep here." "Then you can leave us alone."

"But, Monsieur," I said when the page had gone, "you are too kind; one volume of Bergotte will be quite enough."

"That is just what I was thinking, after all." M. de Charlus continued to walk up and down the room. Several minutes passed in this way, then after a few moments' hesitation and several false starts, he swung sharply round and, in his earlier biting tone of voice, flung at me: "Good night, Monsieur!" and left the room.

After all the lofty sentiments which I had heard him express that evening, next day, which was the day of his departure, on the beach in the morning, as I was on my way down to bathe, when M. de Charlus came across to tell me that my grandmother was waiting for me to join her as soon as I left the water, I was greatly surprised to hear him say, pinching my neck as he spoke with a familiarity and a laugh that were frankly vulgar: "But he doesn't care a fig for his old grandmother, does he, eh? Little rascal!"

"What, Monsieur! I adore her!"

"Monsieur," he said stepping back a pace, and with a

glacial air, "you are still young; you should profit by your youth to learn two things: first, to refrain from expressing sentiments that are too natural not to be taken for granted; and secondly not to rush into speech in reply to things that are said to you before you have penetrated their meaning. If you had taken this precaution a moment ago you would have saved yourself the appearance of speaking at cross-purposes like a deaf man, thereby adding a second absurdity to that of having anchors embroidered on your bathing-dress. I have lent you a book by Bergotte which I require. See that it is brought to me within the next hour by that head waiter with the absurd and inappropriate name, who, I suppose, is not in bed at this time of day. You make me realise that I was premature in speaking to you last night of the charms of youth. I should have done you a greater service had I pointed out to you its thoughtlessness, its inconsequence, and its want of comprehension. I hope, Monsieur, that this little douche will be no less salutary to you than your bathe. But don't let me keep you standing: you may catch cold. Good day, Monsieur."

No doubt he felt remorse for this speech, for some time later I received—in a morocco binding on the front of which was inlaid a panel of tooled leather representing in demi-relief a spray of forget-me-nots—the book which he had lent me, and which I had sent back to him, not by Aimé who was apparently off duty, but by the lift-boy.

M. de Charlus having gone, Robert and I were free at last to dine with Bloch. And I realised during this little party that the stories too readily admitted by our friend as funny were favourite stories of M. Bloch senior, and that the son's "really remarkable person" was always one of his father's friends whom he had so classified. There are a certain number of people whom we admire in our childhood, a father who is wittier than the rest of the family, a teacher who acquires credit in our eyes from the philosophy he reveals to us, a schoolfellow more advanced than we are (which was what Bloch had been to me) who despises the Musset of the *Espoir en Dieu* when we still admire it, and when we have reached Leconte or Claudel will be raving only about

> At Saint-Blaise, at the Zuecca
> You were well, you were well pleased . . .

to which he will add:

> Padua is a place to adore
> Where very great doctors of law . . .
> But I prefer the polenta . . .
> Goes past in her cloak of velour
>   La Toppatelle,

and of all the *Nuits* will remember only:

> At Le Havre, facing the Atlantic,
> At Venice, in the Lido's gloom,
> Where on the grass above a tomb
> Comes to die the pale Adriatic.

So, whenever we confidently admire anyone, we collect from him and quote with admiration sayings vastly inferior to the sort which, left to our own judgment, we would sternly reject, just as the writer of a novel puts into it, on the pretext that they are true, "witticisms" and characters which in the living context are like a dead weight, mere padding. Saint-Simon's portraits, composed by himself evidently without any self-admiration, are admirable, whereas the strokes of wit of the clever people he knew which he cites as being delightful are frankly mediocre when they have not become meaningless. He would have scorned to invent what he reports as so acute or so colourful when said by Mme Cornuel or Louis XIV, a point which is to be remarked also in many other writers, and is capable of various interpretations, of which it is enough to note but one for the present: namely, that in the state of mind in which we "observe" we are a long way below the level to which we rise when we create.

There was, then, embedded in my friend Bloch, a father Bloch who lagged forty years behind his son and told preposterous stories at which he laughed as loudly, inside my friend's being, as did the real, visible, authentic Bloch senior, since to the laugh which the latter emitted, not without several times repeating the last word so that his audience might taste the full flavour of the story, was added the braying laugh with which the son never failed, at table, to greet his father's anecdotes. Thus it came about that after saying the most intelligent things Bloch junior, manifesting the portion that he had inherited from his family, would tell us for the thirtieth time some of the gems which Bloch senior brought out only (together with his swallow-tail coat) on the solemn occasions on which Bloch junior brought someone to the house on whom it was worth while making an impression: one of his masters, a "chum" who had taken all the prizes, or, this evening, Saint-Loup and myself. For instance: "A military critic of great insight, who had brilliantly worked out, supporting them with infallible proofs, the reasons for which, in the Russo-Japanese war, the Japanese must inevitably be beaten and the Russians victorious," or else: "He is an eminent gentleman who passes for a great financier in political circles and for a great politician in financial circles." These stories were interchangeable with one about the Baron de Rothschild and one about Sir Rufus Israels, who were brought into the conversation in an equivocal manner which might let it be supposed that M. Bloch knew them personally.

I myself was taken in, and from the way in which M. Bloch spoke of Bergotte I assumed that he too was an old friend. In fact, all the famous people M. Bloch claimed to know he knew only "without actually knowing them," from having seen them at a distance in the theatre or in the street. He imagined, moreover, that his own appearance, his name, his personality were not unknown to them, and that when they caught sight of him they had often to repress a furtive inclination to greet him. People in society, because they know men of talent in the flesh, because they have them to dinner in their houses, do not on that account understand them any better. But when one has lived to some extent in society, the silliness of its inhabitants makes one too desirous to live, makes one suppose too high a standard of intelligence, in the obscure circles in which people know only "without actually knowing." I was to discover this when I introduced the topic of Bergotte.

M. Bloch was not alone in being a social success at home. My friend was even more so with his sisters, whom he continually twitted in hectoring tones, burying his face in his plate, and making them laugh until they cried. They had adopted their brother's language, and spoke it fluently, as if it had been obligatory and the only form of speech that intelligent people could use. When we arrived, the eldest sister said to one of the younger ones: "Go, tell our sage father and our venerable mother!" "Whelps," said Bloch, "I present to you the cavalier Saint-Loup, hurler of javelins, who is come for a few days from Doncières to the dwellings of polished stone, fruitful in horses." And, since he was as vulgar as he was literate, his speech ended as a rule in some pleasantry of a less Homeric kind: "Come, draw closer your pepla with the fair clasps. What's all this fandangle? Does your mother know you're out?" And the misses Bloch collapsed in a tempest of laughter. I told their brother how much pleasure he had given me by recommending me to read Bergotte, whose books I had loved.

M. Bloch senior, who knew Bergotte only by sight, and Bergotte's life only from what was common gossip, had a manner quite as indirect of making the acquaintance of his books, by the help of judgments that were by way of being literary. He lived in the world of approximations, where people salute in a void and criticise in error, a world where assurance, far from being tempered by ignorance and inaccuracy, is increased thereby. It is the propitious miracle of self-esteem that, since few of us can have brilliant connexions or profound attainments, those to whom they are denied still believe themselves to be the best endowed of men, because the optics of our social perspective make every grade of society seem the best to him who occupies it and who regards as less favoured than himself, ill-endowed, to be pitied, the greater men whom he names and calumniates without knowing them, judges and despises without understanding them. Even in cases where the multiplication of his modest personal advantages by self-esteem would not suffice to assure a man the share of happiness, superior to that accorded to others, which is essential to him, envy is always there to make up the balance. It is true that if envy finds expression in scornful phrases, we must translate "I have no wish to know him" by "I have no means of knowing him." That is the intellectual meaning. But the emotional meaning is indeed, "I have no wish to know him." The speaker knows that it is not true, but he does not, all the same, say it simply to deceive; he says it because it is what he feels, and that is sufficient to bridge the gulf, that is to say to make him happy.

Self-centredness thus enabling every human being to see the universe spread out in descending tiers beneath himself who is its lord, M. Bloch afforded himself the luxury of being a pitiless one when in the morning, as he drank his chocolate, seeing Bergotte's signature at the foot of an article in the newspaper which he had scarcely opened, he disdainfully granted him a hearing which was soon cut short, pronounced sentence upon him, and gave himself the comforting pleasure of repeating after every mouthful of the scalding brew: "That fellow Bergotte has become unreadable. My word, what a bore the brute can be. I really must stop my subscription. It's such a rigmarole—stodgy stuff!" And he helped himself to another slice of bread.

This illusory importance of M. Bloch senior did, however, extend some little way beyond the radius of his own perceptions. In the first place his children regarded him as a superior person. Children have always a tendency either to depreciate or to exalt their parents, and to a good son his father is always the best of fathers, quite apart from any objective reasons there may be for admiring him. Now, such reasons were not altogether lacking in the case of M. Bloch, who was an educated man, shrewd, affectionate towards his family. In his most intimate circle they were all the more proud of him because if, in "society," people are judged, in accordance with a standard scale which is incidentally absurd and a series of false but fixed rules, by comparison with the aggregate of all the other fashionable people, in the subdivisions of middle-class life on the other hand, dinner parties and family reunions turn upon certain people who are pronounced agreeable and amusing but who in "society" would not survive a second evening. Moreover in this social environment where the artificial values of the aristocracy do not exist, their place is taken by even more stupid distinctions. Thus it was that in his family circle, and even to a fairly remote degree of consanguinity, an alleged similarity in his way of wearing his moustache and in the bridge of his nose led to M. Bloch's being called "the Duc d'Aumale's double." (In the world of club bell-hops, is not the one who wears his cap on one side and his tunic tightly buttoned so as to give himself the appearance, he imagines, of a foreign officer, also a personage of a sort to his colleagues?)

The resemblance was of the faintest, but it seemed almost to confer a title. Whenever he was mentioned, it was always: "Bloch? Which one? The Duc d'Aumale?" as people say "Princesse Murat? Which one? The Queen (of Naples)?" And together with certain other minor indications it combined to give him, in the eyes of the cousinhood, an acknowledged claim to distinction. Not going to the lengths of having a carriage of his own, M. Bloch used on special occasions to hire an open victoria with a pair of horses from the Company, and would drive through the Bois de Boulogne, reclining indolently, two fingers on his temple, two others under his chin, and if people who did not know him concluded that he was an "old humbug," they were convinced in the family that in point of elegance Uncle Solomon could have taught Gramont-Caderousse a thing or two. He was one of those people who when they die, because for years they have shared a table in a restaurant on the boulevard with its editor, are described in the social column of the *Radical* as "well known Paris figures." M. Bloch told Saint-Loup and me that Bergotte knew so well why he, M. Bloch, always cut him, that as soon as he caught sight of him, at the theatre or in the club, he avoided his eye. Saint-Loup blushed, for it occurred to him that this club could not be the Jockey, of which his father had been president. On the other hand it must be a fairly exclusive club, for M. Bloch had said that Bergotte would never have got into it if he had come up now. So it was not without the fear that he might be "underrating his adversary" that Saint-Loup asked whether the club in question were that of the Rue Royale, which was considered "degrading" by his own family, and to which he knew that certain Jews were admitted. "No," replied M. Bloch in a tone at once careless, proud and ashamed, "it is a small club, but far more agreeable: the Ganaches. We're very strict there, don't you know." "Isn't Sir Rufus Israels the president?" Bloch junior asked his father, so as to give him the opportunity for a glorious lie, unaware that the financier had not the same eminence in Saint-Loup's eyes as in his. The fact of the matter was that the Ganaches club boasted not Sir Rufus Israels but one of his staff. But as this man was on the best of terms with his employer, he had at his disposal a stock of the financier's cards, and would give one to M. Bloch whenever he wished to travel on a line of which Sir Rufus was a director, so that old Bloch was able to say: "I'm just going round to the Club to ask for a letter of introduction from Sir Rufus." And the card enabled him to dazzle the guards on the trains.

The misses Bloch were more interested in Bergotte and, reverting to him rather than pursue the subject of the Ganaches, the youngest asked her brother, in the most serious tone imaginable, for she believed that there existed, for the designation of men of talent, no other terms than those which he was in the habit of using:

"Is he a really amazing cove, this Bergotte? Is he in the category of the great johnnies, chaps like Villiers and Catulle?"

"I've met him several times at dress rehearsals," said M. Nissim Bernard. "He is an uncouth creature, a sort of Schlemihl."

There was nothing very serious in this allusion to Chamisso's story, but the epithet "Schlemihl" formed part of that dialect, half-German, half-Jewish, which delighted M. Bloch in the family circle, but struck him as vulgar and out of place in front of strangers. And so he cast a reproving glance at his uncle.

"He has talent," said Bloch.

"Ah!" said his sister gravely, as though to imply that in that case there was some excuse for me.

"All writers have talent," said M. Bloch scornfully.

"In fact it appears," went on his son, raising his fork and screwing up his eyes with an air of diabolical irony, "that he is going to put up for the Academy."

"Go on. He hasn't enough to show them," replied his father, who seemed not to have for the Academy the same contempt as his son and daughters. "He hasn't the necessary calibre."

"Besides, the Academy is a salon, and Bergotte has no polish," declared the uncle (from whom Mme Bloch had expectations), a mild and inoffensive person whose surname, Bernard, might perhaps by itself have quickened my grandfather's powers of diagnosis, but would have appeared too little in harmony with a face which looked as if it had been brought back from Darius's palace and restored by Mme Dieulafoy, had not his first name, Nissim, chosen by some collector desirous of giving a crowning touch of orientalism to this figure from Susa, set hovering above it the pinions of an androcephalous bull from Khorsabad. But M. Bloch never stopped insulting his uncle, either because he was inflamed by the unresisting good-humour of his butt, or because, the rent of the villa being paid by M. Nissim Bernard, the beneficiary wished to show that he retained his independence and above all scorned to seek by flattery to make sure of the rich inheritance to come.

"Of course, whenever there's a chance of saying something pompous and stupid, one can be quite certain that you won't miss it. You'd be the first to lick his boots if he were in the room!" shouted M. Bloch, while M. Nissim Bernard in sorrow lowered over his plate the ringleted beard of King Sargon. (My schoolfriend, since he had begun to grow a beard, which also was blue-black and crimped, looked very like his great-uncle.)

What most hurt the old man was being treated so rudely in front of his manservant. He murmured an unintelligible sentence of which all that could be made out was: "When the meschores are in the room." "Meschores," in the Bible, means "the servant of God." In the family circle the Blochs used the word to refer to the servants, and were always delighted by it, because their certainty of not being understood either by Christians or by the servants themselves enhanced in M. Nissim Bernard and M. Bloch their twofold distinction of being "masters" and at the same time "Jews." But this latter source of satisfaction became a source of displeasure when there was "company." At such times M. Bloch, hearing his uncle say "meschores," felt that he was over-exposing his oriental side, just as a harlot who has invited some of her sisters to meet her respectable friends is annoyed if they allude to their profession or use objectionable words. Hence, far from being mollified by his uncle's plea, M. Bloch, beside himself with rage, could contain himself no longer. He let no opportunity pass of scarifying the wretched old man.

"What! Are you the son of the Marquis de Marsantes? Why, I knew him very well," said M. Nissim Bernard to Saint-Loup. I supposed that he meant the word "knew" in the sense in which Bloch's father had said that he knew Bergotte, namely by sight. But he went on: "Your father was a great friend of mine." Meanwhile, Bloch had turned very red, his father was looking intensely cross, and the misses Bloch were choking with suppressed laughter. The fact was that in M. Nissim Bernard the love of ostentation, which in M. Bloch and his children was held in check, had engendered the habit of perpetual lying. For instance, if he was staying in an hotel, M. Nissim Bernard, as M. Bloch equally might have done, would have his newspapers brought to him by his valet in the dining-room in the middle of lunch, when everybody was there, so that they should see that he travelled with a valet. But to the people with whom he made friends in the hotel the uncle used to say, what the nephew would never have said, that he was a senator. For all that he was certain that they would sooner or later discover that the title was usurped, he could not, at the critical moment, resist the temptation to assume it. M. Bloch suffered acutely from his uncle's lies and from all the embarrassments that they caused him. "Don't pay any attention to him, he's a terrible old yarn-spinner," he whispered to Saint-Loup, whose interest was whetted all the more, for he was curious to explore the psychology of liars. "A greater liar even than the Ithacan Odysseus, albeit Athene called him the greatest liar among mortals," his son completed the indictment. "Well, upon my word!" cried M. Nissim Bernard, "If I'd known that I was going to sit down to dinner with my old friend's son! Why, I have a photograph still of your father at home in Paris, and any number of letters from him. He used always to call me 'uncle,' nobody ever knew why. He was a charming man, sparkling. I remember so well a dinner I gave at Nice: there was Sardou, Labiche, Augier" . . . "Moliére, Racine, Corneille," M. Bloch added sarcastically, while his son completed the list of guests with "Plautus, Menander, Kalidasa." M. Nissim Bernard, cut to the quick, stopped short in his reminiscence, and, ascetically depriving himself of a great pleasure, remained silent until the end of dinner.

"Saint-Loup with helm of bronze," said Bloch, "have a piece more of this duck with thighs heavy with fat, over which the illustrious sacrificer of birds has poured numerous libations of red wine."

As a rule, after bringing out from his store for one of his son's distinguished fellow-students his anecdotes of Sir Rufus Israels and others, M. Bloch, feeling that he had succeeded in touching and melting his son's heart, would withdraw, in order not to "demean" himself in the eyes of a "schoolkid." If, however, there was an absolutely compelling reason, as for instance on the night when his son passed the *agrégation*, M. Bloch would add to the usual string of anecdotes the following ironical reflexion which he ordinarily reserved for his own personal friends and which the young Bloch was extremely proud to see produced for his: "The Government have acted unpardonably. They have forgotten to consult M. Coquelin! M. Coquelin has let it be known that he is displeased." (M. Bloch prided himself on being a reactionary, and contemptuous of theatrical people.)

But the misses Bloch and their brother blushed to the tips of their ears, so impressed were they when Bloch senior, to show that he could be regal to the last in his entertainment of his son's two "chums," gave the order for champagne to be served, and announced casually that, as a "treat" for us, he had taken three stalls for the performance which a company from the Opéra-Comique was giving that evening at the Casino. He was sorry that he had not been able to get a box. They had all been taken.

In any case, he had often been in the boxes, and really one saw and heard better in the stalls. However, if the failing of his son, that is to say the failing which his son believed to be invisible to other people, was coarseness, the father's was avarice. And so it was in a decanter that we were served, under the name of champagne, with a light sparkling wine, while under that of orchestra stalls he had taken three in the pit, which cost half as much, miraculously persuaded by the divine intervention of his failing that neither at table nor in the theatre (where the boxes were all empty) would the difference be noticed. When M. Bloch had invited us to moisten our lips in the flat glasses which his son dignified with the style and title of "craters with deeply hollowed flanks," he showed us a picture to which he was so much attached that he always brought it with him to Balbec. He told us that it was a Rubens. Saint-Loup asked innocently if it was signed. M. Bloch replied, blushing, that he had had the signature cut off to make it fit the frame, but that it made no difference, as he had no intention of selling the picture. Then he hurriedly bade us good night, in order to bury himself in the *Journal Officiel*, back numbers of which littered the house and which, he informed us, he was obliged to read carefully on account of his "parliamentary position," as to the precise nature of which he gave us no enlightenment.

"I shall take a muffler," said Bloch, "for Zephyrus and Boreas are vying with each other over the fish-teeming sea, and should we but tarry a little after the show is over, we shall not be home before the first flush of Eos, the rosy-fingered.* By the way," he asked Saint-Loup when we were outside (and I trembled, for I realised at once that it was of M. de Charlus that Bloch spoke in tones of sarcasm), "who was that splendid old card dressed in black that I saw you walking with the day before yesterday on the beach?"

"That was my uncle," replied Saint-Loup, somewhat ruffled.

Unfortunately, a "gaffe" was far from seeming to Bloch a thing to be avoided. He shook with laughter. "Heartiest congratulations. I ought to have guessed: he has a lot of style, and the most priceless dial of an old dotard of the highest lineage."

"You are absolutely mistaken: he's an extremely clever man," retorted Saint-Loup, now furious.

"I'm sorry about that; it makes him less complete. All the same, I should very much like to know him, for I flatter myself I could write some highly adequate pieces about old buffers like that. He's killing when you see him go by. But I should disregard the caricaturable aspect of his mug, which really is hardly worthy of an artist enamoured of the plastic beauty of phrases, although (you'll forgive me) it had me doubled up for quite a while with joyous laughter, and I should bring out the aristocratic side of your uncle, who on the whole makes a tip-top impression, and when one has finished laughing, does strike one with his considerable sense of style. But," he went on, addressing me this time, "there is something in a completely different connexion about which I have been meaning to question you, and every time we are together, some god, some blessed denizen of Olympus, makes me completely forget to ask for a piece of information which might before now have been and is sure some day to be of the greatest use to me. Tell me, who was the lovely lady I saw you with in the Zoological Gardens accompanied by a gentleman whom I seem to know by sight and a girl with long hair?"

It had been quite plain to me at the time that Mme Swann did not remember Bloch's name, since she had referred to him by another, and had described my friend as being on the staff of some Ministry, as to which I had never since then thought of finding out whether he had joined it. But how came it that Bloch, who, according to what she then told me, had got himself introduced to her, was ignorant of her name? I was so astonished that I paused for a moment before answering.

"Whoever she is," he went on, "hearty congratulations. You can't have been bored with her. I picked her up a few days before that on the Zone railway, where, speaking of zones, she was so kind as to undo hers for the benefit of your humble servant. I've never had such a time in my life, and we were just going to make arrangements to meet again when somebody she knew had the bad taste to get in at the last station but one."

My continued silence did not appear to please Bloch. "I was hoping," he said, "thanks to you, to learn her address, so as to go there several times a week to taste in her arms the delights of Eros, dear to the gods; but I do not insist since you seem pledged to discretion with respect to a professional who gave herself to me three times running, and in the most rarefied manner, between Paris and the Point-du-Jour. I'm bound to see her again some night."

I called upon Bloch after his dinner; he returned my call, but I was out and he was seen asking for me by Françoise, who, as it happened, although he had visited us at Combray, had never set eyes on him before. So that she knew only that one of "the gentlemen" I knew had looked in to see me, she did not know "with what effect," dressed in a nondescript way which had not made any particular impression upon her. Now though I knew quite well that certain of Françoise's social ideas must for ever remain impenetrable to me, based as they were, perhaps, partly upon confusions between words and names which she had once and for all time mistaken for one another, I could not refrain, for all that I had long since abandoned the quest for enlightenment in such cases, from seeking—though in vain—to discover what could be the immense significance that the name of Bloch had for Françoise. For no sooner had I mentioned to her that the young man whom she had seen was M. Bloch than she took several paces backwards so great were her stupor and disappointment. "What! Is that M. Bloch?" she cried, thunderstruck, as if so portentous a personage ought to have been endowed with an appearance which "made you realise" as soon as you saw him that you were in the presence of one of the great ones of the earth; and, like someone who has discovered that an historical character is not up to the level of his reputation, she repeated in an awed tone of voice, in which I could detect the latent seeds of a universal scepticism: "So that's M. Bloch! Well, really, you would never think it, to look at him." She seemed also to bear me a grudge, as if I had always "overdone" the praise of Bloch to her. At the same time she was kind enough to add: "Well, he may be M. Bloch, and all that, but at least Monsieur can say he's every bit as good."

She had presently, with respect to Saint-Loup, whom she worshipped, a disillusionment of a different kind and of shorter duration: she discovered that he was a Republican. For although, when speaking for instance of the Queen of Portugal, she would say with that disrespect which is, among the people, the supreme form of respect: "Amélie, Philippe's sister," Françoise was a Royalist. But above all a marquis, a marquis who had dazzled her at first sight, and who was for the Republic, seemed no longer real. And it aroused in her the same ill-humour as if I had given her a box which she had believed to be made of gold, and had thanked me for it effusively, and then a jeweller had revealed to her that it was only plated. She at once withdrew her esteem from Saint-Loup, but soon afterwards restored it to him, having reflected that he could not, being the Marquis de Saint-Loup, be a Republican, that he was just pretending, out of self-interest, for with the Government we had it might be a great advantage to him. From that moment her coldness towards him and her resentment towards me ceased. And when she spoke of Saint-Loup she said: "He's a hypocrite," with a broad and kindly smile which made it clear that she "considered" him again just as much as when she first knew him, and that she had forgiven him.

In fact, Saint-Loup was obviously sincere and disinterested, and it was this intense moral purity which, unable to find entire satisfaction in a selfish emotion such as love, and moreover not finding in him the impossibility (which existed in me, for instance) of gaining spiritual nourishment elsewhere than in oneself, rendered him truly capable (to the extent that I was incapable) of friendship.

Françoise was no less mistaken about Saint-Loup when she said that he "just pretended" not to look down on the common people: you had only to see him when he was in a temper with his groom. It had indeed sometimes happened that Robert would scold his groom with a certain amount of brutality, which was proof in him of a sense not so much of the difference as of the equality between the classes. "But," he said when I reproached him for having treated the man rather harshly, "why should I go out of my way to speak politely to him? Isn't he my equal? Isn't he just as near to me as any of my uncles and cousins? You seem to think I ought to treat him with respect, as an inferior. You talk like an aristocrat!" he added scornfully.

And indeed if there was a class to which he showed himself prejudiced and hostile, it was the aristocracy, so much so that he found it as hard to believe in the superior qualities of a man of the world as he found it easy to believe in those of a man of the people. When I mentioned the Princesse de Luxembourg, whom I had met with his aunt:

"An old trout," was his comment. "Like all that lot. She's a sort of cousin of mine, by the way."

Having a strong prejudice against the people who frequented it, he went rarely into "society," and the contemptuous or hostile attitude which he adopted towards it served to intensify, among all his closest relatives, the painful impression made by his liaison with a woman of the theatre, a liaison which, they declared, would be his ruin, blaming it specially for having bred in him that spirit of denigration, that rebelliousness, for having "led him astray," until it was only a matter of time before he dropped out altogether. And so, many easy-going men of the Faubourg Saint-Germain were without compunction when they spoke of Robert's mistress. "Whores do their job," they would say, "they're as good as anybody else.

But not that one! We can't forgive her. She has done too much harm to a fellow we're fond of." Of course, he was not the first to be thus ensnared. But the others amused themselves like men of the world, continued to think like men of the world about politics and everything else. Whereas Saint-Loup's family found him "soured." They failed to realise that for many young men of fashion who would otherwise remain uncultivated mentally, rough in their friendships, without gentleness or taste, it is very often their mistresses who are their real masters, and liaisons of this sort the only school of ethics in which they are initiated into a superior culture, where they learn the value of disinterested relations. Even among the lower orders (who in point of coarseness so often remind us of high society) the woman, more sensitive, more fastidious, more leisured, is driven by curiosity to adopt certain refinements, respects certain beauties of sentiment and of art which, though she may not understand them, she nevertheless places above what has seemed most desirable to the man, above money or position. Now whether it concerns the mistress of a young blood (such as Saint-Loup) or a young workman (electricians, for instance, must now be included in our truest order of Chivalry) her lover has too much admiration and respect for her not to extend them also to what she herself respects and admires; and for him the scale of values is thereby overturned. Her very sex makes her weak; she suffers from nervous troubles, inexplicable things which in a man, or even in another woman—an aunt or cousin of his—would bring a smile to the lips of this robust young man. But he cannot bear to see the woman he loves suffer. The young nobleman who, like Saint-Loup, has a mistress acquires the habit, when he takes her out to dine, of carrying in his pocket the valerian drops which she may need, of ordering the waiter, firmly and with no hint of sarcasm, to see that he shuts the doors quietly and does not put any damp moss on the table, so as to spare his companion those little ailments which he himself has never felt, which compose for him an occult world in whose reality she has taught him to believe, ailments for which he now feels sympathy without needing to understand them, for which he will still feel sympathy when women other than she are the sufferers. Saint-Loup's mistress—as the first monks of the Middle Ages taught Christendom—had taught him to be kind to animals, for which she had a passion, never going anywhere without her dog, her canaries, her parrots; Saint-Loup looked after them with motherly devotion and regarded those who were unkind to animals as brutes. At the same time an actress, or so-called actress, like the woman who was living with him—whether she was intelligent or not, and as to that I had no knowledge—by making him find society women boring, and look upon having to go out to a party as a painful duty, had saved him from snobbishness and cured him of frivolity. Thanks to her, social relations filled a smaller place in the life of her young lover, but whereas, if he had been simply a man about town, vanity or self-interest would have dictated his choice of friends as rudeness would have characterised his treatment of them, his mistress had taught him to bring nobility and refinement into his friendships. With her feminine instinct, with a keener appreciation of certain qualities of sensibility in men which her lover might perhaps, without her guidance, have misunderstood and mocked, she had always been quick to distinguish from among the rest of Saint-Loup's friends the one who had a real affection for him, and to make that one her favourite. She knew how to persuade him to feel grateful to that friend, to show his gratitude, to notice what things gave his friend pleasure and what pain. And presently Saint-Loup, without any more need for her to prompt him, began to think of these things by himself, and at Balbec, where she was not with him, for me whom she had never seen, whom he had perhaps not yet so much as mentioned in his letters to her, of his own accord would pull up the window of a carriage in which I was sitting, take out of the room the flowers that made me feel unwell, and when he had to say good-bye to several people at once would contrive to do so before it was actually time for him to go, so as to be left alone and last with me, to make that distinction between them and me, to treat me differently from the rest. His mistress had opened his mind to the invisible, had brought an element of seriousness into his life, of delicacy into his heart, but all this escaped his sorrowing family who repeated: "That creature will be the death of him, and meanwhile she's doing what she can to disgrace him."

It is true that he had already drawn from her all the good that she was capable of doing him; and that she now caused him only incessant suffering, for she had taken an intense dislike to him and tormented him in every possible way. She had begun, one fine day, to regard him as stupid and absurd because the friends that she had among the younger writers and actors had assured her that he was, and she duly repeated what they had said with that passion, that lack of reserve which we show whenever we receive from without, and adopt as our own, opinions or customs of which we previously knew nothing. She readily professed, like her actor friends, that between Saint-Loup and herself there was an unbridgeable gulf, because they were of a different breed, because she was an intellectual and he, whatever he might claim, by birth an enemy of the intellect. This view of him seemed to her profound, and she sought confirmation of it in the most insignificant words, the most trivial actions of her lover. But when the same friends had further convinced her that she was destroying the great promise she had shown in company so ill-suited to her, that her lover's influence would finally rub off on her, that by living with him she was ruining her future as an artist, to her contempt for Saint-Loup was added the sort of hatred that she would have felt for him if he had insisted upon inoculating her with a deadly germ. She saw him as seldom as possible, at the same time postponing a definite rupture, which seemed to me a highly improbable event. Saint-Loup made such sacrifices for her that unless she was ravishingly beautiful (but he had always refused to show me her photograph, saying: "For one thing, she's not a beauty, and besides she always takes badly. They're only some snapshots that I took myself with my Kodak; they would give you a false impression of her") it seemed unlikely that she would find another man prepared to do the same. I never reflected that a fancy to make a name for oneself even when one has no talent, that the admiration, merely the privately expressed admiration, of people by whom one is impressed, can (although it may not perhaps have been the case with Saint-Loup's mistress), even for a little prostitute, be motives more determining than the pleasure of making money. Without quite understanding what was going on in his mistress's mind, Saint-Loup did not believe her to be completely sincere either in her unfair reproaches or in her promises of undying love, but nevertheless at certain moments had the feeling that she would break with him whenever she could, and accordingly, impelled no doubt by an instinctive desire to preserve his love that was perhaps more clear-sighted than he was himself, and incidentally bringing into play a practical capacity for business which was compatible in him with the loftiest and blindest impulses of the heart, had refused to settle any capital on her, had borrowed an enormous sum so that she should want nothing, but made it over to her only from day to day. And no doubt, assuming that she really did think of leaving him, she was calmly waiting until she had "feathered her nest," a process which, with the money given her by Saint-Loup, would not perhaps take very long, but would all the same be an extra lease of time to prolong the happiness of my new friend—or his misery.

This dramatic period of their liaison—which had now reached its most acute, its cruellest state for Saint-Loup, for she had forbidden him to remain in Paris, where his presence exasperated her, and had forced him to spend his leave at Balbec, within easy reach of his regiment—had begun one evening at the house of one of his aunts, on whom he had prevailed to allow his mistress to come there, before a large party, to recite some fragments of a symbolist play in which she had once appeared in an avant-garde theatre, and for which she had brought him to share the admiration that she herself professed.

But when she appeared in the room, with a large lily

in her hand, and wearing a costume copied from the *Ancilla Domini* which she had persuaded Saint-Loup was an absolute "vision of beauty," her entrance had been greeted, in that assemblage of clubmen and duchesses, with smiles which the monotonous tone of her sing-song, the oddity of certain words and their frequent repetition, had changed into fits of giggles, stifled at first but presently so uncontrollable that the wretched reciter had been unable to go on. Next day Saint-Loup's aunt had been universally censured for having allowed so grotesque an actress to appear in her drawing-room. A well-known duke made no bones about telling her that she had only herself to blame if she found herself criticised. "Damn it all, people really don't come to see turns like that! If the woman had talent, even; but she has none and never will have any. 'Pon my soul, Paris is not so stupid as people make out. Society does not consist exclusively of imbeciles. This little lady evidently believed that she was going to take Paris by surprise. But Paris is not so easily surprised as all that, and there are still some things that they can't make us swallow."

As for the actress, she left the house with Saint-Loup, exclaiming: "What do you mean by letting me in for those old hens, those uneducated bitches, those oafs? I don't mind telling you, there wasn't a man in the room who hadn't leered at me or tried to paw me, and it was because I wouldn't look at them that they were out to get their revenge."

Words which had changed Robert's antipathy for society people into a horror that was altogether more profound and distressing, and was provoked in him most of all by those who least deserved it, devoted kinsmen who, on behalf of the family, had sought to persuade his mistress to break with him, a move which she represented to him as inspired by their desire for her. Robert, although he had at once ceased to see them, used to imagine when he was separated from his mistress as he was now, that they or others like them were profiting by his absence to return to the charge and had possibly enjoyed her favours. And when he spoke of the lechers who betrayed their friends, who sought to corrupt women, tried to make them come to houses of assignation, his whole face radiated suffering and hatred.

"I'd kill them with less compunction than I'd kill a dog, which is at least a decent, honest and faithful beast. They're the ones who deserve the guillotine if you like, far more than poor wretches who've been led into crime by poverty and by the cruelty of the rich."

He spent the greater part of his time sending letters and telegrams to his mistress. Every time that, while still preventing him from returning to Paris, she found an excuse to quarrel with him by post, I read the news at once on his tormented face. Since she never told him in what way he was at fault, he suspected that she did not know herself, and had simply had enough of him; but he nevertheless longed for an explanation and would write to her: "Tell me what I've done wrong. I'm quite ready to acknowledge my faults," the grief that overpowered him having the effect of persuading him that he had behaved badly.

But she kept him waiting indefinitely for answers which, when they came, were utterly meaningless. And so it was almost always with a furrowed brow and often empty-handed that I would see Saint-Loup returning from the post office, where, alone in all the hotel, he and Françoise went to fetch or to hand in letters, he from a lover's impatience, she with a servant's mistrust of others. (His telegrams obliged him to make a much longer journey.)

When, some days after our dinner with the Blochs, my grandmother told me with a joyful air that Saint-Loup had just asked her whether she would like him to take a photograph of her before he left Balbec, and when I saw that she had put on her nicest dress for the purpose and was hesitating between various hats, I felt a little annoyed at this childishness, which surprised me on her part. I even wondered whether I had not been mistaken in my grandmother, whether I did not put her on too lofty a pedestal, whether she was as unconcerned about her person as I had always supposed, whether she was entirely innocent of the weakness which I had always thought most alien to her, namely vanity.

Unfortunately, the displeasure that was aroused in me by the prospect of this photographic session, and more particularly by the delight with which my grandmother appeared to be looking forward to it, was sufficiently apparent for Françoise to notice it and to do her best, unintentionally, to increase it by making me a sentimental, gushing speech by which I refused to appear moved.

"Oh, Monsieur, my poor Madame will be so pleased at having her likeness taken. She's going to wear the hat that her old Françoise has trimmed for her: you must let her."

I persuaded myself that it was not cruel of me to mock Françoise's sensibility, by reminding myself that my mother and grandmother, my models in all things, often did the same. But my grandmother, noticing that I seemed put out, said that if her sitting for her photograph offended me in any way she would give up the idea. I would not hear of it. I assured her that I saw no harm in it, and let her adorn herself, but, thinking to show how shrewd and forceful I was, added a few sarcastic and wounding words calculated to neutralise the pleasure which she seemed to find in being photographed, with the result that, if I was obliged to see my grandmother's magnificent hat, I succeeded at least in driving from her face that joyful expression which ought to have made me happy. Alas, it too often happens, while the people we love best are still alive, that such expressions appear to us as the exasperating manifestation of some petty whim rather than as the precious form of the happiness which we should dearly like to procure for them. My ill-humour arose more particularly from the fact that, during that week, my grandmother had appeared to be avoiding me, and I had not been able to have her to myself for a moment, either by night or day. When I came back in the afternoon to be alone with her for a little I was told that she was not in the hotel; or else she would shut herself up with Françoise for endless confabulations which I was not permitted to interrupt. And when, after being out all evening with Saint-Loup, I had been thinking on the way home of the moment at which I should be able to go to my grandmother and embrace her, I waited in vain for her to give the three little knocks on the party wall which would tell me to go in and say good night to her. At length I would go to bed, a little resentful of her for depriving me, with an indifference so new and strange in her, of a joy on which I had counted so much, and I would lie there for a while, my heart throbbing as in my childhood, listening to the wall which remained silent, until I cried myself to sleep.

That day, as for some days past, Saint-Loup had been obliged to go to Doncières, where, until he returned there for good, he would be on duty now until late every afternoon. I was sorry that he was not at Balbec. I had seen some young women, who at a distance had seemed to me lovely, alighting from carriages and entering either the ballroom of the Casino or the ice-cream shop. I was going through one of those phases of youth, devoid of any particular love, as it were in abeyance, in which at all times and in all places—as a lover the woman by whose charms he is smitten—we desire, we seek, we see Beauty. Let but a single flash of reality—the glimpse of a woman from afar or from behind—enable us to project the image of Beauty before our eyes, and we imagine that we have recognised it, our hearts beat, and we will always remain half-persuaded that it was She, provided that the woman has vanished: it is only if we manage to overtake her that we realise our mistake.

Moreover, as I was becoming more and more unwell, I was inclined to overrate the simplest pleasures because of the very difficulty of attaining them. I seemed to see charming women all round me, because I was too tired, if it was on the beach, too shy if it was in the Casino or at a pastry-cook's, to go anywhere near them. And yet, if I was soon to die, I should have liked to know beforehand what the prettiest girls that life had to offer looked like at close quarters, in reality, even if it should be another than myself or no one at all who was to take advantage of that offer (I did not, in fact, realise that a desire for possession underlay my curiosity). I should have had the courage to enter the ballroom if Saint-Loup had been with me. Left by myself, I was simply hanging about in front of the Grand Hotel until it was time for me to join my grandmother, when, still almost at the far end of the esplanade, along which they projected a striking patch of colour, I saw five or six young girls as different in appearance and manner from all the people one was accustomed to see at Balbec as would have been a flock of gulls arriving from God knows where and performing with measured tread upon the sands—the dawdlers flapping their wings to catch up with the rest—a parade the purpose of which seems as obscure to the human bathers whom they do not appear to see as it is clearly determined in their own birdish minds.

One of these unknown girls was pushing a bicycle in front of her; two others carried golf-clubs; and their attire generally was in striking contrast to that of the other girls at Balbec, some of whom, it was true, went in for sports, but without adopting a special outfit.

It was the hour at which ladies and gentlemen came out every day for a stroll along the front, exposed to the merciless fire of the lorgnette fastened upon them, as if they had each borne some disfigurement which she felt it her duty to inspect in its minutest details, by the senior judge's wife, proudly seated there with her back to the band-stand, in the middle of that dread line of chairs on which presently they too, actors turned critics, would come and establish themselves, to scrutinise in their turn the passing crowds. All these people who paced up and down the esplanade, lurching as heavily as if it had been the deck of a ship (for they could not lift a leg without at the same time waving their arms, turning their eyes, squaring their shoulders, compensating by a balancing movement on one side for the movement they had just made on the other, and puffing out their faces), pretending not to see, so as to let it be thought that they were not interested in them, but covertly eyeing, for fear of running into them, the people who were walking beside or coming towards them, did in fact bump into them, became entangled with them, because each was mutually the object of the same secret attention veiled beneath the same apparent disdain—love, and consequently fear, of the crowd being one of the most powerful motives in all human beings, whether they seek to please other people or to impress them, or to show that they despise them; and in the case of the solitary, even if his seclusion is absolute and lifelong it is often based on a deranged love of the crowd which so far overrides every other feeling that, unable to win the admiration of his hall-porter, of the passers-by, of the cabman he hails, he prefers not to be seen by them at all, and with that object abandons every activity that would oblige him to go out of doors.

In the midst of all these people, some of whom were pursuing a train of thought, but then betrayed its instability by a fitfulness of gesture, an aberrancy of gaze as inharmonious as the circumspect titubation of their neighbours, the girls whom I had noticed, with the control of gesture that comes from the perfect suppleness of one's own body and a sincere contempt for the rest of humanity, were advancing straight ahead, without hesitation or stiffness, performing exactly the movements that they wished to perform, each of their limbs completely independent of the others, the rest of the body preserving that immobility which is so noticeable in good waltzers. They were now quite near me. Although each was of a type absolutely different from the others, they all had beauty; but to tell the truth I had seen them for so short a time, and without venturing to look hard at them, that I had not yet individualised any of them. Except for one, whose straight nose and dark complexion singled her out from the rest, like the Arabian king in a Renaissance picture of the Epiphany, they were known to me only by a pair of hard, obstinate and mocking eyes, for instance, or by cheeks whose pinkness had a coppery tint reminiscent of geraniums; and even these features I had not yet indissolubly attached to any one of these girls rather than to another; and when (according to the order in which the group met the eye, marvellous because the most different aspects were juxtaposed, because all the colour scales were combined in it, but confused as a piece of music in which I was unable to isolate and identify at the moment of their passage the successive phrases, no sooner distinguished than forgotten) I saw a pallid oval, black eyes, green eyes, emerge, I did not know if these were the same that had already charmed me a moment ago, I could not relate them to any one girl whom I had set apart from the rest and identified. And this want, in my vision, of the demarcations which I should presently establish between them permeated the group with a sort of shimmering harmony, the continuous transmutation of a fluid, collective and mobile beauty.

It was not perhaps mere chance in life that, in forming this group of friends, had chosen them all so beautiful; perhaps these girls (whose demeanour was enough to reveal their bold, hard and frivolous natures), extremely aware of everything that was ludicrous or ugly, incapable of yielding to an intellectual or moral attraction, had naturally felt a certain repulsion for all those among the companions of their own age in whom a pensive or sensitive disposition was betrayed by shyness, awkwardness, constraint, by what they would regard as antipathetic, and from such had held aloof; while attaching themselves, conversely, to others to whom they were drawn by a certain blend of grace, suppleness and physical elegance, the only form in which they were able to picture a straightforward and attractive character and the promise of pleasant hours in one another's company. Perhaps, too, the class to which they belonged, a class which I should not have found it easy to define, was at that point in its evolution when, thanks either to its growing wealth and leisure, or to new sporting habits, now prevalent even among certain elements of the working class, and a physical culture to which had not yet been added the culture of the mind, a social group comparable to the smooth and prolific schools of sculpture which have not yet gone in for tortured expression, produces naturally, and in abundance, fine bodies, fine legs, fine hips, wholesome, serene faces, with an air of agility and guile. And were they not noble and calm models of human beauty that I beheld there, outlined against the sea, like statues exposed to the sunlight on a Grecian shore?

Just as if, within their little band, which progressed along the esplanade like a luminous comet, they had decided that the surrounding crowd was composed of beings of another race not even whose sufferings could awaken in them any sense of fellowship, they appeared not to see them, forced those who had stopped to talk to step aside, as though from the path of a machine which had been set going by itself and which could not be expected to avoid pedestrians; and if some terrified or furious old gentleman whose existence they did not even acknowledge and whose contact they spurned took precipitate and ludicrous flight, they merely looked at one another and laughed. They had, for whatever did not form part of their group, no affectation of contempt; their genuine contempt was sufficient. But they could not set eyes on an obstacle without amusing themselves by clearing it, either in a running jump or with both feet together, because they were all brimming over with the exuberance that youth so urgently needs to expend that even when it is unhappy or unwell, obedient rather to the necessities of age than to the mood of the day, it can never let pass an opportunity to jump or to slide without indulging in it conscientiously, interrupting and interspersing even the slowest walk—as Chopin his most melancholy phrase—with graceful deviations in which caprice is blended with virtuosity. The wife of an elderly banker, after hesitating between various possible exposures for her husband, had settled him in a deck-chair facing the esplanade, sheltered from wind and sun by the bandstand. Having seen him comfortably installed there, she had gone to buy a newspaper which she would read aloud to him by way of diversion, one of her little absences which she never prolonged for more than five minutes, which seemed to her quite long enough but which she repeated at fairly frequent intervals so that this old husband on whom she lavished an attention that she took care to conceal should have the impression that he was still quite alive and like other people and was in no need of protection. The platform of the band-stand provided, above his head, a natural and tempting springboard across which, without a moment's hesitation, the eldest of the little band began to run; she jumped over the terrified old man, whose yachting cap was brushed by her nimble feet, to the great delight of the other girls, especially of a pair of green eyes in a doll-like face, which expressed, for that bold act, an admiration and a merriment in which I seemed to discern a trace of shyness, a shamefaced and blustering shyness which did not exist in the others. "Oh, the poor old boy, I feel sorry for him; he looks half dead," said a girl in a rasping voice, with more sarcasm than sympathy. They walked on a little way, then stopped for a moment in the middle of the road, oblivious of the fact that they were impeding the passage of other people, in an agglomerate that was at once irregular in shape, compact, weird and shrill, like an assembly of birds before taking flight; then they resumed their leisurely stroll along the esplanade, against the background of the sea.

By this time their charming features had ceased to be indistinct and jumbled. I had dealt them like cards into so many heaps to compose (failing their names, of which I was still ignorant): the tall one who had jumped over the old banker; the little one silhouetted against the horizon of sea with her plump and rosy cheeks and green eyes; the one with the straight nose and dark complexion who stood out among the rest; another, with a face as white as an egg in which a tiny nose described an arc of a circle like a chicken's beak—a face such as one sometimes sees in the very young; yet another, also tall, wearing a hooded cape (which gave her so shabby an appearance and so contradicted the elegance of the figure beneath that the explanation which suggested itself was that this girl must have parents of high position who valued their self-esteem so far above the visitors to Balbec and the sartorial elegance of their own children that it was a matter of the utmost indifference to them that their daughter should stroll on the front dressed in a way which humbler people would have considered too modest); a girl with brilliant, laughing eyes and plump, matt cheeks, a black polo-cap crammed on her head, who was pushing a bicycle with such an uninhibited swing of the hips, and using slang terms so typical of the gutter and shouting so loudly when I passed her (although among her expressions I caught that tiresome phrase "living one's own life") that, abandoning the hypothesis which her friend's hooded cape had prompted me to formulate, I concluded instead that all these girls belonged to the population which frequents the velodromes, and must be the very juvenile mistresses of racing cyclists. In any event, none of my suppositions embraced the possibility of their being virtuous. At first sight—in the way in which they looked at one another and laughed, in the insistent stare of the one with the matt complexion—I had grasped that they were not. Besides, my grandmother had always watched over me with a delicacy too tremulous for me not to believe that the sum total of the things one ought not to do is indivisible and that girls who are lacking in respect for their elders would not suddenly be stopped short by scruples at the prospect of pleasures more tempting than that of jumping over an octogenarian.

Though they were now separately identifiable, still the interplay of their eyes, animated with self-assurance and the spirit of comradeship and lit up from one moment to the next either by the interest or the insolent indifference which shone from each of them according to whether her glance was directed at her friends or at passers-by, together with the consciousness of knowing one another intimately enough always to go about together in an exclusive "gang," established between their independent and separate bodies, as they slowly advanced, an invisible but harmonious bond, like a single warm shadow, a single atmosphere, making of them a whole as homogeneous in its parts as it was different from the crowd through which their procession gradually wound.

For an instant, as I passed the dark one with the plump cheeks who was wheeling a bicycle, I caught her smiling, sidelong glance, aimed from the centre of that inhuman world which enclosed the life of this little tribe, an inaccessible, unknown world wherein the idea of what I was could certainly never penetrate or find a place. Wholly occupied with what her companions were saying, had she seen me—this young girl in the polo-cap pulled down very low over her forehead—at the moment in which the dark ray emanating from her eyes had fallen on me? If she had seen me, what could I have represented to her? From the depths of what universe did she discern me? It would have been as difficult for me to say as, when certain distinguishing features in a neighbouring planet are made visible thanks to the telescope, it is to conclude therefrom that human beings inhabit it, and that they can see us, and to guess what ideas the sight of us can have aroused in their minds.

If we thought that the eyes of such a girl were merely two glittering sequins of mica, we should not be athirst to know her and to unite her life to ours. But we sense that what shines in those reflecting discs is not due solely to their material composition; that it is the dark shadows, unknown to us, of the ideas that that person cherishes about the people and places she knows—the turf of race-courses, the sand of cycling tracks over which, pedalling on past fields and woods, she would have drawn me after her, that little peri, more seductive to me than she of the Persian paradise—the shadows, too, of the home to which she will presently return, of the plans that she is forming or that others have formed for her; and above all that it is she, with her desires, her sympathies, her revulsions, her obscure and incessant will. I knew that I should never possess this young cyclist if I did not possess also what was in her eyes. And it was consequently her whole life that filled me with desire; a sorrowful desire because I felt that it was not to be fulfilled, but an exhilarating one because, what had hitherto been my life having ceased of a sudden to be my whole life, being no more now than a small part of the space stretching out before me which I was burning to cover and which was composed of the lives of these girls, it offered me that prolongation, that possible multiplication of oneself, which is happiness. And no doubt the fact that we had, these girls and I, not one habit—as we had not one idea—in common must make it more difficult for me to make friends with them and to win their regard. But perhaps, also, it was thanks to those differences, to my consciousness that not a single element that I knew or possessed entered into the composition of the nature and actions of these girls, that satiety had been succeeded in me by a thirst—akin to that with which a parched land burns—for a life which my soul, because it had never until now received one drop of it, would absorb all the more greedily, in long draughts, with a more perfect imbibition.

I had looked so closely at the dark cyclist with the bright eyes that she seemed to notice my attention, and said to the tallest of the girls something that I could not hear but that made her laugh. Truth to tell, this dark-haired one was not the one who attracted me most, simply because she was dark and because (since the day on which, from the little path by Tansonville, I had seen Gilberte) a girl with reddish hair and a golden skin had remained for me the inaccessible ideal. But had I not loved Gilberte herself principally because she had appeared to me haloed with that aureole of being the friend of Bergotte, of going to look at cathedrals with him? And in the same way could I not rejoice at having seen this dark girl look at me (which made me hope that it would be easier for me to get to know her first), for she would introduce me to the pitiless one who had jumped over the old man's head, to the cruel one who had said "I feel sorry for the poor old boy," to all these girls in turn of whom she enjoyed the prestige of being the inseparable companion? And yet the supposition that I might some day be the friend of one or other of these girls, that these eyes, whose incomprehensible gaze struck me from time to time and played unwittingly upon me like an effect of sunlight on a wall, might ever, by some miraculous alchemy, allow the idea of my existence, some affection for my person, to interpenetrate their ineffable particles, that I myself might some day take my place among them in the evolution of their course by the sea's edge—that supposition appeared to me to contain within it a contradiction as insoluble as if, standing before some Attic frieze or a fresco representing a procession, I had believed it possible for me, the spectator, to take my place, beloved of them, among the divine participants.

Was, then, the happiness of knowing these girls unattainable? Certainly it would not have been the first of its kind that I had renounced. I had only to recall the numberless strangers whom, even at Balbec, the carriage bowling away from them at full speed had forced me for ever to abandon. And indeed the pleasure I derived from the little band, as noble as if it had been composed of Hellenic virgins, arose from the fact that it had something of the fleetingness of the passing figures on the road. This evanescence of persons who are not known to us, who force us to cast off from our habitual life in which the women whose society we frequent have all, in course of time, laid bare their blemishes, urges us into that state of pursuit in which there is no longer anything to stem the tide of imagination. To strip our pleasures of imagination is to reduce them to their own dimensions, that is to say to nothing. Offered me by one of those procuresses whose good offices, as has been seen, I by no means always scorned, withdrawn from the element which gave them so many nuances, such impreciseness, these girls would have enchanted me less. We need imagination, awakened by the uncertainty of being unable to attain its object, to create a goal which hides the other goal from us, and by substituting for sensual pleasures the idea of penetrating another life, prevents us from recognising that pleasure, from tasting its true savour, from restricting it to its own range. We need, between us and the fish which, if we saw it for the first time cooked and served on a table, would not appear worth the endless shifts and wiles required to catch it, the intervention, during our afternoons with the rod, of the rippling eddy to whose surface come flashing, without our quite knowing what we intend to do with them, the bright gleam of flesh, the hint of a form, in the fluidity of a transparent and mobile azure.

These girls benefited also by that alteration of social proportions characteristic of seaside life. All the advantages which, in our ordinary environment, extend and enhance us, we there find to have become invisible, in fact eliminated; while on the other hand the people whom we suppose, without reason, to enjoy similar advantages appear to us amplified to artificial dimensions. This made it easier for unknown women in general, and today for these girls in particular, to acquire an enormous importance in my eyes, and impossible to make them aware of such importance as I might myself possess.

But if the parade of the little band could be said to be but an excerpt from the endless flight of passing women, which had always disturbed me, that flight was here reduced to a movement so slow as to approach immobility. And the very fact that, in a phase so far from rapid, faces no longer swept away in a whirlwind, but calm and distinct, still seemed to me beautiful, prevented me from thinking, as I had so often thought when Mme de Villeparisis's carriage bore me away, that at closer quarters, if I had stopped for a moment, certain details, a pock-marked skin, a flaw in the nostrils, a gawping expression, a grimace of a smile, an ugly figure, might have been substituted, in the face and body of the woman, for those that I had doubtless imagined; for no more than a pretty outline, the glimpse of a fresh complexion, had sufficed for me to add, in entire good faith, a ravishing shoulder, a delicious glance of which I carried in my mind for ever a memory or a preconceived idea, these rapid decipherings of a person whom we momentarily glimpse exposing us thus to the same errors as those too rapid readings in which, on the basis of a single syllable and without waiting to identify the rest, we replace the word that is in the text by a wholly different word with which our memory supplies us. It could not be so with me now. I had looked at their faces long and carefully; I had seen each of them, not from every angle and rarely in full face, but all the same in two or three aspects different enough to enable me to make the necessary correction or verification to "prove" the difficult suppositions of line and colour that are hazarded at first sight, and to see subsist in them, through successive expressions, something unalterably material. I could say to myself with conviction that neither in Paris nor at Balbec, on the most favourable assumption of what, even if I had been able to stop and talk to them, the passing women who had caught my eye would have been like, had there ever been any whose appearance, followed by their disappearance without my having got to know them, had left me with more regret than would these, had given me the idea that their friendship could be so intoxicating. Never, among actresses or peasants or convent girls, had I seen anything so beautiful, impregnated with so much that was unknown, so inestimably precious, so apparently inaccessible. They were, of the unknown and potential happiness of life, an illustration so delicious and in so perfect a state that it was almost for intellectual reasons that I was sick with despair at the thought of being unable to sample, in unique conditions which left no room for any possibility of error, all that is most mysterious in the beauty which we desire, and which we console ourselves for never possessing by demanding pleasure—as Swann had always refused to do before Odette's day—from women whom we have not desired, so that we die without ever having known what that other pleasure was. It might well be, of course, that it was not in reality an unknown pleasure, that on close inspection its mystery would dissolve, that it was no more than a projection, a mirage of desire. But in that case I had only to blame the compulsion of a law of nature—which if it applied to these girls would apply to all—and not the imperfection of the object. For it was the one that I would have chosen above all others, convinced as I was, with a botanist's satisfaction, that it was not possible to find gathered together rarer specimens than these young flowers that at this moment before my eyes were breaking the line of the sea with their slender hedge, like a bower of Pennsylvania roses adorning a cliffside garden, between whose blooms is contained the whole tract of ocean crossed by some steamer, so slow in gliding along the blue, horizontal line that stretches from one stem to the next that an idle butterfly, dawdling in the cup of a flower which the ship's hull has long since passed, can wait, before flying off in time to arrive before it, until nothing but the tiniest chink of blue still separates the prow from the first petal of the flower towards which it is steering.

I went indoors because I was to dine at Rivebelle with Robert, and my grandmother insisted that on those evenings, before going out, I must lie down for an hour on my bed, a rest which the Balbec doctor presently ordered me to extend to all other evenings too.

As it happened, there was no need, when one went indoors, to leave the esplanade and to enter the hotel by the hall, that is to say from the back. By virtue of an alteration of the clock which reminded me of those Saturdays when, at Combray, we used to have lunch an hour earlier, now with summer at the full the days had become so long that the sun was still high in the heavens, as though it were only tea-time, when the tables were being laid for dinner in the Grand Hotel. And so the great sliding windows remained open on to the esplanade. I had only to step across a low wooden sill to find myself in the dining-room, through which I walked to take the lift.

As I passed the reception desk I addressed a smile to the manager, and without the slightest twinge of distaste collected one in return from a face which, since I had been at Balbec, my comprehensive study had impregnated and transformed like a natural history specimen. His features had become familiar to me, charged with a meaning that was of no importance but none the less intelligible like a script which one can read, and had ceased in any way to resemble those strange and repellent characteristics which his face had presented to me on that first day, when I had seen before me a personage now forgotten, or, if I succeeded in recalling him, unrecognisable, difficult to identify with this insignificant and polite individual of which the other was but a caricature, a hideous and rapid sketch. Without either the shyness or the sadness of the evening of my arrival, I rang for the lift attendant, who no longer stood in silence while I rose by his side as in a mobile thoracic cage propelled upwards along its ascending pillar, but repeated to me:

"There aren't the people now as there was a month back. They're beginning to go now; the days are drawing in." He said this not because there was any truth in it but because, having an engagement, presently, on a warmer part of the coast, he would have liked us all to leave as soon as possible so that the hotel could be shut up and he have a few days to himself before "rejoining" his new place. "Rejoin" and "new" were not, as it happened, incompatible terms, since, for the lift-boy, "rejoin" was the usual form of the verb "to join." The only thing that surprised me was that he condescended to say "place," for he belonged to that modern proletariat which seeks to eliminate from its speech every trace of a career in service. And a moment later indeed he informed me that in the "situation" which he was about to "rejoin," he would have a smarter "tunic" and a better "salary," the words "livery" and "wages" sounding to him obsolete and unseemly. And since, by an absurd contradiction, the vocabulary has survived the conception of inequality among the "masters," I was always failing to understand what the lift-boy said. For instance, the only thing that interested me was to know whether my grandmother was in the hotel. Now, forestalling my questions, the lift-boy would say to me: "That lady has just come out of your rooms." I was invariably taken in; I supposed that he meant my grandmother. "No, that lady who I think is an employee of yours." Since, in the traditional vocabulary of the upper classes which ought indeed to be done away with, a cook is not called an employee, I thought for a moment: "But he must have made a mistake. We don't own a factory; we haven't any employees." Suddenly I remembered that the title of "employee," like the wearing of a moustache among waiters, is a sop to their self-esteem given to servants, and realised that this lady who had just gone out must be Françoise (probably on a visit to the coffee-maker, or to watch the Belgian lady's maid at her sewing), though even this sop did not satisfy the lift-boy, for he would say quite naturally, speaking pityingly of his own class, "the working man" or "the small man," using the same singular form as Racine when he speaks of "the poor man." But as a rule, for my zeal and timidity of the first evening were now things of the past, I no longer spoke to the lift-boy. It was he now who stood there and received no answer during the short journey on which he threaded his way through the hotel, which, hollowed out inside like a toy, deployed around us, floor by floor, the ramifications of its corridors in the depths of which the light grew velvety, lost its tone, blurred the communicating doors or the steps of the service stairs which it transformed into that amber haze, unsubstantial and mysterious as a twilight, in which Rembrandt picks out here and there a window-sill or a well-head. And on each landing a golden light reflected from the carpet indicated the setting sun and the lavatory window.

I wondered whether the girls I had just seen lived at Balbec, and who they could be. When our desire is thus concentrated upon a little tribe of humanity which it singles out from the rest, everything that can be associated with that tribe becomes a spring of emotion and then of reflexion. I had heard a lady say on the esplanade: "She's a friend of the Simonet girl" with that self-important air of inside knowledge, as who should say: "He's the inseparable companion of young La Rochefoucauld." And immediately she had detected on the face of the person to whom she gave this information a curiosity to see more of the favoured person who was "a friend of the Simonet girl." A privilege, obviously, that did not appear to be granted to all the world. For aristocracy is a relative thing. And there are plenty of out-of-the-way places where the son of an upholsterer is the arbiter of fashion and reigns over a court like any young Prince of Wales. I have often since then sought to recall how it first sounded to me there on the beach, that name of Simonet, still uncertain in its form, which I had not clearly distinguished, and also in its significance, its designation of such and such a person as opposed to another; instinct, in short, with that vagueness and novelty which we find so moving in the sequel, when a name whose letters are every moment engraved more deeply on our hearts by our incessant thought of them has become (though this was not to happen to me with the name of the "Simonet girl" until several years had passed) the first coherent sound that comes to our lips, whether on waking from sleep or on recovering from a fainting fit, even before the idea of what time it is or of where we are, almost before the word "I," as though the person whom it names were more "us" than we are ourselves, and as though after a brief spell of unconsciousness the phase that is the first to dissolve were that in which we were not thinking of her. I do not know why I said to myself from the first that the name Simonet must be that of one of the band of girls; from that moment I never ceased to wonder how I could get to know the Simonet family, get to know them, moreover, through people whom they would consider superior to themselves (which ought not to be difficult if they were only common little wenches) so that they might not form a disdainful idea of me. For one cannot have a perfect knowledge, one cannot effect the complete absorption of a person who disdains one, so long as one has not overcome that disdain. And since, whenever the idea of women who are so different from us penetrates our minds, unless we are able to forget it or the competition of other ideas eliminates it, we know no rest until we have converted these aliens into something that is compatible with ourselves, the mind being in this respect endowed with the same kind of reaction and activity as our physical organism, which cannot abide the infusion of any foreign body into its veins without at once striving to digest and assimilate it. The Simonet girl must be the prettiest of them all—she who, I felt moreover, might yet become my mistress, for she was the only one who, two or three times half-turning her head, had appeared to take cognisance of my fixed stare. I asked the lift-boy whether he knew of any people at Balbec called Simonet. Not liking to admit that there was anything he did not know, he replied that he seemed to have heard the name somewhere. When we reached the top floor I asked him to send me up the latest list of visitors.

I stepped out of the lift, but instead of going to my room I made my way further along the corridor, for before my arrival the valet in charge of the landing, despite his horror of draughts, had opened the window at the end, which instead of looking out to the sea faced the hill and valley inland, but never allowed them to be seen because its panes, which were made of clouded glass, were generally closed. I made a brief halt in front of it, time enough just to pay my devotions to the view which for once it revealed beyond the hill immediately behind the hotel, a view that contained only a single house situated at some distance, to which the perspective and the evening light, while preserving its mass, gave a gem-like precision and a velvet casing, as though to one of those architectural works in miniature, tiny temples or chapels wrought in gold and enamel, which serve as reliquaries and are exposed only on rare and solemn days for the veneration of the faithful. But this moment of adoration had already lasted too long, for the valet, who carried in one hand a bunch of keys and with the other saluted me by touching his sacristan's skull cap, though without raising it on account of the pure, cool evening air, came and drew together, like those of a shrine, the two sides of the window, and so shut off the minute edifice, the glistening relic from my adoring gaze.

I went into my room. Gradually, as the season advanced, the picture that I found there in my window changed. At first it was broad daylight, and dark only if the weather was bad: and then, in the greenish glass which it distended with the curve of its rounded waves, the sea, set between the iron uprights of my casement window like a piece of stained glass in its leads, ravelled out over all the deep rocky border of the bay little plumed triangles of motionless foam etched with the delicacy of a feather or a downy breast from Pisanello's pencil, and fixed in that white, unvarying, creamy enamel which is used to depict fallen snow in Gallé's glass.

Presently the days grew shorter and at the moment when I entered the room the violet sky seemed branded with the stiff, geometrical, fleeting, effulgent figure of the sun (like the representation of some miraculous sign, of some mystical apparition) lowering over the sea on the edge of the horizon like a sacred picture over a high altar, while the different parts of the western sky exposed in the glass fronts of the low mahogany bookcases that ran along the walls, which I carried back in my mind to the marvellous painting from which they had been detached, seemed like those different scenes executed long ago for a confraternity by some old master on a reliquary, whose separate panels are now exhibited side by side in a gallery, so that the visitor's imagination alone can restore them to their place on the predella of the reredos.

A few weeks later, when I went upstairs, the sun had already set. Like the one that I used to see at Combray, behind the Calvary, when I came home from a walk and was getting ready to go down to the kitchen before dinner, a band of red sky above the sea, compact and clear-cut as a layer of aspic over meat, then, a little later, over a sea already cold and steel-blue like a grey mullet, a sky of the same pink as the salmon that we should presently be ordering at Rivebelle, reawakened my pleasure in dressing to go out to dinner. Close to the shore, patches of vapour, soot-black but with the burnish and consistency of agate, visibly solid and palpable, were trying to rise one above another over the sea in ever wider tiers, so that the highest of them, poised on top of the twisted column and overreaching the centre of gravity of those which had hitherto supported them, seemed on the point of bringing down in ruin this lofty structure already half-way up the sky, and precipitating it into the sea. The sight of a ship receding like a nocturnal traveller gave me the same impression that I had had in the train of being set free from the necessity of sleep and from confinement in a bedroom. Not that I felt myself a prisoner in the room in which I now was, since in another hour I should be leaving it to drive away in a carriage. I threw myself down on the bed; and, just as if I had been lying in a berth on board one of those steamers which I could see quite near me and which at night it would be strange to see stealing slowly through the darkness, like shadowy and silent but unsleeping swans, I was surrounded on all sides by pictures of the sea.

But as often as not they were, indeed, only pictures; I forgot that below their coloured expanse lay the sad desolation of the beach, swept by the restless evening breeze whose breath I had so anxiously felt on my arrival at Balbec; besides, even in my room, being wholly taken up with thoughts of the girls I had seen go by, I was no longer in a sufficiently calm or disinterested state of mind to receive any really profound impression of beauty. The anticipation of dinner at Rivebelle made my mood more frivolous still, and my mind, dwelling at such moments upon the surface of the body which I was about to dress up in order to try to appear as pleasing as possible to the feminine eyes which would scrutinise me in the well-lit restaurant, was incapable of putting any depth behind the colour of things. And if, beneath my window, the soft, unwearying flight of swifts and swallows had not arisen like a playing fountain, like living fireworks, joining the intervals between their soaring rockets with the motionless white streaming lines of long horizontal wakes—without the charming miracle of this natural and local phenomenon which brought into touch with reality the scenes that I had before my eyes—I might easily have believed that they were no more than a selection, made afresh every day, of paintings which were shown quite arbitrarily in the place in which I happened to be and without having any necessary connexion with that place. At one time it was an exhibition of Japanese colour-prints: beside the neat disc of sun, red and round as the moon, a yellow cloud seemed a lake against which black swords were outlined like the trees upon its shore, while a bar of a tender pink which I had never seen since my first paint-box swelled out like a river on either bank of which boats seemed to be waiting high and dry for someone to push them down and set them afloat. And with the contemptuous, bored and frivolous glance of an amateur or a woman hurrying through a picture gallery between two social engagements, I would say to myself: "Curious sunset, this; it's different, but after all I've seen them just as delicate, just as remarkable as this." I had more pleasure on evenings when a ship, absorbed and liquefied by the horizon, appeared so much the same colour as its background, as in an Impressionist picture, that it seemed to be also of the same substance, as though its hull and the rigging in which it tapered into a slender filigree had simply been cut out from the vaporous blue of the sky. Sometimes the ocean filled almost the whole of my window, raised as it was by a band of sky edged at the top only by a line that was of the same blue as the sea, so that I supposed it to be still sea, and the change in colour due only to some effect of lighting. Another day the sea was painted only in the lower part of the window, all the rest of which was filled with so many clouds, packed one against another in horizontal bands, that its panes seemed, by some premeditation or predilection on the part of the artist, to be presenting a "Cloud Study," while the fronts of the various bookcases showing similar clouds but in another part of the horizon and differently coloured by the light, appeared to be offering as it were the repetition—dear to certain contemporary masters—of one and the same effect caught at different hours but able now in the immobility of art to be seen all together in a single room, drawn in pastel and mounted under glass. And sometimes to a sky and sea uniformly grey a touch of pink would be added with an exquisite delicacy, while a little butterfly that had gone to sleep at the foot of the window seemed to be appending with its wings at the corner of this "Harmony in Grey and Pink" in the Whistler manner the favourite signature of the Chelsea master. Then even the pink would vanish; there was nothing now left to look at. I would get to my feet and, before lying down again, close the inner curtains. Above them I could see from my bed the ray of light that still remained, growing steadily fainter and thinner, but it was without any feeling of sadness, without any regret for its passing, that I thus allowed the hour at which as a rule I was seated at table to die above the curtains, for I knew that this day was of another kind from ordinary days, longer, like those arctic days which night interrupts for a few minutes only; I knew that from the chrysalis of this twilight, by a radiant metamorphosis, the dazzling light of the Rivebelle restaurant was preparing to emerge. I said to myself: "It's time"; I stretched myself on the bed, and rose, and finished dressing; and I found a charm in these idle moments, relieved of every material burden, in which, while the others were dining down below, I was employing the forces accumulated during the inactivity of this late evening hour only in drying my washed body, in putting on a dinner-jacket, in tying my tie, in making all those gestures which were already dictated by the anticipated pleasure of seeing again some woman whom I had noticed at Rivebelle last time, who had seemed to be watching me, had perhaps left the table for a moment only in the hope that I would follow her; it was with joy that I embellished myself with all these allurements so as to give myself, fresh, alert and wholehearted, a new life, free, without cares, in which I would lean my hesitations upon the calm strength of Saint-Loup and would choose, from among the different species of animated nature and the produce of every land, those which, composing the unfamiliar dishes that my companion would at once order, might have tempted my appetite or my imagination.

And then at the end of the season came the days when I could no longer go straight in from the front through the dining-room; its windows stood open no more, for it was night now outside and the swarm of poor folk and curious idlers, attracted by the blaze of light which was beyond their reach, hung in black clusters, chilled by the north wind, on the luminous sliding walls of that buzzing hive of glass.

There was a knock at my door; it was Aimé who had come upstairs in person with the latest list of visitors.

Aimé could not go away without telling me that Dreyfus was guilty a thousand times over. "It will all come out," he assured me, "not this year, but next. It was a gentleman who's very thick with the General Staff who told me. I asked him if they wouldn't decide to bring it all to light at once, before the year is out. He laid down his cigarette," Aimé went on, acting the scene for my benefit, and shaking his head and his forefinger as his informant had done, as much as to say: "We mustn't be too impatient."—" 'Not this year, Aimé,' he said to me, putting his hand on my shoulder, 'It isn't possible. But next Easter, yes!' " And Aimé tapped me gently on the shoulder, saying, "You see, I'm showing you exactly what he did," whether because he was flattered at this act of familiarity by a distinguished person or so that I might better appreciate, with a full knowledge of the facts, the weight of the argument and our grounds for hope.

It was not without a slight pang that on the first page of the list I caught sight of the words "Simonet and family." I had in me a store of old dream-memories dating from my childhood, in which all the tenderness that existed in my heart but, being felt by my heart, was not distinguishable from it, was brought to me by a being as different as possible from myself. Once again I fashioned such a being, utilising for the purpose the name Simonet and the memory of the harmony that had reigned between the young bodies which I had seen deployed on the beach in a sportive procession worthy of Greek art or of Giotto. I did not know which of these girls was Mlle Simonet, if indeed any of them was so named, but I did know that I was loved by Mlle Simonet and that with Saint-Loup's help I was going to try to get to know her. Unfortunately, having on that condition only obtained an extension of his leave, he was obliged to report for duty every day at Doncières: but to make him commit a breach of his military obligations I had felt that I might count, more even than on his friendship for myself, on that same curiosity as a human naturalist which I myself had so often felt—even without having seen the person mentioned, and simply on hearing it said that there was a pretty cashier at a fruiterer's—to become acquainted with a new variety of feminine beauty. But I had been wrong in hoping to excite that curiosity in Saint-Loup by speaking to him of my band of girls. For it had been and would remain paralysed in him by his love for the actress whose lover he was. And even if he had felt it lightly stirring within him he would have repressed it, from an almost superstitious belief that on his own fidelity might depend that of his mistress. And so it was without any promise from him that he would take an active interest in my girls that we set off to dine at Rivebelle.

On the first few occasions, when we arrived there, the sun would just have set, but it was light still; in the garden outside the restaurant, where the lamps had not yet been lighted, the heat of the day was falling and settling, as though in a vase along the sides of which the transparent, dusky jelly of the air seemed of such consistency that a tall rose-tree, fastened against the dim wall which it veined with pink, looked like the arborescence that one sees at the heart of an onyx. Presently it was after nightfall when we alighted from the carriage, often indeed when we started from Balbec if the weather was bad and we had put off sending for the carriage in the hope of a lull. But on those days it was with no sense of gloom that I listened to the wind howling, for I knew that it did not mean the abandonment of my plans, imprisonment in my bedroom, I knew that in the great dining-room of the restaurant which we would enter to the sound of the music of the gipsy band, the innumerable lamps would triumph easily over the darkness and the cold, by applying to them their broad cauteries of molten gold, and I climbed light-heartedly after Saint-Loup into the closed carriage which stood waiting for us in the rain.

For some time past the words of Bergotte, when he pronounced himself positive that, in spite of all I might say, I had been created to enjoy pre-eminently the pleasures of the mind, had restored to me, with regard to what I might succeed in achieving later on, a hope that was disappointed afresh every day by the boredom I felt on settling down before a writing-table to start work on a critical essay or a novel. "After all," I said to myself, "perhaps the pleasure one feels in writing it is not the infallible test of the literary value of a page; perhaps it is only a secondary state which is often superadded, but the want of which can have no prejudicial effect on it. Perhaps some of the greatest masterpieces were written while yawning." My grandmother set my doubts at rest by telling me that I should be able to work, and to enjoy working, as soon as I was well. And, our doctor having thought it only prudent to warn me of the grave risks to which my state of health might expose me, and having outlined all the hygienic precautions that I ought to take to avoid any accident, I subordinated all my pleasures to an object which I judged to be infinitely more important than them, that of becoming strong enough to be able to bring into being the work which I had, possibly, within me, and had been exercising over myself, ever since I had come to Balbec, a scrupulous and constant control. Nothing would have induced me to touch the cup of coffee which would have robbed me of the night's sleep that was necessary if I was not to be tired next day. But when we arrived at Rivebelle, immediately—what with the excitement of a new pleasure, and finding myself in that different zone into which the exceptional introduces us after having cut the thread, patiently spun throughout so many days, that was guiding us towards wisdom—as though there were never to be any such thing as tomorrow, nor any lofty aims to be realised, all that precise machinery of prudent hygiene which had been working to safeguard them vanished. A waiter was offering to take my coat, whereupon Saint-Loup asked: "You're sure you won't be cold? Perhaps you'd better keep it: it's not very warm in here."

"No, no," I assured him, and perhaps I did not feel the cold; but however that might be, I no longer knew the fear of falling ill, the necessity of not dying, the importance of work. I gave up my coat; we entered the dining-room to the sound of some warlike march played by the gipsy band, we advanced between two rows of tables laid for dinner as along an easy path of glory, and, feeling a happy glow imparted to our bodies by the rhythms of the band which conferred on us these military honours, this unmerited triumph, we concealed it beneath a grave and frozen mien, beneath a languid, casual gait, so as not to be like those music-hall "mashers" who, wedding a ribald verse to a patriotic air, come running on to the stage with the martial countenance of a victorious general.

From that moment I was a new man, who was no longer my grandmother's grandson and would remember her only when it was time to get up and go, but the brother, for the time being, of the waiters who were going to bring us our dinner.

The dose of beer, and *a fortiori* of champagne, which at Balbec I should not have ventured to take in a week, albeit to my calm and lucid consciousness the savour of those beverages represented a pleasure clearly appreciable if easily sacrificed, I now imbibed at a sitting, adding to it a few drops of port which I was too bemused to be able to taste, and I gave the violinist who had just been playing the two louis which I had been saving up for the last month with a view to buying something, I could not remember what. Several of the waiters, let loose among the tables, were flying along at full speed, each carrying on his outstretched palm a dish which it seemed to be the object of this kind of race not to let fall. And in fact the chocolate soufflés arrived at their destination unspilled, the potatoes *à l'anglaise*, in spite of the gallop that must have given them a shaking, arranged as at the start round the Pauillac lamb. I noticed one of these waiters, very tall, plumed with superb black locks, his face dyed in a tint that suggested certain species of rare birds rather than a human being, who, running without pause (and, one would have said, without purpose) from one end of the room to the other, recalled one of those macaws which fill the big aviaries in zoological gardens with their gorgeous colouring and incomprehensible agitation. Presently the spectacle settled down, in my eyes at least, into an order at once more noble and more calm. All this dizzy activity became fixed in a quiet harmony. I looked at the round tables whose innumerable assemblage filled the restaurant like so many planets, as the latter are represented in old allegorical pictures. Moreover, there seemed to be some irresistible force of attraction at work among these various stars, and at each table the diners had eyes only for the tables at which they were not sitting, with the possible exception of some wealthy Amphitryon who, having managed to secure a famous author, was endeavouring to extract from him, thanks to the magic properties of the turning-table, a few insignificant remarks at which the ladies marvelled. The harmony of these astral tables did not prevent the incessant revolution of the countless waiters who, because instead of being seated like the diners they were on their feet, performed their gyrations in a more exalted sphere. No doubt they were running, one to fetch the hors d'œuvres, another to change the wine or to bring clean glasses. But despite these special reasons, their perpetual course among the round tables yielded, after a time, to the observer the law of its dizzy but ordered circulation. Seated behind a bank of flowers, two horrible cashiers, busy with endless calculations, seemed two witches occupied in forecasting by astrological signs the disasters that might from time to time occur in this celestial vault fashioned according to the scientific conceptions of the Middle Ages.

And I rather pitied all the diners because I felt that for them the round tables were not planets and that they had not cut through the scheme of things in such a way as to be delivered from the bondage of habitual appearances and enabled to perceive analogies. They thought that they were dining with this or that person, that the dinner would cost roughly so much, and that tomorrow they would begin all over again. And they appeared absolutely indifferent to the progress through their midst of a train of young waiters who, having probably at that moment no urgent duty, advanced processionally bearing rolls of bread in baskets. Some of these, the youngest, stunned by the cuffs which the head waiters administered to them as they passed, fixed melancholy eyes upon a distant dream and were consoled only if some visitor from the Balbec hotel in which they had once been employed, recognising them, said a few words to them, telling them in person to take away the champagne which was not fit to drink, an order that filled them with pride.

I could hear the twanging of my nerves, in which there was a sense of well-being independent of the external objects that might have produced it, and which the least shifting of my body or of my attention was enough to make me feel, just as to a closed eye a slight compression gives the sensation of colour. I had already drunk a good deal of port, and if I now asked for more it was not so much with a view to the well-being which the additional glasses would bring me as an effect of the well-being produced by the glasses that had gone before. I allowed the music itself to guide my pleasure from note to note, and, meekly following, it rested on each in turn. If, like one of those chemical industries by means of which compounds are produced in large quantities which in a state of nature are encountered only by accident and very rarely, this restaurant at Rivebelle assembled at one and the same moment more women to tempt me with beckoning vistas of happiness than I should have come across in the course of walks or travels in a whole year, at the same time this music that greeted our ears—arrangements of waltzes, of German operettas, of music-hall songs, all of them quite new to me—was itself like an ethereal pleasure-dome superimposed upon the other and more intoxicating still. For these tunes, each as individual as a woman, did not reserve, as she would have done, for some privileged person the voluptuous secret which they contained: they offered it to me, ogled me, came up to me with wayward or wanton movements, accosted me, caressed me as if I had suddenly become more seductive, more powerful, richer. Certainly I found in these tunes an element of cruelty; because any such thing as a disinterested feeling for beauty, a gleam of intelligence, was unknown to them; for them physical pleasure alone existed. And they are the most merciless of hells, the most firmly sealed, for the jealous wretch to whom they present that pleasure—that pleasure which the woman he loves is enjoying with another—as the only thing that exists in the world for her who is all the world to him. But while I was humming softly to myself the notes of this tune and returning its kiss, the pleasure peculiar to itself which it made me feel became so dear to me that I would have left my father and mother to follow it through the singular world which it constructed in the invisible, in lines alternately filled with languor and vivacity. Although such a pleasure as this is not calculated to enhance the value of the person to whom it comes, for it is perceived by him alone, and although whenever, in the course of our lives, we have failed to attract a woman who has caught sight of us, she did not know whether at that moment we possessed this inward and subjective felicity which, consequently, could in no way have altered the judgment that she passed on us, I felt myself more powerful, almost irresistible. It seemed to me that my love was no longer something unattractive, at which people might smile, but had precisely the touching beauty, the seductiveness, of this music, itself comparable to a congenial atmosphere in which she whom I loved and I would have met, suddenly grown intimate.

This restaurant was not frequented solely by women of easy virtue, but also by people of the very best society, who came there for afternoon tea or gave big dinner-parties there. The tea-parties were held in a long gallery, glazed and narrow, shaped like a funnel, which led from the entrance hall to the dining-room and was bounded on one side by the garden, from which it was separated (but for a few stone pillars) only by its wall of glass which opened here and there. The result of which, apart from ubiquitous draughts, was sudden and intermittent bursts of sunshine, a dazzling and changeable light that made it almost impossible to see the tea-drinkers, so that when they were installed there, at tables crowded pair after pair the whole way along the narrow gully, shimmering and sparkling with every movement they made in drinking their tea or in greeting one another, it resembled a giant fish-tank or bow-net in which a fisherman has collected all his glittering catch, which, half out of water and bathed in sunlight, coruscate before one's eyes in an ever-changing iridescence.

A few hours later, during dinner, which, naturally, was served in the dining-room, the lights would be turned on, even when it was still quite light out of doors, so that one saw before one's eyes, in the garden, among summer-houses glimmering in the twilight like pale spectres of evening, arbours whose glaucous verdure was pierced by the last rays of the setting sun and which, from the lamp-lit room in which one was dining, appeared through the glass no longer—as one would have said of the ladies drinking tea in the afternoon along the blue and gold corridor—caught in a glittering and dripping net, but like the vegetation of a pale and green aquarium of gigantic size lit by a supernatural light. People began to rise from the table; and if each party, while their dinner lasted, although they spent the whole time examining, recognising, naming the party at the next table, had been held in perfect cohesion about their own, the magnetic force that had kept them gravitating round their host of the evening lost its power at the moment when they repaired for coffee to the same corridor that had been used for the tea-parties; so that it often happened that in its passage from place to place some party on the march dropped one or more of its human corpuscles who, having come under the irresistible attraction of the rival party, detached themselves for a moment from their own, in which their places were taken by ladies or gentlemen who had come across to speak to friends before hurrying off with an "I really must get back to my host Monsieur X . . ." And for the moment one was reminded of two separate bouquets that had exchanged a few of their flowers. Then the corridor too began to empty. Often, since even after dinner there might still be a little light left outside, this long corridor was left unlighted, and, skirted by the trees that overhung it on the other side of the glass, it suggested a pleached alley in a wooded and shady garden. Sometimes, in the gloom, a fair diner would be lingering there. As I passed through it one evening on my way out I saw, sitting among a group of strangers, the beautiful Princesse de Luxembourg. I raised my hat without stopping. She recognised me, and nodded to me with a smile; in the air, far above her salutation, but emanating from the movement, rose melodiously a few words addressed to myself, which must have been a somewhat amplified good-evening, intended not to stop me but simply to complete the gesture, to make it a spoken greeting. But her words remained so indistinct and the sound which was all that I caught was prolonged so sweetly and seemed to me so musical that it was as if, among the dim branches of the trees, a nightingale had begun to sing.

If it so happened that, to finish the evening with a party of his friends whom we had met, Saint-Loup decided to go on to the Casino of a neighbouring resort, and, taking them with him, put me in a carriage by myself, I would urge the driver to go as fast as he possibly could, so that the minutes might pass less slowly which I must spend without having anyone at hand to exempt me from furnishing my own sensibility—reversing the engine, so to speak, and emerging from the passivity in which I was caught and held as in a mesh—with those modifications which, since my arrival at Rivebelle, I had been receiving from other people. The risk of collision with a carriage coming the other way along those lanes where there was barely room for one and it was dark as pitch; the instability of the surface, crumbling in many places, at the cliff's edge; the proximity of its vertical drop to the sea—none of these things exerted on me the slight stimulus that would have been required to bring the vision and the fear of danger within the orbit of my reason. For just as it is not the desire to become famous but the habit of being industrious that enables us to produce a finished work, so it is not the activity of the present moment but wise reflexions from the past that help us to safeguard the future. But if already, before this point, on my arrival at Rivebelle, I had flung irretrievably away from me those crutches of reason and self-control which help our infirmity to follow the right road, if I now found myself the victim of a sort of moral ataxia, the alcohol that I had drunk, in stretching my nerves exceptionally, had given to the present moment a quality, a charm, which did not have the effect of making me more competent or indeed more resolute to defend it; for in making me prefer it a thousand times to the rest of my life, my exaltation isolated it therefrom; I was enclosed in the present, like heroes and drunkards; momentarily eclipsed, my past no longer projected before me that shadow of itself which we call our future; placing the goal of my life no longer in the realisation of the dreams of the past, but in the felicity of the present moment, I could see no further than it. So that, by a contradiction which was only apparent, it was at the very moment in which I was experiencing an exceptional pleasure, in which I felt that my life might yet be happy, in which it should have become more precious in my sight, it was at this very moment that, delivered from the anxieties which it had hitherto inspired in me, I unhesitatingly abandoned it to the risk of an accident. But after all, I was doing no more than concentrate in a single evening the carelessness that, for most men, is diluted throughout their whole existence, in which every day they face unnecessarily the dangers of a sea-voyage, of a trip in an aeroplane or motor-car, when there is waiting for them at home the person whom their death would shatter, or when the book whose eventual publication is the sole reason for their existence is still stored in the fragile receptacle of their brain. And so too in the Rivebelle restaurant, on evenings when we stayed there after dinner, if anyone had come in with the intention of killing me, since I no longer saw, save in a distance too remote to have any reality, my grandmother, my life to come, the books I might write, since I now clung body and soul to the scent of the woman at the next table, to the politeness of the waiters, to the contours of the waltz that the band was playing, since I was glued to the sensation of the moment, with no extension beyond its limits, nor any object other than not to be separated from it, I should have died in and with that sensation, I should have let myself be slaughtered without offering any resistance, without a movement, a bee drugged with tobacco smoke that had ceased to take any thought for preserving the accumulation of its labours and the hopes of its hive.

I ought here to add that this insignificance into which the most serious matters relapsed, by contrast with the violence of my exaltation, came in the end to include Mlle Simonet and her friends. The enterprise of knowing them seemed to me easy now but a matter of indifference, for my immediate sensation, thanks to its extraordinary intensity, to the joy that its slightest modifications, its mere continuity provoked, alone had any importance for me; all the rest, parents, work, pleasures, girls at Balbec, weighed no more than a flake of foam in a strong wind that will not let it find a resting place, existed no longer save in relation to this internal power: inebriation brings about for an hour or two a state of subjective idealism, pure phenomenalism; everything is reduced to appearances and exists only as a function of our sublime self. This is not to say that a genuine love, if we have one, cannot subsist in such a state. But we feel so unmistakably, as though in a new atmosphere, that unknown pressures have altered the dimensions of that love, that we can no longer consider it in the old way. It is indeed still there, but somehow displaced, no longer weighing upon us, satisfied by the sensation which the present affords it, a sensation that is sufficient for us, since for what is not the here and now we take no thought. Unfortunately the coefficient which thus alters our values alters them only during that hour of intoxication. The people who were no longer of any importance, whom we scattered with our breath like soap-bubbles, will tomorrow resume their density; we shall have to try afresh to settle down to work which had ceased to have any meaning. A more serious matter still, these mathematics of the morrow, the same as those of yesterday, in whose problems we shall find ourselves inexorably involved, govern us even during those hours, and we alone are unconscious of their rule. If there is a hostile or virtuous woman in our vicinity, that question so difficult an hour ago—to know whether we should succeed in finding favour with her—seems to us now a million times easier of solution without having become easier in any respect, for it is only in our eyes, in our own inward eyes, that we have altered. And she is as displeased with us at this moment for having taken a liberty with her as we shall be with ourselves next day at the thought of having given a hundred francs to the bell-hop, and for the same reason, which in our case has merely been delayed, namely the absence of intoxication.

I knew none of the women who were at Rivebelle and who, because they were part and parcel of my intoxication just as its reflexions are part and parcel of a mirror, appeared to me a thousand times more desirable than the less and less existent Mlle Simonet. One of them, young, fair, alone, with a sad expression on a face framed in a straw hat trimmed with field-flowers, gazed at me for a moment with a dreamy air and struck me as being attractive. Then it was the turn of another, and of a third; finally of a dark one with glowing cheeks. Almost all of them were known, if not to myself, to Saint-Loup.

He had, in fact, before he made the acquaintance of his present mistress, lived so much in the restricted world of amorous adventure that of all the women who were dining on those evenings at Rivebelle, where many of them had appeared quite by chance, having come to the coast some to join their lovers, others in the hope of finding lovers, there was scarcely one that he did not know from having spent—he himself, or one or other of his friends—at least one night with her. He did not greet them if they were with men, and they, although they looked more at him than at anyone else because the indifference which he was known to feel towards every woman who was not his actress gave him in their eyes a special glamour, appeared not to know him. But you could hear them whispering: "That's young Saint-Loup. It seems he's still quite gone on that tart of his. It's true love! What a handsome fellow he is! I think he's just wonderful. And what style! Some women have all the luck, don't they? And he's so nice in every way. I saw a lot of him when I was with d'Orléans. They were quite inseparable, those two. He was going the pace in those days. But he's given it all up now, she can't complain. Ah! she can certainly consider herself lucky. I wonder what in the world he sees in her. He must be a bit of a chump, when all's said and done. She's got feet like boats, whiskers like an American, and her undies are filthy. I can tell you, a little shop-girl would be ashamed to be seen in her knickers. Do just look at his eyes a moment: you'd go to hell for a man like that. Hush, don't say a word; he's seen me; look, he's smiling. Oh, he knew me all right. Just you mention my name to him, and see what he says!" Between these women and him I caught a glance of mutual understanding. I should have liked him to introduce me to them, so that I might ask them for assignations which they would grant me, even if I was unable to keep them. For otherwise each of their faces would remain for all time devoid, in my memory, of that part of itself—just as though it had been hidden by a veil—which varies in every woman, which we cannot imagine in any woman until we have actually seen it in her, and which appears only in the look she gives us that acquiesces in our desire and promises that it shall be satisfied. And yet, even thus reduced, their faces meant far more to me than those of women whom I knew to be virtuous, and did not seem to me to be flat, like theirs, with nothing behind them, fashioned in one piece with no depth or solidity. It was not, of course, for me what it must be for Saint-Loup who, by an act of memory, beneath the indifference, transparent to him, of the motionless features which affected not to know him, or beneath the dull formality of the greeting that might equally well have been addressed to anyone else, could recall, could see, dishevelled locks, a convulsed mouth, a pair of half-closed eyes, a whole silent picture like those that painters, to deceive the bulk of their visitors, drape with a decent covering. For me, who felt that nothing of my personality had penetrated the surface of any one of these women, or would be borne by her upon the unknown ways which she would tread through life, these faces remained sealed. But it was enough for me to know that they did open in order for them to seem to me to be more precious than I should have thought them had they been only handsome medals instead of lockets within which memories of love were hidden. As for Robert, scarcely able to keep his seat at table, concealing beneath a courtier's smile his warrior's thirst for action—when I looked at him closely I could see to what extent the vigorous bone structure of his triangular face must have been modelled on that of his ancestors, a face designed rather for an ardent bowman than for a sensitive man of letters. Beneath the delicate skin the bold construction, the feudal architecture were apparent. His head reminded one of those old castle keeps on which the disused battlements are still to be seen, although inside they have been converted into libraries.

On the way back to Balbec, of this or that charmer to whom he had introduced me I would repeat to myself without a moment's interruption, and yet almost unconsciously: "What a delightful woman!" as one sings a refrain. True, these words were prompted rather by over-excitement than by any lasting judgment. It was nevertheless true that if I had had a thousand francs on me and if there had still been a jeweller's shop open at that hour, I should have bought the unknown a ring. When the successive hours of our lives unfold as though on too widely disparate planes, we find that we give away too much of ourselves to all sorts of people who next day will not interest us in the least. But we feel that we are still responsible for what we said to them overnight, and that we must honour our promises.

Since, on those evenings, I came back late, it was a pleasure to be reunited, in a room no longer hostile, with the bed in which, on the day of my arrival, I had supposed that it would always be impossible for me to find any rest, whereas now my weary limbs longed for its support; so that, one after the other, my thighs, my hips and my shoulders sought to adhere at every point to the sheets that covered its mattress, as if my fatigue, like a sculptor, had wished to take a cast of an entire human body. But I could not get to sleep; I sensed the approach of morning; peace of mind, health of body were no longer mine. In my distress it seemed to me that I should never recapture them. I should have had to sleep for a long time if I were to find them again. But then, had I begun to doze, I must in any event be awakened in a couple of hours by the symphony concert on the beach. Suddenly I fell asleep, plunged into that deep slumber in which vistas are opened to us of a return to childhood, the recapture of past years, and forgotten feelings, of disincarnation, the transmigration of souls, the evoking of the dead, the illusions of madness, retrogression towards the most elementary of the natural kingdoms (for we say that we often see animals in our dreams, but we forget that almost always we are ourselves animals therein, deprived of that reasoning power which projects upon things the light of certainty; on the contrary we bring to bear on the spectacle of life only a dubious vision, extinguished anew every moment by oblivion, the former reality fading before that which follows it as one projection of a magic lantern fades before the next as we change the slide), all those mysteries which we imagine ourselves not to know and into which we are in reality initiated almost every night, as into the other great mystery of extinction and resurrection. Rendered more vagabond by the difficulty of digesting my Rivebelle dinner, the successive and flickering illumination of shadowy zones of my past made of me a person for whom the supreme happiness would have been to meet Legrandin, with whom I had just been talking in my dream.

And then, even my own life was entirely hidden from me by a new scene, like the drop lowered right at the front of the stage before which, while the scene shifters are busy behind, actors appear in an interim turn. The turn in which I was now playing a part was in the manner of oriental tales; I retained no knowledge of my past or of myself, on account of the extreme proximity of this interposed scenery; I was merely a character receiving the bastinado and undergoing various punishments for a crime the nature of which I could not make out, though it was actually that of having drunk too much port. Suddenly I awoke and discovered that, thanks to a long sleep, I had not heard a note of the concert. It was already afternoon; I verified this by my watch after several efforts to sit up in bed, efforts fruitless at first and interrupted by backward falls on to my pillow, brief falls of the kind that are a sequel of sleep as of other forms of intoxication, whether due to wine or to convalescence; in any case, even before I had looked at the time, I was certain that it was past midday. Last night I had been nothing more than an empty vessel, weightless, and (since one must have been lying down in order to be able to sit up, and have been asleep to be able to keep silent) had been unable to refrain from moving about and talking, no longer had any stability, any centre of gravity; I had been set in motion and it seemed that I might have continued on my dreary course until I reached the moon. But if, while I slept, my eyes had not seen the time, my body had nevertheless contrived to calculate it, had measured the hours not on a dial superficially decorated with figures, but by the steadily growing weight of all my replenished forces which, like a powerful clock, it had allowed, notch by notch, to descend from my brain into the rest of my body where they now accumulated as far as the top of my knees the unimpaired abundance of their store. If it is true that the sea was once upon a time our native element, in which we must plunge our blood to recover our strength, it is the same with oblivion, with mental nothingness; we seem then to absent ourselves for a few hours from time, but the forces which have gathered in that interval without being expended measure it by their quantity as accurately as the pendulum of the clock or the crumbling hillocks of the hour-glass. Moreover, one does not emerge more easily from such a sleep than from a prolonged spell of wakefulness, so strongly does everything tend to persist; and if it is true that certain narcotics make us sleep, to have slept for a long time is an even more potent narcotic, after which we have great difficulty in making ourselves wake up. Like a sailor who sees plainly the quay where he can moor his boat, still tossed by the waves, I had every intention of looking at the time and of getting up, but my body was constantly cast back upon the tide of sleep; the landing was difficult, and before I attained a position in which I could reach my watch and confront its time with that indicated by the wealth of accumulated materials which my exhausted limbs had at their disposal, I fell back two or three times more upon my pillow.

At length I could reach and read it: "Two o'clock in the afternoon!" I rang, but at once I plunged back into a sleep which this time must have lasted infinitely longer if I was to judge by the refreshment, the vision of an immense night outlived, which I experienced on awakening. And yet, since my awakening was caused by the entry of Françoise, and since her entry had been prompted by my ringing the bell, this second sleep which, it seemed to me, must have been longer than the other and had brought me so much well-being and forgetfulness, could not have lasted for more than half a minute.

My grandmother opened the door of my bedroom, and I asked her countless questions about the Legrandin family.

It is not enough to say that I had returned to tranquillity and health, for it was more than a mere interval of space that had divided them from me the day before; I had had all night long to struggle against a contrary tide, and then I not only found myself again in their presence, but they had once more entered into me. At certain definite and still somewhat painful points beneath the surface of my empty head which would one day be broken, letting my ideas dissolve for ever, those ideas had once again taken their proper place and resumed that existence by which hitherto, alas, they had failed to profit.

Once again I had escaped from the impossibility of sleeping, from the deluge, the shipwreck of my nervous storms. I no longer feared the threats that had loomed over me the evening before, when I was deprived of rest. A new life was opening before me; without making a single movement, for I was still shattered, although quite alert and well, I savoured my weariness with a light heart; it had isolated and broken the bones of my legs and arms, which I could feel assembled before me, ready to come together again, and which I would rebuild merely by singing, like the architect in the fable.[12]

Suddenly I remembered the fair girl with the sad expression whom I had seen at Rivebelle and who had looked at me for a moment. Many others, in the course of the evening, had seemed to me attractive; now she alone arose from the depths of my memory. I felt that she had noticed me, and expected one of the Rivebelle waiters to come to me with a whispered message from her. Saint-Loup did not know her and believed that she was respectable. It would be very difficult to see her, to see her constantly. But I was prepared to make any sacrifice: I thought now only of her. Philosophy distinguishes often between free and necessary acts. Perhaps there is none to the necessity of which we are more completely subjected than that which, by virtue of a climbing power held in check during the act itself, brings back (once our mind is at rest) a memory until then levelled down with all the rest by the oppressive force of bemusement and makes it spring to the surface because unknown to us it contained more than any of the others a charm of which we do not become aware until the following day. And perhaps, too, there is no act so free, for it is still unprompted by habit, by that sort of mental obsession which, in matters of love, encourages the invariable reappearance of the image of one particular person.

That day, as it happened, was the day after the one on which I had seen the beautiful procession of young girls advancing along the sea-front. I questioned a number of the visitors in the hotel about them, people who came almost every year to Balbec. They could tell me nothing. Later on, a photograph showed me why. Who could now have recognised in them, scarcely and yet quite definitely beyond the age at which one changes so completely, an amorphous, delicious mass, still utterly childish, of little girls who, only a few years back, might have been seen sitting in a ring on the sand round a tent: a sort of vague, white constellation in which one would have distinguished a pair of eyes that sparkled more than the rest, a mischievous face, flaxen hair, only to lose them again and to confound them almost at once in the indistinct and milky nebula.

No doubt, in those earlier years that were still so comparatively recent, it was not, as it had been yesterday when they appeared for the first time before me, the impression of the group but the group itself that had been lacking in clearness. Then those children, still mere babies, had been at that elementary stage in their development when personality has not yet stamped its seal on each face. Like those primitive organisms in which the individual barely exists by itself, is constituted by the polypary rather than by each of the polyps that compose it, they were still pressed one against another. Sometimes one pushed her neighbour over, and then a giggle, which seemed the sole manifestation of their personal life, convulsed them all together, obliterating, merging those imprecise and grinning faces in the congealment of a single cluster, scintillating and tremulous. In an old photograph of themselves, which they were one day to give me, and which I have kept ever since, their childish troupe already presents the same number of participants as, later, their feminine procession; one can sense from it that their presence must even then have made on the beach an unusual impression which forced itself on the attention, but one cannot recognise them individually save by a process of reasoning, making allowances for all the transformations possible during girlhood, up to the point at which these reconstituted forms would begin to encroach upon another individuality which must be identified also, and whose handsome face, owing to the concomitance of a tall build and curly hair, may quite possibly have been, long ago, that wizened and impish little grin which the photograph album presents to us; and the distance traversed in a short interval of time by the physical characteristics of each of these girls making of them a criterion too vague to be of any use, and moreover what they had in common and, so to speak, collectively, being therefore very pronounced, it sometimes happened that even their most intimate friends mistook one for another in this photograph, so much so that the question could in the last resort be settled only by some detail of costume which one of them was certain to have worn to the exclusion of the others. Since those days, so different from the day on which I had just seen them strolling along the front, so different and yet so close in time, they still gave way to fits of laughter, as I had observed the previous afternoon, but to laughter of a kind that was no longer the intermittent and almost automatic laughter of childhood, a spasmodic explosion which, in those days, had continually sent their heads dipping out of the circle, as the clusters of minnows in the Vivonne used to scatter and vanish only to gather again a moment later; each of their physiognomies was now mistress of itself, their eyes were fixed on the goal they were pursuing; and it had taken, yesterday, the tremulous uncertainty of my first impression to make me confuse vaguely (as their childish hilarity and the old photograph had confused) the spores, now individualised and disjoined, of the pale madrepore.

Doubtless often enough before, when pretty girls went by, I had promised myself that I would see them again. As a rule, people thus seen do not appear a second time; moreover our memory, which speedily forgets their existence, would find it difficult to recall their features; our eyes would not recognise them, perhaps, and in the meantime we have seen others go by, whom we shall not see again either. But at other times, and this was what was to happen with the pert little band at Balbec, chance brings them back insistently before our eyes. Chance seems to us then a good and useful thing, for we discern in it as it were the rudiments of organisation, of an attempt to arrange our lives; and it makes it easy, inevitable, and sometimes—after interruptions that have made us hope that we may cease to remember—painful for us to retain in our minds images for the possession of which we shall come in time to believe that we were predestined, and which but for chance we should from the very first have managed to forget, like so many others, so easily.

Presently Saint-Loup's visit drew to an end. I had not seen those girls again on the beach. He was too little at Balbec in the afternoons to have time to pay attention to them and attempt, in my interest, to make their acquaintance. In the evenings he was freer, and continued to take me regularly to Rivebelle. There are, in such restaurants, as there are in public gardens and railway trains, people enclosed in a quite ordinary appearance, whose names astonish us when, having happened to ask, we discover that they are not the mere inoffensive strangers whom we supposed but no less than the Minister or the Duke of whom we have so often heard. Two or three times already, in the Rivebelle restaurant, when everyone else was getting ready to leave, Saint-Loup and I had seen a man of large stature, very muscular, with regular features and a grizzled beard, come in and sit down at a table, where his pensive gaze remained fixed with concentrated attention upon the void. One evening, on our asking the landlord who this obscure, solitary and belated diner was, "What!" he exclaimed, "do you mean to say you don't know the famous painter Elstir?" Swann had once mentioned his name to me, I had entirely forgotten in what connexion; but the omission of a particular memory, like that of part of a sentence when we are reading, leads sometimes not to uncertainty but to the birth of a premature certainty. "He's a friend of Swann's, and a very well-known artist, extremely good," I told Saint-Loup. Immediately the thought swept through us both like a thrill of emotion, that Elstir was a great artist, a celebrated man, and that, confounding us with the rest of the diners, he had no suspicion of the excitement into which we were plunged by the idea of his talent. Doubtless, his unconsciousness of our admiration and of our acquaintance with Swann would not have troubled us had we not been at the seaside. But since we were still at an age when enthusiasm cannot keep silence, and had been transported into a life where anonymity is suffocating, we wrote a letter, signed with both our names, in which we revealed to Elstir in the two diners seated within a few feet of him two passionate admirers of his talent, two friends of his great friend Swann, and asked to be allowed to pay our homage to him in person. A waiter undertook to convey this missive to the celebrity.

A celebrity Elstir was perhaps not yet at this period quite to the extent claimed by the landlord, though he was to reach the height of his fame within a very few years. But he had been one of the first to frequent this restaurant when it was still only a sort of farmhouse, and had brought to it a whole colony of artists (who had all, as it happened, migrated elsewhere as soon as the farm, where they used to feed in the open air under a lean-to roof, had become a fashionable centre; Elstir himself had returned to Rivebelle this evening on account of the temporary absence of his wife, with whom he lived not far away). But great talent, even when its existence is not yet recognised, will inevitably provoke a few quirks of admiration, such as the landlord had managed to detect in the questions asked by more than one English lady visitor, athirst for information as to the life led by Elstir, or in the number of letters that he received from abroad. Then the landlord had further remarked that Elstir did not like to be disturbed when he was working, that he would rise in the middle of the night and take a young model down to the sea-shore to pose for him, nude, if the moon was shining, and had told himself that so much labour was not in vain, nor the admiration of the tourist unjustified, when he had recognised in one of Elstir's pictures a wooden cross which stood by the roadside on the way into Rivebelle.

"That's it all right," he would repeat with stupefaction, "there are all the four beams! Oh, he does take a lot of trouble!"

And he did not know whether a little *Sunrise over the*

Sea which Elstir had given him might not be worth a fortune.

We watched him read our letter, put it in his pocket, finish his dinner, begin to ask for his things, get up to go; and we were so convinced that we had offended him by our overture that we would now have hoped (as keenly as at first we had dreaded) to make our escape without his noticing us. What did not cross our minds for a single instant was a consideration which should have seemed to us of cardinal importance, namely that our enthusiasm for Elstir, on the sincerity of which we would not have allowed the least doubt to be cast, which we could indeed have confirmed with the evidence of our bated breath, our desire to do no matter what that was difficult or heroic for the great man, was not, as we imagined it to be, admiration, since neither of us had ever seen anything that he had painted; our feeling might have as its object the hollow idea of a "great artist," but not a body of work which was unknown to us. It was, at most, admiration in the abstract, the nervous envelope, the sentimental framework of an admiration without content, that is to say a thing as indissolubly attached to boyhood as are certain organs which no longer exist in the adult man; we were still boys. Elstir meanwhile was approaching the door when suddenly he turned and came towards us. I was overcome by a delicious thrill of terror such as I could not have felt a few years later, because, as age diminishes the capacity, familiarity with the world meanwhile destroys in us any inclination to provoke such strange encounters, to feel that kind of emotion.

In the course of the few words that Elstir came to say to us, sitting down at our table, he never replied to me on the several occasions on which I spoke to him of Swann. I began to think that he did not know him. He nevertheless asked me to come and see him at his Balbec studio, an invitation which he did not extend to Saint-Loup, and which I had earned, as I might not, perhaps, from Swann's recommendation had Elstir been a friend of his (for the part played by disinterested motives is greater than we are inclined to think in people's lives), by a few words which made him think that I was devoted to the arts. He lavished on me a friendliness which was as far above that of Saint-Loup as the latter's was above the affability of a shopkeeper. Compared with that of a great artist, the friendliness of a great nobleman, however charming it may be, seems like play-acting, like simulation. Saint-Loup sought to please; Elstir loved to give, to give himself. Everything that he possessed, ideas, works, and the rest which he counted for far less, he would have given gladly to anyone who understood him. But, for lack of congenial company, he lived in an unsociable isolation which fashionable people called pose and ill-breeding, the authorities a recalcitrant spirit, his neighbours madness, his family selfishness and pride.

And no doubt at first he had thought with pleasure, even in his solitude, that, thanks to his work, he was addressing from a distance, was imbuing with a loftier idea of himself, those who had misunderstood or offended him. Perhaps, in those days, he lived alone not from indifference but from love of his fellows, and, just as I had renounced Gilberte in order to appear to her again one day in more attractive colours, dedicated his work to certain people as a sort of new approach to them whereby, without actually seeing him, they would be brought to love him, admire him, talk about him; a renunciation is not always total from the start, when we decide upon it in our original frame of mind and before it has reacted upon us, whether it be the renunciation of an invalid, a monk, an artist or a hero. But if he had wished to produce with certain people in his mind, in producing he had lived for himself, remote from society, to which he had become indifferent; the practice of solitude had given him a love for it, as happens with every big thing which we have begun by fearing, because we know it to be incompatible with smaller things which we prize and which it does not so much deprive us of as detach us from. Before we experience it, our whole preoccupation is to know to what extent we can reconcile it with certain pleasures which cease to be pleasures as soon as we have experienced it.

Elstir did not stay talking to us for long. I made up my mind that I would go to his studio during the next few days, but on the following afternoon, after I had accompanied my grandmother to the far end of the seafront, near the cliffs of Canapville, on the way back, at the corner of one of the little streets which ran down at right angles to the beach, we passed a girl who, hanging her head like an animal that is being driven reluctant to its stall, and carrying golf-clubs, was walking in front of an authoritarian-looking person, in all probability her or one of her friends' "Miss," who suggested a portrait of Jeffreys by Hogarth, with a face as red as if her favourite beverage were gin rather than tea, on which a dried smear of tobacco at the corner of her mouth prolonged the curve of a moustache that was grizzled but abundant. The girl who preceded her resembled the member of the little band who, beneath a black polo-cap, had shown in an inexpressive chubby face a pair of laughing eyes. However, though this one had also a black polo-cap, she struck me as being even prettier than the other; the line of her nose was straighter, the curve of the nostrils fuller and more fleshy. Besides, the other had seemed a proud, pale girl, this one a child well-disciplined and of rosy complexion. And yet, since she was pushing a bicycle just like the other's, and was wearing the same kid gloves, I concluded that the differences arose perhaps from the angle and the circumstances in which I now saw her, for it was hardly likely that there could be at Balbec a second girl with a face that was on the whole so similar and combining the same details in her accoutrement. She flung a rapid glance in my direction. During the next few days, when I saw the little band again on the beach, and indeed long afterwards when I knew all the girls who composed it, I could never be absolutely certain that any of them—even the one who resembled her most, the girl with the bicycle—was indeed the one that I had seen that evening at the corner of the street at the end of the esplanade, a girl who was scarcely but still just perceptibly different from the one I had noticed in the procession.

From that moment, whereas for the last few days my mind had been occupied chiefly by the tall one, it was the one with the golf-clubs, presumed to be Mlle Simonet, who began once more to absorb my attention. When walking with the others she would often stop, forcing her friends, who seemed greatly to respect her, to stop also. Thus it is, coming to a halt, her eyes sparkling beneath her polo-cap, that I still see her again today, silhouetted against the screen which the sea spreads out behind her, and separated from me by a transparent sky-blue space, the interval of time that has elapsed since then—the first impression, faint and tenuous in my memory, desired, pursued, then forgotten, then recaptured, of a face which I have many times since projected upon the cloud of the past in order to be able to say to myself, of a girl who was actually in my room: "It is she!"

But it was perhaps yet another, the one with geranium cheeks and green eyes, whom I should have liked most to know. And yet, whichever of them it might be, on any given day, that I preferred to see, the others, without her, were sufficient to excite my desire which, concentrated now chiefly on one, now on another, continued—as, on the first day, my confused vision had done—to combine and blend them, to make of them the little world apart, animated by a life in common, which indeed they doubtless imagined themselves to form; and in becoming a friend of one of them I should have penetrated—like a cultivated pagan or a meticulous Christian going among barbarians—a youthful society in which thoughtlessness, health, sensual pleasure, cruelty, unintellectuality and joy held sway.

My grandmother, whom I had told of my meeting with Elstir and who rejoiced at the thought of all the intellectual profit that I might derive from his friendship, considered it absurd and none too polite of me not to have yet gone to pay him a visit. But I could think only of the little band, and being uncertain of the hour at which the girls would be passing along the front, I dared not absent myself. My grandmother was astonished, too, at the elegance of my attire, for I had suddenly remembered suits which had been lying all this time at the bottom of my trunk. I put on a different one every day, and had even written to Paris ordering new hats and new ties.

It adds a great charm to life in a watering-place like Balbec if the face of a pretty girl, a vendor of shells, cakes or flowers, painted in vivid colours in our mind, is regularly, from early morning, the purpose of each of those leisured, luminous days which we spend on the beach. They become then, and for that reason, albeit idle, as alert as working-days, pointed, magnetised, raised slightly to meet an approaching moment, that in which, while we purchase shortbread, roses, ammonites, we will delight in seeing, on a feminine face, colours displayed as purely as on a flower. But at least one can speak to these young vendors, and this dispenses one from having to construct with one's imagination those aspects which a mere visual perception fails to provide, and to re-create their life, magnifying its charm, as in front of a portrait; moreover, precisely because one speaks to them, one can learn where and at what time it will be possible to see them again. Now I had none of these advantages when it came to the little band. Since their habits were unknown to me, when on certain days I failed to catch a glimpse of them, not knowing the cause of their absence I sought to discover whether it was something fixed and regular, if they were to be seen only every other day, or in certain kinds of weather, or if there were days on which they were not to be seen at all. I imagined myself already friends with them, and saying: "But you weren't there the other day?" "Weren't we? Oh, no, of course not; it was a Saturday. On Saturdays we don't ever come, because . . ." If only it were simply a matter of knowing that on black Saturday it was useless to torment oneself, that one might range the beach from end to end, sit down outside the pastry-cook's and pretend to be nibbling an éclair, poke into the curio shop, wait for bathing time, the concert, high tide, sunset, night, all without seeing the longed-for little band. But the fatal day did not, perhaps, come once a week. It did not, perhaps, of necessity fall on a Saturday. Perhaps certain atmospheric conditions influenced it or were entirely unconnected with it. How many observations, patient but not at all serene, must one accumulate of the movements, to all appearance irregular, of these unknown worlds before being able to be sure that one has not allowed oneself to be led astray by mere coincidence, that one's forecasts will not be proved wrong, before deducing the incontrovertible laws, acquired at the cost of so much painful experience, of that passionate astronomy!

Remembering that I had not yet seen them on some particular day of the week, I assured myself that they would not be coming, that it was useless to wait any longer on the beach. And at that very moment I caught sight of them. And yet on another day which, in so far as I had been able to conjecture that there were laws that guided the return of those constellations, must, I had calculated, prove an auspicious day, they did not come. But to this primary uncertainty as to whether I should see them or not that day, there was added another, more disquieting: whether I should ever set eyes on them again, for I had no reason, after all, to know that they were not about to set sail for America, or return to Paris. This was enough to make me begin to love them. One can feel an attraction towards a particular person. But to release that fount of sorrow, that sense of the irreparable, those agonies which prepare the way for love, there must be—and this is perhaps, more than a person, the actual object which our passion seeks so anxiously to embrace—the risk of an impossibility. Thus already they were acting upon me, those influences which recur in the course of our successive love-affairs (which can moreover occur, but then rather in the life of big cities, in relation to working-girls of whose half-holidays we are uncertain and whom we are alarmed not to have seen at the factory exit), or which at least have recurred in the course of mine. Perhaps they are inseparable from love; perhaps everything that formed a distinctive feature of our first love comes to attach itself to those that follow, by virtue of recollection, suggestion, habit, and, through the successive periods of our life, gives to its different aspects a general character.

I seized every pretext for going down to the beach at the hours when I hoped to succeed in finding them there. Having caught sight of them once while we were at lunch, I now invariably came in late for it, waiting interminably on the esplanade for them to pass; spending the whole of my brief stay in the dining-room interrogating with my eyes its azure wall of glass; rising long before dessert, so as not to miss them should they have gone out at a different hour, and chafing with irritation at my grandmother when, with unwitting malevolence, she made me stay with her past the hour that seemed to me propitious. I tried to prolong the horizon by changing the position of my chair, and if by chance I did catch sight of one or other of the girls, since they all partook of the same special essence, it was as if I had seen projected before my face in a shifting, diabolical hallucination a little of the unfriendly and yet passionately coveted dream which, but a moment ago, had existed only—stagnating permanently there—in my brain.

I loved none of them, loving them all, and yet the possibility of meeting them was in my daily life the sole element of delight, alone aroused in me those hopes for which one would break down every obstacle, hopes ending often in fury if I had not seen them. For the moment, these girls eclipsed my grandmother in my affection; the longest journey would at once have seemed attractive to me had it been to a place in which they might be found. It was to them that my thoughts agreeably clung when I supposed myself to be thinking of something else or of nothing. But when, even without knowing it, I thought of them, they, more unconsciously still, were for me the mountainous blue undulations of the sea, the outline of a procession against the sea. It was the sea that I hoped to find, if I went to some town where they had gone. The most exclusive love for a person is always a love for something else.

Meanwhile my grandmother, because I now showed a keen interest in golf and tennis and was letting slip an opportunity of seeing at work and hearing talk an artist whom she knew to be one of the greatest of his time, evinced for me a scorn which seemed to me to be based on somewhat narrow views. I had guessed long ago in the Champs-Elysées, and had verified since, that when we are in love with a woman we simply project on to her a state of our own soul; that consequently the important thing is not the worth of the woman but the profundity of the state; and that the emotions which a perfectly ordinary girl arouses in us can enable us to bring to the surface of our consciousness some of the innermost parts of our being, more personal, more remote, more quintessential than any that might be evoked by the pleasure we derive from the conversation of a great man or even from the admiring contemplation of his work.

I finally had to comply with my grandmother's wishes, all the more reluctantly in that Elstir lived at some distance from the front in one of the newest of Balbec's avenues. The heat of the day obliged me to take the tramway which passed along the Rue de la Plage, and I endeavoured, in order to persuade myself that I was in the ancient realm of the Cimmerians, in the country, perhaps, of King Mark, or on the site of the Forest of Broceliande, not to look at the gimcrack splendour of the buildings that extended on either hand, among which Elstir's villa was perhaps the most sumptuously hideous, in spite of which he had taken it because, of all that there were to be had at Balbec, it was the only one that provided him with a really big studio.

It was with averted eyes that I crossed the garden, which had a lawn (similar, on a smaller scale, to that of any suburban villa round Paris), a statuette of an amorous gardener, glass balls in which one saw one's distorted reflexion, beds of begonias, and a little arbour beneath which rocking chairs were drawn up round an iron table. But after all these preliminaries stamped with urban ugliness, I took no notice of the chocolate mouldings on the plinths once I was in the studio; I felt perfectly happy, for, with the help of all the sketches and studies that surrounded me, I foresaw the possibility of raising myself to a poetical understanding, rich in delights, of manifold forms which I had not hitherto isolated from the total spectacle of reality. And Elstir's studio appeared to me like the laboratory of a sort of new creation of the world in which, from the chaos that is everything we see, he had extracted, by painting them on various rectangles of canvas that were placed at all angles, here a sea-wave angrily crashing its lilac foam on to the sand, there a young man in white linen leaning on the rail of a ship. The young man's jacket and the splashing wave had acquired a new dignity from the fact that they continued to exist, even though they were deprived of those qualities in which they might be supposed to consist, the wave being no longer able to wet or the jacket to clothe anyone.

At the moment at which I entered, the creator was just finishing, with the brush which he had in his hand, the outline of the setting sun.

The blinds were closed almost everywhere round the studio, which was fairly cool and, except in one place where daylight laid against the wall its brilliant but fleeting decoration, dark; one small rectangular window alone was open, embowered in honeysuckle and giving on to an avenue beyond a strip of garden; so that the atmosphere of the greater part of the studio was dusky, transparent and compact in its mass, but liquid and sparkling at the edges where the sunlight encased it, like a lump of rock crystal of which one surface, already cut and polished, gleams here and there like a mirror with iridescent rays. While Elstir, at my request, went on painting, I wandered about in the half-light, stopping to examine first one picture, then another.

Most of those that covered the walls were not what I should chiefly have liked to see of his work, paintings in what an English art journal which lay on the reading-room table in the Grand Hotel called his first and second manners, the mythological manner and the manner in which he showed signs of Japanese influence, both admirably represented, it was said, in the collection of Mme de Guermantes. Naturally enough, what he had in his studio were almost all seascapes done here at Balbec. But I was able to discern from these that the charm of each of them lay in a sort of metamorphosis of the objects represented, analogous to what in poetry we call metaphor, and that, if God the Father had created things by naming them, it was by taking away their names or giving them other names that Elstir created them anew. The names which designate things correspond invariably to an intellectual notion, alien to our true impressions, and compelling us to eliminate from them everything that is not in keeping with that notion.

Sometimes, at my window in the hotel at Balbec, in the morning when Françoise undid the blankets that shut out the light, or in the evening when I was waiting until it was time to go out with Saint-Loup, I had been led by some effect of sunlight to mistake what was only a darker stretch of sea for a distant coastline, or to gaze delightedly at a belt of liquid azure without knowing whether it belonged to sea or sky. But presently my reason would re-establish between the elements the distinction which my first impression had abolished. In the same way from my bedroom in Paris I would sometimes hear a dispute, almost a riot, in the street below, until I had traced back to its cause—a carriage for instance that was rattling towards me—that noise from which I now eliminated the shrill and discordant vociferations which my ear had really heard but which my reason knew that wheels did not produce. But the rare moments in which we see nature as she is, poetically, were those from which Elstir's work was created. One of the metaphors that occurred most frequently in the seascapes which surrounded him here was precisely that which, comparing land with sea, suppressed all demarcation between them. It was this comparison, tacitly and untiringly repeated on a single canvas, which gave it that multiform and powerful unity, the cause (not always clearly perceived by themselves) of the enthusiasm which Elstir's work aroused in certain collectors.

It was, for instance, for a metaphor of this sort—in a picture of the harbour of Carquethuit, a picture which he had finished only a few days earlier and which I stood looking at for a long time—that Elstir had prepared the mind of the spectator by employing, for the little town, only marine terms, and urban terms for the sea. Whether because its houses concealed a part of the harbour, a dry dock, or perhaps the sea itself plunging deep inland, as constantly happened on the Balbec coast, on the other side of the promontory on which the town was built the roofs were overtopped (as they might have been by chimneys or steeples) by masts which had the effect of making the vessels to which they belonged appear town-bred, built on land, an impression reinforced by other boats moored along the jetty but in such serried ranks that you could see men talking across from one deck to another without being able to distinguish the dividing line, the chink of water between them, so that this fishing fleet seemed less to belong to the water than, for instance, the churches of Criquebec which, in the distance, surrounded by water on every side because you saw them without seeing the town, in a powdery haze of sunlight and crumbling waves, seemed to be emerging from the waters, blown in alabaster or in sea-foam, and, enclosed in the band of a variegated rainbow, to form an ethereal, mystical tableau. On the beach in the foreground the painter had contrived that the eye should discover no fixed boundary, no absolute line of demarcation between land and sea. The men who were pushing down their boats into the sea were running as much through the waves as along the sand, which, being wet, reflected the hulls as if they were already in the water. The sea itself did not come up in an even line but followed the irregularities of the shore, which the perspective of the picture increased still further, so that a ship actually at sea, half-hidden by the projecting works of the arsenal, seemed to be sailing through the middle of the town; women gathering shrimps among the rocks had the appearance, because they were surrounded by water and because of the depression which, beyond the circular barrier of rocks, brought the beach (on the two sides nearest the land) down to sea-level, of being in a marine grotto overhung by ships and waves, open yet protected in the midst of miraculously parted waters. If the whole picture gave this impression of harbours in which the sea penetrated the land, in which the land was already subaqueous and the population amphibian, the strength of the marine element was everywhere apparent; and round about the rocks, at the mouth of the harbour where the sea was rough, one sensed, from the muscular efforts of the fishermen and the slant of the boats leaning over at an acute angle, compared with the calm erectness of the warehouse, the church, the houses in the town to which some of the figures were returning and from which others were setting out to fish, that they were riding bareback on the water as though on a swift and fiery animal whose rearing, but for their skill, must have unseated them. A party of holiday-makers were putting gaily out to sea in a boat that tossed like a jaunting-car on a rough road; their boatmen, blithe but none the less attentive, trimmed the bellying sail, everyone kept in his place in order not to unbalance and capsize the boat, and so they went scudding through sun-lit fields and shady places, rushing down the slopes. It was a fine morning in spite of the recent storm. Indeed, one could still feel the powerful impulses that must first be neutralised in order to attain the easy balance of the boats that lay motionless, enjoying sunshine and breeze, in parts where the sea was so calm that the reflections had almost more solidity and reality than the floating hulls, vaporised by an effect of the sunlight and made to overlap one another by the perspective. Or rather one would not have called them other parts of the sea. For between those parts there was as much difference as there was between one of them and the church rising from the water, or the ships behind the town. One's reason then set to work to make a single element of what was in one place black beneath a gathering storm, a little further all of one colour with the sky and as brightly burnished, and elsewhere so bleached by sunshine, haze and foam, so compact, so terrestrial, so circumscribed with houses that one thought of some white stone causeway or of a field of snow, up the slope of which one was alarmed to see a ship come climbing high and dry, as a carriage climbs dripping from a ford, but which a moment later, when you saw on the raised, uneven surface of the solid plain boats drunkenly heaving, you understood, identical in all these different aspects, to be still the sea.

Although it is rightly said that there can be no progress, no discovery in art, but only in the sciences, and that each artist starting afresh on an individual effort cannot be either helped or hindered therein by the efforts of any other, it must none the less be acknowledged that, in so far as art brings to light certain laws, once an industry has popularised them, the art that was first in the field loses retrospectively a little of its originality. Since Elstir began to paint, we have grown familiar with what are called "wonderful" photographs of scenery and towns. If we press for a definition of what their admirers mean by the epithet, we shall find that it is generally applied to some unusual image of a familiar object, an image different from those that we are accustomed to see, unusual and yet true to nature, and for that reason doubly striking because it surprises us, takes us out of our cocoon of habit, and at the same time brings us back to ourselves by recalling to us an earlier impression. For instance, one of these "magnificent" photographs will illustrate a law of perspective, will show us some cathedral which we are accustomed to see in the middle of a town, taken instead from a selected vantage point from which it will appear to be thirty times the height of the houses and to be thrusting out a spur from the bank of the river, from which it is actually at some distance. Now the effort made by Elstir to reproduce things not as he knew them to be but according to the optical illusions of which our first sight of them is composed, had led him precisely to bring out certain of these laws of perspective, which were thus all the more striking, since art had been the first to disclose them. A river, because of the windings of its course, a bay because of the apparent proximity to one another of the cliffs on either side of it, would seem to have hollowed out in the heart of the plain or of the mountains a lake absolutely landlocked on every side. In a picture of a view from Balbec painted upon a scorching day in summer an inlet of the sea, enclosed between walls of pink granite, appeared not to be the sea, which began further out. The continuity of the ocean was suggested only by the gulls which, wheeling over what seemed to be solid rock, were as a matter of fact sniffing the moist vapour of the shifting tide. Other laws emerged from the same canvas, as, at the foot of immense cliffs, the lilliputian grace of white sails on the blue mirror on whose surface they looked like sleeping butterflies, and certain contrasts between the depth of the shadows and the paleness of the light. This play of light and shade, which photography has also rendered commonplace, had interested Elstir so much that at one time he had delighted in painting what were almost mirages, in which a castle crowned with a tower appeared as a completely circular castle extended by a tower at its summit, and at its foot by an inverted tower, either because the exceptional purity of the atmosphere on a fine day gave the shadow reflected in the water the hardness and brightness of stone, or because the morning mists rendered the stone as vaporous as the shadow. And similarly, beyond the sea, behind a line of woods, another sea began, roseate with the light of the setting sun, which was in fact the sky. The light, fashioning as it were new solids, thrust back the hull of the boat on which it fell behind the other hull that was still in shadow, and arranged as it were the steps of a crystal staircase on what was in reality the flat surface, broken only by the play of light and shade, of the morning sea. A river running beneath the bridges of a town was caught from such an angle that it appeared entirely dislocated, now broadening into a lake, now narrowing into a rivulet, broken elsewhere by the interposition of a hill crowned with trees among which the townsman would repair at evening to breathe the cool air; and even the rhythm of this topsy-turvy town was assured only by the rigid vertical of the steeples which did not rise but rather, in accordance with the plumb-line of the pendulum of gravity beating time as in a triumphal march, seemed to hold suspended beneath them the blurred mass of houses that rose in terraces through the mist along the banks of the crushed, disjointed stream. And (since Elstir's earliest works belonged to the time in which a painter would embellish his landscape by inserting a human figure), on the cliff's edge or among the mountains, the path too, that half-human part of nature, underwent, like river or ocean, the eclipses of perspective. And whether a mountain ridge, or the spray of a waterfall, or the sea prevented the eye from following the continuity of the path, visible to the traveller but not to us, the little human figure in old-fashioned clothes, lost in those solitudes, seemed often to be stopped short on the edge of a precipice, the path which he had been following ending there, while, a thousand feet above him in those pine-forests, it was with a fond eye and a relieved heart that we saw reappear the threadlike whiteness of its sandy surface, grateful to the wayfarer's feet, though the mountainside had concealed from us its intervening bends as it skirted the waterfall or the gulf.

The effort made by Elstir to strip himself, when face to face with reality, of every intellectual notion, was all the more admirable in that this man who made himself deliberately ignorant before sitting down to paint, forgot everything that he knew in his honesty of purpose (for what cne knows does not belong to oneself), had in fact an exceptionally cultivated mind. When I confessed to him the disappointment I had felt on seeing the porch at Balbec:

"What!" he exclaimed, "you were disappointed by the porch! Why, it's the finest illustrated Bible that the people have ever had. That Virgin and all the bas-reliefs telling the story of her life—it's the most loving, the most inspired expression of that endless poem of adoration and praise in which the Middle Ages extolled the glory of the Madonna. If you only knew, side by side with the most scrupulous accuracy in rendering the sacred text, what exquisite *trouvailles* came to the old carver, what profound thoughts, what delicious poetry! The idea of that great sheet in which the angels carry the body of the Virgin, too sacred for them to venture to touch it with their hands" (I mentioned to him that this theme had been treated also at Saint-André-des-Champs; he had seen photographs of the porch there, and agreed, but pointed out that the eagerness of those little peasant figures, all scurrying together round the Virgin, was not at all the same thing as the gravity of those two great angels, almost Italian, so slender, so gentle); "and the angel who carries away the Virgin's soul, to reunite it with her body; or in the meeting of the Virgin with Elizabeth, Elizabeth's gesture when she touches the Virgin's womb and marvels to feel that it is swollen; and the outstretched arm of the midwife who had refused, without touching, to believe in the Virgin Birth; and the loincloth thrown by the Virgin to St Thomas to give him proof of the Resurrection; that veil, too, which the Virgin tears from her own breast to cover the nakedness of her son, whose blood, the wine of the Eucharist, the Church collects from one side of him, while on the other the Synagogue, its kingdom at an end, has its eyes bandaged, holds a half-broken sceptre and lets fall, together with the crown that is slipping from its head, the tables of the old law. And the husband who, on the Day of Judgment, as he helps his young wife to rise from her grave, lays her hand against his own heart to reassure her, to prove to her that it is indeed beating, isn't that also rather a stunning idea, really inspired? And the angel who is taking away the sun and the moon which are no longer needed since it is written that the Light of the Cross will be seven times brighter than the light of the firmament; and the one who is dipping his hand into Jesus' bath, to see whether the water is warm enough; and the one emerging from the clouds to place the crown on the Virgin's brow; and all the angels leaning from the vault of heaven, between the balusters of the New Jerusalem, and throwing up their arms in horror or joy at the sight of the torments of the wicked or the bliss of the elect! Because it's all the circles of heaven, a whole gigantic poem full of theology and symbolism that you have there. It's prodigious, it's divine, it's a thousand times better than anything you will see in Italy, where for that matter this very tympanum has been carefully copied by sculptors with far less genius. Because, you know, it's all a question of genius. There never was a time when everybody had genius, that's all nonsense, it would be more extraordinary than the golden age. The chap who carved that façade, take my word for it, was every bit as good, had just as profound ideas, as the men you admire most at the present day. I could show you what I meant if we went there together. There are certain passages from the Office of the Assumption which have been conveyed with a subtlety that not even a Redon could equal."

And yet, when my eager eyes had opened before the façade of Balbec church, it was not this vast celestial vision of which he spoke to me that I had seen, not this gigantic theological poem which I understood to have been inscribed there in stone. I spoke to him of those great statues of saints mounted on stilts which formed a sort of avenue on either side.

"It starts from the mists of antiquity to end in Jesus Christ," he explained. "You see on one side his ancestors after the spirit, on the other the Kings of Judah, his ancestors after the flesh. All the ages are there. And if you looked more closely at what you took for stilts you would have been able to give names to the figures standing on them. Under the feet of Moses you would have recognised the golden calf, under Abraham's the ram, and under Joseph's the demon counselling Potiphar's wife."

I told him also that I had gone there expecting to find an almost Persian building, and that this had doubtless been one of the chief factors in my disappointment. "Not at all," he assured me, "it's perfectly true. Some parts of it are quite oriental. One of the capitals reproduces so exactly a Persian subject that you cannot simply explain it by the persistence of oriental traditions. The carver must have copied some casket brought from the East by navigators." And indeed he was later to show me the photograph of a capital on which I saw dragons that were almost Chinese devouring one another, but at Balbec this little piece of sculpture had passed unnoticed by me in the general effect of the building which did not conform to the pattern traced in my mind by the words "an almost Persian church."

The intellectual pleasures which I was enjoying in this studio did not in the least prevent me from being aware, although they enveloped us as it were in spite of ourselves, of the warm glazes, the sparkling penumbra of the room itself and, through the little window framed with honeysuckle, in the rustic avenue, the resilient dryness of the sun-parched earth, veiled only by the diaphanous gauze woven of distance and the shade of the trees. Perhaps the unconscious well-being induced by this summer day came like a tributary to swell the flood of joy that had surged in me at the sight of Elstir's *Carquethuit Harbour*.

I had supposed Elstir to be a modest man, but I realised my mistake on seeing his face cloud with melancholy when, in a little speech of thanks, I uttered the word "fame." Men who believe that their works will last—as was the case with Elstir—form the habit of placing them in a period when they themselves will have crumbled into dust. And thus, by obliging them to reflect on their own extinction, the idea of fame saddens them because it is inseparable from the idea of death. I changed the subject in the hope of dispelling the cloud of ambitious melancholy with which I had unwittingly shadowed Elstir's brow. "Someone advised me once," I said, thinking of the conversation we had had with Legrandin at Combray, as to which I was glad of an opportunity of learning Elstir's views, "not to visit Brittany, because it would not be wholesome for a mind with a natural inclination towards day-dreams." "Not at all," he replied. "When a mind has a tendency towards day-dreams, it's a mistake to shield it from them, to ration them. So long as you divert your mind from its day-dreams, it will not know them for what they are; you will be the victim of all sorts of appearances because you will not have grasped their true nature. If a little day-dreaming is dangerous, the cure for it is not to dream less but to dream more, to dream all the time. One must have a thorough understanding of one's day-dreams if one is not to be troubled by them; there is a way of separating one's dreams from one's life which so often produces good results that I wonder whether one oughtn't to try it just in case, simply as a preventative, as certain surgeons suggest that, to avoid the risk of appendicitis later on, we ought all to have our appendixes taken out when we're children."

Elstir and I had meanwhile been walking towards the end of the studio, and had reached the window that looked across the garden on to a narrow side-street that was almost a country lane. We had gone there to breathe the cooler air of the late afternoon. I supposed myself to be nowhere near the girls of the little band, and it was only by sacrificing for once the hope of seeing them that I had yielded to my grandmother's entreaties and had gone to see Elstir. For we do not know the whereabouts of what we are seeking, and often we avoid for a long time the place to which, for quite different reasons, everyone has been asking us to go; but we never suspect that we shall there see the very person of whom we are thinking. I looked out vaguely over this rustic path which passed quite close to the studio but did not belong to Elstir. Suddenly there appeared on it, coming towards us at a rapid pace, the young cyclist of the little band, with her polo-cap pulled down over her dark hair towards her plump cheeks, her eyes gay and slightly challenging; and on that auspicious path, miraculously filled with the promise of delights, I saw her, beneath the trees, address to Elstir the smiling greeting of a friend, a rainbow that bridged for me the gulf between our terraqueous world and regions which I had hitherto regarded as inaccessible. She even came up to shake hands with the painter, though without stopping, and I saw that she had a tiny beauty spot on her chin. "Do you know that girl, Monsieur?" I asked Elstir, realising that he might introduce me to her, invite her to his house. And this peaceful studio with its rural horizon was at once filled with a surfeit of delight such as a child might feel in a house where he was already happily playing when he learned that, in addition, out of that bounteousness which enables lovely things and noble hosts to increase their gifts beyond all measure, a sumptuous meal was being prepared for him. Elstir told me that she was called Albertine Simonet, and gave me the names also of her friends, whom I described to him with sufficient accuracy for him to identify them almost without hesitation. I had made a mistake with regard to their social position, but not the mistake that I usually made at Balbec. I was always ready to take the sons of shopkeepers for princes when they appeared on horseback. This time I had placed in a shady milieu the daughters of middle-class people, extremely rich, belonging to the world of trade and industry. It was the class which, at first sight, interested me least, since it held for me none of the mystery either of the people or of a society such as that of the Guermantes. And no doubt if a preliminary glamour which they would never now lose had not been conferred on them, in my dazzled eyes, by the glaring vacuity of seaside life, I should perhaps not have succeeded in resisting and overcoming the idea that they were the daughters of prosperous merchants. I could not help marvelling at what a wonderful workshop the French middle class was for sculpture of the most varied kind. What unexpected types, what richness of invention in the character of the faces, what firmness, what freshness, what simplicity in the features! The shrewd old burghers from whom these Dianas and these nymphs had sprung seemed to me to have been the greatest of statuaries. Scarcely had I had time to register the social metamorphosis of the little band—for these discoveries of a mistake, these modifications of the notion one has of a person, have the instantaneousness of a chemical reaction—than the idea had already established itself behind the guttersnipe ways of these girls, whom I had taken for the mistresses of racing cyclists or prize-fighters, that they might easily be connected with the family of some lawyer or other whom we knew. I was barely conscious of who Albertine Simonet was. She had certainly no conception of what she was one day to mean to me. Even the name, Simonet, which I had already heard spoken on the beach, I should have spelt with a double "n" had I been asked to write it down, never dreaming of the importance which this family attached to there being only one. The further we descend the social scale the more we find that snobbery fastens on to mere trifles which are perhaps no more null than the distinctions observed by the aristocracy, but, being more obscure, more peculiar to each individual, surprise us more. Possibly there had been Simonnets who had done badly in business, or worse still. The fact remains that the Simonets never failed, it appeared, to be annoyed if anyone doubled their "n." They were as proud, perhaps, of being the only Simonets in the world with one "n" instead of two as the Montmorencys of being the premier barons of France. I asked Elstir whether these girls lived at Balbec; yes, he told me, some of them at any rate. The villa in which one of them lived was precisely at the far end of the beach, where the cliffs of Canapville began. Since this girl was a great friend of Albertine Simonet, this was one more reason for me to believe that it was indeed the latter whom I had met that day when I was with my grandmother. There were of course so many of those little streets running down to the beach, and all at the same angle, that I could not have specified exactly which of them it had been. One would like to remember a thing accurately, but at the time one's vision is always clouded. And yet that Albertine and the girl whom I had seen going to her friend's house were one and the same person was a practical certainty. In spite of this, whereas the countless images that have since been presented to me by the dark young golfer, however different they may be, are superimposed one upon the other (because I know that they all belong to her), and by retracing my memories I can, under cover of that identity and as if through an internal passageway, run through all those images in turn without losing my grasp of one and the same person; if, on the other hand, I wish to go back to the girl whom I passed that day when I was with my grandmother, I have to emerge into the open air. I am convinced that it is Albertine whom I find there, the same who used often to come to a halt in the midst of her friends during their walks against the backdrop of the sea; but all those more recent images remain separate from that earlier one because I am unable to confer on her retrospectively an identity which she did not have for me at the moment she caught my eye; whatever assurance I may derive from the law of probabilities, that girl with the plump cheeks who stared at me so boldly from the corner of the little street and from the beach, and by whom I believe that I might have been loved, I have never, in the strict sense of the words, seen again.

Was it my hesitation between the different girls of the little band, all of whom retained something of the collective charm which had disturbed me from the first, that, combined with those other reasons, allowed me later on, even at the time of my greater—my second—love for Albertine, a sort of intermittent and all too brief liberty to abstain from loving her? From having strayed among all her friends before it finally concentrated on her, my love kept for some time between itself and the image of Albertine a certain "play" which enabled it, like ill-adjusted stage lighting, to flit over others before returning to focus upon her; the connexion between the pain which I felt in my heart and the memory of Albertine did not seem to me a necessary one; I might perhaps have been able to co-ordinate it with the image of another person. And this enabled me, in a momentary flash, to banish the reality altogether, not only the external reality, as in my love for Gilberte (which I had recognised to be an inner state wherein I drew from myself alone the particular quality, the special character of the person I loved, everything that rendered her indispensable to my happiness), but even the other reality, internal and purely subjective.

"Not a day passes but one or other of them comes by here, and looks in for a minute or two," Elstir told me, plunging me into despair at the thought that if I had gone to see him at once, when my grandmother had begged me to do so, I should in all probability have made Albertine's acquaintance long since.

She had continued on her way; from the studio she was no longer in sight. I supposed that she had gone to join her friends on the front. If I could have been there with Elstir, I should have got to know them. I thought up endless pretexts to induce him to take a stroll with me on the beach. I no longer had the same feeling of serenity as before the apparition of the girl in the frame of the little window, so charming until then in its fringe of honeysuckle and now so drearily empty. Elstir caused me a joy that was mixed with torture when he agreed to walk a few steps with me but said that he must first finish the piece of work on which he was engaged. It was a study of some flowers, but not those of which I would rather have commissioned a portrait from him than one of a person, so that I might learn from the revelation of his genius what I had so often sought in vain from the flowers themselves—hawthorn white and pink, cornflowers, apple-blossom. Elstir as he worked talked botany to me, but I scarcely listened; he was no longer sufficient in himself, he was now only the necessary intermediary between these girls and me; the prestige which, only a few moments ago, his talent had still given him in my eyes was now worthless except in so far as it might confer a little on me also in the eyes of the little band to whom I should be introduced by him.

I paced up and down the room, impatient for him to

finish what he was doing; I picked up and examined various sketches, quantities of which were stacked against the walls. It was thus that I happened to bring to light a water-colour which evidently belonged to a much earlier period in Elstir's life, and gave me that particular kind of enchantment which is diffused by works of art not only delightfully executed but representing a subject so singular and so seductive that it is to it that we attribute a great deal of their charm, as if that charm were something that the painter had merely to discover and observe, realised already in a material form by nature, and to reproduce. The fact that such objects can exist, beautiful quite apart from the painter's interpretation of them, satisfies a sort of innate materialism in us, against which our reason contends, and acts as a counterpoise to the abstractions of aesthetic theory. It was—this water-colour—the portrait of a young woman, by no means beautiful but of a curious type, in a close-fitting hat not unlike a bowler, trimmed with a ribbon of cerise silk; in one of her mittened hands was a lighted cigarette, while the other held at knee-level a sort of broadbrimmed garden hat, no more than a screen of plaited straw to keep off the sun. On a table by her side, a tall vase filled with pink carnations. Often (and it was the case here) the singularity of such works is due principally to their having been executed in special conditions, so that it is not immediately clear to us whether, for instance, the strange attire of a female model is her costume for a fancy-dress ball, or whether, conversely, the scarlet cloak which an elderly man looks as though he had put on in response to some whim of the painter's is his professor's or alderman's gown or his cardinal's cape. The ambiguous character of the person whose portrait now confronted me arose, without my understanding it, from the fact that it was a young actress of an earlier generation half dressed up as a man. But the bowler beneath which the hair was fluffy but short, the velvet jacket, without lapels, opening over a white shirt-front, made me hesitate as to the period of the clothes and the sex of the model, so that I did not know exactly what I had before my eyes, except that it was a most luminous piece of painting. And the pleasure which it afforded me was troubled only by the fear that Elstir, by delaying further, would make me miss the girls, for the declining sun now hung low in the little window. Nothing in this water-colour was merely set down there as a fact and painted because of its practical relevance to the scene, the costume because the young woman must be wearing something, the vase to hold the flowers. The glass of the vase, cherished for its own sake, seemed to be holding the water in which the stems of the carnations were dipped in something as limpid, almost as liquid as itself; the woman's clothes enveloped her in a material that had an independent, fraternal charm, and, if the products of industry can compete in charm with the wonders of nature, as delicate, as pleasing to the touch of the eye, as freshly painted as the fur of a cat, the petals of a flower, the feathers of a dove. The whiteness of the shirt-front, as fine as soft hail, with its gay pleats gathered into little bells like lilies of the valley, was spangled with bright gleams of light from the room, themselves sharply etched and subtly shaded as if they were flowers stitched into the linen. And the velvet of the jacket, with its brilliant sheen, had something rough, frayed and shaggy about it here and there that recalled the crumpled brightness of the carnations in the vase. But above all one felt that Elstir, heedless of any impression of immorality that might be given by this transvestite costume worn by a young actress for whom the talent she would bring to the role was doubtless of less importance than the titillation she would offer to the jaded or depraved senses of some of her audience, had on the contrary fastened upon this equivocal aspect as on an aesthetic element which deserved to be brought into prominence, and which he had done everything in his power to emphasise. Along the lines of the face, the latent sex seemed to be on the point of confessing itself to be that of a somewhat boyish girl, then vanished, and reappeared further on with a suggestion rather of an effeminate, vicious and pensive youth, then fled once more and remained elusive. The dreamy sadness in the expression of the eyes, by its very contrast with the accessories belonging to the world of debauchery and the stage, was not the least disturbing element in the picture. One imagined moreover that it must be feigned, and that the young person who seemed ready to submit to caresses in this provoking costume had probably thought it intriguing to enhance the provocation with this romantic expression of a secret longing, an unspoken grief. At the foot of the picture was inscribed: "*Miss Sacripant*, October, 1872." I could not contain my admiration. "Oh, it's nothing, only a rough sketch I did when I was young: it was a costume for a variety show. It's all ages ago now." "And what has become of the model?" A bewilderment provoked by my words preceded on Elstir's face the indifferent, absent-minded air which, a moment later, he displayed there. "Quick, give it to me!" he said, "I hear Madame Elstir coming, and though, I assure you, the young person in the bowler hat never played any part in my life, still there's no point in my wife's coming in and finding the picture staring her in the face. I've kept it only as an amusing sidelight on the theatre of those days." And, before putting it away behind the pile, Elstir, who perhaps had not set eyes on the sketch for years, gave it a careful scrutiny. "I must keep just the head," he murmured, "the lower part is really too shockingly bad, the hands are a beginner's work." I was miserable at the arrival of Mme Elstir, who could only delay us still further. The window-sill was already aglow. Our excursion would be a pure waste of time. There was no longer the slightest chance of our seeing the girls, and consequently it mattered now not at all how quickly Mme Elstir left us. In fact she did not stay very long. I found her most tedious; she might have been beautiful at twenty, driving an ox in the Roman Campagna, but her dark hair was streaked with grey and she was common without being simple, because she believed that a pompous manner and a majestic pose were required by her statuesque beauty, which, however, advancing age had robbed of all its charm. She was dressed with the utmost simplicity. And it was touching but at the same time surprising to hear Elstir exclaim, whenever he opened his mouth, and with a respectful gentleness, as if merely uttering the words moved him to tenderness and veneration: "My beautiful Gabrielle!" Later on, when I had become familiar with Elstir's mythological paintings, Mme Elstir acquired beauty in my eyes also. I understood then that to a certain ideal type illustrated by certain lines, certain arabesques which reappeared incessantly throughout his work, to a certain canon of art, he had attributed a character that was almost divine, since he had dedicated all his time, all the mental effort of which he was capable, in a word his whole life, to the task of distinguishing those lines as clearly and of reproducing them as faithfully as possible. What such an ideal inspired in Elstir was indeed a cult so solemn, so exacting, that it never allowed him to be satisfied with what he had achieved; it was the most intimate part of himself; and so he had never been able to look at it with detachment, to extract emotion from it, until the day on which he encountered it, realised outside himself, in the body of a woman, the body of the woman who had in due course become Mme Elstir and in whom he had been able (as is possible only with something that is not oneself) to find it meritorious, moving, divine. How restful, moreover, to be able to place his lips upon that ideal Beauty which hitherto he had been obliged so laboriously to extract from within himself, and which now, mysteriously incarnate, offered itself to him in a series of communions, filled with saving grace. Elstir at this period was no longer at that youthful age in which we look only to the power of the mind for the realisation of our ideal. He was nearing the age at which we count on bodily satisfactions to stimulate the force of the brain, at which mental fatigue, by inclining us towards materialism, and the diminution of our energy, towards the possibility of influences passively received, begin to make us admit that there may indeed be certain bodies, certain callings, certain rhythms that are specially privileged, realising so naturally our ideal that even without genius, merely by copying the movement of a shoulder, the tension of a neck, we can achieve a masterpiece; it is the age at which we like to caress Beauty with our eyes objectively, outside ourselves, to have it near us, in a tapestry, in a beautiful sketch by Titian picked up in a second-hand shop, in a mistress as lovely as Titian's sketch. When I understood this I could no longer look at Mme Elstir without a feeling of pleasure, and her body began to lose its heaviness, for I filled it with an idea, the idea that she was an immaterial creature, a portrait by Elstir. She was one for me, and doubtless for him too. The particulars of life do not matter to the artist; they merely provide him with the opportunity to lay bare his genius. One feels unmistakably, when one sees side by side ten portraits of different people painted by Elstir, that they are all, first and foremost, Elstirs. Only, after that rising tide of genius which sweeps over and submerges an artist's life, when the brain begins to tire, gradually the balance is disturbed and, like a river that resumes its course after the counterflow of a spring tide, it is life that once more takes the upper hand. But, while the first period lasted, the artist has gradually evolved the law, the formula of his unconscious gift. He knows what situations, if he is a novelist, what scenes, if he is a painter, provide him with the material, unimportant in itself but essential to his researches, as a laboratory might be or a workshop. He knows that he has created his masterpieces out of effects of attenuated light, out of the action of remorse upon consciousness of guilt, out of women posed beneath trees or half-immersed in water, like statues. A day will come when, owing to the erosion of his brain, he will no longer have the strength, faced with those materials which his genius was wont to use, to make the intellectual effort which alone can produce his work, and yet will continue to seek them out, happy to be near them because of the spiritual pleasure, the allurement to work, that they arouse in him; and, surrounding them besides with an aura of superstition as if they were superior to all things else, as if there dwelt in them already a great part of the work of art which they might be said to carry within them ready-made, he will confine himself to the company, to the adoration of his models. He will hold endless conversations with the repentant criminals whose remorse and regeneration once formed the subject of his novels; he will buy a house in a countryside where mists attenuate the light, he will spend long hours looking at women bathing; he will collect sumptuous stuffs. And thus the beauty of life, an expression somehow devoid of meaning, a stage this side of art at which I had seen Swann come to rest, was that also which, by a slackening of creative ardour, idolatry of the forms which had inspired it, a tendency to take the line of least resistance, must gradually undermine an Elstir's progress.

At last he had applied the final brush-stroke to his flowers. I sacrificed a minute to look at them. There was no merit in my doing so, for I knew that there was no chance now of our finding the girls on the beach; and yet, had I believed them to be still there, and that these wasted moments would make me miss them, I should have stopped to look none the less, for I should have told myself that Elstir was more interested in his flowers than in my meeting with the girls. My grandmother's nature, a nature that was the exact opposite of my complete egoism, was nevertheless reflected in certain aspects of my own. In circumstances in which someone to whom I was indifferent, for whom I had always feigned affection or respect, ran the risk merely of some unpleasantness whereas

I was in real danger, I could not have done otherwise than commiserate with him on his vexation as though it had been something important, and treat my own danger as nothing, because I would feel that these were the proportions in which he must see things. To be quite accurate, I would go even further and not only not complain of the danger in which I myself stood but go half-way to meet it, and with respect to one that threatened other people, try, on the contrary, at the risk of being endangered myself, to avert it from them. The reasons for this are several, none of them to my credit. One is that if, as long as I was simply applying my reason to the matter, I felt that I cherished life above all else, whenever in the course of my existence I have found myself obsessed by mental worry or merely by nervous anxieties, sometimes so puerile that I would not dare to reveal them, if an unforeseen circumstance then arose, involving for me the risk of being killed, this new preoccupation was so trivial in comparison with the others that I welcomed it with a sense of relief, almost of joy. Thus I find that I have experienced, although the least courageous of men, a feeling which has always seemed to me, in my reasoning moods, so foreign to my nature, so inconceivable: the intoxication of danger. But even if, when a danger arose, however mortal, I were going through an entirely calm and happy phase, I could not, were I with another person, refrain from sheltering him behind me and choosing for myself the post of danger. When a sufficient number of experiences had taught me that I invariably acted and enjoyed acting thus, I discovered—and was deeply ashamed by the discovery—that it was because, contrary to what I had always believed and asserted, I was extremely sensitive to the opinion of others. Not that this kind of unconfessed self-esteem has anything to do with vanity or conceit. For what might satisfy one or other of those failings would give me no pleasure, and I have always refrained from indulging them. But with the people in whose company I have succeeded in concealing most effectively the minor assets a knowledge of which might have given them a less paltry idea of me, I have never been able to deny myself the pleasure of showing them that I take more trouble to avert the risk of death from their path than from my own. As my motive is then self-esteem and not virtue, I find it quite natural that in any crisis they should act differently. I am far from blaming them for it, as I should perhaps do if I had been moved by a sense of duty, a duty which would seem to me in that case to be as incumbent upon them as upon myself. On the contrary, I feel that it is eminently sensible of them to safeguard their lives, while at the same time being unable to prevent myself from pushing my own safety into the background, which is particularly absurd and culpable of me since I have come to realise that the lives of many of the people in front of whom I plant myself when a bomb bursts are more valueless even than my own.

However, on the day of this first visit to Elstir, the time was still distant at which I was to become conscious of this difference in value, and there was no question of danger, but simply—a premonitory sign of that pernicious self-esteem—the question of my not appearing to attach to the pleasure which I so ardently desired more importance than to the work which the painter had still to finish. It was finished at last. And, once we were out of doors, I discovered that—so long were the days still at this season—it was not so late as I had supposed. We strolled down to the front. What stratagems I employed to keep Elstir standing at the spot where I thought that the girls might still come past! Pointing to the cliffs that towered beside us, I kept on asking him to tell me about them, so as to make him forget the time and stay there a little longer. I felt that we had a better chance of waylaying the little band if we moved towards the end of the beach.

"I should like to look at those cliffs with you from a little nearer," I said to him, having noticed that one of the girls was in the habit of going in that direction. "And as we go, do tell me about Carquethuit. I should so like to see Carquethuit," I went on, without thinking that the novel character which manifested itself with such force in Elstir's *Carquethuit Harbour* might belong perhaps rather to the painter's vision than to any special quality in the place itself. "Since I've seen your picture, I think that is where I should most like to go, there and to the Pointe du Raz, but of course that would be quite a journey from here."

"Yes, and besides, even if it weren't nearer, I should advise you perhaps all the same to visit Carquethuit," he replied. "The Pointe du Raz is magnificent, but after all it's simply another of those high cliffs of Normandy or Brittany which you know already. Carquethuit is quite different, with those rocks on a low shore. I know nothing in France like it, it reminds me rather of certain aspects of Florida. It's very curious, and moreover extremely wild. It's between Clitourps and Nehomme; you know how desolate those parts are; the sweep of the coast-line is exquisite. Here, the coast-line is pretty ordinary, but along there I can't tell you what grace it has, what softness."

Dusk was falling; it was time to be turning homewards. I was accompanying Elstir back to his villa when suddenly, as it were Mephistopheles springing up before Faust, there appeared at the end of the avenue—like a simple objectification, unreal and diabolical, of the temperament diametrically opposed to my own, of the semi-barbarous and cruel vitality of which I, in my weakness, my excess of tortured sensibility and intellectuality, was so destitute—a few spots of the essence impossible to mistake for anything else, a few spores of the zoophytic band of girls, who looked as though they had not seen me but were unquestionably engaged in passing a sarcastic judgment on me. Feeling that a meeting between them and us was now inevitable, and that Elstir would be certain to call me, I turned my back like a bather preparing to meet the shock of a wave; I stopped dead and, leaving my illustrious companion to pursue his way, remained where I was, stooping, as if I had suddenly become engrossed in it, towards the window of the antique shop which we happened to be passing at that moment. I was not sorry to give the appearance of being able to think of something other than these girls, and I was already dimly aware that when Elstir did call me up to introduce me to them I should wear that sort of inquiring expression which betrays not surprise but the wish to look surprised—such bad actors are we all, or such good mind-readers our fellow-men—that I should even go so far as to point a finger to my breast, as who should ask "Are you calling me?" and then run to join him, my head lowered in compliance and docility and my face coldly masking my annoyance at being torn from the study of old pottery in order to be introduced to people whom I had no wish to know. Meanwhile I contemplated the window and waited for the moment when my name, shouted by Elstir, would come to strike me like an expected and innocuous bullet. The certainty of being introduced to these girls had had the effect of making me not only feign indifference to them, but actually feel it. Henceforth inevitable, the pleasure of knowing them began at once to contract, to shrink, appeared smaller to me than the pleasure of talking to Saint-Loup, of dining with my grandmother, of making excursions in the vicinity which I would regret being probably forced to abandon in consequence of my relations with people who could scarcely be much interested in old buildings. Moreover, what diminished the pleasure which I was about to feel was not merely the imminence but the incoherence of its realisation. Laws as precise as those of hydrostatics maintain the relative position of the images which we form in a fixed order, which the proximity of the event at once upsets. Elstir was about to call me. This was not at all the way in which I had so often, on the beach, in my bedroom, imagined myself making the acquaintance of these girls. What was about to happen was a different event, for which I was not prepared. I recognised in it neither my desire nor its object; I regretted almost that I had come out with Elstir. But, above all, the shrinking of the pleasure that I had previously expected to feel was due to the certainty that nothing now could take it from me. And it recovered, as though by some latent elasticity in itself, its full extent when it ceased to be subjected to the pressure of that certainty, at the moment when, having decided to turn my head, I saw Elstir, standing a few feet away with the girls, bidding them good-bye. The face of the girl who stood nearest to him, round and plump and glittering with the light in her eyes, reminded me of a cake on the top of which a place has been kept for a morsel of blue sky. Her eyes, even when fixed on an object, gave the impression of mobility, as on days of high wind the air, though invisible, lets us perceive the speed with which it is coursing between us and the sky. For a moment her eyes met mine, like those travelling skies on stormy days which approach a slower cloud, touch it, overtake it, pass it. But they do not know one another, and are soon driven far apart. So, now, our looks were for a moment confronted, each ignorant of what the celestial continent that lay before it held by way of promises or threats for the future. Only at the moment when her gaze was directly coincident with mine, without slackening its pace it clouded over slightly. So on a clear night the wind-swept moon passes behind a cloud and veils its brightness for a moment, but soon reappears. But already Elstir had left the girls without having summoned me. They disappeared down a side-street; he came towards me. My whole plan was wrecked.

I have said that Albertine had not seemed to me that day to be the same as on previous days, and that each time I saw her she was to appear different. But I felt at that moment that certain modifications in the appearance, the importance, the stature of a person may also be due to the variability of certain states of consciousness interposed between that person and ourselves. One of those that play the most considerable part in this respect is belief (that evening my belief, then the vanishing of my belief, that I was about to know Albertine had, with a few seconds' interval only, rendered her almost insignificant, then infinitely precious, in my eyes; some years later, the belief, then the disappearance of the belief, that Albertine was faithful to me, brought about similar changes).

Of course, long ago at Combray, I had seen how, according to the time of day, according to whether I was entering one or the other of the two dominant moods that governed my sensibility in turn, my grief at not being with my mother would lessen or grow, as imperceptible all afternoon as is the moon's light when the sun is shining, and then, when night had come, reigning alone in my anxious heart in place of recent memories now obliterated. But on that day at Balbec, when I saw that Elstir was leaving the girls without having called me, I learned for the first time that the variations in the importance which a pleasure or a sorrow has in our eyes may depend not merely on this alternation of two moods, but on the displacement of invisible beliefs, such, for example, as make death seem to us of no account because they bathe it in a glow of unreality, and thus enable us to attach importance to our attending a musical evening which would lose much of its charm if, on the announcement that we were sentenced to be guillotined, the belief that had bathed the evening in its warm glow suddenly evaporated. It is true that something in me was aware of this role that beliefs play: namely, my will; but its knowledge is vain if one's intelligence and one's sensibility continue in ignorance; these last are sincere when they believe that we are anxious to forsake a mistress to whom our will alone knows that we are still attached. This is because they are clouded by the belief that we shall see her again at any moment. But let this belief be shattered, let them suddenly become aware that this mistress has gone from us for ever, and our intelligence and sensibility, having lost their focus, run mad, the most infinitesimal pleasure becomes infinitely great.

Variation of a belief, annulment also of love, which, pre-existent and mobile, comes to rest on the image of a woman simply because that woman will be almost impossible of attainment. Thenceforward we think not so much of the woman, whom we have difficulty in picturing to ourselves, as of the means of getting to know her. A whole series of agonies develops and is sufficient to fix our love definitely upon her who is its almost unknown object. Our love becomes immense, and we never dream how small a place in it the real woman occupies. And if suddenly, as at the moment when I had seen Elstir stop to talk to the girls, we cease to be uneasy, to suffer anguish, since it is this anguish that is the whole of our love, it seems to us as though our love had abruptly vanished at the moment when at length we grasp the prey to whose value we had not given enough thought before. What did I know of Albertine? One or two glimpses of a profile against the sea, less beautiful, assuredly, than those of Veronese's women whom I ought, had I been guided by purely aesthetic reasons, to have preferred to her. By what other reasons could I be guided, since, my anxiety having subsided, I could recapture only those mute profiles, possessing nothing else? Since my first sight of Albertine I had thought about her endlessly, I had carried on with what I called by her name an interminable inner dialogue in which I made her question and answer, think and act, and in the infinite series of imaginary Albertines who followed one after the other in my fancy hour by hour, the real Albertine, glimpsed on the beach, figured only at the head, just as the actress who "creates" a role, the star, appears, out of a long series of performances, in the few first alone. That Albertine was scarcely more than a silhouette, all that had been superimposed upon her being of my own invention, to such an extent when we love does the contribution that we ourselves make outweigh—even in terms of quantity alone—those that come to us from the beloved object. And this is true of loves that have been realised in actuality. There are loves that can not only develop but survive on very little—and this even among those that have achieved their carnal fulfilment. An old drawing-master who had taught my grandmother had been presented by some obscure mistress with a daughter. The mother died shortly after the birth of the child, and the drawing-master was so broken-hearted that he did not long survive her. In the last months of his life my grandmother and some of the Combray ladies, who had never liked to make any allusion in his presence to the woman with whom in any case he had not officially lived and had had comparatively sparse relations, took it into their heads to ensure the little girl's future by clubbing together to provide her with an annuity. It was my grandmother who suggested this; several of her friends jibbed; after all, was the child really such a very interesting case? Was she even the child of her reputed father? With women like that, one could never be sure. Finally, everything was settled. The child came to thank the ladies. She was plain, and so absurdly like the old drawing-master as to remove every shadow of doubt. Since her hair was the only nice thing about her, one of the ladies said to her father, who had brought her: "What pretty hair she has." And thinking that now, the guilty woman being dead and the old man only half alive, a discreet allusion to that past of which they had always pretended to know nothing could do no harm, my grandmother added: "It must run in the family. Did her mother have pretty hair like that?" "I don't know," was the old man's quaint answer, "I never saw her except with a hat on."

Before rejoining Elstir, I caught sight of myself in a glass. To add to the disaster of my not having been introduced to the girls, I noticed that my tie was all crooked, and my hat left long wisps of hair showing, which did not become me; but it was a piece of luck, all the same, that they should have seen me, even thus attired, in Elstir's company, and so could not forget me; also that I should have put on that morning, at my grandmother's suggestion, my smart waistcoat, when I might so easily have been wearing one that was simply hideous, and that I was carrying my best stick. For while an event for which we are longing never happens quite in the way we have been expecting, failing the advantages on which we supposed that we might count, others present themselves for which we never hoped, and make up for our disappointment; and we have been so dreading the worst that in the end we are inclined to feel that, taking one thing with another, chance has, on the whole, been rather kind to us.

"I did so much want to know them," I said as I rejoined Elstir. "Then why did you stand a mile away?" These were his actual words, uttered not because they expressed what was really in his mind, since, if his desire had been to gratify mine, he could quite easily have called me, but perhaps because he had heard phrases of this sort, in familiar use among vulgar people when they are caught in the wrong, and because even great men are in certain respects much the same as vulgar people, and take their everyday excuses from the same common stock just as they get their daily bread from the same baker; or it may be that such remarks (which ought, one might almost say, to be read backwards, since their literal meaning is the opposite of the truth) are the instantaneous effect, the negative exposure of a reflex action. "They were in a hurry." It struck me that of course they must have stopped him from summoning a person who did not greatly attract them; otherwise he would not have failed to do so, after all the questions that I had put to him about them, and the interest which he must have seen that I took in them.

"We were speaking just now of Carquethuit," he said to me as we walked towards his villa. "I've done a little sketch in which you can see the curve of the beach much better. The painting is not too bad, but it's different. If you will allow me, as a souvenir of our friendship, I'd like to give you the sketch," he went on, for the people who refuse us the objects of our desire are always ready to offer us something else.

"I should very much like, if you have such a thing, a photograph of the little portrait of Miss Sacripant. By the way, that's not a real name, surely?"

"It's the name of a character the sitter played in a stupid little musical comedy."

"But, I assure you, Monsieur, that I've never set eyes on her; you look as though you thought that I knew her."

Elstir was silent. "It couldn't be Mme Swann before she was married?" I hazarded, in one of those sudden fortuitous stumblings upon the truth, which are rare enough in all conscience, and yet suffice, after the event, to give a certain cumulative support to the theory of presentiments, provided that one takes care to forget all the wrong guesses that would invalidate it.

Elstir did not reply. The portrait was indeed that of Odette de Crécy. She had preferred not to keep it for many reasons, some of them only too obvious. But there were others less apparent. The portrait dated from before the point at which Odette, disciplining her features, had made of her face and figure that creation the broad outlines of which her hairdressers, her dressmakers, she herself—in her way of holding herself, of speaking, of smiling, of moving her hands and eyes, of thinking—were to respect throughout the years to come. It required the vitiated taste of a surfeited lover to make Swann prefer to all the countless photographs of the "definitive" Odette who was his charming wife the little photograph which he kept in his room and in which, beneath a straw hat trimmed with pansies, one saw a thin young woman, fairly plain, with bunched-out hair and drawn features.

But in any case, even if the portrait had been, not anterior, like Swann's favourite photograph, to the systematisation of Odette's features into a new type, majestic and charming, but subsequent to it, Elstir's vision would have sufficed to discompose that type. Artistic genius acts in a similar way to those extremely high temperatures which have the power to split up combinations of atoms which they proceed to combine afresh in a diametrically opposite order, corresponding to another type. All that artificial harmony which a woman has succeeded in imposing upon her features, the maintenance of which she oversees in her mirror every day before going out, relying on the angle of her hat, the smoothness of her hair, the vivacity of her expression, to ensure its continuity, that harmony the keen eye of the great painter instantly destroys, substituting for it a rearrangement of the woman's features such as will satisfy a certain pictorial ideal of femininity which he carries in his head. Similarly it often happens that, after a certain age, the eye of a great scientist will find everywhere the elements necessary to establish those relations which alone are of interest to him. Like those craftsmen, those players who, instead of making a fuss and asking for what they cannot have, content themselves with whatever comes to hand, the artist might say of anything, no matter what, that it will serve his purpose. Thus a cousin of the Princesse de Luxembourg, a beauty of the most queenly type, having taken a fancy to a form of art which was new at that time, had asked the leading painter of the naturalist school to do her portrait. At once the artist's eye found what he had been seeking everywhere. And on his canvas there appeared, in place of the proud lady, a street-girl, and behind her a vast, sloping, purple background which reminded one of the Place Pigalle. But even without going so far as that, not only will the portrait of a woman by a great artist not seek in the least to give satisfaction to various demands on the woman's part—such as, for instance, when she begins to age, make her have herself photographed in dresses that are almost those of a little girl which bring out her still youthful figure and make her appear like the sister or even the daughter of her own daughter, who, if need be, is tricked out for the occasion as a "perfect fright" beside her. It will, on the contrary, emphasise those very blemishes which she seeks to hide, and which (as for instance a sickly, almost greenish complexion) are all the more tempting to him since they show "character," though they are enough to destroy the illusions of the ordinary beholder who sees crumble into dust the ideal of which the woman so proudly sustained the figment, and which set her, in her unique, irreducible form, so far outside, so far above the rest of humanity. Fallen now, situated outside her own type in which she sat unassailably enthroned, she is now just an ordinary woman, in the legend of whose superiority we have lost all faith. We are so accustomed to incorporating in this type not only the beauty of an Odette but her personality, her identity, that standing before the portrait which has thus stripped her of it we are inclined to protest not simply "How plain he has made her!" but "Why, it isn't the least bit like her!" We find it hard to believe that it can be she. We do not recognise her. And yet there is a person there on the canvas whom we are quite conscious of having seen before. But that person is not Odette; the face of the person, her body, her general appearance seem familiar. They recall to us not this particular woman who never held herself like that, whose natural pose never formed any such strange and teasing arabesque, but other women, all the women whom Elstir has ever painted, women whom invariably, however they may differ from one another, he has chosen to plant thus, in full face, with an arched foot thrust out from under the skirt, a large round hat in one hand, symmetrically corresponding, at the level of the knee which it covers, to that other disc, higher up in the picture, the face. And furthermore, not only does a portrait by the hand of genius dislocate a woman's type, as it has been defined by her coquetry and her selfish conception of beauty, but if it is also old, it is not content with ageing the original in the same way as a photograph ages its sitter, by showing her dressed in the fashions of long ago. In a portrait, it is not only the manner the woman then had of dressing that dates her, it is also the manner the artist had of painting. And this, Elstir's earliest manner, was the most devastating of birth certificates for Odette because it not only established her, as did her photographs of the same period, as the younger sister of various well-known courtesans, but made her portrait contemporary with the countless portraits that Manet or Whistler had painted of all those vanished models, models who already belonged to oblivion or to history.

It was along this train of thought, silently ruminated over by Elstir's side as I accompanied him to his door, that I was being led by the discovery that I had just made of the identity of his model, when this first discovery caused me to make a second, more disturbing still, concerning the identity of the artist. He had painted the portrait of Odette de Crécy. Could it possibly be that this man of genius, this sage, this recluse, this philosopher with his marvellous flow of conversation, who towered over everyone and everything, was the ridiculous, depraved painter who had at one time been adopted by the Verdurins? I asked him if he had known them, and whether by any chance it was he that they used to call M. Biche. He answered me in the affirmative, with no trace of embarrassment, as if my question referred to a period in his life that was already somewhat remote and he had no suspicion of the extraordinary disillusionment he was causing me. But, looking up, he read it on my face. His own assumed an expression of annoyance. And, as we were now almost at the gate of his house, a man of less distinction of heart and mind might simply have said good-bye to me a trifle dryly and taken care to avoid seeing me again. This however was not Elstir's way with me; like the master that he was—and it was, perhaps, from the point of view of pure creativity, his one fault that he was a master in that sense of the word, for an artist, if he is to be absolutely true to the life of the spirit, must be alone, and not squander his ego, even upon disciples—from every circumstance, whether involving himself or other people, he sought to extract, for the better edification of the young, the element of truth that it contained. He chose therefore, instead of the words that might have avenged the injury to his pride, those that could prove instructive to me. "There is no man," he began, "however wise, who has not at some period of his youth said things, or lived a life, the memory of which is so unpleasant to him that he would gladly expunge it. And yet he ought not entirely to regret it, because he cannot be certain that he has indeed become a wise man—so far as it is possible for any of us to be wise—unless he has passed through all the fatuous or unwholesome incarnations by which that ultimate stage must be preceded. I know that there are young people, the sons and grandsons of distinguished men, whose masters have instilled into them nobility of mind and moral refinement from their schooldays. They may perhaps have nothing to retract from their past lives; they could publish a signed account of everything they have ever said or done; but they are poor creatures, feeble descendants of doctrinaires, and their wisdom is negative and sterile. We do not receive wisdom, we must discover it for ourselves, after a journey through the wilderness which no one else can make for us, which no one can spare us, for our wisdom is the point of view from which we come at last to regard the world. The lives that you admire, the attitudes that seem noble to you, have not been shaped by a paterfamilias or a schoolmaster, they have sprung from very different beginnings, having been influenced by everything evil or commonplace that prevailed round about them. They represent a struggle and a victory. I can see that the picture of what we were at an earlier stage may not be recognisable and cannot, certainly, be pleasing to contemplate in later life. But we must not repudiate it, for it is a proof that we have really lived, that it is in accordance with the laws of life and of the mind that we have, from the common elements of life, of the life of studios, of artistic groups—assuming one is a painter—extracted something that transcends them."

Meanwhile we had reached his door. I was disappointed at not having met the girls. But after all there was now the possibility of meeting them again later on; they had ceased merely to be silhouetted against a horizon where I had been ready to suppose that I should never see them reappear. Around them no longer swirled that sort of great eddy which had separated me from them, which had been merely the expression of the perpetually active desire, mobile, urgent, fed ever on fresh anxieties, which was aroused in me by their inaccessibility, their flight from me, possibly for ever. I could now set my desire for them at rest, hold it in reserve, among all those other desires the realisation of which, as soon as I knew it to be possible, I would cheerfully postpone. I took leave of Elstir; I was alone once again. Then all of a sudden, despite my recent disappointment, I saw in my mind's eye all that chain of coincidences which I had not supposed could possibly come about: that Elstir should be a friend of those very girls, that they, who only that morning had been to me merely figures in a picture with the sea for background, had seen me, had seen me walking in friendly intimacy with a great painter, who was now informed of my secret longing and would no doubt do what he could to assuage it. All this had been a source of pleasure to me, but that pleasure had remained hidden; it was like one of those visitors who wait before letting us know that they are in the room until everyone else has gone and we are by ourselves. Then only do we catch sight of them, and can say to them, "I am at your service," and listen to what they have to tell us. Sometimes between the moment at which these pleasures have entered our consciousness and the moment at which we are free to entertain them, so many hours have passed, we have in the meantime seen so many people, that we are afraid lest they should have grown tired of waiting. But they are patient, they do not grow tired, and as soon as the crowd has gone we find them there ready for us. Sometimes, then, it is we ourselves who are so exhausted that it seems as though our weary mind will no longer have the strength to seize and retain those memories, those impressions for which our frail self is the one habitable place, the sole means of realisation. And we should regret that failure, for existence is of little interest save on days when the dust of realities is mingled with magic sand, when some trivial incident becomes a springboard for romance. Then a whole promontory of the inaccessible world emerges from the twilight of dream and enters our life, our life in which, like the sleeper awakened, we actually see the people of whom we had dreamed with such ardent longing that we had come to believe that we should never see them except in our dreams.

The assuagement brought about by the probability of my now being able to meet the little band whenever I chose was all the more precious to me because I should not have been able to keep watch for them during the next few days, which were taken up with preparations for Saint-Loup's departure. My grandmother was anxious to offer my friend some token of her gratitude for all the kindnesses that he had shown to her and myself. I told her that he was a great admirer of Proudhon, and this put it into her head to send for a collection of autograph letters by that philosopher which she had once bought. Saint-Loup came to the hotel to look at them on the day of their arrival, which was also his last day at Balbec. He read them eagerly, fingering each page with reverence, trying to get the sentences by heart; and then, rising from the table, was beginning to apologise to my grandmother for having stayed so long, when he heard her say: "No, no, take them with you, they are for you to keep. That was why I sent for them, to give them to you."

He was overwhelmed by a joy which he could no more control than we can a physical condition that arises without the intervention of our will. He blushed scarlet as a child who has just been punished, and my grandmother was far more touched to see all the efforts he made (without success) to contain the joy that convulsed him than she would have been to hear any words of thanks that he could have uttered. But he, fearing that he had failed to show his gratitude properly, begged me to make his excuses to her again, next day, leaning from the window of the little local train which was to take him back to his regiment. The distance was, as a matter of fact, nothing. He had thought of going by road, as he had frequently done that summer, when he was to return the same evening and was not encumbered with baggage. But this time he would in any case have had to put all his heavy luggage in the train. And he found it simpler to take the train himself too, following the advice of the manager who, on being consulted, replied that "Carriage or train, it was more or less equivocal." He meant it to be understood that they were equivalent (in fact, very much what Françoise would have expressed as "coming to the same as makes no difference"). "Very well," Saint-Loup had decided, "I shall take the 'little crawler.' " I should have taken it too, had I not been tired, and gone with my friend to Doncières; failing this I kept on promising, all the time we waited in Balbec station—the time, that is to say, which the driver of the little train spent waiting for unpunctual friends, without whom he refused to start, and also in seeking some refreshment for himself—to go over there and see him several times a week. As Bloch had also come to the station—much to Saint-Loup's disgust—the latter, seeing that our companion could hear him begging me to come to luncheon, to dinner, to stay altogether at Doncières, finally turned to him and, in the most forbidding tone, intended to counteract the forced civility of the invitation and to prevent Bloch from taking it seriously: "If you ever happen to be passing through Doncières any afternoon when I'm off duty, you might ask for me at the barracks; but I hardly ever am off duty." Perhaps, also, Robert was afraid that I might not come alone, and, thinking that I was more intimate with Bloch than I made out, was providing me in this way with a travelling companion, one who would urge me on.

I was afraid that this tone, this manner of inviting a person while advising him not to come, might have wounded Bloch, and felt that Saint-Loup would have done better to say nothing. But I was mistaken, for after the train had gone, while we were walking back together as far as the crossroads where we had to separate, one road going to the hotel, the other to the Blochs' villa, he never stopped asking me on what day we should go to Doncières, for after "all the civility that Saint-Loup had shown" him, it would be "too rude" on his part not to accept his invitation. I was glad that he had not noticed, or was so little displeased as to wish to let it be thought that he had not noticed, in what a less than pressing, indeed barely polite, tone the invitation had been issued. At the same time I should have liked Bloch, for his own sake, to refrain from making a fool of himself by going over at once to Doncières. But I dared not offer a piece of advice which could only have offended him by hinting that Saint-Loup had been less pressing than he himself was impressed. He was a great deal too ready to respond, and even if all his faults of this nature were atoned for by remarkable qualities which others, with more reserve than he, would never have possessed, he carried tactlessness to a pitch that was almost maddening. According to him, the week must not pass without our going to Doncières (he said "our" for I think that he counted to some extent on my presence there as an excuse for his own). All the way home, opposite the gymnasium in its grove of trees, opposite the tennis courts, the mayor's office, the shellfish stall, he stopped me, imploring me to fix a day, and, as I did not, left me in anger, saying: "As your lordship pleases. For my part, I am obliged to go since he has invited me."

Saint-Loup was still so afraid of not having thanked my grandmother properly that he charged me once again to express his gratitude to her a day or two later in a letter I received from him from the town in which he was quartered, a town which seemed, on the envelope where the post-mark had stamped its name, to be hastening to me across country, to tell me that within its walls, in the Louis XVI cavalry barracks, he was thinking of me. The paper was embossed with the arms of Marsantes, in which I could make out a lion surmounting a coronet closed by the cap of a peer of France.

"After a journey which," he wrote, "passed pleasantly enough, with a book I bought at the station, by Arvède Barine[13] (a Russian author, I fancy; it seemed to me remarkably well written for a foreigner, but you shall give me your critical opinion, since you are bound to know all about it, you who are a fount of knowledge and have read everything), here I am again in the thick of this debased existence, where, alas, I feel a sad exile, not having here what I left behind at Balbec; this life in which I can find no affectionate memory, no intellectual attraction; an environment which you would no doubt despise yet which has a certain charm. Everything seems to have changed since I left it, for in the interval one of the most important periods in my life, that from which our friendship dates, has begun. I hope that it may never come to an end. I have spoken of our friendship, of you, to one person only, to the friend I told you of, who has just paid me a surprise visit here. She would very much like to know you, and I feel that you would get on well together, for she too is extremely literary. Otherwise, to go over in my mind all our talks, to relive those hours which I never shall forget, I have shut myself off from my comrades, excellent fellows, but altogether incapable of understanding that sort of thing. This remembrance of the moments I spent with you I should almost have preferred, on my first day here, to conjure up for my own solitary enjoyment, without writing to you. But I was afraid lest, with your subtle mind and ultra-sensitive heart, you might needlessly torment yourself if you did not hear from me, if, that is to say, you still condescend to occupy your thoughts with this blunt trooper whom you will have a hard task to polish and refine and make a little more subtle and worthier of your company."

On the whole this letter, in its affectionate spirit, was not at all unlike those which, when I did not yet know Saint-Loup, I had imagined that he would write to me, in those day-dreams from which the coldness of his first greeting had shaken me by bringing me face to face with an icy reality which was not, however, to last. Once I had received this letter, every time the post was brought in, at lunch-time, I could tell at once when it was from him that a letter came, for it had always that second face which a person assumes when he is absent, in the features of which (the characters of the handwriting) there is no reason why we should not suppose that we can detect an individual soul just as much as in the line of a nose or the inflexions of a voice.

I would now happily remain at the table while it was being cleared, and, if it was not a moment at which the girls of the little band might be passing, it was no longer solely towards the sea that I would turn my eyes. Since I had seen such things depicted in water-colours by Elstir, I sought to find again in reality, I cherished as though for their poetic beauty, the broken gestures of the knives still lying across one another, the swollen convexity of a discarded napkin into which the sun introduced a patch of yellow velvet, the half-empty glass which thus showed to greater advantage the noble sweep of its curved sides and, in the heart of its translucent crystal, clear as frozen daylight, some dregs of wine, dark but glittering with reflected lights, the displacement of solid objects, the transmutation of liquids by the effect of light and shade, the shifting colours of the plums which passed from green to blue and from blue to golden yellow in the half-plundered dish, the promenade of the antiquated chairs that came twice daily to take their places round the white cloth spread on the table as on an altar at which were celebrated the rites of the palate, and where in the hollows of the oyster-shells a few drops of lustral water had remained as in tiny holy-water stoups of stone; I tried to find beauty there where I had never imagined before that it could exist, in the most ordinary things, in the profundities of "still life."

When, some days after Saint-Loup's departure, I had succeeded in persuading Elstir to give a small party at which I should meet Albertine, the freshness of appearance and elegance of attire, both quite momentary, which were to be observed in me at the moment of my starting out from the Grand Hotel (and which were due respectively to a longer rest than usual and to special pains over my toilet) were such that I regretted my inability to reserve them (and also the credit accruing from Elstir's friendship) for the captivation of some other, more interesting person, I regretted having to use them all up on the simple pleasure of making Albertine's acquaintance. My brain assessed this pleasure at a very low value now that it was assured. But, inside, my will did not for a moment share this illusion, that will which is the persevering and unalterable servant of our successive personalities; hidden away in the shadow, despised, downtrodden, untiringly faithful, toiling incessantly, and with no thought for the variability of the self, to ensure that the self may never lack what is needed. While, at the moment when we are about to start on an eagerly awaited journey, our intelligence and our sensibility begin to ask themselves whether it is really worth the trouble, the will, knowing that those lazy masters would at once begin to consider that journey the most wonderful experience if it became impossible for us to undertake it, leaves them arguing outside the station, vying with each other in their hesitations; but it busies itself with buying the tickets and putting us into the carriage before the train starts. It is as invariable as the intelligence and the sensibility are fickle, but since it is silent, gives no account of its actions, it seems almost non-existent; it is by its dogged determination that the other constituent parts of our personality are led, but without seeing it, whereas they distinguish clearly all their own uncertainties. So my intelligence and my sensibility began a discussion as to the real value of the pleasure that there would be in knowing Albertine, while I studied in the glass vain and perishable attractions which they would have preserved intact for use on some other occasion. But my will would not let the hour pass at which I must start, and it was Elstir's address that it called out to the driver. My intelligence and my sensibility were at liberty, now that the die was cast, to think this a pity. If my will had given the man a different address, they would have been properly had.

When I arrived at Elstir's a few minutes later, I thought at first that Mlle Simonet was not in the studio. There was certainly a girl sitting there in a silk frock, bareheaded, but one whose marvellous hair, whose nose, whose complexion, meant nothing to me, in whom I did not recognise the human entity that I had extracted from a young cyclist in a polo-cap strolling past between myself and the sea. Nevertheless it was Albertine. But even when I knew it to be her, I gave her no thought. On entering any social gathering, when one is young, one loses consciousness of one's old self, one becomes a different man, every drawing-room being a fresh universe in which, coming under the sway of a new moral perspective, we fasten our attention, as if they were to matter to us for all time, on people, dances, card-tables, all of which we shall have forgotten by the morning. Obliged to follow, if I was to arrive at the goal of conversation with Albertine, a route in no way of my own planning, which first brought me to a halt in front of Elstir, passed by other groups of guests to whom I was presented, then along the buffet table, at which I was offered, and where I ate, a strawberry tart or two, while I listened, motionless, to the music that had begun in another part of the room, I found myself giving to these various incidents the same importance as to my introduction to Mlle Simonet, an introduction which was now nothing more than one among several such incidents, having entirely forgotten that it had been, but a few minutes since, my sole object in coming there. But is it not thus, in the bustle of daily life, with every true happiness, every great sorrow? In a room full of other people we receive from the woman we love the answer, auspicious or fatal, which we have been awaiting for the last year. But we must go on talking, ideas come flocking one after another, unfolding a smooth surface which is pricked now and then at the very most by a dull throb from the memory, infinitely more profound but very narrow, that misfortune has come upon us. If, instead of misfortune, it is happiness, it may be that not until many years have elapsed will we recall that the most important event in our emotional life occurred without our having time to give it any prolonged attention, or even to become aware of it almost, at a social gathering to which we had gone solely in expectation of that event.

When Elstir asked me to come with him so that he might introduce me to Albertine, who was sitting a little further down the room, I first of all finished eating a coffee éclair and, with a show of keen interest, asked an old gentleman whose acquaintance I had just made (and to whom I thought that I might offer the rose in my buttonhole which he had admired) to tell me more about the old Norman fairs. This is not to say that the introduction which followed did not give me any pleasure and did not assume a certain solemnity in my eyes. But so far as the pleasure was concerned, I was naturally not conscious of it until some time later, when, back at the hotel, and in my room alone, I had become myself again. Pleasure in this respect is like photography. What we take, in the presence of the beloved object, is merely a negative, which we develop later, when we are back at home, and have once again found at our disposal that inner dark-room the entrance to which is barred to us so long as we are with other people.

If my consciousness of the pleasure it had brought me was thus retarded by a few hours, the gravity of this introduction made itself felt at once. At the moment of introduction, for all that we feel ourselves to have been suddenly rewarded, to have been furnished with a pass that will admit us henceforward to pleasures which we have been pursuing for weeks past, we realise only too clearly that this acquisition puts an end for us not merely to hours of toilsome search—a relief that can only fill us with joy—but also to the existence of a certain person, the person whom our imagination had wildly distorted, whom our anxious fear that we might never become known to her had magnified. At the moment when our name rings out on the lips of the introducer, especially if the latter amplifies it, as Elstir now did, with a flattering commentary—that sacramental moment, as when in a fairy tale the magician commands a person suddenly to become someone else—she to whose presence we have been longing to attain vanishes: indeed, how could she remain the same when—by reason of the attention which she is obliged to pay to the announcement of our name and the sight of our person—in the eyes that only yesterday were situated at an infinite distance (where we supposed that ours, wandering, unsteady, desperate, divergent, would never succeed in meeting them) the conscious gaze, the incommunicable thought which we were seeking have just been miraculously and quite simply replaced by our own image painted in them as in a smiling mirror? If this incarnation of ourselves in the person who seemed to differ most from us is what does most to modify the appearance of the person to whom we have just been introduced, the form of that person still remains quite vague; and we may wonder whether it will turn out to be a god, a table or a basin. But, as nimble as the wax-modellers who will fashion a bust before our eyes in five minutes, the few words which the stranger is now going to say to us will substantiate that form and give it something positive and final that will exclude all the hypotheses in which our desire and our imagination had been indulging. Doubtless, even before coming to this party, Albertine had ceased to be for me simply that phantom fit to haunt the rest of our lives which a passing stranger of whom we know nothing and have caught but the barest glimpse remains. Her relationship to Mme Bontemps had already restricted the scope of those marvellous hypotheses, by stopping one of the channels along which they might have spread. As I drew closer to the girl and began to know her better, this knowledge developed by a process of subtraction, each constituent of imagination and desire giving place to a notion which was worth infinitely less, a notion to which, it is true, there was added presently a sort of equivalent, in the domain of real life, of what joint stock companies give one, after repaying one's original investment, and call dividend shares. Her name, her family connections, had been the first limit set to my suppositions. Her friendly greeting as, standing close beside her, I once again saw the tiny mole on her cheek, below her eye, marked another stage; finally, I was surprised to hear her use the adverb "perfectly," in place of "completely," of two people whom she mentioned, saying of one, "She's perfectly mad, but very nice all the same," and of the other, "He's perfectly common and perfectly boring." However little to be commended this use of "perfectly" may be, it indicates a degree of civilisation and culture which I could never have imagined as having been attained by the bacchante with the bicycle, the orgiastic muse of the golf-course. Nor did it mean that after this first metamorphosis Albertine was not to change again for me, many times. The qualities and defects which a person presents to us, exposed to view on the surface of his or her face, rearrange themselves in a totally different order if we approach them from a new angle—just as, in a town, buildings that appear strung in extended order along a single line, from another viewpoint are disposed in depth and their relative heights altered. To begin with, Albertine struck me as somewhat shy instead of implacable; she seemed to me more proper than ill-bred, judging by the descriptions, "she has bad manners" or "she has peculiar manners," which she applied to each in turn of the girls of whom I spoke to her; finally, she presented as a target for my line of vision a temple that was somewhat inflamed and by no means attractive to the eye, and no longer the curious look which I had always associated with her until then. But this was merely a second impression and there were doubtless others through which I would successively pass. Thus it can be only after one has recognised, not without some tentative stumblings, the optical errors of one's first impression that one can arrive at an exact knowledge of another person, supposing such knowledge to be ever possible. But it is not; for while our original impression of him undergoes correction, the person himself, not being an inanimate object, changes for his part too: we think that we have caught him, he shifts, and, when we imagine that at last we are seeing him clearly, it is only the old impressions which we had already formed of him that we have succeeded in clarifying, when they no longer represent him.

And yet, whatever the inevitable disappointments that it must bring in its train, this movement towards what we have only glimpsed, what we have been free to dwell upon and imagine at our leisure, this movement is the only one that is wholesome for the senses, that whets their appetite. How drearily monotonous must be the lives of people who, from indolence or timidity, drive in their carriages straight to the doors of friends whom they have got to know without having first dreamed of knowing them, without ever daring, on the way, to stop and examine what arouses their desire!

I returned home thinking of that party, of the coffee éclair which I had finished eating before I let Elstir take me up to Albertine, the rose which I had given the old gentleman, all the details selected unbeknown to us by the circumstances of the occasion, which compose for us, in a special and quite fortuitous order, the picture that we retain of a first meeting. But I had the impression that I was seeing this picture from another angle of vision, very far removed from myself, realising that it had not existed only for me, when some months later, to my great surprise, on my speaking to Albertine about the day on which I had first met her, she reminded me of the éclair, the flower that I had given away, all those things which I had supposed to have been, I cannot say of importance only to myself, but perceived only by myself, and which I now found thus transcribed, in a version of which I had never suspected the existence, in the mind of Albertine. On this first day itself, when, on my return to the hotel, I was able to visualise the memory which I had brought away with me, I realised what a conjuring trick had been performed, and with what consummate sleight of hand, and how I had talked for a moment or two with a person who, thanks to the skill of the conjurer, without actually embodying anything of that other person whom I had for so long been following as she paced beside the sea, had been substituted for her. I might, for that matter, have guessed as much in advance, since the girl on the beach was a fabrication of my own. In spite of which, since I had, in my conversations with Elstir, identified her with Albertine, I felt myself in honour bound to fulfil to the real the promises of love made to the imagined Albertine. We betroth ourselves by proxy, and then feel obliged to marry the intermediary. Moreover, if there had disappeared from my life, provisionally at any rate, an anguish that the memory of polite manners, the expression "perfectly common" and an inflamed temple had sufficed to assuage, that memory awakened in me another kind of desire which, though placid and in no way painful, resembling a brotherly feeling, might in the long run become fully as dangerous by making me feel at every moment a compelling need to kiss this new person whose good manners, whose shyness, whose unexpected accessibility, arrested the futile course of my imagination but gave birth to a tender gratitude. And then, since memory begins at once to record photographs independent of one another, eliminates every link, any kind of sequence between the scenes portrayed in the collection which it exposes to our view, the most recent does not necessarily destroy or cancel those that came before. Confronted with the commonplace and touching Albertine to whom I had spoken that afternoon, I still saw the other mysterious Albertine outlined against the sea. These were now memories, that is to say pictures neither of which now seemed to me any truer than the other. Finally, to conclude this account of my first introduction to Albertine, when trying to recapture that little beauty spot on her cheek, just under the eye, I remembered that, looking from Elstir's window when Albertine had gone by, I had seen it on her chin. In fact, when I saw her I noticed that she had a beauty spot, but my errant memory made it wander about her face, fixing it now in one place, now in another.

Whatever my disappointment in finding in Mlle Simonet a girl so little different from those that I knew already, just as my disillusionment when I saw Balbec church did not prevent me from wishing still to go to Quimperlé, Pont-Aven and Venice, I comforted myself with the thought that through Albertine at any rate, even if she herself was not all that I had hoped, I might make the acquaintance of her comrades of the little band.

I thought at first that I should fail in this. As she was to be staying (and I too) for a long time still at Balbec, I had decided that the best thing was not to make my efforts to meet her too apparent, but to wait for an accidental encounter. But even if this should occur every day it was greatly to be feared that she would confine herself to acknowledging my greeting from a distance, and such meetings, repeated day after day throughout the whole season, would benefit me not at all.

Shortly after this, one morning when it had been raining and was almost cold, I was accosted on the front by a girl wearing a little toque and carrying a muff, so different from the girl whom I had met at Elstir's party that to recognise in her the same person seemed an operation beyond the power of the human mind; mine was, however, successful in performing it, but after a moment's surprise which did not, I think, escape Albertine's notice. On the other hand, remembering the "well-bred" manners which had so impressed me before, I now experienced a converse astonishment at her rude tone and manners typical of the "little band." Moreover, her temple had ceased to be the reassuring optical centre of her face, either because I was now on her other side, or because her toque hid it, or else possibly because its inflammation was not a constant thing.

"What weather!" she began. "Really the perpetual summer of Balbec is all stuff and nonsense. Don't you do anything here? We never see you playing golf, or dancing at the Casino. You don't ride either. You must be bored stiff. You don't find it too deadly, idling about on the beach all day? Ah, so you like basking in the sun like a lizard? You must have plenty of time on your hands. I can see you're not like me; I simply adore all sports. You weren't at the Sogne races? We went in the 'tram,' and I can quite understand that you wouldn't see any fun in going in an old rattletrap like that. It took us two whole hours! I could have gone there and back three times on my bike."

I who had admired Saint-Loup when, in the most natural manner in the world, he had called the little local train the "crawler," because of the ceaseless windings of its line, was daunted by the glibness with which Albertine spoke of it as the "tram" and the "rattletrap." I could sense her mastery of a mode of nomenclature in which I was afraid of her detecting and despising my inferiority. And the full wealth of the synonyms that the little band possessed to designate this railway had not yet been revealed to me. In speaking, Albertine kept her head motionless and her nostrils pinched, and scarcely moved her lips. The result of this was a drawling, nasal sound, into the composition of which there entered perhaps a provincial heredity, a juvenile affectation of British phlegm, the teaching of a foreign governess and a congestive hypertrophy of the mucus of the nose. This enunciation which, as it happened, soon disappeared when she knew people better, giving place to a natural girlish tone, might have been thought unpleasant. But to me it was peculiarly delightful. Whenever I had gone for several days without seeing her, I would refresh my spirit by repeating to myself: "We don't ever see you playing golf," with the nasal intonation in which she had uttered the words, point blank, without moving a muscle of her face. And I thought then that there was no one in the world so desirable.

We formed, that morning, one of those couples who dotted the front here and there with their conjunction, their stopping together just long enough to exchange a few words before breaking apart, each to resume separately his or her divergent stroll. I took advantage of this immobility to look again and discover once and for all where exactly the little mole was placed. Then, just as a phrase of Vinteuil which had delighted me in the sonata, and which my recollection allowed to wander from the andante to the finale, until the day when, having the score in my hands, I was able to find it and to fix it in my memory in its proper place, in the scherzo, so this mole, which I had visualised now on her cheek, now on her chin, came to rest for ever on her upper lip, just below her nose. In the same way, too, we are sometimes amazed to come upon lines that we know by heart in a play in which we never dreamed that they were to be found.

At that moment, as if in order that the rich decorative ensemble formed by the lovely train of maidens, at once pink and golden, baked by the sun and wind, might freely proliferate before the sea in all the variety of its forms, Albertine's friends, with their shapely limbs, their supple figures, but so different one from another, came into sight in a cluster that spread out as it advanced in our direction, but closer to the sea, in a parallel line. I asked Albertine's permission to walk for a little way with her. Unfortunately, all she did was to wave her hand to them in greeting. "But your friends will be disappointed if you don't go with them," I hinted, hoping that we might all walk together.

A young man with regular features, carrying a bag of golf-clubs, sauntered up to us. It was the baccarat-player whose fast ways so enraged the senior judge's wife. In a frigid, impassive tone, which he evidently regarded as an indication of the highest distinction, he bade Albertine good day. "Been playing golf, Octave?" she asked. "How did it go? Were you in form?" "Oh, it's too sickening; I'm a wash-out," he replied. "Was Andrée playing?" "Yes, she went round in seventy-seven." "Why, that's a record!" "I went round in eighty-two yesterday." He was the son of an immensely rich manufacturer who was to take an important part in the organisation of the coming World's Fair. I was struck by the extreme degree to which, in this young man and the other very rare male friends of the band of girls, the knowledge of everything that pertained to clothes and how to wear them, cigars, English drinks, horses—a knowledge which he displayed down to its minutest details with a haughty infallibility that approached the reticent modesty of the true expert—had been developed in complete isolation, unaccompanied by the least trace of any intellectual culture. He had no hesitation as to the right time and place for dinner-jacket or pyjamas, but had no notion of the circumstances in which one might or might not employ this or that word, or even of the simplest rules of grammar. This disparity between the two forms of culture must have existed also in his father, the President of the Householders' Association of Balbec, for, in an open letter to the electors which he had recently had posted on all the walls, he announced: "I desired to see the Mayor, to chat to him about it, but he would not listen to my just grievances." Octave, at the Casino, took prizes in all the dancing competitions, for the boston, the tango, and what-not, an accomplishment that would enable him, if he chose, to make a fine marriage in that seaside society where it is not figuratively but literally that the girls are "wedded" to their "dancing partners." He lit a cigar with a "D'you mind?" to Albertine, as one who asks permission to finish an urgent piece of work while going on talking. For he was one of those people who can never be "doing nothing," although there was nothing, in fact, that he could ever be said to do. And since complete inactivity in the end has the same effect as prolonged overwork, in the mental sphere as much as in the life of the body and the muscles, the steadfast intellectual nullity that reigned behind Octave's meditative brow had ended by giving him, despite his air of unruffled calm, an ineffectual itch to think which kept him awake at night, for all the world like an overwrought philosopher.

Thinking that if I knew their male friends I should have more opportunities of seeing the girls, I had been on the point of asking for an introduction to Octave. I told Albertine this, as soon as he had left us, still muttering "I'm a wash-out," thinking to put into her head the idea of doing it next time.

"Come, come," she exclaimed, "I can't introduce you to a gigolo! This place simply swarms with them. But what on earth would they have to say to you? This one plays golf quite well, and that's all there is to him. I know what I'm talking about; you'd find he wasn't at all your sort."

"Your friends will be cross with you if you desert them like this," I repeated, hoping that she would then suggest my joining the party.

"Oh, no, they don't need me."

We passed Bloch, who directed at me a subtle, insinuating smile, and, embarrassed by the presence of Albertine, whom he did not know, or, rather, knew "without knowing" her, lowered his head towards his neck in a stiff, ungainly motion. "Who's that weird customer?" Albertine asked. "I can't think why he should bow to me since he doesn't know me. So I didn't respond."

I had no time to explain to her, for, bearing straight down upon us, "Excuse me," he began, "for interrupting you, but I must tell you that I'm going to Doncières tomorrow. I cannot put it off any longer without discourtesy; indeed, I wonder what de Saint-Loup-en-Bray must think of me. I just came to let you know that I shall take the two o'clock train. At your service."

But I thought now only of seeing Albertine again, and of trying to get to know her friends, and Doncières, since they were not going there, and my going would bring me back too late to see them still on the beach, seemed to me to be situated at the other end of the world. I told Bloch that it was impossible.

"Oh, very well, I shall go alone. In the fatuous alexandrines of Master Arouet, I shall say to Saint-Loup, to beguile his clericalism:

My duty stands alone, by his in no way bound;
Though he should choose to fail, yet faithful I'll be found."

"I admit he's not a bad-looking boy," said Albertine, "but he makes me feel quite sick."

I had never thought that Bloch might be "not a bad-looking boy"; and yet in fact he was. With his rather prominent forehead, his very aquiline nose, and his air of being extremely clever and of being convinced of his cleverness, he had a pleasing face. But he could not succeed in pleasing Albertine. This was perhaps to some extent due to the bad side of her, to the hardness, the insensitivity of the little band, its rudeness towards everything that was not itself. And later on, when I introduced them, Albertine's antipathy for him did not diminish. Bloch belonged to a social group in which, between scoffing at high society and at the same time showing the due regard for polite manners which a man is supposed to show who "does not soil his hands," a sort of special compromise has been reached which differs from the manners of the fashionable world but is none the less a peculiarly odious form of worldliness. When he was introduced to anyone he would bow with a sceptical smile, and at the same time with an exaggerated show of respect, and, if it was to a man, would say: "Pleased to meet you, sir," in a voice which ridiculed the words that it was uttering, though with a consciousness of belonging to someone who was not a boor. Having sacrificed this first moment to a custom which he at once followed and derided (just as on the first of January he would say: "The compliments of the season to you!"), he would adopt an air of infinite cunning, and would "proffer subtle words" which were often true enough but "got on" Albertine's nerves. When I told her on this first day that his name was Bloch, she exclaimed: "I would have betted anything he was a Yid. Typical of their creepy ways!" In fact, Bloch was destined to give Albertine other grounds for annoyance later on. Like many intellectuals, he was incapable of saying a simple thing in a simple way. He would find some precious qualifier for every statement, and would sweep from the particular to the general. It irritated Albertine, who was never too well pleased at other people's paying attention to what she was doing, that when she had sprained her ankle and was lying low, Bloch said of her: "She is outstretched on her couch, but in her ubiquity has not ceased to frequent simultaneously vague golf-courses and dubious tennis-courts." He was simply being "literary," of course, but in view of the difficulties which Albertine felt that it might create for her with friends whose invitations she had declined on the plea that she was unable to move, it was quite enough to make her take a profound dislike to the face and the sound of the voice of the young man who said these things.

We parted, Albertine and I, after promising each

other to go out together one day. I had talked to her without being any more conscious of where my words were falling, of what became of them, than if I were dropping pebbles into a bottomless pit. That our words are, as a general rule, filled by the people to whom we address them with a meaning which those people derive from their own substance, a meaning widely different from that which we had put into the same words when we uttered them, is a fact which is perpetually demonstrated in daily life. But if in addition we find ourselves in the company of a person whose education (as Albertine's was to me) is inconceivable, her taste, her reading, her principles unknown to us, we cannot tell whether our words have aroused in her anything that resembles their meaning, any more than in an animal to which we had to make ourselves understood. So that trying to make friends with Albertine seemed to me like entering into contact with the unknown, if not the impossible, an occupation as arduous as breaking in a horse, as restful as keeping bees or growing roses.

I had thought, a few hours before, that Albertine would acknowledge my greeting only from a distance. We had now left one another after planning to make an excursion soon together. I vowed that when I next met Albertine I would treat her with greater boldness, and I had sketched out in advance a plan of all that I would say to her, and even (being now quite convinced that she was not strait-laced) of all the favours that I would demand of her. But the mind is subject to external influences, as plants are, and cells and chemical elements, and the medium which alters it if we immerse it therein is a change of circumstances, or new surroundings. Changed by the mere fact of her presence, when I found myself once again in Albertine's company, I said to her quite different things from what I had planned. Then, remembering her flushed temple, I asked myself whether she might not appreciate more keenly a polite attention which she knew to be disinterested. Finally, I was embarrassed by some of her looks and her smiles. They might equally well signify a laxity of morals and the rather silly merriment of a high-spirited girl who was at heart thoroughly respectable. A single expression, of face or speech, being susceptible of sundry interpretations, I wavered like a schoolboy faced by the difficulties of a piece of Greek prose.

On this occasion we met almost immediately the tall one, Andrée, the one who had jumped over the old banker, and Albertine was obliged to introduce me. Her friend had extraordinarily bright eyes, like a glimpse, through an open door in a dark house, of a room into which the sun is shining with a greenish reflexion from the glittering sea.

A group of five men passed by whom I had come to know very well by sight during my stay at Balbec. I had often wondered who they were. "They're nothing very wonderful," said Albertine with a contemptuous snigger. "The little old one with dyed hair and yellow gloves—isn't he a weird-looking specimen, quite an eyeful, what?—that's the Balbec dentist. He's a good sort. The fat one is the Mayor, not the tiny little fat one, you must have seen him before, he's the dancing master, and he's pretty awful too—he can't stand us, because we make such a row at the Casino and smash his chairs and want to have the carpet up when we dance, which is why he never gives us prizes, though we're the only ones who know how to dance. The dentist is a nice man—I would have said how d'ye do to him, just to make the dancing master mad, but I couldn't because they've got M. de Sainte-Croix with them—he's a county councillor, and he comes of a very good family, but he's joined the Republicans, for money, so no decent people ever speak to him now. He knows my uncle, because they're both in the Government, but the rest of my family always cut him. The thin one in the waterproof is the conductor of the orchestra. What, you don't know him! Oh, he plays divinely. You haven't been to *Cavalleria Rusticana*? Ah, I think it's marvellous! He's giving a concert this evening, but we can't go because it's to be in the town hall. In the Casino it wouldn't matter, but in the town hall, where they've taken down the crucifix, Andrée's mother would have a fit if we went there. You're going to say that my aunt's husband is in the Government. But what difference does that make? My aunt is my aunt, but that's no reason why I should like her. The only thing she's ever wanted to do is get rid of me. No, the person who has really been a mother to me, and all the more credit to her because she's no relation at all, is a friend of mine whom I love just as much as if she was my mother. I'll show you her photo."

We were joined for a moment by the golf champion and baccarat player, Octave. I thought I had discovered a bond between us, for I learned in the course of our conversation that he was some sort of relative of the Verdurins, who were quite fond of him. But he spoke contemptuously of the famous Wednesdays, adding that M. Verdurin had never even heard of dress-clothes, which made it a horrid bore when one ran into him in certain "music-halls" where one would very much rather not be greeted with "Well, you young rascal" by an old fellow in a jacket and black tie, like a village notary.

Octave left us, and soon it was Andrée's turn, when we came to her villa, into which she vanished without having uttered a single word to me during the whole of our walk. I regretted her departure all the more because, while I was complaining to Albertine how cold her friend had been towards me, and was comparing in my mind this difficulty which Albertine seemed to find in bringing me into contact with her friends with the hostility that Elstir, in attempting to fulfil my wish, seemed to have encountered on that first afternoon, two girls came by to whom I lifted my hat, the misses d'Ambresac, whom Albertine greeted also.

I felt that my position in relation to Albertine would be improved by this meeting. They were the daughters of a kinswoman of Mme de Villeparisis, who was also a friend of Mme de Luxembourg. M. and Mme d'Ambresac, who had a small villa at Balbec and were immensely rich, led the simplest of lives, and always went about in the same clothes, he in the same jacket, she in a dark dress. Both of them used to make sweeping bows to my grandmother, which never led to anything further. The daughters, who were very pretty, were dressed more elegantly, but it was an elegance more suited to Paris than to the seaside. With their long skirts and large hats, they seemed to belong to a different race from Albertine. She, I discovered, knew all about them.

"Oh, so you know the little d'Ambresacs, do you? Well, well, you do have some grand friends. But they're very simple really," she went on as though the two things were mutually exclusive. "They're very nice, but so well brought up that they aren't allowed near the Casino, mainly because of us, because we're too badly behaved. You find them attractive, do you? Well, it all depends on what you like. They're real goody-goodies. Perhaps there's a certain charm in that. If you like goody-goodies, they're all that you could wish for. There must be some attraction, because one of them has got engaged already to the Marquis de Saint-Loup. Which was a cruel blow to the younger one, who was madly in love with that young man. As far as I'm concerned, the way they purse their lips when they talk is enough to madden me. And then they dress in the most absurd way. Fancy going to play golf in silk frocks! At their age, they dress more pretentiously than grown-up women who really know about clothes. Look at Mme Elstir. There's a well-dressed woman if you like." I answered that she had struck me as being dressed with the utmost simplicity. Albertine laughed.

"She's very simply turned out, I admit, but she dresses wonderfully, and to get what you call simplicity costs her a fortune."

Mme Elstir's elegance passed unnoticed by anyone who had not a sober and unerring taste in matters of dress. This I lacked. Elstir possessed it in a supreme degree, so Albertine told me. I had not suspected this, nor that the beautiful but quite simple objects which littered his studio were treasures long desired by him which he had followed from sale-room to sale-room, knowing all their history, until he had made enough money to be able to acquire them. But as to this Albertine, being as ignorant as myself, could not enlighten me. Whereas when it came to clothes, prompted by a coquettish instinct and perhaps by the regretful longing of a penniless girl who is able to appreciate with greater disinterestedness, more delicacy and discrimination, in the rich the things that she will never be able to afford for herself, she spoke very interestingly about the refinement of Elstir's taste, so difficult to satisfy that all women appeared to him badly dressed and, attaching infinite importance to proportions and shades of colour, he would have specially made for his wife, at fabulous prices, the sunshades, hats and coats whose charm he had taught Albertine to appreciate and which a person wanting in taste would no more have noticed than I had. Apart from this, Albertine, who had done a little painting, though without, she confessed, having any "gift" for it, felt a boundless admiration for Elstir, and, thanks to his precept and example, showed a judgment of pictures which was in marked contrast to her enthusiasm for *Cavalleria Rusticana*. The truth was that, though as yet it was hardly apparent, she was highly intelligent, and that in the things that she said the stupidity was not her own but that of her environment and her age. Elstir's had been a good but only a partial influence. All the branches of her intelligence had not reached the same stage of development. Her taste in pictures had almost caught up with her taste in clothes and all forms of elegance, but had not been followed by her taste in music, which was still a long way behind.

Albertine might know all about the Ambresacs; but as he who can achieve great things is not necessarily capable of small, I did not find her, after I had greeted those young ladies, any more disposed to make me known to her friends. "It's very good of you to attach importance to them. You shouldn't take any notice of them; they don't count. What on earth can a lot of kids like them mean to a man like you? Now Andrée, I must say, is remarkably clever. She's a good girl, though perfectly weird at times, but the others are really dreadfully stupid."

When I had left Albertine, I felt suddenly a keen regret that Saint-Loup should have concealed his engagement from me and that he should be doing anything so improper as to choose a wife before breaking with his mistress. And then, some days later, I met Andrée, and as she went on talking to me for some time I seized the opportunity to tell her that I would very much like to see her again next day; but she replied that this was impossible, because her mother was not at all well and she did not want to leave her alone. Two days later I went to see Elstir, who told me that Andrée had taken a great liking to me. When I protested that it was I who had taken a liking to her from the start, and had asked her to meet me again next day but she couldn't, "Yes, I know, she told me all about that," was his reply, "she was very sorry, but she had promised to go for a picnic somewhere miles from here. They were to drive over in a break, and it was too late for her to get out of it." Although this falsehood was of no real significance since Andrée knew me so slightly, I ought not to have continued to seek the company of a person who was capable of it. For what people have once done they will go on doing indefinitely, and if you go every year to see a friend who, the first few times, was unable to keep an appointment with you, or was in bed with a chill, you will find him in bed with another chill which he has just caught, you will miss him again at another meeting-place where he has failed to appear, for a single and unalterable reason in place of which he supposes himself to have various reasons, according to the circumstances.

One morning, not long after Andrée had told me that she would be obliged to stay beside her mother, I was taking a short stroll with Albertine, whom I had found on the beach tossing up and catching again at the end of a string a weird object which gave her a look of Giotto's "Idolatry"; it was called, as it happened, a "diabolo," and has so fallen into disuse now that, when they come upon the picture of a girl playing with one, the commentators of future generations will solemnly discuss, as it might be in front of the allegorical figures in the Arena Chapel, what it is that she is holding. A moment later their friend with the penurious and hard appearance, the one who on that first day had sneered so malevolently: "I do feel sorry for him, poor old boy," when she saw the old gentleman's head brushed by the flying feet of Andrée, came up to Albertine and said: "Good morning. Am I disturbing you?" She had taken off her hat for comfort, and her hair, like a strange and fascinating plant, lay over her brow, displaying all the delicate tracery of its foliation. Albertine, perhaps irritated at seeing the other bare-headed, made no reply, and preserved a frigid silence in spite of which the girl stayed with us, kept apart from me by Albertine who arranged at one moment to be alone with her, at another to walk with me leaving her to follow. I was obliged, to secure an introduction, to ask for it in the girl's hearing. Then, as Albertine uttered my name, the face and the blue eyes of this girl, whose expression I had thought so cruel when I heard her say: "Poor old boy, I do feel sorry for him," lit up with a cordial and affectionate smile, and she held out her hand to me. Her hair was golden, and not her hair only; for if her cheeks were pink and her eyes blue, it was like the still roseate morning sky which sparkles everywhere with dazzling points of gold.

Instantly aroused, I said to myself that this was a child who when in love grew shy, that it was for my sake, for love of me that she had remained with us despite Albertine's rebuffs, and that she must have rejoiced in the opportunity to confess to me at last, by that smiling, friendly look, that she would be as gentle to me as she was ferocious to other people. Doubtless she had noticed me on the beach when I did not yet know her, and had been thinking of me ever since; perhaps it was to win my admiration that she had mocked at the old gentleman, and because she had not succeeded in getting to know me that on the following days she had appeared so morose. I had often seen her from the hotel, walking by herself on the beach in the evenings. It was probably in the hope of meeting me. And now, hindered as much by Albertine's presence as she would have been by that of the whole band, she had evidently attached herself to us, in spite of the increasing coldness of her friend's attitude, only in the hope of outstaying her, of being left alone with me, when she might make a rendezvous with me for some time when she would find an excuse to slip away without either her family or her friends knowing that she had gone, and would meet me in some safe place before church or after golf. It was all the more difficult to see her because Andrée had quarrelled with her and now detested her. "I've put up quite long enough," she told me, "with her appalling duplicity, her baseness, and all the dirty tricks she's played on me. I've stood it all because of the others. But her latest effort was really too much!" And she told me of some piece of malicious gossip that this girl had perpetrated, which might indeed have injurious consequences for Andrée.

But those private words promised me by Gisèle's confiding eyes for the moment when Albertine should have left us by ourselves were destined never to be spoken, because after Albertine, stubbornly planted between us, had continued to reply with increasing curtness, and had finally ceased to reply at all, to her friend's remarks, Gisèle at length abandoned the attempt and turned back. I reproached Albertine for having been so disagreeable. "It will teach her to be more tactful. She's not a bad kid, but she's so boring. She's got no business, either, to come poking her nose into everything. Why should she fasten herself on to us without being asked? In another minute I'd have told her to go to blazes. Besides, I can't stand her going about with her hair like that; it's such bad form."

I gazed at Albertine's cheeks as she spoke, and asked myself what might be the perfume, the taste of them: that day she was not fresh and cool but smooth, with a uniform pinkness, violet-tinted, creamy, like certain roses whose petals have a waxy gloss. I felt a passionate longing for them such as one feels sometimes for a particular flower. "I hadn't noticed it," was all that I said.

"You stared at her hard enough; anyone would have thought you wanted to paint her portrait," she replied, not at all mollified by the fact that it was at herself that I was now staring so fixedly. "I don't believe you would care for her, though. She's not in the least a flirt. You like girls who flirt, I suspect. Anyhow, she won't have another chance of sticking to us and having to be shaken off. She's going back to Paris later today."

"Are the rest of your friends going too?"

"No, only she and 'Miss,' because she's got to take her exams again; she'll have to swot for them, poor kid. It's not much fun, I don't mind telling you. Of course, you may be set a good subject, you never know. It's such a matter of luck. One girl I know was given: *Describe an accident that you have witnessed.* That was a piece of luck. But I know another girl who had to discuss, in writing too: *Which would you rather have as a friend, Alceste or Philinte?* I'm sure I should have dried up altogether! Apart from everything else, it's not a question to set to girls. Girls go about with other girls; they're not supposed to have gentlemen friends." (This announcement, which showed that I had small chance of being admitted to the little band, made me quake.) "But in any case, even if it was set for boys, what on earth would you expect them to find to say about it? Several parents wrote to the *Gaulois*, to complain of the difficulty of questions like that. The joke of it is that in a collection of prize-winning essays there were two which treated the question in absolutely opposite ways. You see, it all depends on the examiner. One wanted you to say that Philinte was a two-faced socialite flatterer, the other that you couldn't help admiring Alceste, but that he was too cantankerous, and that as a friend you ought to choose Philinte. How can you expect a lot of unfortunate candidates to know what to say when the professors themselves don't agree? But that's nothing. It gets more difficult every year. Gisèle will have to pull a string or two if she's to get through."

I returned to the hotel. My grandmother was not there. I waited for her some time, and when at last she appeared, I begged her to allow me, in quite unexpected circumstances, to make an expedition which might keep me away for a couple of days. I had lunch with her, ordered a carriage and drove to the station. Gisèle would not be surprised to see me there. After we had changed at Doncières, in the Paris train there would be a carriage with a corridor, along which, while the governess dozed, I should be able to lead Gisèle into a dark corner and make an appointment to meet her on my return to Paris, which I would then try to put forward to the earliest possible date. I would travel with her as far as Caen or Evreux, whichever she preferred, and would take the next train back to Balbec. And yet, what would she have thought of me had she known that I had hesitated for a long time between her and her friends, that quite as much as with her I had contemplated falling in love with Albertine, with the girl with the bright eyes, with Rosemonde. I felt a pang of remorse, now that a bond of mutual affection was going to unite me with Gisèle. I could, however, truthfully have assured her that Albertine no longer attracted me. I had seen her that morning as she swerved aside, almost turning her back on me, to speak to Gisèle. Her head was sulkily lowered, and the hair at the back, which was different and darker still, glistened as though she had just been bathing. Like a wet hen, I had thought to myself, and this view of her hair had induced me to embody in Albertine a different soul from that implied hitherto by her violet face and mysterious gaze. That shining cataract of hair at the back of her head had been for a moment or two all that I was able to see of her, and continued to be all that I saw in retrospect. Our memory is like one of those shops in the window of which is exposed now one, now another photograph of the same person. And as a rule the most recent exhibit remains for some time the only one to be seen. While the coachman whipped on his horse I sat there listening to the words of gratitude and tenderness that Gisèle was murmuring in my ear, all of them born of her friendly smile and outstretched hand; for the fact was that in those periods of my life in which I was not actually in love but desired to be, I carried in my mind not only a physical ideal of beauty which, as the reader has seen, I recognised from a distance in every passing woman far enough away from me for her indistinct features not to belie the identification, but also the mental phantom—ever ready to become incarnate—of the woman who was going to fall in love with me, to take up her cues in the amorous comedy which I had had all written out in my mind from my earliest boyhood, and in which every attractive girl seemed to me to be equally desirous of playing, provided that she had also some of the physical qualifications required. In this play, whoever the new star might be whom I invited to create or to revive the leading part, the plot, the incidents, the lines themselves preserved an unalterable form.

Within the next few days, in spite of the reluctance that Albertine had shown to introduce me to them, I knew all the little band of that first afternoon (except Gisèle, whom, owing to a prolonged delay at the level crossing by the station and a change in the time-table, I had not succeeded in meeting on the train, which had left some minutes before I arrived, and to whom in any case I never gave another thought), and two or three other girls as well to whom at my request they introduced me. And thus, my expectation of the pleasure which I should find in a new girl springing from another through whom I had come to know her, the latest was like one of those new varieties of rose which gardeners get by using first a rose of another species. And as I passed from corolla to corolla along this chain of flowers, the pleasure of knowing a different one would send me back to the one to whom I was indebted for it, with a gratitude mixed with as much desire as my new hope. Presently I was spending all my time among these girls.

Alas! in the freshest flower it is possible to discern those just perceptible signs which to the instructed mind already betray what will, by the desiccation or fructification of the flesh that is today in bloom, be the ultimate form, immutable and already predestined, of the autumnal seed. The eye follows with delight a nose like a wavelet that deliciously ripples the surface of the water at daybreak, and seems motionless, capturable by the pencil, because the sea is so calm that one does not notice its tidal flow. Human faces seem not to change while we are looking at them, because the revolution they perform is too slow for us to perceive it. But one had only to see, by the side of any of these girls, her mother or her aunt, to realise the distance over which, obeying the internal gravitation of a type that was generally frightful, these features would have travelled in less than thirty years, until the hour when the looks have begun to wane, until the hour when the face, having sunk altogether below the horizon, catches the light no more. I knew that, as deep, as ineluctable as Jewish patriotism or Christian atavism in those who imagine themselves to be the most emancipated of their race, there dwelt beneath the rosy inflorescence of Albertine, Rosemonde, Andrée, unknown to themselves, held in reserve until the occasion should arise, a coarse nose, a protruding jaw, a paunch which would create a sensation when it appeared, but which was actually in the wings, ready to come on, unforeseen, inevitable, just as it might be a burst of Dreyfusism or clericalism or patriotic, feudal heroism, emerging suddenly in answer to the call of circumstance from a nature anterior to the individual himself, through which he thinks, lives, evolves, gains strength or dies, without ever being able to distinguish that nature from the particular motives he mistakes for it. Even mentally, we depend a great deal more than we think upon natural laws, and our minds possess in advance, like some cryptogamous plant, the characteristic that we imagine ourselves to be selecting. For we grasp only the secondary ideas, without detecting the primary cause (Jewish blood, French birth or whatever it may be) that inevitably produced them, and which we manifest when the time comes. But perhaps, while the one may appear to us to be the result of deliberate thought, the other of an imprudent disregard for our own health, we take from our family, as the papilionaceae take the form of their seed, as well the ideas by which we live as the malady from which we shall die.

As in a nursery plantation where the flowers mature at different seasons, I had seen them, in the form of old ladies, on this Balbec shore, those shrivelled seed-pods, those flabby tubers, which my new friends would one day be. But what matter? For the moment it was their flowering-time. And so when Mme de Villeparisis asked me to go for a drive, I sought an excuse to avoid doing so. I no longer visited Elstir unless accompanied by my new friends. I could not even spare an afternoon to go to Doncières, to pay the visit I had promised Saint-Loup. Social engagements, serious discussions, even a friendly conversation, had they usurped the place allotted to my outings with these girls, would have had the same effect on me as if, at lunch-time, one were taken not to eat but to look at an album. The men, the youths, the women, old or mature, in whose society we think to take pleasure, exist for us only on a flat, one-dimensional surface, because we are conscious of them only through visual perception restricted to its own limits; whereas it is as delegates from our other senses that our eyes direct themselves towards young girls; the senses follow, one after another, in search of the various charms, fragrant, tactile, savorous, which they thus enjoy even without the aid of hands and lips; and able, thanks to the arts of transposition, the genius for synthesis in which desire excels, to reconstruct beneath the hue of cheeks or bosom the feel, the taste, the contact that is forbidden them, they give to these girls the same honeyed consistency as they create when they go foraging in a rose-garden, or in a vine whose clusters their eyes devour.

If it rained, although the weather had no power to daunt Albertine, who was often to be seen in her waterproof spinning on her bicycle through the showers, we would spend the day in the Casino, where on such days it would have seemed to me impossible not to go. I had the greatest contempt for the Ambresac sisters, who had never set foot in it. And I willingly joined my new friends in playing tricks on the dancing master. As a rule we had to listen to admonitions from the manager, or from some of his staff usurping directorial powers, because my friends—even Andrée whom on that account I had regarded when I first saw her as so Dionysiac a creature whereas in reality she was delicate, intellectual and this year far from well, in spite of which her actions were responsive less to the state of her health than to the spirit of that age which sweeps everything aside and mingles in a general gaiety the weak with the strong—could not go from the hall to the ball-room without breaking into a run, jumping over all the chairs, and sliding along the floor, their balance maintained by a graceful poise of their outstretched arms, singing the while, mingling all the arts, in that first bloom of youth, in the manner of those poets of old for whom the different genres were not yet separate, so that in an epic poem they would mix agricultural precepts with theological doctrine.

This Andrée, who had struck me when I first saw her as the coldest of them all, was infinitely more refined, more affectionate, more sensitive than Albertine, to whom she displayed the caressing, gentle tenderness of an elder sister. At the Casino she would come across the floor to sit down beside me and was prepared, unlike Albertine, to forgo a waltz or even, if I was tired, to give up the Casino and come to me instead at the hotel. She expressed her friendship for me, for Albertine, in terms that were evidence of the most exquisite understanding of the things of the heart, which may have been partly due to her delicate health. She had always a gay smile of excuse for the childish behaviour of Albertine, who expressed with naïve violence the temptation held out to her by the parties and pleasures which she was incapable of resisting, as Andrée could, in order to stay and talk to me. When the time came for her to go off to a tea-party at the golf-club, if we were all three together at that moment she would get ready to leave and then, coming up to Andrée, would say: "Well, Andrée, what are you waiting for? You know we're having tea at the golf-club." "No, I'm going to stay and talk to him," Andrée would reply, pointing to me. "But you know Mme Durieux invited you," Albertine would cry, as if Andrée's intention to remain with me could be explained only by ignorance on her part as to whether or not she had been invited. "Come, my sweet, don't be such an idiot," Andrée would chide her, and Albertine would not insist, for fear that she might be asked to stay too. She would toss her head and say "Just as you like," in the tone one uses to an invalid who is deliberately killing himself by inches. "Anyway I must fly; I'm sure your watch is slow," and off she would go. "She's a dear girl, but quite impossible," Andrée would say, enveloping her friend in a smile at once caressing and critical. If in this craze for amusement Albertine might be said to echo something of the old original Gilberte, that is because a certain similarity exists, although the type evolves, between all the women we successively love, a similarity that is due to the fixity of our own temperament, which chooses them, eliminating all those who would not be at once our opposite and our complement, apt, that is to say, to gratify our senses and to wring our hearts. They are, these women, a product of our temperament, an image, an inverted projection, a negative of our sensibility. So that a novelist might, in relating the life of his hero, describe his successive love-affairs in almost exactly similar terms, and thereby give the impression not that he was repeating himself but that he was creating, since an artificial novelty is never so effective as a repetition that manages to suggest a fresh truth. He ought, moreover, to note in the character of the lover an index of variation which becomes apparent as the story moves into fresh regions, into different latitudes of life. And perhaps he would be expressing yet another truth if, while investing all the other dramatis personae with distinct characters, he refrained from giving any to the beloved. We understand the characters of people to whom we are indifferent, but how can we ever grasp that of a person who is an intimate part of our existence, whom after a while we no longer distinguish from ourselves, whose motives provide us with an inexhaustible source of anxious hypotheses, continually revised? Springing from somewhere beyond our intellect, our curiosity about the woman we love overleaps the bounds of that woman's character, at which, even if we could stop, we probably never would. The object of our anxious investigation is something more basic than those details of character comparable to the tiny particles of epidermis whose varied combinations form the florid originality of human flesh. Our intuitive radiography pierces them, and the images which it brings back, far from being those of a particular face, present rather the joyless universality of a skeleton.

Andrée, being herself extremely rich while the other was penniless and an orphan, with real generosity lavished on Albertine the full benefit of her wealth. As for her feelings towards Gisèle, they were not quite what I had been led to suppose. News soon reached us of the young student, and when Albertine handed round the letter she had received from her, a letter intended by Gisèle to give an account of her journey and to report her safe arrival to the little band, apologising for her laziness in not yet having written to the others, I was surprised to hear Andrée, whom I imagined to be at daggers drawn with her, say: "I shall write to her tomorrow, because if I wait for her to write I may have to wait for ages, she's such a slacker." And turning to me she added: "You mightn't see much in her, but she's a jolly nice girl, and besides I'm really very fond of her." From which I concluded that Andrée's quarrels were apt not to last very long.

Except on these rainy days, as we always arranged to go on our bicycles along the cliffs, or on an excursion inland, an hour or so before it was time to start I would go upstairs to make myself smart and would complain if Françoise had not laid out all the things that I wanted. Now even in Paris, at the first word of reproach she would proudly and angrily straighten a back which the years had begun to bend, she so humble, modest and charming when her self-esteem was flattered. As this was the mainspring of Françoise's life, her satisfaction and her good humour were in direct ratio to the difficulty of the tasks imposed on her. Those which she had to perform at Balbec were so easy that she displayed an almost continual dissatisfaction which was suddenly multiplied a hundred-fold and combined with an ironic air of offended dignity when I complained, on my way down to join my friends, that my hat had not been brushed or my ties sorted. She who was capable of taking such endless pains and would think nothing of it, on my simply remarking that a coat was not in its proper place would not only boast of the care with which she had "shut it away sooner than let it go gathering the dust," but, paying a formal tribute to her own labours, lamented that it was little enough of a holiday that she was getting at Balbec, and that we would not find another person in the whole world who would consent to put up with such treatment. "I can't think how people can leave things lying about the way you do; you just try and get anyone else to find what you want in such a pell and mell. The devil himself couldn't make head nor tail of it." Or else she would adopt a regal mien, scorching me with her fiery glance, and preserve a silence that was broken as soon as she had fastened the door behind her and had set off down the corridor, which would then reverberate with utterances which I guessed to be abusive, though they remained as indistinct as those of characters in a play whose opening lines are spoken in the wings, before they appear on the stage. But even if nothing was missing and Françoise was in a good temper, still she made herself quite intolerable when I was getting ready to go out with my friends. For, drawing upon a store of jokes which, in my need to talk about these girls, I had told her at their expense, she took it upon herself to reveal to me what I should have known better than she if it had been accurate, which it never was, Françoise having misunderstood what she had heard. She had, like everyone else, her own peculiar character, which in no one resembles a straight highway, but surprises us with its strange, unavoidable windings which other people do not see and which it is painful to have to follow. Whenever I arrived at the stage of "Where is my hat?" or uttered the name of Andrée or Albertine, I was forced by Françoise to stray into endless and absurd side-tracks which greatly delayed my progress. So too when I ordered the cheese or salad sandwiches or sent out for the cakes which I would eat on the cliff with the girls, and which they "might very well have taken turns to provide, if they hadn't been so close-fisted," declared Françoise, to whose aid there came at such moments a whole heritage of atavistic peasant rapacity and coarseness, and for whom one would have said that the divided soul of her late enemy Eulalie had been reincarnated, more becomingly than in St Eloi, in the charming bodies of my friends of the little band. I listened to these accusations with a dull fury at finding myself brought to a standstill at one of those places beyond which the rustic and familiar path that was Françoise's character became impassable, though fortunately never for very long. Then, my hat or coat found and the sandwiches ready, I went to join Albertine, Andrée, Rosemonde, and any others there might be, and we would set out on foot or on our bicycles.

In the old days I should have preferred our excursions to be made in bad weather. For then I still looked to find in Balbec "the land of the Cimmerians," and fine days were a thing that had no right to exist there, an intrusion of the vulgar summer of seaside holiday-makers into that ancient region swathed in eternal mist. But everything that I had hitherto despised and thrust from my sight, not only the effects of sunlight upon sea and shore, but even regattas and race-meetings, I now sought out with ardour, for the same reason which formerly had made me wish only for stormy seas: namely, that they were now associated in my mind, as the others had once been, with an aesthetic idea. For I had gone several times with my new friends to visit Elstir, and, on the days when the girls were there, what he had selected to show us were drawings of pretty women in yachting dress, or else a sketch made on a race-course near Balbec. I had at first shyly admitted to Elstir that I had not felt inclined to go to the meetings that had been held there. "You were wrong," he told me, "it's such a pretty sight, and so strange too. For one thing, that peculiar creature the jockey, on whom so many eyes are fastened, and who sits there in the paddock so gloomy and grey-faced in his bright jacket, reining in the rearing horse that seems to be one with him: how interesting to analyse his professional movements, the bright splash of colour he makes, with the horse's coat blending in it, against the background of the course! What a transformation of every visible object in that luminous vastness of a race-course where one is constantly surprised by fresh lights and shades which one sees only there! How pretty the women can look there, too! The first meeting in particular was delightful, and there were some extremely elegant women there in the misty, almost Dutch light in which you could feel the piercing cold of the sea even in the sun itself. I've never seen women arriving in carriages, or standing with glasses to their eyes in so extraordinary a light, which was due, I suppose, to the moisture from the sea. Ah! how I should have loved to paint it. I came back from those races wild with enthusiasm and longing to get to work!" After which he waxed more enthusiastic still over the yacht-races, and I realised that regattas, and race-meetings where well-dressed women might be seen bathed in the greenish light of a marine race-course, might be for a modern artist as interesting a subject as the festivities which they so loved to depict were for a Veronese or a Carpaccio. When I suggested this to Elstir, "Your comparison is all the more apt," he replied, "since because of the nature of the city in which they painted, those festivities were to a great extent aquatic. Except that the beauty of the shipping in those days lay as a rule in its solidity, in the complication of its structure. They had water-tournaments, as we have here, held generally in honour of some Embassy, such as Carpaccio shows us in his *Legend of Saint Ursula.* The ships were massive, built like pieces of architecture, and seemed almost amphibious, like lesser Venices set in the heart of the greater, when, moored to the banks by gangways decked with crimson satin and Persian carpets, they bore their freight of ladies in cerise brocade and green damask close under the balconies incrusted with multicoloured marble from which other ladies leaned to gaze at them, in gowns with black sleeves slashed with white, stitched with pearls or bordered with lace. You couldn't tell where the land finished and the water began, what was still the palace or already the ship, the caravel, the galley, the Bucentaur."

Albertine listened with passionate interest to these details of costume, these visions of elegance that Elstir described to us. "Oh, I should so like to see that lace you speak of; it's so pretty, Venetian lace," she exclaimed, "and I should love to see Venice." "You may, perhaps, before very long," Elstir informed her, "be able to gaze at the marvellous stuffs which they used to wear. One used only to be able to see them in the works of the Venetian painters, or very rarely among the treasures of old churches, or now and then when a specimen turned up in the sale-room. But I hear that a Venetian artist, called Fortuny, has rediscovered the secret of the craft, and that in a few years' time women will be able to parade around, and better still to sit at home, in brocades as sumptuous as those that Venice adorned for her patrician daughters with patterns brought from the Orient. But I don't know whether I should much care for that, whether it wouldn't be too much of an anachronism for the women of today, even when they parade at regattas, for, to return to our modern pleasure-craft, the times have completely changed since 'Venice, Queen of the Adriatic.' The great charm of a yacht, of the furnishings of a yacht, of yachting clothes, is their simplicity, as things of the sea, and I do so love the sea. I must confess that I prefer the fashions of today to those of Veronese's and even of Carpaccio's time. What is so attractive about our yachts—and the medium-sized yachts especially, I don't like the huge ones, they're too much like ships; and the same goes for hats, there must be some sense of proportion—is the uniform surface, simple, gleaming, grey, which in a bluish haze takes on a creamy softness. The cabin ought to make us think of a little café. And it's the same with women's clothes on board a yacht; what's really charming are those light garments, uniformly white, cotton or linen or nankeen or drill, which in the sunlight and against the blue of the sea show up with as dazzling a whiteness as a spread sail. Actually, there are very few women who know how to dress, though some of them are quite wonderful. At the races, Mlle Léa had a little white hat and a little white sunshade that were simply enchanting. I don't know what I wouldn't give for that little sunshade."

I should have liked very much to know in what respect this little sunshade differed from any other, and for other reasons, reasons of feminine coquetry, Albertine was still more curious. But, just as Françoise used to explain the excellence of her soufflés by saying simply: "It's a knack," so here the difference lay in the cut. "It was tiny and round, like a Chinese parasol," Elstir said. I mentioned the sunshades carried by various women, but none of them would do. Elstir found them all quite hideous. A man of exquisite taste, singularly hard to please, he would isolate some minute detail which was the whole difference between what was worn by three-quarters of the women he saw, and which he abominated, and a thing which enchanted him by its prettiness; and—in contrast to its effect on myself, for whom every kind of luxury was stultifying—stimulated his desire to paint "so as to make something as attractive."

"Here you see a young lady who has guessed what the hat and sunshade were like," he said to me, pointing to Albertine, whose eyes shone with covetousness.

"How I should love to be rich and to have a yacht!" she said to the painter. "I should come to you for advice on how to do it up. What lovely trips I'd make! And what fun it would be to go to Cowes for the regatta! And a motor-car! Tell me, do you think women's fashions for motoring pretty?"

"No," replied Elstir, "but that will come in time. You see, there are very few good couturiers at present, one or two only, Callot—although they go in rather too freely for lace—Doucet, Cheruit, Paquin sometimes. The others are all ghastly."

"So there's a vast difference between a Callot dress and one from any ordinary shop?" I asked Albertine.

"Why, an enormous difference, my little man! Oh, sorry! Only, alas! what you get for three hundred francs in an ordinary shop will cost two thousand there. But there can be no comparison; they look the same only to people who know nothing at all about it."

"Quite so," put in Elstir, "though I wouldn't go so far as to say that it's as profound as the difference between a statue from Rheims Cathedral and one from Saint-Augustin. By the way, talking of cathedrals," he went on, addressing himself exclusively to me, because what he was saying referred to an earlier conversation in which the girls had not taken part, and which for that matter would in no way have interested them, "I spoke to you the other day of Balbec church as a great cliff, a huge breakwater built of the stone of the country, but conversely," he went on, showing me a water-colour, "look at these cliffs (it's a sketch I did near here, at the Creuniers); don't those rocks, so powerfully and delicately modelled, remind you of a cathedral?"

And indeed one would have taken them for soaring red arches. But, painted on a scorching hot day, they seemed to have been reduced to dust, volatilised by the heat which had drunk up half the sea so that it had almost been distilled, over the whole surface of the picture, into a gaseous state. On this day when the sunlight had, so to speak, destroyed reality, reality concentrated itself in certain dusky and transparent creatures which, by contrast, gave a more striking, a closer impression of life: the shadows. Thirsting for coolness, most of them, deserting the torrid sea, had taken shelter at the foot of the rocks, out of reach of the sun; others, swimming gently upon the tide, like dolphins, kept close under the sides of occasional moving boats, whose hulls they extended upon the pale surface of the water with their glossy blue forms. It was perhaps the thirst for coolness which they conveyed that did most to give me the sensation of the heat of that day and made me exclaim how much I regretted not knowing the Creuniers. Albertine and Andrée were positive that I must have been there hundreds of times. If so I had been there without knowing it, never suspecting that one day the sight of these rocks would arouse in me such a thirst for beauty, not perhaps precisely natural beauty such as I had sought hitherto among the cliffs of Balbec, but architectural rather. Especially since, having come here to visit the kingdom of the storms, I had never found, on any of my drives with Mme de Villeparisis, when often we saw it only from afar, painted in a gap between the trees, that the sea was sufficiently real or sufficiently liquid or gave a sufficient impression of hurling its massed forces against the shore, and would have liked to see it lie motionless only under a wintry shroud of fog, I could never have believed that I should now be dreaming of a sea which was no more than a whitish vapour that had lost both consistency and colour. But of such a sea Elstir, like the people who sat musing on board those vessels drowsy with the heat, had felt so intensely the enchantment that he had succeeded in transcribing, in fixing for all time upon his canvas, the imperceptible ebb of the tide, the throb of one happy moment; and at the sight of this magic portrait, one could think of nothing else than to range the wide world, seeking to recapture the vanished day in its instantaneous, slumbering beauty.

So that if, before these visits to Elstir—before I had set eyes on one of his sea-pictures in which a young woman in a dress of white serge or linen, on the deck of a yacht flying the American flag, put into my imagination the spiritual "carbon copy" of a white linen dress and coloured flag which at once bred in me an insatiable desire to see there and then with my own eyes white linen dresses and flags against the sea, as if no such experience had ever yet befallen me—I had always striven, when I stood before the sea, to expel from my field of vision, as well as the bathers in the foreground and the yachts with their too dazzling sails that were like seaside costumes, everything that prevented me from persuading myself that I was contemplating the immemorial ocean which had already been pursuing the same mysterious life before the appearance of the human race, and had grudged even the days of radiant sunshine which seemed to me to invest with the trivial aspect of universal summer this coast of fog and tempest, to mark simply a pause, equivalent to what in music is known as a silent bar—now on the contrary it was bad weather that appeared to me to be some baleful accident, no longer worthy of a place in the world of beauty: I felt a keen desire to go out and recapture in reality what had so powerfully aroused my imagination, and I hoped that the weather would be propitious enough for me to see from the summit of the cliff the same blue shadows as in Elstir's picture.

Nor, as I went along, did I still screen my eyes with my hands as in the days when, conceiving nature to be animated by a life anterior to the first appearance of man and in opposition to all those wearisome improvements of industrial civilisation which had hitherto made me yawn with boredom at universal exhibitions or milliners' windows, I endeavoured to see only that section of the sea over which there was no steamer passing, so that I might picture it to myself as immemorial, still contemporary with the ages when it had been divorced from the land, or at least contemporary with the early centuries of Greece, which enabled me to repeat in their literal meaning the lines of "old man Leconte" of which Bloch was so fond:

> Gone are the kings, their ships pierced by rams,
> Vanished upon the raging deep, alas,
> The long-haired warriors of heroic Hellas.

I could no longer despise the milliners, now that Elstir had told me that the delicate gesture with which they give a last refinement, a supreme caress to the bows or feathers of a hat after it is finished, would be as interesting to him to paint as that of the jockeys (a statement which had delighted Albertine). But I must wait until I had returned—for milliners, to Paris, for regattas and races to Balbec, where there would be no more now until next year. Even a yacht with women in white linen was not to be found.

Often we encountered Bloch's sisters, to whom I was obliged to bow since I had dined with their father. My new friends did not know them. "I'm not allowed to play with Israelites," Albertine announced. Her way of pronouncing the word—"Issraelites" instead of "Izraelites"—would in itself have sufficed to show, even if one had not heard the rest of the sentence, that it was no feeling of friendliness towards the chosen race that inspired these young bourgeoises, brought up in God-fearing homes, and quite ready to believe that the Jews were in the habit of butchering Christian children. "Besides, they're shocking bad form, your friends," said Andrée with a smile which implied that she knew very well that they were no friends of mine. "Like everything to do with the tribe," added Albertine, in the sententious tone of one who spoke from personal experience. To tell the truth, Bloch's sisters, at once overdressed and half naked, with their languid, brazen, ostentatious, slatternly air, did not create the best impression. And one of their cousins, who was only fifteen, scandalised the Casino by her unconcealed admiration for Mlle Léa, whose talent as an actress M. Bloch senior rated very high, but whose tastes were understood not to be primarily directed towards gentlemen.

There were days when we picnicked at one of the outlying farms which catered for visitors. These were the farms known as Les Ecorres, Marie-Thérèse, La Croix d'Heuland, Bagatelle, Californie and Marie-Antoinette. It was the last that had been adopted by the little band.

But at other times, instead of going to a farm, we would climb to the highest point of the cliff, and, when we had reached it and were seated on the grass, would undo our parcel of sandwiches and cakes. My friends preferred the sandwiches, and were surprised to see me eat only a single chocolate cake, sugared with Gothic tracery, or an apricot tart. This was because, with the sandwiches of cheese or salad, a form of food that was novel to me and was ignorant of the past, I had nothing in common. But the cakes understood, the tarts were talkative. There was in the former an insipid taste of cream, in the latter a fresh taste of fruit which knew all about Combray, and about Gilberte, not only the Gilberte of Combray but the Gilberte of Paris, at whose tea-parties I had come across them again. They reminded me of those cake-plates with the Arabian Nights pattern, the subjects on which so diverted my aunt Léonie when Françoise brought her up, one day Aladdin and his Wonderful Lamp, another day

Ali Baba, or the Sleeper Awakes or Sinbad the Sailor embarking at Bassorah with all his treasures. I should dearly have liked to see them again, but my grandmother did not know what had become of them and thought moreover that they were just common plates that had been bought in the village. No matter, in grey, rustic Combray they were a multi-coloured inset, as in the dark church were the flickering jewels of the stained-glass windows, as in the twilight of my bedroom were the projections cast by the magic lantern, as in front of the railway-station and the little local line the buttercups from the Indies and the Persian lilacs, as was my great-aunt's collection of old porcelain in the sombre dwelling of an elderly lady in a country town.

Stretched out on the cliff I would see before me nothing but grassy meadows and beyond them not the seven heavens of the Christian cosmogony but two stages only, one of a deeper blue, the sea, and above it another, paler one. We ate our food, and if I had brought with me also some little keepsake which might appeal to one or other of my friends, joy sprang with such sudden violence into their translucent faces, flushed in an instant, that their lips had not the strength to hold it in, and, to allow it to escape, parted in a burst of laughter. They were gathered close round me, and between their faces, which were not far apart, the air that separated them traced azure pathways such as might have been cut by a gardener wishing to create a little space so as to be able himself to move freely through a thicket of roses.

When we had finished eating we would play games which until then I should have thought boring, sometimes such childish games as King of the Castle, or Who

Laughs First; not for a kingdom would I have renounced them now; the aurora of adolescence with which the faces of these girls still glowed, and from which I, young as I was, had already emerged, shed its light on everything around them and, like the fluid painting of certain Primitives, brought out in relief the most insignificant details of their daily lives against a golden background. Their faces were for the most part blurred with this misty effulgence of a dawn from which their actual features had not yet emerged. One saw only a charming glow of colour beneath which what in a few years' time would be a profile was not discernible. The profile of today had nothing definitive about it, and could be only a momentary resemblance to some deceased member of the family to whom nature had paid this commemorative courtesy. It comes so soon, the moment when there is nothing left to wait for, when the body is fixed in an immobility which holds no fresh surprise in store, when one loses all hope on seeing—as on a tree in the height of summer one sees leaves already brown—round a face still young hair that is growing thin or turning grey; it is so short, that radiant morning time, that one comes to like only the very youngest girls, those in whom the flesh, like a precious leaven, is still at work. They are no more than a stream of ductile matter, continuously moulded by the fleeting impression of the moment. It is as though each of them was in turn a little statuette of gaiety, of childish earnestness, of cajolery, of surprise, shaped by an expression frank and complete, but fugitive. This plasticity gives a wealth of variety and charm to the pretty attentions which a young girl pays to us. Of course, such attentions are indispensable in the mature woman also, and one who is not attracted to us, or who does not show that she is attracted to us, tends to assume in our eyes a somewhat tedious uniformity. But even these endearments, after a certain age, cease to send gentle ripples over faces which the struggle for existence has hardened, has rendered unalterably militant or ecstatic. One—owing to the prolonged strain of the obedience that subjects wife to husband—will seem not so much a woman's face as a soldier's; another, carved by the sacrifices which a mother has consented to make, day after day, for her children, will be the face of an apostle. A third is, after a stormy passage through the years, the face of an ancient mariner, upon a body of which its garments alone indicate the sex. Certainly the attentions that a woman pays us can still, so long as we are in love with her, endue with fresh charms the hours that we spend in her company. But she is not then for us a series of different women. Her gaiety remains external to an unchanging face. Whereas adolescence precedes this complete solidification, and hence we feel, in the company of young girls, the refreshing sense that is afforded us by the spectacle of forms undergoing an incessant process of change, a play of unstable forces which recalls that perpetual re-creation of the primordial elements of nature which we contemplate when we stand before the sea.

It was not merely a social engagement, a drive with Mme de Villeparisis, that I was prepared to sacrifice to the hide-and-seek or guessing games of my new friends. More than once, Robert de Saint-Loup had sent word that, since I had failed to come to see him at Doncières, he had applied for twenty-four hours' leave which he would spend at Balbec. Each time I wrote back to say that he was on no account to come, offering the excuse that I should be obliged to be away myself that very day, having some duty call to pay with my grandmother on family friends in the neighbourhood. No doubt he thought ill of me when he learned from his aunt in what the "duty call" consisted, and who the persons were who combined to play the part of my grandmother. And yet, perhaps I was not wrong in sacrificing the pleasures not only of society but of friendship to that of spending the whole day in this green garden. People who have the capacity to do so—it is true that such people are artists, and I had long been convinced that I should never be that—also have a duty to live for themselves. And friendship is a dispensation from this duty, an abdication of self. Even conversation, which is friendship's mode of expression, is a superficial digression which gives us nothing worth acquiring. We may talk for a lifetime without doing more than indefinitely repeat the vacuity of a minute, whereas the march of thought in the solitary work of artistic creation proceeds in depth, in the only direction that is not closed to us, along which we are free to advance—though with more effort, it is true—towards a goal of truth. And friendship is not merely devoid of virtue, like conversation, it is fatal to us as well. For the sense of boredom which those of us whose law of development is purely internal cannot help but feel in a friend's company (when, that is to say, we must remain on the surface of ourselves, instead of pursuing our voyage of discovery into the depths)—that first impression of boredom our friendship impels us to correct when we are alone again, to recall with emotion the words which our friend said to us, to look upon them as a valuable addition to our substance, when the fact is that we are not like buildings to which stones can be added from without, but like trees which draw from their own sap the next knot that will appear on their trunks, the spreading roof of their foliage. I was lying to myself, I was interrupting the process of growth in the direction in which I could indeed truly develop and be happy, when I congratulated myself on being liked and admired by so good, so intelligent, so rare a person as Saint-Loup, when I focused my mind, not upon my own obscure impressions which it should have been my duty to unravel, but on the words of my friend, in which, by repeating them to myself—by having them repeated to me by that other self who dwells in us and on to whom we are always so ready to unload the burden of taking thought—I strove to find a beauty very different from that which I pursued in silence when I was really alone, but one that would enhance the merit not only of Robert, but of myself and of my life. In the life which such a friend provided for me, I seemed to myself to be cosily preserved from solitude, nobly desirous of sacrificing myself for him, in short incapable of realising myself. With the girls, on the other hand, if the pleasure which I enjoyed was selfish, at least it was not based on the lie which seeks to make us believe that we are not irremediably alone and prevents us from admitting that, when we chat, it is no longer we who speak, that we are fashioning ourselves then in the likeness of other people and not of a self that differs from them. The words exchanged between the girls of the little band and myself were of little interest; they were, moreover, few, broken by long spells of silence on my part. This did not prevent me from taking as much pleasure in listening to them as in looking at them, in discovering in the voice of each one of them a brightly coloured picture. It was with delight that I listened to their pipings. Loving helps us to discern, to discriminate. The bird-lover in a wood at once distinguishes the twittering of the different species, which to ordinary people sound the same. The devotee of girls knows that human voices vary even more. Each one possesses more notes than the richest instrument of music. And the combinations in which it groups those notes are as inexhaustible as the infinite variety of personalities. When I talked with any one of my young friends I was conscious that the original, the unique portrait of her individuality had been skilfully traced, tyrannically imposed on my mind as much by the inflexions of her voice as by those of her face, and that they were two separate spectacles which expressed, each on its own plane, the same singular reality. No doubt the lines of the voice, like those of the face, were not yet finally fixed; the voice had still to break, as the face to change. Just as infants have a gland the secretion of which enables them to digest milk, a gland which is not found in adults, so there were in the twitterings of these girls notes which women's voices no longer contain. And on this more varied instrument they played with their lips, with all the application and the ardour of Bellini's little angel musicians, qualities which also are an exclusive appanage of youth. Later on these girls would lose that note of enthusiastic conviction which gave a charm to their simplest utterances, whether it were Albertine who, in a tone of authority, repeated puns to which the younger ones listened with admiration, until a paroxysm of giggles took hold of them with the irresistible violence of a sneezing fit, or Andrée who spoke of their school work, even more childish seemingly than the games they played, with an essentially puerile gravity; and their words varied in tone, like the strophes of antiquity when poetry, still hardly differentiated from music, was declaimed on different notes. In spite of everything, the voices of these girls already gave a quite clear indication of the attitude that each of these young people had adopted towards life, an attitude so individual that it would be speaking in far too general terms to say of one: "She treats everything as a joke," of another: "She jumps from assertion to assertion," of a third: "She lives in a state of expectant hesitancy." The features of our face are hardly more than gestures which force of habit has made permanent. Nature, like the destruction of Pompeii, like the metamorphosis of a nymph, has arrested us in an accustomed movement. Similarly, our intonation embodies our philosophy of life, what a person invariably says to himself about things. No doubt these characteristics did not belong only to these girls. They were those of their parents. The individual is steeped in something more general than himself. By this reckoning, our parents furnish us not only with those habitual gestures which are the outlines of our face and voice, but also with certain mannerisms of speech, certain favourite expressions, which, almost as unconscious as our intonation, almost as profound, indicate likewise a definite point of view towards life. It is true that in the case of girls there are certain of these expressions which their parents do not hand on to them until they have reached a certain age, as a rule not before they are women. They are kept in reserve. Thus, for instance, if one were to speak of the pictures of one of Elstir's friends, Andrée, whose hair was still "down," could not yet personally make use of the expression which her mother and elder sister employed: "It appears the *man* is quite charming!" But that would come in due course, when she was allowed to go to the Palais-Royal. And not long after her first communion, Albertine had begun to say, like a friend of her aunt: "It sounds to me pretty awful." She had also inherited the habit of making one repeat whatever one said to her, so as to appear to be interested, and to be trying to form an opinion of her own. If you said that an artist's work was good, or his house nice, "Oh, his painting's good, is it?" "Oh, his house is nice, is it?" Finally, and more general still than the family heritage, was the rich layer imposed by the native province from which they derived their voices and of which their inflexions smacked. When Andrée sharply plucked a solemn note she could not prevent the Périgordian string of her vocal instrument from giving back a resonant sound quite in harmony, moreover, with the meridional purity of her features; while to the incessant japing of Rosemonde the substance of her northern face and voice responded willy-nilly in the accent of her province. Between that province and the temperament of the girl that dictated these inflexions, I perceived a charming dialogue. A dialogue, not in any sense a discord. No discord can possibly separate a young girl and her native place. She is herself, and she is still it. Moreover this reaction of local materials on the genius who utilises them and to whose work it imparts an added vigour, does not make the work any less individual, and whether it be that of an architect, a cabinet-maker or a composer, it reflects no less minutely the most subtle shades of the artist's personality, because he has been compelled to work in the millstone of Senlis or the red sandstone of Strasbourg, has respected the knots peculiar to the ash-tree, has borne in mind, when writing his score, the resources and limits of the sonority and range of the flute and the viola.

All this I realised, and yet we talked so little! Whereas with Mme de Villeparisis or Saint-Loup I should have displayed by my words a great deal more pleasure than I should actually have felt, for I was worn out on leaving them, when, on the other hand, I was lying on the grass among these girls, the plenitude of what I felt infinitely outweighed the paucity, the infrequency of our speech, and brimmed over from my immobility and silence in waves of happiness that rippled up to die at the feet of these young roses.

For a convalescent who rests all day long in a flower-garden or an orchard, a scent of flowers or fruit does not more completely pervade the thousand trifles that compose his idle hours than did for me that colour, that fragrance in search of which my eyes kept straying towards the girls, and the sweetness of which finally became incorporated in me. So it is that grapes sweeten in the sun. And by their slow continuity these simple little games had gradually wrought in me also, as in those who do nothing else all day but lie outstretched by the sea, breathing the salt air and sunning themselves, a relaxation, a blissful smile, a vague dazzlement that had spread from brain to eyes.

Now and then a pretty attention from one or another of them would stir in me vibrations which dissipated for a time my desire for the rest. Thus one day Albertine suddenly asked: "Who has a pencil?" Andrée provided one,

Rosemonde the paper. Albertine warned them: "Now, young ladies, I forbid you to look at what I write." After carefully tracing each letter, supporting the paper on her knee, she passed it to me, saying: "Take care no one sees." Whereupon I unfolded it and read her message, which was: "I like you."

"But we mustn't sit here scribbling nonsense," she cried, turning with an impulsive and serious air to Andrée and Rosemonde, "I ought to show you the letter I got from Gisèle this morning. What an idiot I am; I've had it in my pocket all this time—and to think how useful it can be to us!"

Gisèle had been moved to copy out for her friend, so that it might be passed on to the others, the essay which she had written in her examination. Albertine's fears as to the difficulty of the subjects set had been more than justified by the two from which Gisèle had had to choose. The first was: "Sophocles, from the Shades, writes to Racine to console him for the failure of *Athalie*"; the other: "Suppose that, after the first performance of *Esther*, Mme de Sévigné is writing to Mme de La Fayette to tell her how much she regretted her absence." Now Gisèle, in an excess of zeal which must have touched the examiners' hearts, had chosen the first and more difficult of these two subjects, and had handled it with such remarkable skill that she had been given fourteen marks and had been congratulated by the board. She would have received a "distinction" if she had not "dried up" in the Spanish paper. The essay of which Gisèle had sent a copy to Albertine was immediately read aloud to us by the latter, who, having presently to take the same examination, was anxious to have Andrée's opinion, since she was by far the cleverest of them all and might be able to give her some good tips.

"She did have a bit of luck," Albertine observed. "It's the very subject her French mistress made her swot up while she was here."

The letter from Sophocles to Racine, as drafted by Gisèle, ran as follows:

"My dear friend, you must pardon me the liberty of addressing you when I have not the honour of your personal acquaintance, but your latest tragedy, *Athalie*, shows, does it not, that you have made a thorough study of my own modest works. You have not only put poetry in the mouths of the protagonists, or principal persons of the drama, but you have written other, and, let me tell you without flattery, charming verses for the chorus, a feature which did not work too badly, from what one hears, in Greek tragedy, but is a veritable novelty in France. In addition, your talent, so fluent, so dainty, so seductive, so fine, so delicate, has here acquired an energy on which I congratulate you. Athalie, Joad—these are figures which your rival Corneille could have wrought no better. The characters are virile, the plot simple and strong. You have given us a tragedy in which love is not the keynote, and on this I must offer you my sincerest compliments. The most familiar precepts are not always the truest. I will give you an example:

> This passion treat, which makes the poet's art
> Fly, as on wings, straight to the listener's heart.

You have shown us that the religious sentiment in which your chorus is steeped is no less capable of moving us. The general public may have been baffled, but true connoisseurs must give you your due. I have felt myself impelled to offer you all my congratulations, to which I would add, my dear brother poet, the expression of my very highest esteem."

Albertine's eyes never ceased to sparkle while she was reading this to us. "Really, you'd think she must have cribbed it somewhere!" she exclaimed when she reached the end. "I'd never have believed Gisèle could cook up an essay like that! And the poetry she brings in! Where on earth can she have pinched that from?"

Albertine's admiration, with a change, it is true, of object, but with no loss—an increase, rather—of intensity, combined with the closest attention to what was being said, continued to make her eyes "start from her head" all the time that Andrée (consulted as being the biggest and cleverest) first of all spoke of Gisèle's essay with a certain irony, then, with a levity of tone which failed to conceal her underlying seriousness, proceeded to reconstruct the letter in her own way.

"It's not bad," she said to Albertine, "but if I were you and had the the same subject set me, which is quite likely, as they set it very often, I shouldn't do it in that way. This is how I would tackle it. In the first place, if I had been Gisèle, I shouldn't have got carried away and I'd have begun by making a rough sketch of what I was going to write on a separate piece of paper. First and foremost, the formulation of the question and the exposition of the subject; then the general ideas to be worked into the development; finally, appreciation, style, conclusion. In that way, with a summary to refer to, you know where you are. But at the very start, with the exposition of the subject, or, if you like, Titine, since it's a letter, with the preamble, Gisèle has made a bloomer. Writing to a person of the seventeenth century, Sophocles ought never to have said 'My dear friend.' "

"Why, of course, she ought to have said 'My dear Racine,' " came impetuously from Albertine. "That would have been much better."

"No," replied Andrée, with a trace of mockery in her tone, "She ought to have put 'Sir.' In the same way, to end up, she ought to have thought of something like, 'Allow me, Sir,' (at the very most, 'Dear Sir') 'to inform you of the high esteem with which I have the honour to be your servant.' Then again, Gisèle says that the chorus in *Athalie* is a novelty. She is forgetting *Esther*, and two tragedies that are not much read now but happen to have been analysed this year by the teacher himself, so that you need only mention them, since they're his hobby-horse, and you're bound to pass. I mean *Les Juives* by Robert Garnier, and Montchrestien's *Aman*."

Andrée quoted these titles without managing quite to conceal a secret sense of benevolent superiority, which found expression in a rather charming smile. Albertine could contain herself no longer.

"Andrée, you really are staggering," she cried. "You must write down those names for me. Just fancy, what luck it would be if I got on to that, even in the oral, I should quote them at once and make a colossal impression."

But in the days that followed, every time that Albertine asked Andrée to tell her again the names of those two plays so that she might write them down, her erudite friend seemed to have forgotten them, and never recalled them for her.

"And another thing," Andrée went on with the faintest note of scorn for companions more childish than herself, though relishing their admiration and attaching to the manner in which she herself would have composed the essay a greater importance than she wished to reveal, "Sophocles in the Shades must be well-informed about all that goes on. He must therefore know that it was not before the general public but before the Sun King and a few privileged courtiers that *Athalie* was first played. What Gisèle says in this connexion of the esteem of the connoisseurs is not at all bad, but she might have gone a little further. Sophocles, now that he is immortal, may quite well have the gift of prophecy and announce that, according to Voltaire, *Athalie* will be the supreme achievement not only of Racine but of the human mind."

Albertine was drinking in every word. Her eyes blazed. And it was with the utmost indignation that she rejected Rosemonde's suggestion that they should have a game.

"Finally," Andrée concluded in the same detached, airy tone, a trifle mocking and at the same time fairly warmly convinced, "if Gisèle had first calmly noted down the general ideas that she was going to develop, it might perhaps have occurred to her to do what I myself should have done, point out what a difference there is between the religious inspiration of Racine's choruses and those of Sophocles. I should have made Sophocles remark that if Racine's choruses are impregnated with religious feeling like those of the Greek tragedians, the gods are not the same. The god of Joad has nothing in common with the god of Sophocles. And that brings us quite naturally, when we have finished developing the subject, to our conclusion: What does it matter if beliefs are different? Sophocles would hesitate to insist upon this point. He would be afraid of wounding Racine's convictions, and so, slipping in a few appropriate words on his masters at Port-Royal, he prefers to congratulate his disciple on the loftiness of his poetic genius."

Admiration and attention had made Albertine so hot that she was sweating profusely. Andrée preserved the unruffled calm of a female dandy. "It would not be a bad thing, either, to quote some of the opinions of famous critics," she added, before they began their game.

"Yes," put in Albertine, "so I've been told. The best ones to quote, on the whole, are Sainte-Beuve and Merlet, aren't they?"

"Well, you're not absolutely wrong," Andrée told her. "Merlet and Sainte-Beuve would do no harm. But above all you ought to mention Deltour and Gasq-Desfossés."

Meanwhile I had been thinking of the little page torn from a scribbling block which Albertine had handed me. "I like you," she had written. And an hour later, as I scrambled down the paths which led back, a little too vertically for my liking, to Balbec, I said to myself that it was with her that I would have my romance.

The state of being characterised by the presence of all the signs by which we are accustomed to recognise that we are in love, such as the orders which I left in the hotel not to wake me whoever might ask to see me, unless it were one or other of the girls, the throbbing of my heart while I waited for them (whichever of them it might be that I was expecting), and, on those mornings, my fury if I had not succeeded in finding a barber to shave me, and would make an unsightly appearance before Albertine, Rosemonde or Andrée, no doubt this state, recurring for each of them in turn, was as different from what we call love as is from human life the life of the zoophytes, in which existence, individuality if we may so term it, is divided up among several organisms. But natural history teaches us that such an organisation of animal life is indeed to be observed, and that our own life, provided we have outgrown the first phase, is no less positive as to the reality of states hitherto unsuspected by us through which we have to pass, even though we abandon them later. Such was for me this state of love divided among several girls at once. Divided, or rather undivided, for more often than not what was so delicious to me, different from the rest of the world, what was beginning to become so precious to me that the hope of encountering it again the next day was the greatest joy of my life, was rather the whole of the group of girls, taken as they were all together on those afternoons on the cliffs, during those wind-swept hours, upon the strip of grass on which were laid those forms, so exciting to my imagination, of Albertine, of Rosemonde, of Andrée; and that without my being able to say which of them it was that made those scenes so precious to me, which of them I most wanted to love. At the start of a new love as at its ending, we are not exclusively attached to the object of that love, but rather the desire to love from which it will presently arise (and, later on, the memory it leaves behind) wanders voluptuously through a zone of interchangeable charms—simply natural charms, it may be, gratification of appetite, enjoyment of one's surroundings—which are harmonious enough for it not to feel at a loss in the presence of any one of them. Besides, as my perception of them was not yet dulled by familiarity, I still had the faculty of seeing them, that is to say of feeling a profound astonishment every time that I found myself in their presence.

No doubt this astonishment is to some extent due to the fact that the other person on such occasions presents some new facet; but so great is the multiformity of each individual, so abundant the wealth of lines of face and body, so few of which leave any trace, once we are no longer in the presence of the other person, on the arbitrary simplicity of our recollection, since the memory has selected some distinctive feature that had struck us, has isolated it, exaggerated it, making of a woman who has appeared to us tall a sketch in which her figure is elongated out of all proportion, or of a woman who has seemed to be pink-cheeked and golden-haired a pure "Harmony in pink and gold," that the moment this woman is once again standing before us, all the other forgotten qualities which balance that one remembered feature at once assail us, in their confused complexity, diminishing her height, paling her cheeks, and substituting for what we came exclusively to seek other features which we remember having noticed the first time and fail to understand why we so little expected to find them again. We remembered, we anticipated a peacock, and we find a peony. And this inevitable astonishment is not the only one; for side by side with it comes another, born of the difference, not now between the stylisations of memory and the reality, but between the person whom we saw last time and the one who appears to us today from another angle and shows us a new aspect. The human face is indeed, like the face of the God of some oriental theogony, a whole cluster of faces juxtaposed on different planes so that one does not see them all at once.

But to a great extent our astonishment springs from the fact that the person presents to us also a face that is the same as before. It would require so immense an effort to reconstruct everything that has been imparted to us by things other than ourselves—were it only the taste of a fruit—that no sooner is the impression received than we begin imperceptibly to descend the slope of memory and, without realising it, in a very short time we have come a long way from what we actually felt. So that every fresh glimpse is a sort of rectification, which brings us back to what we in fact saw. Already we no longer had any recollection of it, to such an extent does what we call remembering a person consist really in forgetting him. But as long as we can still see, as soon as the forgotten feature appears we recognise it, we are obliged to correct the straying line, and thus the perpetual and fruitful surprise which made so salutary and invigorating for me these daily outings with the charming damsels of the sea shore consisted fully as much in recollection as in discovery. When there is added to this the agitation aroused by what these girls were to me, which was never quite what I had supposed, and meant that my expectancy of our next meeting resembled not so much my expectancy the time before as the still vibrant memory of our last encounter, it will be realised that each of our excursions brought about a violent change in the course of my thoughts and not at all in the direction which, in the solitude of my own room, I had traced for them at my leisure. That plotted course was forgotten, had ceased to exist, when I returned home buzzing like a bee-hive with remarks which had disturbed me and were still echoing in my brain. Every person is destroyed when we cease to see him; after which his next appearance is a new creation, different from that which immediately preceded it, if not from them all. For the minimum variation that is to be found in these creations is twofold. Remembering a strong and searching glance, a bold manner, it is inevitably, next time, by an almost languid profile, a sort of dreamy gentleness, overlooked by us in our previous impression, that at the next encounter we shall be astonished, that is to say almost uniquely struck. In confronting our memory with the new reality it is this that will mark the extent of our disappointment or surprise, will appear to us like a revised version of the reality by notifying us that we had not remembered correctly. In its turn, the facial aspect neglected the time before, and for that very reason the most striking this time, the most real, the most corrective, will become a matter for day-dreams and memories. It is a languorous and rounded profile, a gentle, dreamy expression which we shall now desire to see again. And then once more, next time, such resolution, such strength of character as there may be in the piercing eyes, the pointed nose, the tight lips, will come to correct the discrepancy between our desire and the object to which it has supposed itself to correspond. Of course, this fidelity to the first and purely physical impressions experienced anew at each encounter with my young friends did not only concern their facial appearance, since the reader has seen that I was sensitive also to their voices, more disturbing still, perhaps (for not only does a voice offer the same strange and sensuous surfaces as a face, it issues from that unknown, inaccessible region the mere thought of which sets the mind swimming with unattainable kisses), those voices, like the unique sound of a little instrument into which each of them put all of herself and which belonged to her alone. Traced by a casual inflexion, a sudden deep chord in one of these voices would surprise me when I recognised it after having forgotten it. So much so that the corrections which after every fresh meeting I was obliged to make so as to ensure absolute accuracy were as much those of a tuner or singing-master as of a draughtsman.

As for the harmonious cohesion into which, by the resistance that each brought to bear against the expansion of the others, the several waves of feeling induced in me by these girls had become neutralised, it was broken in Albertine's favour one afternoon when we were playing the game of "ferret."[14] It was in a little wood on the cliff. Stationed between two girls, strangers to the little band, whom the band had brought in its train because we wanted that day to have a bigger party than usual, I gazed enviously at Albertine's neighbour, a young man, saying to myself that if I had been in his place I could have been touching my beloved's hands during those unhoped-for moments which perhaps would never recur and which might have taken me a long way. Already, in itself, and even without the consequences which it would probably have involved, the contact of Albertine's hands would have been delicious to me. Not that I had never seen prettier hands than hers. Even in the group of her friends, those of Andrée, slender and far more delicate, had as it were a private life of their own, obedient to the commands of their mistress, but independent, and would often stretch out before her like thoroughbred greyhounds, with lazy pauses, languid reveries, sudden flexings of a finger-joint, seeing which Elstir had made a number of studies of these hands; and in one of them, in which Andrée was to be seen warming them at the fire, they had, with the light behind them, the golden diaphanousness of two autumn leaves. But, plumper than these, Albertine's hands would yield for a moment, then resist the pressure of the hand that clasped them, giving a sensation that was quite peculiar to themselves. The act of pressing Albertine's hand had a sensual sweetness which was in keeping somehow with the pink, almost mauve colouring of her skin. This pressure seemed to allow you to penetrate into the girl's being, to plumb the depths of her senses, like the ringing sound of her laughter, indecent in the way that the cooing of doves or certain animal cries can be. She was one of those women with whom shaking hands affords so much pleasure that one feels grateful to civilisation for having made of the handclasp a lawful act between boys and girls when they meet. If the arbitrary code of good manners had replaced the hand-shake by some other gesture, I should have gazed, day after day, at the untouchable hands of Albertine with a curiosity to know the feel of them as ardent as was my curiosity to learn the savour of her cheeks. But in the pleasure of holding her hand unrestrictedly in mine, had I been next to her at "ferret," I did not envisage that pleasure alone; what avowals, what declarations silenced hitherto by my bashfulness, I could have conveyed by certain pressures of hand on hand; for her part, how easy it would have been, in responding by other pressures, to show me that she accepted; what complicity, what a vista of sensual delight stood open! My love would be able to make more progress in a few minutes spent thus by her side than it had yet made in all the time that I had known her. Feeling that they would last but a short time, were rapidly nearing their end, since presumably we were not going on much longer with this game, and that once it was over it would be too late, I could not stay in my place for another moment. I let myself deliberately be caught with the ring, and, once in the middle, when the ring passed I pretended not to see it but followed its course with my eyes, waiting for the moment when it should come into the hands of the young man next to Albertine, who herself, convulsed with laughter, and in the excitement and pleasure of the game, was flushed pink. "Why, we really are in the Fairy Wood," said Andrée to me, pointing to the trees all round us, with a smile in her eyes which was meant only for me and seemed to pass over the heads of the other players, as though we two alone were intelligent and detached enough to make, in connexion with the game we were playing, a remark of a poetic nature. She even carried the delicacy of her fancy so far as to sing half-unconsciously: "The ferret of the Wood has passed this way, sweet ladies; he has passed by this way, the ferret of Fairy Wood!" like those people who cannot visit Trianon without getting up a party in Louis XVI costume, or think it amusing to have a song sung to its original setting. I should no doubt have been saddened not to see any charm in this realisation, had I had time to think about it. But my thoughts were all elsewhere. The players began to show surprise at my stupidity in never getting the ring. I was looking at Albertine, so pretty, so indifferent, so gay, who, though she little knew it, would be my neighbour when at last I should catch the ring in the right hands, thanks to a stratagem which she did not suspect, and would certainly have resented if she had. In the heat of the game her long hair had become loosened, and fell in curling locks over her cheeks on which it served to intensify, by its dry brownness, the carnation pink. "You have the tresses of Laura Dianti, of Eleanor of Guyenne, and of her descendant so beloved of Chateaubriand. You ought always to wear your hair half down like that," I murmured in her ear as an excuse for drawing close to her. Suddenly the ring passed to her neighbour. I sprang upon him at once, forced open his hands and seized it; he was obliged now to take my place inside the circle, while I took his beside Albertine. A few minutes earlier I had been envying this young man, when I saw that his hands as they slipped over the string were constantly brushing against hers. Now that my turn had come, too shy to seek, too agitated to savour this contact, I no longer felt anything but the rapid and painful beating of my heart. At one moment Albertine leaned her round pink face towards me with an air of complicity, pretending thus to have the ring in order to deceive the ferret and prevent him from looking in the direction in which it was being passed. I realised at once that it was to this ruse that the insinuations of Albertine's look applied, but I was excited to see thus kindle in her eyes the image—simulated purely for the purposes of the game—of a secret understanding between her and myself which did not exist but which from that moment seemed to me to be possible and would have been divinely sweet. While I was still enraptured by this thought, I felt a slight pressure of Albertine's hand against mine, and her caressing finger slip under my finger along the cord, and I saw her, at the same moment, give me a wink which she tried to make imperceptible to the others. At once, a multitude of hopes, invisible hitherto, crystallised within me. "She's taking advantage of the game to make it clear to me that she likes me," I thought to myself in a paroxysm of joy from which I instantly relapsed on hearing Albertine mutter furiously: "Why can't you take it? I've been shoving it at you for the last hour." Stunned with grief, I let go the cord, the ferret saw the ring and swooped down on it, and I had to go back into the middle, where I stood helpless, in despair, looking at the unbridled rout which continued to circle round me, stung by the jeers of all the players, obliged, in reply, to laugh when I had so little mind for laughter, while Albertine kept on repeating: "People shouldn't play if they won't pay attention and spoil the game for the others. We shan't ask him again when we're going to play, Andrée, or else I shan't come." Andrée, with a mind above the game, still chanting her "Fairy Wood" which, in a spirit of imitation, Rosemonde had taken up too, without conviction, sought to take my mind off Albertine's reproaches by saying to me: "We're quite close to those old Creuniers you wanted so much to see. Look, I'll take you there by a pretty little path, while these idiots play at eight-year-olds." Since Andrée was extremely nice to me, as we went along I said to her everything about Albertine that seemed calculated to endear me to the latter. Andrée replied that she too was very fond of Albertine, and thought her charming; nevertheless my compliments about her friend did not seem altogether to please her. Suddenly, in the little sunken path, I stopped short, touched to the heart by an exquisite memory of my childhood. I had just recognised, from the fretted and glossy leaves which it thrust out towards me, a hawthorn-bush, flowerless, alas, now that spring was over. Around me floated an atmosphere of far-off Months of Mary, of Sunday afternoons, of beliefs, of errors long since forgotten. I wanted to seize hold of it. I stood still for a moment, and Andrée, with a charming divination of what was in my mind, left me to converse with the leaves of the bush. I asked them for news of the flowers, those hawthorn flowers that were like merry little girls, headstrong, provocative, pious. "The young ladies have been gone from here for a long time now," the leaves told me. And perhaps they thought that, for the great friend of those young ladies that I pretended to be, I seemed to have singularly little knowledge of their habits. A great friend, but one who had never been to see them again for all these years, despite his promises. And yet, as Gilberte had been my first love among girls, so these had been my first love among flowers. "Yes, I know, they leave about the middle of June," I answered, "but I'm delighted to see the place where they lived when they were here. They came to see me at Combray, in my room; my mother brought them when I was ill in bed. And we used to meet again on Saturday evenings, at the Month of Mary devotions. Can they go to them here?" "Oh, of course! Why, they make a special point of having our young ladies at Saint-Denis du Désert, the church near here." "So if I want to see them now?" "Oh, not before May next year." "But can I be sure that they will be here?" "They come regularly every year." "Only I don't know whether I'll be able to find the place." "Oh, dear, yes! They are so gay, the young ladies, they stop laughing only to sing hymns together, so that you can't possibly miss them, you can recognise their scent from the other end of the path."

I caught up with Andrée, and began again to sing Albertine's praises. It was inconceivable to me that she would not repeat what I said in view of the emphasis I put into it. And yet I never heard that Albertine had been told. Andrée had, nevertheless, a far greater understanding of the things of the heart, a refinement of sweetness; finding the look, the word, the action that could most ingeniously give pleasure, keeping to herself a remark that might possibly cause pain, making a sacrifice (and making it as though it were no sacrifice at all) of an afternoon's play, or it might be an "at home" or a garden party, in order to stay with a friend who was feeling sad, and thus show him or her that she preferred the simple company of a friend to frivolous pleasures: such were her habitual kindnesses. But when one knew her a little better one would have said it was with her as with those heroic poltroons who wish not to be afraid and whose bravery is especially meritorious; one would have said that deep down in her nature there was none of that kindness which she constantly displayed out of moral distinction, or sensibility, or a noble desire to show herself a true friend. When I listened to all the charming things she said to me about a possible attachment between Albertine and myself it seemed as though she were bound to do everything in her power to bring it to pass. Whereas, by chance perhaps, not even of the slightest opportunity which she had at her command and which might have proved effective in uniting me to Albertine did she ever make use, and I would not swear that my effort to make myself loved by

Albertine did not—if not provoke in her friend secret stratagems calculated to thwart it—at any rate arouse in her an anger which however she took good care to hide and against which, out of delicacy of feeling, she may herself have fought. Of the countless refinements of affectionate kindness which Andrée showed, Albertine would have been incapable, and yet I was not certain of the underlying goodness of the former as I was to be later of the latter's. Showing herself always tenderly indulgent towards the exuberant frivolity of Albertine, Andrée greeted her with words and smiles that were those of a friend; better still, she acted towards her as a friend. I have seen her, day after day, in order to give this penniless friend the benefit of her own wealth, in order to make her happy, without any possibility of advantage to herself, take more pains than a courtier seeking to win his sovereign's favour. She was charmingly gentle and sympathetic, and spoke in sweet and sorrowful terms, when one expressed pity for Albertine's poverty, and took infinitely more trouble on her behalf than she would have taken for a rich friend. But if anyone were to hint that Albertine was perhaps not quite so poor as people made out, a just discernible cloud would overshadow Andrée's eyes and brow; she seemed out of temper. And if one went on to say that after all Albertine might perhaps be less difficult to marry off than people supposed, she would vehemently contradict one, repeating almost angrily: "Oh dear, no, she'll be quite unmarriageable! I'm certain of it, and I feel so sorry for her." As far as I myself was concerned, Andrée was the only one of the girls who would never have repeated to me anything at all disagreeable that might have been said about me by a third person; more than that, if it was I who told her what had been said she would make a pretence of not believing it, or would furnish some explanation which made the remark inoffensive. It is the aggregate of these qualities that goes by the name of tact. It is the attribute of those people who, if we fight a duel, congratulate us and add that there was no necessity to do so, in order to enhance still further in our own eyes the courage of which we have given proof without having been forced. They are the opposite of the people who in similar circumstances say: "It must have been a horrid nuisance for you to have to fight a duel, but on the other hand you couldn't possibly swallow an insult like that—there was nothing else to be done." But as there are pros and cons in everything, if the pleasure or at least the indifference shown by our friends in repeating something offensive that they have heard said about us proves that they do not exactly put themselves inside our skin at the moment of speaking, but thrust in the pin-point, turn the knife-blade as though it were gold-beater's skin and not human, the art of always keeping hidden from us what might be disagreeable to us in what they have heard said about our actions or in the opinion which those actions have led the speakers themselves to form, proves that there is in the other category of friends, in the friends who are so full of tact, a strong vein of dissimulation. It does no harm if indeed they are incapable of thinking ill of us, and if the ill that is said by other people only makes them suffer as it would make us. I supposed this to be the case with Andrée, without, however, being absolutely sure.

We had left the little wood and had followed a network of unfrequented paths through which Andrée managed to find her way with great skill. "Look," she said to me suddenly, "there are your famous Creuniers, and what's more you're in luck, it's just the time of day and the light is the same as when Elstir painted them." But I was still too wretched at having fallen, during the game of "ferret," from such a pinnacle of hopes. And so it was not with the pleasure which otherwise I should doubtless have felt that I suddenly discerned at my feet, crouching among the rocks for protection against the heat, the marine goddesses for whom Elstir had lain in wait and whom he had surprised there, beneath a dark glaze as lovely as Leonardo would have painted, the marvellous Shadows, sheltering furtively, nimble and silent, ready at the first glimmer of light to slip behind the stone, to hide in a cranny, and prompt, once the menacing ray had passed, to return to the rock or the seaweed over whose torpid slumbers they seemed to be keeping vigil, beneath the sun that crumbled the cliffs and the etiolated ocean, motionless lightfoot guardians darkening the water's surface with their viscous bodies and the attentive gaze of their deep blue eyes.

We went back to the wood to pick up the other girls and go home together. I knew now that I was in love with Albertine; but, alas! I did not care to let her know it. This was because, since the days of the games with Gilberte in the Champs-Elysées, my conception of love had become different, even if the persons to whom my love was successively assigned remained almost identical. For one thing, the avowal, the declaration of my passion to her whom I loved no longer seemed to be one of the vital and necessary stages of love, nor love itself an external reality, but simply a subjective pleasure. And I felt that Albertine would do what was necessary to sustain that pleasure all the more readily if she did not know that I was experiencing it.

As we walked home, the image of Albertine, bathed in the light that streamed from the other girls, was not the only one that existed for me. But as the moon, which is no more than a tiny white cloud of a more definite and fixed shape than other clouds during the day, assumes its full power as soon as daylight fades, so when I was once more in the hotel it was Albertine's sole image that rose from my heart and began to shine. My room seemed to me to have become suddenly a new place. Of course, for a long time past, it had not been the hostile room of my first night in it. All our lives, we go on patiently modifying the surroundings in which we live; and gradually, as habit dispenses us from feeling them, we suppress the noxious elements of colour, shape and smell which objectified our uneasiness. Nor was it any longer the room, still with sufficient power over my sensibility, not certainly to make me suffer, but to give me joy, the well of summer days, like a marble basin in which, half-way up its polished sides, they mirrored an azure surface steeped in light over which glided for an instant, impalpable and white as a wave of heat, the fleeting reflexion of a cloud; nor the purely aesthetic room of the pictorial evening hours; it was the room in which I had been now for so many days that I no longer saw it. And now I was beginning again to open my eyes to it, but this time from the selfish angle which is that of love. I liked to feel that the fine slanting mirror, the handsome glass-fronted bookcases, would give Albertine, if she came to see me, a good impression of me. Instead of a place of transit in which I would stay for a few minutes before escaping to the beach or to Rivebelle, my room became real and dear to me again, fashioned itself anew, for I looked at and appreciated each article of its furniture with the eyes of Albertine.

A few days after the game of "ferret," when, having allowed ourselves to wander rather too far afield, we had been fortunate in finding at Maineville a couple of little "governess-carts" with two seats in each which would enable us to be back in time for dinner, the intensity, already considerable, of my love for Albertine had the effect of making me suggest successively that Andrée and Rosemonde should come with me, and never once Albertine, and then, while still inviting Andrée or Rosemonde for preference, of bringing everyone round, in virtue of secondary considerations connected with time, route, coats and so forth, to decide, as though against my wishes, that the most practical policy after all was that I should take Albertine, to whose company I pretended to resign myself willy-nilly. Unfortunately, since love tends to the complete assimilation of a person, and none is comestible by way of conversation alone, for all that Albertine was as nice as possible on our way home, when I had deposited her at her own door she left me happy but more famished for her even than I had been at the start, and reckoning the moments that we had just spent together as only a prelude, of little importance in itself, to those that were still to come. Nevertheless it had that initial charm which is not to be found again. I had not yet asked anything of Albertine. She could imagine what I wanted, but, not being certain of it, surmise that I was aiming only at relations with no precise objective, in which my beloved would find that delicious vagueness, rich in expected surprises, which is romance.

In the week that followed I scarcely attempted to see Albertine. I made a show of preferring Andrée. Love is born; we wish to remain, for the one we love, the unknown person whom she may love in turn, but we need her, we need to make contact not so much with her body as with her attention, her heart. We slip into a letter some unkind remark which will force the indifferent one to ask for some little kindness in compensation, and love, following an infallible technique, tightens up with an alternating movement the cog-wheels in which we can no longer not love or be loved. I gave to Andrée the hours spent by the others at a party which I knew that she would sacrifice for my sake with pleasure, and would have sacrificed even with reluctance, from moral nicety, in order not to give either the others or herself the idea that she attached any importance to a relatively frivolous amusement. I arranged in this way to have her entirely to myself every evening, not with the intention of making Albertine jealous, but of enhancing my prestige in her eyes, or at any rate not imperilling it by letting Albertine know that it was herself and not Andrée that I loved. Nor did I confide this to Andrée either, lest she should repeat it to her friend. When I spoke of Albertine to Andrée I affected a coldness by which she was perhaps less deceived than I, from her apparent credulity. She made a show of believing in my indifference to Albertine, and of desiring the closest possible union between Albertine and myself. It is probable that, on the contrary, she neither believed in the one nor wished for the other. While I was saying to her that I did not care very greatly for her friend, I was thinking of one thing only, how to become acquainted with Mme Bontemps, who was staying for a few days near Balbec, and whom Albertine was shortly to visit for a few days. Naturally I did not disclose this desire to Andrée, and when I spoke to her of Albertine's family, it was in the most careless manner possible. Andrée's direct answers did not appear to throw any doubt on my sincerity. Why then did she blurt out suddenly one day: "Oh, by the way, I happen to have seen Albertine's aunt"? It is true that she had not said in so many words: "I could see through your casual remarks all right that the one thing you were really thinking of was how you could get to know Albertine's aunt." But it was clearly to the presence in Andrée's mind of some such idea which she felt it more becoming to keep from me that the phrase "happen to" seemed to point. It was of a kind with certain glances, certain gestures which, although they have no logical rational form directly devised for the listener's intelligence, reach him nevertheless in their true meaning, just as human speech, converted into electricity in the telephone, is turned into speech again when it strikes the ear. In order to remove from Andrée's mind the idea that I was interested in Mme Bontemps, I spoke of her thenceforth not only absent-mindedly but with downright malice, saying that I had once met that idiot of a woman, and trusted I should never have that experience again. Whereas I was seeking by every means in my power to meet her.

I tried to induce Elstir (but without mentioning to anyone else that I had asked him) to speak to her about me and to bring us together. He promised to introduce me to her, though he seemed greatly surprised at my wishing it, for he regarded her as a contemptible woman, a born intriguer, as uninteresting as she was self-interested. Reflecting that if I did see Mme Bontemps, Andrée would be sure to hear of it sooner or later, I thought it best to warn her in advance. "The things one tries hardest to avoid are those one finds one cannot escape," I told her. "Nothing in the world could bore me so much as meeting Mme Bontemps again, and yet I can't get out of it. Elstir has arranged to invite us together." "I've never doubted it for a single instant," exclaimed Andrée in a bitter tone, while her eyes, enlarged and altered by her annoyance, focused themselves upon some invisible object. These words of Andrée's were not the most reasoned statement of a thought which might be expressed thus: "I know that you're in love with Albertine, and that you're moving heaven and earth to get to know her family." But they were the shapeless fragments, capable of reconstitution, of that thought which I had caused to explode, by striking it, against Andrée's will. Like her "happen to," these words had no meaning save at one remove, that is to say they were words of the sort which (rather than direct assertions) inspire in us respect or distrust for another person, and lead to a rupture.

If Andrée had not believed me when I told her that Albertine's family left me indifferent, it was because she thought that I was in love with Albertine. And probably she was none too happy in the thought.

She was generally present as a third party at my meetings with her friend. There were however days when I was to see Albertine by herself, days to which I looked forward with feverish impatience, which passed without bringing me any decisive result, without any of them having been that cardinal day whose role I immediately entrusted to the following day, which would prove no more apt to play it; thus there rose and toppled one after another, like waves, those peaks at once replaced by others.

About a month after the day on which we had played "ferret" together, I learned that Albertine was going away next morning to spend a couple of days with Mme Bontemps, and, since she would have to take an early train, was coming to spend the night at the Grand Hotel, from which, by taking the omnibus, she would be able, without disturbing the friends with whom she was staying, to catch the first train in the morning. I mentioned this to Andrée. "I don't believe a word of it," she replied with a look of annoyance. "Anyhow it won't help you at all, for I'm quite sure Albertine won't want to see you if she goes to the hotel by herself. It would be against 'protocol,'" she added, employing an expression which had recently come into favour with her, in the sense of "what is done." "I tell you this because I understand Albertine. What difference do you suppose it makes to me whether you see her or not? Not the slightest, I can assure you!"

We were joined by Octave who had no hesitation in telling Andrée the number of strokes he had gone round in, the day before, at golf, then by Albertine, who came along swinging her diabolo like a nun her rosary. Thanks to this pastime she could remain alone for hours on end without getting bored. As soon as she joined us I became conscious of the impish tip of her nose, which I had omitted from my mental picture of her during the last few days; beneath her dark hair the vertical line of her forehead controverted—and not for the first time—the blurred image that I had preserved of her, while its whiteness made a vivid splash in my field of vision; emerging from the dust of memory, Albertine was built up afresh before my eyes.

Golf gives one a taste for solitary pleasures. The pleasure to be derived from diabolo is undoubtedly one of these. And yet, after she had joined us, Albertine continued to play with it, just as a lady on whom friends have come to call does not on their account stop working at her crochet. "I gather that Mme de Villeparisis," she remarked to Octave, "has been complaining to your father." (I could hear, underlying the "I gather," one of those notes that were peculiar to Albertine; every time I realised that I had forgotten them, I would remember having already caught a glimpse behind them of Albertine's determined and Gallic mien. I could have been blind and yet have detected certain of her qualities, alert and slightly provincial, in those notes just as plainly as in the tip of her nose. They were equivalent and might have been substituted for one another, and her voice was like what we are promised in the photo-telephone of the future: the visual image was clearly outlined in the sound.) "She hasn't written only to your father, either, she wrote to the Mayor of Balbec at the same time, to say that we must stop playing diabolo on the front as somebody hit her in the face with a ball."

"Yes, I was hearing about that," said Octave. "It's ridiculous. There's little enough to do here as it is."

Andrée did not join in the conversation; she was not acquainted, any more than was Albertine or Octave, with Mme de Villeparisis. She did, however, remark: "I can't think why this lady should make such a song about it.

Old Mme de Cambremer got hit in the face, and she never complained."

"I'll explain the difference," replied Octave gravely, striking a match as he spoke. "It's my belief that Mme de Cambremer is a society lady, and Mme de Villeparisis is just an upstart. Are you playing golf this afternoon?" And he left us, followed by Andrée. I was alone now with Albertine. "You see," she began, "I'm wearing my hair now the way you like—look at my ringlet. They all laugh at it and nobody knows who I'm doing it for. My aunt will laugh at me too. But I shan't tell her why, either." I had a sidelong view of Albertine's cheeks, which often appeared pale, but, seen thus, were flushed with unclouded blood which lighted them up, gave them that brightness of certain winter mornings when the stones catching the sun seem blocks of pink granite and radiate joy. The joy I felt at this moment at the sight of Albertine's cheeks was as keen, but led to another desire which was not the desire for a walk but for a kiss. I asked her if the report of her plans which I had heard was correct. "Yes," she told me, "I shall be sleeping at your hotel tonight, and in fact as I've got a bit of a cold I shall be going to bed before dinner. You can come and sit by my bed and watch me eat, if you like, and afterwards we'll play at anything that you choose. I should have liked you to come to the station tomorrow morning, but I'm afraid it might look rather odd, I don't say to Andrée who is a sensible person, but to the others who will be there; if my aunt got to know, I should never hear the last of it. But we can spend the evening together, at any rate. My aunt will know nothing about that. I must go and say good-bye to Andrée. Till we meet again then. Come early, so that we can have a nice long time together," she added, smiling.

At these words I was swept back past the days when I loved Gilberte to those when love seemed to me not simply an external entity but one that could be realised. Whereas the Gilberte whom I used to see in the Champs-Elysées was a different Gilberte from the one I found within me when I was alone again, suddenly in the real Albertine, the one I saw every day, whom I supposed to be stuffed with middle-class prejudices and entirely frank with her aunt, the imaginary Albertine had just been embodied, she whom, when I did not yet know her, I had suspected of casting furtive glances at me on the front, she who had worn an air of being reluctant to go home when she saw me making off in the other direction.

I went into dinner with my grandmother. I felt within me a secret which she could never guess. Similarly with Albertine; tomorrow her friends would be with her, not knowing what new experience she and I had in common; and when she kissed her niece on the forehead Mme Bontemps would never imagine that I stood between them, in the shape of that hair arrangement which had for its object, concealed from all the world, to give pleasure to me, to me who had until then so greatly envied Mme Bontemps because, being related to the same people as her niece, she had the same occasions to put on mourning, the same family visits to pay; and now I found myself being more to Albertine than was the aunt herself. When she was with her aunt, it was of me that she would be thinking. What was going to happen that evening, I scarcely knew. In any event, the Grand Hotel and the evening no longer seemed empty to me; they contained my happiness. I rang for the lift-boy to take me up to the room which Albertine had engaged, a room that looked over the valley. The slightest movements, such as that of sitting down on the bench in the lift, were sweet to me, because they were in direct relation to my heart; I saw in the ropes that drew the cage upwards, in the few stairs that I had still to climb, only the machinery, the materialised stages of my joy. I now had only two or three steps to take along the corridor before coming to that room in which was enshrined the precious substance of that rosy form—that room which, even if there were to be done in it delicious things, would keep that air of changelessness, of being, to a chance visitor who knew nothing of its history, just like any other room, which makes of inanimate things the obstinately mute witnesses, the scrupulous confidants, the inviolable depositaries of our pleasure. Those few steps from the landing to Albertine's door, those few steps which no one could stop, I took with rapture but with prudence, as though plunged in a new and strange element, as if in going forward I had been gently displacing a liquid stream of happiness, and at the same time with a strange feeling of omnipotence, and of entering at last into an inheritance which had belonged to me from time immemorial. Then suddenly I reflected that I was wrong to be in any doubt; she had told me to come when she was in bed. It was as clear as daylight; I pranced for joy, I nearly knocked over Françoise who was standing in my way, and I ran, with sparkling eyes, towards my beloved's room.

I found Albertine in bed. Leaving her throat bare, her white nightdress altered the proportions of her face, which, flushed by being in bed or by her cold or by dinner, seemed pinker; I thought of the colours I had had beside me a few hours earlier on the front, the savour of which I was now at last to taste; her cheek was traversed by one of those long, dark, curling tresses which, to please me, she had undone altogether. She looked at me and smiled. Beyond her, through the window, the valley lay bright beneath the moon. The sight of Albertine's bare throat, of those flushed cheeks, had so intoxicated me (that is to say had so shifted the reality of the world for me away from nature into the torrent of my sensations which I could scarcely contain), that it had destroyed the equilibrium between the immense and indestructible life which circulated in my being and the life of the universe, so puny in comparison. The sea, which was visible through the window as well as the valley, the swelling breasts of the first of the Maineville cliffs, the sky in which the moon had not yet climbed to the zenith—all this seemed less than a featherweight on my eyeballs, which between their lids I could feel dilated, resistant, ready to bear far greater burdens, all the mountains of the world, upon their fragile surface. Their orb no longer found even the sphere of the horizon adequate to fill it. And all the life-giving energy that nature could have brought me would have seemed to me all too meagre, the breathing of the sea all too short to express the immense aspiration that was swelling my breast. I bent over Albertine to kiss her. Death might have struck me down in that moment and it would have seemed to me a trivial, or rather an impossible thing, for life was not outside me but in me; I should have smiled pityingly had a philosopher then expressed the idea that some day, even some distant day, I should have to die, that the eternal forces of nature would survive me, the forces of that nature beneath whose godlike feet I was no more than a grain of dust; that, after me, there would still remain those rounded, swelling cliffs, that sea, that moonlight and that sky! How could it have been possible; how could the world have lasted longer than myself, since I was not lost in its vastness, since it was the world that was enclosed in me, in me whom it fell far short of filling, in me who, feeling that there was room to store so many other treasures, flung sky and sea and cliffs contemptuously into a corner. "Stop it or I'll ring the bell!" cried Albertine, seeing that I was flinging myself upon her to kiss her. But I told myself that not for nothing does a girl invite a young man to her room in secret, arranging that her aunt should not know, and that boldness, moreover, rewards those who know how to seize their opportunities; in the state of exaltation in which I was, Albertine's round face, lit by an inner flame as by a night-light, stood out in such relief that, imitating the rotation of a glowing sphere, it seemed to me to be turning, like those Michelangelo figures which are being swept away in a stationary and vertiginous whirlwind. I was about to discover the fragrance, the flavour which this strange pink fruit concealed. I heard a sound, abrupt, prolonged and shrill. Albertine had pulled the bell with all her might.

I had supposed that my love for Albertine was not based on the hope of carnal possession. And yet, when the lesson to be drawn from my experience that evening was, apparently, that such possession was impossible; when, after having had no doubt, that first day on the beach, that Albertine was licentious, and having passed through various intermediate assumptions, it seemed to me to be established that she was absolutely virtuous; when on her return from her aunt's a week later, she greeted me coldly with: "I forgive you; in fact I'm sorry to have upset you, but you must never do it again"—then in contrast to what I had felt on learning from Bloch that one could have all the women one wanted, and as if, instead of a real girl, I had known a wax doll, my desire to penetrate into her life, to follow her through the places in which she had spent her childhood, to be initiated by her into the sporting life, gradually detached itself from her; my intellectual curiosity as to thoughts on this subject or that did not survive my belief that I might kiss her if I chose. My dreams abandoned her as soon as they ceased to be nourished by the hope of a possession of which I had supposed them to be independent. Thenceforward they found themselves once more at liberty to transfer themselves—according to the attraction that I had found in her on any particular day, above all according to the chances I seemed to detect of my being possibly loved by her—to one or other of Albertine's friends, and to Andrée first of all. And yet, if Albertine had not existed, perhaps I should not have had the pleasure which I began to feel more and more strongly during the days that followed in the kindness that was shown me by Andrée. Albertine told no one of the rebuff which I had received at her hands. She was one of those pretty girls who, from their earliest youth, on account of their beauty, but especially of an attraction, a charm which remains somewhat mysterious and has its source perhaps in reserves of vitality to which others less favoured by nature come to quench their thirst, have always—in their home circle, among their friends, in society—been more sought after than other more beautiful and richer girls; she was one of those people from whom, before the age of love and much more still after it is reached, more is asked than they themselves ask, more even than they are able to give. From her childhood Albertine had always had round her in an adoring circle four or five little girl friends, among them Andrée who was so far her superior and knew it (and perhaps this attraction which Albertine exerted quite involuntarily had been the origin, had laid the foundations of the little band). This attraction was still potent even at a great social distance, in circles quite brilliant by comparison, where, if there was a pavane to be danced, Albertine would be sent for rather than another girl of better family. The consequence was that, not having a penny to her name, living, not very well, at the expense of M. Bontemps who was said to be a shady individual and was anyhow anxious to be rid of her, she was nevertheless invited, not only to dine but to stay, by people who in Saint-Loup's eyes might not have had much distinction, but to Rosemonde's mother or Andrée's, women who though very rich themselves did not know these people, represented something quite extraordinary. Thus Albertine spent a few weeks every year with the family of one of the Governors of the Bank of France, who was also Chairman of the Board of Directors of a railway company. The wife of this financier entertained prominent people, and had never mentioned her "day" to Andrée's mother, who thought her wanting in politeness, but was nevertheless prodigiously interested in everything that went on in her house. Accordingly she encouraged Andrée every year to invite Albertine down to their villa, because, she said, it was a charitable act to offer a holiday by the sea to a girl who had not herself the means to travel and whose aunt did so little for her. Andrée's mother was probably not prompted by the thought that the banker and his wife, learning that Albertine was made much of by her and her daughter, would form a high opinion of them both; still less did she hope that Albertine, kind and clever as she was, would manage to get her invited, or at least to get Andrée invited, to the financier's garden-parties. But every evening at the dinner-table, while assuming an air of indifference and disdain, she was fascinated by Albertine's accounts of everything that had happened at the big house while she was staying there, and the names of the other guests, almost all of them people whom she knew by sight or by name. Even the thought that she knew them only in this indirect fashion, that is to say did not know them at all (she called this kind of acquaintance knowing people "all my life"), gave Andrée's mother a touch of melancholy while she plied Albertine with questions about them in a lofty and distant tone, with pursed lips, and might have left her doubtful and uneasy as to the importance of her own social position had she not been able to reassure herself, to return safely to the "realities of life," by saying to the butler: "Please tell the chef that his peas aren't soft enough." She then recovered her serenity. And she was quite determined that Andrée was to marry nobody but a man, of the best family of course, rich enough for her too to be able to keep a chef and a couple of coachmen. That was the reality, the practical proof of "position." But the fact that Albertine had dined at the banker's country house with this or that great lady, and that the said great lady had invited her to stay with her next winter, invested the girl, in the eyes of Andrée's mother, with a peculiar esteem which went very well with the pity and even contempt aroused by her lack of fortune, a contempt increased by the fact that M. Bontemps had betrayed his flag and—being even vaguely Panamist, it was said—had rallied to the Government. Not that this deterred Andrée's mother, in her passion for abstract truth, from withering with her scorn the people who appeared to believe that Albertine was of humble origin. "What's that you say? Why, they're one of the best families in the country. Simonet with a single 'n,' you know!" Certainly, in view of the class of society in which all this went on, in which money plays so important a part, and mere charm makes people ask you out but not marry you, an "acceptable" marriage did not appear to be for Albertine a practical outcome of the so distinguished patronage which she enjoyed but which would not have been held to compensate for her poverty. But even in themselves, and with no prospect of any matrimonial consequence, Albertine's "successes" excited the envy of certain spiteful mothers, furious at seeing her received "like one of the family" by the banker's wife, even by Andrée's mother, whom they scarcely knew. They therefore went about telling mutual friends of theirs and of those two ladies that the latter would be very angry if they knew the truth, which was that Albertine repeated to each of them everything that the intimacy to which she was rashly admitted enabled her to spy out in the household of the other, countless little secrets which it must be infinitely unpleasant to the interested party to have made public. These envious women said this so that it might be repeated and might get Albertine into trouble with her patrons. But, as often happens, their machinations met with no success. The spite that prompted them was too apparent, and their only result was to make the women who had perpetrated them appear rather more contemptible than before. Andrée's mother was too firm in her opinion of Albertine to change her mind about her now. She looked upon her as "unfortunate," but the best-natured girl living, and one who was incapable of making anything up except to give pleasure.

If this sort of popularity to which Albertine had attained did not seem likely to lead to any practical result, it had stamped Andrée's friend with the distinctive characteristic of people who, being always sought after, have never any need to offer themselves, a characteristic (to be found also, and for analogous reasons, at the other end of the social scale, among the smartest women) which consists in their not making any display of the successes they have scored, but rather keeping them to themselves. She would never say of anyone: "So-and-so is anxious to meet me," would speak of everyone with the greatest good nature, and as if it was she who ran after, who sought to know other people. If someone mentioned a young man who, a few minutes earlier, had been in private conversation with her, heaping the bitterest reproaches upon her because she had refused him an assignation, so far from proclaiming this in public or betraying any resentment she would stand up for him: "He's such a nice boy!" Indeed it quite annoyed her to be so attractive to people, since it obliged her to disappoint them, whereas her natural instinct was always to give pleasure. So much did she enjoy giving pleasure that she had come to employ a particular kind of falsehood peculiar to certain utilitarians and men who have "arrived." Existing, incidentally, in an embryonic state in a vast number of people, this form of insincerity consists in not being able to confine the pleasure arising out of a single act of politeness to a single person. For instance, if Albertine's aunt wished her niece to accompany her to a not very amusing party, Albertine by going to it might have found it sufficient to extract from the incident the moral profit of having given pleasure to her aunt. But, being courteously welcomed by her host and hostess, she preferred to say to them that she had been wanting to see them for so long that she had finally seized this opportunity and begged her aunt to take her to their party. Even this was not enough: at the same party there might happen to be one of Albertine's friends who was very unhappy. Albertine would say to her: "I didn't like the thought of your being here by yourself. I felt it might do you good to have me with you. If you would rather leave the party, go somewhere else, I'm ready to do anything you like. What I want above all is to see you look less unhappy" (which, as it happened, was true also). Sometimes it happened however that the fictitious aim destroyed the real one. Thus Albertine, having a favour to ask on behalf of one of her friends, would go to see a certain lady who could help her. But on arriving at the house of this lady—a kind and sympathetic soul—the girl, unconsciously following the principle of the multiple utilisation of a single action, would think it more affectionate to appear to have come there solely on account of the pleasure she knew she would derive from seeing the lady again. The lady would be deeply touched that Albertine should have taken a long journey out of pure friendship. Seeing her almost overcome by emotion, Albertine liked the lady even more. Only, there was this awkward consequence: she now felt so keenly the pleasure of friendship which she pretended to have been her motive in coming, that she was afraid of making the lady suspect the genuineness of sentiments which were actually quite sincere if she now asked her to do the favour for her friend. The lady would think that Albertine had come for that purpose, which was true, but would conclude also that Albertine had no disinterested pleasure in seeing her, which was false. With the result that she came away without having asked the favour, like a man sometimes who has been so kind to a woman, in the hope of winning her favours, that he refrains from declaring his passion in order not to deprive his kindness of its appearance of nobility. In other instances it would be wrong to say that the true object was sacrificed to the subordinate and subsequently conceived idea, but the two were so incompatible that if the person to whom Albertine endeared herself by stating the second had known of the existence of the first, her pleasure would at once have been turned into the deepest pain. At a much later point in this story, we shall have occasion to see this kind of contradiction expressed in clearer terms. Suffice it to say for the present, borrowing an example from a completely different context, that they occur very frequently in the most divergent situations that life has to offer. A husband has established his mistress in the town where he is quartered with his regiment. His wife, left by herself in Paris, and with an inkling of the truth, grows more and more miserable, and writes her husband letters embittered by jealousy. Then the mistress is obliged to go to Paris for the day. The husband cannot resist her entreaties to him to accompany her, and applies for a twenty-four-hour leave. But since he is a good-natured fellow, and hates making his wife unhappy, he goes to see her and tells her, shedding a few quite genuine tears, that, dismayed by her letters, he has found the means of getting away from his duties to come to her and to console her in his arms. He has thus contrived by a single journey to furnish wife and mistress alike with proofs of his love. But if the wife were to learn the reason for which he has come to Paris, her joy would doubtless be turned into grief, unless her pleasure in seeing the faithless wretch outweighed, in spite of everything, the pain that his infidelities had caused her. Among the men who have struck me as practising most consistently this system of killing several birds with one stone must be included M. de Norpois. He would now and then agree to act as intermediary between two of his friends who had quarrelled, and this led to his being called the most obliging of men. But it was not sufficient for him to appear to be doing a service to the friend who had come to him to request it; he would represent to the other the steps which he was taking to effect a reconciliation as undertaken not at the request of the first friend but in the interest of the second, a notion of which he never had any difficulty in persuading an interlocutor influenced in advance by the idea that he had before him the "most obliging of men." In this way, playing both ends against the middle, what in stage parlance is known as "doubling" two parts, he never allowed his influence to be in the slightest degree imperilled, and the services which he rendered constituted not an expenditure of capital but a dividend upon some part of his credit. At the same time every service, seemingly rendered twice over, correspondingly enhanced his reputation as an obliging friend, and, better still, a friend whose interventions were efficacious, one who did not simply beat the air, whose efforts were always justified by success, as was shown by the gratitude of both parties. This duplicity in obligingness was—allowing for disappointments such as are the lot of every human being—an important element in M. de Norpois's character. And often at the Ministry he would make use of my father, who was a simple soul, while making him believe that it was he, M. de Norpois, who was being useful to my father.

Pleasing people more easily than she wished, and having no need to trumpet her conquests abroad, Albertine kept silent about the scene she had had with me by her bedside, which a plain girl would have wished the whole world to know. And yet for her attitude during that scene I could not arrive at any satisfactory explanation. As regards the supposition that she was absolutely chaste (a supposition to which I had first of all attributed the violence with which Albertine had refused to let herself be taken in my arms and kissed, though it was by no means essential to my conception of the kindness, the fundamentally honourable character of my beloved), I could not accept it without a copious revision of its terms. It ran so entirely counter to the hypothesis which I had constructed that day when I saw Albertine for the first time. Then, so many different acts of affectionate sweetness towards myself (a sweetness that was caressing, at times uneasy, alarmed, jealous of my predilection for Andrée) came up on all sides to challenge the brutal gesture with which, to escape from me, she had pulled the bell.

Why then had she invited me to come and spend the evening by her bedside? Why did she speak all the time in the language of affection? What is the basis of the desire to see a friend, to be afraid that he may be fonder of someone else than of you, to seek to please him, to tell him, so romantically, that no one else will ever know that he has spent the evening in your room, if you refuse him so simple a pleasure and if it is no pleasure to you? I could not believe, after all, that Albertine's virtue went as far as that, and I came to wonder whether her violence might not have been due to some reason of vanity, a disagreeable odour, for instance, which she suspected of lingering about her person, and by which she was afraid that I might be repelled, or else of cowardice—if for instance she imagined, in her ignorance of the facts of love, that my state of nervous debility was due to something contagious, communicable to her in a kiss.

She was genuinely distressed by her failure to gratify me, and gave me a little gold pencil, with the virtuous perverseness of people who, touched by your kindness but not prepared to grant what it clamours for, nevertheless want to do something on your behalf—the critic, an article from whose pen would so gratify the novelist, who asks him to dinner instead; the duchess who does not take the snob with her to the theatre but lends him her box on an evening when she will not be using it herself. To such an extent are those who do the minimum, and might easily do nothing, driven by conscience to do something!

I told Albertine that in giving me this pencil she was giving me great pleasure, and yet not so great as I should have felt if, on the night she had spent at the hotel, she had permitted me to kiss her: "It would have made me so happy! What possible harm could it have done you? I'm amazed that you should have refused me."

"What amazes me," she retorted, "is that you should find it amazing. I wonder what sort of girls you must know if my behaviour surprised you."

"I'm sorry to have annoyed you, but even now I cannot say that I think I was in the wrong. What I feel is that all that sort of thing is of no importance really, and I can't understand a girl who could so easily give pleasure not consenting to do so. Let's be quite clear about it," I went on, throwing a sop of sorts to her moral scruples as I recalled how she and her friends had scarified the girl who went about with the actress Léa, "I don't mean to say that a girl can behave exactly as she likes and that there's no such thing as immorality. Take, for example, what you were saying the other day about a girl who's staying at Balbec and her relations with an actress. I call that unspeakable, so unspeakable that I feel sure it must all have been made up by some enemies of the girl and that there can't be any truth in the story. It strikes me as improbable, impossible. But to allow oneself to be kissed, or even more, by a friend—since you say that I'm your friend . . ."

"So you are, but I've had other friends before now, I've known lots of young men who were every bit as friendly, I can assure you. Well, not one of them would ever have dared to do such a thing. They know they'd get their ears boxed if they tried it on. Besides, they never dreamed of doing so. We would shake hands in a straightforward, friendly sort of way, like good pals, but there was never a word said about kissing, and yet we weren't any the less friends for that. Why, if it's my friendship you're after, you've nothing to complain of; I must be jolly fond of you to forgive you. But I'm sure you don't care two hoots about me, really. Own up now, it's Andrée you're in love with. Besides, you're quite right; she's ever so much nicer than I am, and absolutely ravishing! Oh, you men!"

Despite my recent disappointment, these words so frankly uttered, by giving me a great respect for Albertine, made a very agreeable impression on me. And perhaps this impression was to have serious and vexatious consequences for me later on, for it was around it that there began to form that feeling almost of brotherly intimacy, that moral core which was always to remain at the heart of my love for Albertine. Such a feeling may be the cause of the greatest suffering. For in order really to suffer at the hands of a woman one must have believed in her completely. For the moment, that embryo of moral esteem, of friendship, was left embedded in my soul like a stepping-stone in a stream. It could have availed nothing, by itself, against my happiness if it had remained there without growing, in an inertia which it was to retain the following year, and still more during the final weeks of this first visit to Balbec. It dwelt in me like one of those foreign bodies which it would be wiser when all is said to expel, but which we leave where they are without disturbing them, so harmless for the present does their weakness, their isolation amid a strange environment render them.

My longings were now once more at liberty to concentrate on one or another of Albertine's friends, and returned first of all to Andrée, whose attentions might perhaps have touched me less had I not been certain that they would come to Albertine's ears. Undoubtedly the preference that I had long pretended to feel for Andrée had furnished me—in habits of conversation and declarations of affection—with, so to speak, the material for a ready-made love for her which had hitherto lacked only the complement of a genuine feeling, which my heart, being once more free, was now in a position to supply. But Andrée was too intellectual, too neurotic, too sickly, too like myself for me really to love her. If Albertine now seemed to me to be void of substance, Andrée was filled with something which I knew only too well. I had thought, that first day, that what I saw on the beach was the mistress of some racing cyclist, passionately interested in sport, and now Andrée told me that if she had taken it up, it was on orders from her doctor, to cure her neurasthenia, her digestive troubles, but that her happiest hours were those which she spent translating one of George Eliot's novels. My disappointment, due to an initial mistake as to what Andrée was, had not, in fact, the slightest importance for me. But the mistake was one of the kind which, if they allow love to be born and are not recognised as mistakes until it has ceased to be modifiable, become a cause of suffering. Such mistakes—which may be quite different from mine with regard to Andrée, and even its exact opposite—are frequently due (and this was especially the case here) to the fact that people take on the aspect and the mannerisms of what they are not but would like to be sufficiently to create an illusion at first sight. To the outward appearance, affectation, imitation, the longing to be admired, whether by the good or by the wicked, add misleading similarities of speech and gesture. There are cynicisms and cruelties which, when put to the test, prove no more genuine than certain apparent virtues and generosities. Just as we often discover a vain miser beneath the cloak of a man famed for his charity, so her flaunting of vice leads us to surmise a Messalina in a respectable girl with middle-class prejudices. I had thought to find in Andrée a healthy, primitive creature, whereas she was merely a person in search of health, as perhaps were many of those in whom she herself had thought to find it, and who were in reality no more healthy than a burly arthritic with a red face and in white flannels is necessarily a Hercules. Now there are circumstances in which it is not immaterial to our happiness that the person we have loved for what appeared to be so healthy about her is in reality only one of those invalids who receive such health as they possess from others, as the planets borrow their light, as certain bodies are only conductors of electricity.

No matter, Andrée, like Rosemonde and Gisèle, indeed more than they, was, when all was said, a friend of Albertine, sharing her life, imitating her ways, to the point that, on the first day, I had not at once distinguished them from one another. Among these girls, rose-sprigs whose principal charm was that they were silhouetted against the sea, the same indivisibility prevailed as at the time when I did not know them, when the appearance of no matter which of them had caused me such violent emotion by heralding the fact that the little band was not far off. And even now the sight of one of them filled me with a pleasure in which was included, to an extent which I should not have found it easy to define, that of seeing the others follow her in due course, and, even if they did not come that day, of speaking about them, and of knowing that they would be told that I had been on the beach.

It was no longer simply the attraction of those first days, it was a genuine wish to love that wavered between them all, to such an extent was each the natural substitute for the others. My greatest sadness would not have been to be abandoned by whichever of these girls I loved best, but I should at once have loved best, because I should have fastened on to her the sum total of the melancholy longings which had been floating vaguely among them all, the one who had abandoned me. It would, moreover, in that event, be the loss of all her friends, in whose eyes I should speedily have forfeited whatever prestige I might possess, that I should, in losing her, have unconsciously regretted, having pledged to them that sort of collective love which the politician and the actor feel for the public for whose desertion of them after they have enjoyed all its favours they can never be consoled. Even those favours which I had failed to win from Albertine I would hope suddenly to receive from one or other who had left me in the evening with a word or glance of ambiguous meaning, thanks to which it was towards her that, for the next day or so, my desire would turn.

It strayed among them all the more voluptuously in that upon those volatile faces a comparative fixity of features had now begun, and had been carried far enough for the eye to distinguish—even if it were to change yet further—each malleable and elusive effigy. The differences that existed between these faces doubtless bore little relation to equivalent differences in the length and breadth of their features, any of which, dissimilar as the girls appeared, might perhaps almost have been lifted from one face and imposed at random upon any other. But our knowledge of faces is not mathematical. In the first place, it does not begin by measuring the parts, it takes as its starting point an expression, a sum total. In Andrée, for instance, the fineness of her gentle eyes seemed to go with the thinness of her nose, as slender as a mere curve which one could imagine having been traced in order to pursue along a single line the notion of delicacy divided higher up between the dual smile of her twin gaze. A line equally fine cut through her hair, as pliant and as deep as the line with which the wind furrows the sand. And there it must have been hereditary; for the snow-white hair of Andrée's mother rippled in the same way, forming here a swelling, there a depression like a snowdrift that rises or sinks according to the irregularities of the land. Certainly, when compared with the fine delineation of Andrée's, Rosemonde's nose seemed to present broad surfaces, like a high tower resting upon massive foundations. Although expression may suffice to make us believe in enormous differences between things that are separated by infinitely little—although that infinitely little may by itself create an expression that is absolutely unique, an individuality—it was not only the infinitely little differences of its lines and the originality of its expression that made these faces appear irreducible to one another. Between my friends' faces their colouring established a separation wider still, not so much by the varied beauty of the tones with which it provided them, so contrasted that I felt when I looked at Rosemonde—suffused with a sulphurous pink that was further modified by the greenish light of her eyes—and then at Andrée—whose white cheeks derived such austere distinction from her black hair—the same kind of pleasure as if I had been looking alternately at a geranium growing by a sunlit sea and a camellia in the night; but principally because the infinitely small differences of their lines were enlarged out of all proportion, the relations between one and another surface entirely changed by this new element of colour which, in addition to being the dispenser of tints, is a great generator or at least modifier of dimensions. So that faces which were perhaps constructed on not dissimilar lines, according as they were lit, by the flames of a shock of red hair, with a pinkish hue, or, by white light, with a matt pallor, grew sharper or broader, became something else, like those properties used in the Russian ballet, consisting sometimes, when they are seen in the light of day, of a mere paper disc, out of which the genius of a Bakst, according to the blood-red or moonlit lighting in which he plunges his stage, makes a hard incrustation, like a turquoise on a palace wall, or something softly blooming, like a Bengal rose in an eastern garden. And so when studying faces, we do indeed measure them, but as painters, not as surveyors.

The same was true of Albertine as of her friends. On certain days, thin, with a grey complexion, a sullen air, a violet transparency slanting across her eyes such as we notice sometimes on the sea, she seemed to be feeling the sorrows of exile. On other days her face, smoother and glossier, drew one's desires on to its varnished surface and prevented them from going further; unless I caught a sudden glimpse of her from the side, for her matt cheeks, like white wax on the surface, were visibly pink beneath, which was what made one so long to kiss them, to reach that different tint which was so elusive. At other times, happiness bathed those cheeks with a radiance so mobile that the skin, grown fluid and vague, gave passage to a sort of subcutaneous glaze which made it appear to be of another colour but not of another substance than the eyes; sometimes, when one looked without thinking at her face punctuated with tiny brown marks among which floated what were simply two larger, bluer stains, it was as though one were looking at a goldfinch's egg, or perhaps at an opalescent agate cut and polished in two places only, where, at the heart of the brown stone, there shone, like the transparent wings of a sky-blue butterfly, the eyes, those features in which the flesh becomes a mirror and gives us the illusion of enabling us, more than through the other parts of the body, to approach the soul. But most often it too showed more colour, and was then more animated; sometimes in her white face only the tip of her nose was pink, and as delicate as that of a mischievous kitten with which one would have liked to play; sometimes her cheeks were so glossy that one's glance slipped, as over the surface of a miniature, over their pink enamel, which was made to appear still more delicate, more private, by the enclosing though half-opened lid of her black hair; or it might happen that the tint of her cheeks had deepened to the mauvish pink of cyclamen, and sometimes even, when she was flushed or feverish, with a suggestion of unhealthiness which lowered my desire to something more sensual and made her glance expressive of something more perverse and unwholesome, to the deep purple of certain roses, a red that was almost black; and each of these Albertines was different, as is each appearance of the dancer whose colours, form, character, are transmuted according to the endlessly varied play of a spotlight. It was perhaps because they were so diverse, the persons whom I used to contemplate in her at this period, that later I developed the habit of becoming myself a different person, according to the particular Albertine to whom my thoughts had turned; a jealous, an indifferent, a voluptuous, a melancholy, a frenzied person, created anew not merely by the accident of the particular memory that had risen to the surface, but in proportion also to the strength of the belief that was lent to the support of one and the same memory by the varying manner in which I appreciated it. For this was the point to which I invariably had to return, to those beliefs which for most of the time occupy our souls unbeknown to us, but which for all that are of more importance to our happiness than is the person whom we see, for it is through them that we see him, it is they that impart his momentary grandeur to the person seen. To be quite accurate, I ought to give a different name to each of the selves who subsequently thought about Albertine; I ought still more to give a different name to each of the Albertines who appeared before me, never the same, like those seas—called by me simply and for the sake of convenience "the sea"—that succeeded one another and against which, a nymph likewise, she was silhouetted. But above all, in the same way as, in telling a story (though to far greater purpose here), people mention what the weather was like on such and such a day, I ought always to give its name to the belief that reigned over my soul and created its atmosphere on any given day on which I saw Albertine, the appearance of people, like that of the sea, being dependent on those clouds, themselves barely visible, which change the colour of everything by their concentration, their mobility, their dissemination, their flight—like that cloud which Elstir had rent one evening by not introducing me to these girls with whom he had stopped to talk, and whose images had suddenly appeared to me more beautiful when they moved away—a cloud that had formed again a few days later when I did get to know them, veiling their brightness, interposing itself frequently between my eyes and them, opaque and soft, like Virgil's Leucothea.

No doubt, all their faces had assumed quite new meanings for me since the manner in which they were to be read had been to some extent indicated to me by their talk, talk to which I could ascribe a value all the greater in that, by questioning them, I could prompt it whenever I chose, could vary it like an experimenter who seeks by corroborative proofs to establish the truth of his theory. And it is, after all, as good a way as any of solving the problem of existence to get near enough to the things and people that have appeared to us beautiful and mysterious from a distance to be able to satisfy ourselves that they have neither mystery nor beauty. It is one of the systems of mental hygiene among which we are at liberty to choose our own, a system which is perhaps not to be recommended too strongly, but gives us a certain tranquillity with which to spend what remains of life, and also—since it enables us to regret nothing, by assuring us that we have attained to the best, and that the best was nothing out of the ordinary—with which to resign ourselves to death.

For the contempt for chastity, for the memory of casual everyday affairs, I had substituted, in the minds of these girls, upright principles, liable perhaps to falter, but principles which had hitherto kept unscathed those who had acquired them in their middle-class homes. And yet, when one has been mistaken from the start, even in trifling details, when an error of assumption or recollection makes one seek for the author of a malicious slander, or for the place where one has lost something, in the wrong direction, it frequently happens that one discovers one's error only to substitute for it not the truth but a fresh error. I drew, as regards their manner of life and the conduct to be observed towards them, all the possible conclusions from the word "innocence" which I had read, in talking familiarly with them, upon their faces. But perhaps I had carelessly misread it, and it was no more written there than was the name of Jules Ferry on the programme of the performance at which I had seen Berma for the first time, an omission which had not prevented me from maintaining to M. de Norpois that Jules Ferry, beyond any possibility of doubt, was a person who wrote curtain-raisers.

No matter which of my friends of the little band I thought of, how could the last face that she had shown me not have been the only one that I could recall, since, of our memories with respect to a person, the mind eliminates everything that does not concur with the immediate purpose of our daily relations (even, and especially, if those relations are impregnated with an element of love which, ever unsatisfied, lives always in the moment that is about to come)? It allows the chain of spent days to slip away, holding on only to the very end of it, often of a quite different metal from the links that have vanished in the night, and in the journey which we make through life, counts as real only the place in which we are at present. My very earliest impressions, already so remote, could not find any remedy in my memory against the daily distortion to which they were subjected; during the long hours which I spent in talking, eating, playing with these girls, I did not even remember that they were the same pitiless and sensual virgins whom I had seen, as in a fresco, file past between me and the sea.

Geographers or archaeologists may conduct us over Calypso's island, may excavate the Palace of Minos. Only, Calypso becomes then a mere woman, Minos a mere king with no semblance of divinity. Even the qualities and defects which history then teaches us to have been the attributes of those quite real personages often differ widely from those which we had ascribed to the fabulous beings who bore the same names as they. Thus had there faded and vanished all the lovely oceanic mythology which I had composed in those first days. But it is not altogether a matter of indifference that we do succeed, at any rate now and then, in spending our time in familiar intercourse with what we thought to be unattainable and longed to possess. In our later dealings with people whom at first we found disagreeable there persists always, even amid the factitious pleasure which we have come at length to enjoy in their society, the lingering taint of the defects which they have succeeded in hiding. But, in relations such as I enjoyed with Albertine and her friends, the genuine pleasure which was there at the start leaves that fragrance which no artifice can impart to hothouse fruits, to grapes that have not ripened in the sun. The supernatural creatures which for a little time they had been to me still introduced, even without my being aware of it, a miraculous element into the most commonplace dealings I might have with them, or rather prevented such dealings from ever becoming in the least commonplace. My desire had sought so avidly to learn the meaning of eyes which now knew and smiled at me, but which, that first day, had crossed mine like rays from another universe, it had distributed colour and fragrance so generously, so carefully, so minutely, over the fleshly surfaces of these girls who now, stretched out on the cliff-top, simply offered me sandwiches or played guessing-games, that often, in the afternoon, while I lay there among them—like those painters who, seeking to match the grandeurs of antiquity in modern life, give to a woman cutting her toe-nail the nobility of the *Thorn Puller*, or, like Rubens, make goddesses out of women they know to people some mythological scene—I would gaze at those lovely forms, dark and fair, so dissimilar in type, scattered around me on the grass, without emptying them, perhaps, of all the mediocre content with which my everyday experience had filled them, and yet (without expressly recalling their celestial origin) as if, like young Hercules or Telemachus, I had been playing amid a band of nymphs.

Then the concerts ended, the bad weather began, my friends left Balbec, not all at once, like the swallows, but all in the same week. Albertine was the first to go, abruptly, without any of her friends understanding, then or afterwards, why she had returned suddenly to Paris whither neither her work nor any amusement summoned her. "She said neither why nor wherefore, and with that she left!" muttered Françoise, who, for that matter, would have liked us to do the same. We were, she thought, inconsiderate towards the staff, now greatly reduced in number, but retained on account of the few visitors who were still staying on, and towards the manager who was "just eating up money." It was true that the hotel, which would very soon be closed for the winter, had long since seen most of its patrons depart, and never had it been so agreeable. This view was not shared by the manager; from end to end of the rooms in which we sat shivering, and at the doors of which no page now stood on guard, he paced the corridors, wearing a new frock-coat, so well tended by the barber that his insipid face appeared to be made of some composition in which, for one part of flesh, there were three of cosmetics, and incessantly changing his neckties. (These refinements cost less than having the place heated and keeping on the staff, just as a man who is no longer able to subscribe ten thousand francs to a charity can still parade his generosity without inconvenience to himself by tipping the boy who brings him a telegram with five.) He appeared to be inspecting the empty air, to be seeking, by the smartness of his personal appearance, to give a provisional splendour to the desolation that could now be felt in this hotel where the season had not been good, and walked like the ghost of a monarch who returns to haunt the ruins of what was once his palace. He was particularly annoyed when the little local railway company, finding the supply of passengers inadequate, discontinued its trains until the following spring. "What is lacking here," said the manager, "is the means of commotion." In spite of the deficit which his books showed, he was making plans for the future on a lavish scale. And as he was, after all, capable of retaining an exact memory of fine phrases when they were directly applicable to the hotel-keeping industry and had the effect of enhancing its importance: "I was not adequately supported, although in the dining room I had an efficient squad," he explained, "but the pages left something to be desired. You will see, next year, what a phalanx I shall convene." In the meantime the suspension of the services of the little railway obliged him to send for letters and occasionally to dispatch visitors in a carriole. I would often ask leave to sit by the driver, and in this way I managed to be out in all weathers, as in the winter I had spent at Combray.

Sometimes, however, the driving rain kept my grandmother and me, the Casino being closed, in rooms almost completely deserted, as in the hold of a ship when a storm is raging; and there, day by day, as in the course of a sea-voyage, a new person from among those in whose company we had spent three months without getting to know them, the senior judge from Caen, the president of the Cherbourg bar, an American lady and her daughters, came up to us, engaged us in conversation, thought up some way of making the time pass less slowly, revealed some talent, taught us a new game, invited us to drink tea or to listen to music, to meet them at a certain hour, to plan together some of those diversions which contain the true secret of giving ourselves pleasure, which is not to aspire to it but merely to help ourselves to pass the time less boringly—in a word, formed with us, at the end of our stay at Balbec, ties of friendship which, in a day or two, their successive departures from the place would sever. I even made the acquaintance of the rich young man, of one of his pair of aristocratic friends and of the actress, who had reappeared for a few days; but their little society was composed now of three persons only, the other friend having returned to Paris. They asked me to come out to dinner with them at their restaurant. I think they were just as well pleased that I did not accept. But they had issued the invitation in the most friendly way imaginable, and although it came in fact from the rich young man, since the others were only his guests, as the friend who was staying with him, the Marquis Maurice de Vaudémont, came of a very good family indeed, instinctively the actress, in asking me whether I would not come, said, to flatter my vanity: "It will give Maurice such pleasure."

And when I met them all three together in the hall of the hotel, it was M. de Vaudémont (the rich young man effacing himself) who said to me: "Won't you give us the pleasure of dining with us?"

On the whole I had derived very little benefit from Balbec, but this only strengthened my desire to return there. It seemed to me that I had not stayed there long enough. This was not the opinion of my friends in Paris, who wrote to ask whether I meant to stay there for the rest of my life. And when I saw that it was the name "Balbec" which they were obliged to put on the envelope, as my window looked out not over a landscape or a street but on to the plains of the seas, as through the night I heard its murmur, to which, before going to sleep, I had entrusted the ship of my dreams, I had the illusion that this life of promiscuity with the waves must effectively, without my knowledge, pervade me with the notion of their charm, like those lessons which one learns by heart while one is asleep.

The manager offered to reserve better rooms for me next year, but I had now become attached to mine, into which I went without ever noticing the scent of vetiver, while my mind, which had once found such difficulty in rising to fill its space, had come now to take its measurements so exactly that I was obliged to submit it to a reverse process when I had to sleep in Paris, in my own room, the ceiling of which was low.

For we had had to leave Balbec at last, the cold and the damp having become too penetrating for us to stay any longer in a hotel which had neither fireplaces in the rooms nor central heating. Moreover, I forgot almost immediately these last weeks of our stay. What I saw almost invariably in my mind's eye when I thought of Balbec were the hours which, every morning during the fine weather, since I was due to go out in the afternoon with Albertine and her friends, my grandmother, following the doctor's orders, insisted on my spending lying down with the room darkened. The manager gave instructions that no noise was to be made on my landing, and came up himself to see that they were obeyed. Because the light outside was so strong, I kept drawn for as long as possible the big violet curtains which had adopted so hostile an attitude towards me the first evening. But since, in spite of the pins with which Françoise fastened them every night so that the light should not enter, and which she alone knew how to unfasten, in spite of the rugs, the red cretonne table-cover, the various fabrics collected here and there which she fitted into her defensive scheme, she never succeeded in making them meet exactly, the darkness was not complete, and they spilled over the carpet as it were a scarlet shower of anemone-petals, which I could not resist the temptation to trample for a moment with my bare feet. And on the wall which faced the window and so was partially lighted, a cylinder of gold with no visible support was placed vertically and moved slowly along like the pillar of fire which went before the Hebrews in the desert. I went back to bed; obliged to taste without moving, in imagination only, and all at once, the pleasures of games, bathing, walks which the morning prompted, joy made my heart beat thunderingly like a machine set going at full speed but fixed to the ground, which can spend its energy only by turning over on itself.

I knew that my friends were on the front, but I did not see them as they passed before the links of the sea's uneven chain, at the far end of which, perched amid its bluish peaks like an Italian citadel, could occasionally be distinguished, in clear weather, the little town of Rivebelle, picked out in minutest detail by the sun. I did not see my friends, but (while there mounted to my belvedere the shout of the newsboys, the "journalists" as Françoise used to call them, the shouts of the bathers and of children at play, punctuating like the cries of sea-birds the sough of the gently breaking waves) I guessed their presence, I heard their laughter enveloped like the laughter of the Nereids in the soft surge of sound that rose to my ears. "We looked up," said Albertine in the evening, "to see if you were coming down. But your shutters were still closed when the concert began." At ten o'clock, sure enough, it broke out beneath my windows. In the intervals between the blare of the instruments, if the tide were high, the gliding surge of a wave would be heard again, slurred and continuous, seeming to enfold the notes of the violin in its crystal spirals and to be spraying its foam over the intermittent echoes of a submarine music. I grew impatient because no one had yet come with my things, so that I might get up and dress. Twelve o'clock struck, and Françoise arrived at last. And for months on end, in this Balbec to which I had so looked forward because I imagined it only as battered by storms and buried in the mist, the weather had been so dazzling and so unchanging that when she came to open the window I could always, without once being wrong, expect to see the same patch of sunlight folded in the corner of the outer wall, of an unalterable colour which was less moving as a sign of summer than depressing as the colour of a lifeless and factitious enamel. And when Françoise removed the pins from the top of the window-frame, took down the cloths, and drew back the curtains, the summer day which she disclosed seemed as dead, as immemorial, as a sumptuous millenary mummy from which our old servant had done no more than cautiously unwind the linen wrappings before displaying it, embalmed in its vesture of gold.

NOTES · ADDENDA · SYNOPSIS

Notes

1 (p. 5) *Le seize mai*: constitutional crisis in 1877 which eventually led to the resignation of the President of the Republic, Marshal MacMahon.

2 (p. 45) Singers' Bridge: headquarters of the Russian Foreign Ministry in St Petersburg.
Montecitorio: the Italian Chamber of Deputies in Rome.
Ballplatz (more correctly Ballhausplatz): the Austrian Foreign Ministry in Vienna.

3 (p. 49) The tomb of Tourville, the seventeenth-century French admiral, is in fact in the church of Saint-Eustache in Paris.

4 (p. 52) The word is *cocu,* cuckold. Norpois is being comically prudish.

5 (p. 112) August Wolf: German philologist (1759–1824) who was the most notable adherent of the view that the *Iliad* and the *Odyssey* were the work of a number of anonymous bards.

6 (p. 157) The letters p.p.c. stand for *pour prendre congé,* to take one's leave.

7 (p. 207) *Rachel quand du Seigneur* . . . : famous aria from Halévy's opera *La Juive*.

8 (p. 235) Vatel: chef, after the famous *maître d'hôtel* of the great Condé.

9 (p. 313) This is an imaginary work. No such Memoirs exist.

10 (p. 384) Baronne d'Ange: character in *Le Demi-monde* by Alexandre Dumas *fils*—a courtesan who tries to marry into high society without success.

11 (p. 434) *Concours général*: competitive examination open to all secondary schools at *baccalauréat* level. "People's universities" were established between 1898

and 1901 with the object of raising the intellectual level of the workers and bringing different social classes together. They mainly consisted of evening lecture courses.

12 (p. 548) The reference is to Amphion, who, according to Greek legend, rebuilt the walls of Thebes, charming the stones into place with his lyre.

13 (p. 611) Arvède Barine was the pseudonym of Mme Charles Vincens (1840–1908), a French woman writer who published several volumes of critical and historical essays.

14 (p. 680) *Le jeu du furet* is the French equivalent of "hunt-the-slipper."

Addenda

Page 124. *The original manuscript has a more detailed version of the scene, which the Pléiade editors (1954) reproduce in their "Notes and Variants":*

Odette was quite prepared to cut short her visit, but could not leave at once since she had only just arrived. Either to get round the difficulty, or as a studied insult to her niece, "I should be most interested to look over your house," Lady Israels had said to Mme de Marsantes, knowing that the latter had a great regard for her and an even greater need of her. Moreover Lady Israels, who was extremely beneficent and upright, was also very haughty. "I shall be delighted to show it to you," Mme de Marsantes had replied, and at once set off with Lady Jacob [*sic*] as though she felt she had no need to bother about Mme Swann who must be only too happy to be in her house, leaving the unfortunate woman standing there alone, kicking her heels for half an hour. Then Mme de Marsantes had returned and said curtly to Mme Swann: "Excuse me"; whereupon Lady Jacob had raised her lorgnette and looked at Odette as at a person she had not even noticed before and who must have arrived in the meantime, or as yet another feature of the house. This feature no doubt failed to impress her, for it was the only one on which she made no comment, and turning towards Mme de Marsantes she started up a conversation with her in which Odette was not invited to join. "I trust you won't go back there," Swann had said to her afterwards, and this single visit had not encouraged Odette to pursue her offensive in that direction. Let us hasten to add, however, that this was not the world that preoccupied Mme Swann. On matters concerning the nobility, on pedigrees and ducal houses, she lacked even the petty erudition that peaceful bourgeois citizens of Nantes or Tours cultivate night and day, although they may never know anyone from that world. When, as we shall see, it began to flock to the house of the aged Odette, it did not come to fill a void, to gratify a craving induced by the reading of old memoirs and the Almanach de Gotha; it was received without the slightest mental preparation. Mme de Guermantes was for Odette no more than a superior Mme Verdurin whom it was "smart" to have to one's house, and she was far less concerned about who the Guermantes family were than a great many people who would never know them . . .

Page 457. *The manuscript gives a longer and more detailed version of this passage, reproduced in the Pléiade "Notes and Variants":*

So Mme de Villeparisis, who when I used to hear my grandmother talking about her in my childhood had seemed to me to be an old lady of the same sort as her other friends and had always remained so to me—that person who had once given me a box of chocolates held by a duck and was now going out of her way to be agreeable to us—was a member of the powerful Guermantes clan! This change in the value of what we possess, like those old bundles which turn out to be priceless treasures, is one of the things that introduce most wonder, animation, variety and consequently poetry into one's adolescence (that adolescence which, while gradually dwindling until it becomes no more than a thin trickle that often runs dry, is sometimes prolonged throughout the whole course of one's life). The rise or depreciation of one's wealth, the weirdly unexpected reassessments of one's possessions, the misrepresentations of people we know, which make one's youth as fabulous as the metamorphoses of Ovid or even the metempsychoses of the Hindus, derive in part from ignorance—an ignorance that extends to people's names as to everything else. My great-aunt had bought for one of the rooms at Combray some crude painted canvases (perhaps indeed they were only coloured paper) framed in coffee-coloured wood, which represented scenes by Teniers. I had told Bloch in perfectly good faith that we had a room full of Teniers. In the vague world, innocent of any notion of discrimination, that painting was to me then, I could see no difference between a five-franc reproduction and an original work. Similarly in the Army, where one has a captain called Lévy and another called Lévy-Mirepoix: these two names, though the second is longer than the first and therefore a little more ridiculous, appear otherwise interchangeable. When one is a child, certain words placed in front of a name seem funny, except *M. l'abbé* which is respectable; but if Mme Galopin is called Marie-Euphrosine Galopin, or Mme de Villeparisis the Marquise de Villeparisis, this merely adds something rather heteroclite to persons otherwise of the same ilk. For one starts from the impressions one has received, and not from the preconceptions whereby an educated man knows what a painting is, and a man of the world what the Villeparisis are. People have only to present themselves to our eyes in a particularly simple light—which happens especially often with elegant people, like Swann who pushed the piano for my great-aunt and sent her strawberries, or Mme de Villeparisis who had given me a chocolate duck—while being otherwise indistinguishable from the other modest supernumeraries on the family stage, and they will seem to us if anything of a slightly inferior rank. One fine day we are amazed to hear someone we place very high, someone to whose level we seek to aspire, speak of them as people far superior to himself. Thus to ignorance is added, further to mislead us, the homogeneity in one's memory of impressions belonging to the same category, and their heterogeneousness in relation to impressions of another category. This heterogeneousness, in effect, makes it far more difficult for us to calculate value. In order to compare, to subtract, it is first of all necessary to reduce to qualities of the same kind. Those who start from preconceived notions can do so. Childhood, enclosed in its impressions, cannot. Mme de Villeparisis, an old family acquaintance, less brilliant and intimidating than the optician, was further removed from "the Guermantes way" than if she had been confined to "the Méséglise way." But these differences in kind, if they make the assessment of values impossible, are great sources of poetry (all the more so because those beliefs of our youth, like forces that need room in which to deploy, operate over the great, wide surfaces of time that stretch behind us). When we discover that the easy-going captain whom we treated with less respect than Captain Lévy, and who—not content with being nice to us every day—asked us to dinner before we finished our term of service, was the stepbrother of the Duc de Fezenzac (once we have acquired preconceptions and know who the latter is), this sudden displacement—as of a ray of light shifting on the horizon—of a personage who rapidly switches from the vulgar and charming environment in which we have always situated him into a totally different world, acquires a sort of poetic charm. He had become almost unreal, like everything that we once knew in a place to which we have never returned, in a special life intercalated into our very different life for three years, like the officers in our regiment, or long ago the good people of Combray. To learn that these people, as different from real people as pantomime figures, took the train on Saturday, after removing their uniforms or their country clothes, and went to dine with Mme de Pourtalès—how interesting that makes it for us to know Mme de Pourtalès, how we long to get her to talk to us about them! But what she tells us will no more be able to enlighten us than what we ask of people who knew the real people on whom Mme Bovary or Frédéric Moreau were modelled. How could this information elucidate an inner charm which stems from a certain distortion of memory and certain transformations of reality? Thus Saint-Loup could have spoken to me indefinitely about his family without helping me to get to the bottom of the pleasure I had derived from the fact that suddenly, set free from a homely bourgeois prison that had been spirited away as in a fairy tale, Mme de Villeparisis was embarking—or rather (so swift had been the spell) was already awaiting me—on the Guermantes way.

"But how do you know the Château de Guermantes?" Saint-Loup asked me. "Have you visited it—or perhaps you knew my aunt de Guermantes-La Trémoïlle who lived there before?" he added, whether because, finding it quite natural that one should know the same people as he did, he failed to realise that I came from a different background, or because he was pretending not to realise out of politeness.

"No . . . but . . . I've heard of the château. They have all the busts of the old lords of Guermantes there, haven't they?"

"Yes, it's a fine sight . . ."

Page 487. *At this point in the holograph material the Pléiade editors found some loose sheets containing the following passage which Proust failed to complete and incorporate in his novel. (Santois was the name Proust originally gave to the violinist, Morel, who does not make his first appearance until* The Guermantes Way.):

N.B. This, which was originally intended for the last Guermantes party, is for the evening in the Casino at Balbec, but may perhaps be changed. I might split it in two, keeping the quintet for the Guermantes party and the organ for Balbec?

At the back of the Casino's dance hall was a stage from which some excessively steep and widely spaced steps led up to an organ. The "famous Lepic Quintet," composed of women, came in to play *a quintet by Franck (insert another name)*. Although this quintet was her favourite piece, the pianist executed it with the same feverish concentration both on the score and on her fingers as she would have shown had she been sight-reading, and with such a striving towards speed that she seemed not so much to be playing the music as catching up with it as fast as she could go. The piano might perhaps be shattered by the end of it, but she would get there. Since she was a distinguished lady, dressed with studied elegance, she gave her feverish attentiveness a knowing air which from a distance seemed almost mischievous; and indeed whenever she played wrong notes—which happened all the time—she smiled as though she were playing a joke on them, as one laughs when one splashes someone in order to pretend that one has done it on purpose. All the people there were sufficiently elegant and musical not to be paying attention to anything but the music, as would have happened at a bourgeois soirée . . . *Put in here the remarks made to me by Mme de Cambremer about the quintet, perhaps even put in here, to vary it a bit, my observations on art and love . . . and in that case perhaps bring on the man who says "It's devilish fine," who will be a character already introduced but who has gone grey.*

Before putting in Mme de Cambremer's reflexions during the interval, say: Nevertheless the minds of all these people were preoccupied less with what they were listening to than with the way they were listening and the impression they were making all round them. They endeavoured with their boas or their fans to give the appearance of knowing what was being played, of judging the performers and waiting for the extremely difficult *allegro vivace* to compose a satisfying ensemble. The minuet set all their heads nodding and wagging, with knowing smiles which signified both "Isn't it charming!" and "Of course I know it!" Meanwhile my unintentionally ironical smile upset the head-wagging of a few intrepid listeners who replaced the knowing smile with a furious glance and abandoned the head-wagging, though—in order not to appear to be surrendering to a threat—not at once but rather as if under the pressure of Westinghouse brakes, which slow trains down gradually until they come to a complete stop. An artistic gentleman, anxious to show that he knew the quintet, shouted "Bravo, bravo" when he judged that it had reached its conclusion, and began to clap. Unfortunately, what he had taken for the end of the quintet was not even the end of one of its movements but simply a two-bar pause. He consoled himself with the thought that people might imagine that he knew the pianist and had merely wished to encourage her. When the end, longed for by the more musical members of the audience, came at last, I said to Mme de Cambremer . . .

Meanwhile the organ recital had begun. At that moment a paralytic old man, who could walk with some difficulty but was utterly incapable of climbing the steps, conceived the strange intention of going to sit on a chair right at the top beside the organ, and three young men pushed him up. But after a while, as the organ's crisp keyboard notes were executing their pastoral variations, he got up again, with the three young men in hot pursuit. I thought he must have had a stroke, and I admired the obliviousness of the organist who, having ceased to uncoil the spirals of his rustic pipes, covered the descent of the unfortunate paralytic with a thunderous noise. Pushed and carried by the three young men, the old gentleman disappeared into the wings. The pianist, performer turned critic, had now come to sit on the stage. In spite of the suffocating heat, she had donned a white fur coat, of which she was evidently extremely proud. Moreover her hands, so active on the keyboard only a moment before, were buried in an immense white fur muff, either because she simply wanted to show how elegant she was, or in order to enclose the precious relics of her piano-playing in a shrine worthy of them, or to exchange the activity of the keyboard for the motionless but skilful exercise of the muff, which moreover dispensed her from having to applaud her colleagues. No one understood the rôle of this muff, about which Saint-Loup interrogated me in vain. But what surprised me more was that scarcely two minutes had passed before the paralytic old man, evidently warming to the very exercise of which he was all but incapable, returned, pushed by the three young men, to take his useless place beside the organ. He nodded off there for a moment, then awoke and climbed down again, and since the organist was invisible behind his instrument, the stage was to all intents and purposes occupied by the perilous exertions of the clumsy quinquagenarian [*sic*] squirrel. When the organist came down in his turn to take his bow, it was to him that the thankless task devolved of helping down the impotent dotard, whose every step made the frail executant stumble. But with a wiliness that is often characteristic of the moribund, the old man clung to the organist in such a way that it was he who appeared to be supporting the man who was more or less carrying him, to be protecting him, to be presenting him to the audience, and to be receiving his share of the applause, which out of pure modesty he seemed not to wish to take for himself by pointing to the organist, who, tottering beneath his human burden and afraid of falling down the steep steps, could not make his bow.

Meanwhile, I was looking at the programme to see what the next piece was to be when I was struck by the name of the soloist: Santois. "He has the same name as the son of my uncle's former valet," I thought to myself. I heard someone say: "Look, a soldier." I raised my eyes and at once recognised the young Santois, who was indeed now a soldier for a year, or rather disguised as a soldier, so much did he give the impression of being in fancy dress.

He played well, looking down at his instrument with that charming Gallic face, the open yet pious demeanour of some contemporary of St Louis or Louis XI, with the defiance of the peasant who feels that there would be little point in having had a revolution if one still had to say "Monsieur le Comte." To these agreeable features there was added, after the first two pieces, as though to complete the picture of the traditional young violinist, a symmetrical adjunct to the redness of the neck at the spot where the instrument rests (the product of the *allegro* although it was *non troppo*), a curvaceous lock of hair, as round as if it had been in a locket, . . . charming, belated, perhaps not entirely fortuitous, but activated at the appropriate moment by a virtuoso who knew what a contribution it can make to the seductiveness of a performance.

After he had finished playing, I sent a message round to him asking if I could come and pay my compliments. He replied in a few words scribbled on his card saying that he looked forward to seeing me and assuring me of his "amicable regards." I thought of the indignation Françoise would have felt, she who since she had learned, fairly recently it was true, the use of the third person, had prescribed it to the whole of her family, down to the most remote degrees of kinship or descent, every time a young cousin of hers came "to pay her respects to Monsieur." But if I found this deference towards me of the whole of Françoise's family very traditionally domestic, it seemed to me that, although it was at the opposite extreme, there was something no less characteristically French in the cavalier tone of the young Santois, scion of a race that made the Revolution, implying that a peasant's son, educated or not, considers himself nobody's inferior, and when a prince is mentioned insists on showing by his demeanour that such a person seems to him no better than his father or himself—though with a tinge of hauteur in the way he manifests it that betrays the fact that the age when princes were indeed superior is still fairly recent and that he may be afraid that people still remember it.

After the concert I went round to congratulate him, and recognised him without difficulty, not from the face I remembered, since there is always a certain discrepancy, a certain displacement in the memory, but because his appearance accorded with the impression he had made on me in Paris and which I had forgotten. He was doing his military service near Balbec, and he too had immediately recognised me. We had nothing in common save a few mental images, and the memory of the things we had said to one another during the short visit he had paid to me, and which were of little moment. But it would seem that faces are fairly individual, and moreover that the memory is a pretty faithful organ, since we had remembered each other and our meeting.

Santois was presently joined by his colleagues, the other players, for each of whom, as an aeroplane adds wings to an aviator, his instrument was as it were the beak and the throat of a melodious song-bird; a twittering troupe that had gathered for the summer season at this resort and would shortly, with the first frosts, take off elsewhere. I left Santois with his friends, but when I got back to the hotel I regretted not having asked him who the mountaineering paralytic was who had scaled the heights of the organ so many times, and also whether Santois, his father, had ever told him how my uncle had come to have the portrait of Mme Swann by Elstir. I resolved not to forget to ask him these two questions if I saw him again.

Synopsis

MADAME SWANN AT HOME

A new Swann: Odette's husband (1; cf. 112 sqq.). A new Cottard: Professor Cottard (3).

Norpois (5); the "governmental mind" (6); an ambassador's conversation (8). "'Although' is always an unrecognised 'because'" (10). Norpois advises my father to let me follow a literary career (13).

My first experience of Berma (15). My high expectations of her—as of Balbec and Venice (17). A great disappointment (20). Françoise and Michelangelo (21). The auditorium and the stage (24; cf. **I** 100).

Norpois dines at our house (29). His notions about literature (31); financial investments (33); Berma (37); Françoise's spiced beef (39); King Theodosius' visit to Paris (41); Balbec church (48); Mme Swann (49); Odette and the Comte de Paris (58); Bergotte (60); my prose poem (62; cf. 35); Gilberte (65). Gestures which we believe have gone unnoticed (67). Why M. de Norpois would not speak to Mme Swann about me (70).

How I came to say of Berma: "What a great artist!" (72). The laws of Time (74). Effect produced by Norpois on my parents (75), on Françoise (76); the latter's views on Parisian restaurants (78).

New Year's Day visits (79). I propose to Gilberte that we should rebuild our friendship on a new basis (80); but that same evening I realise that New Year's Day is not the first day of a new world (81). Berma and love (83). Gabriel's palaces (84). I can no longer recall Gilberte's face (84). She returns to the Champs-Elysées (85). "They can't stand you!" (86) I write to Swann (86). Reawakening, thanks to involuntary memory, in the little pavilion in the Champs-Elysées, of the impressions experienced in Uncle Adolphe's sanctum at Combray (89, 91; cf. **I** 99). Amorous wrestle with Gilberte (89). I fall ill (91). Cottard's diagnoses (96).

A letter from Gilberte (98). Love's miracles, happy and unhappy (99). Change of attitude towards me of Gilberte's parents, unwittingly brought about by Bloch and Cottard (102). The Swann apartment; the concierge; the windows (103; cf. **I** 500). Gilberte's writing-paper (104). The Henri II staircase (106). The chocolate cake (107). Mme Swann's praise of Françoise: "your old nurse" (110). The heart of the Sanctuary: Swann's library (111); his wife's bedroom (113). Odette's "at home" (114). The "famous Albertine," niece of Mme Bontemps (116). The evolution of society (117). Swann's "amusing sociological experiments" (128). Swann's old jealousy (131) and new love (133).

Outings with the Swanns (134). Lunch with them (135). Odette plays Vinteuil's sonata to me (140). A work of genius creates its own posterity (143). What the little phrase now means to Swann (145). "Me nigger; you old cow!" (149). Consistent charm of Mme Swann's heterogeneous drawing-room (153). Princess Mathilde (157). Gilberte's unexpected behaviour (161).

Lunch at the Swanns' with Bergotte (164). The gentle white-haired bard and the man with the snail-shell nose and black goatee (165). A writer's voice and his style (168). Bergotte and his imitators (169). Unforeseeable beauty of the sentences of a great writer (170). Reflecting power of genius (174). Vices of the man and morality of the writer (181). Bergotte and Berma (183). "A powerful idea communicates some of its power to the man who contradicts it" (186). A remark of Swann's, prelude to the theme of *The Captive* (188). Gilberte's characteristics inherited from both parents (190). Swann's confidence in his daughter (193). Are my pleasures those of the intelligence? (195). Why Swann, according to Bergotte, needs a good doctor (199). Combray society and the social world (199). My parents' change of mind about Bergotte and Gilberte; a problem of etiquette (203).

Revelations about love (205; cf. **I** 129); Bloch takes me to a second-rate house of assignation (205). "Rachel when from the Lord" (207). Aunt Léonie's furniture in the brothel (208). Amatory initiation at Combray on Aunt Léonie's sofa (208). Work projects constantly postponed (210). Impossibility of happiness in love (214). My last visit to Gilberte (214). I decide not to see her again (217. Unjust fury with the Swanns' butler (222). Waiting for a letter (222). I renounce Gilberte for ever (224); but the hope of a reconciliation is superimposed on my resolve (226). Intermittency, law of the human soul (227).

Odette's "winter-garden" (228): splendour of the chrysanthemums and poverty of the conversation: Mme Cottard (234); Mme Bontemps (234); effrontery of her niece Albertine (237); the Prince d'Agrigente (239); Mme Verdurin (239). Painful New Year's Day (251). "suicide of that self which loved Gilberte" (255). Clumsy interventions (256). Letters to Gilberte: "one speaks for oneself alone" (259). Odette's drawing-room: retreat of the Far East and invasion of the eighteenth century (261). New hair-styles and silhouettes (265; cf. **I** 278).

A sudden impulse interrupts the cure of detachment (271); Aunt Léonie's Chinese vase (272). Two walkers in the Elysian twilight (273). Impossibility of happiness (274). The opposing forces of memory and imagination (276). Because of Gilberte, I decline an invitation to a dinner-party where I would have met Albertine (277). Cruel memories (278). Gilberte's strange laugh, evoked in a dream (281; cf. 217). Fewer visits to Mme Swann (283). Exchange of tender letters and progress of indifference (286). Approach of spring: Mme Swann's ermine and the guelder-roses in her drawing-room; nostalgia for Combray (288). Odette and the "Down-and-outs Club" (290). An intermediate social class (295).

PLACE-NAMES · THE PLACE

Departure for Balbec (299). Subjectiveness of love (300). Contradictory effects of habit (301). Railway stations (303). Françoise's simple and infallible taste (309). Alcoholic euphoria (312). Mme de Sévigné and Dostoievsky (315). Sunrise from the train (316); the milk-girl (317). Balbec church (322). "The tyranny of the Particular" (324). Place-names on the way to Balbec-Plage (326).

Arrival at Balbec-Plage (327). The manager of the Grand Hotel (327, 332). My room at the top of the hotel (333; cf. **I** 8).

the sea (523). Dinners at Rivebelle (529). The astral tables (533). Euphoria induced by alcohol and music (534). Meeting with Elstir (553). A new aspect of Albertine (558).

Elstir's studio (564); his seascapes (566); the painter's "metaphors" (567). Elstir explains to me the beauty of Balbec church (573). Albertine passes by (578). The portrait of *Miss Sacripant* (585). "My beautiful Gabrielle!" (586). Age and the artist (588). Elstir and the little band (593). Nullity of love (596). Miss Sacripant was Mme Swann (600) and M. Biche Elstir! (604). One must discover wisdom for oneself (605). My grandmother and Saint-Loup (608). Saint-Loup and Bloch (609). Still lifes (613; cf. 373). Afternoon party at Elstir's (615). Yet another Albertine: a well-brought-up girl (619). Albertine on the esplanade: once more a member of the little band (623). Octave, the gigolo (625). Albertine's antipathy for Bloch (627). Saint-Loup engaged to a Mlle d'Ambresac? (634). Albertine's intelligence and taste (635). Andrée (636). Gisèle (637).

Days with the girls (643). Françoise's bad temper (649). Balbec through Elstir's eyes (651). Fortuny (653). A sketch of the Creuniers (656). The mobile beauty of youth (662). Friendship: and abdication of oneself (664; cf. 430). Twittering of the girls (666). Letter from Sophocles to Racine (671). A love divided among several girls (676). Albertine is to spend a night at the Grand Hotel (695). The rejected kiss (701). The attraction of Albertine (702). The multiple utilisation of a single action (707). Straying in the budding grove (716). The different Albertines (718).

End of the season (724). Departure (728).

A NOTE ON THE TYPE

The principal text of this Modern Library edition
was composed in a digitized version of
Horley Old Style, a typeface issued by
the English type foundry Monotype in 1925.
It has such distinctive features
as lightly cupped serifs and an oblique horizontal bar
on the lowercase "e."